W. James Chan earned a degree in Creative Writing at the University of Wollongong. He currently resides in Sydney, Australia.

Praise for **Blackcloak: A Man of his Sword**

"As if David Lynch rewrote the works of George RR Martin." *KIRKUS*

"An eminently readable novel…no less than thoroughly absorbing…Not just a fun read, *Blackcloak* might be the prelude for a new brand of sophistication in the fantasy genre." *San Francisco Book Review*

"Reads like poetry from its very first line…a book that demands your attention... the urge to read it through again with discovered knowledge is overwhelming." *Self-Publishing Review*

"A hell of a start to an unusual dark fantasy series that deftly combines psychology, magic, and philosophy into a disturbing character study." *Indie Reader*

THE BLOODY TAPESTRY OF KAEF'RE

I The Moon and the Cross

1. Blackcloak: A Man of his Sword
2. Gildenhammer: The Beating of her Heart

Forthcoming

3. Primahriel & Hawkstorm: Jaydemyr, in their own Words

4. Frayed At The Edges

II The Elemental Rapture

5. Embers of the Sun
6. Storms of the Sea
7. Eruption of the Sands

8. Loose Threads

III The Morning Star

9. The First Messiah
10. The Second Sa'ha'khra
11. The Third Revelation

12. Unravelling

GILDENHAMMER
THE BEATING OF HER HEART

W. JAMES CHAN

Table of Contents

First published August 2024
This edition published May 2025

Published in Australia in JSS Press

ISBN 978-1-7640270-4-5

No generative AI tools were used at any stage in the production of this work.

Content warning and cultural context

'Gildenhammer' is an Adult-aimed fantasy book that may contain material inappropriate for younger readers. **Please see the back page for details.**

While I have taken many liberties with the various cultures that inspired the world of this book, I have endeavoured to be respectful to all of them. This is not a historical fiction but it does use some real-world names for its own purposes. The various languages of this book are not meant to be accurate portrayals of real-world languages but instead possible evolutions in an essentially fantastical environment.

For my mother, who taught me to read;
And my father, who enabled me to write.

The Hours of Kaef're

(with approximate 'real world' equivalents)

Highmoon – Midnight to 1am
Lethalmoon – 1am to 2am
Lazymoon – 2am to 4am
Lowmoon – 4am to 6am
Bladesun – 6am to 8am
Morningsun – 8am to 10am
Nighsun – 10am to 11am
Highsun – 11am to 1pm
Aftersun – 1pm to 2pm
Lazysun – 2pm to 3pm
Eyesun – 3pm to 4pm
Fallingsun – 4pm to 5pm
Lowsun – 5pm to 6pm
Dyingsun – 6pm to 7.30pm
Awakenmoon – 7.30pm to 8pm
Risingmoon – 8pm to 9pm
Fullmoon – 9pm to 10pm
Eyemoon – 10pm to 11pm
Nighmoon – 11pm to Midnight

The Twelve Commandments

1. God is The Night. There is no God without The Night. Revere and fear The Night and Her Own.

2. Closest to God are Those Who Dwell in the Night. *Hearken unto Them, cower from Their wrath and exult in Their benevolence. Those Not of the Night are distanced from God and are not to be worshipped or honoured.*

3. The name of God is sacred. Do not invoke the Name of God and Of The Night for any purpose other than praise and worship.
4. Sleep at Night. Do not work while the Moon shines. You may work under the sun for the glory of God, but The Night is for rest, for God and Her Own. The Night is sacred.
5. Honour the way of your parents before yourself. Emulate their lives and perpetuate their beliefs for they are closer to Heaven and to God.
6. Do not kill without the Night's blessing. Life is Given by The Night and only The Night may take it away.
7. Propagate. It is your duty to create children who will serve God and The Night.
8. Do not reach for anything you cannot hold. Ambition is the seed of discontent.
9. Do not hold anything you cannot keep. Blessed are they who know their limits.
10. Do not lie or spread falsehoods to further your own station. The truth is sacred.
11. Do not ask questions if you don't know the answer. Curiosity is a sin beyond Salvation. Thought is the seed of rebellion. The Night provides all you need to know.
12. The word of the Night's Own is holy. They are closest to God and know Her Name and Will. Their command overrides all.

Prologue

The Rouge Eyrie
Risingmoon
6/882 A.R.

"You had to die first."

He looks at her across the room but the lack of reaction from the woman sitting on the bed makes clear she's already expecting his wall-leaning theatrics, his casually devastating deliverances.

"That's what I told myself the first time we 'met', and I couldn't find any reason to disagree. I can say 'I' now, but really it was us. Dog-Ears tried to explain something, but Char wouldn't listen. The third me, the one I accept as closest to who I'm supposed to be, only cared about one thing. Of the seven people in our way, the woman was the only one that might have seen us coming. Chaelle, ever the helpful guide, had said this group would be different, that we weren't dealing with just another handful of Night-bound locals acting on orders they didn't understand. She said: *So now the rivals are involved.* Only Char made the mistake of asking what she meant. The rest of me just did what I always do: we dealt with it. Could I trouble you for some water? It's been quite the run here."

She makes a face he chooses not to read, but obliges by shuffling over the rumpled sheets, reaching for a jug on a side table and pouring it into a cup. He takes it from her outstretched hand, resumes his place against the wall.

"Thank you, Sister. I know it's confusing, but you asked. So try to remember that if you want to see it how it looked to me, I'll have to explain it through the eyes I had then. It's only been a year or so since. Not as if I've changed that much. I, we. We…I've just learned to share with myself. And yes, I'm proud – you should have seen us when we first left Chūnko. Or worse, when I was just leaving Kaifeng. She was all that kept me alive, and naturally She was all that kept me in danger.

"Not that there was ever really much danger. Normally, people investigated what we'd done after we'd done it. Your group decided that 'aftermath' just wasn't soon enough for them. You weren't there to look at the corpses, to stare at each other and ask how this was possible. Didn't matter whether it was a cave, a castle, or just a cottage: those sent to assess the situation always had that same incredulous disposition. I doubt many of them had ever seen a dead Noble, let alone a live one. Kas'Daen Nobles are even more elusive than the ones back home, and I guess our actions weren't making things any easier for them. As far as we were concerned, it was nothing special. We'd just taken our show on the road, although She wouldn't tell me where that road went.

"Sometimes I made myself relive that last night just outside of Kaifeng, when my brothers and sisters-in-arms revealed themselves to be Night's Own and turned on me. I think. Dead is dead. If…re-enacting how I felt then allows me to make dead those who must be dead now, then I will. She helped, sometimes in person, but usually in Her lack of resistance when I sent Her to work. Maybe not sent. Followed. I was just holding the hilt, holding my breath, and holding on."

Her expression does change then, conveying well-deserved doubt at this implication of his role as anything other than the man who wielded the sword that cut her off from almost everyone she'd known that day.

He sees it, and responds by shifting the blame.

"Char declared that your heavy armour and well-worn weapons made you mercenaries. We watched from behind a tree as the party spread around the cottage, Morningsun's rays marking the steel, almost setting alight the golden fists on the cuirasses, sharpening the folds of seven uniformly violet capes. Violet, almost…orchid. No. Violet. More importantly: seven of them. I felt my fingers clutching the bark as I wondered what I'd done to attract this sort of attention. Village authorities, militia, the occasional stray Peddler – yes. I could accept these getting themselves involved after I'd done my job, but an entire group of warriors, before I'd even started? They were waiting for something terrible; I couldn't see their faces for the helms. Not even the resolute samurai of Tsukamoto wore that much gear outside of full-pitched battle. They were waiting for me.

"Seven of them in a rough semi-circle around the cottage's only entrance. A deformed hand with uninvited fingers, or clumsy with too many thumbs. The claw of some demon I'd yet to encounter and figure out how to slay. All we cared about was how to bring down the enemy, known or otherwise. It was right to care about only that. Char continued to dig his nails into the tree; Dog-Ears thought seven was higher than five and that five was the most we'd managed to kill at any one time so far, and even then probably just by luck. Not including Havens. What of Havens, coward? We hate it when Char calls Dog-Ears that, because we know who ran away from Kaifeng eight years ago, who couldn't bear to fight Hua-Shi and reclaim the sword. We know who Char begged to become after the reality of what I'd done battered down the walls of Her soft labyrinth. Dog-Ears is a constant reminder to Char: to become a real weapon, a bully needs to feel and understand what pain he is inflicting and choose to do it anyway, when it is necessary. When is it necessary? When you're razing a Haven to the ground? When it's kill or be killed? When you have seven well-armed geared-for-war foes in your way?

"Charan just watched as the two of them bickered with knuckles and tears.

"The warriors didn't say a word. Didn't fold their arms: that'd mean time wasted unfolding them to draw swords. Just stood there, seven sentinels guarding something we were sure they didn't understand. Wouldn't guard the damned beast if they did. Didn't matter to me. That much crap on, they'd be like statues in a garden. A Garden with a Rose. That's all I wanted. A single flower to cut down so that the weeds could flourish. The Peddlers were so wrong. She taught me that. We must cull this garden. Kaef're is the Garden. Singular illusions of beauty must not outshine the necessary masses. But what was that she said about how worthless mortals are? When we'd started, destroyed the House, ruined Happy's…oh, stop blubbering, you half-wit Dog-Ears. Not like you actually killed the old man. Any of them. Except in the village. Which one? My point exactly. Fine! Victim of circumstance, that's all we are. That's all they are, were. The Peddlers are not wrong. Some weeds give nourishment to the Wild Roses. We must remove them too, before they can do that, and make way for the rest, who will, slow as the tide, sure as the tide, move as one and tear at the Roses, despite the thorns. Thorn. Hua-Shi. Have I killed any Thorns since? Don't ask me that, She said. She said that a lot. And she said this a lot, too: wait.

"We waited. Veteran though the company may have been, we had staked out Noble dwellings for days, weeks, until she said it was time to let Char's philosophy rule and guide. Do unto others before, her way of putting it. We no longer had to wait. It only took an hour before the fist-clad warriors started to get restless. Must have been sweltering in all that metal; didn't see any of them working hydrotheurgy to alleviate the discomfort. Shame. Always enjoy taking out the water-wielders before the others. Can't just burn them. Have to get personal. Should do that anyway. No telling what countermeasures these unknown enemies might have against pyroticism.

"They looked at each other, or at least turned their poor metal-covered faces around, and I imagined the questions they might have whispered. What are we facing? Will we walk away from it? Am I about to discover what they mean when they call some enemies 'widow-makers'? Do my children know that the last goodbye is always possibly the *last* goodbye? Are we really just standing here like idiots waiting to be slaughtered by someone who has already proven himself capable of the impossible? Can we maybe just sneak off at some point to relieve ourselves? Are those eggs I had for breakfast really to blame for the churning in my guts?

"I snickered into the homely depths of the hood, as I always do when Charan has the final say. As I always do.

"That's when the woman noticed me. Yes, you were all wearing ridiculously overwrought armour, head to toe like lurching coffins, but one of you clearly wasn't thinking about 'his' wife. Her helm barely moved, but I knew. She'd heard me and she shouldn't have. None of the elemental Talents I'd dealt with so far gave people augmented hearing or anything like that, not even with Halves. Then again, most people are raised to believe that their Talent is good for nothing more than making a little puddle or shaping clay pots. Most people don't stand around in full plate in summer heat waiting to pass out. So if one of them heard my little laugh, it was safe to assume, immediately, that She was right, and this group was unlike most people.

"And because there was contact now, the woman had to die first.

"Dog-Ears winced as she broke rank, not to approach us but to confer with the one of the others, the leader perhaps. Their attention turned inwards and I moved. As usual, I had no idea which way I'd chosen until well into the action. Char had chomped through his bit and saw himself weave between the sluggish, clumsy knights, slicing off limbs and heads and playing kickball with whatever was left. Dog-Ears watched from a safe distance from behind almost-closed hands, almost-closed eyes. And while the two of them stuck to routine, I somehow shifted myself from behind that tree to another, this one to the side of the clearing and the cottage. Like most of the facades used to hide a lair, the cottage didn't have a back entrance, so there was no use in angling for that. I wasn't sure I was still that bent on getting in anymore. The woman had heard me, and she wasn't supposed to be able to do that. If she died first, I wouldn't be able to learn how.

"Her advance to where I had been didn't faze the others. It was, at best, tentative – she didn't draw her sword, although one hand rested on the handle of the other weapon at her right. Dog-Ears whispered about a dream, but by now Char has seen it all before. Chained whips, kusarigama, maces, morning stars, cudgels…flails. Charan almost managed a half-intrigued 'huh' but we remembered what made us move in the first place. Even tried to breathe softer, shallower. What I did next depended entirely on what she did next. I think that can be said of anything in my life; the sad thing is I'd come to terms with it.

"The woman hesitated, glanced back at her comrades, and then took one more step away from them. That was it. I couldn't sever this malformed hand at the wrist, but with the thumb too far away, it wouldn't be able to grasp anything in time. I blinked, assessed the usual details (no need to call it anything anymore, let alone something as pompous as 'The Window') and was already pulling Oni-Goroshi from between the first one's plate armour by the time I'd realised I'd blinked. I suppose the element of surprise can't get much purer than when you surprise even yourself.

"Chaelle had said they'd be different, but the only way that seemed to work was they moved slower than scared peasants or instinctual Elementalists. The last one had his sword half-drawn when I did something to his body that left it disassembled on the ground."

She has listened to all of this without interruption, but now asks her question after his dispassionate, grisly description.

"…Of course I don't know their names, Sister. I didn't even see their faces. You know I'm not proud of it, but I was proud to be that efficient. She pointed and I went. I can't make reparations or bring them back. This is the last thing I want to tell you; it's probably the last thing you want to hear from me. The day I killed your brethren, the day I decided you had to die first. I can say 'sorry' if it will help you, but you didn't weep then and I don't think you will now. We are simply too aware of our differences to them. But you remember their names, their faces. Whisper those names, pray for them if you will. If everyone and everything we know is right, they've gone somewhere better anyway. I wish I didn't have to use 'if', but it was often my only defence against her. I no longer had the energy or will to make it a question. She said: 'when'; I think: 'if'.

"When I blinked once more, I knew it was done. I was yet again the stark stem surrounded by baleful petals: deflowered, desecrated. Detached, I looked at the entrance of the cottage, conscious of the sudden weight of the sword. It's always at its worst before I wipe any slivers of flesh away, as if even a tiny remnant carries all the guilt of the deed. Or something – typical Chaelle babble: moral repercussions manifest; the greatest punishment is always self-administered. Don't know how the bitch could say that and expect me to believe it – not after what she'd done to me. Still, my sword does get heavier afterwards. I try to hide it from Chaelle, that she's right. But only a dream-memory could convince me where a hundred sermons failed. Pumpkin. I'm still doing this for you. My burden, and you'll never know it."

She moves to touch the pendant around her neck at that name; he is staring at the floor and doesn't see this. There is no pause in his narration.

"As I knelt to use one of those almost gaudy, somewhat gory capes to clean the sword, blood slid from her subtle little smile, easing the drag further. She was almost light enough to sheathe when I remembered you. Not remembered you, but you know. That you were there. If there's one weakness to what Chaelle made me (even if there're many, which is more likely), it's that I get lost in the moment, because one blink makes any moment vast and significant. And when I'd blinked before, you were nothing more than a hesitant blur in the corner of my eye. But now you were a lot more than that.

"Do you know what saved your life?"

Now he looks up, but she is looking down. Her answer is half-hearted, a verbal gesture of impatience not to hear more, but for it to end.

"What? No. You absolutely did not 'surprise' me. I saw your shadow, for Eph's sake. Good idea, trying to take me while I was kneeling with my back turned. Not a good idea, screaming and charging at me with the sun at *your* back. You howled, a hollow shriek tearing at the inside of that silly helmet."

She mumbles a few words, but otherwise doesn't interrupt.

"That silly helmet that saved your life. After you'd missed, and I was in the corner of your eye, Char saw the gap between your head and shoulders; Dog-Ears said to him, 'it's her neck, she's sticking it out for you', maybe forgetting that the self-styled Scourge of Kaifeng (and so many other places now, Char wants to add) doesn't exactly do figures of speech. Practical as ever, Charan allowed Oni-Goroshi to hum towards some point past your neck, not much caring what was in the way. Your flail was stuck in the ground, and I don't imagine that helm gave you much room to see us coming. If you had, maybe you'd have raised your left arm by reflex, and my desire to destroy a hand would have been anything but metaphorical. Or if you'd ducked, I wouldn't have seen it. Your blindness to me saved you.

"The woman didn't have to die, but now she would, and we'd never find out how she heard us. Maybe Chaelle could teach us.

"Dog-Ears wanted to close his eyes again but Char said, oh look, what a pretty pendant. Charan gagged on a guttural scream and, in rare lucidity, appealed to Dog-Ears to do what he never could. But poor, dumb Dog-Ears of Swimming Carp was already remembering an arm etched with deliberate cuts, describing the horror of his not-dreams in shallow, sharp red. He chanted her name, that first sacrifice who preached of beads and destiny: Plumptreat-plumptreat-plumptreat, and tried to ignore Charan who corrected him sarcastically: Chaelle-chaelle-chaelle. No, no it wasn't, and this isn't, so it has to stop, she must not take this one, not this time – all the while, Dog-Ears tried to wrench the too-fast, too-easy sword back, up, away. Anything that wouldn't give the Goddess what She wanted. Char-the-Scourge was sedated by Char-the-thief, who wanted to look at the pretty-shiny more, a lot more, but didn't really want to kill to get it. All three of me needed to save this woman's life from everything I'd been created to do.

"Oni-Goroshi has tested the mortality of my enemies, my friends, my teachers and complete strangers. And because She is the Goddess of Swords, Hers is not a test designed to be passed. You can only delay your failure by surviving a little longer. But Dog-Ears, in his stupid, brave way, decided that he was going to help you cheat. He demanded that Her edge turn and rise, and although we knew there'd be retribution for our disobedience later, She indulged us. What should have been your death turned into a ringing concussion as the sword smacked into the side of your helm. Good thing I only add Fire to Her bite when I know I'm facing at least a Half.

"And who'd presume to find one among the Tantamonian Brethren?

"Just before you fell away from me, I grabbed the pendant, and your staggering combined with my grip snapped the chain and made it mine. Not that it wasn't mine before that. You collapsed in what I suppose was a helpless heap. I stared down at the circle in my right hand, and had lowered my left before I even noticed it trembling, before I heard the steel rattle. I looked at my sword's guard, then back at the medallion. For the first time in my life, I held the Cross and the Moon in both hands.

"I almost took a step towards whoever you were, but of course she wouldn't allow that.

"'Why are you just standing there, Half? Cat got your balls?' As usual, I wasn't immediately sure if it were Vachaelle, Oni-Goroshi or just me, using her voice to pull myself back into line. But then I felt her touch my back, curl around me and stand on her tippy-toes to peck me on the shadow of my right cheek. She never needed to say 'job well done' or 'this is why I love you'. I never wanted her to say it, either. She moved to take hold of my right hand and I pulled it away, shoving it under the untold folds of my tell-tale cloak.

"'I'm not finished.' I took that step, but towards the cottage, not you.

"She kept up – no, she was waiting there when my feet stopped.

"'What do you have in your hand, Charan?'

"'Nothing. I am not finished.' As though that were excuse enough.

"'Take one more step and I will turn your blood to water.' As though that were threat enough.

"But I stopped. Didn't turn around. Was done with that years ago.

"'That is better. Now show me what you had in your hand.'

"It's obvious now – she knew. All I could think about then, however, was what happened to those who deny her. And she'd indulged me more than she had or would anyone else. That was her love for me.

"I pulled the pendant out and looked down at it again. The crescent was golden, the cross black. Opposite of mine. And unlike the tsuba of Oni-Goroshi, the rest of the moon was a solid grey circle. Fingers occasionally unfortunate in their sensitivity felt irregularities about the back of the small disc. I turned it over.

"'Show me.' Her, in Jaydemyrian.

"'Pumpkin'.' Me, in Ziegerian-Common. I almost choked at what I saw next. "CJ.""

"'What?' Chaelle recoiled from me. I felt myself starting to fall, and of course she wasn't there to catch me. Not this time, not ever again. 'What the fu—…what downright nonsense is that you are on about?'

"All I could do was stare at that name, at the initials written in crude Ziegerian. At the simplified crossed-moon that formed the C. The very symbol I now used as my signature, tagging the Night's Own corpses with audacity and mocking.

"It was like seeing my reflection in the water from under the surface.

"'Are you alright, Charan?' Wrong tone, Nightsong. This wasn't about Lily at all.

"'I have to know.' I kept mumbling to myself I as let the damned icon fall from my right hand, even as I raised its familiar twin in my left. Pendant down, sword up. Chaelle bent to retrieve it; I strode towards the unmoving enigma, she who had heard me where no other could, she who wore something no one should. Dog-Ears scanned her body, looking for even a hint of what he remembered from the dream, where she had told him that no excuses were needed. Char, hurled back into a very different dream, sought braids of blonde but saw nothing. Charan allowed them this moment before sinking to his knees to remove her helm.

"'…And as you know, I didn't actually get to do it. You came to with your helm still on and your pendant in your hand? All because of her. I said the helm saved your life, and it's true in many ways; all good truths work like that.

"'Stop, Dog-Ears.' She was right behind me, gripping my right shoulder with Miss Master's severity. Dog-Ears stopped. Dog-Ears winced. Dog-Ears pissed me off. But I'd given him control to stop the sword, and he can be surprisingly stubborn once he has the reins. 'You must not see who she is.'

"'But why?' I lent Dog-Ears a little of my courage. He still almost stuttered. 'I have to know…'

"'You already know.' She sighed and disengaged her talons. 'It is not yet time to see her face.'

"'WHY?' Dog-Ears was using the borrowed bravado like an alcoholic upending an empty bowl of wine. 'If it's her, then… maybe this is just a dream and it will end and I'll finally wake up and none of this—'

"'Oh. Oh…it is not her, you silly boy.' She laughed her brittle attempt at relief. 'She was not real. That was just a dream.'

"'But the word, the initials…'

"'I said, it is not yet time.'

"She leaned over my shoulder and whisper-sang something, snatches of a tune I'd heard either side of falling asleep. And then I was in a room at an inn, telling her excitedly about how the job went, and how her warnings of a 'different' group were all piss and wind. And she was very happy with me.

"I didn't think about you again for what, a whole year, more or less. It was only after Mother kicked down all the doors in my head she herself had locked (and gave Vachaelle the key, for God-knows-what reason) that I even remembered that encounter. After we'd fended the Kas'Daen assault, little more than a scouting party as you know, I went to Mother and asked. But she didn't have to tell me. All she said was that I didn't have to ask for permission. That she wasn't the same as 'certain others'. I was free to go. To do as I please. As I must. Some freedom.

"And by then, you'd remembered too, I suppose. Did you hear me say my name, almost nine years ago? Mother said that she did, and Mentor Arius as well. Of course no one knew what it meant, especially not me and I'd been the one to say it. More than just The Night knew my name after that."

She nods by way of answer.

"….So I found you, on schedule, although I don't know whose. Not mine. I gave myself a year to track you down, but once I left the tower, I knew the right direction. South-west. And the more I travelled that way, the more I knew not just where I was going but *where I intended to go*. Chaelle had called it her home, as safe a place in Kaef're as any, which meant it had ties to us. To Jaydemyr. The path straightened between the roads and highways, until I was no longer taking the long way around as quickly as possible. And then last night, I saw the impossible: our name flying over the walls of that place. This place. This bastion of what was and would yet be."

She shrugs off this little speech.

"I'm done, I think. I've talked of our last, our first, meeting, since you asked. Now it's time for you to talk my ear off. Tell me how you came to be there, and here. Tell me all you can. Just remember: I'm not like either of them, no Dreamwarper or Mindsinger, or maybe I have those the wrong way around…Either way, I can't play tricks with your head and memories, Sister. I can only ask, and you can answer. I know a little about how our trips down someone else's memory lane works, and that if you can disentangle what was imposed from what we used of our real memories to fill the gaps, there's a lot to be learned even from fake lives. Real lessons. It doesn't have to be all in one session. Take it from me: not advised. We'll have time on the long road back north to Vizstrahtza…but your story has to start somewhere—"

"No." Her glare presages the amendment of terms, and he can do nothing but listen by his own request for her testimony. "I am not a character and my life isn't a story. Not yours, and certainly not hers. If you want neat and clean, Brother, you've come a long way to be disappointed. And you will be disappointed if you expect anything but my truth. In truth, little about my life has been satisfying or just. People I thought of as significantly other simply came and went, while others I barely noticed may yet shape the course of future history. Events that seem pivotal now were little more than noise at the time. They will not be convenient markers on this journey. The pace will be uneven, but it must be kept nonetheless. You want meaning, Brother? Meaning is yours to find in the reading, not for me to deliver in the telling. Maybe in a retelling, but that's not what you requested. Retelling is *her* business, her endless need to revise. Manipulate. Refine. Corrupt. Control. *Eph that.*"

Sariana Jaydemyr rises from the bed and begins to gather what little she'll need on the road home.

"So this will be messy." She hefts the odd weapon about which he spoke so oddly. For months, it has rested beside a gauntlet atop beige and grey travelling clothes within one chest of many in this converted storeroom. As with her, its time of rest is done. "But it will be honest. If you want my story, I am sure she can tell you many, all of them beautiful bullshit. What you'll get from me, as best I can do, is the one thing she can't tell you about me. What it feels like to be on the edge of everyone else's lives. Yours, especially." She straightens, wearing now that gauntlet, bearing now that weapon whose name she did not choose but was still hers to give. "The edge, Brother. Neither inside nor outside, which can be made an inside of its own. Her story for me wasn't even about me, but 'who I could be'. Her song. Maybe she never really sang my song. Certainly, she never did. Too busy with yours, I'd say. But if she did anything important with me, it was to convince me otherwise. To make me believe the song was about me, and it was really the first thing I remember believing. So let's start there. Not a where, but a when."

She waves at the door with her gauntleted hand, the other still testing the familiarity of the flail's grip. "I'd say after you, but that's a given now, isn't it?"

But before he can say a thing, she begins her defiance, and goes first, at last.

40 days until the revelation

I. Sarah-Jade Falkenstrom

4/868 A.R.

Chapter 1: What Mother Sang About

When it happened, the baby girl who made it all possible suddenly stopped crying. In a village not an hour away from Teristra, the capital of Teriss-Luniir, the child of a famous singer no longer wailed for her absent mother. Her father, tired from another day in the workshop and another night dealing with the baby's demands, caressed her still-soft forehead as she lay silent in her crib. She'll have been too young to remember the weathered feel of his skilled, gnarled fingers. Being told, years later, what he did for a living won't help make the memories any more real. She'll also be told why her mother was never home, and in much more detail.

Like everything else in her mother's world, the newborn girl soon lost importance other than as an idea for the next crowd-pleaser. But that's not what the mother told the little girl, when the child finally learned how to ask, when it was too late for any answer to matter. Instead she told her daughter how fast it all went, how it seemed like just yesterday. Now crawling, now walking, now talking, now stop asking questions! The mother's delight at her girl's growth was like lightning, but she was always far more interested in the rain. All that mattered was that her Great Work, the song, gained new verses as the girl grew.

But the girl didn't know that she didn't matter, and entered childhood much the same way as other children: knowing she was the centre of her world, not knowing how small it was. It was then that she asked her mother, because she couldn't ask anyone else. When was I born? What was it like? Why do you have to do my ears? Where's Daddy?

How did the song begin?

And Mother, on the few nights she had time for me, would assume a wistful expression a child mistakes for love, an adult for thoughtfulness. At such times, I was her only audience, and she indulged me by indulging herself. Ignorant to this and almost everything else, I just listened as she told me, although I didn't understand much at first. Like everyone else, I heard her song without really thinking about the words. And after I did, I started to add my own lines, shared with her only in the fury of argument and spite. She wasn't there for me, not back then. Not for Father either. That selfish bitch. Singing, dancing, whoring. Night after night. Eph 'n' Shyn, I'm sorry, Brother. That's…that's not what she told me. Well, true. She sang. But it's only the words that I can relate; you'll just have to imagine the music that accompanies them. Imagine, then. Close your eyes and—

Imagine a great hall, a dense expanse of flagstone floors, drunken fists pounding wooden tables, and balconies running the walls, tiers upon tiers, each crammed with sweat, laughter and beer. From the middle of the ground floor, a single fire spread its light and heat; a ring of benches huddled around the pit, and not one was unoccupied. Smoke obeyed an occasional wave of a lazy hand; the fire, although tempted to flare into a blaze, cowered within the stony circle. Only the gust from the main doors opening and closing affected the flames.

It might have been snowing outside; new arrivals stamped their feet and shook the cold from their shoulders. Some but not all deposited the tools of their trade at the counter near the entrance; all were stopped for a moment by the amiable but insistent giant of a man not exactly guarding the entrance. After being cleared by a beaming nod of the stocky man's bald head, newcomers headed down the few steps from the landing into the main room proper. The remains of their frosty breath dissipated like doubt in the smiling face of an old comrade. Now they were part of the everything that never stopped.

A serving girl with curly, bouncy red hair and fulsome bodice threaded her way between patrons and chairs; she was saucy and sassy but never salacious. Now and then she got a pat on her passing rump, but the rules of this Haven were the same as any other, and enforced more strictly than in most others: the Watch were welcome here when off-duty, and even then they were the Watch. Despite being maybe Teristra's largest public house, the Haven was unusually untroubled; all who entered were there for civil, congenial things. There were other places in the city for other desires, places the Watch were far less likely to watch. Citizens of Teristra came here for food, drink, company. Distractions all, but none rivalled the promise of hearing Chantal sing.

Whether they knew it or not, they were there to hear someone take the stage, take that one deep, infinitely potent breath and then fill it with song, taking them away.

To fall under Chantal's spell once again, sometimes for the first time.

For years, a slight young woman with simple blonde hair in a plain white dress had been taking her place on that stage at the front of the Haven's main room. Maybe. Maybe it was the back. She may or may not have carried an instrument, but if so, it was a comfortable, worn thing, a lute or maybe a lyre, looking only slightly out-of-tune, only a little weary. If not, the audience noted the same qualities about the woman, and they knew her songs had aged her, that while her body might have looked innocent, her voice was rich with experience. There was a small stool upon which she arranged herself, regarding the revellers around and above her 'til they recognised her poise; she would remain seated only until the audience realised she was seated. Surging beats of lyrical wings soon returned her to inspired heights, but first the air had to be cleared. She sat there, inhaling the staleness of the hour, exhaling the immortality of the moment. She waited with the certainty of a historian, a prophet, a visionary. Hers was the patience for the inevitable.

The hush began with those who knew the ritual and reduced their own banter to incomplete mumbles. A caught glance here; a frigid flicker of lashes there. The louder people, less attuned to the gradual convergence of attention on the stage, found themselves burping at turned heads and chuckling alone. The woman might have inclined her own head, not so much curious as amused. She knew that none of them, not even the most blustery of boors, would have done as she had done and will do again. With a single suppressed sigh, she declared every man in the establishment a craven beast, announced herself as the maiden who shall lay with the beasts, or at least lull them back to sleep. And she was right. Hers was the generosity for the implacable.

When she could hear her own breathing, the woman gave her name.

"I am Chantal." *The* Chantal. Even the regulars thought of her that way, although in such a busy city there were always new faces upon which her songs could create a hearty flush or streak effortless tears. What few women occupied the Haven any given night usually reacted poorly to the focus, rolling their eyes or slumping back in resignation.

None of the *other* performers received such reverence, so why should this one? Look at her, their scornful glances wanted to say, a slip of a thing timid as a rabbit; you can almost see her shivering in fright. She isn't wearing finery, hasn't even gone to the effort to rouge her cheeks – well, her shameful blush is enough there. And of the few ladies present, maybe one or two reserved their disdain for the others, because they knew. They had heard the songs. This was Chantal. Hers was the serenity for the irascible.

Some nights she started by talking, revealing just enough of herself to set the audience at ease. Tonight will not be a gruesome, bawdy, rollicking mess of repetitive rhyme and catchy chorus, but she didn't say that. Chantal would look at the carpenters, the cobblers, the dock workers and the hunters, and tell them about a long-forgotten kingdom made of shining stones and full of happy, hard-working men and women, about a king who loves his subjects so much he moves among them in disguise and helps those who have given themselves selflessly to crown and country. And then she sang about a carpenter, or a cobbler, or a dock worker, or a hunter who received such secret blessing and fortune. And by the end of her first song, someone in the audience was ready to go home, and left without a word, as though both driven and drawn. Chantal's song had renewed whatever spark of enthusiasm for life itself that the bustling, cloying trade capital of Teriss-Luniir could often sap. And for everyone remaining, Chantal always had one more song. She could sing them into the dawn, but never did. The next night, there was always at least one returning member of the audience, someone who thought it was just because they liked her music, or maybe her face, but she knew. This person had seen others receive that glow, but couldn't put it into words. All they could do was listen and hope.

But one night, not long after I was born, a slight young woman with simple blonde hair in a plain white dress does not take the stage in Teristra's largest Haven, just as she hasn't for the past six months. Outside, the moon will be full and round; people do not come and go. The doorman looks sullen but alert, waiting for desperate knuckles to rap against unyielding wood; the lantern on his counter is cold and dead. Saucy-Sassy-but-never-Salacious is on healing duty, and no one pats her rump this night. The balconies are quiet and the firepit crackles low and cautious. The Havenkeeper, a portly man with cheeks good for both grinning and glowering, holds back a constant sigh; it is barely Eyemoon, so reveals a glance at the notched candle melting in its saucer on a shelf behind him. He is polishing the same glass he's been polishing most of the afternoon, and trying not to look at the door. Havens outside the city keep their entrances open, always, but here in the civilised heart of Teriss-Luniir, the concept of 'Haven' has dwindled and actual refugees from the Hunt are almost just a memory. It isn't even called a Haven anymore by most of the locals, who have named it for another function, this one neither archaic nor official: The All-Trades Inn.

Other than the woman in a dull ruby dress, rumpled and wrinkled with rivulets of radiance, the bar is bare. Behind her slumped back, she can hear only sporadic half-sentences. Grunts. Sighs. Verbal shrugs. She can feel the fire prickling warmth against her back, but it's hardly what's keeping the chills at bay this evening. You could say she's nursing that glass of wine but I think it's safe to say it's the other way around.

"Do you know what might be good?" Jerich grinds his cloth into a glass. She doesn't look up from her own glass, which is half-empty and possibly has been for a very long time. He's asked this before and when she doesn't answer, he says the same damn thing. "A bit of a song. Cheer things up. Just because it's quiet doesn't mean it has to be…y'know, quiet. Isn't that why you're back?"

But it is more than her charming voice that makes her 'The' Chantal. Her smile is never simple, and people always say too much when she lets it out to play.

"Well, isn't it?"

She only stares up at him through scraggly hair, lips wolfish and never far from the glass's rim.

"You couldn't stay home even tonight. Knew it'd be an off-night, didn't you? I know I said you had open tap as long as you worked here, but…look, why won't you accept just a little pay, Chant?" Jerich tries not to sound smug, but it's difficult to remain humble when you think you're helping someone out of their spiral. "Now there's the baby to think about. And carpenters aren't exactly paid like lords. And you *can* draw the biggest crowds in the city—"

"Shut your fucking mouth." Ladies and gentlemen, I give you *The* Chantal. "Was never about the money. Just about the song. And how much of that do you think I can do now? My gut's a big empty bag and my boobs hurt night in, night out. And yeah. I *have* brought the crowds in for you, Havenkeeper, and all I ask is a night or two to regain my rhythm, get back into the feel of it. Tell me, something, Havenkeeper

Jerich." She narrows her eyes around a wicked thought. "How's business been for the past six months or so?"

"…Fair enough." Jerich refills her glass.

Outside, the wind gathers strength and rattles the few windows visible from the great hall of the All-Trades. One of the less-subtle distinctions of the place is that it keeps its own time, ruled only by the ebb and flow of custom. Not even the small gap in the ceiling, five stories directly above the firepit, easily reveals whether it's day or night out there. Despite that, Chantal sings only at night.

Sang.

"Thank you." She takes a slow swallow of the wine, sniffs and turns her bleary eyes downward again. It's almost contrite. "I'll be at it again before long. I promise. It's just so…hard to think about anything."

"Why don't you just go home and be with your family? For Eph's bloody sake, Chant…hmph, forgive my language."

"Forgiven, Jerich." The devout and pious Chantal, on behalf of Her Most Holy. "You're worried the Trades might be losing its local celebrity. Pffft. No need to blaspheme for that. The thing is out now. God knows I was done with it well before that. Would that I had the strength to be done with it now…Great, now I'm the one spouting sacrilege. Like I said, I'll be back in form soon enough." She drains the glass to half-way again.

" 'The thing.' "

Chantal draws a breath, sniffling again. "Has a name, right? Of course she does."

The main doors shudder and before anyone has time to look, the deep boom of impact awakens the Haven and its keepers. The very polished glass slides from Jerich's hands and no one notices. The doorman grabs his lantern and it flares in response. Thus armed, he leaves his post. Jerich catches Saucy-Sassy's eye, and she storms down the stairs, dodging furniture and the few stunned customers without so much as looking away from the door.

"It's a good name too." Chantal breathes this onto her drink.

Doorman and healer heave the great wooden doors open and the chill rushes in, blasting both of them back. Veterans, they maintain their footing and look down at the body that has come in with the cold, then back at the doors. The doorman steps forwards, holding the lantern before him. He waves it left, then right, then left again, but the flame doesn't yield. This is where he remains as Saucy-Sassy exerts a strength reserved just for this occasion and drags the inert man away from the door. One last glance and the Doorman is satisfied. He closes the doors with his free hand and looks down at what must be done.

Saucy-Sassy is kneeling beside the body, touching it with a care and attention many of her patrons would give almost anything to receive. This person has, unfortunately, paid a higher price than she'd ask of anyone. Her expression, unlike her fiery hair, waxes ashen as the futility of her efforts becomes clear.

"Drained?" The Havenkeeper looks across the room.

"Almost." Chantal upends her drink. "Now it is."

"Not you!"

"Drained." Saucy-Sassy drags her feet back towards the stairs and her less sacred duties. "At least he's at peace now."

"*Vahm En.*" Chantal thumps her empty glass on the wooden bar a few times. "*I'm* not dead yet, so keep 'em coming eh?"

The Doorman lumbers into a side room, the body slung over his shoulder like a slab of meat wrapped in rags. The clothing of the Hunted is tattered, mismatched. Only the poorest, loneliest Teristrans would be out there this night.

Jerich pours Chantal another drink, watching the scene play out as it has before but not so recently.

"Stop, Jerich. It's full! You're going to spill it—"

Jerich's instincts pull his hand before the drink can overflow. Chantal is forced to lean over the rim and lap at the wine before she can lift the glass. I wish I could have seen that.

The Doorman closes the side room off and returns to his post after retrieving the lantern, which of course flickers to life the moment his living hand touches it, and flickers away the moment he places it on the counter. Saucy-Sassy stays out of sight, busy somewhere above and far from eager to return to the dreariness blanketing the ground floor.

"Shit. Look at you lot." Chantal licks her lips as the liquid's level lowers. "The Haven's finally doing its job and you're all shocked and shaken. Better than the alternative, I say."

"You're not here to *say* things, Chantal." That's not really what Jerich wants to say. Or even do. He really wants to say, 'you're not here to drink yourself to death.' He really wants to grab her and shake her. He really should have.

"I even gave her a wonderful name." The songstress ignores him. "Eyes like...I don't know. Green. Peas. Spinach. Moss. Snot. You couldn't call them Jade, but I did."

"It is a beautiful name." After a brief pause, he adds, "The Adventures of Princess Jade. That could work."

"Adventure? All she does is cry, shit and cry some more. You want me sing about *that?*"

"Don't think about what she is. Sing about what she could be."

And I think it was just like the Doorman's lantern. The moment something living and warm touches it, it too becomes warm and living. Before the baby, Mother was vivacious, energetic, frenetic. But it was a hollow, inflated sense of being, held afloat only by the collective life of those she could captivate. With me within her, Chantal's too-selfish heart swelled to painful capacity as it tried to keep up with her too-fertile womb. She could no longer perform but she didn't need to: her Great Work was about to be realised. Then I was without her, and she was without me. And the realisation left Mother cold, dead, flat. Not even her professional tendency to exaggerate could pretend this fatty little frog, with its head the shape of a bruised melon and its fingers chubby and clumsy, was the gift from God for which she'd waddled, vomited and yet still prayed. There was no song powerful enough to make me anything more than what I was.

And of course, there was the matter of my ears.

"Because she could be anything." Jerich scoops the last of the shattered glass into a pan. "If you let her be."

Chantal knew the fat would eventually be filled or fall away; the fingers would lengthen and learn. But there was no explanation for those monstrous ears. Daddy couldn't even accuse her of the obvious, because everyone knows that any woman foolish enough to lie with a Fey dies about nine months later. My parents didn't consult any priests, and kept the nature of me naturally out of sight, if not out of mind. Daddy called me a miracle and said that even if the child wasn't his or even hers, at least everyone was alright. This only made Mother angrier, but even she didn't want to make a fight of it. She just wanted to get back to life as usual. Unfortunately I had other ideas, and my rejecting her suckle was all the encouragement she needed to drown it all out, night after night. Inside her or out, seems all I could do was make her throw up in the morning.

"Think about those who aren't as fortunate as you." Jerich, for all his wisdom, pushes too hard and my mother, likely biting back snidery about 'fortune', empties her glass but places her hand over the rim. Jerich hasn't reached for the bottle anyway. "Think about—"

And whatever else he has to say, she doesn't hear it and won't remember it. Chantal just slinks from her stool and steers herself towards a door deeper into the Haven. It's far from her first trip to the waterroom, but this time it's not to be sick; if anything, her squatting over the scented hole is exactly the opposite.

That's how epiphanies work. Just like peeing. You can drink water, beer, wine, even milk, but what comes out is always the same golden stream. And only you know when it's ready to come, when the process of transformation is done and it's time to release. Pressing, urging, demanding. Also, best to do it in private, because even a trickle of relief can turn into a gush of embarrassment. Even though everyone does it; you die if you don't. But no one does it quite the same as anyone else. I've seen her scribbling frantically, the final step in her mystical, forbidding art. She never looks so vulnerable, so open to everything as when she's bringing it all together and letting it all out for the first time.

And by the time Chantal's finished, when the faint odour of urine stings her nose, that door is almost ready to be opened. She stands, steps away and listens to the silence of the hole as it works its magic. You can't drink Holewater, not even from the really expensive, private stalls of the All-Trades, but it's definitely not piss anymore. Even that banal fact feeds into Chantal's current state and will later emerge as an image worthy of poetry…or perhaps even song.

She exits the waterroom with the same dazed, entranced expression so common to her audience. She's too dazed and entranced to enjoy what this means, but she's enjoying being dazed and entranced.

"Feel better?" Jerich lets the words play themselves into whatever shape she needs to hear.

"I will." Chantal retrieves her satchel from under the stool. She holds onto the bar with her left hand after straightening.

"What are you doing? You can't go home now." The Havenkeeper almost leans into the last word.

"I'm going to need water, Jerich." Chantal regards him, and then looks away at a table in the shadows under the multi-tiered stairway. "Water and bread. And that's all."

He knows not to say anything, to do nothing more than nod at her back as the faded songbird seeks a new perch. You can run a lamp on alcohol if you have to, and you can make alcohol from all sorts of things through fermentation. And Chantal is nothing if not a master of fermenting things. But to really keep a fire burning, you have to dig deeper, tap some heavy, primal oil thick with dormant darkness. You can't just boil a few potatoes and use a few tricks when you want to feed the sober, frenzied flame that both schemes and dreams. It demands sacrifice, just like the nurturing Night Herself, hungry and holy. So when Chantal takes her leave, when she takes only bread and water, what she's really doing is taking herself apart, apart from everyone, and reconstructing all the unrelated ideas, notions and whims of the world, and she's using the only glue that suffices. She might as well be writing each verse with her blood, her spittle, her piss, coating her nails with all the precious ink her body can spare and tear into the paper her reckless, helpless release.

Saucy-Sassy keeps the bread and water coming; Jerich keeps to himself; the Doorman keeps his eye on the main doors. All three pay no real attention to Chantal, now that she's not drinking or feeling sorry for herself or exploding her vitriol in someone's face. Truth is, she's not really there anymore, which is why no one notices when she finally leaves.

Against all evidence and fact, against everything she told me, let me tell you: *that* was the night I was born.

Mother stayed out until just after dawn. As I said earlier, Daddy was exhausted from both work and having to take care of me. I was due to feed, and the moment she stepped in the door, I stopped crying. On some whim no one will understand, she took the milk from Daddy right as he was about to dribble some into my mouth. She even kissed him, licked the milk from his now-speckled beard and drank the bowl herself. She just smiled at him, tired but full, wordless but complete. As though this all made sense, he left for work and I finally accepted Mother as my cow, accepted it as readily as Daddy accepted her absences and arrivals, her movement in and out of our world.

Chantal was not seen at the All-Trades for three months. Maybe her audience wondered, but the truth was probably too simple and nice for them: she was at home. Her husband went to work. They cooked together. Slept together. All three of us. For a tiny while, it seemed as though Chantal had been rewarded for her decision to come home, to stay home. To choose home.

But if it ended there, there'd be no use in me telling you. This is what she told me: once she understood who I really was, it was time to tell everyone else. That respite was hers to savour, but it was never more than a pause and a preparation. It was a held breath. And when Chantal let it go, she wouldn't just tell. She would share. She would teach.

She would sing.

One night, a woman who was once slight but now carries a domestic heartiness takes the stage in the All-Trades Inn. She wears white, red and black: dress, sash and shawl. Her hair is highlighted with blonde, rich with hazel and wispy with grey. She has tied most of it back in a practical tail, but also braided part of the fringe, which seems almost at war with the widow's peak. Her eyes under dark brows do not land on any other pair belonging to those who have noticed her presence; in fact, her gaze doesn't seem to rest anywhere at all, other than in itself. Attention upon her rises like a seamless scale, building into a furore, where before it was a decrescendo of respect and awe. Whispers of who-is-that precede gasps, themselves just intakes of necessary breath to carry the cries of her name. Tonight, as the crowd realises just what it has been missing, she will not have to tell them who she is…but she does anyway.

"Hi, folks." The timeless she stands in front of her stool, in front of her audience, in front of everything. "I'm Chantal."

She smiles at the cheering, somewhere between the loved triangle of humility, acknowledgment, and impatience. She moves her hands from perching upon the memory of a motherly swell to bring her fingers together, to her lips, as though she's holding back the tears. No one would imagine it's part of the act, least of all she. The chorus of clapping and cascading calls quietens at this gesture. The women in the audience aren't holding back *their* tears: look at that, she's human after all. The mothers, maidens and even the oldest there admit it to themselves. Chantal has become a real woman; but she's so pretty still; oh, but she's seen it all. She's one of us now.

"Well, as you can see, things are a bit different since the last time we saw each other…but I hope that what I sing for you tonight will share some of the wonder, joy and pain of being the maker of a miracle, as all mothers are."

Of course the women eat it up, there and then. The men, a little uncomfortable, a little baffled, just wait; she might be Chantal, but this isn't normal. She's never sung about herself, nor any of her feelings. She'd always made clear the music was the magic, not her. Can she be trusted to be not only the instrument but also the subject of the song? This is what the men are feeling but not expressing. To them, it's just wariness and doubt, never to know the genuine clarity of a very valid concern.

"Tonight I will debut 'The Curse of Princess Jade'."

Chantal subsides into the anticipated if initially hesitant applause, which grows more fervent even as the men relax: she won't be singing about herself or her daughter after all. Chantal is no queen and her baby is no princess. This will be an epic. This will be fun. It will make no sense and they won't care, because real life makes sense and that's not why they're here. They want to hear about everything they'll never experience for themselves. All the adventures. The glory of conquest. The courage and the hope, the romance and the redemption. Revenge. Justice. Joy. Satisfaction. Exultation. You know, the same Ephing crap she's always fed them and God how they've missed it.

This is all the fantasy they can accept, but the glint in her eye is the truth: this is all real, and they'll almost believe it by the time she's done.

Hers is the ember for the incendiary.

Here's where you'll have to imagine her voice. The singing, the flow. Words in waves. The art and artifice. I remember bits and pieces, and will probably fall into some horrible imitation now and then. But you understand, don't you? I want to tell you what she told me, not sing it. Not…make it any more than it really was. Yes, I knew you'd know exactly what I mean. Just how easy it is to allow her song to become something you can't hear anymore and yet can't resist. But we do, and we did. I think…

Very well. The Curse of Princess Jade. Sort of.

Prologue. Two warring fiefdoms. An ancient struggle, so bitter and spiteful it was said that the children were born with swords in their hands. Really. I think it made more sense when people didn't have a chance to think about the actual words, Brother. And yes, very painful. And messy. Let's just agree it's a metaphor and move on, because there's a lot to cover. So, you had the two realms. She often changed the names in repeat performances and I'm sure people just substituted their own in once the Curse really made the rounds, but we'll use the two she never dared to but always meant. *Jaydemyr* and *Kas'Daen*. A tale of birds and foxes, finally retold.

Ah, now I have your attention…good.

The whole thing started at a dinner party, like most wars and illicit affairs. Like most wars and illicit affairs, there was no telling which was to blame for the other. The Lady of Kas'Daen, Dhivashes, was ruling in her husband's stead, because the Lord Xenides was off fighting the great fight with his Jaydemyrian neighbours. Now, this dinner party was a grand event, no less part of the age-old feud than the crash of steel on the battered field. Battered. It's poetry, Brother. I don't get it either. Just…go with it. So, it was customary to invite a Jaydemyr delegate to these balls, because everyone was civil and beautiful. And it was customary that one be sent, usually some stuffy old politician or young, pointless court fop.

Usually.

The guests entered the ballroom to the fanfare and announcement of their famous names. They bowed and bantered, nibbled and minced. They danced with the grace of pale white swans. Well, no. I haven't. I *have* seen a swan about to be roasted black and eaten though. Probably isn't much of a song in that.

So, the Lady met the Jaydemyrian delegate, a particularly charming captain by the name of Arius Hawkstorm. They were beautiful and civil for precisely as long as they had to be, and the next day Arius was gone and Dhivashes was pregnant. I'm not making that up. That was Mother's way. People didn't listen to her grandiose songs for the sordid details, and I'm not going to fill gaps in the story I know you can fill for yourself. You're leering, Char, and this is possibly our parents I'm talking about here. Try to behave, will you?

Excuses, illnesses and clever choices of garment can only go so far, and court gossip told everyone Her Ladyship was with child long before Dhivashes started to show. Arius had since been recalled to the front, but word travels as fast as the wind that carries it and soon enough both sides of the conflict knew it all. The Lord of Kas'Daen, Xenides who was also known as Redfox, was ensanguined with jealousy…what? It means 'covered in blood and pissed off at his slattern of a wife'. *Obviously*. Anyway, he was left with a choice. Seek Arius of Jaydemyr on the field, challenge him, gut the bastard and restore his honour, or quit the field, challenge his wife, gut the bitch and restore his honour. They were indeed simpler times.

But before he could choose, something else happened: the Fey Folk intervened.

The song splits into three here, and how Mother made it easy for the audience to follow is well beyond me. It happened the same night, at exactly the same time. One Fey visited the Lord Jaydemyr, Charas'z the Primahriel. Another came to the Lady of Kas'Daen, Dhivashes, in her dreams, or maybe just in her bed. A third imposed on Xenides the Redfox during a well-attended bath. After overturing a bit about how sparkly and gorgeous the Night's Own are, the song tells that all three Fey said the same thing: 'You had no choice.' The Lord Jaydemyr heard out what the Night planned and agreed with the logic. Lady Dhivashes, not exactly nimble on her feet, accepted her instructions from the Fey without a word. Lord Xenides, after some thrashing and splashing and cursing, tried to bargain with the lithesome creature, because he didn't want to let his wife go without at least some memento. An ear, maybe a toe. At the very least. But one does not bargain with the Will of God, king or no, and whatever punishment he received for his insolence will remain unsung…but he did not emerge from his battlefield tent the next day, or indeed for several days thereafter.

Of course, it would not do for the nobility of two great realms to admit they'd been puppeteered by the true Nobles, The lofty and ever-elusive Night's Own, so elaborate plans were drawn and treaties drafted. The fighting and the dying continued but that was just for appearances. Reputations. Court gossip again went to work, and this time in the direction both Kas'Daen and Jaydemyr desired. The child of two kingdoms would represent the unification. Re-unification, actually, or so the historians on both sides conveniently discovered. The child would be a blessing, a gift. A miracle. The only person expected to disagree, Lord Xenides himself, had taken ill; his retainers blamed the bath attendants and had them all executed. When he heard about this, a frothing, enraged Xenides had *them* executed and then ordered his army to break camp, mainly because the other army had already done so. With morale flagging, Lord Xenides drove his soldiers home, forced march, swords very sheathed.

Winter didn't impede their fateful stride, for the Fey blessed their feet with feathers and flight. The army of Redfox hastened over plains, crossed rivers, passed through mountains, and arrived home without a single loss. Not even the sly Xenides knew why, but he wasn't inclined to question the Fey a second time. And as he crested that last hill, and as he looked down, Xenides knew that he'd been had, and he'd had no choice…but he smiled anyway and ordered that swords be drawn.

The sapphire banners of Jaydemyr's Primahriel encircled the deep-dug fortress Rosenbara, his true home, like cold-eyed vultures marauding over a dying vixen.

The Queen's private chambers. By now she was about as agile as an albatross, and there was the Lord Jaydemyr looming at her bedside. At the other side, Captain Arius Hawkstorm. Both knelt, as the Lady of Kas'Daen sat on her bed and listened to what they had to say. When the first treacherous rock from a Kas'Daen catapult crashed into Rosenbara's infamous walls, distant but deep, the two warriors rose from their supplication and began to part ways as brothers-in-arms should: with a wordless, heavy nod.

But that was not meant to be.

Charas'z, Primahriel and Lord of Jaydemyr: "Take care of her."

Arius stopped smiling the moment his Lord's back was turned, and drew his sword. The Lady of Kas'Daen, gripped by spasms, the poor woman, could only watch. The Lord Jaydemyr naturally heard the ominous scrape of blade leaving leathery sheath, but did not look back.

Arius, Hawkstorm and Lord-Captain of Jaydemyr: "I will. I have no choice."

The tip of the sword rose…and stayed there as the Lord Jaydemyr quit the room. What held the captain's lethal hand? Some say it was the command of the Fey, whose plans are as mysterious as the ways of the God they represent. Others say it was love or duty. Others still say they're the same thing. The point is, no one listening to the song wanted Arius to betray Charas'z and so he didn't, at least not in that rendition.

The captain used the edge of his sword to nudge the door closed and then turned to the mother of his child. She, strengthened by the knowledge that to tarry was to die, was already out of bed and wobbling towards her wardrobes. The captain, sword in his right hand, offered the precious woman his left arm. Champion and Lady, they entered the secret passage and escaped the doomed keep of Rosenbara altogether.

That was when it started snowing in Kas'Daen-*desne*, and the snow did not stop until well after it was over. Xenides, Lord Redfox and Charas'z, Primahriel of Jaydemyr, then threw their might at each other. All very typical. First was the siege, then the armies met and the ranks thinned, and then lieutenants shouted their names at each other, declared their deeds, duelled and became momentary legends. The Fey watched and aided neither side. Both the Redfox and the First Among Eagles took this for a sign that the Nobles approved; after all, this was the decisive battle, and the war between the two would finally be over regardless of who won.

…No, Brother, she didn't, but it wouldn't have been a very good song if she'd dwelled on things like battle tactics and cutting off supplies, starvation, logistics, reinforcements, rationing…see, you're bored already. Let's just say it was a wonderful little war right up until Charas'z and Xenides ran out of troops, and then ran out of rocks, and then ran at each other, across the divide and over the mangled remains, the blood of too many heroes to name, and embraced a mutual destiny of skewering one's mortal foe with a gasp and possibly some brief embarrassment at what intimate state they'd be found in afterwards, if indeed anyone did find them.

Mother could make anything funny, and she could make anything sad. She had the entire All-Trades at her whim that night; they'd probably forgotten the name of the song, never mind the fact that it seemed to have nothing to do with a princess or a curse. Chantal evoked not one kingdom but two, raised the very stones with her voice, populated the world with all manner of character and then let it destroy itself, all over a little girl who wasn't even born yet, whose purpose of linking two rival clans now seemed futile.

The one thing she couldn't do was change what happened next. That's the one thing the woman they called The Chantal could never do.

Epilogue. A month or so later. The night she gave birth, the former Lady Dhivashes of Kas'Daen, now answering to the name Dhiana Jaydemyr, having embraced not only the clan name of her beloved but also its femifix, received another visit from the Fey. In that tiny barn, cold with the last flurries of this terrible winter, the glorious presence of a messenger from God was like a steady flame in a blizzard. The midwife did not see or hear the visitor, and Arius was outside standing guard, shivering but stoic. He was to be her Champion first, father of her child second. This the Night had commanded.

Though it is difficult to tell them apart, the Noble that came to Dhiana as she gave birth was the one she'd seen before, perhaps in her dreams. He told her that the child was his, and that her liaison with Arius had produced nothing more than widespread gossip and slaughter.

Dhiana's disbelief, very vocal and unladylike, only prompted soothing pats and reassurances from the midwife. But once Dhiana accepted the Fey's claim, she realised what this meant, because no human woman survives the birth of an abomination. Of a Half. The Noble just stood there as the fallen Lady howled and pushed, and the midwife focused on her work.

And just as the baby made its squawking debut to this tragic world, the midwife saw proof of the claim she hadn't heard and gave Dhiana a horrified stare as she struggled not to stare at the little monster in her arms. The unseen Fey knelt beside the kneeling midwife and eased her terror with a light kiss on the neck. Blissful and rewarded, she returned to God's Dark Breast with a sigh. Dhiana, gritting her teeth, struggled up onto her elbows.

And what did she see?

According to the song, a glowing aura that struck her dumb with awe as the Fey worked a miracle. What did she *really* see? A great deal of blood, probably. A sticky little traumatised tadpole and a pale pair of arms cradling it. And then she didn't see so much as feel what happened next, as the Fey's smile tore through the last link between child and womb. Naturally it did not hurt, but she howled nonetheless, and it was a scream that eclipsed all the other noises she'd produced that night.

The full voice of Dhiana's pain was unlike anything even the battle-grizzled Arius had ever heard, and he rushed into the barn.

And what did he see?

There was no blood, anywhere. What? No, not even on a leaf. What leaves? They were in a barn, Charan. There was hay, dirt, a blanket or two, and the now deceased midwife. But there was no blood. There was the mother of his child, and the child of his loins, one holding the other. Dhiana was sitting up, clothed in her white gown, black hair clammy against her red forehead. And as he came closer, Arius saw the child's pointy ears, and of course he knew what that meant.

But Dhiana was not dead. His child was not dead. And this meant more to him than anything, so he dropped his sword, dropped to his knees and leant in to embrace them both.

Dhiana who was Dhivashes: "You're soaking wet." She pulled away, but only for a little while. "Her name is Jade. Jade Hawkstorm."

Arius held his family in his arms, and did not argue about the name, think about the dead midwife, or ask about the ears. After all his years dedicated to ending life, he was happy to take part in any beginning of it.

And it was not revealed how Dhiana survived that night, or why the Fey didn't take its child from her, although Princess Jade would later go on many, many adventures to learn the answer, to find out who she truly was.

Now I want you to imagine the song ending there. Chantal's voice faded out of the words and into a haunting refrain. The Theme of Princess Jade, they'd call it, and for years it'd be repeated in drunken stupors, in second-rate beer halls, ladies' changing rooms and school courtyards. But like everything else Mother creates, it was only perfect the first time, and even that was probably an imitation, an attempt at what she really intended.

There was no applause, because people weren't aware it was over. The thrall hadn't just affected this carpenter or that cobbler: everyone was slack-jawed, glazy-eyed.

Everyone except Jerich. "What, that's it?"

A different sort of silence followed, refusing to be either insulted or relieved. Then there was a laugh, and the room settled on an air of thankfulness. At some point, a pyrotic in the audience had lowered the flames of the firepit, but now the fire returned to full strength and the gleam in people's eyes was nothing more than reflected light.

"It is until she gets a bit older." Chantal's light counter drew another uncertain laugh. Her voice was even more husky and ravaged than ever, but this was the exhaustion of the triumphant. She clasped her hands and bowed.

The audience had their cue to give vent to what they really wanted to do. They yelled, they clapped, they cheered. The All-Trades Inn erupted with approval until hands throbbed with almost sympathetic pain and throats were as raw as hers, or close enough.

She told me after that night they didn't want to hear anything else, and 'The Curse' became her obsession, our means of survival. I guess sometimes there really isn't a substitute for the real thing, or maybe the song was the reality and I was just there to inspire it, to give the world what it wanted, through her.

They didn't know that Jade was a real girl, and that her name, given to her by her father, was actually Sarah Falkenstrom. She wasn't a princess; the Fey did not attend her birth or harass her upbringing. She wasn't 'a cursed child of the Night' and her beauty did not 'outshine all the trembling stars and mock God's perfect eye'. But you can see that by looking at me now, right? Oh, I'm sure I've changed since then, I was just a little girl, but that's where it started. I grew up in the memory of a shadow of a fantasy, unable to live up to any of it. Your smile tells me you get what that means too.

But do you know, as difficult as Mother's standards might have been, one thing about that night, about that song has long bothered me. If it's all just a fantasy, and she made it all up, that's fine. But if she was cunningly telling the world about our origins and the beginning of the end of our clan…where was she in all that? What terrible role in the whole affair did she leave out of her song?

It was never about what Mother told me. It's what she didn't tell me that really did it. Knowing this at far too early an age. That it made becoming Princess Jade *my* curse, as surely as being called 'Pumpkin' by Daddy was my very brief blessing.

False Idyll

The siblings stay another night at another inn, leaving their room only when necessary. Charan is certain his sister is safe after he eliminated the remainder of the Kas'Daen advance party sent against Viestrada (although, as he notes with typical sardonicism, by then it was more like a withdraw party). Sariana knows her brother doesn't understand how tenacious Xenides-ra can be, but doesn't press the point. They are safe here, and she's only just begun to share with him what only she knows. He suspects she's not so much weaving her tale as quilting someone else's, and if it's Vachaelle's then perhaps he can help her figure it out. She suspects he's too damaged by a more severe version of what she's experienced to be of much assistance, which would bother her more if she felt she needed any.

They eat, read, and reminisce by themselves, but mostly they sleep. It is an interesting quirk of their unique biology that they can elongate waking periods with similarly long intervals of rest. Humans count their sleep in hours; Halves can do it by days. Before too long, when Sariana's wariness proves apt, this will be a very helpful attribute. But for now, there is time for recuperation, hot mugs of tea, and a warm, quiet evening padded comfortably by the next part of her story.

38 days until the revelation

Chapter 2: When Daddy Went Away

Why do we always remember the bad things so easily? It's not fair, that I can't just shut my eyes and feel his hand on my head, or hear his heart beat, feel the warmth of his chest as he pressed me against it. I know these things happened. I'm sure of it. Maybe I was just too young, but I don't have to even close my eyes to vividly recall other things, like the smell of her vomit or the way her eyes would not meet his afterwards. You could blame what I am, what we are, but that just makes the selective clarity even crueller. That we can possess this strength of recollection but only use it to lift the worst crap out of the hazy swamp of memory, or worse, imposed experience. Well, you can call it being human if you want. Or Half. I call it a pain in the arse, but tonight at least it seems to be serving something of a useful purpose.

Yes, Brother. Empowered futility does run in the family. But maybe it's not so futile as long as we keep running.

Well, there. That works. Running. That's one of my first really good memories. Mine, not some jumble of told and imagined. And I don't care if it really happened or not. Like you said, even fake experiences can leave us with real feelings. Lessons, memories. Call them what you like. Scars? Sure, that's not perfectly grim at all. You never fail to remind me that I'm not the only one to have suffered her attention. Love? The fact that you even call it that proves my point. And I thought it was my point you wanted to hear all about?

Running, literally. I can feel the grass swishing against my legs, the dandelions through my hands. If…when I do just that, walk through an overgrown field, and then run, it's like I'm four all over again. I'm Sarah the Princess, princess of all the cows and all the trees and everything I can see. I'm smart, good, brave…all the things I can hear Daddy calling me but can't see him say. I'm alone. Four years old and alone. He's gone and Mother's good-as-gone and I don't know anyone else. Anyone except Mrs. Baker, who looks after me and actually does bake the most wonderful muffins. I've never seen her house so sometimes it's like she just stops existing once she leaves ours. I've seen other people but I don't know them. Sometimes I hear them late at night, outside my room, the nights Mother doesn't go to work. I have my own room now. It used to be his room. Now it belongs to the Princess. Princess of all the hills, all the fields. All the world.

No, Brother. I genuinely had a very poor sense of time. I can't tell you in a nice, ordered fashion when all this happened. Certain things came before others. There wasn't much logic to the order. Mother would say things like 'I will be back before Bladesun' and then tell Mrs. Baker what to do, what not to do, but all I knew was this meant she'd almost certainly be back after the sun rose the next morning. Tomorrow morning. Morning I understood. And night. And in-between was my time, when Mrs. Baker would eventually slump in her chair, her flabby, shiny face snoring so loudly I didn't even have to tip-toe out the back door. As long as I was back before night, she never knew. Well, maybe she did and didn't care. Made no difference to me. The few times Mrs. Baker told Mother I'd been naughty, the gentle and noble Chantal had spared no efficiency and, I think, pleasure in the laying of hands on bare backside. Mine, Charan. Not hers. Shyn's Tits but you're weird sometimes.

But those times were too rare to have much effect. Off I'd sneak…preferably with one of Mrs. Baker's muffins. That, too, was a slight challenge. When she brought a basket full of those warm handfuls, so fragrant with apple and sugar, she'd slap my hand before I even had a chance to make a grab for one. This struck me with awe at the time. Mother had gone to work and left her mind-reading friend to torment me. After one time, when she'd cracked my hand so hard her nails drew blood, I thought at her, as loudly as I could, I HOPE YOU GET STUNG BY A BEE UP YOUR NOSE YOU MEAN OLD WITCH…and she didn't say or do anything, so that was the end of that brief delusion. Definitely not a mind-reader. And, as it turns out, a very deep sleeper, because I'd actually *say* things like that to her after she'd passed out, just to make sure. Any and all fear of Mrs. Baker walked out the door right before I did, with a nice warm muffin in my red hands and crumbs all over my happyface.

No, I don't think Teristra had many real Maliscients, even back then before the Guilds and the war. And I know you're assuming what I have no choice but to believe: the Teristra of my youth, of a youth that almost certainly wasn't real, was itself real in the details. When I 'go back' there someday, I fully expect to know certain streets, landmarks, statues, with the same confidence of someone who was raised there but moved away years ago. But if you're asking about the city's now-famous anti-Talent position, it was all just a distant thunderhead. A city founded on trade and sustained by the fallacy of a good hard day's work being the very height of fulfilment never looked favourably on Talents but their practicality was difficult to deny. We'll get to that soon enough, because I was there…well, Sarah-Jade was, at least in part. I promise I'll get to it. If you remind me. Which I know you will.

Why would you care about Maliscients anyway? Had a run-in with a few, I suppose. Eh? "Fat Delight?" What does that mean? Oh, sorry. My Chūnko-go is more than a little rusty. Plump Treat then. You're mumbling. I can't understand you…

Oh, don't worry. I'm more than used to it, your ramblings and your half-sentences and your rude-as-Eph interjections…but not when you've asked me to tell you my story. You had your chance to tell yours, didn't you? Don't blame me if you told it 'to the darkness'. Whatever that means.

Back to me and my ill-gotten muffin, please. Stealing away to tramp about the fields and woods. I knew the other direction, back into the village, was where I was not allowed to go. Not if I Knew What Was Good For Me. Which I clearly didn't. But there was nothing that way to interest me. I'm sure the village didn't have vast expanses of grass to run through or trees to climb. But no matter how high I climbed, it was never high enough. It just didn't look the same as when Daddy used to take me there, me propped on his shoulder and only a little bit afraid. He needed one hand to keep me steady, but with the other he'd point at different things.

"What's that, Pumpkin?" I imagine him smiling, but not because he knew the answer. He was proud of me, his little miracle, because I always looked where he was pointing, and I always answered.

I wish I'd looked at him instead.

"Thatta cloud!" I was somewhere between two and four years old and squarely in the middle of Knowing Everything.

"And that?"

"Tree!"

"And that thing?"

"Cow, Daddy. Cow!"

"Ah, you're so smart, Pumpkin."

"Don't be smart!"

He'd pause then, as if aware of who was actually answering him.

"Then…what do you want to be, Pumpkin?"

"…Good girl."

I think he let me down then, and we started to walk home. And it might have been a certain time, or all of them, or none. Maybe I was sitting on his knee at home near the fireplace in the middle of one of those harsh Terissian winters. Either way, the conversation didn't end there.

"You can be both smart and good, Sarah."

"But mummy said don't be smart—"

"Your mother is going through a hard time, Pumpkin."

"But Daddy, Mummy—"

"Sarah."

I don't remember what followed that, which means something good. We went home and had dinner, or he hugged me. Typically? Beef stew, bread, maybe oats. I used to like the lamb, if you must know, not that we had it that often. Ate it a lot more later, though.

Another time, another walk.

"What that, Daddy?"

"You know what that is, Pumpkin. You told me before."

"What is it?"

"It's a cow."

"Oh. Doesn't look cow."

"Doesn't look *like a* cow. Come on, let's go."

"That's not cow."

"It's definitely a cow, Sarah. Just…a very sick one."

"So give cow soup?"

"Different sort of sick."

"Worser?"

"Worse. Looks like the cold got it. Poor thing's good as gone."

"Went gone?"

"It's just gone, Sarah. Same as we need to get going."

"Gone means what?"

"Gone. Never coming back. Ever."

"Where?"

"Away. Enough. Your mother's waiting. We'll have soup."

I remember looking back at that cow, but I probably didn't. It wasn't there the next time we went for a walk, but I guess that's assuming we even took that route again. There was a lesson, and I didn't yet know I'd learned it.

One time, when Daddy was at work, and Mother was home. Unusual, yes, but so was the fact that her belly had been getting bigger than normal. And you know that when I say 'one time' what I really mean is 'that very particular time' because I wouldn't bring it up otherwise. I was playing on the floor, fumbling about with some sticks or blocks or whatever, and Mother was sitting at her desk, somewhat closer to the fire. She was bigger, and slower, but she was still Mother, and any movement she made was a flinch I had to resist.

But.

"What's that?"

"Don't point like that, Jade."

Daddy had his names for me. Mother had hers. And that was that.

"What's that, Mummy?"

"You mean this? It's my belly. And before you ask, I'm going to have a baby."

"But you already—"

"Don't be smart, Princess. I'm having *another* one. This time, God willing, a boy. One girl is more than enough…What are you looking at, Jade?"

"You, Mummy."

"What did I say about being smart?"

"Don't be smart. But…"

"Don't make me come over there."

"Sorry."

I imagine that look of hers, the one that desperately wants to forgive but doesn't think it's time for that yet. Mother was all about teaching but sometimes I think she never quite believed anyone ever learned anything.

I know, and it doesn't really make sense to me either. If she was so put out of sorts by having me, why in Eph's wounded hell did she want another? Was it something as simple as me being a girl, thus a mistake? Did Daddy want a son that badly? Or were they hoping the next one would prove that my ears really were just a curse, just for me?

Where did I fit into the picture of two happy parents and their very normal, round-eared little boy?

See, it always comes back to those damn ears. *These* damn ears. They'll never heal properly, not now. Of course I regret it, but it's not like I knew any different. You thought yours were misshapen, wrong somehow, but least you had a chance to learn otherwise. Thanks to Mother's…love and my idiocy, my stubbornness, this is normal now. I haven't put a knife near them in almost ten years, but it's far too late.

I suppose not, not that first time. Too young again. But I definitely remember what it was like each time after that. Every year, when the growth became too hard to hide. Yes, just like a birthday, Brother. No, I can't. I don't want to. Words aren't enough to describe it. Look at them, won't you? Just Ephing look. I know you have. Everyone does. Of all the things we're raised to very carefully ignore, a pair of mutilated ears is still too out-of-place to not notice. Well, that's very kind of you, but if you think 'they're not so bad', why do you wear a hood all the time, Dog-Ears? Hm?

Okay, fine. I'll try. You say you've had your ears pinched, pulled, tugged. And that it was agony. Pfft. That's just the start. That's like a bucket of water to bring you around just so you can be tortured some more. And you want me to describe the actual torture?

Fine.

Here's how I think it might have gone.

"Come here, Jade."

I didn't. Just kept doing whatever I was doing.

"I said, *come here*."

I stopped doing. Looked at the floor near her. Took one step. Two. Bit my lip, probably. Harder than just a gesture. Thought about running. She wasn't in any shape to give chase.

"Jade. Don't make me tell your father that you've been naughty again."

Not that he'd punish me. He'd just look at me. Look at me looking at him, both of us covered in guilt and shame.

I walked to her desk, stood next to her. Looked up at her, sitting on her stool. She was holding a small knife.

"There's a good girl. Now, close your eyes."

I did. The threat of Daddy learning about my disobedience was in full effect now. She'd tell me and I'd do. It was that simple.

I felt her cold fingers touching my ear. Left, not that it matters. I pulled away. Got tugged back into place. More touching, probing. Muttering.

"Do you want Mummy to sing you a song, Jade?"

'No." I was really answering different questions, questions I wanted her to ask. Are you okay? Can I do this to you? Is this right?

"Are you sure? I promise it'll help."

"NO!" I pulled away again. Opened my eyes, just in time to have them forced away by her slap.

I cried.

"Fine. I can wait."

I made her wait. Bawled. Screamed. Stamped my feet. Rolled on the floor. Screamed some more.

And when I was all out of energy, she picked me up, wiped my fatty little cheeks and held me close. I don't remember the sound or the feel of her heartbeat, only that I had trouble breathing. Terrified. She hadn't punished me for the tantrum. Didn't say a single word. Just squeezed.

Then she held my shoulders, pushed me back and shook her head.

"Well, that didn't do much good, did it, my girl?"

I stared at her. Deflated. Broken. Lower lip nibbling. Eyes hot and full but well past tears.

"Want to do it again? Got more?"

"...No."

"Close your eyes then."

I did, and there was no song. She'd offered, and I'd refused. She never makes the same offer twice, even if you sometimes fool yourself into thinking you've been given a second chance.

She was not quick about it. And she talked the whole time, like she was chatting with herself. How I know that despite my howling is baffling, but I know. It's the sort of thing she'd do. And that day I learned just how isolated our house was, because no matter how much noise I made, no one came to my rescue. Especially not Daddy, who might have been in his workshop on the moon for all I knew or cared.

There was one small mercy in this, Brother. It was a very sharp knife, and she never used it for anything else. But it was a very small mercy. After that day, the sight of it alone sent me to my knees, crying and begging. You're right. I *am* avoiding the details. I told you words wouldn't be enough. Agonising? Unbearable? A world of suffering and horror and despair and helplessness, endless in that moment? KillmenowpleaseGodnowpleasepleaseplease? All just parodies of what it's like. Insults. But I can tell you what made the process of getting my ears trimmed worse than all of those.

Chantal Falkenstrom might have been famous for her singing, but no one ever considered it her Talent. And they were right. God, in Her boundless wisdom, gave Mother the perfect Talent for someone who believed in the curative properties of a knife. She'd make a fast, deft cut, and just before I could really feel the pain, press her fingers into the blood and…well, you know what healing feels like. Fire, then ice. Both burn.

And, as I wailed, that happened over and again. Cold nails, cool knife, quick slice, hot rush, freezing sting. I would have lost count even if I'd tried to keep it.

Eventually…

"You can stop crying now, Jade."

I didn't. Just waited for the next.

"Stop crying. You're not hurt."

How *dare* she say that?

And yet I felt no pain. I only remembered it, and even that was fading.

"Give me your hand."

"No…"

"Open your eyes."

"NO!"

She shook me. Had to open my eyes to see her, and I saw something I didn't understand.

Had this hurt her too? Did she feel pain whenever I did?

"It has to be done, Jade. You are not normal. I won't let you…you won't have to put up with it…I'll make things right."

She'd offer variations on this reasoning and this promise over the years, as predictable and inexplicable as those tears lying down her face.

"Touch your ear, Jade."

I did. Felt the changed shape, the roundness and the softness. It didn't hurt. Then I looked at her ears. Round and soft.

"Like yours, Mummy."

"That's right. Just like mine. Now, let's do the other one."

After that, the walks were different. More frequent, but shorter. Different.

"Pumpkin."

"Huh?"

"You know your mother loves you very much."

"Yes Daddy."

I think I was looking at everything. Trees, hills, sky, clouds, birds. Grass. Dirt. Cow shit. Everything but what he was pointing out.

"And so do I. You're my smart princess."

"And brave and good?"

"…All those. And more."

We walked.

He pointed.

"What's that, Pumpkin?"

"Silly Daddy. That's a cow!"

"Are you sure?"

"Sure! But not a gone one."

"Dead, Sarah. The word for it is dead."

"Dead, gone, not comin' back never."

"Happens to everyone…but not us! Not for a very, very, very long time."

"Kay. Daddy?"

"Yes?"

"Are my ears good too?"

To this day I can't remember his answer.

Now that I was getting bigger, I started spending time with Daddy in his workshop. Even if he'd been a Holecleaner or something nasty like that, I probably would have clung to him every second I could. I remember what the workshop was like from later visits, but that was after. I can still smell sawdust and varnish when I think, 'Daddy's workshop', but I've been around carpenters since, so…more assumptions and deductions. He'd tell me not to touch anything and I didn't, and when I didn't he'd tell me what I could touch, what I could hold. Feel. I…I can feel his hand wrapped around mine, him standing behind me. Shadowing me, his shadow over the wood. He says something. Go. Go with. Without? No. Eph damn this, he said…go with…

"Go with the grain, Sarah."

He pushes my hand forward, pulls it back. Not much pressure, but both of our hands press against the block. We both press the glass paper along the wood. Back and forth. I could go to sleep doing this. Maybe I am asleep doing this. His breath on the top of my head measures the movement. He is everything steady and stable and reliable. I want to lean back against him, into him, but we have work to do, to do together.

"Touch this. Here."

I do.

"And now here. What's the difference?"

I move my hand from one patch to the other, back and forth. I squint, trying to think. I've felt this difference before, but the words aren't there when I want them.

"Diffent."

"That's right. Different."

He takes my hand again, guides it left.

"Here it is rough."

"Ruff."

And then right.

"And here it is smooth."

"Smoov."

"And that's the difference. We made the wood go from rough to smooth."

I want him to do it again, for us to do it again, but there it stopped. I wasn't yet big enough to help with what he had to do next.

Oh, Eph 'n' Shyn. The hammer. I just remembered. That's where it all started. All of it. This came a bit later, a different time certainly. When I thought I was big enough. I think it was after…yes. Because he had a harder grip now, more forceful. Determined. The warmth of the woodwork had become something stronger, more heated. I had to say something because he wouldn't. Just kept at it, dragging my hand up, pausing, slamming straight down. Bang. For the first time ever, I didn't want to be there. He wasn't going to let me go, and I couldn't ask. But. Had to tell him.

"Daddy, my hand. It hurts."

Bang. The force jars my wrist, my arm. But I won't let go of the handle. He won't be able to do it without me. Or he'd do it without me.

"We have to do it this way, Sarah. It requires this much effort. If you want the nail to go in cleanly, you can't be weak. Do you want me to let go of your hand? You can watch if you'd like."

Tap, tap. Another nail in place.

"No…but…"

"No buts, Sarah. If you want me to teach you how to do this, this is how I will teach you."

"Why?" I've discovered this word. It's better than 'what' because I get different answers no matter how many times I use it.

"Just the way it is. It might hurt, but you need to be brave. Ready for another?"

"I guess." Discovered that one too. It means yes-but-not-really-I'll-leave-it-up-to-you-no. And not even Daddy's clever enough to figure it out.

Up. Down. Bang. This time I uncurl my fingers from the hammer's grip, look at them. Soft, pink. A little sore.

"Got a blister?"

"What's blisted?"

"Give me a look."

He goes to touch my hand. I flinch. One thing to be held, another to be poked, prodded.

"I don't see anything, but if it hurts you should stop."

"No, I can help! I am brave!" I might be in trouble. If he doesn't need my help, then he might take me home. To her.

"You can just watch for now, Sarah."

"…Okay. I'm sorry, Daddy."

"It's alright, Pumpkin. Nothing to be sorry for. Watch. I'll show you."

So he did. It wasn't like being there with him, a part of him, coordinated and merged, his hand my arm our will driving nails into the wood so deep you couldn't feel where they were. But each time he lifted the hammer, and each time he brought it down, I regretted giving up. Maybe I swore that next time I wouldn't, but that's the sort of stupid promise you make when you're older and know about the fragile nature of 'next time.'

…Oh, so you noticed. Do you really want the gory details then? Too bad, because I don't have them. I didn't stand behind a door and peek at the scene. For all I know, it all happened somewhere else. I don't recall a Sister of the Liquid Night visiting. Maybe there was an abbey near the village. Or I was somewhere else. Maybe I was in Daddy's workshop. Maybe I was asleep. What matters is I wasn't there. But I've taken part in…oh, a few deliveries since, so I can easily make up a story if you'd like. Yes, Charan. Even *those* sorts of deliveries. Let's not though. Not yet. Maybe never. Let me decide that. Suffice to say that for whatever reason, the version of you that would have taken part in the joyous event that was my childhood decided to just say Eph It and skipped the whole debacle.

As I said, the walks were now shorter but much more common. We were just as likely to spend hours in that workshop. The silence between my parents was…more pointed, like neither of them wanted to break it for fear of never being able to repair it. Because something else had broken. Something had gone wrong and Mother was no longer going to give Daddy a son. That's all I knew.

Well, I knew one other thing.

I wasn't anyone's Princess anymore.

"What's the fucking racket!?"

Mother, somewhere just out of sight where I would not look but could always hear. I didn't understand the words, but the tone was enough. It made the storm outside sound almost tame. I stopped, stared at what I was doing. The blocks of wood, made for me by Daddy of course, were scattered across the floor. One was in my hand.

"For God's sake, woman. Watch the language."

"Not like she's old enough to understand it, Arius. My head's murder and I'm trying to write. And she's…"

I wanted to be old enough. Something wasn't right and it was my fault. I needed to become old enough. To be a good girl. Brave. Smart. Good. What Daddy told me to be.

"It's not her fault, Chant. Like you said, she's not old enough. She's a kid, being a kid. Take it out on me all you want, but she's your daughter too. It's not her fault."

"She might not have done it on purpose but that doesn't mean she didn't do it. Keep her quiet. I've got *work* to do. Take her for a walk or something."

"In this weather? Seriously?"

He approached me. Close now. Squatting beside me. Giant. Protective. Respectfully feared and loved.

"What are you doing, Sarah?"

"Hamm'rin woods."

He laughed, and I imagine Mother lancing him with one of her famed venomous glares.

"Well, how about we do that a bit later, and for now, you just be a good girl and play quietly. Not so loud, okay? No hammering."

Oh. So that's what being a good girl meant. I could do that. "Kay."

He might have kissed my hair, or touched my shoulder. I don't remember flinching though.

I fiddled with the blocks. No hammering. Hammering was loud and loud was head murder. What else could I do? I arranged them like clouds. And then like bricks. Bricks went up, became houses. I started to stack them. Three, then two, then one. Triangle. Neat. Decided to try it the other way around. One…two…three? Didn't work so well. The blocks tumbled down when I let them go. Well. Lesson learned. Good girl. Learning is smart.

So why'd she come over and hit me?

I cried out but hardly reacted beyond that. What's a swat on the arm compared to the yearly ritual of ear trimming? I decided to give up trying different ways of building block pyramids for the time being. That wasn't being a good girl. Tried to think of other things.

Too late.

"You little bitch. You're doing this on purpose. Pushing me…"

She hit me again, over the head.

Started shoving me about.

"How do you like it when I push back, huh?"

Above and outside my cowering arms, I heard her screech, felt her grab my arm, dig her nails in. Shaking. Stinging.

"Chant!"

Bang. Or something like it.

And then she let go, and I scrambled away to the wall, and I tried to climb it, clinging to it, blurry and thoughtless. Wouldn't look. If I looked, she'd see me and it'd happen again.

"I'm sorry I'm sorry I'm sorry…" I blubbered to the wall, but it didn't say it was okay. Then again, it wasn't hitting me either. Sanctuary enough.

"I'm…sorry, Chant, I didn't mean to—"

"Oh, didn't you? You never do anything you don't mean, Ari. It's what they always so admired about you. Of course you meant it."

"I meant to stop you, nothing more. Just that."

"You'd side with her over me?"

"Side with…Chant, who exactly do you think is against you? She's. Four. Years. Old."

I peeked around, saw him, now just a hulking shadow of anger and hurt, over her. And she was there in front of him, angry and hurt too. He was holding her wrist, and her hand wasn't far from his face. His other hand was up, back. A fist. Like he was holding a hammer. But he wasn't holding a hammer at all, so he lowered it.

"I'm sorry I'm sorry I'm sorry…" I lay on the floor, feeling the smooth wood and my tears soaking into the grain. Or maybe against it.

"The girl is a curse. A mistake. She was never meant to happen. She isn't meant to exist. And now I'll never have the chance to make up for that. To be right in God's eyes…"

"A curse? The only mistake was you writing that God-damned song. Spin your lies for the crowds all you want, Chantal, but it's not true. None of it."

"What is true is that we have no idea *whose* child she really is!"

Not true, not true, not true…

"Why why why why…" Cheeks flat against the floorboards, eyes on the wall. I got no different answers each time. I got no answers at all, so I kept asking. And kept listening.

"I…she's ours, Chantal. You carried her to term and then you gave birth. I don't understand how you could say otherwise. There's no way in Eph's Seven Hells she's not your child. But am I the father? Those ears…"

Always back to the Ephing ears.

"Yes, that's right. Accuse me of that. Go on. You've taken to beating me and blaspheming, so why not find bone before blood and just call me the cheating whore you clearly believe me to be. Cheating, barren, useless whore."

"It was only once. I didn't mean it. Never again. Ever."

"What if I said the same then? Just once. Never again. Even if sleeping with a Noble was a damn good fuc—GO ON, do it again. Even so much as think about raising that fist and I'll know. And then others will know, because I have *lots* of friends who don't think well of men who treat women this way."

"…Don't make your war with me, Chant. Don't even threaten it."

"Oh, look at you. So tough. So staunch. Mr ex-Captain of the Guard, all puffed up and pompous. I haven't told them where you are, so don't worry. Shit, you're too blue in the blood to even go near the city. Face it. You're hiding, Arius Falkenstrom, and it's all you know how to do. You've been hiding behind me for years, and now you're hiding behind a little girl. Well maybe I'm tired of hiding you. I certainly see no reason to hide this. How'd you get that bruise, Chant? Oh, you know. My husband, he's a good man, but times are hard and he has a bit of a temper…"

"You bitch. You absolute snake. You can have your crowds, your adoring legion. You can have all of Teristra for all I care."

Then I heard his heavy footsteps come towards me. I curled into a ball, smaller and smaller. So small no one could see me. So small I went into myself, and then I went away. Gone. Not coming back never.

"You can have the world at your beautiful feet, Chantal, but you won't do any more harm to my girl.

"Sarah, honey. It's okay."

Not true, not true, not true…

He touched my arms. I whimpered and tried to sink deeper into the floor. But waves of something determined wrapped around me. Rough and smooth all at once. Different.

"Get your hands off her, you monster!"

"Give it up, Chant. You're the one who butchers her ears, slaps her around, calls her every name under God's cursed sun, and I'm the monster?"

If he was, I would never be afraid of monsters again. I was sitting up, rocking away the tears, and he was behind me. Breathing on my hair. One huge arm around my chest, not stopping me but not letting go either.

"We can't keep her hidden forever, Arius. Surely you can imagine how people would treat us if they knew. I did it right. Ask her! Healed every single little cut straight afterwards. She probably didn't even feel a thing."

He leaned closer, breathed on my ear. I stiffened, stop rocking. When I felt something touch me there, where nothing was welcome, I screamed. Had to get away. Not the fire and the ice. Not again.

"Sarah! God, what's…" I felt the grip tighten. Whatever was keeping me from getting away, I threw my everything against it. I scratched. I ripped. Kicked and squealed. And when that didn't work, I bit down on the nearest thing that wasn't me.

That worked.

I was free and, on my hands and knees, looked around for Daddy, who would tell me it's okay, nothing to be sorry for. But there he was, bleeding through the sleeve of his shirt, staring down at me as though I wasn't me. I couldn't say anything. It was all my fault and 'sorry' hadn't done any good. It hadn't made me a good girl.

And despite how clearly I remember all this, one thing still stands out. As I was backing away from my father, hands and feet all shoving me towards the wall again, she laughed. If I say it was *her* laugh, would you understand? Yes, just like that. That was the first time I heard it and somehow every time she did it after that I relived the night Daddy went away. This was her victory, and it was as hollow as that triumphant laughter.

"Looks like she doesn't want you touching her either, Arius."

"What have you done to her, Chantal? What have you done?"

"I told you, she's a curse. But she's *my* curse to live with. To take care of. You will just have to accept that."

He looked away from her and at me. I trembled, turned to the wall, started nodding my head against it. Bang. Bang. Bang. And I rubbed the wood. Rough, smooth.

"My poor darling." Heard him come closer, but then the sound of footsteps stopped.

"I think you should leave, Arius."

"Leave? And leave her with you? You're mad."

"I'm also the only person who can take care of her. Who will. Do you have the strength to do what I've done? You just spoil her. You might accept what she is, but no one outside that door is going to see what you see. They will see those ears and they will know. A Half. And *you* know what they do to Halves, eventually. What I do I do for her. Because God knows whatever I do isn't good enough for you. Is it?"

He should have answered. He should have defended himself. Defended us.

"I think we've seen more than enough proof of that, husband."

He should have said something.

I just kept nudging my forehead against the wall.

"Walk out that door, Arius Falkenstrom. Take time to think things through. When you come back, we'll talk things out rationally. Realistically. Like adults."

Bang.

"Just one night. Please, Ari. That's all I'm asking. I don't care what you get up to. Just…go."

I am smart. Bang. I am brave. Bang. I am good. Bang.

"Sarah."

Smart.

"Pumpkin..?"

Brave.

"Listen to me."

Good.

"I'm not going anywhere. Not tonight."

Touching me, holding me. Hand against my forehead, between bone and wall. Slick. Slippery.

"I'm sorry Daddy sorry sorry sorry…"

Tighter. Warmer.

"Shh."

Far away, Mother says something sharp and unforgiving. I hear the front door open. I hear the front door close.

He is still here.

And the storm has passed.

"Not tonight."

The warmth is everywhere. It's stroking my hair. It's enfolding my arms. It's burying my fears. I'm going to die someday and it's going to feel just like this. I'm not on fire. I'm not freezing. I am everything balanced, not by excess of extremities but through their absence. There is nothing left to do but silently thank God for this moment, say goodbye to all the woes, the confusion and the pain, and then surrender with neither defeat nor loss.

Goodnight.

Disorientation is coming out of sleep alone when you went in with someone else. It's like they somehow got lost in there and now will never escape, and even if you go back in, you won't find them again. I was in bed. Definitely didn't remember getting there. And not my bed.

"Daddy?"

I sat up too fast. Blood rush. Thumpthumpthump. Woozy. Didn't care. Looked around. This wasn't my room. His bed. Chest of drawers, made by him. Decorations, collected over the years. All him. A strangely out-of-place smiling portrait of Mother on one wall. Not him.

"Daddy!?"

I was in the main room, looking. Searching. Trying very hard not to think about the closed front door. Mother had left through it. He couldn't have. I wasn't alone.

"…Daddy?"

"He's not here." Mother emerged from my room.

"Daddy?"

"Told you, not here."

"THEN WHERE IS HE?!"

"Oh, great. Another tantrum. Get it over with then." She sat at her desk and began to write.

But there was no tantrum. Tantrums and crying were last night, back when Daddy was here. When I was a different person.

"At work?"

"Maybe. Maybe not."

"I want to go there."

"Not likely. It's just you and me now, Jade my girl."

"I want. To see. Daddy."

She finally put down the quill, and looked at me as I just stood there.

"He's gone, Jade."

I widened my eyes. That word.

"Gone?"

"Yes."

Gone. Went. Not coming back. Never.

Dead.

"No. Not gone. No."

"Yep. He'll never hurt you again. The bastard."

…Fine, I had one last great outburst left in me, and there it was. I fell to the floor, lashing out and punching and kicking and lashing out some more.

"Well, get it all out. I have a friend coming over this afternoon and I want you on your best behaviour. You'll like her. She bakes the most excellent muffins."

Familial contempt

One more night they'll linger here, in this inn with a name neither will remember. Charan has spent little time in their room today, sensing with his typical abundance of acumen that she needed less of his demanding presence than usual. Sariana had ended last night's session in ugly, heaving dry sobs and had, upon awakening sore and listless around Eyesun, asked him to kindly fuck off with his incessant probing, if only until evening. Her hours alone are precious few, but she needs them between what is fast revealing itself to be a much less amusing affair than she'd imagined. Maybe she does need the help; maybe he can provide it. But she is a long way from either admitting that or confirming otherwise. She knows there's only one way to do that, but not yet. Now is too soon, but soon now may be too late.

They take repast in their room in silence. Neither is much interested in the dish's particulars. Human enough to enjoy the flavour, but enjoyment is not sustainment. Besides, he seeks more nourishing fare and requests it when he feels she might not refuse. She believes the worst is over and steadily if warily provides. She is, of course, wrong.

36 days until the revelation

Chapter 3: Why the Dumpling smiled

How cruel, that things became clearer after that, at least for a while. It's as though losing him, the man who at once had all the answers and yet knew exactly what to ask, made room for all the future memories I had to collect and puzzle over. I envy you, Dog-Ears, when you say you don't remember what it was like when your mother left. That you could just stare out a window at night, up at the moon or some other vague, romantic, naïve symbol and construct her as an ideal. Because I will tell you, it's neither the start nor the middle of a relationship that defines how we think of people we've lost. It's always, always how things ended. It can be a single breath, or it can be years. It is still what we think of as 'the end.' And the night Daddy left, or was taken, was the end of knowing there was someone in my life who even cared about questions and answers.

Oh, some tried I suppose. The visitors Mother entertained (yes, you may smirk at that choice of words, Brother) typically came and left without fuss, treating me with no more attention than a curious piece of furniture – some weird, squat chair with silent, staring eyes and expressionless lips. At most they'd pat me on the head or rub my cheek with the back of their hand in passing. But now and then there'd be a small toy or a treat, which I usually ignored. I might have half-heartedly played with the toy or nibbled the treat. But it was certain even then that these people were not Daddy, and that their place was much like Mrs. Baker's. To come, stay a while, and then go.

No, if anyone tried to fill his place it was of course *her*, and that's why she made sure I was in his workshop that day. I've managed to give you a few glimpses of my toddler years, but like I said: his absence threw everything into harsh clarity, and I can tell you all about this event or that. The nitty-gritty, as you say. You might enjoy this, but if so, please at least attempt to pretend otherwise, because I sure as Eph didn't and won't.

Maybe Mrs. Baker was busy that day. Maybe some part of me knew where Mother was going and refused to be left behind. Either way, we went back to the workshop just once before moving to the city, to do all the things that need to be done when someone has…is gone.

The workshop was even farther from the city than our house. I remember. When Daddy and I would take those rambling walks, it was always out the back door. Mother was of course less concerned with staying out of sight. The first time we stepped out of the house and into the muddy road, I looked right, and saw the city, past some hills. The road itself didn't go that far, and it was as though you had to break some sort of rule to get to the city from the village. Find your own road, or make one. I thought it was a magical castle, that maybe I'd get to go there someday. I remember, too, Mother cuffing me for just standing there and then dragging me by the arm, to the left. Away. I tried to look over my shoulder. Another cuff. Cursing. Princess Jade gave up and followed Mother through the damp, destitute streets of the village, and into Daddy's workshop.

Mother was strangely comfortable in Daddy's workspace. No, not comfortable. *Satisfied.* I saw her walk around the big table in the middle of the room, fingers idle over the sawdust, leaving more of a mark than she might have intended. And even now I can't tell you what she was feeling. I mean, of course she didn't cry or anything like that. She saved her precious tears for a better audience than her stupid, half-wit daughter. I want to say she was dead, or at least she wanted to be. Her expressions, her movements. How can either be called 'lifeless' when the dead have neither? And yet, as she circled that table, taking in the workshop for the first time in a long time, I hope she felt something behind her unchanging face, under her stray nails scraping the dust.

I watched all this from the door, clutching the strap of my patched-up carry bag. By then she knew better than to expect me to answer, which could be why she'd really started talking to me. Or maybe just to herself, around me.

"Smells in here."

Prompted, I began to list all the smells in the room in my head, tapping my forehead against the doorframe to keep count. Sawdust. Paint. Wood. Grease. Lacquer. Leather. Daddy.

Mother hitched up her skirt, strode to the far wall, flung open a window. Countless flecks danced in the light. She coughed and waved her hands as she walked through the drifting multitude.

"Better. Jade, my girl, we have work to do."

Not there, not then. Not without him.

"Come on, help Mummy over here." She was gathering jars full of little bits of clinking mystery. Not carefully or deliberately, no. Like they were bothering her, in her way. The tinkle of nails and screws, once a chime announcing Daddy and I were about to make something Together, was too loud, too much. Tapping of forehead became thumping.

"Stop that, Jade. You'll damage the wall."

No. This made sense. Something in the air. There was more to Daddy's workshop than the smells or the sights. It had to sound a certain way.

"...Fine then."

But I wasn't so young anymore, and I knew that knocking my head on the wood wasn't helping anyone. I kept it up as she fussed with Daddy's stuff, trying to maintain the smooth-rough rhythm. It started to hurt. I was hurting myself. He wouldn't want that. Had tried to stop it at the end. So I slowed, eventually turning my head to rest my cheek against the doorframe, watching her once more.

Efficient. That's the word you're looking for, Brother. Waiting to hear perhaps. Chantal did everything according to her agenda, whether it was the careful progression of a song or the itemisation and planned disposal of her absent husband's belongings. She had her back turned, hands shoving this and that around the main worktable. I remembered her face after she'd first done my ears and imagined that it looked much the same now. That she was doing-what-had-to-be-done-even-if-it-hurt-her-too. I smiled where she could not see me smile.

Then she moved to another set of shelves, and I could see her profile. Of course not. The imagined and the real rarely aligned. Maybe even now. No, she wasn't even grimacing. Just...bored.

"What are you smiling at?" Her profile saw me back and became a glare. Caught me before I could catch myself.

"Not." I did everything I could to prove it. Frown. Stare at floor. Bunch fists. Anything short of looking her in the eye.

"You were. Don't think I don't see everything, Jade. Why don't you go outside if you're not going to help me?"

"No!" Hard head shake. Made me dizzy. Being here without Daddy was bad enough. But her being here without Daddy or me? No. "Just gonna watch."

You know, she never did *make* me help her. Just kept saying the word in the tone of someone who never in their whole life received any help whatsoever. I suppose she expected a five-year-old to ask 'how?', and probably would have chastised me for not figuring it out for myself. It wouldn't surprise me, Brother. Either she never was or it'd been so long she'd forgotten what it was like to be a child herself. Is it that easy to get caught up in being an adult that you lose touch with how you thought and felt as a child? Maybe letting go of that need to be told 'how' is what it means to be an adult? Eh?…No, me either.

"You lazy little dumpling." She shrugged, turned back to her work.

That wasn't my name. Not here. But neither was Jade. And if I had to choose, I'd take Dumpling. It sounded closer. Close enough, anyway.

I crept over the floorboards. Bits of mud clogged each step.

"I can hear you, Jade."

I stopped, heard my heartbeat and remembered something. The wood.

"Why are you so scared? Thought you liked it here."

I touched a leg of the worktable. Rubbed it gently. Smooth. Rough. Of course I couldn't feel the nails holding it in place. I raised my hand, made a fist again. Hit the wood. Thud.

"Mummy…?"

"Hmm?"

"…Nothing."

"Hm."

But it never is. I did it again. And I knew what I wanted.

I half-climbed onto a stool to better see what Mother was doing.

"Mu—"

"Out with it, Jade!" Thankfully she didn't look at me.

"…Why are you cleaning Daddy's stuff?"

She just turned and glowered at me, Daddy's hammer clutched in her bony fist.

I half-fell off the stool.

"I swear." The hammer in her hand became a threat. "Sometimes I have no idea where you came from, babbling like that. Your father was useless but he wasn't an idiot. Slow down, speak clearly. Use your words."

But I…exactly! Yes, that's precisely how she makes you feel. Except it's not a piece of meat she's treading on, it's your heart…yes, okay, that was a little melodramatic. Fine, it was a lot. Stop rolling your Ephing eyes, Brother. Let's just say I'm fairly sure I was making sense, that I was using my words, and that for whatever reason, she didn't understand. Couldn't. Refused to.

So I gave up on words and reached back to what I knew worked.

I pointed at the hammer, sort of whimpered. Tried to look pleading.

"Eh?" The hammer went down, and my gaze, my fingers, my need went with it. And my hopes. "This? What does a little girl need with a hammer? You'd just hurt yourself, or worse, someone else."

Then she walked over to me, so close I saw almost nothing but her thin cotton dress, almost not even her smirk, and placed what I wanted just out of my grasp, just out of my sight. On the table, right above me. The moment my eyes flickered up to see, hers bore down at me, into me. Something inside me fell back, fell over. Thud.

"Don't even think about it."

And since Mother wasn't anything like Mrs. Baker, I tried very, very hard not to think about it. I looked for distraction. I knew she'd offer none, nothing other than ostensibly returning her attention to the task of swapping all evidence of Daddy's existence out of existence. Ostensibly, because if I so much as stood on tippy-toes to get that bit closer to what I wanted, she'd snake around and send me flying. I knew it. Hell, Brother, I'd already taken a few steps back to reduce *any* temptation she might have.

"That's better. You may have your muffin now, for being a good girl."

I smiled and smiled and smiled and didn't even bother trying to hide it. Muffin! I was pulling it out of my bag before she even finished her sentence.

Oh. Forgot to explain those, didn't I? Having proven herself totally incompetent in the area of child-minding, Mrs. Baker's role in my life had been reduced significantly…but not outright removed. Every few days she'd drop by, drop off a load of those incredible muffins, then drop out of our life once more. And let me tell you, those muffins were bloody good. Funny you'd ask that, but maybe I expect it by now. Yes, I mean literally. Apple, berries, sometimes cinnamon…these were just sugary flavours failing to mask the soggy dark truth. Oh yes. That is indeed how Mother works. Why blood muffins? Ephed if I know. The usual mixture of cruelty and consideration. Trying to cultivate a taste for our ancestral nourishment? An acceptance, perhaps. All I can say is those muffins were pretty much everything I lived for back then.

Ugh. I make it sound like an addiction, but really it was just the one sweet, satisfying, and more importantly consistent thing in my life. And is there really anything wrong with obsessing over something that keeps us going, despite it all?

Are you seriously comparing muffins to a *sword*? Fine. I'll eat one, you eat the other. No flesh from my bones either way. But let me ask you, Dog-Ears, surely there was something as simple as a favourite food in your childhood. Hah, I like that. "Food was a favourite." And you, Char Ah-Ran? What would delight a savage little street rat of Kaifeng? Something meaty, I suppose. Rabbit stew maybe? Ha, knew it. Don't feel bad. You're not that transparent. Most times. And there's no need to ask you, Charan Jaydemyr, brother of my blood. There's the answer right there. Just like you. Never in an age would you know or understand why a muffin could bring a smile to a dumpling's face.

And yet I can tell you know what was really happening. That Mother waited until I was well into devouring the muffin, both consuming and consumed by it, to almost accidentally sweep back to the table, her hand just happening to knock the hammer to the floor. And no, she didn't bend to pick it up or even say anything.

She just watched me. Daring me to defy her will. To choose the forbidden desire over the granted one. Mouth full of mushy joy, I just watched her back.

Three seconds later she seemed to relent, gave out a theatrical cry. "Oops! Clumsy me!"

And then she took the hammer up.

Only to leave it on the stool.

And then she resumed her observation of me.

Never in the history of God's Blessed World has a quarter of a muffin lasted so long. I nibbled. I picked. I turned chewing into a game of meticulous division years before I'd learn either word.

"Oh, just finish the fucking thing." Graceless in defeat, she turned back to her work. Thankful for her absent gaze, I complied with relish, shovelling and mashing now that I had no one to fool. Well, yes. Try to fool.

That's when she began to hum. No, not quite sing. That she yet reserved for the appreciative crowds. Just a pointless little melody cribbed from any number of her pieces and pasted together for one simple purpose. To create a beat.

Maybe she knew. Eph knows I made no effort to hide my habit of retreating into raw rhythm when the world didn't make any sense, and her world so rarely did. A light tapping joined her wordless tune, first nails then pads of fingers.

She glanced back at me, the humming done but the drumming incessant.

I didn't move.

Then she glanced at the hammer, now well within reach.

It didn't move either.

Mother resumed her song and sent her attention elsewhere. The hum became vocalised notes, and the beat became a pulse, heel of palm against age-grained wood. I wasn't even vaguely able to tell that the thumping was precisely the same tempo as my own instinctive impact, but it was. I only knew that it resonated with me, aligned everything back towards that which she had denied me. I needed. I wanted. It was his and it was ours and she'd stolen it and the hammer could give it back. Had to take it back. Yes, Brother…there are some things you can never take back.

This time she didn't look around.

Thud. Thud. Thud. Thud.

"You really want to take it, don't you, Dumpling? To hold it."

Thud. Thud.

Nope. Nopenopenopenopenopenope—

"Yes, Mummy."

Thud-thud. Thud-thud.

"And what did I say?"

"Don't even think about it."

"And did you do what I said?"

Thud-thud-thud-thud-thud-thud…

"…Yes, Mummy."

Thud.

"You didn't even think about it, not even once? But it's right there.
You could take it and I wouldn't see. Not with my back turned. Maybe
you already have. Have you, Jade?"

Of course not. But had I thought about it?

Of course.

Which answer did she want?

"NO!"

Thump.

"No, you haven't thought about it? You're lying, little princess. What
happens to children who lie?"

She'd told me, once maybe, twice even, but what did it have to do
with any of this? Think. Think real hard, Sarah. Children who lie…did it
rhyme? Everything important rhymed. Like 'when the moon is round,
sleep safe and sound'. And so…Children who lie…cry? Sigh? Get no
pie?

If I couldn't remember and I lied, or guessed, which was the same
thing really, maybe I'd find out. Didn't want that…

"I don't know."

She laughed. I almost cried, sighed, got no pie'd. Almost *died.*

"Finally telling the truth. Did you pick up the hammer yet?"

"No you said not to so I won't."

Laughter stopped. Tone shifted. Whoever said what came next, it
wasn't Mother or Mummy. It was someone who always got what they
wanted at the expense of someone else desperate to give it to them.

Chantal Falkenstrom had arrived.

"I suppose you don't really want it that badly then."

Cry? Sigh? Get no pie? Go bye-bye?

"No, not that badly, not at all nope."

Lie.

"Let me tell you then, little princess. Let me teach you what no one
else will ever teach you because they don't love you the way I do. Let me
tell you what happens to children who lie.

"Children who lie, little princess, get what they want."

Eph's Wrinkled Sac, it didn't even rhyme. And yes, Brother.
Completely. Ten: 'The truth is sacred'. It's probably the most cited
Commandment, and yet almost certainly the most violated. Well. Maybe
not 'and yet'. Maybe 'because it is'. Because for all her performative
piety, Chantal Falkenstrom had a spectacularly flexible relationship with
the truth. And yet she said:

"Tell me the truth now. Why haven't you picked up the hammer yet?"

Like I had a choice at that point.

"Because I'll get in trouble."

"Only if you get caught."

"But…but you…"

What? Why are you looking at me like that, Brother? Your smile right now is her smile.

…That's better.

"But I might not turn around."

"You will." I didn't know the word *eventually* but she'd taught me the meaning well enough.

"Are you thinking about it right now?"

"Yes, Mummy."

"And didn't I tell you not to think about it?"

"Yes…"

Another tonal shift. Now we were conspirators, solitary bearers of the black and white flame of truth in a world of dark grey deceit.

"Then you're already doing what you were told not to do. You're already in trouble, little Jade."

No sigh. No lack of pie.

Just cry. Soft and helpless and completely guilty.

"Have I hit you, Jade?"

I sobbed a no.

"Have I told you you can't have a muffin?"

I sobbed another no.

"And have I said you can't take the hammer?"

In grownup language, 'don't even think about it' meant 'no'. Surely.

I sobbed a third, very confused no that really meant 'please stop this.'

"No. I have not. I never said that. I said don't think about it, which you still did. And you are in trouble for that. A little bit. Do you think you'll be in bigger trouble if you take the hammer?"

"Yes…"

I was dry now, now that 'in trouble' didn't mean absolute retribution in the form of a quick backhand, as it more than occasionally did.

"Maybe. Or maybe you'll just get what you want."

And that was what she left me with. Her implicit invitation and the hammer so close I wouldn't even need to stand on my tippy-toes to get it.

I waited. She kept working, humming. No beat this time.

Hmmm..hmmm-hm-mm-mm…

I slid one foot a tiny bit forward, eyes locked on her treacherous back.

Hmmm-mm-mm-mmmm

I gently, so gently put my carry bag on the floor.

Hm-hm-hm…hmmmhmmm…

My right hand became the slow, slow reach towards wrath, ruin and really, really want…

Mm-mmmmm-hm

Fingers so close they could almost tap in time on the handle…

MmmmMmmm

Knuckles creaked into a possibility of motion, and I felt the rough-smooth wood of the—

"O, Accurs'd was the Princess Jade!"

She started to turn.

I couldn't even pull my hand back. I was done. Done done done. All I could do was *not* take the hammer. That was what would get me in bigger trouble, right? Just trying, she didn't say I couldn't do that.

Not that it really marked anything but yes, I did. A little bit. Bladder control is hardly a priority for any five-year-old, Charan, and I wasn't just any five-year-old.

Her voice echoed away and she didn't turn around. Just reached for something to her right.

Resumed humming.

Was this a hint that she would turn around for real? Or proof that she never would?

My five-year-old self said a five-year-old version of 'To Eph with it' and just snatched the hammer off the stool.

That was when I realised the only thing I wanted to do with it was bash something. Bash something really hard. Make the loudest, angriest, happiest, rudest thumping sound ever.

Actually, that's a lie. I realised it was the only thing I wanted to do right after I'd done it against the wooden floorboards.

Mother definitely turned around.

I froze, resisting an incredible urge to smash the hammer against my stupid, stupid head.

Her too-fast, too-slow open-handed swat made sure I didn't have to resist for very long. It wasn't a slap, and it wasn't a shove. It was…a dislocation. I saw it coming and simply didn't move. The hammer might as well have been nailed to the floor…and yet after the initial splash of pain, the momentary darkness, the shock of being moved from *here* to *where!?*, and then of course the boiling tears as I scrambled for the door, it was only the realisation that my right hand was not empty that gave it all any semblance of meaning.

It was my triumph and even then I knew it. Even as I cowered against the door frame, I knew I didn't have to use my head this time. With what I imagine was a feral sneer, I brought myself to my knees, forced myself to return Mother's furious glower and deliberately cracked the hammer against the floor again. And again. And each time, I heard it speak in my stead.

Mine.

Now.

Again.

MINE.

…And you know what happened next, don't you?

She laughed.

But it was a different laugh. It didn't mock or scathe. It wasn't released to cut or sever. This was the first time I'd hear that laugh, and it was the last.

Chantal Falkenstrom subsided into giggles, then sniffled, and then wiped a tear that came from nowhere and went to much the same place. I have no Ephing clue what any of it meant, but when she was suddenly *there* wrapping her arms around me, it didn't matter at all.

Whatever I'd felt before, it was nothing more than suggestion and assumption. I didn't know terror or awe or stupefaction until the moment she enfolded me and said, "Yes. *Yes.* You took it and you held it no matter what." Horror of horrors: she stroked my tangled, knotty hair as though that might soothe my bile-clenched guts, my shredded nerves. And the worst thing is it almost did. "You lied and you did not get caught, not until you were able to hold onto what you wanted. Only then, my sweet Princess, only then did you make your move, loud and clear. Mummy is proud of you, darling girl. I am so…*so* fucking proud of you."

I was just so…*so* Ephing grateful she wasn't hitting me.

Mother pulled back, holding me at arm's length so that our eyes had to meet. Hers, now hardening once again and mine, still blurry but quickly, too quickly reflecting my grasp of the situation, a situation in which I was getting what I wanted, not just for myself but from her. Things locked into place, a crass causality that relegated empathy to nothing more than a redundant detour.

"What happens to children who lie, little princess?"

I grinned, fierce and strong. I knew. *I knew.*

"They get what they want!"

"Unless?"

Without even a hint of considerate hesitation:

"Unless they get caught!"

I see you get it now, Charan. Yes. She wasn't content to just tell me the Commandments. That's not her way of teaching, is it? Things told can be ignored. Things read can be forgotten. Things experienced, things felt, never go away. They possess you, own you. They claim you and never let go.

"That's my girl. Now give me back the hammer and let's get back to work, eh?"

So I held it out to her without a single thought.

She smiled, took it off me, and then moved to the next Commandment.

It takes a lot of skill to knock someone on the head with a hammer without really damaging them, but that's just what she did. Right on the forehead, just hard enough to ring my senses and shatter that moment, shatter all moments. I knew the feeling because it was only the tiniest bit worse than what I'd done to myself earlier. And because I knew it, it didn't really surprise me other than the awareness that someone else could grant it. That my self-punishment, so righteous and indignant in its calculated weakness, could be turned into something threatening just by removing that small but crucial measure of restraint. It was, plainly put, a brilliant violation. That's what she stole from me that time, and forever after. How could I ever return to careful displays of self-abuse now that she'd revealed them to be nothing but a farce?

"Never give back what you have worked so hard to take, Jade." She put the hammer on the floor. Mother straightened her legs, drove her disappointment down at me. "It is yours until someone else can take it from you. Don't let them."

I was beyond tears. Beyond grovelling. Beyond anything you could call rational. My lips buckled towards words but produced only a groan swollen with inexpressible frustration. Even a newborn baby knows to cry, to wail, to shudder and squirm. I was before all that, reduced to some state that feels everything and says nothing.

What could I do? Something.

And that something was, of course, to snatch up the hammer, rise to my feet and dare her with everything I was, everything I could be, to come closer, to try to take what was mine. All I had left.

"Okay, Jade. Enough games." She held out her hand. "Hand it over now."

"Okay, Mummy." Just as she started to scowl at my failure, I tucked the hammer away into my bag and grinned. My teeth were shiny fangs. My lips were thin and bloodless. My cheeks ripened and my eyes…hardened into cool, opaque jade.

No laugh this time. No smile. Just a quirk of her own lips and one last question. And like everything else she said, it was a sentence.

"Good. I've let you have a muffin and taught you a few things. Now, what do you say?"

Yes. The bitch tapped the earliest call-and-response, the this-leads-to-that that makes no sense and made no sense but made it all make sense. Finally.

"Thank you, Mummy."

I didn't stop smiling, if that's even what it was, even as she went back to work.

By the time she was done, the place was clean and orderly and devoid of anything that marked it as Arius Falkenstrom's workshop. We left and never looked back, and I never returned to that place, that place where he taught me about rough and smooth things, about the value of being honest and the necessity for perseverance…and where Mother took it all away…and even made me thank her for it.

You seem dissatisfied, Brother. I can't blame you. I wish I could say something profound like, "and yet some part of me hardened inside, the part that could hear Daddy saying how wrong this was, how this was not the way to be, and I'd never, ever forget what he taught me!" but to be completely Ephing honest, all I knew was that I had taken and I had held and I had kept what little of him remained.

And that I would crush, pulverise and destroy anyone who'd try to take it from me again.

Breaking Ground

They find themselves between settlements when the sun starts to fall. Charan is far more accustomed to life on and off the road alone, having spent weeks at a time tracking his prey. Sariana has had few extended periods of true isolation, and one of those was with well-stocked and paced caravans for over a year. Though both of them are naturally (or perhaps unnaturally) resilient and hale, and can likely keep moving until they reach the next Haven or inn, they acknowledge the fattening of the unfull moon, and save the notion of being sequestered indoors again for when they won't have the luxury of doing aught else. She casts about for a large tree a safe distance from the high road despite their solitary presence so far, seeking to huddle at its base in her woolen cloak. He, still feeling the rebuke of his prying into her troubled origins, disappears for a while, having muttered something about rabbits or birds and stew.

She is still wide awake when he returns a few hours later, that being his default 'is it safe to come back yet?' duration of absence. Rather than dinner, he brings back a bundle of sticks. Branches, almost. She watches as he rams them into the dirt near her, curious at first but then, when he completes the lean-to with a stretch of canvas from his pack, she is grateful. There'll be nothing to cook tonight and so no need to risk a fire, and even slightly inclement weather would obliterate the shelter. But for someone accustomed to urban comforts, even his desperately pitched tent is much better than her cloak and a tree.

33 days until the revelation

Chapter 4: How my torment endured

Which brings me neatly to the biggest real change in my pre-awakened life: moving to the city. To Teristra, into the All-Trades Inn itself, and smack-bang into the early days of what was later called the Purge.

What term? Purge? It's one of a few titles given to what happened when the guilds went to war and forced pretty much everyone to sign up or get the Eph out of town, especially those who used their Talents as anything more than daily-life tools. I wasn't really there for the worst of it, so if you want a comprehensive account of how bad it was, ask someone else.

Oh, you meant 'pre-awakened life'? It seems a good way to look at it, doesn't it? What she did. It's not a dream, even if she calls it that. Dreams end. You can look back and say, that was a dream. Weird things happened and it was all in my head and it didn't really make sense and it doesn't really matter. So I hear. I know you've had your share of it, but I think mine was different again. After all, yours was all about teasing out both her idea of you and Mother's plans…I'll call her that for now, to save complication. Two very different personalities, one hiding the other, almost representing fragments of the third, the real you Father intended to use. No need for that sort of complex layering with me. You were the dangerous one, after all. The honest-to-God prodigy with an ego to match. Oh, they had to hide me too, but one constructed history of utter obscurity and insignificance was more than enough. I've no idea why our real mother left it in her hands, and it's hard for me not to resent her for it. I'm sure I'll get the chance to ask her about it sooner rather than later.

Assuming we don't get our arses squarely kicked between now and then. Not an assumption I'm willing to make yet.

All of which is to say, to reinforce: what I'm telling you is as real to me as anything that came after. I had not yet awakened, but it was life. So: pre-awakened life. Not a dream. No more a dream than a mountain is just a very big rock.

Yes, Brother. It is a *very* you thing to say. Don't let this go to your head but that's not so bad. You're not always just some twit waving his sword around like it makes everything right. Now and then, you...well, it's not you I'm worried about sounding like.

"Weapons?"

"Weapons? Churna Mountain, seriously." Mother glared up at the very large, bald man standing between outside and in. "Do you see either of us carrying anything vaguely resembling a weapon?"

A pause.

"The Chantal: I do not."

"Good, so let's get this over with."

Another pause.

"Weapons?"

"...No, Churna. No weapons. I have no weapons to hand over."

No pause at all.

"Good! The Chantal: who is this with you?"

"This is my daughter. Jade."

Definitely a pause then. And then, very softly: *"The Princess Jade?* The princess...Jade?"

Half-right. Too close. Far too close.

"Close enough." Mother tugged my hand a bit. "Jade, say hello to Mr. Mountain."

If only I'd been paying more attention.

"Hello to Mr. Moun—"

She did that thing. Squeezed my hand tight enough to hurt, not tight enough to do any damage. I looked up at her. She was smiling at the giant man barring our way. I know now how strained that smile was. She was smiling the apology she'd never make.

"She's a very shy princess, Churna. Aren't you, Jade?"

If you say so, Mother. "Hello."

I stared at his very large knees as he grumbled very deep sounds from far above. Then something touched me on the head and I almost screamed. That wasn't meant to happen anymore. Thankfully Mother was holding my hand so tight I knew any sudden noises would bring out her nails. Didn't want that.

I endured in silence until the hand resting on my hair went away.

"Your Highness." His entire body folded down. Knees became waist. Waist became chest. Then his face was almost level with mine. A moment of scrutiny between fear-frozen eyes and his awfully, wonderfully hairy chin.

Another grunt. Then a smile emerged from the dark thicket, all yellow teeth, crooked but somehow straight too. "The Princess Jade: don't be afraid." A laugh, almost infectious. "The Princess Jade: Not afraid?"

"Jade not afraid." Almost true. Still not my name.

"Good." Good enough.

"Get on with it, you lug." Her grip was now inescapable. "I've no time for your stupid little drama."

Smile gone. Laugh gone. Almost-moment gone.

"Weapons?"

To me this time. And I had no idea what to say.

Curse my name, I almost said the truth.

"...No." Then I remembered the rest of what she'd said. "I have no weapons to hand over."

"Good!"

Good. Yes.

The man then put something in front of my face, between us. "This is The Lantern. The Princess Jade: stand still please." I'd seen it before, or something like it. At night, mostly. But then, like the magic it was, a pale green light appeared in the glass, grew into a firefly, and zipped about its cold confines.

"See? She's fine. We're all fucking just fine." Mother's grip loosened just a bit. Not quite enough.

Churna...Mr. Mountain smiled again but in the strange glow, he didn't seem very happy this time. He returned to normal height, straightening his knees. I looked up, watched the lantern lose its light as he pulled it away from me.

"The Chantal: stand still please."

"Clearly not going anywhere..."

Once again the lantern burst into life, this time much brighter. And the light was yellow. White. It wasn't green.

"Get that shit out of my face, Churn! It worked yesterday, it's working now, it'll work tomorrow."

Seemingly immune to my mother's charms, the doorman stepped aside, making a clumsy but clearly practiced gesture of entry.

"Welcome-To-The-All-Trades-Inn-Have-A-Nice-Stay."

"Every bloody time." Mother rolled her eyes and dragged me inside.

Of course it was a lie. Jade very damn afraid. I was terrified. I knew, even as she hauled me further into the preserved gloom of mid-afternoon All-Trades Inn, what was banging against my hip inside my bag. Every step. That illicit relic, stolen and reclaimed, never to be taken again. Even if asked for. It was a weapon. It had to be. It's all I had.

"Mummy."

"What?" She didn't stop. We were much closer to the bar by then.

"Is Mr. Mountain a good person?"

"He does his job."

Oh. So, that's…good.

"Why do you ask that, Jade?"

Huh? This was…*new.*

"Hammers. On the wall. He took them?"

"People gave them to him. They'll get them back when they leave." She stopped then. "You will learn, Jade. Some people can't be trusted with what they hold. Sometimes what they use for good can very easily be used for bad. That's the difference between a tool and a weapon. Understand?"

Nope. "Kay. Mummy, I'd never. Ever."

Lie. If anyone tried to take it from me…

"Of course, Jade. That's why I let you keep it."

Another lie. She didn't let me keep it. I didn't let her take it.

"Kay."

I lied and I got what I wanted. Good. I wasn't sure I wanted to try to crush, pulverise or destroy Mr. Mountain. He seemed nice enough. Just doing his job. His job did not involve taking my hammer away from me. Phew.

"Anyway, here we are."

Where, I was nowhere near asking.

"So *you're* the famous princess!"

Before I registered anything close to my usual resistance to being touched let alone moved by anyone other than She Who Did Whatever The Eph She Wanted With Me, someone had hoisted me onto a bar stool. For the first time, I was given an adult's eye view of the place. A huge counter stretched away in both directions. It felt so warm to my cheeks and smelled like Daddy in the best of ways. And Mother in the worst. Lamps lined the walls, so much more familiar in their gentle glow than the *wrong* thing Mr. Mountain called a lantern. Between the lamps hung all sorts of decorations, from animals heads on plaques to paintings of people doing everyday things I'd never imagined. Such strangely animate things trapped in happy unfulfillment. Chasing each other, never to be caught. Sharing food, never to actually eat. Smiling at each other, forever. The only other painting I'd seen was that of Mother looking so composed and placid. This wasn't like that. These could be true. Forever. I smiled back at them, maybe.

"Jade?" That man's voice again.

Huh. I sat up, reverie broken and hair clumped against soppy forearms.

He was standing in front of me, looking down with a smile of his own. And when it came to Jerich, everything was his own, even though if I were to describe him to you in greater detail, you'd probably say every Haven in the world has someone just like that. And it's true, except he was the first. Every time I'd see a broad grin from a shopkeeper later, it was his they borrowed. Every barrel-chested merchant hitching their thumbs into their belts and looking contemplative over a sale learned that pose from my Jerich. Men who were comfortably balding and absolutely not compensating in the form of grandiose waxed moustaches, and I'd meet so many of those over the years, they were just sad pretenders to the original.

And when they'd ask, "What would you like?" I always told myself it was with the same sincerity and genuine concern as Jerich showed for me, right from the start.

Unfortunately, no one had asked me that before so I didn't have an Ephing clue how to answer. What he was even saying. It was almost gibberish after life under her.

"Huh?" Ow. Sorry Mother. The back of my head deserved that one. "I mean, pardon?"

Bless the man, he actually scowled over my shoulder. "I asked, what would you like to drink, young Jade. We have milk, fresh juice, water if those don't take your fancy."

Too much. Again. I felt my face twist around the questions I knew now not to ask, and just turned to Mother, who was standing behind me no doubt ready to play her role should I dare to ask anyway.

"Mummy? Which?"

"He didn't ask me, silly. He asked you. Have whatever you like."

Yes, well, *she'd* never asked me, so how the Eph was I supposed to…fine. "Juice."

OW.

"Please."

"Just for that, she'll have water, Jerich."

"Hm, you've certainly worked hard on her manners, Chant." Jerich turned away. "What a good mother you are."

No, Charan. Years and years too early to understand what a difference inflection can make. I just heard those words and sagged inside. Even strangers called her that. Good. Why would they lie? So this is what a good mother is. This. Alright.

"Oh, you know, we all do our best."

"*Vahm en.*" That was the first time I heard the second-most useful phrase in the world, just after 'Eph this shit'. "Performing tonight?"

"No, Jerich Bielsen, I just came here to drop my kid off and go running around town naked for a lark."

SHE WHAT?

"…I don't think the little Miss appreciates your refined humour, Chant." He put the mug in front of me and patted my head with a wink. "There, there."

Third most useful phrase.

I sipped the water although I should have asked first. No slap this time.

It tasted an awful lot like juice for water.

"I'm sure she's just joking." Jerich moved to stand in front of the empty stool next to me. She wasn't joking about what drink I was going to get. She was just wrong. Somehow. I didn't have to lie to get what I wanted that time. Was hard not to smile. She'd see *that* truth for sure. And she'd punish it.

"Joking? Me? Hm. I suppose I am." Sigh. Grumble. Plumping of rump upon stool, just in time for the glass of red wine placed there.

What a coincidence. "This time." Smile. Wink of her own. Both pointless. Long drink from the glass. Pointed.

"Good. That's good." He seemed to use that word a lot. Did that make him good too? "And you, Jade. Ready to hear the song that has the same name as you?"

"She is not. She will be in bed hours before then. She's far too fucking young for what goes on here at night."

Jerich laughed at an irony I was far too Ephing young to get...or, more likely, I was far too Ephing accustomed to Mother's unironic usage of language to get that anything unusual had even just happened.

"If you say so, Chant. As to that matter, will she be attending school?"

"As much as is possible. Oh most definitely. There's a reputable establishment up in Parelle I've an eye on."

I took another sip of the world's juiciest water. Orange. Fresh. Reminded me of the orchards Daddy and I used to pass. Of seeing the dead fruit on the ground under the trees. The bad ones. Even I knew that's what they were. And the ones to be picked, eaten. The good ones. This was what I was drinking. This was what Jerich gave me.

"Parelle. Fancy part of town. She's what, six now?"

He looked at me, as though I was meant to say something. Make a face maybe.

"Almost seven." Mother drank. "Where do the years go."

Of the things gone from my life at that point, 'the years' were not something I worried about.

"Close enough to Levi then. He can show her where it is. Maybe help her settle in here."

"Are you sure you want to bother him like that? Bright kid. The chubby little dumpling would probably just slow him down. Hold him back. Doesn't seem fair."

Jerich looked at her as though she hadn't just said the truth. "That's *horrible*. Your jokes are unusually spiteful today, even for you. And Levi could probably do with a bit of grounding. He's always running around. Head in the rafters, feet tripping over the floorboards. He doesn't exactly have many friends himself. Not since the guilds started working their way through his classes." Jerich shook his head, looked down and turned away to do stuff with the bar.

"No fear of that happening with Jade. She's talent for little more than getting on my nerves and eating muffins. Lots of muffins."

Because she gave me *so many* chances to grow and learn…

"Well, let's hope that between my boy's whimsy and your girl's love of muffins, those thugs going around calling themselves 'Mentors' find more tempting recruits elsewhere. Hmph, they're still just kids themselves."

And if they were anything like me, they'd have found that conversation incredibly boring. The mention of muffins pricked my interest but I had no intention of bringing any further attention to myself while I was drinking water-that-wasn't-water-at-all. Would Mother have cared? No, but she might have dragged me through yet another 'lesson' about lying and truth. Better to just enjoy what I had and let them go on about whatever they were going on about. Kids and thugs and guilds and stuff.

After I finished my drink, I slid off the stool, almost wrecking my ankles with the landing.

"Bored already?" Mother glanced at me over her shoulder. "This place isn't safe for you to explore alone. Stay close."

I padded around a bit, caught in the gravity of Mother's commandment not to wander off. Before I knew it I was pacing behind her, five steps this way, five steps back. Staying close.

"Right, enough of your shit." Mother raised her hand and I cringed, but she just snapped her fingers and looked around the room. "Bells!…Where is that useless…Jade, Bells can take you to your room, where you hopefully won't cause any trouble."

But…my room was so far away, all the way out of the city and back down that road and around the corner and—

"Yes, Chantal?"

Behind me was the woman you already know to be the All-Trades' long-time resident healer and sufferer of drunken breaches of personal space. She looked neither saucy nor sassy, but instead tired and a little distracted. I hadn't noticed the place getting busier, but it had. And despite her name, she most definitely didn't jingle.

"Would you kindly show my daughter to her room? Jerich should have told you which would be ours. Jade, go with her and do whatever she says, there's a good girl, I'll be up to check on you…later." Mother gave me a shove towards the woman and turned back to her drink and the bar without waiting for an answer.

"As you wish, Chantal." Bells pursed her lips and regarded me. I regarded my hands holding my bag. Breathing out very slowly through her nose, Bells offered her hand. I relinquished my grip on the bag with just one hand and reached out to her.

Years of having had my knuckles pressed together by Mother's tendency to treat hands like the straps of a leash prepared me for an unpleasant but necessary first contact.

"Come on then, *Princess*." She took hold of my fingers in a way that was both light and firm. I did my best to keep pace with her through the room, which wasn't quite full of legs. We came to a long set of stairs and I stopped despite myself.

"What's wrong?" I got the feeling she actually wanted an answer.

Still, the answer did not come easily, because that feeling was still new and difficult to figure out. "That's a lot of stairs." Far more than I'd ever climbed in the village. And these steps weren't solid, just slats of wood with huge gaps between them. Huge enough for a little girl to fall through.

"I suppose it is. Would you like me to carry you then?"

Of course. Yes. Please. "No. I mean, no thank you."

But I didn't move. This felt like an impossible situation now. Tell the truth and be punished for giving in. Lie and stand there all day…or…try?

"Alright. Let me know if you change your mind. Here we go."

I tried. The first step was okay. The second was good too. The third caught my foot and I tripped, one hand held by hers and the other dropping the bag, which made a very dull thud but miraculously didn't fall between the steps.

"Oops-a-daisy." I had no idea what that meant. She reached over and, clearly far stronger than anyone I'd ever met ever except of course Daddy, scooped me up, held me in place with just one arm as I clung to her.

Then she bent and picked up my bag.

"Goodness me, Jade, this thing is heavy. What do you keep in it, rocks?" There was laughter in her question. Too many new laughs today, but this one was part of her words rather than after them. I liked that then, and have ever since.

Still, I said nothing because while I didn't keep rocks in it, I didn't want to ruin this by either lying *or* telling the truth. That and I was very quickly coming to enjoy being held this way.

"I suppose a girl has to have her secrets." Bells adjusted her grip on me and handed me my bag, which I then held much as she held me. "Right then. Let's go."

I let her take me, trying not to look around as we went higher than I'd ever been before, at least inside a building. I'd climbed hills and rocky paths with Daddy but if you tripped down those, there was ground all the way. Trip from the second floor walkway of the All-Trades and there was only ground after a lot of falling.

And there were two more floors to go. Naturally Mother would insist on being placed at the top.

Bells put me down after we reached the last floor but I didn't let go of her hand.

"It's okay, just remember there are railings but stay close to the walls if you can." Despite Mrs. Baker's failures, apparently adults really could read my mind that easily. That or maybe I was gripping her hand just a little bit too tightly. "You'll get used to this soon enough. Here we are. Your room, Your Highness." Another laugh, this one after her words.

She turned the handle and ushered me through the first door after the stairs.

This was *not* my room. My room was far away and safely on the ground and I missed it fiercely already. It was also much smaller, didn't have a curtained window, a large bed, a trunk at the foot of the bed, a partition for changing clothes, a chamberpot…or any of the other things I'd come to understand as basic Haven room features.

"Oh, look, all your stuff is already here. Your mother's good."

And it was. And she was. People kept saying so.

I looked in a closet and drawers, and saw familiar clothes. I opened the trunk, and saw a few familiar toys. But they were mixed with unfamiliar everything else, like the red rug covering a lot of the floor and the decorative dresser with a very large mirror. And that awfully big window.

"Well this *is* impressive." Bells even whistled, a sound I'd only heard from Mother but there was no song to follow. "Jade? What are you doing down there?"

"Nothing." I crawled further under the bed. Tried not to look at the wall with the drawn curtains exposing the window. I did try to bury my head into the floorboards. I don't remember if they were smooth or rough…just cold.

Bells sighed. "You don't have to be afraid. You're safe here. Very safe. And your mother's room is right next to this one. See? It's just through this door." I didn't look up, so I didn't. I'd *know* soon enough, oddly not by its proximity but its lack of use. "Are you hungry? I imagine it's almost that time."

I don't know if I was or not, but I knew the right answer to that question. I elbow-kneed out from under the bed.

"Hungry. Yes, please."

"Alright then. I'll fetch you something. Don't go anywhere." Another speaking-laugh. "Other than to use the waterroom, of course."

And she left me alone.

I don't really remember how I felt or acted other than I tried to skirt around that window as much as possible. I had no idea how high up we were and it might spring open at any moment, and the wind might pull me out and down.

Nope. I didn't try, neither the window nor either of the doors. She said don't go anywhere so I didn't. And I had no idea what a waterroom was or what I'd use it for, so that didn't stick either. The closest I came to 'going anywhere' was pacing the room for a while before flopping on the bed and marvelling at how soft it was. How soft and warm and...

The wall lanterns were lit when I woke up. There was food on the table beside the bed. Good food. *Really* good food. Roast meat and baked vegetables and buttered bread and tasty broth. And there was drink. More water-that-tasted-a-lot-like-juice from Jerich. And best of all, best of all, there were muffins. *Two* muffins. One to eat, one for the bag. This was...just wonderful.

Not too long after I finished, someone who wasn't Bells knocked and entered and took the tray. The All-Trades had a large number of workers, and I didn't really get to know many of them. I can't even tell you if she were old or young, happy or sad. She was just there and then not.

A while after that I heard cheering and applause. Then there was silence for some time, and then more noise. This went on and on. I admit, I wanted to open the door to see what was happening but 'don't go anywhere' was still the last thing I'd been told by someone Mother said to obey. And it was dark outside the window. Night-time. I was meant to be asleep at night. So I peed in the potty under the bed and then— well, no, I took it out from under the bed first, Brother. The bed wasn't *that* big. Nor I that small. Oh. Another of your jokes. Oh. Ha, ha.

No, it wasn't the last thing I did before going to sleep. The last thing I did was drag those thick curtains to conceal the window. Wait, no. The *last* thing I did was pull Daddy's hammer from my satchel and curl up with it on the bed, tearless and silent, as I would for many nights to come.

Despite the noise and the light, I had no trouble passing out. I do remember waking up once, into darkness and solitude; somehow those lanterns must have gone out. I do not remember Mother coming in through that other door to check on me, but that's not to say she didn't.

Hey, don't make that face. A girl can hope.

"I believe this is the right room!"

Levi Jeriksen believed a lot of things. He believed in not knocking before bursting into people's rooms first thing in the morning. He believed that saying what he thought was usually the best course. He believed in thinking about what he said. Shyn', I think he believed in believing. Mostly, he believed in starting almost every sentence with two words that make most people doubt whatever comes after.

I believe I was too busy shying away from the suddenly open door full of someone I didn't recognise to do much more than stand there. I'd been looking out the window having finally come to terms with it, or something close to that. Outside was still daunting, but much easier to take with a mouthful of muffin.

I'll spare you the obvious: yes, he looked a lot like an eight-year-old version of his father, which means full head of red hair, ruddy cheeks, a body shape somewhere between comfortably round and actually fat, and eyes sparkling with a vigour I wouldn't have recognised a day ago.

"And I believe you are Jade. Like the song. *The Curse of Princess Jade.* But I believe that's all made up. You don't look like a princess, but bless my eyes if this isn't a room fit for one!" I still didn't move, not even to finish chewing the rest of the muffin I'd crammed in my mouth just before he appeared. Now he entered and closed the door behind himself. Slammed it, really. Leaned against it. And looked at me. "So, whatcha' eating?"

Funny thing about the word 'muffin'. When you say it with your mouth full of muffin, it still sounds a lot like 'muffin'.

Or so you'd think.

"Nothin'? I believe that's a lot of nothing you've got in your cheeks!"

I know now that he was grinning and that he meant very well because that's just who he was, but at the time I didn't know how to read any of that. I *did* know that he was calling me a liar, so I proved it wasn't 'nothing' by opening my mouth very wide, then chewing and swallowing the remains of the ever-so-delicious: "Muffin."

I stated that very decisively at his feet. Or the floorboards near them.

"Oh. Guess you got one from downstairs. We get fresh baked muffins all the time. And bread. And pastries. I like the apple ones. I believe they're my favourite. What's yours?"

Halfway through this sunny barrage I'd moved away from the window, closer to the bed, but still pressed against the wall. Despite the boy believing this was the right room, I was pretty Ephing sure that right then it wasn't. He was looking for some other Jade, someone who was fine with being ambushed mid-breakfast for lively chats about baked sweets.

"Why are you here?" I managed to say this at his knees. At the ragged, beige pants covering them. Then, in a rare fit of social dexterity, I looked at his round face. "Who are you?"

Yes, 'how do you know my name?' would have been good and made more sense, but I knew from Mother that her six-year-old daughter was rarely good and rarely made any sense at all.

"Why, it's Offday!" I took his obvious tone as more mockery of my ignorance, a rebuke that I even had to ask. "Otherwise I believe I'd be at school and definitely not here. But it's Offday so I can do whatever. Except Dad said I should come say hello to you. So, hello to you! He also said we can play all day, if you want. Can't go too far but I can show you some really interesting things outside. Do you like dresses? I believe the girls at school like dresses. I'm not supposed to because I'm a boy but I know some places we can look at them. "

And then, mercifully, he stopped. Maybe it was the look of terror in my eyes. Maybe it was the realisation that this wasn't a conversation but a monologue. Maybe he just needed to catch his breath.

"Oh, Dad's right. I'm such a dunderhead. Forgot to introduce myself. Hi. I'm Levi. I live here. But I don't work here. Not yet. Dad does. I will, someday. So, what flavour muffin?"

And maybe none of those things.

Thankfully his last question allowed me to answer everything else he'd asked.

"I don't know." And then I said something I never thought I would. Ever. "I want my Mummy." So I can ask her what the Eph to do about any of this. About this boy. About Offday. About 'school'. About dresses. About muffin flavours.

"You shouldn't say that, not like that." The boy pushed off the door and sat on the wooden chair next to the bed. He looked down and wrinkled his nose. "Oh. You still use a pot. That's right. Are you sure you're six years old? Only babies use a pot and ask for their Mummy."

I turned my head and felt the wood of the wall rub against my damaged, painless ear. Smooth. Just smooth. "I *am* six years old."

"Okay. Just…" He seemed to think about that for a bit, long enough for me to skitter along the wall and towards my bag, so carelessly left beside the bed but on the opposite side to the chair. "You can bring that if you want. You should, in fact. Who knows what we might find?"

I wasn't about to tell him it already had everything I'd ever need inside. Although it had run out of muffins for now, I'd shoved the hammer back into it upon awakening. Another instinct that soon became habit.

"Bring it where?"

"Wherever we end up, I guess! Your mother, she's famous you know, well of course you know, she's your mother, she's downstairs having breakfast. A real breakfast. Not just muffins. If you want her, downstairs. You should get dressed first though." He laughed after saying that.

I grunted before I could catch myself, but mostly down at the bag in my hands.

"I mean, your nightgown is okay." I know now he was blushing. But then? The only time I'd seen a face that red was when it was flushed with rage. "For sleeping, anyway. Sorry, I'll…yeah." Levi stood, looked around the room again, and slunk out the door with just one sentence left to add to the already confusing pile of things added to my suddenly flustered morning. "I'll be, uhm, waiting just outside, don't take too long getting dressed okay bye then."

Click.

'Don't take too long' meant 'do it right fucking now' so the moment the room was mine again I did just that, despite a lingering urge to crawl under the bed and wait for Mummy to return. Levi had said she was downstairs. No telling when she'd be back up here then. Somehow I knew after just one day: this place was *different*. They called me Princess Jade here, which made her…the queen. A queen with no king, whose petty rule had been absolute in that little cottage for years. A queen who had finally taken her rightful place in this vast, terrifying palace full of intimidating, imposing subjects.

But if this were her rightful place, which would be mine?

Working Together

They agree on one last evening in the wild, safe from the potential threats any sort of 'haven' in Kas'Daen territory might incur. Charan sleeps most of the day, taking his turn in that makeshift shelter. Sariana forages and, despite his claims that he is the superior in this area (and most if not all others, owing to the unfair abundance of experience afforded by several fully-lived-through lives), it is she who brings back not mere sticks but a wild duck, fungus and some dirt-crusted root vegetables. When he finally admits to being awake, neither raise the matter of the duck's horribly misshapen skull. Oni-Goroshi has surely removed stranger heads from their perch atop equally strange bodies. She enjoys watching him have to use his beloved partner (she cannot believe it might be the other way around) to do the base work of a cleaver. He enjoys her watching him employ Dog-Ears' grisly yet gentle expertise.

The moon is barely a nick of black off full but visible only when the clouds see fit to permit it. Tonight they will need a fire, and he provides. They also need more water than usual, and she provides. He suggests roasting, but she did not collect those ingredients without a plan. Later, as they sup upon duck stew, she picks up her story with no overt prompting. Perhaps it is the eager way he asks for a second helping, but she knows otherwise. She's been waiting for this. She feels what comes next are the best few years of her best life. And when he fails to hide how much her exuberant storytelling hurts him, she realises her error and renders her childhood joy a mere segue. She understands. Reviewing fabricated torture is cathartic; reliving fabricated happiness is true torture.

30 days until the revelation

Chapter 5: Which me to be

Who could miss that spirited young lady, golden hair pulled in slightly messy pigtails, bursting from the waterroom and dashing down the stairs, face fresh and eyes aglitter with excitement for the day ahead? Who could even glimpse her, clad in the notable and distinguished black, silver, and red uniform of the prestigious South Parelle Respite Girls Academy and not think, 'there goes the very embodiment of youth and happiness!'?

Surely not the woman busy tending to the many lights, lamps and lanterns about the third floor of the Trades. Not that much older than the girl herself, she paused in her duties, hands still lit by the glow of her Talent.

"Hey, not so fast!"

The girl skidded to a halt on the landing between flights of stairs. "Oh, good morning, Agnis!"

"Good morning to you too. I meant to ask, would you like the heat on in your room when you get home from school? When? Eyesun? Fallingsun?"

The girl hummed in thought before nodding. "Thank you, Agnis, that'd be great. But goodness knows when I'll be back. Maybe just wait until I *am* home? It never takes that long to warm my room up."

"I can do that. But you know I'm off at Dyingsun, so I'll do it before I go either way. Well, whatever you get up to, have a wonderful day."

"You too, Miss Agnis! Don't work too hard."

Agnis looked down at her then-dim hand, made a fist, held it for a second, and then loosened her fingers. The soft aura returned. "I'm sure I'll manage."

After a nod and a wave, the girl resumed her descent. With effortless grace she reached the next landing, flung out one hand to grip the polished post and seemed to glide around it like a pendulum, only to resume with renewed pace. And when she finally came within distance of the ground floor, the sprite sprang off the flight four steps up, with just the most jubilant smile lighting the way. She barely lost momentum when the balls of her feet pounded against the floor and propelled her towards a long table laden with food for breakfast.

And who would have thought *this* was the same girl who, not so many years ago, had cowered in her mother's shadow for months after arriving, speaking rarely when rarely spoken to, seen to smile only in the confounding company of the Havenkeeper's lackadaisical son, and even then only as though trying to mimic the boy?

Who would have guessed this lively young woman so quick to giggles and grins now all but charging for the morning spread…was *me?*

Bells was already there, deliberating over pastries and gruel, as she did most mornings.

"Mmmmm, those apple turnovers look scrumptious." I took a deep breath. "And they smell even better. Excuse me."

I reached past her to pick up a handful of the pleasantly warm muffins, which were 'for royalty only' and so mine and mine alone, wrap them in a fresh napkin, and tuck them into my bag.

"They do, don't they? But maybe I should have something healthier this morning?"

"Oh…" I paused to look at the woman's mid-thirties full figure. "I think you're a long way from worrying about that. Go on."

"Maybe you're right, one won't hurt."

"One won't be as good as two."

She frowned, but not at me. "…Two. Just today." Again, something she said more days than not.

"Enjoy! See you this afternoon."

She had already taken a large bite of the first pastry, so her reply was muffled but the wave was clear enough.

I then broke into a run for the exit. I was more than ready to face the day ahead.

"Hey! Aren't you forgetting something?"

I pulled to a stop and looked back at the person who'd called out as she cradled a mug of coffee.

"Huh?"

"Don't 'huh' me, Jade. Breakfast?"

I sagged, all evidence of my great mood flagging only a little. "Grabbed a few muffins. Can I go now? I'm late."

"You're *never* late, and I'm pretty sure Levi's still in the kitchen. Come now, spare a little time for your mother, eh?"

"Shit." I made my hiss loud enough to make sure she knew I wanted her to hear it. Her smile faltered only a bit as I shuffled back towards her table and slumped into a chair. "I'm home aaaall night, every night, and most Offdays, and *now* you want to talk to me."

"Don't be a snooty little brat. I always want to spend time with you, but you know how it is."

"Suppose. Sorry, Mum."

"Pigtails again?"

"Mmhmm."

"I'm glad you're not hiding your face anymore. No princess, but pretty enough." She appraised me with both eyes and hands. "That tie really does bring out the best of your eyes. I named you well. The hair though. Aren't you ready for something a bit more mature? Do you want me to braid it?"

"Maybe tomorrow. I gotta go. Really."

"Don't you walk to school with Levi anymore?"

I looked at her then, but she was just curious and tired. Mostly tired.

"Sure. Sometimes."

"Today?"

"I'm going to be late, Mum."

"He's a good kid. Probably take over from his father someday. And it's not as though they're going to be falling over themselves for someone like you…"

"Just stop, alright?"

"Fine, fine."

"Definitely going to be late now. Fuck…"

She feigned offence, but laughed anyway.

I smiled.

"Who taught you to speak like that?"

"Same bitch who taught me everything I need to know about this shitty fucking world."

"That's my girl."

We both laughed.

Then she stopped and looked genuinely irate. "So what did you think of my latest addition to the song?"

"What song, Mum? You sing so many of them."

"You really think I don't know that you sneak out of your room to listen? You can't fool me, Jade. But I understand your curiosity. It's all about you, after all."

I didn't reply for a few seconds, then shrugged. "If I had, I'd say the bandits were idiots and should have set a better trap for the ever-cunning Princess Jade. But I didn't hear a thing, so…" I shrugged again, this time with just one shoulder. And I smiled, this time with just one side of my mouth.

And from her, yet another laugh, this one seemingly delighted, impressed and a little…cautious. "Of course you didn't. Okay, give me a kiss and off you go."

I looked around, saw Levi talking to Mr. Mountain near the door. Appearing defeated, I stomped over to her, leaned in and obliged her the least-committed peck on the cheek I could offer. The little golden *f* pendant that, as far as she knew, I never took off, hung between us. Before I pulled away she reached out and touched one of my ears. I paused as her fingers travelled the uneven, recently resculpted curvature, seeming to suppress a sigh.

"Looks good. I'm glad you're not hiding them anymore. Be proud of who you are. Who your mother is. I work hard for both of us. Please appreciate that, Dumpling."

"You know I hate it when you call me that, Mum." Despite my protests, I took the chance to give her a very quick hug and a long-suffering, "Bye…" before retrieving my bag and heading over to Levi and the way out.

Mr. Mountain frowned at my approach. "The Princess Jade: Good morning."

"Morning, Mr. Mountain." I grinned up at him. His gruffness, all part of the job, fell away and he reached over his counter, ruffling my not-so-carefully arranged hair with one of his gargantuan hands. I laughed and shied away after a few seconds.

"Oh, there you are, Dump—Jade." Levi wore the much more drab uniform of Oakenstage Common School, greys and blues mostly. Other than that, he looked much the same as he always had, ever since I'd first met him. Maybe a little taller, maybe a little less pudgy. Maybe a few more spots on his face. Hard to notice these things day-to-day, so I didn't really try. Levi was Levi. "I was waiting for you. Shall we?"

He stepped aside, sweeping his hand in a you-first gesture and bowing more than a little.

"Why, thank you, sir." I latched onto his proferred arm as we left The All-Trades Inn together.

It was brisk and overcast at early Morningsun. I stayed close to Levi as we passed under the All-Trades Inn's solitary sign, a painted white hand catching a drop of red blood, and walked beside the bustling Estenthric Highway, eastbound and a little deeper into the city proper. We dodged hurried adults on the path, everyone seemingly eager to avoid the thunderous passage of horses and carriages. Then, when we reached the fountain with its statue of some famous dead person speechifying silently in the middle of the crossroads, we turned left off onto the quieter Russet Street and headed north out of the AllTrades district and into Parelle.

That's when I disengaged the contact and moved to a more relaxed distance. Both of my hands could now grip the bag's strap, and did so, quite firmly. The weight of the bag almost hurt as it thudded against my left thigh.

"That Ephing *gash*." I felt my breath through these words: rough. Definitely not smooth. "'All about me.' Shyn's Ravaged Slit it is."

"Sarah?" Levi gave chase but I was seeking solace in the various shopfronts and stalls of Parelle's main street. The Whimsyway Markets were mostly in AllTrades and covered anything from fruit to frying pans but this northernmost end specialised in all forms of clothing. Most but not all of the shops had some sort of needle-and-thread sign. Many were still closed and wouldn't open until late Morningsun, even early Nighsun. On Offday they'd open much earlier, of course. This is where Levi brought me that first day, making good on his offer to show me a lot of dresses, which I hadn't liked then but made sure to like now, despite not owning many.

"Ooh, look at this one." I picked a random window display and skipped over to it. I think the dress, snug over a petite mannequin, was yellow, but it might have been black or pink. "I really like it."

"You've been fuming ever since we left. You might fool everyone else but I believe I know you better than that. Talk to me, Sarah."

"That's not really my name." The shop window held my attention until I felt his hand touch my shoulder from behind. I shrugged it away as gently as I could. "I wish I hadn't told you about it. Say, would you get me this dress, Levi?"

"Uh, maybe when the shop isn't closed." He stepped around to stand on my right, maybe an arm's length away. "And I'm not sure it'd fit...Sarah."

"Why? Because I'm fat?"

"What! No. Because it's for grown-ups."

"So it's not because I'm a fat Dumpling?"

"I didn't...sorry."

"Oh but it was close. Because it's true. I'm a fat Dumpling so the dress wouldn't fit."

"No, it's not because you're fat!"

"Did you just say I'm fat?"

No quick answer that time. "...Why are you so mean sometimes, Sarah?"

"Maybe because I'm fat. I've never seen a skinny dumpling." I laughed it off and leaned forward, breathing on the frosty glass. I doodled something with a crooked finger. Might have been a moon. Might have been a cross. Might have been both.

I think it was a hammer.

"I don't call you that and I don't think you're fat okay? Okay?"

I wiped away whatever it was when I heard giggling and half-whispers. A small group of girls maybe around my age, maybe a bit younger, and dressed in a uniform I didn't recognise paused not far from our little altercation. As one, they decided to cross the street before getting too close. I didn't have to look to know they were wearing matching engraved wooden badges. Flowers maybe. Probably passing through Parelle to reach Servandish to the east, the closest the Trades quarter had to real affluence. Mother had opened herself to more than a few men from Servandish during those years when *The Curse of Princess Jade* had yet to really catch on...and occasionally afterwards.

I lowered my gaze from the dress (or maybe it was a skirt) and stared at the concrete underfoot, scuffed at it with one well-polished black shoe then spat emphatically. "Eph her and Eph it all."

"E...Eph who?" Levi lowered his voice to a whisper. "Your mother?"

I straightened and turned my head his way. He looked confused and agitated. He was Levi, then and always. "Sorry. She just gets me so angry. You didn't deserve any of this. Thanks for being my friend, Levi." I opened my arms towards him. The hug was brief and awkward, with my arms enfolding him. I don't remember what he smelled like.

"Are you okay, Sarah?"

Not even close to it, Levi, but it wasn't your fault and I had just enough self-awareness to hold it back. "Yeah. I'm alright now. Let's go."

"I don't believe that." He fell in step beside me as I adopted a pace that left no room for straggling. "But I do believe you'll feel better once you're at school. A new year, new friends. Must be nice."

"You get to stay with *your* friends though, Levi, year after year."

"Not really my friends. Not like you are."

I said nothing more about friends. The word alone was fast losing what little value it had to begin with.

The colourful veneer of Parelle gave way to Oakenstage's more honest tones of wood, iron and grease. Just west of here was where a world of elaborate costuming folded into a world of base trickery. Oakenstage was once true to its name, a district dedicated to makeshift street performances of all nature. Anything from pantomime to not-so-playacted punishment. With certain guilds sweeping in to gather up those with real aptitude for more permanent positions in richer districts to the east, Oakenstage was left little more than a rotten pile of brothels, bars and flophouses; its occupants pronounced the name 'Ohkenstidge', perhaps forgetting the origin altogether. But one element resonant with the place's name remained: where the needle-and-thread was everywhere in Parelle, in Oakenstage it was wise to ware the cloak, the dagger, and the mask.

I imagine Levi and I chatted along the way. Silence never sat well between us, or at least so he seemed to believe.

We came to the familiar intersection, as we had for years. We stopped, as we always did.

Anticipating the usual words of parting, I made sure to say something unusual first.

"Levi, I didn't mean it, you know."

"What?"

I took a few steps closer to him, to the left and away from my next destination. "Any of it. Except the part about being your friend. I meant that. That's all. I gotta go."

I didn't move. He did, however. To his right, toward me and my next destination, where we knew he could not follow.

"See you this afternoon back at the All-Trades then." He reached out and patted my arm a few times. "And I know. Friends. I just wish…blah, doesn't matter." He looked away, down the street towards his school. "Better go myself."

"Kay then." When I saw that I had his attention again, I tapped my cheek. "Kiss for good luck? New year and all."

He bent down slightly and obliged as though he'd done this many times before, which of course he had. "I'm sure it'll be fine and everyone will be just like always. What difference will being in a new year make?"

"Probably none. You're right."

"Still." He wavered, as though measuring the weight between his belief and my feelings. "Maybe it wouldn't hurt if you, if you…I don't know, tried to be a little less—"

"Fat?"

"Mean! I mean…Mean."

"No idea what you're talking about, I'm always nice." I added a pout.

"Of *course* you are. God's Love but I hate to think how you treat the girls at that school. They truly do not deserve such scathing."

"Go on with you!" I made a shooing motion. "I'll see you this afternoon."

He went his way with a wave and a laugh. I went mine with the same.

A few minutes after that, when the chance of being seen by someone else from school was too high, I stopped, yanked out the pigtails, covered my ears and most of my face with my lanky hair, stuffed the ribbons in my little bag of things, put my head down and shuffled the rest of the way to school.

I was neither early nor late. No one bothered me as I made my way under the gate, across the courtyard and into the somehow never-not-cold stone building. There were other girls all around. I knew some of their names. If they noticed me, they didn't act on it. I may have returned a Flail here and there.

There were a few classrooms per year. Parelle Girls, to use the abbreviation, was both prestigious and selective, which meant most of the students were there either because of wealth or ability, and neither were in great abundance in West Teristra. But of what there was, it was reflected in how the students behaved, how they cliqued. Which guilds they were considering, and which guilds were considering them.

When I could, I looked around my new class, trying to spot who was sporting which badges. Nothing out of the ordinary or surprising. Feathers. Flowers. Coins. Instruments. And at least half displayed no badge at all.

I suppose you would think that, but no. The lessons were incredibly specific and most of them, in hindsight, useless for a girl growing up in Teristra. At the time, however, I just took for granted that along with grammar drills, Book readings and local history, we were learning stuff like Kakanic, the language of the lands between Kas'Daen and Chūnko. And the geography of south-east Kas'Daen. A smattering of Chūnko-go. The tenets and ways of a fanatical Tantamonian sect in the Faighana Valley called the Swords of Heaven…Now you see. Now you see.

And yet I never thought about any of it once the classes were over. Honestly, I didn't pay that much attention at all. Why would I? Teristra was my world entire. Barely a fifth of Teristra, at most. And here they were trying to get me interested in far-off lands and languages I'd never need. Waste of my Ephin' time.

After the morning block of lessons, just around the start of Highsun, the Master dismissed class for lunch and left us to our own devices for half the Hour. Another distinct division: those with wealth gathered in the catering hall, those without ate their brought lunches either in the room or around the grounds. Mother had offered me the chance to eat with the rich girls. We could afford it, certainly. But I said no. They rarely served muffins, and when they did they weren't very good. She accepted this reason.

"Uh, hi, uhm, Jade, we're in the same class now?" I heard this from somewhere nearby. A few desks away maybe. I didn't look up from picking at one of my muffins. Whoever said it sounded almost as timid as I probably looked. I didn't know her voice.

"You have to say her full name if you want her attention." Someone else, louder and brasher. I knew *that* voice. "*Princess* Jade." A slight pause. "Just like the song."

I still didn't look up.

"I know who she is, Tia. And you're not even supposed to be in here. Your class have their own room."

"There's no Commandment against spending lunch wherever the hells I or anyone else should please, Little Lu." Tia was fifteen years old.

One of the big girls. She didn't really need to use the word 'little' but people don't really need to brush dust from their shoulders either. "This might not be my room but I still have friends in here. Right, Princess?"

"Mmhmm." I finished the muffin, folded the napkin and dabbed at the crumbs around my lips. Someone snickered. I then used the same napkin to try to sweep my desk clean, gathering the mess in a cupped hand.

"Saving a little for later?" No one snickered at Tia's barb, but a few girls let out something close to a gasp. I didn't know them, and they didn't know her.

"That's not funny, Tia." Lu managed to rally some quiet if careful agreement.

I looked at the little pile in my hand. The bin was near the entrance to the room. My desk was not. So I just poured them back into the napkin and scrunched it up. I then reached down to place the napkin back in my little bag of things and looked at what else was in it. After a second or two, I flipped the bag closed and sat there, elbows on desk and chin cupped in hands.

"Well, I was in this class last year, and let me tell you, she really is a princess. A princess of stuffin' muffins." Tia snorted with something probably meant to be laughter, but no one joined in. "Well, *I* thought it was funny. So did the girls last year. We had a great time. Right, Abs?"

So she'd come too.

"Sure, Tia. Last year was great. Hi, Jade."

"Mmmmhey Abby. How's the world of meat and bone?"

"Same as always. Sharp and blunt. You join a guild yet?"

"I was considering the bakers."

I could hear the easy smile in her voice and allowed one of my own, mostly eaten by the flesh of my palms.

"Bakers?" Tia knew better than to let us banter for long. We might have forgotten she was there. "Oh. I get it! Muffins." She brayed in a way that wanted to sound forced. I had to look at her then, almost expecting her unfortunately attractive face to look like that of a horse.

"That wasn't funny." Thanks Lu, but I wish you hadn't.

"Shut it, squeak. The adults are talking." Tia blinked, as though realising she'd missed something, which she had. "Well *I* joined a guild. Shall I tell you which, Princess Muffmuncher?"

"I reckon I can guess, Tia-mutt."

Tia made another noise, but it was even further removed from a laugh than before. "See, that was funny too. I can take a joke. But here's another, a real good one." Tia wandered closer to my place near the window, but remained near the front of the room. "This princess here, girls. You heed her words. Do what she says. She's the head girl of this class. Because she's older than you. By a whole year. Older? Silly me, I meant *bigger*."

"Leave her alone, Tia." Lu's tenacity was going to get her into trouble one day, but I can't say I didn't like it.

"Yeah, that's enough, Tia." Someone else.

"I'm going to tell the Master…" Someone else again.

"Do you little ones know that Princess Jade isn't even her *real* name?" Tia leaned against the slate chalk board. "Anyone care to guess what it might be?"

Abby didn't need to guess, but she knew not to say.

Everyone else didn't know what to say.

"I'll give you a hint, girls." Tia's arms pressed into her breasts, her fashionably wavy hair obscuring the lightning bolt-shaped wooden badge she was almost certainly wearing. "You can eat it. And I bet she does. All the time…"

"Shit?" Someone who had already decided who would win this little spat drew appropriate nervous laughter.

"Er, ew? I feel sorry for whoever's sitting next to you then." The collective laughter at Tia's rejoinder then was more thankful than nervous.

"Probably not 'string-bean'." This earned a few titters from the quicker ones before the others followed suit. I swung my head her way. Round wire spectacles. Fairly short. Feather badge. Little smartarse.

And that really set them off. "Muffin's the obvious choice, but muffins are sort of cute."

Tia rewarded that one with a delighted squeal. "Now you're getting it!"

I leaned back in my chair and looked over at someone saying nothing. Abby the fiery-haired, almost as slow in rising to temper as she was in simmering down, now so proud with a wooden cleaver pinned to her chest. And she looked back at me from her place near the door. I tilted my head. She shook hers in a way that didn't want to look like she was shaking her head, then broke eye contact.

I smiled the same way, leaned forward, lay my forearms against the desk and let my face press into the wood. I sighed and felt my smile change as one cheek caressed the rough, smooth texture. In my head now, I spoke to other voices than the ones in the room, which were both getting louder and more distant.

"Pumpkin. You are smart. You are brave. You are good."

"Daddy. You are gone. Not coming back, ever."

"So listen to *me*, Jade. Good children lie. Good children get what they want. But this is the truth: you don't let people take things away from you."

"Is happiness a thing?"

"The most important thing, Sarah."

"And you let them take it, Jade. So maybe you need a new lie, princess. This sulking, bullied act? Not working anymore, not now that Tia's left you behind."

"So who should I be now?"

He didn't answer.

She did. "That's up to you to figure out, my little—"

"Dumpling!" I clutched the sides of the desk and stood with this cry, shoving the chair back so hard it clattered over. I glared right at Tia and killed her gloating expression with the full force of my indignation. "My real name is Dumpling, and I know I'm fat and stupid, but I was only your friend because no one else in your class would put up with your crap but you're not in my class anymore so just *Eph off, Tia!*"

Tia recoiled, moved her mouth a few times, but then recovered with a flick of her lustrous chestnut hair, revealing something very deliberately. I'd been wrong. The lightning-bolt shaped wooden badge wasn't there anymore.

Now it was metal. The silvery glimmer of it seemed to catch everyone's eye, to catch everyone's breath.

"Oh, *crap*." Abby acted when no one did. "Someone get the Master. Now. Fucking *run*."

Lu fucking ran. Little and hopefully Very Fast Lu.

"Jade Falkenstrom. You'd truly speak to a Mentor that way?" Tia's harsh volume was gone; her voice was soft, almost delicate. Had she been wearing gloves, they'd be off now. "You. Untalented. Unguilded. Or…am I wrong? Are you hiding something, my not-so-little friend?" Tia lifted her right hand, and everyone saw the blue and white flashes of light playing between her slender fingers. "I've shown you mine…show me yours."

I didn't move. Just held onto the sides of the desk, although maybe by now it was more for support than anything else.

"Tia." Abby adopted a tone designed to talk cats down from trees. "No one's questioning your status. I'm sure everyone's very impressed that you made Mentor so quickly, but this isn't…For Eph's sake, Ti, if the Master catches you using at school, you won't be a Mentor for long."

Tia glanced at her, then down at her still-crackling fingers, and started to say something.

Three things happened then, all at once, or very close to it:

I picked up my chair and sat down, not in defeat but to reach into my little bag and take hold of something that I might or might not have considered slamming into Tia's face repeatedly, and it was very hard not to smile now;

the door flew open and the dark shape of the Master, about whom I remember very little other than what I'm about to describe, filled the doorway. "Tiamat! Jade! Explain yourselves!";

and, by the time the door was open and the Master was one step into the room, Tia had dismissed any sign that she was about to abuse her newly-revealed status.

Whatever claustrophobic sense of doom had descended onto the classroom was gone, lost in a rush of excuses.

I lifted my empty hand from the bag. "I was just trying to eat my lunch, minding my own business, when—"

Tia gestured with her equally empty hands. "I was just trying to tell Jade and everyone some really exciting news but—"

Lu did her best, despite being out of breath. "That's not true you just came in insulting Jade and—"

And now the chorus.

"We didn't know she was a Mentor, Miss!"

"It was all just talk, no one was gonna—"

"Jade didn't mean what she said…"

"Oh, I meant it." But there was no chance I'd be heard now.

Abby knew this too, and said nothing.

The Master did that thing with one word that made her the Master. "*Enough.* Tiamat, why exactly are you in my classroom?"

"Like I said, Miss, I wanted to tell my friends that—" Tia was never one not to come undone under the gaze of her true superiors.

"I will repeat. Why exactly are you in *my* classroom?"

Tia looked wonderfully confused. "I, well, there's no Commandment against it, is there?"

"There is not. There is however Commandment Ten, which I shall not ask you to recite, in light of your excellent Book grades in my class last year. What is the essence of the Tenth, Tiamat?"

"Don't lie for your own benefit, Miss." She was mumbling by this point.

"Jade." The Master looked my way with eyes I remember as very unsettling. No colour, no shape beyond that. They might have been pure black for all I know. Well, no, of course she wasn't one of Them. It was the middle of the day. But still. "When Tiamat says that she was just here to tell you some 'exciting news', was she lying for her own benefit?"

The Master, true to her calling, was turning this into a lesson.

"I don't know, Master. Maybe that's all she came here to do."

"Is it all she did when she came here?"

"No, Master. And she didn't actually tell me or anyone any news."

"I was going to but everyone kept making jokes—"

"*Tiamat.*"

"Sorry miss."

"So Jade, what did she do?"

I paused and looked at Tia. Her misery was not as pleasant as I expected, but it was expected. No need to lie to get what I wanted then. I lied for a different reason. "We did make fun of each other, Master, but only because we haven't talked since the break. We're not always like this. We're just catching up."

The Master looked as though she was about to say something else, to contradict me perhaps. She turned to Lu, who'd resumed her seat and clearly wanted to be anywhere and anyone else. "That's not quite how you told me events transpired."

"I was excited. Upset. They seemed so serious…I'm sorry for lying." And yet she hadn't, because she didn't get what she wanted either.

From the Master: more silence full of contemplation. Of judgment.

Then.

"Tiamat."

"Miss?"

"Congratulations on your promotion, which was no doubt the 'exciting news' you came to deliver. I imagine you will be a great credit to the Guild of Talents." Tia preened, massaging the shiny badge on her left breast with her right hand. "…Provided you do not forget that part of being a Mentor is wisdom and guidance, not merely displays of power. Now, if you've nothing more to say or do with my class, I'd like to commence Aftersun lessons."

"No, I think we might continue this later." Now we locked eyes one last time. "Dumpling."

"Or never, Tia-mutt."

Her left eye twitched at this final swipe but then she swept out, pride fully restored and status as Someone Best Not Fucked With clarified.

"…Abby?"

"Miss?" Abby had somehow found an empty desk and was doing her best not to be noticed.

"Need I even say it? You too. Go on. Out."

"I don't wanna. Tiamat scares me." If you didn't know Abby or Tia, you'd probably think she was just pretending.

"As she should." The Master knew them both. "So watch yourself, young Abbadonna. She is one step closer to being Of The Night than you are now."

Abby's face took on a downcast shade of Oh Fuck Me before she slunk out.

The moment Abby was gone, the Master all but folded into herself and sought refuge at her desk. She looked as though she were about to put her face in her hands, but settled on steepling her fingers before it. And that's where the classroom stayed for a good minute, silent but for our breathing and the Master's private ruminations.

Until.

"Jade, I know you were not innocent in this matter." She peered at me over her hands. I didn't keep her gaze for long. This new self might have been able to stare down the old self's friendlyish oppressor, but there was no need to apply the same resistance to real authority. "Would you not think it best you stay after class as penance?"

This was not how punishment was administered. Even if 'the' Chantal Falkenstrom had not been my mother, that much I would have known. Still, I didn't answer immediately and when I did, I chose my tone very carefully.

"If you say so, Miss." A glance askew, then down at my hands. "But I think I'd rather take my chances and be home on time, like my Mum says. She is sort of fond of the Fifth over the all the others, and sort of not fond of me breaking it."

I cracked a nervous smile and everyone laughed. Even the Master raised her eyebrows. It was a slight blasphemy but one familiar to anyone with parents.

"Truly your mother is known to God's Dark Heart. Heed her and make haste home when the day is done." Thankfully the Master was still visibly amused.

"*Vahm en.*" I maintained a straight face, and that was that.

The Master stood to begin the Aftersun lessons. "Let us use this little incident to review something of increasing importance in our city. The Guild of Talents is unlike any other in Teristra. It is the only guild that is not concerned with a trade or profession. The Talents have direct ties to sacred organisations such as the Peddlers, the Sisters of the Liquid Night and the Imperial Watch. And yet so many other Guilds see them as a threat to our way of life. Who can tell me why?"

I could have. But the answer I'd have given wouldn't have left anyone smiling, so I said nothing and someone else responded. Now that I'd embraced a new self, I had some serious planning to do. While it had everything to do with what the lesson was about, it had nothing to do with anything anyone in that class had to say about it.

When class ended at Eyesun, some of the girls, including Lu, came up to me and offered a balance of sympathy at my impending demise at Tiamat's hands, and sincere gratitude for doing what they'd always wanted to do. I somewhat expected this.

What I didn't anticipate, despite my very deliberate duplicity, was what was lurking behind Lu's hesitant fawning.

"It's funny. I feel like it's all my fault." She dawdled and lingered after the other girls had said their piece and left the room. I made to follow them after retrieving my little bag and bidding the Master a good afternoon. Lu was right behind me. "You know. If I hadn't said anything to you at lunch, she might not have singled you out."

I stopped, and she bumped into me.

I whirled on her.

"This had nothing to do with you." I wanted to cut her out and off for her own good, but then saw all I'd done was cut her down. I sighed, and tried again. "Don't blame yourself, Luce. The moment Tia stepped into the room, she had her target. One way or another, it was going to happen."

"Still." I waited for her to say more, but more was not forthcoming. At least, on that subject. "Uhm. Can I walk home with you? Just in case."

I made a baffled face, because I almost was. "Just in case what? She's not going to come after you. Besides, we don't live anywhere near each other I imagine. Unless you're from the Trades area as well." Didn't mean to add that last part, but I thought nothing of it at the time.

"Well, no." She looked around, even though it was evident we were alone in the hallway. "Between you and me, I'm from the Con." Only a slight pause, a considering look. "Don't tell anyone. Please."

"Convergence? Well, what do I care where you're from?" I honestly saw no connection between her living in a poor district up north and whether or not she'd walk home with me. Again I realised it wasn't the right way to say it only after her hurt silence told me so. This wasn't working. Tiamat had done too good a job forcing me to realign. This new self was strong and forthright and oh I liked it. But Lucy didn't. I pretended she was someone else then. "Eph me, I'm sorry, you didn't deserve that. What I meant was, does it matter? We can still be friends."

She smiled and I figured it was now okay to return to the newer self and resumed my walk towards the stairs down and the way out.

Lu chattered as we went. "I remember last year, watching you three and thinking you guys were just so untouchable. So confident. What I wish I could be."

"That was stupid." Now we were friends, it was okay to say it like that.

"I know. She's a horrible person and I had no idea you were just another of her victims."

I thought about this as we trotted down the staircase.

"But now she's a Mentor of Talents." We reached the ground floor. "She's not just horrible; she's dangerous. And she's after me. Do you really want to get caught up in this?"

"Jade, I already am. Look."

I turned to look at her. First her face, which seemed as mousy and harmless as ever. Then down, at the wooden badge she held in one outstretched hand.

It was a lightning bolt, impossibly lit in the briefest flash of intensely hot blue flame flaring from her other hand. It was only there for a second, and I felt like I'd thrust my face into a forge. My turn to recoil in shock.

"Oh, you stupid, Ephing…Fuckcuntshitfuck…Ah, *Bitterspite!*" No self of mine was ready for this complication, so the real one took over, invoking a Heavenly name never to be used outside of Book readings. Mother would have blackened my eye for that one. Lu's fierce look didn't change, not even at that unfettered outburst. I had to explain then what this really meant. "You're *one of them.* That's all the more reason for you to stay away from me. If Tiamat so much as says 'get her', you'll turn on me. You'll have absolutely no fucking choice."

Once again I thought about my bag, what was in it. Whether or not I could use it here, and not be caught. And some part of me, the same part that had, so long ago now, been glad that Mr. Mountain didn't try to take it away, just didn't want to have to do that to Lucy as well as Tiamat. They weren't exactly the same, but now they had enough in common. Too much.

"True…unless I make Mentor myself, and I will, very soon." Lucy closed her fist around the badge. I chose to believe her, and stopped thinking about what I might have to do. For now. "Then I'll be able to take care of her. No money or family name can save her from a formal challenge. And I'm such an easy target, she won't be able to resist."

"I still think you should keep your distance."

"No, Jade. Mentor or not, if her lightning comes at you, my fire will be ready."

"Not so loud." We were getting close to the exit. "You just had to be a pyrotic, didn't you?" Somehow I'd earned myself an overzealous bodyguard with fire at her command. I'd been planning on recruiting Abby against Tia; her skill with various sharp objects as a Butchery Guild recruit and her even-headedness struck me as a useful combination in a fight. But Little Lucy? Even she knew she was an 'easy target'. Not even given a second thought. Now I was giving her potency a lot of second thoughts.

We came to the main doors. It was busier here than elsewhere. Not quite so safe for that sort of talk. Lucy had wisely put away her badge. It wasn't really a bad thing in itself, but it would attract attention. Tia's was the only lightning bolt I'd seen in any of the classes so far.

Lu kept going as we crossed the crowded courtyard. "Let me help you. I can. I will. You did something truly good today. No one in class will call you Princess or Dumpling now. Not after that. Let me help, and others will too. You stood up to Tiamat. Fucking Tia-mutt." She giggled as though it was the dirtiest joke she'd ever heard.

"I just spoke my mind." I made another thoughtful face, as though pondering what 'help you' entailed. "You can accompany me until we reach Russet Street. That's where I figure we'll be splitting up, and if Tia's going to act, it'll be before that."

"And after that? Still a long walk from there to the Trades."

"It's fine, I'm meeting my boyfriend in Oakenstage."

"You…you have a *boyfriend?*" She was a little more awestruck than I expected. "Well, of course you do. You would. And from Oakenstage. Wow."

"Sort of. He's a boy. We're friends."

"Uhuh. You'll tell me about him on the way? Please?"

"Sure." I had absolutely no intention of letting this world even come within spitting distance of that one. "But it doesn't matter. What matters is that we stay alert. Let's go."

So we did. There was no sign of Tia outside the gate, along the street. Her idea of 'later' was not as immediate as 'right after school' then. That meant, like me, she was probably planning something bigger.

When we reached the intersection with Russet Street, Lucy tried to enter my world one last time. "Are you sure you're okay alone?"

"I should be asking you that. Heading that way." I tilted my head to the north. "No one's idea of safe."

Her laugh was haughty and carefree. "They'd be very glad to know you feel that way. But I live there, Jade. It's my home. They're my people. And a lot of them are proud to finally have a Bolt emerge from the shit-stink of the Con."

I realised that I wasn't the only one putting on an act at school. Which meant everyone could have been. Even Tia. I didn't like that thought.

And Convergence *did* stink. The name said it all: not every building had a waterroom but every street had a gutter, and by some strange curse of geography, the Con is where a lot of the filth ended up. Somehow Lucy's family had gotten her into Parelle Girls. Her story to tell, and she would or she wouldn't.

"Fair enough. See you tomorrow." I made to walk away.

This was apparently not how newfound elementalist bodyguards say goodbye, because she fair threw herself at me through tears I should have anticipated but did not. "Sorry, I was just, so scared she was going to. Any moment." She probably sniffled and dribbled all over my uniform. I liked the idea of that. So I returned the embrace, pushing her further into my chest. Let it soak right in, all of it.

"There, there. It's okay." I let her snuffle and snivel a bit more. "Tia's going to lick her wounds for a while…Okay, that's enough now Luce. Wouldn't want my boyfriend seeing this and getting the wrong idea."

Or the Watch seeing it and getting possibly the right one.

"O-Of course." She pulled back and swiped her face with the back of her hands. "Sorry."

"It's fine. I was scared too." I couldn't decide if that was true for any part of me. Especially not the one I was trying to suppress now. Lucy had kept me too long. "But I wasn't joking. He's probably waiting. Tomorrow, okay? Tomorrow we'll see what happens."

"Tomorrow. I'm glad we're friends now, Jade."

And that *was* how this particular elementalist bodyguard said goodbye.

I watched to make sure she didn't turn around. More than three times, anyway. When she was finally out of sight, I turned south as I told her, and definitely didn't meet my boyfriend. I made it to the fountain that marked the intersection with the Estenthric Highway. To my right, only a block down, was the imposing shadow of the All-Trades Inn; to my left, the straight line east into the Imperial Quarter, where I would never go.

I turned neither way and crossed the Estenthric, into my favourite part of the whole city: Hammerdin. The district where honest folk made wonders from nothing but raw materials and very hard work. A few blocks south of the Estenthric, I stopped, as I almost always did, and took it in, letting it take me away. The heat of the smithies enfolded me; the scent of sawdust left me feeling almost light-headed. I ducked into a side alley, one of a few that had served a very specific purpose over the years. I removed the crimson tie that marked me as a student of Parelle Girls and shoved it into my bag. I then pulled out two things. The first I pinned proudly to my chest, the other I used to tie my hair up in a bun, exposing my savaged ears for the first time since parting ways with Levi. Next came a leather apron the colour of woodchips, which I tied around my waist by reflex alone; the hammer came with it, tucked into the largest pocket. Finally, I withdrew a cap from my bag that concealed my long hair nicely. After returning to the busier streets, I looked at myself in a shop window, distracted by the tools displayed behind it.

Gripped by the same sense of being actually real I always felt after this ritual, I loosely folded my arms and stooped over a bit. I nodded at my reflection. Yes. This was me. This was which one I wanted to be.

Sarah-Jade, child of Arius Falkenstrom, was home.

The Way Station

They hasten and arrive by Lowsun. One to another, these nests of mercantile activity resist much in the way of distinction, following a similar practical pattern despite regional architectural methods: a Haven at the heart of whatever dwellings its operation demands. Charan regards the square structure's integrity, hooded eyes measuring its every dimension from the moment they spy it as though already dismantling the building stone by stone. Sariana hopes it has a heated Waterroom with private stalls, but suspects that is the sort of unlikely excess that cushioned the dream she did not choose. Neither give voice to these urges, not even after passing the Doorman (who is a Door*woman*, Sariana notes) and into a large open common area courtyard. They leave three things at the entrance: a short, curved sword, a strange spiked-ball-on-a-chain, and the memory of the Lantern glowing a dull orange.

Charan secures their rooms, which Sariana knows by the layout will be in the outer wall itself but allows him to guide her. Despite the oppressive moonlight, there should be no outside threat to this place. Their presence ensures that, although none of the people taking refuge within these walls may know it. But as the siblings dine in the busy common area, what starts as polite privacy over their food turns into uncomfortable hunching and eventual slinking away. Behind them, travellers and merchants stir their family name into gossip as easily as salt into soup. As though the name had not been completely absent from their collective awareness until a few months ago. To them, Kas'Daen has always been at war with Jaydemyr, Kas'Daen has always won, and Jaydemyr has always quietly plotted revenge. To this reminder of their Father's failure and their Mother's power, the siblings neither stay nor listen.

29 days until the revelation

Chapter 6: Who really knew me

"Where in the Seven Wretched Hells have you been, Boy?" Three-Fingers Bob, whose name wasn't Bob and who had all of her fingers, was typically the first person I ran into upon sneaking into the guild hall from a side entrance. No one who came and went used the front door. She'd also been the first person I'd seen in here, ever. She was imposing then, and imposing now. Folded arms, mistrustful glare, shaven head. A bit like Jerich in appearance but all Mr. Mountain in function, if attitudes could be considered weapons.

Not that long ago a question that open-ended would have left me in a panic – Where had I been? Where to start? I'd been lots of places. I was thirteen years old. I'd been *so* many places I'd definitely forgotten some of them. How could I tell her about those? Maybe they didn't matter. But *maybe they did.* And I'd have failed to answer because unlike you, Brother, I don't have straight lines in my head when it comes to indecision. So I'd have lied, probably, because that's the next best thing. As far as I knew.

Except, and this is part of why the Headquarters of the Teristran Guild of Construction Labour and Services in Hammerdin was my home, people here had a different sort of straight line. They called it 'common sense' and of course even after years of running with and for them, it was too wondrous for me to consider it 'common'.

"School. Also, I'm not a boy."

As she well knew, and yet a name's a name. Here I was Boy, had been from the first time I'd barged in, not really expecting to see Daddy but mostly eager to be part of whatever world had been his before

Mother and me. Seven years later I was fairly sure this world wasn't that, but here Boy was treated a lot better than Dumpling elsewhere. So I liked Boy. A lot.

"Jack's been waiting. Needs to send a message. School ended hours ago. Liar."

"Fine, I lost track of time talking to my girl friend." Not a lie.

"Shame I can't be in there when you try that pissant excuse with Jack." Grunt-snort-laugh.

"Maybe someday you can. That'd be nice." I tried to move forward. For most, any attempt to get past Bob would be a waste, but for me she stepped aside, gestured with a scarred and scorched arm towards the boss' office. As if I didn't know exactly where it was.

Left Bob to her singular purpose, trying to pretend I wasn't wary of her marauding gaze.

It was a fairly normal guild hall. Long tables, hearth, boards with posters for news, work opportunities. Bar. Chatter. And yet even I knew by now that it wasn't normal at all. I mean, they…we were meant to be craftsfolk, carpenters and smiths and tanners. And I still believed, before my stumbling upon them, they'd been just that. But now the whole place quivered, like someone holding their breath against their will.

And then there were the occasional cries and shrieks coming from Jack's office, from behind that closed door off to the side. Sounds to which no one paid any attention, as though they were nothing more than the ringing of hammers or the scraping of leather. And they were not quite screams, not yet. Last time it'd been someone from the Fish Market. Some complaint about the wood rotting or something. Time before that, some shop owner from Whimsyway whose finances didn't take into account the need to pay on time. Idiots who had no business dealing with us, in other words.

Fools who don't pay attention to messages.

Per routine, I waited outside until the latest yelp became a whimper. I used that time to pull out my hammer, heft the weight once or twice. Just in case someone in the hall wasn't a regular. Some first-timer seeking the illustrious services of Teristra's finest construction workers. I once asked Jack if that'd just scare them off, but Jack had half-shrugged a reply: 'and where would they go?' Jack had also said that was a very smart question for a seven-year-old floor-scrubber to ask. I knew what smart meant. Of course.

Or thought I did. Because apparently 'not crossing the line with us' was also smart. I still wasn't sure what that line was, but since I was a part of 'us', it didn't really matter. What mattered was I liked Jack's idea of smart a lot more than Mother's. If you were smart with her, you got hurt. Smart with Jack, others got hurt.

The meaty slap of the hammer's head against my palm felt great.

The whimpering trailed away.

I broke the silence by tapping the hammer's head on the door. Three times. Then two. Then two more. Then, after a count of four, one last time.

It didn't mean anything, but Jack had asked me to make up new ones each time, and it was fun. One time I tried knocking just once, and had to wait at least a minute for Jack to open the door. Hahaha. Not this time. This time she answered almost straight after the last knock.

"Ah, the Sender has arrived." Jack's weathered face looked a little weary from what I suspected was a lot of talking. I could see someone tied to a chair behind her. Just as Bob wasn't really Bob and didn't have just three fingers, Jack wasn't just Jack. But when the person in charge tells you what to call them, it's best to call them that and not much else. I'd seen people put into that chair for being…too smart, I guess.

"Sorry I'm late." Lie. It had been worth it, as Jack would soon find out. "Was spending time with my girlfriend." Let's see if Bob was right.

"Oh, that's fine, enjoy it while you can." Nope, guess not. The boss returned to her desk to the left of the entrance. The chair, and its unfortunate occupant, were in the centre of the room. Jack was, naturally, an exquisite craftswoman and refused to ruin the walls of her office, built by her own hands she said, with junk like paintings or trophies. A well-made wall speaks for itself. And a whole room of them, that's something special indeed.

Jack propped her boots onto her desk. "This is messenger Fifty-Six. Boy, say hello to Fifty-Six."

"Hi." I leaned against the door, half-crossed my arms and tapped the hand holding the hammer against the other elbow. I'd practised this a lot. Just so.

Fifty-Six wasn't really code either. Probably just the messenger count. Fifty-Five had been a few days ago, after all. Fifty-Four, a week or two. Fifty had been at least a few months back now. Jack had taught me how to count properly long before Parelle Girls did. Some kids there had struggled to get past Twelve. Haha, little joke. Yeah, I know you've heard it before, Brother. Just trying to…eh, Eph it. Point being, some people had names I needed to know. This person didn't.

Fifty-Six looked a little younger than that age. Male. Bit pudgy. Unharmed, of course. Just very, very scared. Thankfully Jack had already gone through the part where they learn there's no use making noise or threats or begging. I won't lie; I was more often than not 'late' to let that stuff happen without me. I think Jack understood that too. There'd been other smart questions about the talking beforehand and how I felt about it, out of my mouth before I could stop them, and her even smarter question in response: 'Would you rather do it?'

"Story or not, Boy?"

There was only one answer. I smiled. "Story please, Jack."

"Right! So, Fifty-Six here is a florist. You might have seen his shop, probably on the way to school—"

Yeah, I know. I should have realised what *that* statement really meant. But it was story-time. Shh. Don't interrupt.

"—and it's quite popular with the young ladies from East Teristra. Which is to say, Fifty-Six here has esteemed clientele and a respectable location. A few years back, we were delighted to create not just a sign for Fifty-Six's wonderful shop, but an entire store front. Window dressing, racks, curtains, the lot. And we did a pretty good job, didn't we, Fifty-Six?"

Sometimes they didn't respond immediately, because the number isn't their name. These days, the talking part made clear that while they were in this room, however, the number *is* their name. Fifty-Six nodded, face towards me but eyes, so wide and so earnest, towards Jack. Fifty-Six nodded and nodded and said nothing.

"That job brought us quite a lot of business too. We were most appreciative. But then something very sad occurred the other day. The sign we made fell from its place above the door. These things happen, especially if you don't occasionally ask the good people who make these things to check the sign is still secure. Unfortunately someone was underneath it when it fell. Someone important, I'd say. Because all of your clients are important, aren't they, Fifty-Six?"

Another nod as Jack leaned forward to take a drink from her mug.

"And when that sign fell, and when someone was hurt, who did you blame, Fifty-Six?"

Oh, you poor bastard. Your first and last words to the Sender and they're that obviously guilty. Even then, I felt a little sad.

"Y-you, Jack."

"*Me?*"

"The T-Teristran Guild of Constru—"

"The. Teristran. Guild. Of. Construction. Labour. And. Services. The whole blessed guild." Jack flashed a smile that wasn't, and gave off a laugh that was. "All of us. And you didn't even use our proper name, did you? How did you put it? 'Those Ephing useless Nailbiters', was it? But you were upset and surprised. We all say regrettable things in vulnerable moments. But even after that, you neither took responsibility nor sought our assistance. And once those words left your mouth and entered the world's ears, they became a public attack. On my guild, Fifty-Six. On all of us. We lost business and, worse, found ourselves in…difficult situations. Several of my associates have been forced to defend themselves against aggressive competition and…well, angry florists who question our integrity. I hardly need to tell you, Fifty-Six, what sort of damage a sharp pair of shears can do to a fellow. Can…and did."

The guildmaster stood up and planted her fists on her desk. She looked over the scattered papers before her, as though the instructions for what came next were in that mess somehow. As she leaned forward, the medallion that marked her unique station in the guild slipped out, a neat hammer in a golden circle pendulating above the mess of her work. Apprentices wore wooden badges. Mentors, metal ones. There were other ranks after that, but only one Pendant in any guild. Only one Master. Let the Messenger see that, just in case they had any doubts left who they were dealing with.

Jack resumed her seat to start writing out what I would do. "Message begins."

Finally. I shoved off the wall, moved to stand behind the chair and Fifty-Six. Put the hammer on the floor, all but dropping it. This close, I could smell the sweat I'd been watching. I think I did expect some sort of floral whiff, or at least dirt and fertiliser. When I wasn't Boy, I'd spent enough time in florists and vegetable gardens with Levi to know. But no rosy scent, not here. No safe aroma of soil and manure.

"For besmirchment of an allied Guild to the public, one bruised arm."

I nodded and took the Parelle Girls tie from my bag.

"For directly involving an allied Guild in another Guild's conflict, one bruised leg."

I pulled the tie taut.

"And for indirectly causing serious injury to an allied Guild's members, two broken hands. End of message."

I stepped forward and gagged Fifty-Six from behind. I'm sure he knew not to make much noise but sometimes knowing isn't enough to stop it.

Then I picked up the hammer again, felt his arms a few times, and got to work.

As Jack found out not long after I'd found the Guild, I was useless at anything resembling carpentry. Too impatient. Too clumsy. No real head for dimensions. Not strong enough to be a labourer. But as *I* found out, there's so much more to a Guild than what it says on the sign. And of all the weird tasks assigned to me, as someone who just wouldn't accept that there wasn't a place for me in that world, delivering messages was by far my favourite.

I want to make this clear: I didn't like the actual hurting people part. But hurting is better than killing. Like you, I don't really care for the Twelve all that much but that doesn't mean it doesn't make sense. Killing is bad. Hurting to prevent killing is good. And I was good at it. Genuinely good. No one else in the Guild was any good at it. Messages One through Fifteen died within minutes of their creation. I think the next ten or so were just given written warnings to hand to their leaders. Clearly the Construction Guild had a problem adequately expressing its displeasure. And then one day some other young hopeful in the Guild, as eager for their wooden badge as anyone else, had pissed me off and I'd sort of just whipped out the hammer and bruised their arm a couple of times, very quickly. A couple, maybe more. I think they were trying to take the hammer away from me. The kid, or someone else. And you know that wasn't going to happen.

Jack broke it up, sent the kid to the Hammerdin Haven (never been there myself, but I suspect they knew of my work) and asked me if I could do that again if I tried. Do what, I asked. Hit someone with the hammer but not break bones or kill them. Turned out I could.

Here's the thing about our messages: they're generally too petty for major healing, too significant to ignore. Word got around that our Guild was neither a dire threat nor to be taken advantage of. Good place for an association just trying to do some business to occupy. My messages were effective…so why, I wondered as I finished up with Fifty-Six by way of a single measured drop of the hammer onto his strapped hand, were people needing more of them lately?

The best thing about being the one who crafted messages, a Sender, was it gave me private time with Jack. I didn't take it often, because once I found out she knew almost nothing about my father other than he'd once been Captain-Guard of the All-Trades district and a social member of the Construction Guild, there wasn't much to discuss. Grandiose though the titles might sound, all it meant was that my father had been in charge of about fifty men keeping the peace in a ridiculously peaceful part of the city and paid to use the Hammerdin establishment for personal projects. And the hammer itself, so hard won and kept…just another hammer.

And by then I was so involved with the Guild myself the reason for forcing my way into their roughshod world was all but irrelevant. They'd given me purpose and I knew it was good. No complaints, no questions.

Until that day.

"Jack? May I sit and talk to you?"

You'd think I'd avoid that chair given I knew what it represented but it was the only other chair in the office and had very likely accommodated far more important rumps than mine.

"By all means, Sarah-Jade. Sit. What's on your mind?"

Alone and no more need for pretence. She'd used the other name, the one I'd given when she'd first asked, the one none of the others felt suited me as much as 'Boy'. But that's why she was the boss and they were…whatever they were. Soon enough, it wouldn't matter.

I sat, fidgeted with the hammer. Was that a speck of dried blood? Ugh. "You know those speeches you and the others give, about how the Guild of Talents is…uh…impinging on our way of life?"

"I do write them myself, so surely I know them, yes." Contrary to the snappish response, Jack's tone was steady, encouraging. Because oh, did she ever give speeches about Talents, or more specifically the idea of a Guild dedicated to nothing but turning our God-given gifts into weapons. "Although you know that stays here, right? Just like everything else we do. You school girls do love to chat and gossip."

"Not me. Who would I talk to? Parelle girls are serious bitches. All of them."

"And some of them are already Talented…is that where this is going?"

Smart. She was just so blessedly smart.

"Yeah, but…one of them. She's not just Talented. She's trained. Already a Mentor."

"At your age? Shyn', that's scary." Jack poured on the theatrics for others. Right now, she looked genuinely concerned, shaking her head.

"I was wondering. Maybe a message?"

"Oh, Sarah-Jade Falkenstrom. No. Nonono. There are forces with which we mere craftsfolk do not meddle. The Night's Own. The Imperial Teristran Guard. The Watch. The Sisters. Blood Peddlers. And most importantly, people who can shoot lightning from their fingers or make the blood boil under our skin at a glance. No. We stay out of their way. Blessed Mother, have I truly misled you so?"

The last question seemed less about me and more about anyone she might have tried to teach. Still, she was talking to *me* there and then.

"No. Of course. You're right, Jack. Foolish of me to suggest it." Careful. Not too thick, Sarah. Be smart. Just… "Just thought I'd ask. I'm afraid she's going to come after me anyway. That's all."

"…What have you done?"

"Nothing. Really. We just had a fight. With words, I mean. And she might have threatened to get me later. Whatever the Eph that means."

Jack stroked her chin, picked up her pen. "What's her name?"

"Tiamat. Tiamat Fourneval."

She hesitated. "Oh. She's one of them. That's…tricky."

"Yep." Self-involved idiot that I was, I didn't think that Jack's 'them' and my 'them' might be very different indeed.

"Alright. Since you're so good at your job, I'll look into this, just for you. See if she's a problem or just a big mouth. I'm reckoning the latter, but mostly for your sake. Last thing we need is friction with the Fournevals. You stay well clear of her. Got it?"

"I promise."

"No, Sarah-Jade. I mean it. Swear to me you will not provoke this girl or anyone else in the Guild of Talents. Just go about your life, pay no heed to their intrigues and drama. If I…encourage her Guild to check Tiamat's reins, you will respect that and mind your own. This is not your fight, so stay out of it. Swear to me on the memory of your father."

I don't know what my face was doing in reaction to this, but it must have been at least a shade of the turmoil clutching every other part of me.

Jack relented. "That was. I'm sorry. Unnecessary. Of course you'll do the right thing. You *did* the right thing, telling me about this bully from that…*Guild*. Eph curse the lot of them. I said this is not your fight, but that doesn't mean one isn't coming. Oh, it's coming…"

I said nothing. Just stood up. Hefted the hammer. Made for the door.

"Hey. Don't forget your school tie."

I looked over my shoulder. "Why would I forget it? I know exactly what it was used for. What and whom." And then I left.

I rarely lingered in the Guild Hall. A full day at Parelle Girls was usually exhausting enough, so when I say Hammerdin was my home, I don't mean in the sense that I felt welcome or loved. I felt needed and used, and saw absolutely no reason to spend any time there that didn't reinforce this. Artisans are usually independent and self-driven. Set them a task and they'll do it, but leave them alone and they'll probably still be unable not to make something, design something. But even now, as you can tell, I'm not inclined to self-motivation. I have trouble answering questions that aren't asked. So you *could* ask me who else was in there, what I thought of them. If they meant anything to me. They might have. But when you asked what led up to the Purge, I talked about Jack and the messages and Tia and Lu, because as Mother might put it, what does the fire care for the kindling?

It was mid-Dyingsun when Dumpling skipped back into the All-Trades Inn. The heat was on in my room. Reminded myself to be extra-thankful to Agnis in the morning. Dinner arrived shortly after I did, brought by Mother herself. The visit was brief but pleasant enough, because it was going to be another busy night down there. And if Levi was upset that I'd done my own thing yet again after school, he didn't show it. We talked a bit, watching the growing crowd from well above, and then said goodnight. Just like that. We'd been playing this game of unannounced avoidance for years, ever since he'd failed to show me around Hammerdin himself seven years ago, so why would he fuss now? And yet, as I lay in bed, in the slightly stifling warmth, buffeted by the muffled, distant music about a me that never was, I sort of wished he'd say or do something. Let me know if I was *really* doing the right thing or not. Tell me what he believed. Send me a message of his own.

The next day and for many days afterwards, nothing unusual happened. Just everyday deceptions. Levi and I continued to hold hands and peck cheeks and deceive Mother; I continued to gawk at dresses and deceive Levi; and whoever they thought I was at school continued to flourish in the wake of prolonged but now quashed bullying and deceive the other girls…including, it seemed, Tia, who acted more like a normal person than any of them. There was just one awkward moment of sizing up before we exchanged casual greetings almost simultaneously and engaged in pointless banter, with Abby completing the triangle in her clownish way. No more snide needling; no veiled threats. Absolutely no issued challenges, and no follow-through on her sinister declaration of 'later'. I figured everyone assumed this sudden change was because I'd stared Tia down, humbled her during what was now a vaguely legendary confrontation at the beginning of the year. I knew better, but nothing indicated that what I *did* know was any closer to the truth. Jack had said she'd handle it, and I owed her my restraint. But each day that passed that didn't end with Tia showing her hand was like another pat on the head when you're expecting a thumping. Sooner or later you get tired of shying away and instead just let it happen. And then you start to get used to the pats…

Lu remained wary though, and I was thankful for it, but even she started to buckle. Her advancement in the Guild of Talents increasingly occupied her time, as it should have. The impending but largely sanctioned clash with Tia as a fellow Mentor at Parelle Girls dominated the gossip; of course word was out that Lu was in the Guild of Talents not long after she'd revealed it to me. By then most of us had our Talents anyway, and they were no longer some source of pubescent mystery or anticipation. Not all, but most. Eh, much as it is now, for me. A little water when necessary. No threat to anyone. Only Tia and Lu were worthy of wearing the Bolt.

Even down at the Construction Guild, Jack had said nothing more on the matter I'd raised that day. The frequency and severity of messages decreased. The Hammerdin Hall seemed to breathe out slowly, as though something terrible had just been averted.

Things appeared to be becoming just fine.

And all I could do was wait, wait for the so-called fight against the Guild of Talents Jack had promised. For Tia's 'later'. For Lu's ascension to Tia's rank so that she no longer posed a threat to me if Tia's 'later' became 'now'.

I could do nothing but wait for the hammer to fall and, as Teristra's greatest Sender of messages written in fluent Hammerdinian, it was *agonising*.

The next year, what was left of my old 'friends' circle crumbled when Abby left Parelle Girls to fully commit to her future as one of Teristra's only lady butchers – her term for it, always said with a solemnity that failed to match the self-mocking arch of her severe ginger brows. On top of this, I was in a different class to either Tiamat or Lu, which may or may not have been a coincidence; if Jack was still not-meddling, then I'd be silently thankful. Due to her status as the only Mentor of Talent at Parelle Girls and, of course, being a Fourneval, Tiamat all but ran the school by then. Lucille and I rarely spoke now, partly because of what Jack said but mostly just because that's how things go sometimes. Her infatuation with me had peaked with my seeming desire to make Tiamat my nemesis, and ebbed with my making clear that I'd been acting almost totally in desperate self-defence and had no interest in any of their 'stupid Talent guild shit'. Not to say she didn't still seem to look up to me, but if so it was mostly from afar and only when she wasn't busy threading her way through Tiamat's network of antagonism. It wasn't bullying so much as…provocation. To Lucille's credit, she never rose to it, but she also never went out of her way to hide that she had her own intentions regarding Tiamat Fourneval's future as a Mentor in the Guild of Talents. Or lack therof. If she tried to talk about it with me, I changed the subject. Made clear I thought the whole thing was dumb and dangerous and dumb. Fucking drama queens, the lot of them. I probably said something like this when she wouldn't shut up about it: *I know you're strong, Lu, so how about you leave me alone and just show them already? It's none of my business, alright?*

Eph yes it was awful and I could tell I was hurting her feelings. I was one of the only girls not to be under Tiamat's thumb, and probably one of a very few to have seen the unnatural hue of Lu's pale fire. She was so powerful, and so lonely, and I could have been there for her. But when Jack said to do something, I damn well did it as best I could. In case that wasn't already perfectly clear.

Inevitably the day came, when neither Tiamat nor Lucille were at school. It's all any of the girls could talk about, because surely it could mean only one thing. But for me, I who strove so hard to pay no attention to these 'intrigues and dramas', it was just another day at school, and another day for me to wear whatever masks I needed to before I could slip out. Slip into Hammerdin, into the easiest, least-ornate mask and into the Construction Guild hall. Slip past Bob's japes and jabs, and head for Jack's office, eager to be the world's greatest Sender yet again. To be what I was truly meant to be.

Unsafe Haven

They should have stayed and listened. Maybe not all night, but certainly a while. Charan thumps on her room's door, an incessant rhythm rivalling the one she cannot otherwise deny in her chest, her ears, her head. Sariana follows him down the dim corridor, barely dressed and deeply aware of how little that matters. He rants a little about the idiocy of letting Dog-Ears make any sort of decision, and she does not pursue this. It is difficult enough to keep up with his urgent stride towards the entrance of the Haven. Or, she amends under her breath, probably better to think of it as the exit given her brother's pace.

Waystations are noisy by nature. Safety after the solitude of a journey energises a person's desire to interact. Unfortunately, this also greatly increases their vulnerability, especially with all that drinking. So she isn't surprised to see the unconscious bodies sprawled about the courtyard at first, because she doesn't yet know they actually are bodies and not merely unconscious, and that they're not sprawled but arranged. Charan assumed it was a brawl over clan ideologies at first, since there isn't much blood or mess and a wave of anti-Jadeymyr sentiment was cresting when they retired last night. Then he saw what prompted him to drive her out of bed at Nighsun, what she sees now. She looks at him and says one of his names as an accusation, but even Char denies it. Besides, he signs their name in little bloody slices, because of course he does. Whoever did this used the Haven itself as the message. Kas'Daen Havens are no longer safe and your precious Lantern is now useless. Signed, Clan Jaydemyr. Whether the author was actually one of theirs or someone fomenting further anti-Jaydemyr fervour, neither of them much care. They do, however, care that such a message exists, and perhaps not only here. Destroying it before they leave the lifeless building behind is no effort. The real problem is now they not only can't avoid Havens and inns, they need to actively seek them out all while avoiding anyone who, rightfully, might think to blame two Halves of Jaydemyr, one of whom has a long history of turning Havens into giant funeral pyres.

As they travel, she continues her telling, for she knows her time is short.

28 days until the revelation

Chapter 7: Where it all went…Wrong.

What I first noticed: the chair was empty. I'd entered the room wondering what Messenger Sixty-Three was going to be like, given Sixty-Two, some wily brat from the Calculators making a skim, had been literally a slap on the wrist and not much else…and I'd heard not a single cry, whimper or protest from within.

"Sit." Jack closed the door behind me. Something she'd not done personally…maybe ever. And I didn't move at first, because surely she was talking to someone else. But whom? It was just us.

I sat, the chair facing her desk, hammer in hand.

Was it darker in there than usual?

Jack didn't sit. She strode towards me. Stopped. Glared.

"Hand it over. No trouble now."

It. I didn't doubt what she meant. Nothing else made sense yet. For the first time, I looked at her middle-aged body the same way I looked at almost everyone else. I considered bones. Joints. Forehead. Cheek. Face.

I thought about the door, and what lay beyond it.

Mostly, I thought about how if she'd wanted to, Jack could. Anytime.

"Will I get it back?"

"We'll see. What will you do if you don't?"

"I'll take it back."

"With what, Sarah-Jade?"

So there it was. In that room, in that Guild, the hammer was all I had, probably all that I was.

Never let anyone take it from you, Mother had taught me. But in here, I realised, it wasn't mine. It was Jack's. I'd given it to her when I'd given myself to the task she'd set it.

So I held the hammer out, limp and confused.

I figured everyone else who'd been told to sit in that chair asked what or why. Because they didn't know none of that mattered. The answer was going to be the same if you asked or not. Idiots.

Jack knew that too, which is why she did the talking. Even now that I was the one in the chair, I was appreciative of that.

She started to pace, toying with the hammer. "I've been mulling how to say this, but you don't really care how, so here it is. You're out."

"What? Why?"

Oh come on, you saw that coming. I didn't though.

"Because I clearly can't trust you. Because I asked you to do one thing. I said. Do not provoke Tiamat Fourneval—"

"I didn't! She's been—"

"—or *any other girl* in the Guild of Talents. Why didn't you tell me about Lucille Loudair?"

Ah. Why, yes, Brother. That name *does* sound familiar, doesn't it?

And yet my response, because at the time she really was nobody:

"Who? Oh. You mean Lu. She's not a problem, in fact she's on my side…"

"No, you fool. You're on hers. Your 'girlfriend', you called her that day when you asked me to interfere with Tiamat. When you asked me if you could send a Message to the Guild of Talents. Oh, you sent a message alright."

"Oh Jack, I was just fucking kidding with that. Come on. There was nothing to tell."

Obviously Jack knew Lu was a candidate for Mentor rank in the Guild of Talents. So it wasn't that that I was meant to tell her. Was I meant to tell her that it was very likely that Lu's promotion had been today? But if I did that, I'd be admitting I hadn't stayed out of it after all. I obeyed what I considered the one rule of that chair: I shut the Eph up.

"Are you absolutely sure of that? Can you recall with clarity every word you've said to her, every conversation you've shared, in the past four months?"

Of course it was an unfair question, but it was also a terribly *fair* point. Bereft of the one thing that gave me any semblance of purpose, the relic that made rigid all of my long-running lies, I sagged into the truth.

"No."

"No? Just no? Not even going to try?"

So I stayed silent and I did try. That was the depth of my desperation to appease Jack. I indulged in the futility of trying to remember it all. The banter. The daily exchanges. The furtive and yet seemingly empty promises and threats. The name-calling that confirmed amicable separation, denied earnest intimacy. But the truth into which I'd slumped was one I now know to be anything but unique or special. We simply have no idea of knowing at the time what events we will *need* to remember later, and what can be safely allowed to rot into harmless mush. So there was every chance I'd said something harmless, thoughtless to Lu that to her ears might have been an instigation to enact her terrible plans. Because Jack had said 'do not provoke them', and because by some miracle they hadn't provoked me, I had simply distanced myself from their situation. And it had been easy, since Tia and Lu's volatile dance had become so much more significant than either girl's interaction with me. Until that moment, I'd believed I'd done precisely what Jack had asked of me. I'd stayed out of their way effortlessly because their way had moved away from mine. But it was impossible to just avoid them entirely. We went to school together. We were acquaintances. Friends. Rivals. Enemies. From Morningsun to Eyesun, for most of most days, we were all each other had.

"I…What did I do, Jack? What did I say?"

"Honestly, Sarah, it's what you *didn't* say."

The magnitude of trying to remember everything I'd said to Luce in four whole months had almost crushed me. The impossible scope of its opposite, everything I *hadn't* said to her, just left me groaning with my eyes closed, as though I'd been kicked a hundred and six times in the gut. The groaning gave me something to focus on that wasn't retching, that wasn't screaming.

"No. That's what you didn't say. You didn't say no."

To what to what for Eph's everloving sake to what?

I opened my eyes, looked up at her and hoped my expression asked something like that. Something.

"I'm tired of that word. 'No'. So let me ask you something to which you should have a different answer. Did you know Lucille Loudair's promotion to Mentor was today?"

"Yes!" I nodded, because I was tired of that word too. "I mean, I learned it was today, today. She'd said it was coming up. This week. Or something like that. She wasn't at school today, so we all assumed."

"And do you know who her opponent was?"

Opponent? For a promotion? The test was a *fight*?

"Tiamat Fourneval?" Why did I make it a question? Who else could it have been?

Jack laughed and shook her head.

"You really thought it'd be that simple? That of all the potential examiners, they'd go with another neophyte who clearly doesn't know her place? Shit, Sarah. You have no idea how large that Guild is. How many people of power, real power, flock to its sanctified ranks. So we're back to the 'no', aren't we? No, you didn't know who her opponent was, and I know you didn't."

"Should I ask who?" Because a simple 'who?' might be wrong. This seemed…safer. Seemed.

"Blessed Mother, you aren't even listening. When I say real power, I mean names you wouldn't recognise. But that doesn't matter. What matters is Lucille Loudair's promotion duel was today and she won. Her victory was, I hear, devastating. Absolute. Now *her name* will be one of power, and even you know it."

What did those words mean? For that matter, what exactly was this duel anyway? Gosh, if only Jack hadn't told me to stay away from it all, to essentially pretend none of it had anything to do with me, I might have listened and learned.

"But it's not her name we need to worry about. Not yet. It's yours. Your name that tumbled from her ecstatic, jubilant lips right after she…won."

I just shook my head. Why in all the hells would Luce say anything about me? In her moment of ascension, I should have been far away, as far away as Parelle Girls was from wherever the Eph the Guild of Talents held its illustrious gatherings. Far away.

"When she said you, her best friend, Jade Falkenstrom, were her courage. Her inspiration to do her best, and then do even better. That was her victory speech, you see. They don't normally do those, not for a mere Mentor promotion, but this was no mere anything. A pauper nobody from Convergence had annihilated the Mentor she only needed to incapacitate to advance. That's the word my friendly witnesses used. Annihilated. Anyway, congratulations. Your name is now a big fat question because this little prodigy is claiming you're the one who drove her to win by way of turning her opponent into a brief statue of ash."

Jack sat behind her desk and laid the hammer upon it. I tried not to visibly relax, but a solid, well-made wooden *thing* now lay between her ire and me, the target of it. Now I was trying to imagine Little Lu as a killer. Had there been any sign of it? Was she *that* powerful? If so, why was Tiamat the one everyone feared? Why had Tiamat been made a Mentor first? Had Lu lost control? Or was this just her way of showing Tiamat how serious she was? And why had she said *my* name at the peak of her exultation?

…And then I thought I realised what Jack was trying to tell me. This wasn't about me. It wasn't even about my hammer. This *was* all about Lucille Loudair, the newly-revealed terror of Talents. Yet one more formidable enemy in the 'fight' Jack and the other Construction Guild higher-ups kept speeching about. And apparently one of their own, a Sender no less, had made her.

"So, Sarah, whenever she asked you for help. For kind words. For this so-called inspiration and courage. Whenever this 'best friend' from whom I expressly told you to stay the fuck away came to you for anything more than to borrow a fucking pencil, *why didn't you just say no?*"

Didn't I? Hadn't I been the very model of passivity?

For *every single conversation* in what, four months?

I started to turn inward again to test this, knowing already that I'd almost certainly encouraged Luce at least a few times to rise to the challenge of taking Tiamat down a notch or ten when the time came, and Shyn knew it didn't take much. Then Jack really brought home how totally Ephed I was.

"We might call you Boy but bless me if you aren't truly a girl. Remember what I said? Girls gossip. Laugh if you want but I'm not so old to forget what it was like, trying to impress each other, put others down. And it seems one way you tried to impress this Lucille Loudair was telling her that you're a member of a certain guild yourself. At least, so she said. Repeatedly. To a whole bunch of Talented aristocrats, scholars and well-to-do types. So now we have an out-of-control pyrotic from Convergence of all the Eph-forsaken places blabbering about, what was it?" Jack's expression grew radiant as she delivered a scathing imitation of a young woman at her most exuberant, shrill and breathless. "'My best friend, her name's Jade Falkenstrom, she gave me the inspiration to be the best I can, and she's not even one of us but a lowly

Builder and oh I'm from the Con so goshness knows I know all about lowly!'"

I laugh-hiccup-convulsed, just as I'd seen other Messengers do when it was their turn in this chair, listening to Jack's comical condemnations. And when I heard myself making that awful noise, I thought, *Holy Ephing Shyn. I am a Messenger.* I was Sixty-Three. I glanced at the hammer that had been mine, and wondered to whom Jack would be sending me, and in what state.

And she saw this, and she knew. "Oh, please. I wouldn't waste the time or effort. Whatever I'd do to you, nothing compared to what *they* will. This connection to our guild? That's my problem. Yours is much worse. Because it's going to take absolutely no time at all for them to figure out who you are, and what. Or did you really think everyone believed your ridiculous stories about how your ears got that way…Half?"

The spiral resumed. I doubled over, clasped my stomach. I didn't even really know what 'Half' meant, only that Jack had brought up my mutilated ears. My deepest shame everywhere but here. Until now.

"The Peddlers will be after you, 'Princess Jade', daughter of Chantal of the All-Trades Inn and Eph-knows-who-else because it sure as fuck wasn't the very human Captain-Guard Arius Falkenstrom. Yes, I know who you really are. As if I wouldn't. Who you are and what you are. Right now, they're the same thing to me: gone. So…here. Your retirement gift." Jack picked up the hammer. Picked herself up. Dropped the thing on the floor in front of me. Stood over me. "You might need this. Now give *me* what I asked for, Boy. And get it right this time. And then get out."

It was a purely symbolic surrender and that's why it hurt so much. Just a badge. Just a stupid little piece of wood. Just everything I'd believed I was, really was. After accepting it, she sat down again and I retrieved the hammer, dismayed at how little comfort its return brought.

"I…had a plan, Jack. That day I told you about Tiamat…but not about Lucille. I had a reason for that. But then Tia's 'later' never happened so I just let it go."

"What? Still here?" She sounded irritated. Just irritated. "Still sitting *there*?"

"I was going to set up a fight." I had to say it now. All of it. Last chance. And too late, of course. "Me and Abby…and Lucy, maybe. We'd take down Tia. A genuine Mentor of the Talents, but only just coming into her own. Not there quite yet. Surely we could have taken her. Especially with one of them on our side. This is a war, right? And they are the enemy. Them. Not the sad shits you have me torture so lightly for being sad shits. I wanted to do more than just…" I waved feebly at the room in which I'd pretended to be so important, so tough. Nothing more than her tool, in the end. Her hammer, wielded in self-interest. Hers…and mine. "I wanted to really earn my place in the guild."

"Sarah, you *had that already*. So many other members would climb over each other to be where you were. Here, in this room you so glibly dismiss. What exactly do you think we were doing? Every move against or for another guild is a preparation for what's coming. But you Halves, never content with your lot. That, what you just said. An afterschool fight turned pitched battle. That's not a plan. That's a fantasy. A daydream. A delusion. We're realists, we Builders. And realistically, your 'plan' would probably have just been a slaughter and *not* of them. Hammers and sticks against a storm. Even a fledgling like Tiamat is dangerous…and say you 'take her down', by some Eph-blessed miracle. Say you *killed* a Mentor of the Talents. The reprisal would be devastating. They'd raze this place in an instant, and the Watch would just sit and…watch."

There I sat, chastised in a way none of Mother's scathing lessons could come close to matching. One of Father's own had laid it all out: I wasn't smart. I wasn't brave. I definitely wasn't good. Just a useless Dumpling resisting, yet again, the urge to drive the hammer's head squarely into her own skull. But I knew that wouldn't fix anything either. What would? This, at least, might be a start:

"I'm sorry, Jack."

But whatever it started, Jack had already decided to finish.

"Don't be sorry, Just be gone. Please. Quietly, quickly. And then, for Eph's sake, for your own sake, hide those damn ears, keep your damn head down, and run. Far away. Not even the Haven will be a haven for you now."

So I did exactly that. Well, most of it. I wasn't ready to run, not with what little I had on me. Not with how little I really knew or understood. And, as Dyingsun deepened into Awakenmoon and I trudged back to the All-Trades Inn, I simply couldn't accept that things were as bad as Jack had said they were. People were still going about their business under an indifferent sky. No one looked at me. No one said my name. Great gouts of blue flame, exaggerated from what little Lucy showed me that day, did not pour down the streets, and sturdy Construction Guild members did not charge from alleyways, ready to make their mundane war on the focused forces of nature. If I was fucked, no one had told the world in which I lived. So all that fear, terror, tension…everything Jack had infused into my naïve bones and blood, it all just receded from a shore of certitude that in no way could The End come from so uneventful an evening's walk home. And I felt that way right up until I stepped into the All-Trades, down the few steps into Churna Mountain's checkpoint.

Where Mother was waiting.

Dressed for work.

Calmly chatting with Churna.

See? I told myself before she saw me. Everything's normal. Everything's fine.

Then she did see me, and she smiled, and I knew that, if anything, Jack had understated the situation.

"My goodness, look at you. What in the world are you wearing, Dumpling?" Because of course I hadn't had time to switch back to the Parelle Girls uniform, nor to let my hair down only to tie it up again. She was looking at Boy, and she'd seen straight through it. "You look like some street urchin. Like someone who'd spend their time skulking about Hammerdin. Associating with…guildsfolk there. Let me guess." She put on a big show of touching her fingers to her lips and not guessing at all. "Construction Guild? Trying to follow in your father's footsteps, Jade Falkenstrom?"

"He wasn't my father and you know it."

"Well, close enough. Churna, she's all yours. See you inside, Dumpling."

She swept away.

"Weapons?" I couldn't tell if he knew it was me or not.

I deposited the hammer for his collection. It was nowhere near as momentous an occasion as I'd long anticipated. He grunted, tossed it in a box where it kept other tools…weapons company.

The Lantern glowed at my touch, same pale green as usual.

"Welcome-To-The-All-Trades-Inn-Have-A-Nice-Stay."

"Not Ephing likely."

As outside, so inside. The crowd was typical for Awakenmoon: not yet ready for Chantal's gift of rapture, but palpably building towards it. I could easily have skipped upstairs and into my room, where no doubt things would be even more bafflingly normal. Where I could have changed into Dumpling properly. Boy had no place here. But, and you knew this already, she had the answers and Jack had left me with an uncomfortable burden of questions. She'd either provide or not, regardless of my appearance.

Jerich ignored me when I came to a halt next to her at the bar. Ignored me with a scowl.

"Another drink if you would, Bielsen." Mother pushed the base of her wine glass, the contents barely touched, my way. At my puzzled expression, she shrugged. "You want to act like a grown-up, you get to drink like one."

I didn't. Of course. Didn't drink, didn't understand what she meant. I'd acted like a stupid little girl according to Jack. Gossiping and bragging and impressing my way into strife when I'd thought I'd made every effort to stay out of it.

"I'm sorry." I couldn't even tell you what I meant by that. It might as well have been a burp or a fart. Anything to get this started.

"For what? You've done nothing more than be exactly who I know you to be." She sipped her new glass of wine. "Although I'm surprised how little effort you've put into chasing him down, learning about who he really was. Who you really are."

"It didn't matter." I tried to look enthralled by the lack of reflection in the dark wine before me. "I was whoever I needed to be. I am. A lie? Yes, and a good one. I got what I wanted." Past tense. As was everything else about me. "Mother, what's going to happen now?"

She cough-laughed, as though she'd already been singing for hours and was reduced to guttural stutters. But then, much clearer and declared with the belief of a prophecy on the verge of fulfilment: "The Peddlers are going to come for you tonight and take you away. I'm going to mourn very openly, probably through a new and spectacular rendition of 'The Curse'. People you know will wonder what went wrong, for a little while, but they'll tell themselves you were always a little strange, a little...not-right. Before long, your removal as a disturbance and disruption will make sense to them. Bells is finally going to lose some weight." Another jagged laugh. "But she doesn't matter. Who does matter is the one who's going to make you a martyr, a symbol, for her cause." She drank a little more, a little more like her usual self. "And you know, Dumpling, I'm genuinely stunned it's not me."

"Lucy." I simply had to prove that I knew at least something. Or prove that I didn't know a damn thing. "Lucille Loudair. The Pauper-pyrotic."

"What? No. She's going to be a different problem. Bigger, certainly, but bigger doesn't concern you. No, I meant that annoying busybody down in Hammerdin. The one you chose over me. A God-forsaken revolutionary."

I guess I did, but at no point in all seven or so years had it felt like a choice. More like a lack of. Yes, Brother. That *is* how she works. "You chose a fucking song version of me over *me*."

"That song put a roof over your head, food in your belly, and you into a good school." This was almost a mere mimicry of indignation. "But we both know that's not why. I did it because I *love* my song, love it in ways I could never love you or anything else. That's just what I am. The way I was made. We can none of us fight that."

So flat, so honest. So I didn't believe it, but I'd never give her the pleasure of knowing that. I groped for practicality. "Jack told me to run. Should I?"

"You'd be dead in days. Not a good idea."

"I'm dead anyway, aren't I? The Peddlers are coming. Something I said. Something I did. Something I am. I just don't fit, so they're going to cut me away, just like you do my ears."

"Oh, Jade. I would never let that happen." She turned on her stool and reached out for my arm. I didn't flinch, because there was none of the usual intensity or desperation in her expression when she gripped me for stability. Both her look and touch were soft, but not drunk-soft. Sad-soft. Goodbye-soft. "When they come, you have to trust me. Trust that your old mother knows what she's doing."

Of the many doubts I'd had about her, that she knew exactly what she was doing was not one. I just never figured that any of it was for my benefit. Especially when she said it was.

"So what do I do?"

"Simple. Go to your room, pack that carry-bag of yours. Wait."

"And I guess I'll be clutching that bag right up until the Bluehands thrust me back into God's dark embrace."

Her hand fell away. "I won't keep telling you that this is not how you're going to die. And I won't keep pretending that asking you to trust me means anything. You don't have much choice here. Your guild has quietly disavowed you, your schoolfriends are about to be caught up in a not-so-civil war, and the only thing keeping you safe, insignificance, has been blown away like a statue made of ash." I pulled away from her. "Or so I imagine." She smirked a little.

"Eph's Balls and Shyn's Cunt but I hate you."

Not even that provoked her. "That's not going to stop you from doing exactly as I said, is it?" She glanced at the notched candle behind the bar. Jerich had made himself busy elsewhere a while ago. "Time for me to do what I do. Do I at least get a goodbye hug or kiss? We are not going to see each other for a while."

There were ways she could have acted that I wouldn't have been able to resist. I'd have fallen back into that role, for both of us. But this? This matter-of-fact dismissal of hope? This complicit extraction of me from…everything?

"Save it for then, then." I left her there.

I managed to dodge anyone on the floor who even vaguely knew me, feigning a shitty mood, or so I told myself. But when I saw Levi cleaning a table on the mostly empty third floor balcony, I paused. He was, as usual, very attentive to his work, and I could have slipped by, up into my lavish room to await my fate. Was it fair of me to just disappear without at least…? People taken by the Peddlers rarely if ever knew it was coming. I tried being philosophical about it, considering it a gift that I at least could say goodbye. To say the things that needed to be said now, because otherwise wasn't 'later'; it was 'never'.

I approached him, stopping to grip the back of a chair at the table he was so furiously wiping down.

"Hey you." Calm. Casual. Normal. Everything was normal.

"One moment." Levi finished with one last satisfied swipe. Then he threw the rag over his shoulder, and looked up at me. He'd been crying. Who I was then could see it and felt the pain behind it. "Is there something I can do for you?"

His tone wasn't meant for me, or who I was. Didn't he recognise me dressed like this? I mean, Boy wasn't *that* good a disguise. "It's me, Levi."

"Who?" Too emphatic to be anything but rhetorical. "Honestly. Who are you? I believe I have no idea."

"Me. Sarah. Jade. Dumpling."

"So you have four names. At least." He now refused to meet my gaze. "I have just one. Leviathan Jeriksen."

"And it's a good name." I fumbled for connection even as I tightened my grip on the back of the chair. "It's you, and you are enough. More than. Levi. You know…I'm…Fuck…I'm…"

"Sorry. Yes, I know. I believe I should say the same but I can't think of a single thing I've ever done wrong to you. And I know you've a lot more to be sorry about than anything to do with me. So I'll take that last little 'sorry' you can't say and keep it where you can't betray it." He smiled in a way I'd never seen before, a way I was strangely thankful I'd never seen before. Who knew he was capable of such bitterness? Not selfish little me, that's for sure.

"Levi, I…I think I need to run away. You know, don't you? What's coming for me."

He said nothing. Either those drying tears from the eyes that wouldn't look at me were for me and he knew, or they weren't and he didn't.

"Come with me. Big world out there. There's gotta be more than just…this shitty fucking city. These shitty guilds and their Ephing shitty conflicts. It's going to get bad. Very bad. Teristra is going to burn and I've seen the flame that's going to start it. Come. Please. Won't you come with me?"

He blinked, started a little. And then he looked at me, bewildered, like I'd just proposed he cut off his own hands, one at a time.

And then he nodded…and I knew it wasn't in answer to what I'd proposed.

"Dad said you'd be desperate, dangerous. But crazy? I don't believe I saw that coming. Leave? Why would I leave? This is my home. And even if something awful did happen to Teristra, I'd stay and fight alongside Dad, and Agnis, and Churna, and Bells, Frey, Verdande, Kharyb…and everyone here. I believe that's what it means to love someone. To be there for them, and they'll be there for you. I don't believe you can understand any of this. No Dad to love you. That…loveless woman for a mother. There's something *wrong* with you, always has been, and I don't believe I can fix it.

"Leave, you say. And with you. *You*. And do what? Play at husband and wife? I don't believe you have the first idea of what that would mean. It means being reliable. There for each other. It means being true to your word. You were *never* around when you said you would be, and I don't believe how many times I waited for you, and believed you when you said sorry, so quickly and so often. When you say that now, I don't believe you. When you say anything to me now, and it's not very often, *I don't believe you.*"

I'd started crying midway through this, and convulsed with palm-faced, snot-slickened sobs by the time he reached that final eviscerating iteration of 'you'.

"I don't believe you, and I never will."

Then, and only then, did I know I was alone. Beyond salvation. That it had all caught up to me, the lies that got me what I wanted. I wasn't crying for Levi as he may have cried for me. For all my effort at being myself, whatever the Eph that meant from one person to another, at not being like *her,* I'd fallen into the only trap any too self-conscious brat falls into. And there I was, mourning the loss of me even before she would, if that's what it was really going to happen.

And when I looked up, he'd moved to another table. Not that far away. I could have chased after him, tried again. But I wasn't that me anymore. She was useless. She was gone. Not coming back never. They all were. All except for the me who remembered Daddy's workshop, remembered Mother's proudest moment. Remembered not what rhymed with 'lie', but that which follows 'what do you say?'

"Thank you." I tried to memorise the shape of him, and moved off to my room, to sit on my bed and wait to be taken to my death. Or not. Didn't matter anymore.

You want me to say I did anything else? That I opened the window and jumped out to some miraculous landing, or fashioned a rope from my blankets and climbed down to freedom? Made a weapon of the cutlery left with the dinner that was waiting for me there? There was a knife already. Quite sharp. And no doubt Princess Jade, about whom Mother was already singing downstairs, would have done all of those at some point. Or charmed those coming for her. Or used that convenient cloak of invisibility she stole from the wicked queen to simply disappear.

The closest I came to disappearing was crawling under the bed at some point, but the smell of the chamberpot drove me back to just lying on the quilt in the darkness. Couldn't even do that right.

I wondered if Princess Jade were rousing a rebellion down there, encouraging her best friend to exercise her vast power to turn against the oppressive aristocrats. I wondered what Lucy was doing then. What

Tiamat was doing. Abby. People who had been friends with someone I wasn't. Who definitely wouldn't have been friends with who I really was. Well, Lucy maybe. I should have been me around her, to Eph's Heaven with Jack's orders, for all the good obeying those did. Probably still would have ended up the same way. Was it all over the moment Little Lu noticed me? And…how far back had that been? So much further back than when I noticed her. Years, maybe. Didn't matter.

It didn't matter so much that I started mumbling that to myself.

It was only when I was falling asleep that I realised I hadn't packed any sort of bag and I'd left the hammer with Mr. Mountain. Or maybe I realised that I'd known all along that I wouldn't need any of that soon enough.

The biggest surprise is that they *did* come and that Mother hadn't lied, and the Peddlers arrived much in the way you've described from your time in the same organisation. I woke to mostly darkness, stained with shifts of movement, whispers and then a silence that made both seem like a delusion. I just lay there, no longer indulging in the internal frenzy of self-pity but instead resigned to this ultimate proof that Jack, Mother, Levi…they'd all been telling some sort of truth. Enough of a truth for it to come to this. For strangers to steal into my bedroom as I slept and remove me from the world, like a splinter from a calloused sole.

Then one of the masked, hooded, cloaked shadows spoke quite clearly. Well, I assumed they were masked, hooded, cloaked. Wouldn't you be?

"Wake up, Sarah-Jade Falkenstrom." It was a woman's voice. Fairly deep. Deliberate.

I said nothing. Did nothing. Whatever happened next, I had no intention of hurrying it along.

"She's awake, I can hear it." A man this time. Youngish voice. After a little while, there was a flare of light and I flinched. Absolutely I did. Were they going to burn me to death? That'd be appropriate.

But all it was was one of them using their talent to light a few of the wall fixtures, just as Agnis would. Exposed as awake and aware, I sat up, still dressed like Boy, and saw that there were only two of them, and the male's hands were still aglow. Again, just like Agnis. I was really, really going to miss her. Eph me, I was going to miss them all. I didn't cry then, but it was very close.

"There we go." The woman left her mask, cloak, hood…all of that, firmly in place. She was otherwise wearing, well, black. Leather and cloth. There was absolutely no doubt: these were Peddlers. And they were acting very strange.

"Grab her bag." Him to her. "As for you, Princess. Up. We're not carrying you."

"You're not?" I complied regardless.

"This bag?" The woman picked up my carry satchel. "Seems light for travel."

"I didn't pack one. Didn't think I'd need it. You *are* Peddlers, right? "

"But she *told* you to pack a bag." The woman was irate, and I was then very aware of the sword slung over her back. "Make a habit of disobeying Sisters, do we?"

"Uh." Then, more or less as eloquently: "Uh?"

"Time enough later to talk about that." She threw the strap of my bag over her shoulder. "Let's go."

"Honestly, we'd rather you walk." The man followed her to the door. "But we *will* carry you if we have to. You wouldn't enjoy what we'd do to you before that. Your decision."

I was still fully clothed when they'd entered. So other than my hair being mussed from the cap, I was ready to go. Consciously, as much as possible.

"You won't have to walk far. We've made arrangements."

Yes, I know. *Very* reassuring of him.

They led me out of my bedroom and into an eerily quiet hallway. Why wasn't Mother still performing? Was it that late? Was there such a thing as too late for her performance? God, was tonight's song *that* different?

"Do you need to use the waterroom?" The woman turned her masked face towards the end of the hall. I gaped at her. "Long journey ahead. Five minutes won't make any difference, and it's not as though you can climb out the window on the fifth floor."

"No. I mean, no I don't." I had no idea what to call these people, and no desire to call them anything at all if possible.

So we trudged down flights of stairs I never thought I'd ever stop using. The All-Trades Inn was dead. Not abandoned. I knew there were people in their rooms, and I saw some sort of activity at the bar once we reached the ground floor. The firepit looked cold. We proceeded almost casually to the exit, where I could see the most alarming thing of all: No

Mr. Mountain and no lantern on his desk. This was a Haven, and *every* Haven had to have two things: a doorman and his lantern.

I glanced back, one last time, and Jerich was staring back at me from the bar. He didn't seem angry. He didn't look upset. He just looked like he always looked when no one was looking: a little sad, a little tired. He looked like the veteran Keeper of Teristra's largest Haven, a role so solemn and important only the next of kin could take it up when the solemnity and importance grew too much for old bones to bear. I hoped that Levi would be spared that for many years yet.

"Jerich!"

"Sarah." His arms remained folded across that wonderful barrel chest that was his and would always be his and his only. "May I have a moment with her, good servants?"

The man shrugged, leaned against Churna's desk. "Of course. We are all very pleased with your work here, Jerich Bielsen. Have your moment. Have two."

The woman sat at one of the tables not far from her partner, toying with a small dagger she produced from…somewhere. I wasted no time getting to the bar, but just stood there. I knew better than to do something so pointless as pull up a stool.

"I'm not going to say anything astounding or pivotal, Sarah." Jerich tapped himself a mug of beer. I'd never seen him drink, but that doesn't mean he never did either. I'd just never seen it. "No revelations about your father, or your mother. You'll learn all that soon enough. But I will say a few things, two things, and let you be on your way. Best you be gone before long, before what's coming."

I really wanted to know. Of course I did. And there was no time, not to ask. Only to listen.

"Firstly, I'm…really disappointed that you're not who my son thought you were. Or maybe, you're that but you're something else too. You lied to him, to us both, for years. I don't know what you really feel for either of us, but we really did think the best of you, saw the best in you. They all said, don't trust her. She's a Half. They're mad in the blood. Can't help it, just what they are. And her damn witch mother. That's what they said, Sarah. Not me."

Again, they who? Not the others in here. The Peddlers themselves? They knew him. Their work somehow coincided with his. I wasn't the first Weed they'd taken from this place, I knew then. And Jerich was so…so much more than I'd known. They all were. Everyone. I'd treated them all so glibly, so lightly. Like they were all so easy to fool, when I'd been the one fooling myself. I didn't matter, and this wasn't my story. It was theirs. All of them. My removal from Teristra? The tiniest of erasures. Mother had been right. And yet:

"And secondly, I want you to know this is very much my fault. It was so simple in the moment, so easy to say, I was just being nice. Trying to encourage her. One night, not long after you were born, and she was here. Drunk as usual. You know how it goes. She hadn't sung in months, and I…felt sorry for her. Thought if she found a new song, maybe things would be better." He looked down, drank deep. Didn't look back up.

Wait. I *knew* this story. She'd told me. And not once had I thought about his role in it, not in terms of blame and guilt. She's the one who sang it. She's the one who made of me, *me*, nothing more than a childish fairy tale. So…why, Jerich? Why would you do this to yourself?

"If only I'd just kept refilling her drink, let her ramble about the baby, about her woes. If only I'd never said 'make a song about her, about what you'd like her to be, and love at least that much.' Damn, what a stupid thing to say to a woman like her."

"You didn't say that." He'd never said that in her version of the story, so…it wasn't possible. It just wasn't. "All you did was guide her to do what she was always going to do."

He grunted, as though refusing to commit to disagreement. "Maybe. Still, I was there that night when everything started to go wrong for you, and I said things I wish I could take back…and yet would probably say again, if I were in the same situation. Like you said, Sarah. We do what we're always going to do. I just couldn't help it."

One of the Peddlers cleared their throat. We both looked over and saw the woman replacing her mask. "Sorry. Kind of stuffy in here. Don't let me interrupt."

I looked back at Jerich. We finally had that moment, and we knew it, because the real moment had passed and we could just smile at the inevitability of people being who they are, nothing more, nothing less.

"Goodbye and good luck, young Sarah-Jade." Jerich offered his hand as one would a fellow grown-up. No hug then. No kiss on the cheek. No ruffling of hair. Something better, in its way.

"Thank you, Jerich." I accepted his hand with my own. It was the most intimately simple touch I'd ever felt. "Good luck to you too. Whatever's coming."

"Ah, I'm fine. We're taken care of. Aren't we, my friends?"

"Absolutely, Havenkeeper Bielsen." The man pushed off Mr. Mountain's counter. "The All-Trades Inn will be the last building standing should the entire city go up in a blaze. Which it might, but somehow I reckon otherwise. We're off then?"

The rapport between these people, between the man I respected the most and these reputably terrifying strangers who were meant to come and take me to some gruesome end, convinced me at last: *I wasn't going to die. Not like this.* Now I could say it.

"I'm ready to go."

The three of us left The All-Trades Inn. I didn't even think about the hammer until much later, when it seemed right that something I'd been given, had taken and fought to keep…but then gave away anyway, should remain in the city that gave it any meaning at all.

Because it was obvious, the moment we emerged from the All-Trades, that the city was already moving beyond anything I knew of it. Even if you consider that I rarely ventured out at night, especially not on certain fullmoonlit ones, and so wouldn't know normal from not, this just didn't seem right. There was a crowd in the middle of the Estenthric Highway, denser towards the crossroads fountain and, by my guess, coming from Hammerdin. Many of them bore torches, although by the faint glow to the sky I figured the time was already Lowmoon; daybreak was not far off. They were mostly quiet, as though still waking up to the irritation of being awake so early. But a few people were not quiet, were in fact directing them. The silhouette of a stout woman stood on the fountain's ledge, gripping the arm of the statue with one hand, gesticulating with the other. I couldn't hear her voice, but her body language was all rouse, rally and muster. I had a feeling that whoever she was, she was wearing a very familiar pendant around her neck, and I hoped she didn't look our way. Didn't see I wasn't keeping my head down, hadn't run. Hadn't been smart or brave. Definitely not good.

"Crap. It's already started." The male Peddler ushered me away from all of that, towards the less-crowded Westgate.

"Chantal wasn't going to wait. Not now that Princess Jade's fiery little friend has manifested."

I lost view of whatever *it* was; any attempt to glance back just found the female Peddler's body, which she seemed to have positioned precisely for that purpose. I focused on keeping pace with the man in front of me.

"Hey. Wait. Did Mother sing about Lucy? Lucille Loudair?"

"In here." The man guided us down an alley to the right. I knew this particular little street, as I knew most of the nooks of the AllTrades district. And not once had I seen it as anything but a dead end in the shadow of Westgate's imposing wall. "And yes, she did. Although typically more about who Lucille is going to be, which people found a lot more exciting and inspiring. Wait there."

We waited as he disappeared into a doorway, and I tried to think about what he'd just said. Tried to even begin.

"He won't be long. I recommend you keep calm, Sarah-Jade." She gave me no reason to do anything other than that, and that was enough. "Did you honestly never consider why your mother's singing was so popular, so…influential?"

Ever? Not even once in a whole four months?

How about almost eight years?

"I must have, but I don't remember it really mattering to me. I listened sometimes but never for long. I didn't want to know too much about this made-up version of me that everyone loved. That everyone seemed to lose their wits over."

She sighed behind the mask. "You poor thing. It wasn't a version of *you* they loved. It was *her* singing. Her power, not yours. The Havenkeeper was right in that the blame is his, if he really did encourage her to sing about Princess Jade. Perhaps it would have been better had he not encouraged her to use your name that way. Perhaps not."

"What's *your* name?" I was *that* calm then? To forgot that Peddlers very likely didn't converse with Weeds very often.

"Chrys."

"Kris?"

"Short for Chrysanthemum."

"Oh." I regretted asking only after she answered. What did my knowing this secret mean? "And him?"

"*I* am called Pricker." He emerged from the doorway. "We're clear. Let's go."

I didn't know what 'clear' meant, but when we approached Westgate, it was abandoned but for one guard, who didn't even look at us. More precisely, he was looking past our shoulders. The noise behind us, deeper into Teristra, was growing; the crowd was fast becoming a mob. The

Peddlers noticed too; Chrys and 'Pricker' hurried me through the archway. Near its mouth, on a stone bridge leading out into a world I'd not returned to once since entering the city nine years ago, was a black carriage. Four sleek black horses. Hat-and-caped driver. Coachman, I later learned was the word for it. Fancy. I'd occasionally seen these thunder down the Estenthric into the East Quarter, but rarely the other ways.

"Wow. Guess we aren't walking then."

Chrys laughed; the man just shook his head and opened the door to the carriage. "*You* aren't. In."

I did as he bid, still marvelling at the luxury of it all.

Chrys took a seat opposite me, placed my carrybag beside me and closed the door for us both.

Pricker reached one hand up through the window, and she gripped it briefly. "Don't dally, Chrysanthemum. We have days at most."

"I *never* dally, Nicholai. The nerve of you. Right then. We're off." Odd name, I thought, before wondering why. No weirder than Pricker, but then he'd worded it weirdly too: 'I am called' is not necessarily 'my name is'.

And then we were off, just like that. I wasn't sure, but I could have sworn I heard the first explosion of what would become known as the Purge of Teristra in the distance not long after we left.

"I have something for you. Two somethings." Chrys hadn't taken off the mask or removed her hood. Sitting this close though, I couldn't but notice the lingering tension in her hazel eyes. "First, this."

I glanced down at what was in her gloved hands, cupped as though holding water, or a rare flower. Or a large pendant, which I picked up by its thin golden chain as cautiously as I would very fine fabric.

"Your mother said you'd need it, but not to wear it yet. That you'd know when."

For one disgusting moment, I actually allowed myself to believe it might have been Jack's. That any circular medallion could be a Guildmaster's symbol of authority, and that somehow despite everything that had happened, I coveted, no, *deserved* that role. It made no sense, of course – none! – but maybe I really *was* Princess Jade. Maybe all those ludicrous twists of fate and as-luck-would-have-it heroics that saw Princess Jade overcome all sorts of calamity were meant for me after all. I *wasn't* nobody. Oh, I was being saved for now, but really I was also being saved *for later.* I would, someday, be called back to Teristra and some grander purpose as the true Construction Guildmaster. Against all logic, that was my first reaction.

Then I remembered just how terrible I was at nailing two pieces of wood together, and almost laughed. Me, Construction Guildmaster. Yeah. Right.

As good a shattering of a stupid dream as any.

No, this pendant was something else. If it were a guild's device, I didn't recognise it.

I don't have to describe it to you, but at that point, it was just unfamiliar and beautiful. I'd never really had any jewellery other than the obligatory *f* necklace, and I only wore that when the guise demanded it. As opposed to that crude little thing, this was…art? Yes, as good a word as any, Brother. Though I suspect you've said the same thing about swords, so as usual I'm left questioning your standards.

"Was this my father's?"

"No idea. Who's your father?"

I didn't know what she meant by that question. Who was he supposed to be? Who was he to me? To others?

Was he anyone at all, really?

"Doesn't matter, I guess. 'Pumpkin'." I read the word aloud after examining the engraving on the reverse side. "'CJ'."

"CJ. That your father? Do you recognise it at all?"

"No. But he did call me that. Pumpkin."

"Eh, common enough pet-name for little girls. Anyway, you keep that hidden. I suspect to reveal it before its time would be a very bad idea."

Still holding it, I grabbed my satchel, pulled out the same napkin I'd use to hold the muffins, shook some crumbs out and wrapped the beautiful, dangerous thing up and stashed it in the bag. "Chrys?"

"Hm?"

"Do…you wear a badge like other guilds?"

And is its symbol a moon and a cross?

She laughed a little, and I chose not to try to understand it. "Of course not. We're not a guild. We're more like…hm, a team. Intermediaries. Messengers. You'll see." She said that in a way that discouraged further questioning. I would see…but right now, I would not.

"As to the other thing I have for you, it's not from your mother, but us. The best we can do to ease your troubles. We usually use this for something else, but…trust me, it'll help. You've a long journey ahead, and you'll need your energy for what's at the end of it."

"Some kind of sleeping aid?"

"Of a sort. Dreaming, too. Good dreams, or so I hear. Or hope." She proffered the small vial. Its fluid contents could have been anything, but going by her words, chances were it was something very specific.

A drug. Was this how they subdued Weeds before spiriting them away? "You ever use it?"

"Sometimes we need good dreams too, Sarah-Jade. But not this time. This time, mine is to watch over yours."

I *was* tired, and yet felt unable to sleep. And she'd probably just force me to take it anyway. I saved her the effort, swallowed the mixture. It was intensely bitter, and that's how I knew it was going to work.

"I've heard of stuff like this, down at the guild." I handed back the vial.

"I highly doubt that, Sarah-Jade. As with everything else tonight, your mother ensured you receive the best care. I am proof of that."

"Chrys…" I felt the descending heaviness lull me in tandem with the rhythm of the road. I still tried to fight it, just because that's what I do. Because I'm the same girl who always refused Mother's numbing song when she did my ears. "Who the *fug*…iz she…reeeeally?"

"You'll see, and you'll be so very astonished. Terrified, but mostly astonished."

"Oooohng."

And then I was out.

And that's all I remember of being Sarah-Jade Falkenstrom. Of that life, if you can call it that. We both know it wasn't what happened to me, but you know, even if it were, I don't think I'd remember it any clearer. And we also both know that those things really *did* happen one way or another, the big ones in Teristra, the ones she wouldn't let me be a part of. The Purge of the Talents and the rise of Jacqueline Wright. Lucille Lourdaire, Tiamat Fourneval, and their shared foil Abaddonna Kaufmann…although I doubt they went to the same school. Strange fantasy, that. Still, strange fantasies are *her* favourite coin.

And remember how I wondered what her part in that song was? The song that began with a none-too-subtly manipulated version of the beginning of our downfall? I think the Sarah-Jade Falkenstrom scenario was like that for me. Not to be in it, but to simply know it intimately. To experience it without being really affected by it. To witness it from within. The difference is, of course, she had choice, power, control. I only had the illusion of those, and realising that essentially freed me from it. From the moment that song began, its ending was decided: Teristra would be on the brink of a guild war, the Fey would intervene just a little, and I'd be whisked away safely before it all went boom. Safe not from the events but from learning I was a nobody caught up in the fringe of them.

Or so she wanted me to think, feel, believe. A pity she couldn't control what came next, what I really experienced, whether it was induced by the belief I'd been drugged into visionary torpor...or the hope that there is no fringe, and no one is safe from the event of their own life.

W. James Chan

His Dream

The (final?) Garden
Moonsun…moon?
??? A.R. WHAT IS A.R. ???

It started as it ended as it always did: endless, precipitative, momentous.

Where I was alone in the grey. There was nothing in the sky above me and nothing on the ground below me. There was no sound, not even my heartbeat which I knew was wrong. I knew that and I knew one other thing. I knew the word for that. All of it. A title for that state of being before and after and in-between.

Lapsarian.

If I could have laughed I would have, because then I knew a third thing: I was Lapsarian. Ah.

Then that was gone.

Because then I knew another thing. I was not naked. I knew this because then I was clothed in something that at first was very heavy, very hollow, something in which I felt encased, but soon went unnoticed because it had always been there. Armour. Plates of it. Layers and layers. I could name every piece, some with old words, some with words that would only have existed had any of that been real. So. I knew it was not real. Important to remember. I knew, though, that I would forget this one thing, because I knew something else: *I could be wrong.*

I would have been wrong if there was a before in which I could be wrong, but there wasn't. There was then, and then I looked and saw variance in the sky, little explosions of creation within what might have been clouds and I thought the world was starting to know things too. Silence, and then not.

THUMP!

The first thud caught my breath.

Thumpthump.

Oh. Or was it…? Ah, it was *both*. Thunder and my heartbeat. There they were, and that was right.

They. Did I ever think I was alone? I was not, would never be. *Could* never be.

After all, were I alone, why would I have been holding a weapon? It was like a hammer. I knew hammers. Oh, did I know hammers. Well, it was like a hammer but with a chain between the handle and the other part. It was…a flail. A scourge? No. It was a hammer. Golden…no…

It was the *Gildenhammer.*

Seriously, you named it?
No more than you named yours, Brother.

And it was going to be very handy when They approached.

Who then did. No. Different them. This they hadn't approached. They were just there, gathered in some loose formation that seemed to be around me but really just happened to contain me. Some wore the same armour as me. Some did not. Some human, some not so much. All were armed, but not all bore arms. They were there for what was coming. All were ready. *All are welcome here.* No, that one wasn't mine. But they were, so it might as well have been.

We had a name. The last name for the last forces at the last stand. Jaydemyr. There was a longer name but it wasn't necessary anymore. And we were by no means Jaydemyr alone. But we were Jaydemyr and we were alone.

Then I also knew: in a different then, there had been talk. A lot of talk. Planning. Preparation. Not too far from here had been our home, home because there had been nowhere else left. A camp, nothing more. Temporary, like everything else in that world, that…what was the word again? *Falling* world. Like that world. There only as long as needed. Massive but limited. Everyone in the world in one place was only an impressive concept when everyone was many people at all. But we were here, waiting, as we had been and as we would be, until this then had passed, replaced by something equally timeless, equally endless.

That something had a word too. I knew it, but it was not my place to say it. It was hers. That one, suspended above and before the gathering on a pedestal of ice. She was short, with blonde hair in a single defiant braid. She wore a simple white dress, stained from our long, long journey to now. I hadn't known her but then I did and always had. Her name was Vachaelle, and she would lead him to lead us.

The sight of her painfully familiar hair prompted me to check my own. Two braids, same colour as hers. Yes, of course it was. No princess, but pretty enough to…was I? Was I what? No. Was I *who*?

The word interrupted that thought; it pealed forth from her distant lips and assaulted the desaturated storm gathering overhead.

"*Sa'Ha'Khra!*"

I knew what that meant. Everyone there did, but she wasn't saying it to us. Or for us.

We responded anyway, cheering and screaming and shaking our various arms at the sky, at what we knew it concealed. Some of us yelled the word as well, but I did not. I just adjusted my grip on the weapon, breathed in and braced myself for what would befall that falling world.

That is why those assembled had formed no battle lines, no ranks. The Garden was nothing but starved, desperate weeds, and the cleansing rain of Roses and overbearing will brought not nourishment but annihilation. As it was always going to do.

Oh, such things had passed to put us there. The advent of Crucinacht. The war that had been so encompassing we called it the Worldwar. The Rapture of the Four: Kaaji's modifying flame; Talize's maddening bolt; Fallyn's muffling tear; Alisan's muting tremor. The sword they had become, wielded by he to whom she would lead them, he who could not but love the sword. A fearsome thing that had cut away continental chunks of an already broken world, and provoked Their belated but terrible response. The First and the only. The world had been made smaller and smaller. Those who had fought over it, fewer and fewer. Until that concentrated, narrow then, when the division was done and we who remained were immune to the simple logic of 'we' as a thing that could be reduced. And the concept of the world entire was nothing more than 'there'.

There. Then.

The heaving, swollen maelstrom above, lit with more and more flickers and cracks, seemed to pull into itself, and then burst, expelling its horrific cargo of heavenly hate-made-flesh. Like filthy screeching fireworks, I thought, and then thought, no. No comparisons, no metaphors, no similes.

They came, and the Second *Sa'Ha'Khra* was upon us.

If Their twisting, barrelling bodies made any sound as They dove, it was vastly quieter than Their polyphonic shrieks. Somehow over that piercing opening strike I heard and saw some of us, Us I thought but then thought no, just us, drop to our knees and clutch blood-gushing ears. We had all heard that before, but not in such unison, because never before had there been such a choir, and there would never again be such a choir. But most of us endured the divine wail, because most of us hadn't been made to be destroyed by it.

If They had wings, we could not see them. Some of us did. Some of us were half-Them, and some of us were half-Something Else. But even those who could have did not take to the skies, because as more and more of Them emerged from the tumbling, awesome tempest, we knew the heavens were Theirs. The Garden, onto which the monstrosities were now pouring down, was ours.

Kaef're had been ours and would be ours until the end.

Then it was clear: we had expected some sort of uniform area of arrival, of impact. We had ignored the expanse of Their host; we had gathered and waited together. Children anticipating a deluge obedient to gravity. So when the first wave defied that straight line between above and below, spread out and veered away but still in descent, seemingly intent on flanking us, we scattered and were no longer immune to division. Vachaelle remained poised, waiting for him, but others I knew led their own groups to intercept. Zhao La-Ahn, another Half but one of his oldest companions, peeled away with a keen cry, the air around her highmoon-robed figure distorted as it was so often then. I knew what she looked like not by face but by presence. We none of us had looked at each other's faces much by then, entirely uneager for the questions waiting there, equally uneager for the answers folded underneath. So we had developed other means of identifying each other, identifying *with* each other. La-Ahn was still La-Ahn over there, but she was also a blur accentuated with razor-thin curves of air and light, integrating what she was with what one of Them used to be. She didn't even stop before seeking another.

And I knew there was Pai Hei-Wah, a healer bathed in warmth and love for us, all of us and even him, she the big sister he never knew he had had. *There* was Pai Hei-Wah, with her own entourage, because anyone that had really known him or knew him or would yet know him led as well. Not far from her: Ishida Koh-Cho, all swords and twirls and devotion, etching her way through the madness, ignored then as before as ever. Ming Tou-Fah trailed, behind but always so close to her, gyrating chains perforating the difference between sense and senselessness. And of course Chang Tong-Kut, his endless typhoon generating a hailstorm of daggers. Yes, all there. But he wasn't. Still, he wasn't.

I turned my attention elsewhere, a different point of this uncentred star. Littleknife was one of the stronger ones, retaining a distinct human form and face that I thought was crying, even as she flipped and zipped about, nothing but a namesake leaving a wake of delicately stripped limbs. How well he must have remembered her, for her to still be that, after almost everything had fallen out of place, into place, until it was no place at all.

I had a rare twinge of uncertainty: what of me? I disengaged my attention from the storm that wasn't around me, and considered me. Still armoured. Still female. Still two arms, two legs. I used my free hand to gauge my face, and was jealously exultant to discover it was there. He would remember me too then. Of course he would. He was fighting for me, wasn't he? I knew exactly who he was and so didn't stop to wonder who 'he' was.

Or why Vachaelle was waiting for him. Why it seemed like until he was there, it all felt just like arrangement. Place-setting. Background. Past-tense waiting to become, never to become. If the world was falling, it was falling towards the devastating finality of his arrival.

The battle continued without me. I was excluded for now. I knew that to surrender myself to the same savagery absorbing my comrades, my fellow final inhabitants of the world, would be to expend unnecessary energy, energy I'd need to play my role soon enough. Very soon. Imminently. As soon as he fell into our falling…Lapsed into it.

"Lapsarian…Aaaahshit." Then I laughed. Yes, that was me, exactly. Falling, fallen, fell, aaaahshit. My heart jittered with a flutter of epiphany. I said it again, but this time with a different stress, a new pause. Louder. Clearer. So not really saying anything again after all. "Lapse. Sariana…? *Shit.*"

The moment that was her turned to me at that, all of her bearing down on all of me. I dared look back at her, up at her, on her crystal cold stand. I was not laughing now. Her expression I knew, although I wasn't sure if it was hers. Whatever she'd been building (writing? Singing?), I'd almost torn it down. Laughing.

"No. You are too close." Maybe Vachaelle was talking to herself, but was definitely talking *about* me. I was too far away to see her lips move but too close if I could hear and understand that. Then she, as ever unmoved, made me move. Away just enough. Still in the frame of that last of all battles, but distinctly 'There!' rather than everyone else's all-encompassing 'here'. I was in the distance to anyone truly in the throes of it. As he would be, soon, so very soon. I would otherwise be in the corner of the eye, and so that was how I watched those who would not be, who would be noticed and thus fall so gloriously first: punishment presented as privilege. As they fought, as they played it all out, I felt an urge to join them, but she would just remove me again. So I stood there, in armoured, armed frustration. I was reserved for some important after-the-fact function. Privilege presented as punishment. It was enough that I knew what that fact was, and so would recognise it when it happened.

Thump!

When it happens, it is neither thunder nor my heartbeat, but a landing. An arrival. Silence imposes as anticipation, as though by the lifting of a curtain from a cage, and now unleashed is a scream that is unlike any of the countless this world has heard. A wail. I look because there is nowhere else to look, and I see him, there. In the middle of everything, all of everything. He clenches his eyes against the sudden deluge of exploding gore. His sword, which has a name but only he knows it because She is not an it, is embedded in the ground. He does not let Her go. Then a lonely crash of thunder shatters the thickened air. It is his heart breaking, and I understand, we all do. The world aligns itself instantly.

Vachaelle attends to him now that he is here, and my attention is no longer welcome. It is needed elsewhere, or rather, here and now, because one of Them has noticed me, somehow spared the slaughter otherwise engaging any of us, any of Them. It is a nightmare thing that turns towards me, though I do not remember any dreams or nightmares plagued by so defined a horror. That, I realise, is because this isn't *my* nightmare. No time to dwell on what that means. It approaches. Its arms are too long; its legs are too long. It walks and scrambles and strides and leaps, and its maw pulls back and back, as though to swallow me whole from above. I know something else, though: nothing with that many teeth ever swallows anything whole. My pulse jumps ahead, becomes palpable pain not in my chest but in my head. I can…*hear* it, demanding that I keep up.

There is no way I can fight this divine monstrosity. I am here to be devoured, unnoticed and irrelevant. I remember something else, and realise that not even being unimportant can save me here. Wait. No. This is not as was; this is not *her* nightmare either. It is his dream, and I do have a role to play, because I am here. Ah! Once I accept this, things move so impossibly fast, catching up to where I should have put them much sooner. Down it comes, this first Fey, this poor Rose, and *up it goes,* my fist which is not empty, will never be empty. The cruel head of the Gildenhammer, my flail, slams into the monster's jaw. I hear the thing's chin crack right before it flies off. The impact sends the Fey's head around until its gaze finds the sky. I step back, and the mutilated Fey falls at my feet. I am smashing the Gildenhammer into its face before it can even begin to recover. I take a knee, take hold of the flail's desecrated head in one hand and use the other to drive the spiked pommel through the Fey's pure black eyes, taking one at a time. I have done all of this before. There is no effort, only muscle, metal, and memory. I will do all of this again.

Right now. I know I am welcome now to join the fray, and I do it again. And again. My whirring flail seeks skulls, driven towards nothing else. Now and then bits of jagged Fey bone ping against my armour, but it is the traditional vestment of the Jaydemyrian Eagles, and the bone might as well be pebbles against a fortress wall. I kill and I kill, knowing that sooner or later I will be noticed, and then I *will* be the most important person in this entire tiny shard of the world, in all of this fracture of existence. But…he won't know my name. He sees me, and I *matter,* more than anyone and anything, but he doesn't know my name, and so neither do I. And even when he does, he won't get it quite right. I know this too, even as I am as good as gone, absorbed into the melee.

This goes on and on, the Gildenhammer expressing my endless offence, ancestral plate declaring my unbreachable defence. But I am tired and sore and the horde just keeps coming from above. I forget what it was like before I had to look up, always looking up, ready to sidestep the terror tumbling from the wringing clouds. Now that he has seen me and put me into perspective, I do not know whether or not I am still safe. Is my part done? Can I now be killed off, conveniently out of his notice? Others have fallen already, having been acknowledged, named and cast aside. Surely my turn approaches. Yet another Fey comes too close, loses its features to the Gildenhammer's relentless rhythm of impact, a beat kept by the sharp pulse endless in my ears.

Thumpthump. Thumpthump.

I am done with this. Please, let this be done. Somehow I turn just in time to both dodge whatever was coming and send my flail into whatever is going. Exhausted. Beyond exhaustion. I kill and I don't die and I kill. I cannot wait, I must wait. I wait to hear what must come next, oh for the love of Eph and Shyn, Brother, *say it already!*

"Itohshihitohnohtamehni!"

Finally. The magic word. I don't understand it, don't even know if it's even really a word, but I know what it means. *For the one I love.* I almost sob with relief and the thudding in my chest and ears subsides. He has said it, and now he will do what he is here to do, and it can end. I can end.

I try to watch it end for the others, but I'm already feeling myself start to disentangle from this place. It is enough that I can see him become some sort of fury, a form of perfect murder. The Fey bear down on him and him alone, and I sag in relief, released from that unbearable present.

I surrendered to this conclusion. It was all about him, and now he had accepted that, and could die a hero. And I am...was his Talon, though I didn't know what that meant. He had another name for me, for who he thought I was. I knew it then. Tzara-Min Jaydemyr. And it was close. Oh it was so close. But he couldn't have known what my real name meant.

I fell to my knees with a gasp. It was supposed to end there, so why was there now this sudden blossoming of agony? Perhaps I hadn't noticed when it happened. Adrenaline, or something even more potent. I looked down and saw blood seep from between the segments of metal that, for all their worth, had failed to protect me after all. The stain spread, and I felt as though my guts had already spilled out and were being cradled by the curvature of the cuirass. So...I would not survive his dream after all. Always knew it. Still...did it have to be so Ephing painful?

I choked out one last bloody laugh. Of course it had end like this. Because it was his nightmare, but *her* dream. And that bitch never made

it easy for anyone. For me. Fading now. Fading…toppling over…breathing, and hearing only the beating of my heart…slowing.
Thumpthump.
And slower.
Thump…thump…
And…
Thump…

II. Tzara-Min

Mothers Abbey

868 - 875 A.R.

Chapter 8: Scarlet Survival
4/868 A.R.

Gasp.

Eventually I did wake up, of course. It likely wasn't even that long after my arrival. I hardly need remind you of the inefficacy of traditional sedation techniques on the likes of us. Splendid for placing difficult cases into a more agreeable state, but nothing in comparison to the narcotic embrace of Dreamsong; I defer to your sadly superior experience regarding that. So it was not some mesh of memory and whimsy from which I emerged on that bed in that room, and yet:

The first thing I saw after that one intake of breath, vague but distinct, was a woman wearing red sitting next to the bed, and I almost panicked. *She* was here, of course she was, who else would it be!? She'd said we'd see each other again but not for a while, oh Eph she's going to hug me and everything will be fine but nothing will be *right* and Chrysanthemum oh Chrysanthemum no Chrys—

And then, like an intense ache in a fleeting dream, that was all gone, and I was me again.

I gave myself time to come to. I was lying on my left side but found the view disagreeable. So I rolled onto my back. Took in the room, itemised its unadorned details. The bed was just a cot, wedged against a stone wall. Above it, a single indented square. A window? I naturally recoiled but then relaxed upon realising no light passed through it. Not a window, no. Just a recessed shelf. Above and around it, just more stone, a uniform colour I could only think of as 'dismay'. And head back to the left: a simple desk in the far right corner, the few candles upon its stark surface somehow providing more shadows than light. The only door to the room was closed, wooden, no bars…and there was the woman in red, sitting on that stool. I could not see anything in the far left corner behind her.

I went back to looking at her, not her eyes but everything else. The red robe put one word in my head: 'ritual'. I didn't care for that so I tried to think of other things a similar hue. Cherries. Tomatoes. Wine. Wounds. I felt my face wrinkle in distaste, and forced myself away from the red, seemingly against its every intention of being seen and not ever unseen. Her hair, then: brown. Wavy. Long. No fitting replacement as far as notable features go, but surely less temporary than one's choice of clothing. I was determined not to leave it at 'the woman in red'. Eyes. Grey. Face. Composed. Ears. She had two, small and round. I almost laughed, bitter with a thought I buried immediately because Father would not have been amused, but will faithfully excavate and put on display for you now: *nse'ante* all look alike.

"Good evening, Rose." The woman's words had been far too congenial, and that name a mistake.

"Tell me who you are to address me so." Mortal.

She did not answer immediately, which meant she was either fatally ignorant as to who I was, or 'who I was' was now 'who I had been'. I felt my upper lip twitch, annoyed at these two possibilities with a shared conclusion. That gesture, mostly reflex but not entirely undeliberate, did what my words could not:

she stood from the stool,

(how dare she force me to look up at her!)

only to sink to her knees,

(better…)

make the sign of the Flail,

(such a sorry little habit…)

and then prostrate herself at my feet.

(there: balance restored. Perhaps she does know after all.)

But she still said nothing.

I glared down at her back, waiting. I had told her what to do, as clearly as one could, but instead she chose a different sort of submission. Disobedience enveloped her obeisance, repackaged it somehow. I did not understand, and I had very little patience for mortals doing things I did not understand. "Reply. But do not raise your head."

Reply she did, soft and deferential. Exactly as commanded.

"I said lower your head." I was aware that both I hadn't said that and she'd be a fool to point this out. "Not your voice."

"Sister Cass. This one is known as Sister Cass."

"A name. Meaningless." To me. "Very well. Tell me what you are. No. I expect you'd just waste my time again. Woman, recite the Twelve."

She had pushed me far enough. Time for a standard test. I cannot express how much I wanted her to pass.

She began to speak the Twelve, and I listened not to the words but the tone and delivery. As she proceeded through the only thing mortals should really care about, I conjured visions of the woman, or at least as close to her as I could manage given how singularly immemorable she was, being violated in all possible manner. It would be pointless for me to recount even many of them, so I present only one. A simple example. Gone was that pretentiously coloured robe, pitiful denial of her vulnerability as it was. They are all naked before our eyes. Something cut her skin, pulled it apart, peeled it, bit into the revealed muscles, ground its teeth trying to find the bones. I imagined her pain, as best I could, and the behaviour befitting it. Screams, writhing, whimpers. A desperate need for it all to stop. It did not stop. The body struggled to find a configuration that would ease the suffering. No such configuration existed. As something widened the body's entrances and exits, passages natural and otherwise, the limbs folded to deny the insertion. Futile. I heard laughter, as I was taught to do, but did not understand why. They said it enhanced the subject's perception of agony. I perceived no such enhancement but regarding this exercise, mine was not to perceive, only to project.

What I did have to perceive was any change in the recipient. Should the test prove successful, such a change would be not be slight. For whatever reason, those who can receive what we can project usually mimic the projection. Such is the sensitivity of the reception. Or perhaps the strength of the projection.

I withdrew the projection. The woman kept reciting. No contortion, no sudden exhalations. No screams. I resumed the projection. No change. I withdrew the projection again.

The woman was mundane. Banal.

Good. Loathsome obscenities, those Maliscients, if convenient for expedited communication. I was disappointed that she failed, that the test did not end this inappropriate encounter with her violent demise, but it meant that something more intriguing than the arrogance of maliscience was behind her lack of compliance.

And then, although I knew I'd performed this test many times, I found myself unable to do anything. A moment of weakness, no more.

"Stop."

She stopped.

"Tell me where I am."

"You are in an isolation cell."

Insolence! Again, that bothersome 'either' business: either she cared so little for her life that she dared such a pointless response, or a higher command than mine kept her from being more specific. I needed to know the answer, and so she needed to be alive.

"Tell me the name of the building. The nearest town. The local Nobility." Tell me why you are making this so difficult.

"No."

She would deny me? ME?

Of course I killed her.

No. Of course I didn't. I tried. Or, I did something without thinking that should have killed her but did not. And that 'should have' was so natural, so lacking in exception, that I saw it happen. It is possible that I was still aligned with projection, with visualisation. There is always a risk of letting it overrule reality, that's what I was taught, but I was not one for losing myself in forceful imagination. Indeed, it would have taken a stronger imagination than mine to conceive what actually did happen.

"No."

"Rika Fasz!" Her denial drew that from me, and I was only half-aware that while the words were mild, the switch in language was an error, and then…blood did not seep from her ears. Pain did not fuel her scream. She reacted no more to those two words than she did the projection of her ruin.

I blinked. I blink so little it felt like a grand surrender, a total loss of composure. She had not responded to the projection, which gave a clear and very likely result: that she was not Maliscient, and my unvoiced thoughts were not hers to peruse. But at immediate exposure to the Tongue of Revelation, she had not so much as squeaked, when any mortal would have died. That meant she was not mortal. Yet not one of us. And not one of those mad things condemned to dwell between, She be praised for that much.

I had not meant to deploy our sacred language as a weapon, so when it failed to operate as one, I did not try again. But it had also failed to communicate my disgust and wrath, so I reverted to what they call Ziegerian-Common. "You're useless!"

First blinking, now ceding this bewildering confrontation with such obvious feebleness. I started to slip off the bed, contemplating deploying something else as a weapon, but held myself. If words that should have killed did not, then other methods I expected to be similarly effective might also be just as shamefully dull-toothed. Perhaps the insult hadn't been directed at the woman at all.

She did not respond. After all, I hadn't given her a command.

"Tell me what you are."

"I'm useless."

I ignored this facetiousness. Any reaction to her impudence would just have confirmed my impotence. "Repeat your name and state your role in this place."

"I am Sister Cass, Second Hand of the Liquid Night."

Whatever force had restrained her from being more helpful thus far, its suppression seemed to have missed a crucial angle. I now knew a lot more than any captor would deem intelligent. Not quite my location, no. But my situation, absolutely. And there was only one possibility in which that situation was not to my advantage. A possibility crystallised by the fact that this woman was impervious to the lethality of our words.

"You serve Vachaelle then."

She said nothing. Of course. I was musing, nothing more. Unwilling to be specific myself.

"You called me 'Rose' before. The Liquid Night does not use that particular designation, nor engage with Roses. Tell me why you are performing Peddler duties."

"I cannot."

Again. That wall. These were reasonable demands. Although part of the same process of mortal management, Vachaelle's Liquid Night Sisterhood and Father's pet project the Blood Peddlers were separate and a member of either order would know that. She should have just done as I said. Surely she grasped how easily a Rose, as the woman seemed to consider me, could wring the answers from her. Or at least wring her until forced to find the answers elsewhere. Surely she realised how likely it was that a Rose, as I understood them to be based on the full name 'Wild Rose', would indeed do just that with no concern for its own safety. Same conclusion, another 'either' to annoy me: this woman was fearless, or she was powerless.

I chose. "Tell me why you are here. Tell me what you intend to do with me."

Fearless.

"I am here to fetch you. I am to prepare you for your audience." She remained prostrate, but something changed nonetheless, confirming my choice. No one truly powerless would so confidently declare: "I intend to do nothing with you. I attend to the Liquid Night. As will you."

My audience. My audience with. So my audience, as someone else's audience.

I did not choose.

Powerless.

"Describe the preparation for this audience."

"If you will permit me, I shall show you, and then we may proceed."

All that resistance and resilience, and still she sought my acquiescence. Very well.

"I do not permit you. Describe it, and then I will decide."

The woman sighed.

The woman…sighed.

At me. Someone she had called a Rose. A Fey who has lost faith in all of God's teachings, in the power of the Twelve, in anything but the fact that *nse'ante* are just squishy toys full of food.

A Fey, I realised then, who was quite hungry.

So be it. Enough of this farce.

I was out of the bed in nothing close to a flash. By all that was meant to be, Meant To Be, I should have been pressing the woman against the wall, my grip cracking her head against the ceiling, my teeth to her throat, and me enjoying with unremitted delight that vital tap. Action followed desire. Think, do. This sorry gap in which I found myself pulled between the two, pulled so hard and sharp I was on the floor, hands and knees, barely able to support my own body, was not for me. I knew the word 'heavy' but never, ever had I experienced it. Not the way mortals seemed to, shuffling about until it was time to run and be caught. Run. I could not even crawl. Running, just running, was in that moment as beyond my grasp as frolicking in the sun or immersing myself in a river.

"I would speak, if you permit it."

With immense effort, I fought this force eager to drag me ever downwards and struggled back onto the bed, onto my back. The woman did not look up, but no doubt she heard it all. I was definitely going to kill her now. Once I—I admitted it, finally. I was definitely going to kill her…once I could.

"Speak."

"I am to prepare you for your audience. To explain what has happened to you, as a Rose. To dress you as is correct. To convey you to Mother's presence. I am to do so with all haste, and merely describing it is not at all hasty."

Mother's presence. The Mother's presence. Your Mother's presence. MY Mother's presence.

NO.

"No. You must not. Not her." Full sentences eluded me. That weakness I'd discovered leadening my limbs combined with a terror I was only just remembering as entirely appropriate. Appropriate because I now also remembered why I was here, or at least somewhere stripped of my birthright and natural supremacy. "I…beseech you. Keep me away from her. If you knew what she planned, what she can do. No one believed me."

The woman sighed again and this time I heard not scorn but hope. I heard not exasperation but shared resignation. Perhaps we were powerless together. "I cannot keep you from her. I cannot know what she planned. I am to explain to you what has happened. Prepare you for the audience. Convey you to her. With your permission."

Perhaps not.

I closed my eyes. The words had come out, all but begging to be spared Mother's attention, and the slivers of recollection followed. Sliced into the skin of happy ignorance, but not through it. Father was gone. Mother had ascended. And her plan was not supremacy. Not familial perpetuation. Her plan was total obliteration. Obliviation. Of all of us. I'd used those words to describe it, to anyone who would listen, and then…nothing. A void in memory I could not measure. As though merely speaking of it brought it about.

And now…

Now I was here. Humiliated. Stripped of all potency.

Being prepared for my audience with 'Mother'.

I groaned onto my left again, opened my eyes and regarded her inert form. So submissive…and completely in control.

"I grant you permission. Yes. Proceed." And please make it as slow as possible.

The woman…Sister Cass, then, since who she was now figured into me finding out who I had become, unfurled and seemed to evanesce into that darker corner between where she had been sitting and the door. I strained to see…and that was wrong too.

I should not have needed to strain to see. This room should not have been dark to me at all. The candle light should have been the problem, not the shadows they cast. I knew this the way a bird knows how to fly, or a cat how to stalk. But then not all birds know how to fly. Not all cats know how to stalk. Not the ones kept in cages or pampered by their owners. I had simply known what I was, and taken for granted that I was an exemplary version of it. That was now evidently untrue, so as Sister Cass 'prepared', I tried to remember a more solid reason why I was not perfectly what I should have been. Nothing. I just went to sleep one morning and woke up here. That gap in my recollection. A nothing that was something. This was…new.

"I will now explain what has happened." Her voice was getting harder to make out.

I think I nodded.

"You have not been fed for a long time. Longer than considered safe. You are past the madness, past the loss of control. You are, in fact, very close to ascending to Her eternal domain. This is why you are so weak. This is why you are unable to think clearly. To remember much at all. Your vision is failing. You are a wilting Rose about to wither. I am the only source of sustenance in this room, and I am entirely beyond your faltering reach. You must accept all of this. Your body will die here, as is your final divine right. I am here to witness it."

Her tone had changed again. As with the Twelve, she'd been reciting. She'd said all of this before. I did accept that. But then she emerged from the dimness carrying a robe. Red. Like hers. But not quite. Red.

"But Mother has interceded. She will receive you. Heal you. Restore you. For as she does say, not all Roses are Wild. The Garden must be cultivated. *Vahm En.*

"Now, put this on."

That is when I really gave up. Stopped trying to figure any of it out. To remember. To end this bothersome knew-too-much mortal. To resist this idea of avoiding 'Mother'. Because it all made sense, even this Sister talking like a Peddler. It all made sense because none of it did.

"I will need your assistance."

"I will provide it."

The first few times she touched me were a violation. Of course they were. We touched the *nse'ante*. They didn't touch us. We helped them. They didn't help us. We supported them. They didn't support us. No one doubted that. No one questioned it because it was never even a necessary statement. But no, someone had. Father. He had challenged all of that, exposing what he called a master-slave relationship as a farce, and then proposing…no, that was lost to me too. But oh I remembered that much. Sariana, he had said and I could hear it then, they touch us. They help us. They support us. Without them we would not be. So stop calling them that awful word. I don't care that others do. Not even your Mother. You will not.

And somewhere between being stuck on that rough bed commanding Sister Cass over and again to no useful end, and being on my feet, held up by her, clad in that red robe, I knew Father had been right about it all. Maybe that's why he was gone. And now I knew it too, and I'd be gone as well. Was already gone.

And Sister Cass was the only person who could help me find out what happens after that.

"Steady now." We shuffled towards the door. I dreaded even a slight distance from her, that it might send me to the floor once again. And then it occurred to me that we were going somewhere beyond that door. Down a hall perhaps. Stairs. Please God, no. Let me end as a Wild Rose before demanding that much of me.

"Now, sit." She turned me towards the door. I knew not on what, only that the curt offer was by then all-too-welcome so sit I did. Fine. Yes. Not an offer. A command. And I obeyed.

Sister Cass opened the door. She was just a blurry mass by then, but I suspect she checked both directions after doing so. Then she returned and stood behind me.

A few moments later, the chair started to move forward. Such a miracle. You may laugh now, but for a creature who never knew illness, could all but fly and move miles in a minute, a wheeled chair is a thing of stupid wonder. Fortunate, then, that I had not the energy to question it.

I could do nothing more than let my head drop forward, my eyelids droop, then flutter, then droop, and then not flutter. I knew I'd been stuffed into a wheeled chair with someone else guiding it, able to do naught but listen to the captivating friction of the wheels grinding against the seemingly endless floor. And I knew that I should have been revolted, not…relieved.

One last proud thought then: I was not opening my eyes enough for it to count as blinking. Ha.

Before long, I was not opening them at all.

I still didn't open my eyes when I came to. Was brought to, by a voice and maybe something else. A scent. A slap. A kiss?

"Will that be all, Mother?" A voice. Sister Cass. Behind me, even then.

"That shall be all, Daughter." Another voice. Before me, of course.

"She has not been given any sustenance, per your orders, but is it really…safe?" Talking about me. So this overpowering malaise was not the fatal conclusion she'd described. I tested it, first by trying to make a fist. The most I could manage was a frail grip on the wheeled chair's arm. I could have opened my eyes, but I wasn't ready to face who was facing me.

"For us, Daughter? Safe as Havens. For her…well, that is what I intend to find out. That *shall* be all."

A door creaked opened. A door clicked closed.

And by then, I knew the second voice. Not Mother's…but possibly worse. Someone to whom you always left the first move.

So my eyes remained shut, but she knew the rest of me was open to her.

"Looks to me like Chrys' little gift worked a tad too well, eh Jade?" The strangeness of the query, and that she asked it in what mortals called Ziegerian-Common disarmed me so thoroughly I did open my eyes. And of course that left me looking straight at Vachaelle the Nightsong, Witch-Seer of Clan Jaydemyr, in her well-lit, windowless chamber. If Sister Cass' robe had been a cup of blood, and the one she'd helped me into a fresh cut, then the witch's elaborate combination of formal dress and ceremonial garb was much closer to the black of a dried, crusty scab. I hadn't seen her wearing that particular garment before; at court she knew to play the role of demure but compelling advisor, and most other times she seemed comfortable in drab clothing befitting her fellow servants. She sat there, in a high-backed chair, hands folded on a desk messy with whatever mess desks are messy with. From the slight leaning forward to the cant of an angular face, the half-smile and the unwavering gaze of those chipped ice eyes, her body language said it all: your move.

I said nothing, because not a word of what she'd said made sense.

She sat back, hands now in her lap.

I returned her stare.

And stared some more.

And then I blinked.

She nodded. Correct move.

"I know you're angry with me, Dumpling, but you know now I did the right thing. I had to get you out of there. Shit was on fire. I'm sorry I made it all so scary. You didn't exactly give me much notice."

"Who." I faltered over a single word. It happens a lot with her but you always expect that next time you'll be ready. It wasn't just what she'd said, but how. The familiarity and the crassness. Common rather than Jaydemyrian. Who was she trying to fool? But yes, I started with what she'd said. With something that should be immutable. My identity. My name. "Sister Cass tells me I'm a Rose. You call me Jade and Dumpling. Who do you mean?"

At this she looked confused. Not a new expression for her, but rare in regards to me. Then she nodded again, slower. "Hm. Not as strong as his. No surprise. Gently does it, then…" I didn't have to pretend she was talking to herself. Again, one of her more frequent traits. "I imagine you're hungry. I can have some of your special muffins sent down."

"Vachaelle." I spoke in Jaydemyrian, of course. "Your underling called me a Rose. She told me in no uncertain terms what had happened to me, so you know very well that I am extremely hungry, and not for…a muffin."

Her body convulsed a little. Were I not distracted by the quickening of my own, I could have sworn I heard her heart punch against her ribs. Satisfying. "…You." Her turn to trip over single words. Then, also in Jaydemyrian, very softly, very cautiously: "It's you."

"I am indeed me." And despite what Sister Cass had said about me being close to death, starving, wasting away, it seemed finally being acknowledged for who I was provided energy enough to sit up and smile. To stop wondering if Father had been right when he'd said one did not consume the blood of the Liquid Night. No, I wasn't that desperate. I think. "Hello, Aunty Chaelle."

"Sariana-ra." She was still muddling through all of this, as though that wasn't my purported role in the situation. "You do know you're supposed to be dead, don't you?"

She laughed, light and untouchable. Back in control. Maybe.

"I'm no Rose. And I don't plan to wilt like one. But I find myself at a loss." We knew each other now, but that didn't mean the game was done. Merely reconfigured. "We are in an abbey of the Sisterhood. I have been brought here, weak and powerless. How came I to be in such a state and why here? Has something happened to our home?"

"It's gone." She wouldn't give more than that. Not so freely.

If so, it must have been her. Mother. No one had listened to me, not even Aunty Chaelle, whose will so often met Mother's with a passion many Fey would consider self-destructive, never mind mortals…or whatever the Nightsong really was. And if no one managed to stop Mother, then I already had my answer. The abbey was to be my physical hiding place; 'Jade' or 'Dumpling' was my personal one. 'Chrys' was likely who I'd remember as my escort here. Her 'gift', some means of making me conveniently unconscious for the journey. And Chaelle, as the 'Mother' to this abbey, would serve as my protector until…until something. "Her plan worked."

"*The* plan worked, Sariana. Your brother is also safe, far from here. He has no idea who he is. No one does. No one should. Oh, Sari, this is really bad. You honestly shouldn't be here. Maybe if I gave you a really solid whack over the head?"

"Try it, mortal." I shook my head. Be smarter than that, Pumpkin. "If I'm not supposed to be here, then why are you? The obfuscation should have been total."

"Because I am *very good* at being who I'm not supposed to be. Once Dhiana realised she couldn't Delve me, my role became clear. To me, if not necessarily to her. Not at first. But this isn't about who I am, supposed or otherwise. It's about who you are supposed to be. Need to be."

"Who am I supposed to be, and what will happen if I reveal the truth?" As ardently as I'd tried to thwart Mother's plan to erase all knowledge of our existence from the world, I knew she'd only enact it if left with no option. That, as well as 'it's gone' being my family home's status, made clear that if 'Sariana' were supposed to be dead, then it was for only the direst reason.

"I can answer the second one, but who you are supposed to be is…well, it's a whole other person, Sariana. I don't doubt your ability to absorb whatever I throw at you, but it'll still take time to impart and even more time to integrate since you're still you as well. Unless…you want to do it my way?"

"And end up like Uncle Arius? No thank you very much."

"Ouch. How little you know, to be so flippant. Fine, I shall answer that second question and with no small delight: you squeak, you die. Actually die from actually being killed. You're a Half now, or something like it. Actually dying from actually being killed is something people do very easily. You will learn to fear the certainty of that. As much as you've feared, say, the sun until now."

"Half? That's ridiculous, Aunty."

"Just Chaelle for now. Aunty is a title you'll use for others here."

"More underlings?"

"As you have seen, I prefer to call them Daughters."

"Underlings then. Very well, Chaelle. How could I, true daughter of Dhiana-ra Jaydemyr and…Father—" He had a name; why couldn't I say it? "—be a Half? Mother is or was alive after my birth. And yet…hm." If I could accept this one crazy truth, that I wasn't entirely Fey, then it explained almost everything else: why my usage of the Tongue of Revelation didn't end Sister Cass; why I was unable to effortlessly destroy her; why I wasn't feeling as ravenous as she'd said I should, not when I really thought about it. And why Sister Cass might actually be a Maliscient after all. Only Fey can project well enough to sunder a Maliscient's mind. No. I'd allocated that woman more than her share of maybes.

"Ah…So that's where the block is. My, that's a lot. You didn't completely fail, Dhiana. In fact…oh. Bless me. You made a spare. You clever, clever bitch."

"Spare? Because my perfect brother's the heir, right? If he somehow doesn't survive this awful plan, there's always good old Pumpkin. She'll do." I wasn't bitter. Not at all.

"What? No. Yes. Not important." Hesitancy. An overtly bad move. Why? "So yes, you're Half now. You can go for a picnic at Highsun without combusting, take a dip in the local river without sinking, eat normal food without vomiting and move quite fast…for a mortal. And you've a Talent. Lucky you, it's the rarest known type. Hydrotheurgy. You're one in thousands, Sariana. Still, I may know someone who can help you work through it."

Another bad move, playing so many pieces at once. I wasn't going to respond to any of it. Yet. "You say I'm Half, but I've been classified as a Rose. A Wild Rose. Roses are never Half. That's essentially tautology.

And…oh." For the first time since this all started, I reached up to feel my ears. "Oh, no."

"It was no effort to convince the Daughters you're a Rose." She seemed to be ignoring my horror at what my fingers found. "In fact, they needed no convincing. Mother says, 'this is a Rose', it is a Rose. No matter what it looks like. They've not seen every Rose in existence, so they lack my proof that one that looks just like you cannot exist. And I doubt any of them have thought that much about it. Yet. Which means yes, you are also a Rose here, and until I say otherwise, your death is only postponed. One way or another, you must let Sariana-ra Jaydemyr be as dead to the world as your mother wanted."

Unspoken: why wasn't I? The so-called Mindwarp would not have made a mistake. And even Chaelle had seemed surprised. I would pursue that later. "I can't believe you let them cut my ears. They'll just grow back, you know. And if I'm meant to be Half, you could have just left them alone. I know they have them too. Like we do. Did."

"You know about Halves, but not about Roses. Clipping a Rose's ears marks the final step in their progression towards the end. It's one of the last things the Peddlers do for them. Also, no. They won't just grow back. Half, remember? Maybe once a year or so we will have to give them a trim. It won't hurt. Much."

"Hm. I don't know what power you and Mother employed to achieve this, but I accept it as given and proceed from there. I'm Half. Will I also end up the way they do?" I was fourteen years old, I knew that much. Not yet old enough as a Fey to learn how to stop counting or caring, and maybe four years away from the age at which a Half needs to be taken care of. And even if I somehow survived past that and regained my sanity, I'd have…a hundred years, maybe a bit more. I would, I had to admit, count them all with a miser's intensity. "Do I truly have so little time left?"

"I don't know." Her smugness was gone. "I hope not."

"I appreciate your concern."

"You know I care. And do you accept the rest of what I've said?"

"I'll need you to set about teaching me who I'm supposed to be, but yes. And I imagine that who I'm supposed to be has a few layers. Not as many as him." I said I wasn't bitter! I'm not… "But a few. What name would she use here?"

"Not Jade or Dumpling. She'll hate those." So why was she smirking again? "Not Sarah either. No, she knows she's supposed to be hiding. How about…Tzara-Min?"

"Oho, so you remember that one too. What an interesting journey that was. Charan wouldn't stop calling me that, after hearing someone mispronounce my name. His unerring ability to nettle irritated me then, but…I miss it now."

"It certainly showed us all how much your brother loved everything Mifūné. I doubt more than five people in existence know of Tzara-Min. So you will be Tzara-Min, Daughter of the Liquid Night, born Sarah, cursed as Jade, occasionally a Dumpling, someday to again be Sariana-ra Jaydemyr. Well, this shall be fun."

"Wait. Daughter? Hmph. I suppose it only makes sense to commit that much to the ploy. Is Mother out there somewhere, waiting for me to 'remember' at some special time when it's time to do so?"

"No, Tzara-Min. Not you. Him. And when he does remember, when the key turns and the lock loosens, so will everyone else. At their own pace. Well, maybe not you, it seems. The eventual goal is, of course, a full-scale return of the clan. One hopefully with neither clipped wings nor ears this time."

"And you'll be helping him?"

"I can't. I'm to look after you. I might visit him from time to time, when he seems in need of my love. For now, he's in good hands." One side of her mouth quirked up a little at this. "But enough of him. As a precursor to our forthcoming sessions, I will say this: you must not give any indication to anyone that you're anyone but a carpenter's daughter from a big city making a new life for herself in the service of the Night. No mention of clans, no doodling of the crux et luna as you daydream. No talk of plans to leave and seek anyone out, especially not your brother. You are, to my knowledge, the only person in the world to remember Jaydemyr in any detail, and while I am sure anyone unfortunate enough to hear the truth would dismiss it as nonsense, I'd still have to kill them and that's a bother. So let's not do any of that."

"You're already treating me like her." I was unsure whether to be impressed at the sudden shift or bothered that she seemed to have forgotten I was not 'some carpenter's daughter'. Even as a Half, I was smart enough not to do any of that. Tzara-Min (no family name; let people decide for themselves) would be precisely the blank slate 'Jade' needed her to be. And 'Jade', 'Dumpling', or 'Sarah' would be the rest of me. Perhaps only in dreams would Sariana-ra Jaydemyr wait, wait for the sign that she was once more welcome in the world. Dreams, now at night. How fitting.

"You're already wearing the Scarlet, but there are a few small things to take care of before I can revoke your status as a Rose and instate you as Daughter of the First Order."

"Why that name, First Order?"

"Sounds rather pompous, doesn't it? But I assure you, it's practical: you will see to the first order of business of the Liquid Night. Daughters learn, Sisters serve, Aunties teach, and Mother…mothers. More on that later."

"Does this mean I'll have to call you 'Mother'? Not Chaelle?"

No smirk this time. Outright hearty laughter. "Officially I'm Sister of the Third Eye, Chantal Falkenstrom, but yes, here I am known as Mother. Oh, don't make that face, Dumpling. You'll get used to it. After all, it's what Sarah-Jade calls me. Sarah-Jade *Falkenstrom.*"

"…WHAT?" I had to pretend to be someone pretending not to be the actual daughter of the head of a matriarchal society in which everyone called her actual mother…Mother? But this was the Witch-Seer of Jaydemyr. The shock of her was that one never quite stopped finding what she did shocking. "Seriously, Chaelle. What?"

"What do you mean what?" One last twinkle in her delighted eye. "Oh, the small things I mentioned?"

No but she clearly wasn't going to answer the question. And I'd need to know this, so: "Yes."

"Shouldn't take more than a day or two." She shrugged. "Just girly things. Well, humany things really. For a start, let me tell you about something called 'defecation'."

Not Exactly Haven-trained

"Yes, we understand the next full moon isn't for almost another three weeks, and yes we know that means it's probably going to be fairly quiet in here until then. Havenkeeper Fyodor, both my brother and I are experienced travellers. That is not why we are here. As I tried to explain to your Doorman, there is a credible threat to your establishment, and we don't believe it's going to wait until the next Hunting night. But a week ago we were staying in another Haven, quite a ways south-west of here, and as we slept something attacked it, slaughtered its occupants. No, there was no fire, and didn't you hear? The Scourge has stopped doing that, ever since good Lord Xenides-ra Kas'Daen declared that the evil Jaydemyr clan was again on the rise and he, The Scourge that is, is busy leading it. Oh, no. My brother just likes to wear black. Keeps him cool he says. Isn't that right, Ahran? Yes, thank you, good Havenkeeper. We promise we will be no trouble. Just let us stay here and keep an eye on things. Please do let us know if anyone suspicious arrives. Especially a Half. Okay, yes, other than us, hahaha."

"Eph's sake, Brother, could you maybe look a *little* less like the shadiest bastard in all of Kaef're? No? Fine. You stay in the room then. I'll get us some dinner, and if you eat all your vegetables I might tell you the next part of the story. IF. There's a good Dog-Ears."

20 days until the revelation

Chapter 9: Amber Acclimitisation
5-11/868 A.R.

Shiver.

We sat there, Sister Cass and I, she on a stone bench in the scathing sun assaulting the courtyard of Mothers Abbey, me on the stone floor in the homely shade of the open corridor enclosing the grassy square. It was Highsun, a near-mythical apex of unrelenting light from which even the most obstinate shadows shy away. I had been awake during that time before, but never awake *and outside*. I'd loathed the chilly little cell in which Chaelle had kept me but I now could think of nowhere else I'd rather be.

I was weak and frail. I was dying.

I was *starving*.

"We can do this all day." Sister Cass barely managed to get this out around a mouthful of bread. "Rather, *I* certainly can."

"Pray God you do not." I refused to look her way. "It is most foul."

"How is me enjoying my lunch in this lovely weather 'foul'?"

"You know how. I have told you. I refuse to believe you might have forgotten."

I heard her swallow and glanced up in nascent hope that it might be the last.

She was taking another bite and caught my furtive eye. I broke the contact. "Mmm. Blessed be the breadmakers. Mm." A foolish, meaningless quip, but she laughed anyway.

"Do keep talking." Anything to help mute the noise of her mushy mastication.

Sister Cass said nothing more.

A few weeks ago, give or take whatever void of memory lay between, I'd not once have thought to be subjected to any of this. It had been simple enough when I'd seen mortals as something other, something else…something *less*. Some served us: servants; some were served *to* us: vessels. That was all. Never in these curated interactions did they themselves *eat* in our presence. Given our predilection for vivid interpretation, it would have been unspeakably offputting. I knew things went limp when they died but never considered what such a slackening might release. I'd always just assumed the vessels were unusually weak and emaciated compared to the servants; perhaps that is why they were vessels in the first place. And, of course, it was poor manners to drain a vessel entirely. Hardly noble to act so desperately, so uncontrolled. But now, thanks to…Mother, I knew why.

Even at that distance from Sister Cass' consumption, I could not but imagine the hollow need to engorge, the uncomfortably violent sensations in the gut afterwards, and then lower, all the churning and bubbling leading towards the rank, base eventuality. Sooner or later I'd have to feed; they wouldn't let me subsist on water and a few slices of what they called 'black sausage' forever. No. Not feed. Eat. The word for it was 'eat'. I would need to eat and then experience…all that happened after that.

I shivered again.

"Do I have to, though?" I feigned indecision. "The Blood sustains nonetheless."

"The Blood sustains *Roses*, Tzara-Min." I looked up to see her rise from the bench, pad barefoot over the grass in the robes of what I knew now to be the Crimson of the Second Hand, and crouch on the threshold of the shaded corridor. "And you are not a Rose. Mother told me so. Every moment you spend in the dark, denying the needs of your body, you accuse her of breaking the Tenth Commandment."

Another reinforcement embedded in her response: the Twelve dictated my behaviour here as much as anyone else's, because I was not a Rose…anymore. I was to be a Daughter. One of them.

I chose not to answer.

"But still you demand proof. Still you doubt." She produced an ornate knife and pulled it across the palm of her other hand. She winced at the well of blood and made a fist which she held out to me. "Owfuckinnng. Nnngg!"

I watched the precious trickle fall from that fist onto the sheltered stone. Did any of the Twelve cover wastefulness? Surely. And for this grand transgression, Sister Cass was risking great castigation. I, however, would not.

"The stronger the doubt expressed, the stronger the faith impressed. Thus spake Kashensan." I barely heard this, while each drop pounding against the stones underfoot echoed in my ears. "The Blood sustains Roses and Nobles, Tzara-Min. Not ordinary people, not even half-ordinary people. Sunlight and food sustain us. So I'm offering you all three, but if you choose one, you choose them all, and then you will learn the truth. Come now, Tzara-Min. We're so very close to the beginning of your redemption." She shook her fist for emphasis. I tracked the movement's effect on the trajectory of the vessel's...of her blood. Found myself crawling towards the sorry little accumulation, so little and so much. Licked my lips.

She moved back at my approach, held her forearm upright so the blood no longer dripped but instead scrawled down her paperthin skin. "One more step. Just one. Join me. Join us. The Blessed Mother's night is no longer for you."

Or I could stay in the shade, safe and cool, and 'accept' that which she'd already offered. Like a *Rika Fas'z* settling for what they can get. Thought, action. I glanced up at her on my hands and knees, through the curtain of unkempt hair, tongue waging war between the dignity of restraint and the impulse of indulgence. No. Not indulgence. This was need.

And the woman knew it. "Well go on then. Start with that. See if you can stop."

So I did, before it could dry any further. I heard myself make a frustrated grunt and snarl; I could barely discern even a tingle of the blood from the grit and the dust. Only a few drops, after all.

More.

I reached for the human's blood-streaked limb, shuffling my knees across the flagstones, but stopped just shy of the lethal bath of sunfire within which it floated.

"By Her Love, you're so *pathetic.*"

"You will *die* for that, nse'ante." I felt the weakness of this threat in the back of my throat. "Come to me."

The vessel relented a little, leaning forward and opening its hand. I lunged, but somehow this vessel was faster than me, than *me,* and now all but the hand was lost to the vicious glare. The hand then. I clutched and fell upon it, employing every faculty at my disposal to extract the sensation denied of me by the contaminated sample underfoot. The twinge was there, but the relief, the satisfaction, was not.

More.

I tried the arm itself, but couldn't puncture the stone-like skin; not so paperthin after all. The vessel reacted as expected, pulling away but I wouldn't allow that, not when I was so close, so I went with it, taking what I could from the vastly inadequate slice in the vessel's palm. Finally, after some scramble and pursuit, I felt it. *Finally.* I closed my eyes and pulled and pulled. The hot flush and the pleasure washed over me, enfolded me back into the shudder of fulfilment.

But even that wasn't enough. As the sensation began to subside, I succumbed to instinct and tried for more. Not even a slight sip further and I realised that the taste in my mouth was wrong. Rather, there *was* a taste where there should have been nothing but bliss. There was something tainted about this vessel. *Vachaelle.* The Witch-Seer had starved me to the brink of utter desperation and then, when I was at the bottom-most pit of deprivation, presented a fouled vessel. Of course she did.

I relinquished the mangled hand and spat, gagged, retched.

Mid-expulsion I opened my eyes and saw the brilliant green grass beneath my feet, so sharp and so fresh, and knew something even more alarming: my taking of the offering *wasn't* the source of the warmth.

Everything I was wanted to retreat back under the corridor before inevitable eradication. When would this reassuring cocoon tighten and sear me with its intensity, corrupt comfort into constriction, and then consume me altogether?

And, despite it all, I froze.

"There, there."

I looked up and saw the vessel…Sister Cass with blaring clarity, wrapping a bandage around her hand. The bite marks on her exposed arm were already bruising. "You're alright, Tzara-Min. Just close your eyes again and take a deep breath."

Maybe the effect was delayed. But everything I was also knew that wasn't how it worked, had seen exactly how quickly and suddenly and completely it *did* work. There was never a delay. Not when it came to solar exposure. So I did as she said, and the sunfresh air in my body felt almost as good as the blood should have.

"Good. Breathe. And when you are ready, open your eyes again."

I did not rush to be ready, but each inhalation, each exhalation, flooded me with scents new and glorious. Who could have known? Who could have told me? I gasped at the perfume from flowers blooming in a light the moon could never provide. The slight breeze delivered that and more, nameless stimulations that I yearned to know. Even the trimmed grass smelled like...like life incessant and irrepressible. And if the mere aroma could grant me this rapture, then...

I opened my eyes.

And it was amazing what those eyes beheld, a world illuminated and exploding, vivid and pulsating. I swung my whole face towards those flowers and realised I needed a whole new vocabulary. Red, yellow, orange, green, blue, purple, white? Dull. Insufficient. Flat. The Tongue of Revelation, stripped of projection, was shallow, functional. Forget words; I needed a whole new *language*, one that didn't rely on shared impression and collective accumulation of meaning. Something that would allow me to take it all in and understand it as mine, mine alone, and express it only when I was ready. I would learn every word for every hue the sun could show me.

And as my squint became a hungry gaze, I blinked with one last realisation: I was no longer seeing the sunlight.

If something can end you in a moment and your only defence against it is to avoid it, you only see *it*, the overwhelming threat it is, and you fear it, rightfully. But if by some act of God, in Her eminent providence, you are granted safety from that thing, and you can find solace in it, you stop seeing it as a thing, and then you stop seeing it altogether. And then all you see is the beauty in what it shows to you. An end has become a means. With that epiphany, I knew there wasn't a single creature in the world who appreciated the sun that day more than I.

I tried to drink it all in, but one glance at the boundless blue overhead and I was on the ground, convulsing and helpless. I'd seen vessels and servants do this, but only when making displays of fear or suffering. I knew it never helped them, so why would I...?

"What?" I made the vibrant grass my focus. "What is this? What is my...what am I doing?"

"Hold still." She came close and took my cheeks in her almost too-warm hands. "You are learning the truth, Tzara-Min. You have opened yourself to the light, touched its grace, and are now able to feel what it is to be human. Forever weak. Overwhelmed. Vulnerable. Inferior.

Forever at the mercy of your senses. Forever…until that body dies and the spirit called 'you' is free of this fallen world, and may once again be united with Her Eternal Majesty."

"Oh, God." I lowered my head. That was the balance. That was the price of all this glory. Of life. And I had no choice but to pay it. "I'm going to die."

"Yes."

I fell to rack and ruin once again.

She waited until my tearless sobbing began to subside before wrapping her arms around me, and then I remembered again what Father had said about humans. *They touch us. They help us. They support us. Without them we would not be.* And if that were true, and if I were unique in knowing what it is to be both Them and Us, then I decided, right as I leaned into her hug, that I would complete…evolve Father's belief. *We* touched each other. *We* helped each other. *We* supported each other. Without each other *we* would not be.

"I hate it." I pressed my face into her chest. "It feels…feels like something else is controlling me. Something I cannot stop, but don't want to stop it either. I have known happiness, and sadness, and awe, and humility, and terror, and uncertainty, but this is all of them at once, and it's too much of all of them. It's too much, Sister Cass."

She just patted my back. Rocked me gently.

Eventually she broke the contact, stood up and held out a hand to help me up. The other she kept at her side, fingers and palm bound, sleeve hiding evidence of my temporary insanity. No. I wouldn't hide behind words now. I had threatened her. Hurt her. Injured her. Tried to grievously wound her. Drain her. End her. I remembered wanting to, and not just in that thoughtless episode. From the start, I wanted to take *her life.*

"I had no right. None…I am so sorry, Sister Cass." Still, I accepted her offer and allowed her to guide me to my feet. After that, she let me go and I made my way, at my own pace, back out of the sun and into the shade. She followed.

"You didn't do anything, so there is nothing to apologise for." Sister Cass employed no emphasis and invited no interpretation. "Now indulge me, Daughter Tzara-Min. I might be mistaken but…are you still hungry? How about we nab you something from the kitchen?"

The next time I visited that courtyard in daylight, days and a few muffins later, it was abuzz with scarlet-clad Daughters and crimson-clothed Sisters coming and going. I confessed my enlightenment yet again to my strolling companion as we meandered the cloister. "I still lack the means to describe it, Mother. Any of it. I feel it may take a lifetime to fully acquire the language, and now I have one." I dropped my voice to a whisper. "Chaelle, I'm going to *die*."

"I wouldn't worry about it. You're Half, remember? You'll very likely need to be put down long before that."

I refused to let her logic stay my feelings. "But if nothing else kills me, time itself will. Time seemed so endless but now *my* measure of it isn't. Have there been others? Fey who somehow became mortal? Am I the first?"

"Afraen is The First. I will brook no blasphemy, Tzara-Min. There is only one, and righteous oblivion shall befall anyone who even suspects otherwise."

That was her answer and I understood it. I raised my voice back to a volume betraying no secrets. "As you say. Something else I've been contemplating. Did you somehow keep this whole place clear that day?"

She didn't break her meditative pace. "I felt you would want privacy for the event. I granted my Daughters general permission to visit the village for the day. Few would say no to that even were the weather miserable, and as you keep telling me, that day it was anything but."

Before I could respond, a few Sisters of the Second Hand emerged from a doorway to our left. They stuttered to a halt upon seeing the Mother, and made an almost familiar gesture. They stopped, bowed their heads, and began a Flail. Left hand to forehead, trace across and down one's chest and belly. But instead of finishing the Flail by cutting right to left across the belly, this variant paid ultimate honour to the Liquid Night, before even to Afraen The First, Who Was Ephriem: it ended with both hands cupped in front of one's abdomen. I mirrored their movements, but held the last longer per my inferior station as one robed in scarlet. Mother merely inclined her own head and touched her forehead, as though too busy and important to do the rest. Then they were on their way, and we were back to ours.

"Enough with the distractions, Sarah-Jade. Tell me the name of your best friend."

More drills.

"Lucille Lourdaire of the Convergence, also known as Little Blue, and the Pauper-pyrotic."

"Why is one of her names Little Blue?"

"Because that is the colour of her flame, significantly stronger than the typical red or yellow."

"And who was your worst enemy?"

"Myself."

She sighed. "Clever, very. Seriously now."

"Tiamat Fourneval, Tia-mutt, Stormwitch of Servandish, heir to Fourneval Foundries."

"On which floor and in which establishment did we live?"

"Fifth floor, All-Trades Inn, Teristra. Why did you pick a city I've never visited?"

"I didn't. Wouldn't matter anyway, if Dhiana hadn't…oh, you're doing it again. Hmph. Colour of uniform for Parelle Girls?"

"Blue, no, yellow, wait…red? Black and red." I stopped. "Do I really need to know all of this, Mother?" I lowered my voice again even though we were alone but for a few specks of crimson hurrying across the courtyard in my periphery. "If who I am meant to be is hiding it, then what does it matter? Why not just have a few breezy answers ready to deter further attention and let Tzara-Min be her own person?"

She kept walking just enough to face me. "You seemed fine with the idea before."

"Yeah." I picked a word Sister Cass might have used, not Sariana-ra Jaydemyr. And why stop with just one? Time to build Tzara-Min's persona, one stolen expression at a time. "That was before you forced me to accept what I am now, and what I am is human. Fallible, frail, flatulent fucking human. And let's not forget…forgetful."

I enticed rebuke, which meant I knew to expect anything but. And there was a smile, but it wasn't self-satisfied or smug. It was tight-lipped, and gave away almost nothing. "Fallible, frail, flatulent *Half*-human."

"Close enough, you nitpicky bitch."

"Excellent. Now you are starting to pass for her." The smile widened, revealed a sliver of amusement. "You are wrong, of course. Being Half is something else entirely. But that can wait. We are done for the time being. Daughter Tzara-Min, report immediately to Aunty Sofiya in her office, third floor, end of the hall. She will see to your arrangements on the First Order of business. You may come up to see me in my own offices whenever you have time, but I suspect you won't have much of that soon enough."

When Mother said 'suspect', she meant 'know', and this was to be no exception.

The stairs to the third floor were midway down a large well-lit wooden hallway almost wide enough for a small carriage. I passed quite a few closed doors behind which I could hear muffled voices. Had I stopped and listened I likely could have made out what was being said if not done. It must have been between hours to be that busy behind closed doors. The second floor I ignored and the stairwell stopped at the third. I guessed it wasn't the top floor but had little reason to think on that further. Where the first floor was designed to exude an air of luxury, the third was far less embellished, far less inviting. The 'end of the hall' to which Mother had directed me was easy to find: only one end had a door. The other had a coloured glass window that veritably glowed thanks to the daylight and I very much wanted to examine it, but I knew any more than a cursory glance would become a fascinated stare and there would go the whole afternoon.

Swallowing my disappointment, I made for that door and knocked.

"Do come in, Tzara-Min."

I liked her raspy, curt voice. I didn't like what it had said. I obeyed nonetheless.

Unlike Mother's underground retreat, this chamber revelled in natural light, windows surrounding the interior on all three sides. Very few walls of our now-lost ancestral home had windows, but I recalled that one room defied all logic and considerations of safety: Father's study. We always took for granted it was this dangerous design that made him forbid anyone enter without his permission, without exception. But what I did see of it would have resembled this Sister's workspace in the light of day.

And Aunty Sofiya of the Second Hand herself: as aged and weathered as the voice indicated, but also spry and alert. She gestured from her side of the desk, her back to the largest window. I sat facing her, trying not to be distracted by the view of the clouds crowding the sky behind her.

"How did you know it was me?" A little reckless, but curiosity prevailed.

"Eleven." *Commandment Eleven: do not ask questions if you don't know the answer.* But also:

"'The night provides all you need to know.'" I finished the full description. "You are the Liquid Night, and I need to know."

"Oh, you're a sharp one. Let's waive the Eleventh then, in the spirit of expedience. I knew because Mother Chantal was just here, telling me you were in need of my assistance." How? *How?* Curiosity had its limits, and directly questioning the ways of the Witch-Seer of Jaydemyr was well past them. I held my tongue. "Relax. This won't take long. Would you care for a drink, dear?"

My immediate reaction was that she was somehow poking fun at my now-revoked Rose status, but then I saw the glass on her desk with maybe a finger's width of water. She was already refilling it from a jug before I could answer. "Yes. Please."

"Help yourself to some water then." She gestured with her glass at a side table, upon which I saw a few metal cups and a different jug. I hesitated, and she swallowed a laugh after swallowing her drink. "You've far more years of this boring old life before you've much need of *Akravit*, Tzara-Min. And I'm quite a few past where drinking half as much as I do is very healthy, but someone has to keep the lazy cows downstairs busy. Hahaha."

"What's *Akravit*?" I fetched my water as bid.

"Mmm." She hummed this mid-drink, then swallowed and answered with pedagogic patience. "Akra you should know from The Book of Truth. In the Holy Tongue: Light. Vit? Some other origin, means life or something like it. The Light of Life. Certainly the light of *mine*."

I sat back down. What was it we called the offering of a vessel in the (apparently Holy) Tongue of Revelation? *Vahm'esta.* Darkflow. What lay between the darkness of blood and the lightness of alcohol? I took a sip and found my answer: water. Warm, boring water.

"Let's see now." One last gulp and she set the glass down, flicked through a book on her desk. Ran her forefinger down the hand-written accounts. "Hmm…I will assign you a bed in the Gold dormitory, first floor below. So called for the colour of the door, nice and easy to find; the walls are obviously not gold. You'll share the dorm with eleven other Daughters, all of the First Order, all about your age I'd say. You will find everything you need on the bed." She put pencil to paper, scratched some notes and closed the ledger. Pencil down, glass up. "This will be your daily routine. Bladesun: Lamps on. Breakfast in the first floor below dining hall. Morningsun: Lessons. Highsun: lunch, which you may take in the abbey's main hall or anywhere on the grounds. Aftersun: Talent training. Lazysun onwards: Duties. Dinner and personal time after that. Tomorrow, and every seventh day, is Offday, just like anywhere else, which means there's a chance you'll get to sleep in. There is no bedtime, and you will be called on to the break the Fourth far more than you'll like in the greater service to Her glory. But if you sleep through the Bladesun bell, miss breakfast and find yourself struggling through lessons on an empty stomach well m'love that's your fucking problem any questions?"

Fourth Commandment: Sleep at night.

"No." I was already overwhelmed and didn't want to make this any more confusing, then realised my mistake and amended. "Wait, yes. A few. I didn't see any coloured doors on the first floor, just varnished natural-coloured wood." Sarah-Jade would have known that, so I let it 'slip' out.

"First floor *below*. First floor above, or just first floor, is for Deliveries And Services. Second floor is guest accommodation. Third, administration. You'll be working on all three. Fourth is for Third Eye operations. You will definitely not be working there. Any higher than that and you're on the roof. First through fourth floors below, however, that's where we live. Come summer you'll appreciate this, and come winter, well, let me think, Gold dorm…I suggest you don't antagonise a Purashenan girl called Sister Viera before that." Laugh, cough, drink, clearing of throat. "You said you had a few questions."

Third Eye operations on the fourth floor. Mother did say 'come up to see me', but wasn't her office somewhere down below, below even the living quarters? "I still don't know what the First Order of business is, Aunty Sofiya. Will that be part of my lessons?"

"Not directly, no. Potential Daughters are told on or before induction, but I hear your arrival was…unusual. So let me prepare you for what the lessons will assume you know. The First Order of business for the Liquid Night is seeing to the needs of our guests during their stay. You fetch their meals, beverages, any herbal concoctions prescribed. You bring them a healer of the Second Hand should they need it, or a Maliscient of the Third Eye should one be required. You comfort and counsel them. And after their procedure, a Sister of the Fourth Going will see them home safely with their newborn child. It's all quite menial but when you see how flustered the Second Hand Sisters are, you'll be grateful for that."

I chose my next question carefully, because probing most of what she'd just said would expose me to scrutiny up to which my recent decision to not torture myself memorising every tiny detail of Sarah-Jade's life would not stand. "Ah, this is making a lot more sense now. I am from a city, Teristra, but only really heard about the Liquid Night in passing. I guess things were a bit different there, and any Sisters visiting for a Delivery were of the First Order. The other ranks? Second Hand, Third Eye, Fourth Going…never heard of them. But even a girl growing up in a big city has a small world, I suppose." I smiled in a way I hoped was disarming in its artlessness.

"No, you've the right of it." She refilled her glass again. "Outside of isolated abbeys such as this one, we maintain a secrecy equal to the Blood Peddlers. Teristra certainly has a Sisterhood branch or two for discreet home Deliveries, I'd say. As to what the other ranks mean, *that* you will learn through fulfilling the First Order if not direct lessons. All in time, Tzara-Min. Any other questions?"

"No. I will make my way down to first floor below, look for a gold door and then an empty bed with some clothes on it. And then try to not to offend the Gold dorm's pyrotic, who I will recognise for her brown skin."

She cocked a smile as I rose. "I *do* like the sharp ones. Ah, pyrotic. That reminds me. *I* have a question before you go."

"Hm?" I turned back to her, hand still gripping the doorknob.

"What is your Talent?"

I had to think a bit to remember this, because Mother had only told me once and I hadn't seen any evidence of it so far. "Hydrotheurgy. But I only gained it recently."

She clapped her hands. "Ah, a truly rare sort then. Firestarters, zappers, and rockshifters are always so aggressive, don't you think? So eager to fight and show off. And healers, well, *everybody* loves them." She raised her glass and I watched it fill of its own accord. "But us? We're the unsung heroes of Mothers Abbey, Daughter Tzara-Min. I will see you at Aftersun Talent training. I do hope you enjoy cooking and cleaning."

The Gold dorm on first floor below was empty and, as she'd said, one bed alone looked unclaimed. The others were made, give or take, and each had a chest at its foot. Six beds a side, with a washing room at the end. I moved the Book of Truth on top of the bed to the side table and dumped everything else in the chest (a few spare robes and other sundries I'd care about later), and then lay down for what would be the first of many snoozes far shorter than I would have preferred.

"Tzara-Min?"

I opened my eyes and glared at a tired, somewhat angular face, visible only for the glow from her slightly shaky hand. She was right to be scared and shaky. I'd been on call for fifteen guests the night before until Highmoon and it wasn't yet Bladesun. Anyone would be irritable in my situation.

"Which is it?"

"I'm sorry to wake you but—"

"It's fine, Viera." I slumped out of bed and into my slippers. "Which is it? Hole or bath?"

"Bath please." She displayed the towel in her other hand, and I was thankful for that much. It didn't happen often but when there was a problem with the Hole, I usually had to be sick afterwards. As good a test of the facilities as any.

"Okay."

A few beds were empty, but most of the other girls were snoring away, no doubt exhausted by their own duties of the First Order.

I adjusted my nightshift, grabbed my own towel from on top of the trunk and followed her little guiding light into the washroom. She closed the door behind us and lit the wall lamp. As usual, the floor was slippery, someone had left a bloody rag near the Hole stall, and the inside walls of the empty bath were smeared with scum.

"Early start?" I tiptoed over the slick stone and up the few steps leading into the bath and then sat on the ledge.

"Not especially. I just haven't had a chance to wash for a few days. Slept in my robes and all."

"Explains why I was awake before you said a thing." I pinched my nose at her. She shrug-wince-smiled another apology and I set to work. The first stream from my hands washed some of the scum off, which I wiped down with my much-abused towel (I cleaned it whenever I could). I then put the towel down and used both hands to fill the bath. Easy at first, but a few minutes of continual Talent usage when you don't exactly get much time to train it is exhausting. I paused when the bath was half-full and flexed my fingers.

"You're good. Sometimes I can barely manage a few seconds."

"Lucky for you setting things on fire is usually instant then." I resumed filling the bath, finding the word 'good' distasteful for some reason. Once it was full enough for comfortable submersion, I stopped pushing and shook my hands out, patting them dry with the now dirty towel. I sighed.

Viera had peeled off her soiled robe and undergarments and moved closer. Sat her brazen, bronze butt on the ledge near me and ran her own hand over the water. True to what I said, there wasn't much time between the passage of her warm fingers and the steam rising from the surface.

I stood up and went to retrieve the reddened rag. Lizaveta again, no doubt. Healers were simply the worst. Far past squeamish, I just carried it into the stall, held it over the Hole, and gave it a quick wringing. One last surge of water and it was almost white again.

I hung the rag on a rack and made my way to the door.

"Oh…but I made the bath so nice and warm."

"And come winter, I'll really appreciate that. But let's be honest, Viera. I'd probably just fall asleep and drown."

Also, you filthy brat, I am extremely tired, you've just used me as a hose, and that sloven Liza owes me yet again. Forgive me if I'm not in the mood for spontaneous intimacy.

"I would never let that happen!…But thank you, Tzara-Min. I'm sorry I woke you." She slipped into the water.

"Me too, but I know you'll make it up to me." I slipped out of the room.

Not for the first time I was grateful the floors below had no windows. I could at least pretend the night had barely started.

But by the time I was lying down again, ready to succumb to sleep, the Bladesun bell tolled high above. Five disgustingly lively clangs. The lamps came on and the room was abuzz with Daughters chatting, yawning, and dressing their way to breakfast.

"Thanks again." Viera passed by, hair still wet and wearing what was probably a clean robe. I just rolled over and moaned her away.

Six months ago I'd discovered the wonder of daylight, of mortality, of life infinite and ephemeral, fragile and enduring. I'd felt like there was no possible way to ever tire of its offerings, even if embracing it meant forgetting what I'd been before: indefatigable; endless; impervious. And, in far too many ways, good as dead.

But that morning, I had my first true teenager thought, and gave voice to it into a damp smelly pillow. "Fuuuuuck, just kill me already."

Rethinking Rolemodels

"Shyn's Tits but I swear there must be some unspoken code that secret Jaydemyrian agents stand out as much as possible. The Keeper has informed me that a Half male wearing black leather armour and a hood just entered the place. Let's go."

"Well met, fellow mongrel. My brother and I would like to speak to you in private. Our room, or outside. Your choice. We'd prefer outside though, just in case this gets complicated. Don't...damn it, he ran. Come back!"

"Right. Now that we've clarified which of the three of us is the slowest and weakest, let's try that again. How about we start with your name? No, Brother, don't hit him again. Just hold him still. Now, 'Get Fucked Kas'Daen Scum', I'm Sariana and this is Charan. Can you possibly guess our last name? Nope, not 'Bullshit You Are', but close enough. Okay, see this? The pendant? And...well, alright, you can't see his sword and trust me you really don't want to, but they're the same. Clan Jaydemyr. Also, did you miss that we've been speaking in Jaydemyrian all this time?

"I think you can release him now, Brother. Let's...oh, come on. Stop that. Get up off the ground and just listen to me. Yes, it's okay. You're forgiven. On one condition. Stop. Fucking. With. Havens. I don't care that The Scourge used to do it. He's an idiot, aren't you Brother? In fact, stop killing people at all. Wait. Was it you? Radomyr's Rest village, Half. Not far from here, a year ago. Destroyed. Its Haven torn down, everyone inside...true, how would you know? One much like another, right? A conversation for later then. Now do you remember where Vizstrahtza is? Go there. Right now. Arius Hawkstorm should be there, if you're lucky. Our mother, Dhiana-ra Jaydemyr, if you're not. We will see you there soon enough for that chat about Radomyr's Rest. Well? Get moving!"

"Thank you again, Havenkeeper. That was close. For you. So what's for dinner?"

18 days until the revelation

Chapter 10: Auric Openings
10/869 A.R.

Whisper.

"Tzara-Min?"

I looked up from whatever I was reading in the first below library and wondered if she started conversations with others the same way. I'd known her over a year now and it was always like this. Mother had told me that another pyrotic, Lucille Lourdaire, would have been similarly timid around Sarah-Jade, at least in public, which made me wonder if Sarah-Jade ever reached some point of complete and total intolerance and given her a good shaking. Tempting, but that was something else I'd learned: Half might not be Fey, but compared to normal humans we were still superior in almost every useful way: faster, stronger, healthier. Useful…Until we reached early adulthood, when we inevitably go from 'handy' to 'handled'. But until then, I could try for a light slap and end up breaking someone. So I restrained myself. For now.

"What is it, Vi?"

"I'm sorry for bother—"

I slammed the book closed. Not getting back to studying recipes for the guests now. The library was just a single room barely half the size of a dormitory, and the slam was louder than I'd intended.

"Funny how you only say 'sorry' when you want something."

She sat in the comfy reading chair opposite me at the little table, nonplussed and apparently a little hurt. "You looked busy."

"Clearly not anymore. Consider me bothered *and* intrigued. So...what is it?"

She played with her raven ponytail a bit. Seemingly no end to this one's nervous habits. "I know I owe you, so much, honestly everyone in Gold does, so...you know the harvest festival?" She didn't pause to let me answer, maybe worried I might not give the one she needed to hear to proceed. "Of course you do. And you know it's later this month. I was...we were wondering if you'd come with us? There's so much food, and dancing, and music, and markets...Mother gives us an allowance and—"

"IF Mother allows me to I would be very happy to go." I hoped, in her excitement, she'd not notice how odd it was that I'd need permission to do what any other Daughter is actually encouraged to do. "And I'd let you buy me birthday gifts from the market. And we'd dance until we cannot stand. And eat until we cannot move."

"It'll be near your birthday? Yay!" She moved to stand and do something else, but I just raised a hand.

"If."

"Promise you'll talk to her about it soon."

"Promise."

"Wonderful. A whole three days! Food. Music. Dancing. And...ooh." She all but sparkled with glee now. Where had all that shyness gone? "Maybe there'll be some Tantamonian acolytes there. Thank the Blessed Mother they don't have to take vows of purity like those poor Respite attendants."

"Wait. Acolytes. Purity...do you mean...with boys?"

She stopped, and the absence of shyness became an abundance of disbelief. "Of course I mean boys, silly. How else are we to honour the Seventh!?"

And off she went with a laugh that made clear I wasn't meant to answer that either.

The Seventh. The only one of the Twelve with a single word commandment. One simple, terrifying demand.

Propagate.

Vachaelle gaped at me, and then burst out laughing in her high-back chair. We were once again in her chambers on sixth floor below, since I felt this matter should be discussed with no chance of clerical interruption.

"You requested a private audience for *this?* Of course you can go, you ninny. Can and should. The Liquid Night might seem isolated to you now but we are ultimately very worldly women. It does my girls good to…get to know the very folk they serve. And while I advocate *responsible* honouring of the Seventh, it's not a problem for you anyway."

"Why not?"

"Don't the other girls talk about their monthly cramps and taking Second Hand remedies, or needing Lizaveta to touch their bellies? How they produce blood, y'know, down there? Hopefully collecting it for the Third Eye?"

"Mother, I *do* know what moonflow is. I'm not completely ignorant." Of course I missed how easily she named the healer in my dorm out of dozens of dorms and what that signified.

"Moonflow? Is that what the girls call it these days? That's touching, if a little inaccurate. Anyway, if you're so aware of it, how you could not get that *you don't get it?*"

"I…I just assumed it was part of being Half. Being different. In this case, a good one. Moonflow seems quite unpleasant."

"A correct assumption, but you don't know what your inability means."

"I think I am getting close, but you know what? Do what you do best, Witch-Seer."

She inclined her head at this incomplete suggestion, but knew better than to ask for the rest.

"You *can't* honour the Seventh, Sariana. Not properly. Halves are an affront to God, an aberration She tolerates for only so long. Only so short. But She adores balance. For every gift, a price. In this instance, you are spared 'moonflow' because you cannot give birth. You can certainly *fornicate* but you cannot *propagate.* And those other gifts, you know the price for those already. You only have about three years left until it is demanded, so you should probably get to the fornicating while you can. Just…don't tell me any of the details."

This all made sense. I wondered if Viera had known. The dorm knew I was Half, of course. That I wasn't part of the 'we'.

I then asked something that, in my pride, I'd avoided all this time. "Would Sarah-Jade do it?"

She drew a deep breath, leaned back. "I believe she'd pretend not to care and then when she failed to realise no one noticed her not caring, she'd throw on a poorly-conceived disguise and throw herself at whoever would accept her."

I could do that. Or at least pretend to. But then again, I wasn't her. I was Tzara-Min, a Half born not of doomed human mother and reckless Fey father but…some other unspeakable Jaydemyrian conception (and literally unthinkable, still), who would never bear children and be dead within five years. A glutton for daily life and all that it can offer in the way only someone who until a year ago didn't *have* a daily life can be, especially since for most of that year daily life was seeing to the needs of others. There was no way I would 'pretend' any of it. "Is there anything about these Tantamonian acolytes I should know beforehand?"

"They're good boys. Men of the Tantamon travel in small parties to wherever they're needed, working for basic needs and little else. Travel guards. Labourers. Messengers. Farmers. Cooks. Conveyors of goods. Anything that doesn't force them to directly disobey the Twelve. The Tantamon is a flexible approach to the practical limitations of Eight and Nine, lending aid to those who reach for what they cannot hold, and those who find themselves holding what they cannot keep. Funny story, actually. Two of them carried you to your cell when you arrived. They tried to keep their complaints about how heavy you are quiet, and failed gently. Imagine if they were to…oh, far too much of a coincidence. And they likely wouldn't remember you anyway."

I had wondered about that; whoever had done it would have struggled. There's a reason Fey don't swim. It's not that we'd die drowning…if anything, it's that we wouldn't. I mean they. Not we. "Why haven't I seen any followers of the Tantamon around the abbey?"

"Do we *look* like we need help, Tzara-Min?"

I shrugged a 'how-would-I-know' at her but otherwise didn't respond.

"Besides, those of the First Order are too busy to leave the main compound much, and not even Tantamonian brothers are welcome here unless it's absolutely necessary. Say when we need an unconscious Fey carried to her room. Then we invite two of them. Fine young exemplars of the Tantamon they were, too. Well worthy of the Violet mantle."

"Twice, Mother? Really?"

She just lifted her eyebrows.

I then remembered why I was there. "Mother Chantal, does a Daughter who…honours the Seventh get treated here like a guest?"

"Not as such. Have you noticed any absences from the dormitories? Heard any whispers or gossip about a Daughter being deemed unfit to serve, perhaps due to an unwise dalliance, and so sent home?"

"I have. It's rare but it happens."

"Well all of that is true, but for the last bit."

"...Oh."

"That's why I said do it 'responsibly'. And they will. We never let Daughters off the grounds without a stern talking-to and some very specific herbs. The Tantamon isn't the only flexible approach to the Twelve. When The Book says 'propagate', it is in the aim of populating the world for, among other things, the Night's needs, what you and I and no one else here may know to be Vahm'esta. The Liquid Night in all its facets serves the meaning behind the Twelve rather than the words. Daughters work at night. They ask questions to which they don't know the answers. Daughters are not following in their parents' footsteps. And so the Seventh: a woman might directly bring one or two children into the world at a time, a humble contribution to propagation. But in all that time when she is unable to meet the demands of service, a Daughter can help Deliver dozens of babies who may have otherwise not survived: a significantly greater offering to the Night. So for a Daughter of the Liquid Night to allow herself to fall pregnant is an act of supreme selfishness and blasphemy. They deserve all that comes their way, and so much more."

At some point in this tirade she'd developed a fervour I wanted to believe was as feigned as anything else the Witch-Seer did. Wanted and actually failed. She was...trembling with what definitely looked like barely-contained rage.

Interesting. Scary, but interesting. "So if, for example, and this is just if, a Daughter says she wants to honour the Seventh and goes to the festival next week intending to engage the interests of a boy and...succeeds, she knows that 'honouring the Seventh' means honouring the act that embodies it?"

Vachaelle rolled her eyes. "You know what Sarah-Jade *wouldn't* do?"

"What?"

"Waste time talking around the point. I thought I was clear enough. If a Daughter has told you that she plans to honour the Seventh, then she was just being polite or humble about her carnal appetite. You can either assume she knows to be careful *or* you can tell her yourself. Don't be surprised if she's offended that you'd think her that naïve though."

I didn't bother to hide my relief, but also decided Viera and I would have a chat before the festival. "I will try to be careful about it. Intimacy with boys might be practical, but I'd rather not lose any opportunities for intimacies of the impractical kind."

"Well, neither Commandment nor Sisterhood rule against that. Again, spare me further details."

"Gladly." One last thought occurred to me, and I had to share it with her and her only. "Aren't you concerned I might go to this festival and run away? Look for anyone else who might remember the truth? Or at least my brother?"

"Not at all. You're not a prisoner here. You've been with us a year and to my knowledge have never shown an inkling of rebellion, even posing as Tzara-Min – who would be a real pain in my arse were she actually Sarah-Jade. You know that your situation is unique because if anyone else remembered, anyone less important, I'd have dealt with them. As for your brother, you don't need to 'look' for him. I'll tell you exactly where he is. Physically, he's in a Blood Peddler house far, very far to the east. The Malevolent Hand, in Kaifeng, Chūnko. Didn't I tell you this at some point? Closest to his beloved Mifūné we could manage. It'd take you almost a year to get there by caravan. Mentally he's a street rat, ran away from abusive parents, raised by an old thief in a sort of orphanage for young ones. Now he's being trained by the Peddlers to carry out their sacred tasks but they already know he's capable of much more. And emotionally, he's a total disaster."

I would remember this. All of it. "If he's so far away, how can you know all of this? You speak of it as though you can see it happening."

"What exactly do you think the Third Eye is for, Tzara-Min?"

At a guess, Vachaelle? I'd say hiding your true powers as the Witch-Seer of Jaydemyr. "I see…He's a lot farther from home than we are, isn't he?"

"That honestly doesn't matter anymore. He'll return when he's ready, and so will we. I think you know this, and you know that here is about as good a place to wait as any other. Food, shelter, companionship, education. I suppose I could encourage Sofiya to reduce your Duties if you can't handle them. Might look like favouritism to the others in your room though, and then they'd start wondering why…"

"Point made and taken, Mother Chantal." I scraped my chair back. "Speaking of said duties…"

"One last thing." Here it came. "Your ears are getting a bit long there. Let's give them a trim so you look at least a little less of a beast and don't scare the poor villagers, hm? Not to mention any handsome young men. Unless…you'd rather just not go?"

After all that? This was the price she wished to exact? "I'm a big girl who knows her way around a knife and isn't afraid of a little pain. I'll get it done in no time." I stood up. "Maybe I'll let you do it next year."

Curse the woman, she actually looked disappointed before waving me out.

It was the day of the festival, first Offday after my otherwise uncelebrated birthday. I'd just heard the Nighsun toll and I was fairly sure I was screwed. The room was mine but for Lizaveta passed out in her scarlet on her back on top of her bedsheets. I'd been lying on my bed when she crept past me, used the washing area, and collapsed. Lying on my bed and lying to myself that I could do my own ears any time I wanted to. That I didn't need Chaelle to do it. That it wasn't going to really, *really* hurt. That maybe I could do it alone.

Ah, but what luck! Now…I wasn't alone.

"Lizaveta?"

"Mmf?"

"This yours?" I held the wet strip of fabric over her face and then dragged it down her freckled cheeks. She tried to bat it away, as though it were an insect crawling over her skin or a stray strand of that scraggly flaxen hair. I just let a few more drops fall onto her nose, took a breath, and then gave the rag a good old squeeze.

Her milk-sour face flushed, and not just with the bloody water. She spluttered and sat up. I dropped the rag in her lap and stepped back.

"ThefuckTzara!" She hurled the cloth onto the floor. "I was asleep, you Ephin' gash."

To so easily break the Third, she must have been quite upset. Good.

Not quite upset enough to try more than words though. Not against me. Also good. "Oh, Liza, it's not my gash that's the issue here."

"No Eph—fucking idea what you're on about. Ghastly freak. Just leave me alone."

"I mean *that*." I nodded to the offending article. Of course I'd already washed it. Again. Mostly. "You're going to do something for me, or I'm going to tally up every time you left one of those for me to clean up. And then I will wake you up just like this, for ten times that number of mornings. You *do* know that I'm up before the rest of you. We 'ghastly freaks' barely need to sleep, after all." I smiled with all my teeth. Not Fey, but not quite human either. "Oh, and before that, I'll report you to the Third Eye for wasting resources. And just for good measure I might mention to the Head healer of the Second Hand that you have a habit of invoking a Name of the Night inappropriately. Aunty Nadzia, isn't it?"

Strange how pale she could look despite the thin pink veneer.

Pale but oh, very awake now.

"It's not always mine!" As if that made any difference.

"The blood or the rag?"

She said nothing.

"I always take care of it anyway. Look. Do what I ask and we will be even. Maybe I'll run a bath or two for you now and then. But I am *done* cleaning up after you."

Fear ebbed into wariness, and then re-emerged as cunning. She wiped her face dry with the sleeve of her robe. "Must be serious if you can't ask someone else."

Serious? Sure. Mostly desperate, Lizaveta, but you are far too conceited to say that. "Not serious, but you're like me. You're the only one in our dorm who can do what you do and everyone takes it for granted. I assure you, I will not." *And anyone else has already made plans for the day.*

"Healing?" She straightened up, preened a little. Reached for the knife any good healer would keep on hand, and she certainly wasn't that. "Sister Nadzia says I'm the cleanest at incisions and sutures in her class, and she once worked in a Haven so she'd know."

An Aunty would have flayed you alive had she known a Daughter dared call her 'Sister'. "Of course. And that includes the healing after, right? You can make it painless?"

"*No one* can do that, stupid…but I can make it very, very quick. I practice on myself sometimes. Oh." Her cunning misread the sign and trotted alone into the cave of conspiracy. "Is that what this is? Why you can't ask someone else? You want to feel it too?"

I whistled at her dedication, and upon seeing her smile formed a new theory about those discarded rags. Not my business. "That's actually quite reassuring, and flattering, but not the point here."

"Oh." She looked down at her knife as though suddenly unsure what it was, what to do with it.

I sat down on her bed, tilted my head away from her, and pulled the loose hair back. "I'm tired of being a 'ghastly freak'. I want you to make my ears as round as you can before Highsun. Any longer and I chat with Aunty Nadzia."

"Why Highsu—oh, Shyn's Tits, it's Festival Day!"

"Uh, don't you need a bowl and a cloth or something?" I was annoyed at this reminder of what sort of slummock I was dealing with. "I can provide the water."

"I suppose. You're no fun…"

"Highsun. Get to work."

The bell overhead ringing in a bright Lazysun made it easy for us to sneak out of the abbey and into the assembly. Mother Chantal had just concluded her speech to the hundreds of Daughters and Sisters gathered on the hill facing north, leading down from the abbey's front entrance to everywhere else in the world. She invited each Daughter to approach her individually while the remaining handful of Sisters left for the village ahead of us. There was no queue but somehow still order. I joined the waiting throng and nodded to the others from Gold as I saw them, each focused almost completely on seeing Mother and hurrying off down the road by foot or gig, a road usually used for those coming rather than going.

When I shuffled into her presence, she bade me kneel, so I did.

"Receive this as your reward for service, my Daughter." As she intoned this, Mother handed me a little pouch that jingled into my waiting palm. Then she bent over a bit, scrutinised me and lowered her voice to a private offering. "The healing is quite adept but those cuts are horrendous. Oh dear. Stay away from knives, Tzara-Min. Stick to blunt objects. Trust me."

"Thank you very much Mother, and fuck you too." I hid Lizaveta's otic obscenity with my hair once more.

"Have fun." Beneficent smile, shooing gesture. "Next!"

Abbey's Village was barely a few miles from home, an easy stroll for a girl run off her feet most days. The staggered procession of Daughters threaded the woods, hillocks and fields with steady purpose. I started alone, content to take in the verdancy of the path at my own pace, but before long the dorm girls found me and their chatter added an air of urgency to the jaunt. Soon a few buildings, accommodation for those who would be or had been our guests I assumed, became a few more. A sturdy stone bridge over the Little Tranquil river replaced the meandering road, and the village itself swallowed us like a sponge soaking up spilt wine.

Structurally it didn't look much different to any other village or hamlet would in moonlight, of which I'd…seen more than a few. The only real distinction was one I'd been anticipating: it seemed half the local businesses were either cart rides between Abbey's Village and its namesake, or inns. And even those were functional rather than fancy.

But the festival gave everyone a chance to embrace the fancy. The villagers and the Daughters fawned over each other, the former eager to sell typically austere girls all sorts of trinkets and treasures, and the latter more than happy to be served for once.

Viera had, of course, been right. There was food, food everywhere. I think at some point she shoved a muffin in my hand, having decided from observation they were my favourite repast. I liked them just because they were easy to eat in a hurry. I was just as fond of the pies, sausages and fruit that also made their way to my eager hands. And there was dance, people spinning and whirling with an abandon that either belied what I knew to be their fate or absolutely embodied it. I marveled at how easily some Daughters picked up the rhythm, but found the music itself rudimentary and crass. Or so I told myself as a reason for not joining in.

Also true to Viera's word, the dorm girls saw to it that I didn't have to open my allowance pouch even once. Even Liza managed to buy me something: a set of ear cuffs, so I wouldn't be the only one without some sort of earrings. I very kindly thanked her and said I'd try them on later, and surprised myself by not throwing them away.

As we wandered and wondered, I did notice, scattered throughout the polychromatic commotion, a few grey and beige-dressed women set to watch, lightly armed and armoured, aware perhaps of how quickly a spirited disagreement can become a melee. The only hint as to their true nature lay in the travel-worn carmine cloaks and how well they hooded their watchful eyes. And, of course, I caught glimpses of fit young men trailing mauve capes; those Vachaelle had made absolutely sure I wouldn't not notice. Now and then I pulled my attention back to Viera and the others. They were even more distracted by the festival's friendly merriment than I, and a healthy distance remained between the Daughters of the Liquid Night and the sons of the Tantamon.

That is, until the friendly merriment died down, and something far more primal took its place.

Because what Viera hadn't mentioned was just how much drink there'd be later on. Kegs and casks of the stuff, tankards and flasks, goblets and horns. As the afternoon cavorted into evening and bonfires replaced sunlight, the mood shifted entirely. Children dispersed, the music became slow and somber, and smaller groups formed for more intimate interaction. I saw a few huddles of scarlet and violet at tables and around fires, laughing, drinking, and flirting. Seeing no real opening and unready to see just how far Vachaelle's power reached, I took a position on a log at the edge of it all. Now and then one of the boys would glance into the dark, maybe seeing me, maybe not.

Of course, Vi eventually noticed and came over.

I really wish you hadn't, love.

"Here. You look thirsty." She plonked down onto the coarse wood.

I accepted the mug but didn't think I did. As far as opening moves go, though, it was a solid step up from 'sorry for bothering you.' "Not as thirsty as some." I sipped the drink anyway. Cool. Sour. A little sweet. A little fruity. Mostly sour. Infinitely bland compared to the sensation of a single drop of *Vahm'esta* but…tingly enough, I suppose. "Is this *Akravit?*"

"Just wine." She looked a little taken aback. "Didn't think you'd know about *Akra.* Can get some if you want but if you don't know what it tastes like, you proooobably don't want it. Actually, even if you do you don't." She paused having confused herself. "Yeah. Don't."

I took another taste of the wine, then nodded at the table from which she'd lurched. "So who are they?"

"Who?"

"Very funny, Vi."

She nudged me so I'd look away from the hushed simmer and see her flushed, radiant expression. "They're all a bit curious about you but two of the boys, deeeeefinitely more than justa bit." She upended what was absolutely not her first mug of the wine. "Oh shit, lookitat, all gone. Come on, I want a refill and *they* want to ask you something."

Two of them.

Boys.

Tantamonian acolytes.

Viera stood, yanking me with her to the long wooden table. For a fairly short, slender girl, she did a good job barging her way in. "Shove over, bitches!" Two Daughters from different dorms whose names I didn't know and would never learn protested and tried not to spill their own drinks, but shuffled on the bench enough for the two of us to fit between them.

"Sorry. She's, you know…" I made a helpless wave at Viera for the Daughters' benefit, but they just rolled their eyes and turned back to whatever didn't involve me or my extremely tipsy friend.

"Now, these two are—" Said extremely tipsy friend gesticulated across the table with her mug. "—Fuck, almost spilled my drink—"

"It's empty." I didn't really expect her to hear this murmur and I was too busy appraising who 'these two' were to care. Both boys wore the tell-tale Tantamon cape, and both boys were otherwise dressed like villagers: tunic, jerkin, caps failing to contain their hair. On the left in front of me, long curly blond locks. On the right, shoulder-length brunet.

"—Anywoo, this is Daughter Tzar—" Wave of empty mug at me. "Oh, it's. Must have spilled. Weird. More please." She stood up and staggered off.

"Hi." I attempted an apologetic smile at the two amused young men facing me. "I'm Tzara-Min. My rather useless friend says you have a question for me."

The hale boy opposite me shot his startlingly green eyes at his slightly smaller, twitchier companion, who looked like he was trying to grow a beard. It lent his jaw a fuzzy glow when it caught the lanternlight. Which it did now, because he leaned forward a bit, hands around his drink on the table, and looked at me with an unsettling intensity.

"It's her. Pay up, Kendahl." His voice sounded like it was at least a few years off growing a beard, despite its owner's best efforts.

"Not yet. Not until she answers. And Night take us, how rude we've been. This grumpy little weasel is Brother Huysman and, as he said, I'm Kendahl."

"Call me what you like, I'm still right."

Kendahl might have been posturing because Huysman was definitely not a weasel. Certainly, Kendahl was, as Vachaelle put it, a fine specimen but both of them had a weathered, wasteless vitality that stirred something in me that I thought long gone. Desire? Longing? Lust? Thirst? Maybe Vi was right. To cover any chance of the pair seeing any sign of this twinge, I drained the wine and set it down. The tingle from before lasted longer and spread further. Familiar. Nice.

"Allow me." Kendahl slopped something else into my mug. I hadn't noticed how many bottles were on the table. "Least I can do for bothering you like this." His smile was stupid and forced and he knew it and it was nice too.

I drank that as well. All of it. Richer than the other. Deeper. Warmer. I looked into the mug and saw traces of thick claret.

Vahm'esta!

"Wh—what is this?" I looked back up. They were both completely focused on me now. We could have been alone for all I knew.

In fact, when I looked around, we were. I tried to find Viera, called her name, tried to find Lizaveta, called her name too. And then I was just calling for anyone at all.

Huysman chuckled, and Kendahl reached for his purse, clicking his tongue. "It's exactly what you think it is." He placed a few silver coins in his friend's outstretched hand. "And you've just answered our question. But now we have another."

They both stood up and levelled swords they'd somehow drawn from nowhere down at me. I tried to move but couldn't, instead pulled to somehow lick whatever was left in that mug. Empty. I tossed it aside and stared up at them, and knew how I'd get more.

Before I could stop their impossible question with a lunge of fingers, nails and of course teeth, Huysman unleashed a searing accusation. "You're a useless, barren Half with only a few years to live. How did an immortal Noble, Sariana-Ra of Jaydemyr, fall so far?"

I realised the question *was impossible*. Only I knew any of that, and only I would wonder what it meant. So I very deliberately shut my eyes, told myself it was just red wine, and that maybe drinking when drinking meant losing control and losing control meant forgetting who I'd become, and that who'd I become was someone who *didn't drink other people's blood,* was a very bad idea indeed. I told myself all of that with a slow, careful breath and opened my eyes right as I heard the raucous noise once more.

Kendahl and Huysman were still staring at me but less in judgment and more with concern. They had no idea how warranted that concern was: what I'd done to myself was not entirely unlike what I'd tried to do to dear Sister Cass that first night. Sariana-Ra Jaydemyr and Tzara-Min could not, I finally decided, co-exist.

I was still clutching the mug. I set it down and pushed it not towards them but away from me.

"I'm…shit, this is so embarrassing." What had my unhinged fancy looked like to them? I hazarded a likelihood. "I don't normally drink, and I fear it's got me quite addled. What did you say, sorry?"

"I said it was the least I could do." Kendahl's fine straw brows lowered in guilt. Likelihood confirmed, but that didn't make me feel any better for making him think it was his fault. "I probably shouldn't have. I assumed you were as…like the other Daughters."

"How curious." Huysman left it at that.

"No one is like dear Daughter Viera." I kept it as light as possible. "Speaking of whom, I should go. She shouldn't be alone. It's a long way back." I made to stand then paused, as though remembering. "Oh. What were you going to ask?"

"It's of no matter now." Kendahl found his charming smile again just in time to convince me maybe someone else might/could/would/should find Viera and help her home. "Just two idiots too deep in their cups not minding their own business."

This was the local village, not some Lybichmisto slum. Viera would be *perfectly safe.*

I sat back down. "Let me guess." It *was* them, so why not. "You carried a certain unconscious girl to an isolation cell deep under Mothers Abbey late one night about a year ago, didn't you? How is that not your business? And I'd like you to know that whoever that girl is, she's quite grateful."

Huysman smirked and held out his hand to a taken-aback Kendahl, blessedly not quite in the way I'd made myself imagine.

Kendahl shook his head. "No. The wager's void. We shouldn't have done this. We know better, Huysman. Respect the Tantamon. We assist. We do not ask. We provide. We do not probe. And we…" He took his friend's cup and his own and set them aside. "Have had far too much of this. Come, let's hie to camp, Brother."

My self-inflicted vision of the two of them somehow finding me out and reacting with vicious accusations couldn't have been more misplaced. Chaelle had been right: these were good boys, and I felt like I owed it to them to show them I understood that. That pleasant feeling from before, the one I mistook for Sariana's ancestral craving, was back, and Tzara-Min knew what it was.

"You know, uh…" I frowned my way through what came next. "I would not mind your company a while longer." Having negotiated that, I found my own smile at the other end of the admission. "I'd love to hear more about the way of Tantamon and some of your tasks. Surely they've seen you all over the land."

"Well…" Kendahl puffed up in a way that made me far too proud of my approach. "The folks of Kas'Daen never lack for our—"

Kas'Daen-desne!? That's where you've put me, Vachaelle?

I swallowed and ignored that for now. Do go on, good sir.

But Huysman had little time for our might-be-flirting. Aunty Sofiya would have liked him. "Thought you were concerned about your own friend?"

"I…We could look for her together? I'm not sure I'd trust myself to do it alone in my current state." Why not just throw yourself at them, Tzara-Min?

I really wish I had.

"I suspect you'll manage." Huysman stood up. "You don't seem all that drunk to me."

"Likewise." His acuity aroused my irritation…and admiration.

His own smile might not have lit up like Kendahl's but it contained a glint of respect for this barb that told me if we were ever to speak again, there was a lot about myself I wouldn't have to tell him, some of it I wouldn't mind him knowing.

Kendahl, meanwhile, seemed to realise he had a choice now. The same choice Viera hadn't let me make when she'd so conveniently wandered off in a stupor. When he looked at me, there was a reciprocal desire to stay. When he looked back at Huysman though, there was a question, but then also an answer. "My brother is right. She will be safe in this village, or on the road back. As will you." Kendahl had convinced himself. Damn it. "She has you and your many Sisters on the same path. Our path takes us elsewhere, for now."

I almost corrected him but then remembered that to outsiders, all servants of the Liquid Night were 'Sisters'.

"The festival has another two days. It is possible I'll see you again." I wanted this to come out like a fact, but I heard the desperation and hated it. And hoped it worked.

"It wounds me greatly to admit that is unlikely." He rose and looked for Huysman, who'd already headed off through the sparse scattering of tables. The festival did have two days to go, but for now the party was over. "We have been here a week already, and our reward for that was tonight. It was not at all unpleasant."

There was that thrice-cursed smile again. Put it away, you tease. Please.

"It was not. Do look me up if you're ever at Mothers Abbey again. I promise you'll not be quite so unfairly burdened next time."

Where the fuck was I pulling this crap from?

But he nodded. "That much is possible. We are sometimes tasked with teaching Sisters of the Fourth Going various physical skills they may need while travelling. I hear the training can be quite…intense. But I see you are a Daughter of the First Order, so…"

"So clearly I need to consider a change in vocation."

"That would be most agreeable. Until then, Tzara-Min of the Liquid Night."

"Yes, until then, Kendahl of the Tantamoh fuck it he's gone." I reached for my mug, remembered it was empty. Now what?

I helped myself to whatever was in the nearest bottle and nursed it for a few very long, deflated minutes. Sweet. Honey. Syrupy. Ah. Mead.

"That was Ephin' beautiful." Someone leaned over my shoulder and attacked my face with a fruity, sour breath. I almost folded under her careless weight. "You coulda landed two of 'em, but oh, off they go, noble riders seeking more appropriate mares."

"Oh, go fuck a horse, Lizaveta." Seemed I'd burned whatever wit I had on the now-departed brothers. All that was left of me was unclever and in no mood for her shit. I pushed her away a little too hard (but not *too* hard, not even then) and stomped off.

The village square and the path leading south back to the bridge weren't busy but I did see couples lolling about. When I made my periphery my focus I couldn't ignore the occasional tangle of vermilion robes, exposed limbs and low heaving. I tried to be disgusted at the oddly unfrantic orgy but as usual Vachaelle knew all too well that I'd just be fascinated. I dared not tread too close because even I knew that'd be rude, but I did pause and stare quite a lot. I told myself it was because one of them might be Viera, but so far, none of the flashes of flesh in the torchlight were quite the shade I associated only with her.

"Hey."

I looked at whoever had spoken behind me. He was a scrawny kid, a villager or some farmer's son. Skin the colour of a pig's underbelly. Face roughly the shape of a melon and almost as pocked. No cape, violet or otherwise.

"Hello." I went back to watching my fellow Daughters hopefully not honouring the Seventh too thoroughly.

"You're one of them Halfs, aren't ya?"

Thanks to Lizaveta's overwhelming enthusiasm and underwhelming skill, my ears weren't distinctly pointy but not even a lackwit would confuse them for normal.

"Yep."

"Can't have babies, they say. Don't get sores down there neither. That true, Half?"

"Yep. I can also punch you hard enough to turn your face into a bowl of gruel and do it so quickly you wouldn't have time to piss yourself."

"Yeah but you won't. Not tonight."

"Nope." Astute bastard.

"So, Half...you wanna go cunt?"

"I...what?" Did he actually call me that...or did he just turn a word for vagina into a *verb*?

I didn't want to look at him, but I simply had to after *that*.

"No risk of baby and no cuntsores." His not entirely toothsome grin almost said it all. "Reckon you get no proper fucktumbling with all them Sisters, but tonight's a proper gorgy and all ya doing is watching everyone else cunt?"

Yep, definitely a verb. And 'gorgy'? I almost swooned at the brilliance of it. And he was right; I couldn't see Viera but that didn't mean I *couldn't* see her doing precisely what she'd made her main objective of the festival. And what would have happened had I found her anyway? I imagined no possible outcome that didn't leave at least one of us feeling almost irrevocably awkward about the other.

I sighed. Get it over with, Mother had said. What would Sarah-Jade do? 'Throw herself at whoever would accept her'. "Fine."

"Fine what?"

"Fine...Let's go cunt."

Now maybe sex is good. Maybe fornicating is a lot of fun. I'm sure fucking is fucking great. But cunting was absolutely miserable. I suspect this is just God's inexorable demand for balance again; it would stand to reason that someone who cannot conceive or catch any diseases and thus can safely copulate as much as they want would be completely incapable of enjoying it. There is so much balance in *that*, I realised as he worked himself into a frenzy on top of and inside me, it made me want to scream right as he did.

At least he had the courtesy to take me to a barn on the outskirts of Abbey's Village first and used the hay as a sort of bed. At least it had been quick.

"Ah…Ah." He panted with typical eloquence, and rolled off me.

I straightened my robes and wondered what to do with whatever the hells he'd squirted into my nethers. "Ah…huh?"

"I gotta go or me Mam'll notice." He was dressing with surprising haste and efficiency. Welcome, but surprising. And then sickening: *he had done this before.* "You can sleep here. Too late to go back up there tonight."

And there was no way I'd be the only Daughter sleeping off the festivities celebrating the annual harvest. "Thank you. I'm Tzara-Min, by the way. What's your name?"

"Yeah, not gonna remember that. Or this. You were really shit at it but at least you're safe. Bye, shit cunt."

"Bye quick prick." I lay back and tried to think of Kendahl, blanketing myself in the knowledge that he'd be nice enough to at least keep to himself how awful someone might be at this. And maybe I wouldn't be as 'shit' at it with him. Or was it Huysman's unnerving inability to conceal that he was one of those very special few who just *know?* Both at once, my imagination decided, or maybe a perfect combination of the two. Riding this fantasy was as good a passage to sleep as any.

"Where the FUCK is he?"

The screech didn't rouse me, but something hitting my thigh had me on my feet very quickly.

"Who?"

The girl facing me down was probably my age, maybe a bit older. At first all I could make out in the dim of dawn was her slight frame, braided blonde hair and very red cheeks. "Roderic, you simpleton. Who else?"

Then I saw the short sword in her hand. I tried very hard to take in the details of the barn, wishing to the Blessed Mother I'd done that last night before, or even after, 'Roderic' did me. One entrance. Closed and her blocking it. Windows. Too high to reach without a ladder. No animals for distraction. A lot of wood and straw.

Please don't be a pyrotic, please don't be a pyrotic...

"I'm sorry I don't know who—"

"Of course you don't. He wouldn't bother telling someone he doesn't really care about. But he cares about ME, because he told me..." She stepped forward, and I stepped back. "His fucking name!"

Now I could see her face. Her clear eyes bore their dark grey rage at me. The honey hue of her hair was delicate and nuanced. A tiny smattering of freckles. Subtle dimples on her cheeks. Small, gently upturned nose. Straight, slightly off-white teeth. Two nice little young round pink human fleshy ears. She was, despite her exasperation and desperate state, and my assumption based on last night's ugly anticlimax, quite beautiful.

"Look." I raised my hands in an attempt at placation, but also because that was the only way I knew how to use my own Talent. "I am sure he loves you very much and I promise you this is a huge mistake—"

"I assure you it is not. Roddy might seem a bit touched but he knows exactly what he's doing. He picked *you* because *I* am not ready to honour the Seventh. He made no mistake." She pointed at me with the blade – maybe it was just a very long knife? "You made the only mistake here, in not realising how clever my man is."

"Why are you punishing me? I'm the victim here."

"I *was* looking for him, but you're here now, and while I am not ready to honour the Seventh, I think this is a clear case of the Ninth." *Do not hold anything you cannot keep.* "I have held him and I *will* keep him."

"Don't you think that's his choice?" Maybe if I distracted her with a hard spray and dashed around her? I couldn't afford to fight her directly, not as both a Half and a Daughter. What if I soaked the dirt under her feet so she'd sink into it? Or just splashed her dress to increase its transparency, which would be so shameful she'd drop the sword and run away in a fit of pique? I almost laughed at how bad these ideas really were.

"You were his choice and I think we can both agree how poorly that turned out. You are stalling." She smiled as if realising what she'd just said. "That's a good idea."

She splayed the fingers of her free hand. The ground gave under me as though loosened to sand. I was quicker than her, stronger, but apparently not smarter, because neither speed nor strength worked with nothing solid beneath one's feet. I sank into the strange dry mire up to my knees when she raised that same hand and snapped her fingers into a fist. Loose grains became dirt, then clods, then solid rock.

A pyrotic would have been dangerous in a wooden building with a lot of hay. Dangerous for both of us. But a geomancer this creative? I could have gone full force as a Half and still struggled.

Could I produce a jet of water strong enough to send her flying? Certainly, with years of training and a daily regimen that wasn't almost exclusively running baths, cleaning bloody sheets, and washing tiles. A daily life as…A Daughter. A servant of…

"The Liquid Night!" She cocked her head at my cry, as though ignorant to the colour of my disheveled robe. "Do anything to me and my Sisters *will* bring their full power to bear. I am a precious resource to those who serve the Night. They will notice my absence."

After the scum and bloody rags build up too high, anyway…

"Maybe." She stepped even closer to me. "But there's another Commandment that takes precedent. The Second."

Oh shit oh shit oh shit. So it fucking well did.

"The Nobles are of the Night, so we humans hearken unto them." The paraphrased sanctity spun light like drunken stars into her eyes. "Halves are Not of the Night and not to be worshipped or honoured. Nor do they hearken unto the Nobles."

"I can't help what I am!"

"No, but you can help what you do, and what you've done has put you here, with me." She moved even closer, to press the swordtip against my chest. I noticed a slight unsteadiness to her grip, but that didn't make the point any less of a threat. If anything, more so. "Thank the Blessed Mother; Her will be done."

I thought about screaming, and then remembered where the barn was. I could be lucky; someone might hear it. They would not be quicker than this horrifically smart, pious, good-looking girl, her heart scorned and blade drawn. I thought about somehow using my hands to fight her off, but I'd likely just overextend with no means of regaining my balance.

I thought about screaming. I thought about fighting back. And that is all I did. Think about it.

That's when I peed myself. Or that sticky problem from last night had found its solution. Maybe it was a mixture of both.

She pulled the sword away to pace around me.

"Think of it as a coup de grâce." How did a mere villager learn these words? "A quick, merciful end to the madness awaiting you. I am sparing those who revere the Night all that effort of stopping you once you can no longer stop yourself. I suppose, by this reading of the Second, we could consider this sanctioned by the Sixth too." *Do not kill without the Night's blessing.* Would the converse hold?

"No, it doesn't work that way…"

"All I'll have to say is a Half attacked me out of nowhere." Now she was behind me, and I resisted turning around; very bad idea with my feet stuck like that. "You lot go crazy all the time. You are not of the Night, so I need not submit. I pray for the strength to resist your foul charms. And glory be, She hears and grants this humble servant the courage and power to survive."

I felt the beating of my heart, used it to measure the quickening of my time, so fast approaching its end. By some small miracle, she completed her circle instead of giving me a 'quick, merciful end' in the back. I'd held some hope that she'd talk herself out of it. Realise that Roderic, of all people, was not worth actually trying to assault a Half. Surely she knew this. It was stupid of me, but I couldn't get past the idea that someone this attractive, smart, eloquent, and Talented could also be this…*fucking insane.*

In front of me once again, she stepped back, gripped the sword in both hands and pulled it back over her shoulder, looking like a lumberjack driven to wits' end by a stubborn trunk.

Something was wrong with her poise. She was undeniably good with her Talent and able to support her violence with a robust faith, but I knew from watching my brother train under Uncle Arius and any number of experts that she did not know much about swords. A two-handed grip on something that short might give her enough power to do some real damage to a Half, but she'd have very little control or flexibility. She was sacrificing speed for power, because even now she knew a Half wasn't some lamb to be slaughtered.

"You don't want to do this." I was clawing for the seconds I could feel falling away with each thunderous thud behind my ribs. "You don't *have* to do this."

There she stayed, either by my words or some precipitous realisation of what she was about to do.

Stayed but did not stay. "Funny." She blinked a few times, and then her too-wide stare was back. "You're half right." And with an animal grunt, she committed to the swing that would carve through my neck and place even a Half beyond the realm of healing.

Before the pull became a push, I narrowed my eyes and told myself a series of unassailable truths, starting with hers.

You're half. Right.

The sword came in wide, slower than it could be but still faster than it needed to be.

No. Not just Half. You are Sariana-Ra Jaydemyr.

Now I could see the edge and began to judge how far it was from impact.

Noble blood yet flows through your veins.

The fury on her face started to freeze in a hateful portrait, and the sword was now maybe a foot from my neck.

You are Half not by birth but by design.

I could see individual muscles adding deeper lines to her now very ugly expression, and the sword was still a foot from my neck.

And that design will not be stopped here.

Now she was all but still, caught before me, fragile and vulnerable. And the sword was a whole foot away from my neck.

So put this nse'ante in her place already, Rika Fas'ʒ!

I thrust my left hand out to grab her wrist and shove it away. I lacked the balance to do much more than push it down. I could have ducked but I didn't trust her ability to aim properly, in which case an anticipated decapitation would turn into a very messy downward chop. No, the sword had to go somewhere and stay there. I braced for that inevitability but used what I knew to be the last of the moment to push my other hand at her open mouth and run a bath straight into it.

As though the usage of Talent was too much for the slowed time to bear, the instant the water sprang from my hand it all happened and happened so quickly.

The short sword pushed into my flank, and the pain added to the scream I finally let loose as the gush punched into her face and drove her back. The two-handed grip combined with the sudden slickness from the water meant she had to let go of the sword as she staggered back, gagging and hopefully choking. It also meant that instead of the sword burying itself deep into my body, it cut just enough to get stuck. She screamed too, but nothing even close to what I was letting loose.

Instinct and so much pain took over and I reached for the hilt of the sword to yank it sideways and out, still using my right hand to drench her with as much force as possible. The sword came free and I tossed it aside with a voiceless gasp, pressing the same hand to what certainly felt like a huge, lethal gape. It throbbed hot and slick in vile synchronicity with what I yet heard in my ears. The blast of hydrotheurgy began to falter because running a bath essentially relied on gravity; sustaining a high-pressure flow defying gravity was well beyond my skill.

The girl recovered with a frustrated yowl, spat one last time, and strode back towards me, saturated but otherwise quite capable of picking up her sword and finishing God's good work. Then she stopped, her malice and my last splutters dripping down her face as she raised her hands as though lifting a rock over her head.

I just screamed in primitive, non-verbal denial again, now trying to stanch the wound with both hands.

"Stop!" The barn's door crashed open as though hit by a boulder, but the command came too late. My assailant threw her hands down and the world rose to eat me. I thrashed and floundered in the mud, and then thought: mud?

You imbecile, Sari. Any wonder she looked so satisfied. You made the ground the one thing a geomancer can't. You made it wet.

But even as the sloppy, squelching pit pulled me down, I saw someone dressed in grey and beige and just a flutter of red tackle that geomancer to the ground and pin her there with ease. That did not stop the girl's exultant laughter; she lifted her head just enough to grant me one last look at her manic eyes and gleefully twisted mouth. Then her subduer pushed that mad face into the dirt with a single choice. "Stay still or I twist, Zlatina Ciobanu."

She stayed still.

I continued to sink, bleeding into the slurry.

A second woman came in, dressed not unlike the first. She stood next the one kneeling on Zlatina's back, took one unimpressed look at me (now over waist-deep), raised a leather gloved hand, and flicked it as though brushing away a fly. I felt the glop around me dry and harden. Then she used the same hand to make two more gestures, one a small sweep of her palm to the left, the other the same to the right. And suddenly I was standing in a square hole surrounded by piles of dirt. Even the original shackles about my feet were gone.

The woman looked down at Zlatina, devoid of anything but contempt. "Amateur. Stab first, preach later." Then she tucked her hands into her red-brown cloak and walked out.

"Why didn't you call out sooner?" Before I could respond, or even figure out if the voice was talking to me, I keeled under waves of nausea.

oh I'm actually dying from actually being killed

His beating of her Heart

"What do you mean, there's no tension because you know I didn't actually die because I'm sitting here telling you all this? Of course you know that, but if the only thing keeping you interested is whether or not I was killed before sitting here telling you all this, Brother, I have some very bad news for you about how time works. Forget your shallow need for tension and theatrical plot twists. Spare a thought about the sheer volume of pain your sister was going through. Was going to go through. It might not be as interesting as the shocking death of the narrator-protagonist, but what happened that morning meant the world to me. It was the world to me. It changed my world entirely. Death only changes your world once. Almost dying, that one you can do over and over and it's never the same twice and you never get used to it.

"No Brother, you don't get to say that when you had your turn. And if it is 'me too', if you truly understand that not-dying is sometimes almost-dying, then why did you say that? It wasn't funny. It wasn't smart. It was dismissive and condescending. And it really hurt.

"But you know what, it's fine, I needed to take a break anyway. Go…I don't know, terrorise some rabbits with that stupid sword and leave me to figure out how to make my life less boring for you. Maybe I'll kill off some of my Sisters. Let them be brutally raped and slaughtered. After a gruesome battle and razing of Mothers Abbey. Thus began my bloody tale of bloody revenge. Doesn't that sound *tense* and *exciting* and oh-so-*titillating*? Fuck off."

"I told him this wouldn't be satisfying, that I wouldn't make it a story. But of course I can't help it. Even sitting here talking to myself, I…scrounge for meaning. For self-importance. For anything other than being his excuse to resist her doctrine. Father, forgive me. Mine will be the beating of his heart as you asked of me, but…must I endure his beating of mine?"

17 days until the revelation

Chapter 11: Verdant Verisimilitude
3/870 to 2/872 A.R.

Whimper.

When I opened my eyes, it was Chaelle's attentive face waiting to be seen. Who else could it have been, really?

"So here we are. I told you to stay away from knives." That was all I wanted to hear from her before figuring out what 'here we are' meant. As though I actually had been killed and actually had died (as she'd warned me I actually might do), and then somehow been pulled into a loop of time to maybe not do that again, I was back in an isolation cell suspiciously similar to the first one. Identical room, right down to the amount of light given off by the time-marking candle on the table.

The only differences were who was on the stool, and how aware…afraid of my own mortality I now was.

"Sword. Not knife. Long long knife. You wait there all this time?" Not that I had the foggiest idea how much that was.

"You're special, Tzara-Min, but not *that* special. A few of the Sisters took turns, when Cass could be pulled away. It was in fact she who informed me you were awake."

"But…" I paused as the pain in my side caught up with the gargantuan effort of remaining coherent. "…But didn't I just…wake up?"

"Didn't I just say otherwise?"

"Yes but don't remember. Hope I didn't say anything weird."

"For Cassandra's sake, so do I."

So much to ask, so much to do. And yet I knew even a slight movement could be too much. At best I could close my eyes and just…breathe. In. Out. Ow. In. Ow. Out. In. Ow. Ow. Ow.

"Is this a bad time? Should I come back later? You've been more or less out for five months, what's another day or two I suppose."

I gave off a single snort of amusement despite or at her indignation, and then even that little twitch of laughter turned to a cry of pain. I started to curl up into a ball but as soon as my knees bent and my body folded, the heavy dull ache erupted into what felt like a lance through my chest. A lack of crying turned to an excess of dry sobbing.

I heard her say something but only really picked up on the tone, which was about as understanding and compassionate as one would expect of either the enigmatic Witch-Seer of Jaydemyr Vachaelle the Nightsong or the pragmatic Mother Chantal Falkenstrom of the Liquid Night. Through the feeling of meat and bones still figuring out which went where, a crunch pulling me into myself where there was only more pain, the same pain, I felt her lift my head and push something against my spit-slick lips. "Drink this."

I knew what it was the instant the spoon tapped my teeth, and I accepted the offering because I had no choice. The *Vahm'esta* tasted like Zlatina's sword had looked after it tried to make a sheath just under my heart. Rusty. Old. Both dull and sharp in unfortunate places. Then the taste stepped aside as the priceless panacea galloped through me. It could have tasted like used Holewater and I still would have melted in the singular pleasure not of elevated joy but of quelled pain. I could almost feel my distressed innards arrange themselves in proper order once more.

"Can I…More?" It was there, but it wasn't *there*. Not yet.

After a few more softened spasms, I sensed the spoon again and opened my mouth wider. The syrup slicked my tongue and numbed my throat. The waves of affliction receded even further and before long were mere splashes of discomfort against the fortification granted by the sacred sap. I exhaled the last of the suffering and just lay there, basking in numb reprieve.

"Feel better?" I watched her place the half-darkened phial on the desk. "No sickness in the gut, no urge to retch?"

"No, everything is…" I sighed for lack of words. To think I once compared something as commonplace as sitting in a garden at Highsun to *this*. How could I so thoroughly forget who and what I truly was?

"Having trouble answering? Understandable. Let's try something easier. What's your name?"

"Sariana-Ra Jaydemyr. Aunty Chaelle, can I have…just a little more? Please?"

"Well, that is a shame." I lolled my face towards her, but there was no gloat or sarcasm. Through the enraptured haze, she really did look disappointed. "Here we go again."

"What…"

And then she turned in a circle, the creases of her blood-black vestment undulating and oscillating in ways that pulled me over and in and under and out. There was a brief sparkle the colour of a cloud veined by lightning. Only my addled detachment from all things material kept me from believing this was what the madness would feel like, and even then I had to shut it out with a stinging squint. Had it truly always been this much, from so little *Vahm'esta*? This much, so much. All much.

"Keep your eyes closed, Sariana." I wanted to, I wanted to cling to her sensible words, but my eyelids jumped as though surprised from behind. There was no more enchanted shadow or untethered clothwaves. A different Chantal just stood there, looking a little shorter in a dress the colour of cheapened ruby, heartwood hair streaked with the ashen fatigue of a life that had flirted with the dark end of a street one too many times. Her skin was not as age-stressed as before, but her lips were pinched with ancient jealousy.

"Where'd the other Chantal go?" This was Chantal and this was not Chantal. *We all have more than one side*, I thought through *Vahm'esta*'s epiphanic vapour, *and she means to take them all.*

"Little trick I made up. I call it a job change. It's rather fantastic." She verged on self-panegyrical. "White Mage to Songstress. One of my deeper secrets, but you won't remember anyway."

But in that very moment I *did* remember and tried to block my ears, knowing it wouldn't help as she began to sing.

Whimper.

I woke up and opened my eyes. Of course it was Mother Chantal in her blood red robes sitting before me. I was in an isolation cell, maybe the same one as before, when I first arrived…last year? In a cell, in a bed, dressed only in a nightshift.

"I send you off to find a figurative sword to sheathe and you go get poked with a real one."

I knew why I was here. Not how, not when, but at least why. "It was both." I was surprised at the strength of my voice. "And I'd rather remember neither. How did I get here?"

Her attentive glare mirrored some of my surprise with a faltering of its own. She almost smiled. "Two heroic acolytes of the Tantamon carried you all the way back here."

"Oh no…Nonono…"

Then she did smile, and it wasn't entirely cruel of her. "No indeed. That would be ridiculous. Almost as ridiculous as an heir to Jaydemyr thinking she wasn't being watched the whole time she was let out of my domain. Almost the whole time. Sister Hedwig will long regret that 'almost'. Carting you back and keeping you alive for the trip was the least of her penance. At least Sister Teadora was alert and stopped that bothersome bumpkin."

"Zlatina." I remembered more of what happened, the fragments of nightmare in which she was always the last thing I saw. "And Roderic. What of them?"

"What of them? One took a Daughter against her will and the other tried to kill her. And that should be the end of their part in your story."

"It wasn't against my will. It was foolish and very dangerous but I wasn't rape—"

"That's not how he remembers it. Or her, for that matter."

I snapped my mouth shut.

"Or would you rather I'd have them executed and their remains given over to the Third Eye?"

"Did…did anyone else hear about it?"

She shook her head. "You really need me to spell out what we had to do? Very well. Yes. They did. It's a small village and the boy who…took you had a big mouth. My Maliscient Sisters were busy for days. None of us equal your mother, or even come close, but we managed."

Had?

"Did you…" I hesitated. "Did you have to work on any of the Tantamonian acolytes?"

"They'd moved on the very same day, so no. Daughter Viera did tell me you and a certain two of them were quite cosy. Although given what happened next, clearly not cosy enough."

Of course Vi was just fine. Of course she told Mother Chantal all about it. Of course she wouldn't exaggerate *at all*.

I started to ask something else when the ache in my lower chest erupted in pain, sharp and unannounced. "Ow. Ow…Owwwww! Nnnnng…"

"Do you need more time to rest? You've been in a healing sleep for just over six months now. A day extra won't change much."

"Six months?" The taut cramp faded a little. Helped if I lay still. "Who took care of me? And no, no more sleep. Just talk to me."

"Sister Cass, of course, was your main caretaker. Sister Teadora from time to time. Nadzia took care of the immediate wounds. None of your fellow Daughters were involved, since I know you wanted to know. We *are* on sixth floor below. All they know is you almost died, and we're trying to save you."

Trying. So…still. And with that thought the pain returned, far worse and far more dominating. I bore down against it, but it wasn't enough.

"Drink this." Mother Chantal poured a little of the dark, sludgy liquid from a bottle she'd been holding into a spoon. I waited for the spasm to ease enough to peer at it, inches from my mouth.

"What is it?" But I knew. How could I not?

"Medicine." She pushed it between my hesitant lips.

I held the viscous dram behind the grimace the grotesque flavour evoked. The stabbing pressure peaked, and then as it began to withdraw, I spat the 'medicine' on the floor next to her booted feet.

"It hurts, Mother, but it doesn't hurt so much that I'd need that. Are you trying to fucking poison me? I *know* human blood when I see it, and I remember what happened last time I tried to take it."

She leaned back on the stool, appraising me. "I'm sure you do." Then she rose and put the bottle and spoon on the desk near the door. And picked something else up. When she sauntered back, I saw what dangled between her raised hands.

"I had no idea that was here."

"You wore it that night." She widened her hands such that the chain might be easily slipped over someone's head. The crux et luna pendant spun a little, sparkling with the tiniest glimmer of its stolen glory. "And now that you've proven that letting you off the abbey grounds was a very poor decision on my behalf, you may have it back. In fact, I am going to make you a one-time offer, Tzara-Min."

She didn't move any closer, so I assumed my reply would govern whether or not the pendant would return to its proper owner.

"As you say, Mother." I forced myself to sit up, swing my legs off the bed and be ready nonetheless.

"One question then. Did Daughter Tzara-Min of the First Order, Sister of the Liquid Night, born Sarah-Jade Falkenstrom of Teristra, die of her grievous wounds despite the Sisters' best efforts?"

I almost responded with the obvious truth, and then left my mouth hanging open. This was not something Tzara-Min alone could answer. Sariana-Ra Jaydemyr took over, and disassembled the question to find the offer. She…I knew that to return to being the daughter not of Chantal, or the First Order, or even the Liquid Night, was to be sent away, out into a world I knew nothing about. And not as a Fey per my birthright but a doomed Half, with no real skills, no family, and no friends. Then again, there was no proof that life in the abbey (and only the abbey, as Chantal had made very clear) would lead to anything but the same conclusion: me, dead, not even twenty years old. After possibly losing my wits and hurting any number of people I had come to know and like, maybe a few even love. Vachaelle would not make this offer if she didn't already believe…or even *know* what answer I'd give. Which in turn meant that it wasn't about 'yes' or 'no'; it was about her asking me this *now*. Something about where I was, what I was. What I'd said. Done. She had been waiting to make this offer because it was no offer at all. It was a test.

And saying just 'yes' or 'no' would have been me failing it.

So I looked away from the hypnotic waver of my most prized possession, and addressed those narrowed eyes of coldest ice. "She did not. She recovered after half a year of intensive healing and rest, returned to her Duties healthier and happier than ever. She reunited with her dorm Sisters, who treated her with newfound respect at her miraculous recovery. She excelled at her work, and before too long was promoted to the rank of Sister of the Fourth Going. In the course of her martial training with some visiting Tantamonian brothers, she fell in love with one of them and he fell in love with her and they got married and travelled all over Kaef're and lived happily ever after the end yay."

She didn't so much as blink the whole time, but after the deliberately deadpan 'yay', Chantal's mouth tilted upwards on just one side, pulled by mirth…I hoped. "The ending's unfortunately not right but the rest?" She stepped forward and returned my father's gift to where it belonged.

"I rather liked it. Fourth Going, you say. That can be arranged…although you do realise a condition of fulfilling those duties is, well, to go forth? And you, Tzara-Min, are not going anywhere until I say so. And if you ask, I will say 'not yet". Every. Time."

"I am sure I've much to learn from the First Order." I ran one index finger over the arc of the moon and the intersecting lines of the cross within it. "I see no reason to rush."

"That is because you don't know how much can happen in half a year."

I heard both a threat and a warning in this, but kept quiet. Yet another spasm was threatening my flank but as I braced, it only pinched for a count of two before returning to the very acceptable state of a flat ache.

"Half a year and a lot of healing. And you do know what healing is, don't you, Tzara-Min? It's accelerated growth. Forced. Teaching the body to try to return to its natural state."

I listened but didn't see her point, but then I let my head sag. Not one point. Two of them.

"Is this a condition of me going 'free'? Finally indulging your twisted desire to carve my ears?"

"Yes." No point in her denying it. "It's not quite your sixteenth birthday, but you denied me on your fifteenth, so this is late rather than early. And there is no chance of me letting you do it yourself. Not after…that."

I could have told her it wasn't me, but I knew it *was* my fault and I also knew even Lizaveta did a better job of it than I would have. I surrendered. "Okay, but not right now."

"Let's give it a few days, just for good measure." Chantal stood up with this generous acquiescence. "Lie back. I'll have some books brought for you to pass the time, and meals now that you're with us once more. There's a waterroom down the hall. And should you have any visitors, do remember what I said to you when you first arrived here. No talk about your past. No exposing anyone to any evidence of it…especially what's around your neck. If you are smart you will hide it and hide it well. And you will know when to wear it openly, because you will be far, far away from here by then.

"Now gather your strength, Daughter. I suspect you'll be needing all of it soon enough. And I don't mean for the clipping."

For once she was wrong. Correction: she was right about the ear clipping (far less painful than last time; Mother was almost habitually deft with her knife and a hundred times the healer Lizaveta would ever be) and she was right about hiding my beloved pendant (very bottom of my chest, wrapped in the smelliest socks I had) but she was wrong that I'd be needing all my strength anytime soon. After I was discharged from the depths of Mother's true workplace, I was placed back in Gold dorm and allowed only light Duties for a month. If I showed any discomfort, a healer was never far away. Oddly this didn't include Lizaveta, who mysteriously kept to herself most of the time and definitely no longer left any used rags lying around. Viera tried hugging me the moment I entered the dorm but I was nowhere near ready for that. She remained observant and concerned, but she never asked me what had happened, not even regarding the two boys to whom she'd introduced me. And I didn't have the courage to ask her *what* she thought happened that night or the day that followed. The courage or the desire to undo whatever it was Mother and the Maliscients of the Third Eye had so carefully arranged. That, I decided, would be ungracious.

Perhaps what surprised me most wasn't that others had been made to 'forget' the details, but that my body also showed little sign of remembering it. We spoke of lessons and scars not so long ago, and it seemed the only thing I had learned was how to hide there'd been a lesson in the first place. By the time my seventeenth birthday sauntered by, there wasn't a trace of puckered tissue or misaligned skin. Chantal might not give second chances, but somehow I felt like I'd been rewarded with one anyway. A reward for passing her test, perhaps.

Come Festival Day just after that, the Aunties made sure I was simply too busy to leave the grounds. I peered down at the assembly, a blend of familiar faces and fresh recruits, as I cleaned a window on the third floor. I spied Viera milling about, and hoped she remembered to be *responsible* when she honoured the Seventh.

Not long after that, I decided to warm our bath after she did.

Why no, Brother, I don't think I will. If I skip over something or sanitise it with matter-of-fact distance, please understand that I bring it up only to provide context for that which I *do* want you to know and understand. While they meant so much to me at the time, they don't mean anything to us now, and I'd rather not have to be reminded of that. My history is not yours to vivisect; it is mine to sift through and present based on pertinence. These are the lines between which you must read. And then keep your conclusions to yourself.

Although I yet resided in the Gold dorm, my Duties transitioned from First Order lessons to Second Hand services; I relinquished the bright fresh scarlet for the worn fade of crimson. Now I served the guests not before Delivery but during and after. I saw then why the first floor was so quiet despite frequent Procedures: Second Hand Maliscients and healers invariably rendered the guest insensate before making the two necessary incisions of the Delivery. I knew from lessons that we used that word, Delivery, because in some long-dead language, it meant 'to set free', but I'd always assumed it meant either liberating the child from the mother's womb, or the mother from the burden of the child in her womb. It wasn't until my task was to deliver the blood gathered during the Procedure and the precious pouch we called Mothergift to the Third Eye healer in attendance that I understood 'Delivery' had a third meaning.

Wait, so my abbreviated intimacies with my girlfriend wasn't enough carnal detail for you, but even a brief overview of something completely natural that women experience all the time is too much? Something far safer and kinder than what happens *without* Sisterly care, I should note. I could describe that next. We had a few where the baby came out as it does in most animals, through the vagina…no, really, it's quite interesting. We even had a word for it. Labour. As in work. Imagine having to *work that hard* after nine months of…work. But…actually, you're right. Now isn't the time. Later. I promise. Steel yourself, Mr. Badass of Fire and Steel. You'll know when, and I won't tolerate your squirming next time. Who knows, you might actually learn a thing or two about women most men never do. If they did, maybe they wouldn't be quite so overtly…what word did I use before to not describe a woman? Salacious. Or maybe they would. Ugh. Never know until it's too late, really…

You know! Now I think about it, I never did learn *what* the Third Eye did with what we Delivered them other than a notion of what they did with everything else: macabre rituals for divination and long-distance communication. So at least I can spare you *those* details, but given what we do know of Vachaelle, I can safely conclude they'd be…very detailed.

But that's really the issue with her, isn't it? She's never sparing with details. She's downright generous with information and instructions. They're just rarely the ones you want, need or can use.

"Still sane, Daughter?"

This time she was waiting for me at the front entrance. The newly-promoted Aunty Cass of the Second Hand herself had tapped me in the dining hall during lunch to tell me of the appointment. I remember thinking *why don't she and I talk much anymore?* and then watching her dash off as an unspoken, implicit answer. We were all so occupied, all the time. And yet somehow the highest authority of the entire abbey, the entire organisation for all I knew and suspected, occasionally 'requested' my company. If this struck the other Sisters as odd, none mentioned it. Maybe they envied the break from one's Duties these sporadic audiences with Mother Chantal granted. If so, I envied their ignorance.

"Am I still sane? Well, I haven't tried to eat anyone or dash about the grounds naked in the moonlight so I suppose so." I fell in step just behind her as we began to wander the perimeter of the abbey compound. "I also suppose this is about my ears again."

She clasped her hands behind her back. "I wouldn't suggest a stroll taking in the spring air were that my intention, although it is nice of you to remind me." As if she'd ever need that. "No, today I want to ask you another single question."

"It always starts there, doesn't it, Mother?"

"Would you rather it didn't?"

"Please don't tell me that's the single question."

I watched her grip tighten a little as we made our way around the path dividing the longest wall of the abbey and the hill supporting it. And then she stopped. "Look to your left, Tzara-Min. But don't tell me what you see. Instead, answer me this: do you still lack the language to describe it?"

I was already doing that, since it was a great deal more interesting than anything else. I searched for the right words to capture and share the tone of the tufts and the bushes, the hue of the woods at the base of the hill, the precise expression for that cloudy yet light afternoon sky. Many came close, but the moment I decided on one, the colour of what I saw seemed to bend away from it.

"No, but who am I to decide? I don't own the world. If I say the grass is green, the trees are brown and darker green, and the sky is grey,

I trust whoever's listening to have their own vivid idea of what that means. There are times when it's good to be specific, but for something most people have already seen for themselves? Probably only necessary when things are unusual or noteworthy."

"That was quicker than I expected." She turned towards the abbey. "Report for Fourth Going training next offday at Morningsun in the back field. You are still to stay within abbey grounds, but I wish to be sure that should the day come that I deem otherwise, you will be ready. You know not to ask, so I'm going to set a goal for you. If you somehow remain yourself by the age of twenty, you will be invested as a Sister of the Fourth Going. And then likely sent on some one-way trip far away so that when you do turn, no one will know or care. But until then, you will remain a Sister of the Second Hand.

"Oh." She paused before opening and disappearing through one of the many doors back into the abbey. As though anything she does is spontaneous. "Make sure to bathe, do your hair and wear your nicest robe. This will be the first time brothers of the Tantamon join us in training in over a year and you *do* want to make a good impression, I imagine."

Ever the fool me, I took her advice, believing it to be a hint that a familiar handsome young man or two might be part of the training. Instead I spent quite a few offdays being thrown around, bruised and banged up by grizzled old brothers with shaven heads and fearsome walking sticks. So much for the infamous durability of Halves. They taught us how to fall, how to roll back to our feet, and then how to fall again. Do that enough, it's onto simple Talentless self-defence. Mostly quick blows to soft spots. Nothing I'm sure you don't know far more about than I, but enough to fend off a ruffian or two. One time I accidentally went a little too fast with the strikes and put another Sister out of Duties for a week. The next offday I was partnered up with a brother who told me to try that again. He was slower, older, and weaker…but he proved that none of that mattered if you knew where the opponent was going to strike and simply waited for it. He said he'd seen wanted posters more difficult to read than me. I didn't tap my abnormal advantages in training again, deliberately or otherwise.

Most importantly, we were not allowed to wield any sort of weapon until we managed to disarm an opponent during sparring, and only received one of our own upon being made a full Sister of the Fourth

Going. You were the one who received all of the attention there; I had been expected to rely on my instincts as a young Fey who'd never have to deal with anything more threatening than a stubborn vessel or undisciplined servant. So it didn't bother me to have to learn how to face various everyday weapons unarmed. Mother Chantal had told me to stay away from sharp objects and I found it sound advice. But not even blunt ones really called to me. Not yet.

There were other considerations handled by Aunties of the Fourth Going back inside the abbey, such as how to dress for different weather; how to survive alone with nothing but a knife and one's given Talent; etiquette on the road, amid minor nobility, and in towns; cooking game and scavenging plants; and folk dancing. The last one surprised me but every Sister of the Fourth Going had stories about how dangerous situations and tense negotiations could be softened considerably by a jovial turn, a silky smile, and a proffered hand.

At some point I realised that lovely long hair was a liability in a fight, and one that men in particular would reach for when dealing with an obstreperous woman, and I quite liked being both. So I had Mother cut it short the next time she did my ears. Somehow, almost another year had passed and I simply hadn't noticed. The joys of a hermetic, physically grueling daily routine.

Almost eighteen and still sane, Mother. Perhaps I would prove her wrong again, but I'd be lying if I said the thought of visiting brothers and Sisters having to incapacitate me after I'd lost all reason didn't worry me very much.

"I didn't recognise you."

I was sitting on a log facing the back field, sweating out the morning sparring. I was too sore to turn to look, so I just sat there, hunched over and happy to let whoever it was that said that speak their piece. Probably wasn't even talking to me. Still, the nature of the words and something about the voice, deep though it was…

I saw him swing one leg over the log and then the other, and take a place farther down it from me, a distance that respected training that taught a person to respect distance as much as balance and timing. That's when I turned to look at him without lifting my head.

I didn't recognise him either, not with that full bushy brown beard and dressed as though he'd just divested a set of plate armour. Not so tall. Not with a shaven, sun-leathered scalp. But then my eyes caught his, and I knew.

And he knew.

"Short hair, somewhat taller, and dare I say more full-bodied." Huysman still had that wry lack of triviality I remembered quite well. Remembered liking it quite well too. "And your ears seem to have found a gentler knife for the clipping. How fare you, Sister Tzara-Min?"

"Well enough to handle whatever your bastard-strong brothers throw my way." I had just as little concern for small talk as he. "Here to join them, Brother Huysman?"

"It's Jorik. Call me Brother should we be paired off out there." He nodded at the field, where both Sisters and brothers were embroiled in various forms of mock fighting. "But otherwise, I'd rather you not call me Brother, or merely by my family name."

"Oh." I thought about how little could change in almost three years, and yet I'd never even known his given name. "Well you can omit the Sister as well, but I'm afraid I've no family name worth sharing."

"So I've heard every Half say, and it's always both lie and truth. Are you scared?"

"Yes." It didn't matter that I didn't know what he meant. He knew.

"So I've heard every other Half say." The easy smirk was barely visible under that beard, and I realised then why he'd grown it. "And it's always the truth. Are you training so that you can run away before it happens?"

Eph me but you don't waste time finding bone before blood.

"No." Lie and truth. "I am doing this because Kendahl told me it was the most likely way I'd see either of you again."

He grunted a single laugh and shook his head, hands folded between his knees. "Flattering, but…find another reason. While it's true, he has taken the tonsure too. Do you know what that means?"

"I can guess." I was disappointed and yet certain I'd never try to honour the Seventh with either of them. Or anyone. "Viera did say you didn't have to take vows of celibacy, although that might have just been her eager naivete speaking."

Another laugh, this one somehow even bitterer than the first. "That's true too. To do otherwise would countermand the Seventh. What we can't do is fall in love with a woman or raise a family. Rather, we can do either of those, but only once as followers of the Tantamon."

I tried to cover my imbalance at his unswerving reading of me. "So we could have sex, but not cuddle afterwards. Works for me."

No laugh this time. "You're Half, so yes, it would. But for normal people, it's not that simple."

Maybe it should have been him I faced in that barn. He'd have done a better job of killing me, and with his words alone.

I had to retake control, and immediately. "So you knew I was Half that night. Incapable of getting drunk. Incapable of conceiving. Acting all the way. And yet the creature you and Kendahl struggled to carry down all those steps into the heart of Mothers Abbey, she was not Half. She was a Rose. Isn't that what Mother Chantal told you? So who are you to judge me without knowing who I really am?"

He whistled softly, and I enjoyed a flutter of satisfaction. "We assist. We do not ask. We provide. We do not probe. And the Mother was not forthcoming at all. As I recall, she said 'carry this' and we did. 'This' was a box. Long, wooden. It was very heavy, too heavy for what Henri…Brother Kendahl suggested it might be. And it wasn't us alone. Two Sisters helped. I was just thankful that at least some of the floors were connected by an upndown. We only caught a glimpse of what was inside when our task was nearly complete: putting what was inside on the bed. What, well, who. That was when we knew the weight wasn't just the box. Kendahl assumed Rose, since it was indeed sometime after Highmoon, but I only saw…you."

Aaaand we were back to me reeling and fumbling. "You saw me at the festival. Well before I saw you."

"I saw you *arrive* at the festival. Mid-afternoon. Rather sunny day." He scuffed the dirt of the largely grassless field. "Henri didn't believe me. Hence the wager. If it was the girl and she was Half, I won. If it was not, he won. Coaxing your genuinely drunk friend to introduce us wasn't difficult for him. And of course he knew that Halves resist poison, so despite what was by that night evident, he still tried to serve you some wine as a final test. As though the ears were not sufficient proof."

"Thank you for indulging my act then."

Jorik shrugged his now-broad shoulders. "As you've just revealed, yours is a story well beyond the best interests of any humble follower of the Tantamon. Let the Sisters and the Peddlers handle the likes of Roses and Halves. Although I have seen a few more of both recently, even near Abbey's Village. I pray God they mind their own but we must watch them nonetheless. As you are watched here, no doubt. Curious times in which we find ourselves."

Other Halves? This close to my chosen sanctuary in exile? *And Roses?*

"You!" One of the Brothers called from the field, pointing with his quarterstaff. We both stood almost to attention. "Train on the training field, or take your lallygagging off it."

We shared a glance that suggested more 'lallygagging' later and trudged across the slightly baked mud in different directions. I didn't look back as I sized up potential partners, and I don't imagine he stayed to watch.

But he was gone from the abbey within days, drawn by the calling of the Tantamon I supposed. And enough time passed with well-tuned monotony that I genuinely started to wonder if I'd imagined it out of boredom or some longing for whatever spark I'd almost caught that one night. I asked around but no one else remembered seeing a Brother of his description that day, but I knew how poor my memory was; it would have been folly to think theirs any better. Still I wondered, in silence and solitude even when I was neither quiet nor alone, was this the beginning of it? Was I already forfeiting the chance to meet Mother's ultimatum?

Had it been him, or just who I thought he'd become? Did either of them even remember me? Why would I give him the name 'Jorik'? Or Kendahl 'Henri'?

Did madness always introduce itself with a friendly face?

If so, I was well and truly doomed.

Three or four months after I'd decided it didn't *really* matter since I was not, to my knowledge, trying to hurt anyone and only bit Viera when enticed to do so (there, happy?), something happened that both reinforced Huysman's visit and assured me I wasn't going mad, at least not yet. Something that still gives me waking nightmares, the significance of which you should grasp given how Vachaelle loves to turn mere dreams into lifetimes.

I was cleaning up after an Eyesun Procedure when a Daughter of the First Order forced the door open. Puffs of hot air gathering in front of her glistening red face as she struggled to catch her breath.

"Sister Tzara-Min?...Mother Chantal wants you at the front entrance."

"You ran here to tell me this?"

"Yes, Sister. She told me to." Another heave, hand on belly. "Give or take."

Naturally she'd know where I'd be. This was her abbey, and her abbey was my entire world. I knew not to ask.

"Thank you."

I made haste as bid, if only so Mother would know the poor girl had done her best.

But Mother was nowhere to be seen in the reception hall when I arrived. Crimson and Scarlet robes but no blood black dress. I pecked about the throng for a face more than just passingly familiar, but was left bewildered. No Mother and no commotion. Business as usual.

Then I saw one Sister pushing a wheeled chair towards me from the front doors. Behind her through the windows I noticed it had started to snow. I really should have not noticed that, given who was in the chair.

"Blessed Sister Tzara-Min." She was very, *very* pregnant and still attractive: Zlatina Ciobanu listless and clammy in a thin white dress. Despite what Mother had said, I stepped back and almost tripped on the hem of my robe. I sought escape but the steady tide of red around me denied any such egress. Her voice, so familiar and so strange, demanded my attention. "I didn't dare hope that you'd see me. Not after what we…I did. I know it is improper of me to ask now, but it has to be now. Before my Delivery, I must ask: can you forgive me?"

All Relief is Temporary

"You know what? You're right. I *was* happy until that point. I'd found purpose, something I was good at, quite a few somethings. I hadn't yet remembered that during the long healing process, I'd somehow reverted to something I would never actually be again, and it was good seeing Jorik once more, one last time before neither of us were the same. I doubt Vachaelle really cared either way, but she didn't seem to actively contrive situations that converted my contentment into adversity. Not during those few years of Tzara-Min's maturation. She never went out of her way to separate me and Viera, or to complicate matters any more than I already had. The impending threat of insanity aside, I'd say those were the best days of my best life. I know, I said the same of my childhood in Teristra, but I realised as I recounted those that I was only meant to think that, to feel that. Part of the Sarah-Jade Falkenstrom persona preceding the Tzara-Min façade. Sarah-Jade of Teristra never existed. At all. Tzara-Min of the Liquid Night, however, did. An act, but one so natural I couldn't tell if it was incredibly shallow or incredibly deep. What else could you call that but 'real'?

"And yes, Brother. That is precisely why it couldn't last."

10 days until the revelation

Chapter 12: Turquoise Truthfulness
2/872 to 4/873 A.R.

Shudder.

I knew that this made sense. That whatever Zlatina remembered, it wasn't what had haunted me. But there is a vast chasm between knowing something makes sense and confronting the proof of it when it disproves everything you've felt for years. I waited for her face to lose its desperation, its imploring wideness, to once again mould its hate around her statistically validated prejudice, her personally validated jealousy. Her scripturally validated vengeance. To leap out of that chair and claw at my terror-taut throat. To raise but one hand and send me down into the dark of rock and worms where I belonged.

But then I weighed her words as she waited for mine, and decided, actually, yes, she should beg my forgiveness. Attacking me with her Talent and a sword was a bit over the line even if I had unknowingly forced her to reckon with the Ninth while catastrophically failing to even slightly enjoy honouring the Seventh. She might be weak for now, but I knew, somewhere under all of that, was the person who had used the Twelve to justify ending my life. Let her apologise for *that*.

I willed myself to kneel down and reach for her hand. The skin felt as thin as recently dried paper, as damp as recently soaked. "Forgive you? For what, Zlatina? Truly, for what?"

"No time." She turned her hand over so that her fingers could grip mine. Frail. So pitiably frail. "Not for all of it. But for me. For trying to kill you. For not listening when you tried to tell me. For breaking the Second. Third. Fourth. Sixth. Eighth. Ninth. Tenth…Eleventh…" Her eyelids fluttered and that weak grip became momentarily the claw I'd feared.

The Second Hand attendant behind the chair tried her best not to intrude. "Sister, we must not delay. Mother awaits on the fourth floor."

Fourth floor…for a Delivery?

"This cannot wait." I looked straight at Zlatina's pinched eyes, her pain-flared nostrils, and tried to give her what she seemed to need there and then. "For all of your transgressions, lesser child of God, you are forgiven. *Vahm En.*" And then, less formally: "You have suffered enough for that night." I…supposed. "Whatever happens next, know that I wish you well. God absolves those who admit the filth of their slate."

Zlatina peeled her eyes open with a bearing-down grunt. "Even for what I did to Roddy?"

"That I cannot say." I had no idea what she meant and the Sister was already wheeling her back to veer around me. "But I believe Her mercy is boundless for those who submit."

"Sister…" Her hand left mine. "I." Another spasm. "I gave him the chance to submit to Her first. If She can forgive him…then…anyone."

The Second Hand Sister started to wheel her past me, when Zlatina's hand shot out to grab my arm. "Be with me. Until."

I looked up at the Sister.

"Mother will say if you're not welcome. Come then."

So I straightened up and followed them down the main hall. Corners. Off the main hall. We stopped before a set of two sliding doors, and entered the surprisingly large updown. So this was how Third Eyes came and went without using the stairways. Hidden mechanisms? Third Eye potency? I never learned. As long as the blessed thing worked, then if no other time. It *was* weird watching the stonework of the abbey as it seemed to crawl down the walls around us.

We stopped and a different set of doors slid open. No fewer than seven Sisters were waiting, crimson clothed and wearing black leather masks depicting the Third Eye with a blue blooddrop iris on their foreheads. Seven masked Sisters, and one Mother in not only her clot-dark vestments but a white linen gown.

"Tzara-Min?" She looked surprised, and the lack of sterile title proved it. The other Sisters rushed Zlatina's chair down a well-lit hallway. "You should not be here, Daughter."

"Zlatina requested I stay with her and, given the lie my actions made of her life and the sincerity of her repentance, I felt I'd at least try. Besides, I'm *incredibly* curious why she's acting like this is her last chance to speak to me."

"That is regrettable." Mother marched off. The upndown was gone, so I chased after her. "You will observe, speak only if addressed, do as you are told, and *anything* you see or learn stays on this floor, but I think you know why we are up here. Why *you* are here. Zlatina Ciobanu is five months pregnant and has less than five hours to live."

"Five months? That is far too soon! She might make it, but the baby..."

"The child will be fine. It's she that won't make it. On the fourth floor, five months is always too late."

It started like a normal Procedure. Mostly. The Sisters left their Third Eye masks on, the surgical equipment bore markings and details I'd associate with ornaments rather than operating tools, and Mother was there. She stayed next to me, by the double doors to the small, windowless chamber. Lamps bathed the room in cold blue-white, denying the comfort of warm shadow.

Two devices dominated the middle of the room, one I recognised and one I did not. The table upon which Zlatina panted, naked but not yet torn, was metal rather than wood. It was wrought with various cogs and levers, and I realised it was designed to lift and tilt, as though the guest might at some point need to slide off. It also had restraints for all four limbs; they were unused for now. Beneath the table was not solid floor but grating and gutters. Resource recovery, I figured. And off to the side was a sort of stool, horseshoe-shaped and low. There was a more conventional chair behind it. I didn't have to push my imagination to see how that thing would work either.

Maliscients whispered into Zlatina's ears and massaged her skull, and she was calm. Healers tended to the rest of her body, hunched over the belly to make their assessments. A hydrotheurge kept the exposed skin wet and clean. A pyrotic applied measured heat to the instruments. All of them tried to stay on one side of the table, such that we were afforded clear view of the Procedure. It all felt just a little bit performative, and I doubted that was for my benefit.

So far, so normal.

Mother murmured something beside me I didn't catch. The Sister designated to make the primary Sacred Cut held her knife as though about to sift through sand for shells. The only person in the room breathing regularly was probably Zlatina herself; everyone else seemed caught between tight inhalation and welcome exhalation. The razored edge touched the shiny skin. Nothing. The surface of Zlatina's distended belly did not give. The Sister pushed down and pulled back, but the blade just slid over the carapacial curvature. She tried again, now pressing with otherwise inadvisable force.

Against logic I expected the blade to snap, but instead it just skidded away again. It sounded like she was trying to cut glass with a nail.

Mother actually winced at the stony screech.

And then she was gone from my side, and nothing about this Procedure was normal.

It was hard to make out one Sister from another as they moved in eerie silent concert, turning the bed to face the weird stool. Mother was in the fray as well, whisper-hissing aggressive commands while assisting whoever seemed to be less than completely with the program. And, for no reason I could conjure other than it was simply part of the ritual, one of the Sisters stepped back, steepled her fingers and began singing. No, not singing. Keening. Ululating. Beseeching some aspect of God to intervene, perhaps. Others joined in even as they laboured.

…Labour? Oh…Zlatina, not even you deserved this.

The Maliscients backed off, and Zlatina's eyes inched open once she emerged from their hushed oblivion. Then she howled, and the walls of the chamber amplified the volume of her distress to piercing nausea. The Sisters' wailing deepened to a hum, as though supporting Zlatina's cry just as they supported her body towards vertical orientation. After tilting the bed they caught her, guided her over to the stool. Something close enough to blood trailed her every step; I saw only some of it fall between the grates. Zlatina collapsed onto the stool, and then her true labour began.

I watched in rising horror as most of the Sisters fell silent and left once Zlatina was seated and supported. All but one of the Maliscients. The pyrotic. The hydrotheurge. Even the healers.

I failed to notice that the last to leave locked the doors behind us.

"Should I go as well, Mother?" I was grateful for the absence of the Sisters' discordant chorus. It would have been dramatic, certainly, but very distracting and eventually quite annoying.

"No, Daughter." She knelt between Zlatina's spread thighs. "We'll need water, and you need to see what's about to happen. Sit behind her. Massage her shoulder. Let her lean on you. Pretend she's Viera. Run her a gentle bath. Say lovely things."

Not a few times during this labour, as I did precisely what Mother instructed, I wondered if Zlatina and I might have had a different relationship had we met under less volatile circumstances. Just one more reason for me to regret lingering that night. I didn't have to pretend she was Vi; she was Zlatina, whose passion almost ruined me, and now was certain to ruin her. Commiserations, sympathetic breathing, cooling down, and reassurances were such a poor substitute for the conversation we should have had years ago. Such was not Mother's will, however. This, here and now, was. So as I held Zlatina and spoke lovely things into her left ear, I pretended every word was 'sorry'.

The sole remaining Maliscient crouched besides Zlatina's other ear and worked her Talent to keep the woman sedate. It might have been wishful thinking but I felt the Sister's power too. That or I was just in shock.

So it proceeded: breathing, whispering, rubbing, breathing. Any time I caught Chantal's eye, she frowned as though to tell me to ignore her and focus on the woman about to honour the Seventh as her final, filial act to the Blessed Mother. She knew I had questions; how could I not? I knew they'd have to wait.

And anytime Zlatina tried to look at me, to start that too-late-and-now-never conversation, I shook my head and reminded her why we were here. It seemed idiotic, that she might forget, but she reached for distraction anyway. I would not be it. She rocked side to side, and even stood up a few times, leaning on Mother for a few waddling steps. Most of the time, however, was as you'd imagine: her seated, me serving as her backrest, the Maliscient reducing stress of all present, and Mother...mothering.

"It is time, Zlatina Ciobanu." In the end, it was the only thing Mother could have said. She delivered the ultimate command of this labour: "Push."

Zlatina Ciobanu pushed.

This much I knew from the few labours I'd seen: not long now. And indeed, the baby's head emerged within minutes, and the rest followed. Its skin was not pink but almost white, etched with veins under the film of its former home. And even then, its poor little ears were decidedly wedged-shaped, removing any doubt what Zlatina had done. Or what had been done to her. She knew, surely, what happened to those who took Noble seed. Just another question I felt unqualified to ask.

Mother cradled the thing and I couldn't but stare at it. That had been me, or something close to that, eighteen years ago. But no, impossible. My true mother was Noble; my father was as well. Unless he wasn't, in which case her holyfleshed body should have cleansed itself of his piddling squirt immediately. Unless *she* wasn't Noble…in which case…

"Tzara-Min." Mother used my name for the first time since it all began. "Is she still alive?"

I checked Zlatina's pulse, listened to her breath. "Barely."

"Come then, hold this." But…but my place was back here. For Zlatina. I stood up anyway and Zlatina just sagged forward a bit.

The Maliscient straightened her legs, dragged the chair I'd been sitting on over to the wall and sat in it herself. She removed her mask and revealed a young face lathered in sweat and possibly tears.

Released from the Maliscient's thrall, Zlatina gasped and reached for the child, but Mother denied this of her. Even this. "No. You are too weak. Just breathe."

Still, I saw the surprise on Mother's face, and greatly feared what it portended. I shuffled around the stool and accepted the baby.

Mother took hold of the cord with one hand and squeezed tight. At the same time as I was marveling over how *soft and wet* the baby was, Mother returned to examining what was now Zlatina's birth canal. She clucked her tongue. "Some tearing, nothing I couldn't fix." Then she severed the cord and took the child back from me.

"Why don't you?"

"Because I'd have to cut it anyway for the Mothergift." Mother seemed mildly angry that I'd asked, as though this were a simple classroom exam and not the worst labour I would ever see. She looked over at the exhausted Maliscient. "Enough rest, Sister Bianka."

The Maliscient replaced her mask and strained to her feet.

So it resumed. Again, this is 'normally' the simple part. The Mothergift should be easier to liberate than a complex, living bundle of bones, muscle, limbs and skin. Sister Bianka remained standing and just kept her left hand on Zlatina's right shoulder. Mother cradled the baby with an ease born only of experience, and coaxed the Mothergift free of its now-redundant womb. One last grunting effort and it was out. The splashing sound it made on the floor was far…far too loud.

And the whole thing was just far too red.

"And now you may rest, Zlatina Ciobanu, and may She forgive you this grave transgression. *Vahm En.*

"Right. Pick that up and give it to one of the Sisters in the hallway, Tzara-Min." Mother idly rocked the baby. "Then come back in to help with clean-up. Bianka, assemble a team of healers to begin resource recovery. Idiot woman can at least be that useful."

Bianka went to the doors and knocked. I heard them unlock, roll open, and then close again.

I went to stand, to retrieve a cloth from the Procedure table in which to scoop up and deliver the Mothergift when Zlatina moaned ever so softly.

"Uh, Mother?"

"What?" She was intent on the baby, which had changed positions and seemed to be trying to suckle her breast. Instead of exposing her nipple, she just pulled the fabric down a bit and let it try there. "Ow…little monster. Anyway, what is it?"

"She's still alive. Zlatina is alive. We can save her."

I expected Mother to show at least a little of the surprise I felt, but instead she just raised one disappointed eyebrow. "No woman survives the birth of a Half, Tzara-Min. You know that. Everyone knows that."

"But—"

She came closer and, because I'm such a habitual liar, ascertained for herself by listening. By noticing the waver to the woman's hair. "This is exceedingly rare, but not without precedent. Tilt her head back please, Tzara-Min. It will help open her airway. Her breathing is far too shallow."

I did, and the girl still groaned a little.

Then Mother adjusted her grip on the baby, which was still nibbling at her chest, and inserted her knife under Zlatina's chin. In almost the same motion, she withdrew it, tossed the bloodied weapon away and pressed her hand against the wound. I didn't even have time to let go of Zlatina's head in shock.

"No woman survives the birth of a Half. You know that. Everyone knows that."

"We could have saved her…"

"No, Daughter, we could not. Never mind the Mothergift or the cleaning. Clean yourself up and return to the dormitory. And remember what I said before. This is the fourth floor's business. You know I can make you forget all of this, and I will if you break my trust. Otherwise, I am happy to answer your questions later.

"Go get something to eat. Have a nice long bath. It's been a long evening, but for you at least, it is over."

"Sister Viera?"

"Mmf?"

"I need my bath heated."

"But…" She breathed her way out of the darkness of sleep. "Okay. Let me get dressed."

"You don't have to."

"…Tzara-Min, it's been a really…*really* long day, and—"

"You're right, I'm sorry. It has been a long day. And night. Please at least make sure I'm not soaking it out in bone-cold water."

"Alright. I can do that." She sat up in her nightgown, stretched a bit and yawned. Then she saw me, and she knew. Not everything, but enough. She just took my hand and I followed her.

I tried to enjoy her ministrations, but each press of her knuckles into back muscles and each kneading of obdurate shoulders put me back into that room, except it was me on the labour stool and she infinitely incapable of touching more than my detached, numb skin. I stayed in the water long after she'd gone back to bed, waiting for the tears I knew I could not cry or the Bladesun bell, whichever came first.

"It's barely Morningsun. Have you even slept? That eager for answers then. Very well. Ask about last night, or anything I suppose. Then take the day off. I will authorise it. You look a perfect wretch, dear."

Now that I'd experienced hopefully the worst of the fourth floor's business, I was welcome to revisit it (even via the upndown) and see Mother in her office there. Unlike the underground quarters, it was just another room. Desk. Shelves. Chairs. Window. What I took to be a closet or storeroom door. No one in there had time for any more than that, because she clearly didn't.

"What happened to Zlatina's belly?"

"It hardened to protect the child. A human body infected, rather, *infused* with Fey potence can't tell a helpful knife from a dangerous animal's teeth and claws."

No, Brother. She never, ever 'slipped her tongue'. But I almost never, ever let her distract me with her not-slips either.

"And once it goes that way, that's it?"

"Yep. There is no cure for it, no fix. That's why we couldn't save her. That's why she didn't survive. Had we not been there, the child would probably have made its own way out, and not through the va—"

"Was she raped?"

"—gine what?"

"Was Zlatina Ciobanu raped or was this of her own free will?"

Mother tamped down her annoyance at my interruption with a scowl. "When it comes to male Roses at the height of their unbridled power and no respect for the system of the Twelve, Tzara-Min, there is very little difference. But in her case, I suspect it was one last act of self-punishment. She's gone. Does it matter?"

Of course it mattered, you loathsome witch. "What will you do with the child?"

"Adopt it out to a Peddler house, of course. Halves make excellent Peddlers. Your presence here is strictly due to your true identity."

"My true identity. My true *nature*. You wanted me in there as much as Zlatina did. To show me how it really works. And so, one last question: I'm not Half, am I?"

"No, Tzara-Min, you're not. But whatever you and your brother are, Dhiana made you forget for good reason. And you're close enough to Half that the label fits."

"I'm not going to turn into a thoughtless beast and hurt those I…love. Not before twenty, maybe not ever."

"Correct. But you fearing it has been to your advantage. Now I think you are self-restrained enough to know the truth."

"You are going to grant me permission to join the Fourth Going."

"I intend to."

"To find Charan."

"I expect so. You know where he is. Plan well; it's a very long journey."

"I intend to."

"Are you sure you don't have any more questions? I will be less available soon. Events are in motion and will require my personal attention."

"You are going to him."

"At some point."

"Soon."

"Not that soon. A year or two perhaps. Depends on how long it takes him to figure out he needs me. To ask for me. To pray for me."

"You will not be there by the time I arrive. If."

"That is up to him, but I wager he'll be very eager to leave Kaifeng behind. An unexpected by-product: I think I've finally rid the boy of his puerile Mifūné infatuations."

"Alright, one *final* question, then I expect to see you when or if *you* want to see me. Who runs Mothers Abbey in Mother's absence?"

Mother finally smiled. "You."

"What?" She just *had to* make sure I was a liar about that final question.

"I jest, Daughter. The place mostly runs itself. Sofiya keeps everyone and everything in their place. And if you need someone to talk to, don't forget who has been there for you all this time, from the very start. If anyone here can be trusted with your deepest and darkest, it's Cassandra. Just as long as you remember the usual rules.

"Anyway, this place doesn't really need me. I'm just here for the hugs and the heals. Occasional words of encouragement. And handing out allowances come Festival Day."

"Like fuck you are."

"As good a goodbye as any."

Another year passed in which nothing worth noting occurred, and that was fine by me. A winter that hadn't once beared its fangs slouched into a chilly spring. Fourth Going training resumed every offday, but I didn't see Jorik Huysman again, or Henri Kendahl even once. Spring baked into summer. I heard tell Mother was in and out, but mostly out as she'd told me. Summer wrinkled into autumn. Viera became personal assistant to a pyrotic Aunty of the Fourth Going and her own departure seemed inevitable; our relationship cooled from that ephemeral intensity only cooped-up, overworked teenage girls can really experience to a frictionless lack of time for each other. This meant I was getting a bit more sleep at night, which was good because what happened next wouldn't have happened otherwise.

I knew I was dreaming because nothing made sense and that made sense. It didn't start logically or with any build-up. Before, I was lying down to sleep, and now I was standing in a world of white. It reminded me of that chamber of horror on the fourth floor, only where there should have been walls, there was just more space. Very much unlike that room, however, were the snarls and growls around me. And a chant underscoring both, a word that sounded like my brother's name as though spoken by Mifūnjin, the 'r' much closer to an 'l'. So I knew I was dreaming and dreaming about him. But from which corner of my imagination and experience could this have come?

I felt drawn to look down and saw two things: a young man kneeling at my feet, and a sword between us. Not just a sword, though. The sword. The only sword I'd ever put in the same dream as him: *Oni-Goroshi*. And in such detail! Certainly more than I thought I knew, back when he was told it was his only if he could take and keep it, a sly appropriation of the Twelve by Uncle Arius. Had anyone asked me about it, I'd have said, 'Curved. Sword' and that was about it. But here it was, the hilt wrapped in highmoon and highsun, the edge gleaming like an inviting smile. And the guard, which I knew somehow was called a *tsuba*, was of course the crux et luna. I received the pendant from Father; he received the sword. We had a cross to bear, a cross and a moon. And if that was indeed the precious blade 'Demon Slayer', then the young man…

He was just a young man but also here he was a Great Scholar named Wong Shah-Long, once known as Dog-Ears of Swimming Carp Village, a sage risen from filial iniquity to enlightened grandeur at the end of his venerable life. He was meant to die today. Graceful, grateful. Farewelled by those now who had turned his name into a goad. By some dint of destiny obeyed for decades, the boy who was once my arrogant, insufferably gifted younger brother had been allowed to become a man of talent and wisdom. I thought I would chafe at this but I also knew that something had gone awry. Some ancient flaw in his pacific mien had at the very last second demanded his attention and reckoning. And he had reacted very poorly. He had used that sword, which he'd sworn to never lift in anger ever again. Used it to murder…his father. Not our father, but the man who Dog-Ears believed was his, the way I was supposed to believe Vachaelle was my mother. And this father, Wong Chu-Deng, had been bad. Very bad. Did that excuse it? This final stumble on the path to enlightenment and eternity?

That was how I found him, and I knew exactly what he needed to hear.

"There is no excuse needed." I tried to sound soothing but couldn't hold back some undercurrent of rage and disappointment. I hadn't wanted to add that last word, and yet there it was, turning condemnation into consolation. So be it.

I rested my hand upon his poor tortured head, and he looked up at me. The face was not his, not the gaunt, ebon-eyed slate-skinned enigma that knew exactly how enigmatic it was, but instead who he thought he was. Round face, bruised and misshapen. Ears like that of a dog. And of course he'd be Mifūnjin, or perhaps Chūnkojin. Which meant he'd probably find my own blonde hair very strange indeed. We were both hesitant, curious. Me, because I couldn't believe that I'd just absolved him of patricide, and him because…I had the disturbing idea he thought I was his mother.

I shook my head at *that* ridiculous notion and floated backwards by will alone. And that's when I lost all control. The dream took over and I became but its puppet. It pulled my arms up and out, as though to suspend me in mid-air. My head fell back, eyes to what passed for a sky in this dreadful nowhere. I remembered Zlatina and wondered if he would then ram his sword into *my* skull as well. But no, this wasn't one of her dreams. This was all him: self-serving, self-aggrandising, and turning his older sister into some sick, sickening mother surrogate.

Yet helpless, my spine bent backwards. I knew I'd been contorted to some limit, and wondered if this were perhaps very belated punishment for what I'd tried to visit upon Sister Cass five years and so many lifetimes ago. But no. Even then, this was about him. It was *all* about him.

"It is time to reclaim what is ours, Charan." It was still someone else's script, sharp and demanding. but at last there was some harmony between how I truly felt and how this farce was playing out. I was Sariana-Ra Jaydemyr and more than ready to 'reclaim what is ours'. If that meant going along with the little shit's sorry attempt at overcoming his egotism, if this were somehow the key about which Vachaelle had spoken, then I would turn it gladly.

I started to look down at him again when—

I woke with an almost irresistible desire to see if Vachaelle were back. Back from using her Dreamsong on my brother. A year by caravan she'd said, but I could not put it beyond the powers of the Witch-Seer of Jaydemyr to cover that distance, any distance, in well-folded time. I knew she'd be around, if not now, then in the morning. Or the day after. Soon. Soon enough. I fell back to sleep, and if I dreamed, it was but the healthy purge of excess from a brain too full of unknowable, unattainable things.

She summoned me two days later to her depths by way of yet another poor First Order waif.

She must have been in a serious hurry because for the first time she wasn't wearing her Mother Oh-So-Superior black-red attire. Instead she was dressed a little like a Sister of the Fourth Going: little red cape, and a slightly dirty white dress.

"We haven't long." She confirmed my assessment as I sat opposite her. "A week, perhaps. You need to be ready for…anything. I have no idea what will happen to you."

"I knew you'd say that, Mother. I knew you'd call for me. And I know I'm not going to see you again for a very long time." I delivered this with such flat confidence even she paused.

"Well? Go on."

I described the dream, as clearly as I saw it, then decided to ask something I normally wouldn't. "Was this one of yours? Because it felt like him, like the sort of self-aggrandising fantasy he'd crave, but the convoluted yet precise method…that was all you."

Joys of joys, I left her dumbstruck *twice* in one conversation. "…Have you had any other dreams like that, Tzara-Min? Dreams of him, where you just know certain things, or have a role to play out?"

"I would have told you if so. It was just too unnerving not to share with the one person I'm allowed to."

She failed to hide her relief at this answer. I hid what I thought about that. Mother steepled her fingers in a very clear gesture of restored self-assurance. "Well this is certainly vexing. Perhaps it's some unusually strong link between you and him, given not even I know what you are, not fully. Perhaps your dreams draw from the same well. I will have to ask him about this, see if he remembers any of it. Even if not, I believe he'll be remembering more before long."

"I need to find him, Mother. Take me with you. Please."

"No. I cannot."

"Why not!?"

"It's a seeeecret."

I huffed and slumped back in the chair. What did I expect, really? "Fine. At least let me join the Sisters of the Fourth Going early. I want to be as close to reaching him as possible no matter what happens. If this dream signifies our return…and his otherwise utterly unbelievable discovery of humility and consideration for others, then I *should be with him.*"

"There are no exceptions when it comes to Fourth Going. Even if I said so, it takes time to prepare for a Sister's promotion. So again: no. You will remain here until you turn twenty. You will earn your beige-and-greys and your weapon. You are not that far off. Six months, no more. But also, Tzara-Min…no less."

"I'm going to be too late. I'm going to miss him because you'll have already dragged him into the storm of our resurgence. I do not want to be just tossed about by the fringes of the whirlwind, *Vachaelle.* Not this time."

"And you won't be, *Sariana.* You will have your own storm to weather, that I promise. Isn't it time you outgrew his?"

Curse the serpent-tongued faterigger, she'd finagled me into silent fuming again. Agree and she won: I would do as she said. Disagree and I lost: I would be admitting that as much as I scorn my brother's egocentricity, I'd just be legitimising it by committing my life to find him.

But I had to say something. "I hope he remembers everything you did and shoves that sword of his down your twisted throat, Nightsong."

"I'm sure he'll want to, little Talon." I knew she was invoking something else I'd been made to forget with that title. But it meant nothing, like so much of what she said. Life would be simpler without her. Better. My life. So off you kindly fuck, Witch-Seer. I've my own path to create.

"However long it is until I see you next, Vachaelle, it'll be centuries too early." I stood up. Turned to go. Was halfway through the door.

Naturally it couldn't end there. "You're going to miss me, and you won't even realise it. So one final gift then: before entering Kaifeng, look for a Haven called The House of Happy's Departure. You're a smart girl; you'll figure out what to do next. Goodbye, Tzara-Min. You'll never know how much I liked you."

I almost took her seriously, almost thanked her, but then just left and closed the door behind me.

We were just finishing a long, indulgent lunch soaking up the spring sunlight in the courtyard. Two Sisters and a rather young Aunty formed a comfy if too rare triangle. Not long ago, Aunty Cass might have been a little too much company for Viera and I, but not long ago, Viera and I had been just company enough. Since Mother's definitive absence, Cass had really gone out of her way to spend more time with me, as though she sensed how lost I was without Mother's guidance: a fucking ridiculous thought but…it was true.

"By Her Love, I've really missed this." I favoured Cass with a fond glance to my right between bites.

"Me too, Tzara-Min. Me too."

"And I am going to *really* miss you!" I nodded at Vi, admiring the way the grey and the beige travelling clothes sat on her well-defined features.

She just smiled and shrugged. We had been good, but this was always what was going to happen.

I listened as they prattled and joked, just basking in the warmth and appreciating that, at least for now, life was more than good. It was damn near perfect. No Mother to complicate things; delicious hamper lunch from the dining hall; and enjoying it with my two favourite people in this admittedly tiny world.

"She probably just wants you to heat her bedroll every night." Viera's musing on what a seasoned Sister of the Fourth Going might need from her attracted all sorts of quips. Happy to provide. "With your hands, I mean."

Cass chortled, shoved me away as Viera's mahogany cheeks fair glowed with a blush. "Not in front of your elders, you filthy brat."

I kept giggling but her words resonated; not all that long ago I'd almost dismissed Viera with those very two words. I'd been right, but it would have been the wrong thing to say.

Vi rolled right with it. "Well, you do hear stories, of what might transpire between we Sisters of the Fourt—"

My name is Charan Jaydemyr

Oh no not now not with them not NOW

NO

Thump.

Thumpthump. Thumpthump. Thumpthump.

I just lay there listening to the beating of my heart in my ears. It had almost stopped, but now it was strong, regular. The armour was gone. The screaming. The end of the world…had just been a dream, some Ephed up vivid-as-Shyn's-tits hallucination from the sleeping potion Chrys gave me. I should have known better.

Chrys!

I sat up, realising quite a few things at once. I was not in the carriage; I was sitting on a lawn in an enclosed courtyard. Stone building, not unlike Parelle Girls. It was bright, so daytime. Not only was I not wearing the armour from the drug-induced vision, I was wearing…red. Robes or a smock or something. As were the two women sitting near me. A slight Purashenan like I sometimes saw in Hammerdin, smiling the same way Lu smiled when she heard a naughty word, and a more full-bodied Kas'Daenne with lightly-tanned skin and mid-length curly brown hair. They both looked older than me, significantly. Young adults.

"Tzara-Min?" I knew the 'sheen meant me. Name from the dream. Tzara-Min Jaydemyr. Was this just the next step of the too-real hallucination? Was I still unconscious in the carriage thundering to Shyn-knows-where? She moved to touch my shoulder. "You okay, love?"

I recoiled, as much from the word as her reach. I looked at each of them, back and forth. "Who the Eph are you, how do you know that name, where's Chrys, is Mother here, and…" I trailed off, having looked down at myself to avoid their bewildered faces. "Wow, they're almost as big as Bells'. When did *that* happen?"

Her beating of His Heart

"Yes, I can see why you'd consider it a power of sorts, but I have no control over it, so what is a power over which you have no power? An Ephin' inconvenience, that's what. But sure, let's dwell on this a bit, because I'm fairly certain you don't need me to elaborate on what happened on the Fourth Floor of Vachaelle's Abbey of Abominations. I can enter your dreams. I can see parts of your dreams that even you can't. Provided those dreams are not normal dreams but instead pre-constructed experiences imposed by the Nightsong. I can, it seems, even enter dreams that you have within dreams, which is just fucking crazy. You say I have the power but Brother, you're the one with a mind so powerful it can play host to dreams within dreams so complete not even you can see all of them. We are neither of us human but you are less human than anyone I've ever known. Human, Half, Fey. Less human, more something else.

"Still the world's biggest idiot though. Thinking I was somehow your mother. Forgiving you for murdering your father. How is it even your humblest, most downtrodden aspect still has the arrogance to *make his own mother* forgive that? That powerful mind has nothing on the power of your ego, and the really pathetic thing is it's not even in *your* power to stop her from making you the centre of everything. At least pretend not to enjoy it so much from time to time, please?"

7 days until the revelation

Chapter 13: Purple Preparation
4-10/873 A.R.

Start.

"When they happened for the rest of us, silly." The Kas'Daenne was acting far too familiar. "Although for some of us, a little more so. Bells might be pushing it though, heh."

The Purashenan remained quiet. I felt her concerned stare. She knew me, or thought she did. Knew and cared for.

"Eph me. A sheen and a kasser. Let's sort this out."

But before I could do anything more, the Kas'Daenne and the Purashenan both curled Flails, of a sort (what was with the belly cup bit?), and pulled away from me.

The sheen looked as though I'd cut *her* across the belly. "Mother might not be here, but that's no call for blasphemy, Tzara-Min. And...you know I don't like to be called that."

I did recall Mother's great dislike for my breaking the Third, which is precisely why I did it. Which means if these two were similarly upset, they might be working for her, answer to her. And given their familiarity with me, and what I was wearing, I wondered if I'd also been made to believe the great Chantal was some sort of leader or figure of authority. Where the Eph did someone as busy as she'd been, singing and whoring in The All-Trades, find time to do something like this?

Not to belabour the obvious but I was far from the world's quickest thinker, and probably just sat there slack-faced as I went over all of this.

"Something's wrong, Cass." The sheen...Purashenan was a sharp one. "Fetch a Maliscient."

"No!" I knew nothing of anything of this new here and now, but I knew plenty about that old there and then. Mother's usage of the Curse to incite a rebellion. Jack's plan to start a war against the Guild of Talents. Lucille's immense power and her decision to wield it in my honour. Tiamat representing a frightening new prodigy from the well-to-do but stagnant Fourneval bloodline. All culminating in Teristra engulfed in flames. The Peddlers were supposed to take me somewhere safe from that, and here I was, years missing from my memory and being threatened with Maliscient attention by two red-robed…Priestesses. *Liquid Night*. They had to be. "I'm fine, don't need a Maliscient. I promise…Cass. And I'm sorry for what I said." I made sure to look at the Kas'Daenne woman as I said this. Tried a smile.

She glared at me, but then nodded. "Nevermind, Viera. Sit down." The sheen…Viera crossed her legs and looked almost as lost as me. "We can talk this through. Sudden short-term memory loss isn't unusual in Halves. Ask your questions, Tzara-Min." At the mention of 'Half' I reached up and stroked my left ear. Round. Soft. A little bumpy. Just like yours, Mummy. So whatever else had happened between then and now, someone had been doing my ears.

"Where are we?"

Viera's eyes widened and I thought, Eph it all, that was a very poor start. Careful does it, Sarah. Tease through this.

"An abbey of the Liquid Night, near Abbey's Village. western Kas'Daen. A long way from Teristra. A very long way."

How'd she know that was my next question? Well Eph's shiny balls to your face, lady, it won't be now. So this is where Mother sent me. A backwaters baby institute in the middle of Teriss-Luniir's rival territory. Now, why can't I remember anything from the carriage ride to now? I was being hidden. Did she hide me…even from myself? I needed to know, then, who had been 'me' in my stead. Why the name from the dream. Why not Sarah-Jade Falkenstrom. Or Dumpling…or Pumpkin? I fumbled for my throat, and found nothing there. No chain, no pendant.

Alright. Next. "Was there anyone with me when I arrived here?"

"It was just you when you came to. I was the first person you saw when you woke up." She laughed. "That, let me tell you, was a very rocky start. You thought you were a Noble, a Wild Rose. Oh, Tzara-Min, you almost killed me!"

Assuming I woke from that far-too-real dream, then this made sense. I had felt...other in that endless grey battlescape, fallen and falling and...oh, so powerful. My fingers remembered the heft of that weapon, and I remembered its name. Was I meant to acquire it at some point? Learn how to fight like that? Was that why I was Half? And if it was more than a dream, but instead some brief glimpse into what may be, was everyone else in it real too? Was...*he?* He for whom it was all staged, arranged, executed. He whom I had thought of...as brother.

I only had a vague idea what a Wild Rose was, and me...a Noble? Laughable. And so she had laughed. I echoed with a few huffs of disbelief. "So no Peddler was with me. No one called Chrys."

They looked at each other, seemed to weigh up the import of these names, and shrugged.

"Is Chantal Falkenstrom here?"

This time they didn't shrug but did something worse: they shared a different look, one even I could read as 'this is worse than we thought'.

"Not at the moment, but she's been here most of the time you have."

So they knew the name. Chrys had said when I found out who she really is, I'd be 'astonished'. And terrified. Time to find out. "What does she do here?"

"She's...well..." Viera answered this time. "She's Mother. How could you possibly forget that, Sister?" Shared attire's purpose confirmed: I was one of them. A Priestess of the Liquid Night. She looked around as though any of the few other Sisters coming and going might notice something very wrong happening. I hoped she was just being paranoid. "I *really* don't like this, Cass. Is this how it starts?"

"I don't think so, Vi, and I don't like it either, but...oh, fuck it. Come here, my dear." She opened her arms to Viera, who crawled across the grass in front of me to collapse into her embrace. Cass stroked her hair and whispered vapid 'there theres' at it.

Or so I assumed, which, as usual, was me being the dumbest bitch in the world.

Cass eased Viera down to the grass, leaving her prone as though asleep. Affection suffused her every gesture and look at the girl...but then she turned to me and all of that was gone. I straightened up at the intensity of her expression.

"This timing is terrifically lousy, Sariana, but obviously it's not your fault." She raised a hand to stifle anything I might have said in protest or surprise. Had I known that name in the dream too? *Lapsarian…ah. Lapsed Sariana…shit.* "Vachaelle warned me this might happen, but thankfully you're not him and she's not Lady Dhiana. And until just now, her cryptic task for me made about as much sense as anything else. Anyway, we don't have long." She idly rubbed Viera's thigh that whole time, but didn't pause in her speech otherwise. "You think you're Sarah-Jade Falkenstrom, daughter of the singer Chantal and the carpenter and former guardsman Arius. Ah ah, let me finish. You're from Teristra. You were caught up in the start of a conflict between a guild that taught people how to make weapons of the Talents and, it seems, everyone else. Your last memories are of being whisked away from the city, age fourteen. A Talon…sorry, Peddler named Chrysanthemum accompanied you. You were not told where you were going, and Chrys drugged you on the way. Nod if this is all true."

Like I had an Ephin' choice.

"Good. Now I have a question. How did you know your name is Tzara-Min here?"

"It came to me in the dream." True, but somehow insufficient. I considered lying, but if she knew this much, being honest might lead to her saying even more. "The drug Chrys gave me. It was so real. I don't know how to say this without sounding like I was on some seriously strong intoxicants which I was…but…I think I saw the *end of the world.* Angels of He Who Shines battled Nobles and Halves and…And my brother was the absolute centre of it. Forget it. I don't have a brother. It was all Eph…fucking ridiculous. I don't even read the Book that much. No idea why I'd dream anything like that."

"It's an interesting way of connecting dots. Probably irrelevant. Now I will tell you who you really are, and you will know it. Give me your hand."

"Okay…" Again, like I had an Ephin' choice.

Her hand, having just now massaged Viera's prone leg, was warm, her voice warmer still. "Your name is Sariana-Ra Jaydemyr. You are the exiled heir to a Noble clan, and you are Half. You came here when you were fourteen, in the year 868. I don't remember or know the details, only that Vachaelle, the woman you and I and presumably everyone else here knows as Chantal Falkenstrom, brought you here for your own safety. She told you that you must pretend to be her daughter Sarah-Jade Falkenstrom, pretending to be not-her-daughter, Tzara-Min. And you've done an excellent job of it. The year is now 873. You are nineteen, a skilled hydrotheurge who assists with the delivery of children, and in six months you will turn twenty and leave this place. You love Sister Viera but she will be leaving very soon and you doubt you'll ever see her again. Your road will take you away soon as well, across the plains and steppes of eastern Kas'Daen, through the desolation of Karakan and into Chūnko, where you know your brother to be. Nod if this is all true."

I nodded. The moment she said it, I knew it. Remembered it. Moreover, I remembered a lot of what she hadn't said as well. How I'd treated Cass at first. Vachaelle's ploy. The sun, oh dear Mother of All, the *sun*. Eating. Pooping. Learning. Sofiya. Lizaveta. The brothers of the Tantamon. The festival. Roderic. Zlatina. The Fourth Floor. I wasn't actually Half, not like her heretical get. The other dream, a week ago, in which I'd been compelled to forgive Charan his patricide. At first it was like recalling a *different* dream from days ago, weeks ago, and then wondering if it actually happened, or something like it, at some point. Some similar event to inspire that dream. And what started as suggestion became possibility and then fact and oh my Ephin' God I had been right all this time *this clever bitch* was *a Maliscient*.

"No need to call me that. But yes. I was…am, one of the Nightsong's servants. Not just here, but there. Before. You're not the only remnant she placed here in her personal stronghold. And here is further proof for you that I am telling the truth despite my kind's reputation to the contrary: I could not read you until now. Not Sariana, not Tzara-Min. But the girl who thinks she's Sarah-Jade? It is difficult *not* to read her. But then again, perhaps the reason I couldn't read you before was because I, too, had no idea who I was. 'My name is Charan Jaydemyr'. It was like someone whispering it into both of my ears at once, somehow. And it wasn't in any language I knew."

Yes, just like that. Hearing without sound. Understanding without comprehension. Knowing without learning.

"Please don't do that. Just talk out loud. That way I can actively block the rest. You deserve your privacy and, in case you've not noticed, Viera and I care very deeply for you. For Tzara-Min."

"I know. If you block what I'm thinking, does that mean you're done…influencing it?"

"I am. It doesn't take much. A nudge or two. Your mind will do the rest. It has to. It will decide which you to be. But since Sarah-Jade is a fabrication and Sariana has spent years trying to forget who she is, I would be very taken aback were you not to remain Tzara-Min, Sister of the Second Hand and soon the Fourth Going."

I looked down at Vi's slumbering body, remembered and remembered and remembered…and then nodded. "I dislike how the name came to be, but now that I've had not one prophetic experience about him but two, I see no choice but to stay the course. Six months is not much time, but I've attained most of what I'll need. I may come to you for help, as Mother has suggested time and again, but I am sure you have your own…occupations now. Did Mother bring anyone else here from before?"

"I don't believe so. Too many in one place would be an easy target. At the risk of sounding self-inflating, I think she chose us because we would be of the highest value upon the weakening of Lady Dhiana's lock. You at the very least."

"Cass." I pivoted about a point neither of us likely wanted to consider. "Do you think Vachaelle's used her song on us since we came here?"

The Maliscient, my first friend here and almost certainly my closest, smiled ruefully as she started to rouse Viera, who was making cute little snorts of resistance. "I've just used something similar on Vi. She'd consider it a violation and a betrayal if she knew. I know I did it for her own good…but also my own convenience. You know Vachaelle well enough to even *doubt* she's done the same."

Viera stirred, rolled over.

I had to say one last thing then. "I suppose it doesn't matter then. We are, as ever, in her hands."

"She's called Mother for a reason, Tzara-Min." Cass poured her love into Viera, and I so very much wanted to do the same. "Wake up, you. Come on, you have to get packed and go show the world how wonderful you are."

"…Mm." She sat up, and the way she knuckled sleep from her eyes almost made me weep. "Nice nap. Needed that."

"That or just too much food, a little drink, and a lot of sun."

She yawned. Stretched. Killed me over and again. "Also a prossibility. Pobable. Eh, you know. Blessed Mother but I'm worn out."

That was my cue to reset the tone and the mood. "Better get used to that. Aunties of the Fourth Going don't massage themselves, Vi."

Cass spared me the tiniest look of approval before launching herself at Viera for another hug.

I wondered if Vi had noticed her cheeks were wet when she woke up.

After we saw Viera off, I spent at least an hour in Gold dorm, sitting on my bed fondling the pendant under the sheets. I couldn't let them see it, not now that I knew what it was, to both of me. Us? Me. Sariana knew who'd given it to her and why; Sarah-Jade still thought of it as her only proof that she did, in fact, exist and had seen Jack's own hammer-engraved pendant and had met Chrys and Pricker (Nicholai was it?), and received two gifts in the carriage. Tzara-Min was pretty sure that to anyone else it would have looked like we were taking care of our carnal needs, which wouldn't be out of place given I'd lost my well-known bedwarmer, possibly forever.

All three of me (see, Brother, I can do it too) knew that the time was coming when I'd be able to wear that pendant proudly, which meant I'd need something else in hand, because there'd always be someone who disagrees. And I'd need to know how to use it.

"I'm sorry, you want a what? Tell it to me again, step by step." The stocky blacksmith of the abbey's outer grounds, bald as a Tantamonian monk but nowhere near as reserved, looked up at me from his anvil as though I'd just asked him to stick his hands into the fire and wiggle them about a bit. I sighed and leaned against a post supporting the awning of his workspace. The day was hot enough, but the constant radiation of heat from the forge turned explaining it even once into a crushing chore.

"A wooden steel-reinforced handle roughly the length of my forearm."

He hunched over the anvil, visualising my request with a chalk sketch. "Right."

"Leather wrapping for the grip."

"Mhm."

"A metal spike for the pommel."

"Can do."

"A length of chain maybe half as long as the handle attached to the other end."

"So *like* a small flail…"

"And then a metal ball on the end of the chain, maybe about so big."
I demonstrated by touching my fingertips to form a sphere. "Covered in
small metal spikes the length of my finger, and just a bit thicker."

He shook his head, and pointed at his sketching on the anvil. "That,
Sister, is not a flail. That's not even a morningstar. That's just some sort
of ball-and-chain thing and, from what I can tell, a very quick way to
catastrophically hurt yourself. I can't in good faith make that knowing
it'd harm the wielder. Why not a good old battle hammer or mace? You
hold the safe end and make a glorious pulp of whatever or whoever eats
the other."

"Master Smith, the Sisters do pay handsomely for a Fourth Going
weapon and once I'm off abbey grounds, any and all misuse is my
responsibility." I was well-aware that this was his forge and I was in his
domain. "If you are truly so concerned I can have Mother Chantal
Falkenstrom see you personally." No I couldn't, but pray God he didn't
know that. "And please, that's not a threat. Were she displeased with the
idea, it wouldn't be you confined to the abbey for Holecleaning duties
until the Second Coming of Afraen Who Was Ephriem, *Vahm en.*"

Also I was an Ephin' Half-monster who remembered using a 'ball-
and-chain thing' to slaughter Angels in a real dream but I couldn't tell
him that.

He worked the sketch again, started to tinker with it, mumbling
about materials and weight and whatever else. "Do you plan to travel
with this thing?"

"I am receiving it for becoming a Sister of the Fourth Going, Master
Smith, not a Sister of Not Going Anywhere. So yes, I do."

The smith gave me a sour look at this, and I tried smiling. He
lowered his head again, muttering something I'm glad I didn't hear. "In
that case, Sister, you'll need to see a leatherworker to fashion a belt for
it. Strap. And as for that spiked head, maybe a pouch lined with steel or
chain. Or just a thick layer of…something down your right thigh?"

"I shall take all of this under consideration."

"Still think you're gonna just conk yourself in the gourd first time
you try to use it, but I like a challenge. When do you need it?"

I pretended to think and try to remember. "Three months from now
at the latest."

"A dedicated weaponsmith could probably bang out a work of art in
a week or two, but I'm far from that. Not when you Sisters need
anything from horseshoes to hanging hooks. And for a sword I'd just

head down to see someone in the village or…" I tolerated this, because I knew what he'd eventually say. "Look. Come back in just under three months and, if I haven't completely discredited my profession, I will deliver this…weapon to your specifications. I might even request a demonstration."

"I'll bring some melons."

My next few stops in the workshop area were to acquire the means of fashioning and testing a relatively harmless simulacrum of what I'd explained to the smith: a few pieces of wood, some thin rope. Here Sarah-Jade's years spent lurking in Hammerdin came quite in handy. The abbey didn't have a ropewalk to make its own bindings but I was able to procure a small length from the head carpenter. Also had him use his brace and bit to make a hole in the makeshift handle, through which I threaded the rope. For the head, just a block of wood, similarly attached. In the end it was ugly as Shyn's Plundered Slit but Jack would have given me an Ephin' medal, given how little actual crafting I did while spending so long in a guild dedicated to it.

It occurred to me that I probably should have done all this *before* visiting the smithy, but then perhaps he would have requested that demonstration up-front and I would have…catastrophically hurt myself. Then he never would have made the real thing for me, because I'd be either dead or dead embarrassed. Not sure which was worse.

Now it was time for the other part: seeing if I knew how to use it. The nearby training field was empty; offday was half a week away. It was also sweltering that mid-summer Highsun; I imagined most Sisters taking refuge indoors, particularly on the floors below. So I had the dry, well-trodden enclosure to myself, which was just as well given what I expected to happen. I'd learn next to nothing about the real thing with this crude device, but at least I could test to see if Tzara-Min's battle in the Final Garden imparted any sort of muscle memory.

Not at first. One swing I knocked into my knee, and down I went. Another hit my shoulder. The spectrum of the bruising later would be magnificent. But that's when I realised I was still thinking and acting like Sarah-Jade, she who had made this tool. But she'd made it for someone else, and I had to let that someone else take her turn. So I closed my eyes to the heat and tried to visualise that dream again. The momentous grey; the armour weighing me down, holding me up; the deformed thing of claws and teeth swirling around and around and then diving…and me…

The harmony was missing but the movement was right. I opened my eyes and was crouching on the ground, left hand gripping the wooden weight, right plunging the end of the handle through the hot, crusty dirt. Satisfied, I close my eyes and played through the rest. Sariana mused at how, as a Half or something like it, she was able to draw on the Noble facility for compressing a deluge of meaning and moment into a singular point of presence. What did you call it? The Window? Yes, something like that. That combined with perfect recollection of the dream of the end.

And as though I really were following some lethal pattern, some prescribed dance, I finished not gracefully but in a position of projected pain, clutching my abdomen.

After I'd felt myself spin and twirl and leap and dive…and die, I tried it with my eyes open. Nope. Planted my face in the dirt on the third spinning jump. Too distracting to see the world that was when I was trying to re-enact my choreographed routine from a world that never yet would be. Still, I was satisfied. For a first attempt, it was more than enough. I had my proof. The dreamborn Tzara-Min Jaydemyr of the Final Garden, wielder of the Gildenhammer, and the realgirl Tzara-Min of The Liquid Night, a living evolution of both Sariana and Sarah-Jade, of Fey and human, were one and the same. And they were all me.

I resolved to repeat this exercise whenever I could, preferably when the field was abandoned…which, thankfully, was six days out of seven. I could only improve each time.

I wrapped the weight around the handle and marched back up the hill to the abbey proper, at peace with the world within me.

The blacksmith saw me coming that autumn, a Sister striding in slightly soiled Crimsons that would soon be washed and passed on. He waved me over to his forge. "I don't see you carrying any melons, Sister."

"You know what? In my excitement to see your masterpiece, I just didn't have time to get any."

He grunted his approval of my playing along, and then lumbered over to a mess of weapons. "Won't be needing a demonstration anyway." He kept his back turned. "Fool me for underestimating a Half." Of course he'd noticed my ears and height, but if he showed any fear at my age and what that meant, he hid it with professional curtness.

But…"What do you mean by that? Underestimating."

"We aren't that far from the training grounds, Sister. A curious fellow could easily watch the Brothers and Sisters prepare their bodies to wield his work. We tradesfolk are all quite curious by nature. When you do test this, know that at least one person will be admiring it."

He turned around and held his attempt at my chosen weapon out to me, one hand gripping the handle, the other cradling the chain near the head.

It was exactly as I'd imagined it. He'd met my requirements *and* added a few details I didn't bother to mention because I figured what I'd asked for was weird enough. The way he'd wrapped the leather. The colour of it. The length of the spikes. It was all too perfect. But had he somehow represented it from the dream, or did the dream represent what he'd made?

Either way, he'd done it.

"I still say it's not a flail." Despite his achievement, the smith remained disgruntled. "And I still wouldn't make one unless I knew the wielder wasn't going to brain themselves. Now that I've seen what you'll do with it, I am honoured to have been given the chance to create it. Whatever you decide to call it."

I reached out and copied the positions of his hands, and breathed out in wonder as he laid the weapon onto my waiting palms. "Gildenhammer. You've made the Gildenhammer."

"A Gildenhammer, surely, but 'The'? Better than ball-and-chain-thingy I suppose. And Mother forbid we call it The Gildenhammer Flail…So this thing takes my name. Always thought it'd be a sword, my legacy, but perhaps the world has enough of those."

"Wait, that's *your* name?"

"Ah, shit on a stick." He was taken aback and then annoyed at his own lack of manners. "We've only met a few times. 'Sister' and 'Smithy' did just fine for business. I just assumed you knew my name, and I know better than to ask a Sister hers…"

I took the weapon in my left hand and held out my right. "Easily rectified. I am Tzara-Min, Daughter of the Liquid Night, and it is my pleasure to have met you and received your work."

He blushed furiously, wiped his hands down on his apron, and met my offer with predictable firmness. "You are well met here, Tzara-Min of the Liquid Night. I am Harald Gildenhammer, Kas'Daen-verified Mastersmith and Forge head of Mothers Abbey." He shook my hand a few more times, and then pulled his away. "Even if it was not on purpose, I am glad my name will be associated with so memorable an invention."

"Oh, I'm sure someone else has made one somewhere." I was unable to comprehend what this tiny little 'coincidence' really meant, and just blurted out this the thoughtless dismissal of Master Gildenhammer's ingenuity. Then I realised I'd just been a callous shit again. "But none like this. Thank you. I take it payment has been—"

Another faux pas. He waved his hands in dismissal. "Not an issue. The Fourth Going Sisters and I have an agreement. But I do have something else here, made it on a whim, no great effort…" He pottered about the forge for a bit, and then came back with a…metal-studded glove? "I see you took my advice with the belt and leggings, but something else occurred to me. You may need to actually hold that ball at some point, and not even a Half could do that safely barehanded. I only guessed your size and can adjust for comfort but let's just try it first."

I hadn't thought of this at all because in the dream, I'd been wearing more than just a single gauntlet, and in practice the 'ball' had been just a block of wood. Harald's foresight likely saved my fingers many times after that day, but what really struck me at the time was that he'd made it for the correct hand, and that I knew just by looking at it that I was meant to wear it.

"I suspect it'll fit quite snugly." I shifted the Gildenhammer to my right hand to slip the left into the opening of the glove. My suspicions proved true. I turned my forearm a few times, flexing and clenching. "I…don't know what to say." Because I really didn't. Sometimes it's just true and you have to say it.

"Hrm…How about if anyone asks why it's called a Gildenhammer, you tell them my name."

"I will. I will regale them with tales of a legendary artisan toiling away in a secluded castle called Mothers Abbey, supplying the servants of God with the finest weapons in the world. And when they ask, I will say his name is Harald Gildenhammer, Mastersmith."

"Oh-ho, that would be grand. I may not deserve such praise, but I do feel the world might be a better place if people sung less about heroes and villains, and a little more about those who make their deeds possible with good old-fashioned hard work."

How like Jerich he was, and yet how like Jack too. And, I had to admit, not unlike the inspiring songstress 'The Chantal' that Mother…Vachaelle pretended to be. I dismissed a pang of longing I knew to be unjustified.

"Well then, I shall present both hammer and glove to the Office of Fourth Going for my graduation next week…in a few days after I've had a little play with them, should you be 'curious'. Thank you again, Harald."

"My pleasure."

I started to walk off, once again holding the Gildenhammer in both hands, with my well-gloved left close to that wickedspike head to keep it from swinging dangerously. Then I stopped. The day had one more jaw-slackening surprise for me.

"Mastersmith?"

"Sister?"

"What's this you've carved on the handle below the wrapping?"

"Oh, that." He laughed and rubbed his head. "I have no idea, but it looks right, don't you think?"

"It doesn't just look right. It *is* right. Thank you…again." I tucked the new weapon into its strap at my right side and ensured the head was bobbing against the moulded leather thighguard, naked fingers of my right hand still tracing the curved groove, the two intersecting trenches within it.

He might not have heard you say our name as Cass and I did, but somehow, the way it was written was slowly, unstoppably emerging back into a world that been made to forget it. How could I not see this as my final and irrefutable sign that it was time to rejoin that world too?

Almost needless to say, I spent quite a while in the training field the next few days. The heavy gauntlet provided a wonderful counterweight, and I no longer had to close my eyes to perform the patterns, which meant I did notice when I had an audience. Not always, but often. I imagine they were as curious about the weapon as its maker; I was just another Sister preparing for her Fourth Going. Most importantly, I was able to draw on a competence and skill that possibly never existed: that of Tzara-Min Jaydemyr, wielder of the Gildenhammer and one of the final survivors of…everything. I didn't have her memories beyond the ability to string together new training patterns, but I had more than enough conflicting memories clamouring for domination anyway. For as long as I was following the weapon's lead, 'who' I was didn't matter at all, and that was also just fine by me.

"I graduate to Fourth Going tomorrow, Aunty Sofiya."

"I'm well aware of this, Sister Tzara-Min. I have arranged for your provisions after all. That is what I do here. That and…everything else."

"I know, I just wanted to come up and…tell you."

"You'd be stunned by how many other Sisters about to go forth have done this. Sometimes I pretend to be as excited and overwhelmed and breathless as them, but these days…I'll still be here afterwards, doing what I can to make sure they don't go out there unprepared for what's ahead."

"Maybe you should be called Mother."

"Still your sacrilegious tongue, child. Here, if you're going to open that fool mouth of yours, at least put something good in it."

"…ACK! Is this…?"

"Now you *really* know why it's called *Ak-ravit*. Heheheh. I *know* you can't get drunk but if anything can challenge that knowledge it's *Akravit*. To call it booze is to call the sun 'warm and yellow'. *Akravit* loosens tongues, trades well anywhere, fuels fires, melts ice. Truly the light of life. Never freezes either."

"And it's almost potable."

"We would waste it were it any more so. Now, regarding that 'what's ahead' I mentioned, I usually give a word of advice for outgoing Sisters. Here's yours: don't."

"Don't…ugh, this stuff is vile…don't what?"

"Go. I know, it's the great dream to leave this stuffy old place behind, see the world, help others. I *have* been there, Tzara-Min. The problem is there's no place on the road for people like you or me. Your Sister Viera, on the other hand, will not lack for opportunity; people always need fire for something. And they need someone to fan their flames. And someone to make a place for them. And then someone else to heal the idiots when they get burned. But us? There is no shortage of water out there, not unless you go deep, deep into the East and few Sisters are welcome there. And winter is not far off; the last thing anyone needs when snow is everywhere is more ice."

"Aunty Sofiya, surely…surely that's just the *Akravit* talking."

"Witless child, I wouldn't tell you this *but* for the honesty the drink demands, so shut up and receive what I am offering. We are not, despite all that, useless. Hydrotheurges are unmatched in our domestic usefulness, and there is *no shame* in accepting that. We are not heroes but the people heroes need. When they are out hurting others in the name of this cause or that, we're here hurting no one. Helping many, in fact. There is *nothing* wrong with that. Not a damned thing…"

"And what if I do intend to go deep, deep into the East?"

"Then nothing I say can save you. You'll either die spraying your water at a Karakani's bent sword or, far more likely, spend the rest of your life taking care of it. Not even the Brothers of the Tantamon venture far into the desert. Have you not heard its names? Expanse of Ruins. The Abandonment. Certainly, a desert called 'Waterless Place' might seem to demand our Talent, but where we are of no use here in Kas'Daen, we are something worse there: a rare treasure to be claimed, kept, used. If you truly mean to trek there and, I assume, into Chūnko beyond, do *not* reveal your Talent to anyone better armed than you…and from what I've heard about your Fourth Going gift, that's everyone."

"The *Takhla*." I suddenly realised how thoroughly Sarah-Jade had squandered yet another of Mother's attempts at preparing me for what lay ahead.

"Indeed. There aren't many texts on the deserts in our library but it seems you've found one of them. I am impressed. At least you'll know the local name for your place of demise."

"I can't take all the credit." I fumbled for the thread of the conversation, too close to losing myself in conflicting strands of what-was-real. "Am I to assume anyone bearing a weapon on the road is a threat, Aunty?"

"Mostly, mostly. A few groups who have mastered life in the wastelands might aid you. There's a branch of…liberated Tantamon followers among the Karakani. You'll find them in the Faighana region for certain, but they roam the major roads and routes picking off bandits, protecting caravans, helping people as is their wont. Unsurprisingly, they tend to wear something lilac. And they'll be bald. Call themselves the Swords of Heaven. They may help you but don't expect them to like you: any love they had for Kas'Daen dried up long ago like a forsaken oasis. Or maybe it was always just a mirage."

"I read about them too. *Jenetchen Kulutchara*, in Kakanic."

"Glad to see that sharpness hasn't dulled after years of watery drudge."

I knew this too: the Jenetchen Kulutchara had an unknown quantity of chapterhouses in and around the lush Faighana Valley. The chapterhouses were autonomous but each had an authority called Father: a now-familiar operational structure. They held similar beliefs to the Kas'Daenne Brothers of the Tantamon but with a lesser emphasis on individual acts of benevolence and service, more on simply obeying the word of God in all things. They rarely actually cited the Twelve, considering them implicit in their teachings. I knew this and more and I could not let her know I knew because I shouldn't have.

"But what's an oasis? A mirage?" And yet right after asking, I realised I knew those words as well.

"You'll learn. Also, the Swords usually speak both Ziegerian-Common and Kas'Daenne, since they save a lot of idiots from the west. Not that I'm calling you an idiot, but wait yes I am."

"Anything else you can tell me about the places between, Aunty?"

"One last thing. As terrible as they might seem, both winter here and summer there are better than what lies south of the desert, where, so they say, the ground has erupted to gnaw at the clouds. Leave the Skyrend peaks to the goats and the birds."

"Well, I am neither goat nor bird." *Though I might yet be an eagle.* "Thank you, Aunty. For all of this wisdom. I will not waste any of it."

"I doubt that, but your belief otherwise might be enough. Now that you've gone and made me maudlin about my own roaming days, be off with you before I refill my glass, and you'll really regret that.

"Reminds me. Don't forget…this. From my personal stash. For emergencies only. I mean it. I don't bequeath my *Akravit* to any but fellow Waterbringers. The others, too likely to drink it when they're thirsty. I can think of no greater insult to the Light of Life than using it to slake one's thirst. Also it would kill them, and I don't want that on my conscience."

"Don't think it would kill me, Aunty."

"Let's not find out either way, Sister."

There was no final test for taking the beige and the grey and donning the simple red cape of the Fourth Going. You just started training as early as you could and when you turned twenty, well, here's your uniform and weapon off you go hope you were paying attention. And since everyone turns twenty at different times, there was obviously no grand ceremony either. Despite that, I was hoping that

Mother…Vachaelle might have found her way back to see me off. To see me ready, armed and complete. And I knew the moment I had that hope, that desire, I would not get what I wanted. But…yeah, I hoped.

Cass looked me over at the front entrance after I'd received (back) the Gildenhammer and the gauntlet from the Offices of the Fourth Going. She fussed over the sleeves of the shirt—

"I am not fussing. I am *adjusting*."

"I wish you could come with me."

"Sorry to say I have much more important things to do here than traipse about the countryside being a nuisance. Others may come. They'll need my guidance."

"Nothing yet then?"

"It's only been a handful of months, Tzara-Min. I am sure we are scattered all over Kas'Daen if not Kaef're. Do you have your knife?"

"Yes, Aunty Cass."

"Whetstone? Flint? Mug? Plate? Blanket?"

"Now you *are* fussing."

"Remember to draw your hood when passing people on the road."

"So that they know not to disturb me, yes."

"In fact, leave it up just to be safe."

"My ears aren't that ugly."

"…And the pendant?"

"Do you see it? No. Do you think I'd leave it here? No."

"You might see its like out there. Do not initiate contact with anyone displaying it. Let them obey the pull back to what was on their own. But if they do talk to you, mention Abbey's Village in central Kas'Daen and leave it at that."

"Yes, Cass."

"And you've said your goodbyes?"

"The only person left in my dorm I even know anymore is Lizaveta and she's too busy preparing for her Third Eye transfer. Vi's gone; Mother's gone. Time for me to be gone as well."

"Now if for some reason you cannot join your designated party in the village, come back here and—"

"I'm more likely to just take up with some Brothers, Cass. As long as they're headed east, I will go."

She nodded, looked around. "This weather. It reminds me of that day."

"And I won't forget that either. You'll see me again, Aunty Cass. When your calling and mine intersect. When my real mother and your spiritual one look in the same direction. That day will come."

"And on that day you will *not* call me Aunty, and I *will* call you My Lady. Odd how much I look forward to it."

In answer to this, I hugged her long and tight. Then I stepped back, and allowed her some final words. She just smiled as though her status as custodian of the abbey and mine as Sariana-Ra Jaydemyr were already in effect, and withdraw herself with a bow.

And that's how I left Mothers Abbey, which would later become known as the Rouge Eyrie, first stronghold of the Scarlet Sparrows under the command of Lady Cassandra, The Mindchanger.

All Around The Watchtower

"I was worried this place would be abandoned somehow. Then we'd have to just keep going I suppose, north and east and north until we reached even less likely sites of our resurgence. But no, look at that. Vizstrahtza Stronghold, almost miraculously restored after only a few months. Patrolled. Guarded. You say that wall wasn't there before? Those ramparts? I imagine they all went up fairly quickly after you left, if you faced the sorts of forces I suspect you did. Me? Eh, I was nowhere near any of it. Did a little cleaning up on the rear. Why yes, Brother, I do have some experience there, aren't you just clever. Right, let's go."

They approach under the false cover of night, impressed at how many of the guards notice them, and how many wave them on upon seeing his sword, her pendant. Less impressive is the meek but firm servant answering the main door at the base of the tower. He informs them that Lord Arius Hawkstorm, Protector of the Southern Realm, Great Champion of Vizstrahtza, Sworn Brother of the last true Primahriel et cetera, et cetera, is currently absent but will return in a day or two, and would the young sir and madam please follow him to these unfortunately meagre lodgings where they will be given the utmost care and respect until his return.

"Ooh, comfy. For an underground holding facility. Alright, Brother, what would you like to hear next? Looks like we've come this far just to have to wait a little longer."

2 days until the revelation

Chapter 14:
Violet Vacillation, Alabaster Abandon
2/874 to 8/875 A.R.

Tremble.

"If I make it any stronger, it'll burn the Ephin' place down."

"It's made of stone, you f-f-f-f-ckin'…Besides, you can barely keep the w-w-w-wood going, doubt you could even warm the bricks. Look at this poor Sister, catching her death all because you w-w-w-won't do your job."

I pulled the hood deeper over my face and leaned forward on my chair, as close to the hearth as comfortable. The two curious old men, each endowed with a half a head of greying hair and dressed like destitute pilgrims but huddled in thick lavender cloaks, continued to bicker in Ziegerian-Common over the fire. We were almost alone: the doorman was snoring at his station (which had but two objects: a lantern and an almost empty bottle), and the Havenkeeper came and went but mostly stayed in what I presumed was the kitchen. I saw no one else. Other than 'daytime' I had no idea what the time was. I'd take any company, and considered not one but two followers of the Tantamon very welcome indeed.

"Better in here than out there, Brothers." I forced my teeth to almost chatter. "How came you to this place? The followers of the Tantamon rarely find themselves so isolated."

The pyrotic next to me hacked out a cough, and his companion beside him clucked his tongue. "H-h-h-hear that, Volodyk? She called us 'Brothers'. How long has it been, eh? H-h-h-how long it has been."

The beset pyrotic tamed his ravaged bark with one last phlegmy rattle and swiped the back of his hand across his cracked lips. "How long indeed, Miro." He turned to me, and I withered a little at his intense glare under thick, vexed eyebrows. "Has the snow blinded you, Sister? See you not the state of our once-shaven pates?"

I remembered what Kendahl had told me, but had never assumed that *all* Brothers of the Tantamon sacrificed their hair. Or that they stopped being called 'Brother' even after somehow leaving the order. "My apologies, sirs. You wear the Tantamonian vestment, and I figured you hadn't stolen them."

"Only a fool would say no to a cloak in this weather, Sister. As for how we came here, same reason as you most likely. On our way somewhere, our way became impossible."

I held my naked right hand towards the fire, keeping the gauntleted left tucked beneath my own travelling cloak. "We are strangers, and I appreciate your reserve. I am Tzara-Min of the Liquid Night, abroad to assist those who need what little help I can offer." I paused, and then committed to a better truth; maybe they'd reciprocate? "I aim to head east, into the wastelands, and eventually through to Chūnko. "

The pyrotic nodded. "Volodymyr. And he's Miroslav."

"Well met." I nodded back.

They nodded back at my nodding.

And then there was silence.

"I'm sorry if I interrupted something." Their companionable nagging had at least filled the void of whistling wind and the occasional sound of limbs straining under the snowfall outside.

"Nothing of importance, Sister." Miroslav's stammer was suddenly quite gone. Volodymyr just stared into the flames.

"I'm glad to hear that."

And then there was more silence, and clearly I *had* interrupted something.

I tried to think about what to say to them. Naturally, that meant I was mostly dwelling on how the Eph I came to be here, and how much I was willing to tell them.

Two?...I think it was two months into My Grand Adventure and for probably the tenth time that day I wished I'd taken Aunty Sofiya's offer to stay where it was warm, dry, well-stocked, and warm. Two. The first was half waiting for the other Sisters to agree on which direction we'd go in, and half realising by then it was too cold to leave Abbey's Village. Wait, no, it must have been three, because the *next* month was us leaving anyway, forging through the unforeseen plummet in conditions from town to town, hamlet to homestead, helping those who needed it because that's what we did. As long as we stayed off the road we were perfectly adequate, cherished and welcome. A few healers, a few pyros, a geo and me. Of course Aunty Sofiya was right; I could run a bath or fill a cleaning tub, maybe prepare a nice soup in the kitchen, but without heat it was all just ice waiting to happen. Oh shit, you know what, it's more like *four* months, how could I forget those incredible two weeks where Sister Hylia caught cold, never a good thing for a healer to fall ill, and then Sister Gretzyn followed suit so there went our heating, and…look, you asked. I tried to tell you I was miserable and cold and lonely for months after leaving the abbey, but you wanted for examples, so there are a few for examples. I'm not going to go out of my way to make it interesting because it wasn't. I was angry and fed up and happily chose to sneak away the moment the snow cleared.

That afforded me two or three weeks of solitary travel, at a pace closer to Sariana-Ra Jaydemyr's tireless dash than Sarah-Jade's trudging through the muddy slush. I stopped only to eat and sleep, relying on the Fourth Going training for the former, and our accursed nature for the latter.

I agree, it is a strange word for what certainly seemed like a gift. I imagine were it not for that 'accursed' nature I'd have died several times over just from eating or drinking the wrong thing. From exposure. From exhaustion. I discovered, firsthand, why God abhors our kind and drives them into a self-destructive rage: we are otherwise unstoppable. No fear of the sun, no craving for *Vahm'esta*, a Talent, bodies that reject poison and illness, superior speed, strength, we can sleep for days and stay awake for weeks…the more I thought about it, the more I felt such a perfect combination of attributes would be less 'born' than 'made'. And then I thought about the fact that you and I *were not born Half,* but somehow became it…and, as I dashed from one plume of smoke to the next, I wondered just what our true mother and father had meant for us, and I kept circling back to that word: made. Made to be unstoppable.

But not, it seemed, immune to good old-fashioned loneliness.

Uh, of course I didn't. I went east, she went south, I assume. Although she hated being called a sheen (and rightfully so), Viera was a fully-fledged Sister of the Liquid Night *and* a daughter of Purashena. Though she never spoke of it, we both knew that her desire to join the Fourth Going was mostly to do with a Home Coming. So no, Brother. She's not going to conveniently turn up and 'justify her significance in earlier parts of the story' as you so heartlessly put it. She had her own life, and I was grateful enough that she'd shared it for a few years with mine.

Still, we do that thing, don't we? When lost, when alone. We conjure possibilities for our absent friends and loves, first as a happy what-if then as a bitter, envious conviction that they're doing much better than we are. We use the possibility of their success as a blanket to swaddle the reality of our failure. So of course I thought about her basking in the sun with her family, laughing at children running around and eating whatever delicious shit they ate down in Purashena. And of course I thought about Cass, poised in the abbey, waiting in her own office, fireplace ablaze with her impatience for others to come. But y'know, the fact that I didn't bring them up was sort of your clue that I didn't want to admit any of that, that maybe I was strong enough to endure solitary life as a competent Sister of the Fourth Going. Physically, definitely, but emotionally, definitely not, so as always thanks for reminding me of that.

The weather had turned shitty again and proved my delusions of superpotency wrong. Feeling sorry for myself and desperately missing Viera's heat, I'd been forced to house in a Haven, the few occupants of which were none-too-pleased to receive a solitary Sister who couldn't even heal. I imagine they'd have been even less happy to help me were I to lower my hood and expose what by then were my certainly less-than-manicured ears. I had enjoyed the perplexed look on the doorman's face as I handed over the Gildenhammer though.

And now I glanced over at that doorman, and the weapon I knew he was keeping safe behind that desk. The weapon I would wield in the Final Garden…if I ever made it out of this Ephin' snowstorm.

"You know what, fuck this weather. I've a bottle of *Akravit* I've been saving for a truly terrible day. Either of you care for a nip or two?"

Probably not the emergency Aunty Sofiya meant, but these two were the first Tantamonian followers I'd seen in weeks. Something had to give. Something had to be given.

"You're not blind, and neither are we…Half."
Fair enough; it's not always just about the ears.
"More for you then."
"The Sister makes a good point, Volodyk."
"…Eph me." Volodymyr reached for his pack as I reached for mine.

Not really, no; you don't make it to old age in an environment that hostile being a useless drunkard. There was no singing, no cheering, no slobbering, no stumbling and definitely no vomiting. Both of them sipped the precious spirit, respecting it for what it was: strong and in very limited supply. At some point the Havenkeeper even brought over some bread and took a small drink himself. No, I think it was just the nature of the offering itself that eased us into conversation…and kept me constantly in fear of it turning into an interrogation.

Which meant giving more than just a few fingers of *Akravit.*

Miroslav proved to be the more curious of the two. "What business has a Sister in the East, in Chūnko? Awfully long way to help deliver some babies. Tell us your story."

"Now that's very personal." I gave him a smile that was definitely not a no. "You two first. Where were you headed when the blizzard struck?"

Volodymyr raised the flames of the hearth with just a wiggle of his forefinger. I'd seen Viera do something similar, but she'd needed both hands. And she was skilled enough to attract a Sister of the Fourth Going. Or maybe…just hot enough. "Home. We'd been…sent away from our Chapterhouse, a few years ago now, and not for the first time. We are usually welcome to rest there, but not stay. On that, I will say no more."

Miroslav grumbled something while peering into his mug. Volodymyr must have heard and understood it, because he nodded, and then shook his head and patted Miroslav's hunched shoulder. Gave it a squeeze with his gnarled fingers. Something right, and something wrong.

"How far away is 'home'?"

"Miles and miles to the south and east. Roughly your intended direction, I'd say, if your intention includes traversing what the Karakani call *Ozon Yol*…" Volodymyr trailed off. Right. My turn.

"I do intend to take the 'Long Way', yes. I know no better route to Chūnko. I was hoping to travel into Faighana and seek the help of the

Jene…Zhenetch…" I sagged under the weight of my apparent inability to pronounce Jenetchen Kulutchara. "The Swords of Heaven."

"No need to travel that far to find them." Miroslav prompted Volodymyr's gentle admonishment at this but kept going. "No, Volodyk, there's no more hiding it… You're not the only one seeking to go east, Tzara-Min. Word has travelled down the Long Way that something terrible and extraordinary is happening in western Chūnko, even the wastelands between there and here. Havens, razed to the ground. Karavansarays and entire villages left smouldering, ruined. The Swords have cast aside old bitterness and come to us here. That is why we are heading home. A general assembly in the area of all who follow the Tantamon, to decide our course of action."

"Any idea who it might be?"

"Southern Dissidents, Karakani rebels, Roses, Halves…who knows?" Miroslav shrugged, and Volodymyr took a drink. "Most of the attacks might just be rumours, because there is a *lot* of distance between some of them. If you ask me, and you did, I'd say it's some foul machination of He Who Shines, Blessed Mother forfend. Some mad awakening. A call. The millennium approaches and with it the end."

They both Flailed themselves and I followed suit.

"You still haven't told us why *you* want to go into the wastelands and beyond, Sister Tzara-Min." Miro was a sharp old fart, that's for sure.

"Since I am coming with you after this weather clears, we'll have plenty of time to discuss it on the road." Plenty of time for me to make shit up, anyway.

"We have one horse." Volodymyr made one last attempt. "We take turns. Raskol doesn't like women."

I just waved it away. "I have two legs, and this woman doesn't like horses."

A few days later the weather did clear. A few days after that I'd told them some fragile version of the truth in which you were not a Clan heir in hiding but my distant cousin who once took the Long Way. Honestly I doubt they believed me but a Sister who is also Half is allowed her secrets, especially when she reveals her unerring ability to provide fresh water for drinking and cleaning. I'd decided by then they were not better armed than me – after my little trek at superhuman speed through most of western Kas'Daen, I was starting to wonder if anyone was. All that aside, those two old fellows had much more pressing matters on their mind.

This became very apparent a week or so later when we came to one last bridge over the Din river and beheld what the former Brothers called 'home'.

"Uh, this isn't a chapterhouse. This is a fucking city."

Sarah-Jade would have said 'cute little town', and Sariana remembered her childhood home as larger, but Tzara-Min was in charge and compared to Abbey's Village, this place was *immense.*

"Why we were eager to return from our exile." Volodymyr dismounted and urged the blackcoat tarpani Raskol off the bridge, toward the not-so-distant hub. "Welcome to Azak, Sister Tzara-Min. Stay close to us now. More than I've ever seen before. These desert lions hunger with their eyes, and more besides."

Above Azak's civic outline in the rising light of Bladesun, violet banners and flags quilted the persistently grey sky. On those banners, I saw all manner of heraldry: animals, weapons, and flowers denoting various factions I presumed. Before the town proper, ornate tents clustered about the northern outskirts through which we entered, defying the snow as surely as they defied the sands to the east. Brothers bustled about these tents, some as ruddy as those I'd seen in Abbey's Village, some closer to the hue of rich soil and everything between the two. It wasn't hard to spot the Jenetchen Kulutchara, not just because of their desert-tough skin but also, and I found this a little amusing, because they wore hides and furs precisely the way someone unaccustomed to a frigid climate would. Their curved blades made your beloved *Mifūntoh* look like a sewing needle, and I was delighted to see some of them carrying a rougher version of the Gildenhammer, with rope rather than chain and nasty looking bone heads instead of a spiked metal ball. As we passed their camps, some of them noticed us and took to quiet commentary. A few even laughed outright. But none of them fastened me with the sort of lustful look Volodymyr had proposed. If anything, both he and Miroslav received the bulk of the unpleasant leering, and I remembered Aunty Sofiya's words. No love lost between these very divergent followers of the Tantamon.

"Should have shaved our heads anyway." Miroslav's breath visibly carried the querulous sentiment.

Ah, so that was the reason for the Swords' animosity. Not only because my companions were Kas'Daen Tantamon, but also because they weren't anymore.

"Commander Vadim would confine us to our old cells, Miro. Until the truth grew back. Now is a very bad time."

I picked up on something there. "Commander? Not 'Father'?"

"Commander. As I said: Very. Bad. Time."

It must have been the bitter cold that drove the two of them to be so quarrelsome a week ago. Since then, they'd been much more harmonious, and it was obvious they'd learned to communicate with an intimacy born of years of close if not outright isolated company. Volodymyr had headed off my curiosity on that front immediately and I sought not to push their hospitality. Not when I'd all but forced my way into it.

Not when I'd decided it was time to say goodbye to it.

I waited until we'd entered the permanent town, with the Kakanic encampment behind us and the grandeur of a Kas'Daen-funded Tantamonian fortress above us. It seemed both Sisters of the Liquid Night and the Brothers of Tantamon had a penchant for nesting on hills. I had absolutely no desire to get caught in this one. If they were preparing to investigate what I took to be the first haphazard blows struck against the Overclan by those who now Knew Your Name, that seemed very likely given my obvious status as a Sister of the Fourth Going and a Half. The Karakani might view me as a treasure to be won, but I'd take that over a Kas'Daenne Tantamon 'commander' deciding I was worth the risk, a very bad weapon to be wielded in very bad times.

"I have imposed on you both greatly." I slowed my pace and then killed it altogether. Raskol just kept plodding along, and Volodymyr had to tug the reins to change his mind. Or try to. "But we are here now. You have solemn business with your brothers – no, it's the right word, Volodymyr. They've recalled you, so I think they at least see you as brothers still. At any rate, I said no lie when I said I mean to head into the wastelands, towards the Faighana and the Long Way. And eventually Chūnko. Our paths thus split, Brothers."

They both stood there, slightly hunched over with age and trepidation, starkly aware of how much they stood out...but not as much as me.

"She just went the same way as us, Volodyk. We cannot stop here."

"True, Miro. Our way remains that way."

I nodded. They nodded. Raskol probably daydreamed about kicking me in the chest.

"Farewell then."

"May The Holy She see you safely through the deadlands, so that you find your…cousin." Volodymyr Flailed and Miroslav bowed his head before following suit.

"*Vahm en*." I mirrored the benediction, and off they went.

I strolled back towards the northern part of Azak, the serendipity of these circumstances supporting the easy gait. Until that very morning I had been certain that finding any Jenetchen Kulutchara outside of their home realm the *Takhla* of Karakan would be very difficult. And normally, that was probably true; I was fully prepared to just keep racing east from Azak, following any guidance from fellow travellers and locals towards towns along the Long Way. But during 'very bad times', it seemed even a secretive sect rumoured to rarely leave its paradisiacal enclave in any great number obeyed an imperative to present a significant show of force. Rather than struggling to make contact with them, I was actually struggling to decide with which of them I would engage.

I then stopped at one of the larger tents with a handful of men loitering about its entrance. Rather, it stopped me. The black flag snapping above the lilac pavilion bore two images that by themselves would have been negligible but together cried out for my attention: a red crescent moon, and a white sword within its curve, blade piercing the lower part of the arc.

That settled that.

As I approached, I noticed something even more interesting about the Jenetchen Kulutchara than their excess of furs. Just as the Karakani themselves hailed from the foreboding wastelands between Kas'Daen and Chūnko, their armour was a functional mismatch of leather, chain and lamellar. A few wore all three, looking like knights who'd nailed small rectangular metal plates to the chain covering their chest and belly. Some wore steel caps similar to that of their Kas'Daenne brethren, others more ornate, conical helms I'd seen way back when we'd visited Kaifeng and you named me Tzara-Min. Similarly their weapons: 'whatever works' is the shortest description I can give you there. I realised that where Aunty Sofiya and likely anyone enjoying the shelter of Kas'Daen-*desne* saw the *Takhla* as a place of death and abandonment, the Jenetchen Kulutchara had harnessed it.

And there I was, a lone Sister in her red hood and winter-thick beiges and greys, just traipsing up to a group of them like a neighbour about to ask for a cup of milk and maybe chat about the weather.

Almost as though I'd forgotten all about the flail in its strap at my side and the way some of them had eyed it before.

"Mother's Blessing to you, Brother." I approached a broad-shouldered young guard standing next to the loose flaps of the tent's entrance. I hoped I'd managed something close enough to Kakanic – as I said before, Sarah-Jade hadn't been the most studious of girls. I also curled a Flail, which probably lost some of its peaceful intent due to the gauntlet that made even a wave a suggestion of war.

"Greetings." His reply was in only slightly accented Ziegerian-Common. I imagined he was roughly the age Kendahl and Huysman would be, maybe even a little younger. The stubble on his scalp and face mocked the idea of razors. He was only slightly more armoured than me, a mail shirt over his black robe, and of course his thick doublet was some shade of violet. He kept his left hand on the pommel of his longsword, a weapon that wouldn't have looked out of place behind Churna in the All-Trades. The other performed roughly a third of a Flail, little more than a swipe of sweat from his smooth brow. "What business has a Sister of the Liquid Night with the Swords of Heaven?"

I smiled at his casual attempt at asserting a position of superior knowledge, uncertain if he had succeeded or not. "My name is Tzara-Min, Sister of the Fourth Going, originally from Kas'Daen. Might I have your name, Brother?"

"You might, Tzara-Min of Kas'Daen, if you answer my question. You are many, many miles from home."

I let the smile drop. No time for idle chit-chat then. "And I plan to travel many, many more. I seek passage across the Takhla, via the Long Way. I meant to enter the Faighana for aid but, thanks be to She Who Loves, those I sought have met me halfway."

"Halfway." It was almost a question. "It took us five months to get here directly from the Faighana, and Azak, Sister, is over halfway to Kas'Daen from the Faighana. The *Ozon Yol* is a commitment for we who know it well…For those who do not?" He clucked his tongue.

Fuck this smug bastard. I removed my hood, and didn't have to peel back hair I'd kept short ever since training to go forth. "I can travel quite fast."

He gawked at my ears, right before I hid them again. Aunty Sofiya had cautioned against revealing my Talent, but the fact that I was innately cursed and to be reviled, that was mine to disclose, or fail to hide, as had been the case with Volodymyr and Miroslav.

"What I can't do is travel alone for long. Too much time spent in solitude, I start to talk to myself. I get…weird thoughts. Go a little crazy, you might say."

This time the Flail he curled was with the correct hand, and much more complete. He recited a familiar creed in Kakanic. "We assist. We do not ask. Even of those doomed by blood."

"You find bone before blood." Even though he'd just wasted my time trampling the Eleventh. I was in no mood to pretend he was getting away with using a different language to speak truths he'd rather I not understand. "Now may I have your name or shall I wait here for someone more important?"

"Wait here." He ducked into the tent.

"Don't mind him." I glanced over and saw an older man, bald but with a slightly grey beard down to his chest, warming himself at a brazier. Unlike the guard, he was well kitted out for battle; his slouched form made the various layers of leather, metal and pelt look as comfortable as smallclothes. His Ziegerian-Common was more thickly accented than the young guard's, but somehow easier for me to understand. "Djuneht is on guard duty for too much drinking last night. Now he's bored and hungover. Punished and punished again. Unfortunately for you, it has not left him in the best of moods."

"I admire his adherence to duty. Judging by the state of his skull and jaw, I suspect he has not been a Brother for long."

"He has not. And say *kulutch,* or Sword." Same word, different tongues. Strange how exotic one sounded, while the other just sounded lazy and uncreative. "An understandable mistake, but you did not make Djuneht any happier by calling him Brother. Twice. In two languages."

"I will apologise upon his return. Might I know *your* name, Sword?"

"Ehvran." He studied me for a reaction. When I just nodded, he returned his deepset eyes to his hands and the fire they were trying not to touch. "And I say now, little mishap with young Djuneht aside, you are having a fortunate day. Most Swords are here to…work with the

Brothers of the Tantamon. Us, maybe not. And if we leave, you will give a reason to be with us. We are a fighting group far from home, not a caravan of traders and tourists, shuffling over the sands."

I almost gave that reason, or something akin to it, when I paused and realised that he meant not my 'reason' but *a* reason for them taking me along. "If you leave, I will give you a reason to include me."

I saw the fabric of the curtain rustle right before I beheld a man less a 'Sword' in the sturdy but compact Kakanic sense and more a 'Twohander' from Teriss-Luniir. Well, swords did come in all forms, and fool me for forgetting it. He was aged rather than old, a little older than Ehrvan but with a fuller, thicker beard, and wore nothing more than a loose-fitting russet tunic cinched with a fine lavender belt. Sarah-Jade recognised these after a moment: a woolen kaftan, and a silk sash. I felt something hot emanating from him, and for a brief panicked spell thought it was raw masculine lust. Volodymyr and Miroslav had been right. These lions were famished…

Then he beckoned me over to another brazier to the right of the tent and brought it to life with a casual lift of his swarthy fingers. Oh.

I did not see Djuneht exit the tent as I followed this two-legged tower's gesture. I did see Ehvran make himself scarce, however.

"I am Iskendahrl." He stood over his crackling creation as it wavered between us. "*Kuluf* of the Pallid Harriers." *Kuluf.* Sheath. Swords. Uh…don't overthink that one, Sarah. "Tell me, Sister Tzara-Min of the Liquid Night, Halfbreed of Kas'Daen, who seeks the Long Way and beyond. What use are you to us?"

It was more curious than rude or dismissive, but somehow he made even a haughty snot like Djuneht seem courteous.

"What are the needs of your company?"

"Fulfilled."

"And their wants?"

"Unfulfilled, and they shall remain so, Mother willing."

"I can cook."

"We can all cook, Sister Tzara-Min. Better than most and with less."

"I can clean."

He just rolled his eyes.

"Very well. I can *fight*."

"Everyone says that when they are your age. But a Half entering adulthood? Hearing you say you know when *not* to fight would please my ears more."

"I will not turn. I promise you that, Lord Iskendahrl."

"Commander. Or just *kuluf*." He looked at me. "I *have* dealt with your kind before."

"I *know* I will not turn, so I don't think you have."

He sniffed into a frown, his eyes tracking the dancing flames once more. "It is a strange thing, the madness of mongrels. It does not come as a storm. You will not simply lose your reason or become a beast. No, it is more like a siege. One day you will feel everyone is your enemy. Every look your way will seek weakness in your walls; every question will be a rock against them. Feeling becomes knowing. And your only response will be to desire more power. First you will ask, and then you will take. But you will be unable to hold it, because you will be too busy reaching for more. It is surprisingly easy to kill someone whose hands forget that weapons are tools, not treasure."

Weapons. Swords. Moon. *Ephin' Shyn, Sarah, why didn't you open with that?*

"So if I do turn, you will have no trouble dispatching me?" I had to figure out how to veer the conversation away from me and back to them. Them, and that flag.

"If you do?" He snorted a laugh that turned into a throat-clearing. He still did not spit. "Sister-Half, I am saying you possibly already have."

Nope. No subtle way of doing this. "How long have you been *kuluf* of the Pallid Harriers?"

The man raised an eyebrow, but then looked almost relieved to be given a chance to discuss something a little more familiar and safe. "I have been *kuluf* and *kulutch* most of my life." He was back to that odd morosity undercutting what might have been a proud declaration. I started to ask again, aiming to emphasise the latter part of the question, when he raised his hand in placation. "You've either a keen eye or a quick tongue to know to ask this. We *are* new. Not even a year ago I formed the Pallid Harriers. This does not speak to our collective experience as Swords."

"And the design on the flag? Yours?"

"Mine."

"You saw it in a dream, didn't you? A vision?"

He recoiled a whole step. "Maliscience..." Then he recovered, assumed an entirely pointless stance of defiance. "I've nothing to hide, Liquid Eye."

Liquid Night. Third Eye. Interesting contraction. Also, nothing to hide? Huge lie. "Why did you choose the name Pallid Harriers?"

"I…like birds?"

I…tried not to laugh at his helplessness. "Do you remember what you were before you were *kuluf* or *kulutch*?"

"A child. A boy. Happy. I was happy." I exulted in how smoothly he was breaking, but then he rallied. "I was ignorant and weak too. Powerless to stop what happened. No longer. And no more. Sister, I have no need for a Maliscient prying into my company. Nor just another fighter. And absolutely not a bloodmongrel. Give your reason or leave us in peace…please."

It was tempting, yes. Show him the pendant, see if I could really pick through his place in Vachaelle's tapestry. Had he been some frontier guardsman for us? A Peddler? Or had Jaydemyr held dominion over some of the Swords of Heaven? But then I considered the risk: what if he had been an enemy? Surely the Mindwarp's plan had included them. There was every chance he'd dreamed our name not in allegiance but in opposition, and taken the device simply because he'd known it was important.

Sorry, Aunty Sofiya. Again.

I held my right hand out towards his fire and pushed until it hissed, sizzled and steamed, and then died. "When I said I can cook and clean, I meant I can do both alone."

Please don't have a hydro already, please don't have a hydro already…

His shoulders slumped. "Balance is the curse that keeps on giving."

"Kashensan?" I shook a few droplets from my fingers.

"Could have been. True whoever said it. So you are not a Maliscient. How did you know then?"

"Accept my reason and I will tell you when we part ways in Khovokand."

"You need not make such conditions, waterwitch. I accept your reason. You will…cook and clean if you wish. Provide as the company needs. You will *not* assist any of my Swords in the fulfillment of their desires, and they may try despite my orders. I trust a Half who says she can fight will have no issue dissuading them without doing serious harm."

"Only two people have confused me for someone eager to honour the Seventh, and they both died in truly horrible ways. Be sure to include this in your warning to them. I would not want to have to become a permanent member of the Harriers because I somehow reduced your ranks."

I saw that he believed me, because he still believed he'd 'dealt with our kind before'. Thank Eph. Thank Shyn'. Thank Her. "We will convey you to Khovokand. Our duties as *kulutchara* are above all else. If we are called elsewhere, we will see you safely to a karavansaray of the Long Way and then we will be gone."

"And what if the company becomes too accustomed to a regular water supply in the wastelands?" See, Aunty Sofiya, I was listening.

"Do not overestimate your value, Sister-Half. A few months for your Talent is worth the risk of your volatile presence. But no longer than that."

It wasn't worth trying to convince him again that I was anything but volatile, and if it kept him and his away from me, all the better. "May I set up camp here?"

"I'll have you in my tent tonight before we leave tomorrow. I sleep very light." He still looked as though he really wanted to spit but was holding himself back. "Tomorrow we leave and no later. These Brothers, I tell you. Villages burn, bandits assault caravans, and now word of rogue Halves openly attacking karavansarays and Havens. And they cower in their comfortable Respite, arguing over a single word in the Twelve for days." Here the *kuluf* sighed, and it robbed him of much of his gruffness. "But as they do, we assist. We aid. We help…even *Kutsahl Melyaz*." And then, finally, he did spit, his mouth having reached its limit for distasteful things, and strode back into his command tent. A heroic effort of restraint until that point nonetheless. A minute later, Djuneht returned to his post, looking a little chastised.

Kutsahl Melyaz. 'Holy Mongrel'. It seemed a contradiction, but what is balance if not the delicate resolution of contradiction?

The Pallid Harriers were a decent sized company, maybe thirty members. Most were travel-hardy; Djuneht was younger, stronger, and faster, but still clearly their runt. Let's say Ehvran, flexible in his beliefs but unswerving in his devotion, was as good an example of a *kulutch* as any. They only had a few riding horses for the scouts, so we travelled by foot and cart. But they knew these roads and the frequent pockets of safety found on them, and with me in their number we didn't have to stop for water. White melted into green, and green gave way to ochre.

Certainly 'things happened', but nothing so dramatic that they can't be dismissed as 'things'. But go on, ask. I'll give you two questions, then we have to proceed past the rest of my trek on the Long Way. I made it to Kaifeng, after all, and I've no doubt that's what you'll want to hear about most. Two. Ask.

First, Dog-Ears. Yes, to my surprise. Better than you or I, that's for sure. Iskendahrl hadn't been merely bragging on that point. We ate well, even on the road. And at Havens and later karavansarays, much better. If this was the 'wasteland' Aunty Sofiya so dreaded, I believed she'd made too much of stories meant to scare the foolhardy milkskins of Kas'Daen away. I'll give you that one for free: Eph no it wasn't. There's a reason Faighana is considered the last bastion of safety before tackling the *Takhla*.

And second. No, Char Ah-Ran. *Kuluf* Iskendahrl must have really drilled it into them that the waterwitch Half was not for their 'desires'. But even if one of them had tried, do you honestly think I'd tell you?

Really? One more? Okay, that's only fair, Brother. And that was actually a good question, the answer to which I learned the first time we happened upon some bandits posing as toll collectors – lucrative if the road is peopled by traders and stragglers. Big problem if a party of Jenetchen Kulutchara march your way. With a swiftness that spoke to his experience, Iskendahrl drew his weapon, a plain old scimitar, and used the sheath to direct just how his Swords would set about encouraging the bandits to seek other means of employment.

Again, if I did learn there *were* other meanings to his title, I have no desire to share them with you.

And here, something you didn't ask but should have: yes, the *kuluf* did remember my promise, about revealing to him how I knew the source of his flag's design, and no, I did not tell him the truth. A few months is nowhere near long enough to learn if someone can be trusted with a secret of that magnitude. No, I lied and said I too had seen it in a dream, but passed it off as it being a sign that I should seek *his* usage of it. This appealed to the man's ego, of course, and made our parting that little bit sweeter.

Would that I had a map here and now, so that I could just draw you a nice set of lines connecting the dots, charting my travel on the *Ozon*

Yol[1]. Would that we had much more time so that I could regale you with the wonders of Khovokand in the outer reaches of the Faighana valley, which is where the Pallid Harriers left me per our agreement. I knew better than to ask to go with them deeper into their valley where the Jenetchen Kulutchara kept their own secrets. Towers and spires of a style I'd never seen before and would never see again, wrought for the glory of some civilisation likely mentioned in the *AkraVahm* but now long gone. Khovokand is a hub through which the Long Way threaded, bringing all manner of people – but not a single Sister other than me. Going by Aunty Sofiya's opinion of this part of the world, I wasn't that surprised, and the simplicity of the hood, the travelling clothes, meant that I drew no attention. And the food. Blessed Mother, I had never eaten better and I haven't since. Giant melons sweeter than any Kas'Daenne berry. Flat bread laced with garlic and some sort of heavy butter. Noodles spiced with all manner of curry and aromatic pastes. Khovokand was a haven of its own that summer and I stayed there until the weather eased into autumn and the caravans resumed. I simply had to seek one out that needed a hydrotheurge and off I went, left alone but for when someone wanted a drink or help with the usual domestic duties. I was able to keep the Gildenhammer concealed on my camel. It was slow, barren and mostly dull. But unlike the first part of this journey, I wasn't angry or frustrated. I could have moved a lot quicker, but only alone, and I'd take the plodding pace of shared introspective silence between each karavansaray and then listening to banter and gossip, idle talk of future and past, at each waystation, over lonely expedience anyday. And I did, for many, many days.

36 hours to the revelation

---

[1] See "Appendix: The Known Timeline of the Siblings Jaydemyr" for details of Sariana's journey to the East.

Her Dream

Vizstrahtza (Jaydemyr Stronghold)
Lowmoon
9/882 A.R.

"The night before I was due to leave Zheng City, last stop on the Imperial Highway only a few dozen miles west of Kaifeng, I was having trouble getting to sleep.

"They say The Long Way is not a place for dreams or restlessness; when it was time to sleep, to regain energy and stamina, the body just took over and stayed as still as possible for as long as possible. It wasn't uncommon for a caravan guide to have to wake we less-accustomed travellers and even then some people resisted. But ever since crossing the Jade Gate and entering the much more developed final stretch of the *Ozon Yol* of western Chūnko, I'd become increasingly tense and wary. I put it down to the proximity of my brother's last known location, but it could easily have been the fact that the days on the road here were nowhere near as intense or exhausting. Probably both. Might have even been that Chūnko was so populated, getting a room to one's self in any given dosshouse was an unusual treat.

"So was it a dream? I don't know. When you lie in the darkness and go into your thoughts deep enough, deep enough to block out the snoring, farting and occasional crying, there's no great difference between imagination, rumination, recollection, and dream. Lucidity retreats to the last illuminated corner of your mind and puts out the light. What remains is unrestrained negative space, and an instinctual yearning for definition. So you fill it, starting with shapes, sounds, concepts, ideas. In that or any order, or all at once. No, that's not right either. *You* don't fill it, because that would require conscious thought. It just fills, empties, fills. Or so I assume, because the only dream I could and can remember other than what happened that night, well, they were yours. Didn't I deserve one as well?

"Fine. It was a memory. But one so fragmented, so divorced from continuity, and yet so committed to chasing its own narrative logic, it bore almost no value as a memory. But I have to tell you anyway, because had I not had whatever it was, a lot of what came after wouldn't have.

"Bet you're really wishing you had those Mindwarp and Dreamsong powers about now, huh? Me too.

"Running. Familiar place to start, familiar place to end. But this feels like a middle – we've already been running, and we'll continue running. Through hallways, around corners, down stairways. She's holding my hand, pulling me along. I know this is strange because I'm the strong, fast one and she's just a servant. Still, she leads and I follow because she's taller and older and because Father said to. Not tonight. Long ago. If anyone comes to my room dressed like her, he said, I am to go with them. Do as I am told. Do not eat them. Not even a little bite. Are they going to inherit the world, Father? I hope so, he said. Them, or those like them. I used to disobey Father but not when he was Serious. And not afterwards.

"We're near the exit of the house now. One of the exits. House, keep, mansion, castle. How big does a house have to be before it's not a house anymore, Charan? How small does it have to be to be a home? You ask the weirdest questions, Sister. Charan. Hey, where's my brother? Someone else is taking care of him, Lady Sariana. Who? Please just keep up here, Lady Sariana. Where is Mother? We will see her later. Then what about Fath—No, wait, Sari, don't ask that. Father's dead. Gone. Not coming back, never. Are we going to die?

"The masked woman stops then, and so do I. I can hear people yelling, but not understand the words. That is strange. I speak all the languages I've ever learned. The woman bends down a little. I am fourteen so she isn't that much taller than me. My brother is only eleven no not twelve next month eleven, and he is taller than me. A bit. That's not fair. She is too but she's older so that's fair. She puts her hands on my shoulders, which she's not supposed to do but do as you are told means letting her do what she wants I think. Lady Sariana, listen to me. I listen to her, staring up into her eyes, trying to decide if they are brown or blue or yellow. You are not going to die. Not here, not like this. Do you understand? I nod. Do you believe me? I nod again. Browuellow? Yelluen? Has to be a word for it. Good, now we have to keep going.

"We leave the building and it's darker out here. People are running around. Some of them are on fire. Some of them get flung by some invisible wind off into the night. A lot of them are hitting each other. I want to see more but the masked woman who is not going to let me die keeps me behind her as we creep along the walls. If we keep this up it will take far too long to reach the gates. I ask her if that's what we are doing, but she just shakes her head and stays between me and everything else. There is snow everywhere. It's pretty. White and red and pink. Aunty Vachaelle showed me flowers like that once. Blossoms, she said. Also pretty.

"There is a small building ahead. A guardhouse. Another person dressed like this woman appears from inside it, or behind it, and says in here. In we go, and wait. Not long. Then we are out of the building. Don't dally, Chrysanthemum, he says. We have minutes at most. I never dally, Nikalay, the woman replies. I disagree because we are definitely dallying as they waste time saying not to waste time. Humans are stupid. I don't say any of this because Father would not have liked it. Let my brother say the things Father didn't like.

"They embrace and we move closer to the gateway. If someone comes close the masked woman, Chrysanthemum that is a type of flower like a blossom, she waves her hands and whoever is close is sent away, pulled into the darkness and the snow and the wind. Aerian. What my brother would call a kazeht sky. I think he means *kaze tsukai* but everyone knows his Mifūn-go is better than mine. Chrysanthemum is a kaze tsukai, an Aerian, Sturmmacht, a Feng-sha, and a powerful one. She flicks the violent shades away from us, and we keep running.

"We are close to the gates now. But so are others, humans and Halves and Fey. Around us. We have you, Talon, one of them says. Talons are Uncle Arius' servants. Give up the child, Peddler, says another. Peddlers are…were Father's servants. Is she both? I do not know. All I know is she is clearing a path through the people and to the gates. We run through both, and are then in the outer courtyard of what used to be my home.

"It is clearer here, but not empty. Chrysanthemum stops, pulls me aside again. I can smell something wrong with her. Wrong, and right. I open my mouth, no, my mouth opens itself. She puts her arm near it. Drink. No, I must not. Father said no. Sariana, drink. No. Father said. I don't care. Do as you are told. Oh. I see. I drink, a little. Enough. Chrysanthemum grunts but I say to her it's okay, I won't take any more. Good. Then she pulls out a small vial and fills it with her blood. *Vahm'esta.* If I need it. I nod. If.

"Then she asks a weird question, as weird as any of mine. Do I have the pendant? The one Father gave me before he…before? Yes. I do. I show her. She says good, now hide it. Do not lose it. No matter what. Okay.

"We start running again, and now I am less of a burden. Now she is not leading me. We run together. This is good because someone is closing the outer gates. They are large and heavy with twisted metal, black bars. I have never seen these gates closed and I do not want to see what happens afterwards. I say to Chrysanthemum as we move, now we must really run fast, can you do that? It will be like flying. She says yes, lets go of my hand and we prepare to run. To fly.

"I run, straight through the slow, slow gap between the gates. Nothing could be easier. I laugh and squeal at the chance to stretch my legs, push my body, show the world my brother is not the only one who can fly. I dance and spin in the snow, light and untouchable.

"Then I see Chrysanthemum pressed against the gates. They are closed. She is behind them. Oh. Humans can't really run fast. They can't really fly. Even powerful ones like her, who saved me because I did as I was told.

"I scream her name for absolutely no reason I can understand. Screaming won't open the gates. Screaming won't put her on the other side of those gates. Screaming won't stop all those other people from pushing her against the gates. But still I scream as they flatten her face into the bars, and then overcome her entirely.

"For fucks sake stop that Sariana. I stop it, look at who is speaking although I know. Aunty Chaelle stands there, wrapped in furs and anger as so often she is. But Chrysanthemum Aunty Challe we have to go back she saved me and now. And now we have to keep going because you my dear girl are not saved yet. Go back and you will die just like her. A waste, don't you think? Something in me drops the act then, and call her every name I can think of, every disgusting word and blasphemous curse, but all she does is laugh to herself and drag me away from the gates, from the mob, the fire and the walls falling down, from Chrysanthemum. Even with the *vahm'esta* flowing through me, I can't fight her. I go from screeching to wailing, to mumbling, to just whispering. Always her name, never forget it. Chrysanthemum. Talon. Even when Chaelle begins to sing. Talon. Even as I begin to fall asleep. Chrysanthemum.

"Even as I begin to wake up."

"I lay there the rest of that night, caught in that space between sleep and waking, into and out of which we cannot deliberately go but now and then do slip.

"The next morning, before completing a journey that had taken at least a year, possibly many of my years, I sought a florist's stall on the way out of the city.

"I pointed to a flower and asked the old lady working the stall what it was called, in what was certainly awful Chūnko-go.

"She said it was Fah. Flower.

"I swallowed my frustration and tried again, saying what I hoped was 'this flower. This one right here'.

"She told me, and it was the first word in Chūnko-go I made sure I said perfectly right, because I planned to use it as much as possible.

"*Gukh-Fah*. Chrysanthemum."

III. Talon Gukh-Fah / Sarivashes-ra Kas'Daen

Kaifeng / Kas'Daen-desne

876 - 882 A.R.

Chapter 15: The Proud Mare
9-11/875 A.R.

"Welcome to the House of Happy's Departure."

I lowered the lantern, relinquished the Gildenhammer to the elderly Doorwoman, who handled it as though the spiked head might suddenly bite her, and made for the service bar.

The place was real. Eph me, but Chantal hadn't been lying.

I'd seen the sign above the door, of course. The white-hand-red-blood mark of any Haven, and the name of this one. Written in both Chūnko-go and the language of we who travel, Common (the further east I went, the more frequently its origin was left out). But in the latter, it had read as something else, similar but not quite right: House of Joyful Leave-Taking. A coincidence, I was sure, even as I entered the multi-floor complex maybe ten miles east of Zheng City. There was only one road going that way, and it was conveniently named the Zhengkai Way. So there was, really, no chance of me missing the establishment. Something Vachaelle would have known.

But there seemed to be nothing special about the place otherwise. Sarah-Jade Falkenstrom had already lived in one of the world's largest Havens, and whoever I was now (Talon, I reminded myself, Talon Gukh-Fah) had stayed in dozens of lavish karavansarays and roadstops since. The only thing I really noticed was it looked…recent. You can tell when a Haven has a history; it's soaked into the timber, the furniture. The smell of it is everywhere. This Haven had none of that. It felt more like a stage. Certainly, it was Aftersun and the moon that night would have been half at most: two reasons why any Haven would be quiet. But this wasn't just quiet. This was tranquil…Sterile.

I headed for the bar and looked at the young man slurping noodles behind it. No Havenkeeper he. Maybe late teens. I wondered if he were like Levi, but pushed that one down deep. Very deep. "Who's Happy?"

"What?" He was seemingly vexed that this Kasudenjin loudmouth had interrupted his lunch. He wiped some broth from his lips. "You want something?" His Common wasn't quite as good as the Doorlady's, which told me quite a bit.

"Name of Haven. Who Happy?" This time in Chūnko-go.

He made an 'ahh' sound, threw about five sentences at me in about as many seconds and went back to his noodles. I caught a few words but none that made much sense without context.

From my time on the Long Way, where Common was good enough but rarely used fluently, I knew not to lose my patience, or to raise my voice, or speak…very…slowly…those were not how one bridged linguistic or cultural differences. I also knew not to try to continue this in his tongue, because no one takes someone who talks like a toddler seriously. "Water please?"

Odd asking for that, given my Talent, but another thing I'd learned: sometimes it can be handy to ask for something you can get for yourself if it means giving someone else the chance to provide it.

"Water, okay one moment." He drained the bowl with a mighty gulp and set it aside, then placed a porcelain teacup on the bar and filled it from a jug. For all his sloppy eating, he didn't spill a drop.

"Thank you." I took a courteous sip, maintaining eye contact to make sure he wouldn't slip away. "This Haven is called 'Happy's Departure'. Who is Happy?"

He scratched his stubbled cheek, shrugged. "Someone who left?"

Well, Chantal, as usual you really didn't make this easy.

"Think I'll do the same. Thanks for the water."

"Unh."

I left the water unfinished, and went to retrieve my weapon. The Doorwoman was trying not to laugh. "The Zheng Guard kick Ngaiyeun out few months ago." She thunked the Gildenhammer on the desk. "Boy's been real shit head since. Useless."

"How did he get kicked out out of the Zheng City Guard?"

"Be useless shit head."

I secured my weapon, but wasn't done with her. Not after how unwilling the boy had been to talk. "Are you his mother?"

The wizened crone frowned. "What, you think Chūnkojin all look the same? All related? Keep it in family?"

As if people up and down the Long Way didn't play *this* game all the time. "No, Poh-Poh, I just thought only a mother could sound so proud."

"Ha. Hahahaha." Without even a trace of mirth.

This place was fucking *weird.* "Hahahaha."

"Ngo his aunt. Ngaiyeun mother died in fire. God took wrong one."

"What fire?"

"Go outside. Cross road. Walk around a bit. Find stone. Read it."

And now I knew why this Haven felt so new. It *was.* "One moment. You might know. Who is the 'Happy' in the name of this Haven?"

"Go…Outside…Cross…Road…Walk—"

"I understand." No need to be polite now. "Your Common is good. Get a lot of travellers between here and Kaifeng?"

"Oh, you not coming from Kaifeng? Not leaving?" She both avoided my question and forced me to ask another. Canny old twig.

"Why would I be leaving Kaifeng?"

"You come from west, see people like you going back where you came from, didn't ask them why?"

Eph me, could you stop doing that!?

"Their business was theirs."

She clucked in dismay. "Okay, I help you one time, then you go read about what happened, then good luck with shittown Kaifeng. What you say?"

"Thank you." Because that's what you say.

"Getting into Kaifeng easy. Guards too busy watching other way. Ever since the fire and the big fight, Kaifeng's problem is Kaifeng. Getting out also easy, if Kaifeng has no use for you. And Kaifeng has use for people like you."

'People like you'. The same term again, but very different meaning. "Maybe people like me have a use for Kaifeng."

"See who get used up first then."

"You're…not the most friendly of Havenkeepers." It was entirely obvious that's who she was by that point. Quiet day like that, no reason for the Havenkeeper not to play gatekeeper as well.

"Zhang was most friendly, not very good it did him. Safe travel."

I knew better than to ask who, or to linger. I hefted my pack and left her there to her cryptic evasion and her useless shit head nephew.

I should have noticed it before, but I guess that's why the new Haven was so imposing and impressive: it was a distraction as much as an attraction. Across the road, I walked around a bit in the desolate clearing. A traveller could easily mistake the area for an abandoned or planned construction site, until said traveller realised the stone path leading up to a small roped-off area was leading not to an unfinished future but an unmade one. Within the seal was a single stone marker, maybe waist-high, and quite long. It had to be, to convey the following information in Chūnko-go, Mifūn-go, and Common. I do not presume the last one received the best translation possible. I crouched down and read the blood-coloured engraving.

The Joyful Goodbyes Fire

Late 4th Month, Year 873 AR (4/873), the Haven at this site, The House of Joyful Goodbyes, met with devastating misfortune. A catastrophic inferno engulfed the building, leaving nothing but ashes. There were no survivors. 356 souls returned to God.

The Zhang family had operated the House for over a century. Its final Keeper, Zhang You-Mi, served for 38 years. He would have been succeeded by his grand-daughter Zhang Ping-War had she not also been tragically taken.

The cause remains unknown, although some believe it to be the act by the murderous fugitive 'The Scourge of Kaifeng', a rogue Halfbreed Blood Peddler also known as Chah Ah-Rahn.

The Zhengkai Massacre

A week before the fire, a bloody conflict between members of the Bleeding Darkness gang and the Blood Peddlers of the Spiteful Hand chapter happened on the Zhengkai Way. It is believed that The Scourge was the only survivor of the Zhengkai Massacre and took refuge at the House of Joyful Goodbyes. He then burned the Haven to the ground and fled into the west.

The Joyful Goodbyes Fire is considered the first disaster of the ongoing strife within our blessed city Kaifeng.

The Mother God's Will Be Done. *Vahm En.*

It then proceeded to list known victims, and I'm quite certain neither the death toll nor the details were particularly verifiable.

Okay, Charan, *stop that.* I know what 'Ping-war' means. I know a lot that you still do not, and if you keep interrupting with your helpful 'comments' and 'corrections' it will stay that way.

Thank you.

"Chah Ah-Rahn. The Scourge of Kaifeng. Eph me. The stupid little shit went and burned down the one place you told me to go, Vachaelle. I *told* you I'd be too late." I straightened my legs. "Now what do I do?"

I took another glance behind me, at the new and improved House of Happy's Departure (why couldn't anyone decide on a single translation of that one?), and decided to stay the course down Zhengkai Way. I'd been pushing east all this time. How far I had come. Only a few more hours and I could stop, at least for a while.

I could have done it quicker, but eh, it was nice weather and honestly I wasn't sure if I were in a rush to enter a city so deeply affected by my brother's singular derangement, even if I knew I had no choice.

Now that, Sarah-Jade Falkenstrom of Teristra, is a fucking city.

I stopped and stared at the magnificent western outer wall of Kaifeng maybe a mile away, over a near-still river and beyond the sporadic bursts of foot traffic. How far I had come…and yet how far I had left to go. The Long Way had been true to its name, but there had been a sort of compression of time in the routine of hopping one caravan to the next, stopping when necessary, waiting until I could undertake the next step. Now that I beheld the magnitude of my brother's last absolutely known location, the behemothic capital of Chūnko, I realised I could spend years in there. Eph that; people spent their entire lives probably not setting foot in every street or even suburb behind that imposing bulwark.

I knew you weren't in there. Even if the memorial plaque had somehow been wrong. Vachaelle had swooped in, awakened you and swept you away, off on some turbulent serpentine path of havoc and ruin wending west. Maybe north. Back to Vizstrahtza, and maybe even Kazan.

No, I don't suppose you would remember. She didn't want you to, and it hardly matters now. You usurped the system, regardless of the order of each act of rebellion. But as you likely figured out by how quickly they replaced the Haven you destroyed, that system was not going to go down without a fight. Surely you know by now it wasn't you alone, that others who heard your name or saw the crux et luna were drawn to acts of sedition and disruption, but yes, I think you can claim credit for the state in which I found Kaifeng. Strange, given how much you loved the place when we visited it in that life before. Then again, not so strange, given how often you used to break your toys.

Time to see how you broke this one…or if it broke you.

I took up pace behind a wagon full of hay, wondering if I should try to hide inside it or something. It's the sort of thing Princess Jade would have done. But if the old woman had been telling the truth, then that wouldn't be necessary. I decided to wait until we were closer, and of course by then it was too late.

The guards, four of them, asked a few questions of the driver, then waved the cart through. I secured the hood over my ears and stepped forward.

"Gentlemen." I lowered my voice an octave or two and opened with Common. Couldn't hurt to try.

They stopped a good ten feet from me, such that their halberds could mince me well before I could so much as twitch. "Business in Kaifeng, Half?"

I was sure, after a year or so on the Long Way, I'd look like some quirky mix of sunbaked Kakanic skin and snowfrosted Kas'Daenne hair, were it not for our…biological particulars. On some days near the end there, I peered down at the flesh of my arms and swore it had developed at least some sort of gentle tan, and not remained that damning paleness I tried so hard to conceal. Clearly not the case.

I spread my hands to show that while I was armed, I had no intention of wielding said armaments. "My name is Talon Gukh-Fah. I am a Sister of the Liquid Night, sent forth to assist the Havens of Chūnko with childbirth and any other duties."

The guard who spoke raised an eyebrow under his fur-lined conical helm. "Gukh-Fah? Hm. Sister. Papers? Proof?"

"The red hood and uniform aren't enough?"

"Anyone get those. Easy pretend. You Kasudenjin. You Half."

"Are either not allowed in the city?" Because this sort of challenge is exactly what you should do when a bunch of guards who barely understand you are starting to see you as a problem.

"No welcome, maybe allowed. Two choices. Submit to inspection, or find other city with Havens to help."

Yeah, thanks for the one time help, old woman. Real lifesaver.
"I have to enter, so I submit to inspection."
"Follow. We have held line long enough."
I glanced backwards, saw a merchant with a wooden box slung over his back, smiling with about half a mouthful of teeth, and what was probably his young daughter doing the same.

I tried to apologise to them in hesitant Chūnko-go, but they just kept on smiling. A few of the guards moved in to harass them, while the rest marched me towards the gates.

I wasn't even in yet, and I knew: there was something desperately wrong with this city.

'Submit to inspection' was one way of putting it. Probably a more accurate one would be 'held indefinitely while we figure out whether we need to dispose of you or not'. Because there was no actual inspection; there was just the short tramp through the open gate, into a much more practical doorway on the left halfway under the wall, a number of poorly-lit corridors, corners, a few more doors…and then we were back out in the open.

At last I was in the city. And I had about ten seconds to take any of it in before they led me into a stark stone building with a *lot* more guards about inside. No one bothered to ask my name, nor did anyone ask to see papers that the two escorting me knew I did not have. All around me, people talked with almost grating volume in Chūnko-go, quite unlike the hushed politesse I remembered from my last time here. Of course, the situation had been considerably different, and I had to wonder just how unrealistic that whole visit had been. Was this the real Chūnko? In my conceit, I'd just trotted up to the gate and expected them to just let me in. Hadn't everywhere else? Well, no. The Brothers at Azak would have kept me well away from the inner councils, tucked me in some civil but segregated corner of the city. The Jenetchen Kulutchara had made clear I wasn't getting into their sacred valley. At least a few cities along the Long Way had set up their karavansarays outside their walls. Why had I expected Kaifeng to be any different?

Because, I figured as the Guard confiscated the Gildenhammer and its gauntlet, Vachaelle had told me the place's name and connected it to my brother. It was almost explicit: 'you will go there to see him', or, probably more accurately, 'go after him'. It seemed ridiculous that someone as blatantly potent as she would set me on such a path without lining that path with signs and guidance, if one had but eyes to see them. And so far, so good. But this? Disarmed and in custody in a city where I barely spoke enough of the local language to apologise for not speaking enough of the local language. An obvious threat with no real assurance that I wouldn't go berserk any day. And no proof of who I really was, or who I *really* was, beyond a symbol that by virtue of its enigmatic resurgence could just as easily get me tortured as liberated.

More marching. More corridors. Stairs down.

Rooms with bars for walls. All empty.

Well, not anymore.

"In."

Surely they knew a Half could overpower them, dash past their paltry checkpoints and be free...without even needing to use her Talent. Surely *I* knew that, so why did I let that shove usher me into the cell?

Because, curse the Mother, Ephriem, Shynsa and anyone else I wasn't supposed to curse...I still had faith that this is where I was meant to be. I was in *Kaifeng*, after years of waiting, preparing, travelling. The city in which my petulant, insufferable brother, who cared more for a sword than anything, than other people, than his own family, somehow became a mass murderer, sparking long-running civil unrest, and then just disappeared. Vachaelle was with him, I was sure. Which meant that there was more to the story than she'd ever tell me. Than my brother likely even knew himself. That is why I was there.

"Stay here." Fellow had a real touch for pointless statements. "Someone will come to talk to you."

"Soon, I hope." But he was already walking away.

Still, I had to say it. To prepare myself for the likelihood that it wouldn't be soon at all.

Prison in Kaifeng wasn't that bad if you could make water to wash away the mud you made. The food was passable at first. Some days I received a whole bowl of rice, pork, and vegetables. Stringy shoots and cabbage mostly. I could turn that into several servings of gruel, a dish to which I'd grown accustomed on the Long Way, albeit one that loses most of its appeal with nothing added to it. The meat, once or twice a week.

Other prisoners came and went over the days, and then weeks. I figured out that rather than being some sort of long-term holding facility, this was a guardhouse serving as an intermediary between either more permanent prisons elsewhere or an execution ground. The inmates all kept to themselves, possibly aware that bad behaviour would do them no favours in avoiding either. And of course once they realised what I was, they kept away, as though the solid iron bars were not protection enough from a crazed Half. Perhaps they weren't.

The guards, who mostly stayed upstairs, ignored me entirely other than to deliver food and take away the bowl.

Did I mention the cell had a working Hole? I was impressed. And at each end of the hallway, incense burned with a pleasant enough fragrance in small alcoves. I'd paid for dirtier, stinkier rooms both in Kas'Daen and on the Long Way through Karakan.

And there was a waterroom around the corner, which I was allowed to use once every few days after that first month. Soap. It had *soap*. And a heated bath.

And a bed. They provided clean sheets and a blanket every week.

Other than the Gildenhammer and the gauntlet, they'd let me keep my pack. Even the knife.

The most distinct change in that second month: the meals went from meat, vegies and rice to noodles and dumplings. Three times a day. Some sort of tea. Rice buns. Sweet cakes.

What sort of prison does any of that?

One that isn't a prison at all.

I was incarcerated, yes, but I wasn't being punished. I was simply being made to wait. And whoever was going to come deal with me, they wanted me healthy and clean.

So yes, okay. What I said before about prison in Kaifeng being not that bad? Probably not a claim I can make in good faith, considering all that. In fact, once I realised I was not a typical prisoner, my entire perspective shifted from 'this isn't bad for a prison' to 'if this is just for holding, I dread to think what they do to real criminals'.

That was when I decided to abuse that other quirk of our nature, and just slept for days, sinking into that leaden time-skipping torpor where not even Vachaelle's dreams dared to tread.

"Talon Gukh-Fah."

I was awake, sitting on the bed facing the hallway, head down, forearms on thighs, fingers clasped. I watched my hair sway with each measured breath. I had no idea as to the time, other than by whatever passage my pulse marked, in which case it was somewhere between Eatingmoon and Poopingsun.

"Sister of the Liquid Night. Talon Gukh-Fah."

Her Common was clear but clipped, as if each word were a dead growth being pruned or a patch of mould being sliced off a hunk of bread. Her pronunciation of my chosen Chūnko-go name, so smooth and nuanced, clarified the effort she was making.

I pushed my hair back with both hands, as though just coming out of a bath, and straightened up. The pendant had somehow fallen into view, but she was too far away to see its details. I tucked it away nonetheless.

I regarded the woman fully. She was, at first glance, very average. Average height, build, disposition. Even her hair, that almost-black all but universal in Chūnko, denied scrutiny in its shoulder-length simplicity, the straight-cut fringe. Ovaline face. No visible attempts at make-up. Her light red coat, lapels left loose, didn't try to conceal the loose-sleeved reddish-gold dress underneath. She kept her hands at her side, fingers slightly curled.

And yet there was something familiar about her, for all these immemorable features. An air of resolution. Of enfolding. Confidence and comfort. I decided to take the risk, because were I wrong, well, my circumstances couldn't really be made too much worse.

"That is me, and you are Pai Hei-Wah, the healer."

Her single step backwards brought me more pleasure than anything had in months, and her little gasp was just all sorts of sprinkled sugar on top of the happymuffin upon which my pride was gorging itself. I was cheating but they'd kept me waiting long enough. And besides, I had my sign now. Couldn't have been more noticeable even had the woman turned up waving a crux et luna banner. I *had* made the right move.

"…Where did you hear that name?"

Wait. That wasn't her actual name? Then…oh Shyn'.

It was *his* name for her.

"Would you believe my brother taught it to me?"

She crossed her arms loosely, clenched so hard her jaw muscles stiffened, and for good measure shook her head a few times. "Did he send you? Did *she*?"

Nope. This was not going well at all. If I didn't want to spend another few months in here if not somewhere far worse, I needed to course-correct. Immediately.

"No. Look, I want to tell you the truth but it's very hard to believe. Can I just ask you: is your name actually Pai Hei-Wah?"

"Is your name actually Talon Gukh-Fah?"

"No."

"Then same. Pai Hei-Wah was…work. A job. Duty? Me, not me. Did he tell you about other flowers?"

"Like I said, it's very hard to believe. But if you knew my brother, then maybe you have already experienced things very hard to believe. I've the time, but do you? It's a long story."

She lingered on this, although whether because it was difficult for her to understand what I'd said in Common or just plain difficult to understand I could not tell.

Then she turned, waved over the guard lingering at the bottom of the stairs to her right. "Sister Talon Gukh-Fah, you have been accepted into care of the Helping Hands. Follow me. Don't forget your stuff."

"I will take those."

I figure she said something like this to the guards in Chūnko-go on the way out, keeping the Gildenhammer in one hand, the gauntlet in the other. I suppose I should have just been thankful she hadn't bound my hands or somesuch.

"If you wear the glove on your left hand, you can carry the spiked ball safely." I hadn't learned a word of Chūnko-go since arriving, so Common it was.

I was more than a little surprised when she actually did it; she'd struck me as the sort not to take advice from potentially crazy halfbreeds. You know, the smart sort. "Thank you, that helps."

"You're welcome…"

"Keep hood on, head down."

I had no intentions of doing otherwise anyway, but it was…nice to get confirmation: I was still not welcome here.

She led me out of the guardhouse with no fuss and no effort. There were fewer guards about than when I came here. One or two I recognised as those who had tended to my basic needs but they too avoided eye contact. Couldn't fault them for that.

The sunlight was not as piercing as I'd anticipated; the sky loomed grey and thin and a chilly wind prickled my cheeks. Time wasn't the only thing kept in stasis in the holding cells beneath the guardhouse; it had always been quite warm. Hardy though I was and am, the abrupt change pecked at my skin and bowed my back.

I took in the architecture and general hubbub of what I felt to be mid-afternoon business as I followed her through the streets. Well, you lived there for years so I won't waste time describing it all, but since I've also seen far more cities than you, I can point out that Kaifeng had an unusually high number of walls dividing its areas. And people on top of said walls. With crossbows. I don't imagine you'd be climbing those in a hurry. Or at all.

"Here, take." We'd turned a few corners and reached what I took to be the continuation of the Zhengkai east-west road through the southern half of the city. She seemed a little more relaxed here. "You may need."

I accepted both weapon and gauntlet with equal measures of gratitude and wariness. Why would I need a weapon like the Gildenhammer in a well-guarded city? Surely I had been wrong in my first impressions. Kaifeng was bustling with people, bantering and bartering and eating and chatting. The old Havenkeeper's warning was probably what she told all the stupid gweiloh in the area.

Then I remembered feeling precisely this sort of relief on Sarah-Jade's last night in Teristra. Unwarranted and naïve. Pathetic and hopeful. Dangerously blasé.

"I suppose you didn't want the guards back there to see you letting me have it back?" I kept to the same level of hush. Stood to reason not to go chattering in Common in a city that had, by all appearances, expelled most if not all of its Western foreigners.

"Yes, would look bad. Looks bad enough now."

We soon crossed a small bridge over a canal. By this point the foot traffic had diminished significantly. We still weren't alone, but we could probably speak in Common at a normal volume and not draw strange looks. A large tower above even the walls caught my eye to the left, presumably in the north-easternmost part of the city. Not a tower so much as stacked floors, at least six of them. Kaifeng didn't seem to have many distinct landmarks, but that one alone could tell a person where they were anywhere within the walls just by its location and visibility.

But for the most part I did as she told me to do: kept my hood on and my head down.

"We are entering Munnamdun. Remember this. If you ever get lost, Munnamdun is home."

"Okay." I saw absolutely no difference between these areas. Namdun meant 'south-east'. But... "Mun...Door? 'Opening'?"

"Gate."

Ah. Handy word indeed if this city really was on the precipice of unrest. "What should I call you?"

"Leelee. Hei-Wah, in Common. Leelee Flower."

"You mean Lily?" I berated myself for what I was sure sounded like a condescending correction. Let the woman pronounce her name any way she wishes, Sarah-Jade. Seriously.

"Yes. Lill. Lee." She frowned, and tried it again with a surprising smile. "Lily. I like the sound. Ah. Flowers very important in Kaifeng. You know this I think, Talon. Gukh-Fah."

"I only picked this name because...it belonged to a friend. Chrysanthemum. Gukhfah. Or so I was told in Zheng City."

"Close enough." Lily shrugged, and led us down a side street to the left. The walls here were less pronounced, but I'd seen that had we continued further down that road, we'd have hit another city exit. Another massive obstruction between Kaifeng and everywhere else. "So you did not know that gukhfah is flower most famous in Kaifeng?"

"I really didn't."

Here she glanced at me, as though my expression might tell her the truth my words had not. I didn't even need to try to look ignorant. Lily then switched to Chūnko-go, her tone rising and falling around what seemed to be a statement of awe or reverence. She even Flailed herself afterwards. "Sorry. Can't say that for you. It's okay. You will learn to understand."

"I plan to." Yet again I lamented Sarah-Jade's wasted education. There had been *at least* a year of Chūnko-go lessons in her very tailored experience at Parelle Girls. Could Vachaelle...or Mother not have made her more studious? Or were there limits to the personality manipulation of Dreamsong and Mindwarp? If so, I genuinely had no one to blame but myself for who I'd been, even if it hadn't really been me. Because it had always really been me. Ugh.

"We are here. Gentle Bouquet House. Munnamdun. See? Helping Hands."

I looked up at the sign as she climbed the few stone steps towards the double sliding doors into the standalone structure. I couldn't read the Chūnko-go (I would learn to understand) but the icon either side of the characters was at once recognisable and, to my knowledge, completely unprecedented. A black hand cupped downwards, a drop of blood falling from it; a white hand cupped upwards, a drop of blood falling into it. The blood went from blue to red, with a small but clear band of purple in the middle.

This was neither Haven nor Blood Peddler Chapterhouse, and it was both. This was a resolution of contradictions not even God Herself would tolerate. This wasn't balance…This was *blasphemy*. Beautiful, brilliant blasphemy.

"Come. Inside. We will drink tea and talk. Much to learn."

An Other Way Of Looking At It

"I remember what I said when I first saw that building. All that it represented. When it was just one hand, very much the wrong one. I said, 'I am so, so, *so* fucked.'"

"I felt something similar, Brother, but less 'I' than a more general 'this'. I imagine when it's 'I' you absolutely don't want to know what happens next, but when it's 'this' a sort of gruesome curiosity prevails. You feel safe by detachment, observation. It's a lie, of course, but a meager sense of agency granted by affected distance from the fuckedness is better than none at all."

30 hours until the revelation

Chapter 16: The Jealous Mongrel
11/875 A.R.

"Stay close."

The main hall of the Gentle Bouquet in Munnamdun was almost completely lacking shadow. Large octagonal windows on three sides drew light from outside in, with no shutters to ever block it; small lanterns occupied every table; and overhead, larger paper-enclosed globes hung rosy and bright. I'd seen from the entrance that the building had two or three floors, but in a style reminiscent of the All-Trades Inn, the ground floor of the hall extending at least two stories high. Most of the tables had people, eating, drinking, chatting. Workers came and went through doorless passageways into that fourth wall to roughly the west, opposite the entrance. Lily steered her way through the throng, towards a set of stairs to the right of the only wall lacking windows. We climbed a handful of steps, hit a landing, turned left and finished the ascent to a mezzanine that Sarah-Jade found both familiar and disturbing. Was this design a standard of Havens in major cities or had Vachaelle somehow modelled the All-Trades Inn of Sarah-Jade's childhood around this place? How many times had she been here, moving her pieces and turning them in the desired direction? Surely not that many; it had taken me a good year to get here and she'd been around most of—

"We sit here." Lily eased me into a corner table that looked like it would seat a small party. I placed the Gildenhammer on the floor and slid onto the wooden bench while she took a chair opposite me. "Tea will come."

"Lily…What *is* this place? It's not a Haven. It's not a Blood Peddlers Chapterhouse."

"It is Tsahn-ten." She smoothed her dress a little too self-consciously. "Food hall. Buy food. Drink. Talk."

"So a tavern." I just kept looking around. "What is that written on the walls?" More accurately, painted on yellowed paper stuck to the walls.

She didn't need to follow my gaze. "Food. Dishes. People choose which."

"You don't just eat whatever the kitchen has made?"

She rested her hands on the dark stained wooden table, left forefinger tapping with either impatience or nervousness. "Kitchen makes food, yes."

I just nodded, piecing it together for myself. *Like* a tavern, but somehow so efficient and popular it didn't just serve whatever the kitchen had ready. It made dishes as people requested. I could find no word in Common for this, nor in Kas'Daenne, Kakanic or even Jaydemyrian, so tsahn-ten it was. Gentle Bouquet tsanden.

I tempered my eagerness. If Lily's Common were any indication, I was going to have to learn a lot more Chūnko-go before I could ask the right questions. So we sat there, awkward but amicable.

Not long passed before a serving girl brought the tea and some sweet cakes on a tray. She was probably twelve or thirteen, sharp features, stiff jaw and eyes made for accusation and judgment. Lily helped her set the tea and snacks but, as the girl went to leave, grabbed her sleeve and seemed to chastise her in very quick, very unhappy Chūnko-go. The girl's expression remained fixed somewhere between fury and indignation as she replied just as swiftly. She glanced back at me once or twice, and then just glared at Lily. After an irate twitch of her lips, the healer released the girl, who scampered off.

"Tea for you." As though nothing had happened, Lily placed one of the cups on my side of the table and filled it. "Cake too. Try. It's good."

I forced myself to return to the banality of this afternoon repast rather than track the girl's departure. "Thank you, Lily." I sipped the tea. Similar to what I'd received in the guardhouse, only a bit sweeter and richer. "What is this tea?"

"Gukhfahcha." She took a sip of her own before placing one of the seed-topped cakes onto a small plate and pushing it my way. "Flower tea. Like?"

"Mm it *is* good." And since she seemed determined to keep this polite and civil before explaining what the Eph was going on, I tried the cake too. A little crumbly. Some sort of sweet paste in the middle. The black seeds on top popped between my teeth. "Yum. How do I say 'good food' in Chūnko-go?" Might as well get started.

"Hoh sek. Hoh is good. Sek is food. Meal. If very good, hoh hoh sek. Easy."

Phrases *would* be easy, but the lack of connecting words meant that anything more complex would be relying on tone and context. Not something I'd expect to be easy to learn. For the love of Shyn's Pendulous Tits, Sarah-Jade, try to remember *something* from back then. It wasn't all Tiamat and Lucille and Abby shenanigans, was it? Surely you picked up some basic grammar. "The tea is…also very good."

Lily actually clapped her hands together and nodded.

Alright, did trying this in Chūnko-go mean I'd earned the chance to stop wasting time here? "Who was girl?"

Lily reached for her cup, took another sip as her expression retreated from the joyful moment. "Siusiudoh. Siu. Siu. Doh. You understand this word?"

"Small small sword?" Damn it, Sarah-Jade, why did you have to be so Ephin' indifferent to what really mattered?

"Close. It means knife. Swords are made to cut people, hurt them. Knives? They cut food. Paper. Bandages. The knife is better than any sword, and a little knife is the best of all."

Yep. Shit. Another name from that first dream. Littleknife.   "I understand, thank you. Why…why she look…" No. Too important that I get the right answer. Back to Common. "Why did she look at me like she wanted to kill me?"

"Oh no, don't think she want kill you, Talon Gukh-Fah." Lily shook her head, misunderstanding but still giving an answer that worked. "She just hates clothes. Your clothes. Red." Then another Chūnko-go word as she gestured at my head, and I didn't need her to translate that. I'd just learned the word for 'hood'. "And your hair."

"My…oh." I hadn't really thought about it for a long time, and now it was long enough to be braided or pulled back in a tail. "I suppose I should get it cut."

"Not that, but yes." Lily laughed again. She did that a lot, and somehow it had yet to bother me. "I mean colour. Yellow." Another another new word that no doubt would prove significant: 'blonde'.

How could I have forgotten so obvious an indication of my outsider status? There were the mangled ears, and the curdled skin colour, but those were abnormal, more than just 'outsider'. Normal people distinguish one another almost immediately by their hair. "So blonde hair, red hood. She has met a Sister?" And because it was a title in Common: "A Sister of the Liquid Night?"

"She has. At Haven. Sisters not that rare before." Lily then taught me the title in Chūnko-go. A simple and straight translation.

"When was the last one?"

She shook her head, reverted to Chūnko-go. "That's not my story. It's hers. When she is ready. Only then."

"When I ready. When my Chūnko-go better."

"You will learn. But her Common is quite excellent." Here she switched again, employing her own Common not for my benefit but for hers, and very likely Littleknife's. It then occurred to me I was fluent in a language that could function as code in a city where surveillance in Chūnko-go seemed…Common. And even in this somewhat secretive language, she lowered her voice. "She worked at Haven outside Kaifeng. Before it burned down. Many deaths. Very sad. Her death saddest."

"I must talk to her."

"Later. Have other questions?"

Finally.

"Is Common good?" Contrary to this, I clung to the Chūnko-go. "Questions very secret. Danger." Even though more and more of the language was tumbling into my awareness, I was struggling.

"Yes, you are right. Speaking in Common is good."

"Did you rescue me?"

"Rescue, help?"

"Yeah."

"Talon, there was a big…fight over you. Guards wanted you. Imperial members wanted you. Bloody Shadows. Everyone. We had to use many things to get you. Sent good food. You liked?"

"Very much. Hoh hoh sek. So you saved me. Why?"

"Sister from Kasuden who is Half try to enter Kaifeng. Now, when Kasuden people all left city. My husband heard about this, wanted to know more. We are sorry not…rescue you sooner. Very sorry."

"Helped me in the end. That's enough for me. Does your husband work here too? At this…eating hall?"

"He is coming here soon. Ask him this."

A different serving girl came then and arranged a few dishes onto the table. Took away the empty cake plate. Placed a bowl of rice in front of us both. She left Lily with chopsticks, me with a spoon and fork. Unlike Littleknife, she showed only passing interest in me, which I found very comforting. Then she left.

"These look very good." I heaped some of the vibrant green vegetables onto my bowl. Probably should have eaten some of the rice first to make that 'into' the bowl, but eh, I *was* hungry. "Is this one…sheepmeat?"

"Lamb. And yes. And this one is chicken. It is quite spicy." I wasn't sure about that last word, but the bright red slivers and little yellow seeds told me everything I needed to know. Chili was the fiery heart of Long Way cuisine. Interesting in small amounts, toxic beyond that. Or so my body's reaction told me when I'd popped a whole pod into my mouth early into my journey. No coughing, no vomiting, no hilarious sputtering. Just a curious sensation of anti-flavour for a few seconds and then an urge to spit it out. "The chicken is a favourite of mine."

She picked at both dishes, using the sticks with enviable deftness. Too hungry to try now, but later, I would learn. "Did this place use to be a Haven?"

"No." She finished chewing. "Was Peddler place."

Had to be one of the two. "You were a Peddler?"

"No…and yes. I worked at Haven nearby, but Haven worked with Peddlers. I ask question now. Truthful answer please. You are Char Ah-Ran's sister? Different hair, different much. Same skin. But you knew his name for me. Name I gave him for me."

"I am absolutely *truthfully* his sister. He did not send me though. I had dreams about him. With him in them. And you. And Littleknife. And…others. Are they here too? La-Ahn? Tou Fah? Ishida Kocho? Chang Tong-Kut?"

Her eyes went wide then. Of course they did; who'd believe dreams could be so rooted in reality? Someone who'd dealt with Vachaelle, that's who. I didn't even have to ask. "You come a long way to find him. But he is gone."

"I came *the* Long Way. It took a year. I knew he'd be gone though. Vachaelle took him away, didn't she?"

"Fa Shai-Yeh, yes. Said she was his sister. Never believed it. She was a Sister. I knew that. I thought she was here for Peddlers. For Menu."

"What's a menu?"

Lily paused, ate some more. Chewed as though trying to break her thoughts down into bite-sized pieces. "Sisters send list of people to Peddlers. People who need to be taken away. That is Menu."

And that's how I learned what the Third Eye really did, halfway across the world from where I'd spent years living among them. I'm sure there are dumber people in Kaef're but at that moment, I couldn't conceive of it. "And the people I asked about? Those names."

"They are all dead, Talon Gukh-Fah. Your brother kill them."

The Zhengkai Massacre. So this was the Spiteful Hand chapterhouse once. Now run by a group called Helping Hands. Oh, that made sense. Haven and Peddlerhouse. Why would they merge? Because they'd lost their strongest members? And the Menu? Did Chantal stop sending them out the moment she reconnected with Charan? Surely Mothers Abbey was not the only site of Third Eye operations. Then again, maybe it was so sensitive that's all they did. That and…very special Deliveries. Halves delivered, then delivered to Peddlerhouses. Not all Peddlers were Half. Not even many. So they were the elite. Normal people dealt with Weeds, who were on the Menu. Halves led small parties into more dangerous situations. And sometimes those situations turned very messy. If, say, the leader had his moment, his turn. And then turned on friends and foe alike. And anyone who survived could flee to a Haven, and likely expect special treatment. Havens. Peddlerhouses. Sisters. Distinct but related.

Was this truly all Vachaelle's doing? Something about this triumvirate structure felt off; finding balance in duality was divine, but the rigidity of a triangle? So little room for flexibility, for manipulation. No, this was someone else's idea. She was just using it…and poorly, it seemed. Or breaking it, very well.

"I am sorry, Talon Gukh-Fah. This very upsetting talk." Lily misread my silent contemplation for something much more natural, something I couldn't quite feign because I wasn't anywhere near ready to integrate it into my reasoning. Ignore the three factions for now then. Focus on who was killed, and why. Or rather, why they were no longer alive despite the prophetic nature of the dream. Did Charan kill them to *disprove* the prophecy? Or was that dream 'true' at the time of dreaming but never confirmed beyond that? I needed to master this city's language because no amount of internal rumination could get me closer to the truth…

"It is okay, Lily. Were they your friends?"

They'd be to-the-death allies in the dream, but that had been when Charan was twelve. When he'd barely met them…which confirmed that Vachaelle had indeed imposed it. She'd wanted him to feel a connection to these people before he even had a chance to make one of his own. *Oh, my poor brother, you never stood a chance to become anything but hers.*

"They were Pai Hei-Wah's friends. We work together. People at Benevolent Hand healed them. Malevolent Hand Peddlers brought us people to heal. I tried to warn them that Char would turn."

Ah, Malevolent Hand. Not Spiteful. I knew not to trust that translation on the memorial stone. And Benevolent Hand, a sister Haven to the Peddlerhouse.

"Two of them were also Half, right? La-Ahn and Chang. Maybe they turned on him."

"I think no. Two of them surprise him, he lose. But if he surprise them, and with his sword back, they lose."

"Wait. Sword back? He didn't have it while he was here?"

Lily gestured at the vegetables in front of me, and I nudged the plate her way. Her chopsticks clacked with a pleasant tempo as she plundered the saucy mix. "No, of course not. Danger enough without. Wooden sword, later fire. Husband can tell you more about that."

"How did *you* feel about him? My brother."

She chewed, swallowed. Took another mouthful. Repeat. "He scared me. Fa Shai-Yeh told me, be nice to him. Be a friend. I tried. Hard at first. He kept getting hurt. La-Ahn, Orchid, she didn't try as hard as me. But Talon Gukh-Fah, he wasn't scary then. Just young and eager? Wanted to do things, everything, now now now."

"Eager, yes."

"As Hua-Shi train him, and Chang make him like little brother, and other Peddlers start to try to get him to like them, then he gets scary. Talon Gukh-Fah, I want to say…scary not because angry or wild. Scary because easy to like even though I know how strong he gets." Lily's speech had grown quicker, more confident. And of course, the more fervid she became, the less her grasp of Common could keep up. She switched into Chūnko-go and articulated her thoughts to herself. Then she slumped. "Sorry, hard to explain in Common. I try."

"It's alright. The word you're looking for, if I may, I think it's *charm*. Charm. It means…uh…make someone like you, maybe love you." The last was a risk, but I had to know.

"No, I love husband." *That* was a little too quick to be missed. She caught herself. "Charm. Yes. But not love. For Char, I think I feel…concern. Even in Chūnko-go, I could not say the words before the night of Zhengkai fight. Gave him little present. Said nice words. But not the words in my heart. Not proper goodbye."

"Who is that you mentioned before, the one who trained Char. Wa-Shi?"

"Hua-Shi was Thorn here. Old friend of husband long ago. From same…place for children with no mother, no father."

"Orphanage?"

"That maybe. Hua-Shi and Fa Shai-Yeh were close. Very close." She scooped the last of the rice up, holding the bowl in her other hand, and just looked at me over the rim.

I nodded. Vachaelle 'very close' to Charan's direct mentor. This fit. "Where is Hua-Shi now?"

She set the bowl and chopsticks down in a manner that seemed almost like punctuation. "Died in Haven fire. You know about this?"

"I saw the place on the way here a few months ago. Yes, I know." I didn't recall seeing his name on the plaque, but there had been a lot of names. "So my brother killed him too."

"Maybe. Littleknife knows more, but I do know Fa Shai-Yeh was there that night. I don't think she is dead."

"I am sure she isn't." In what capacity? The beguiling songstress? The merciless healer? Some other guise I didn't yet know? "Did you know what Fa Shai-Yeh's Talent was?"

"Water energy. Shui-chi. Very powerful. Not just water. Hard water…the word…Ice. She could make ice."

That answered that. No one had more than one Talent. But Vachaelle seemed to be able to change them just by changing her name. Then again, changing one's name is no mere 'just'. And which one was her real one? Did she have a real name, or just roles like the rest of us? "Littleknife saw this?"

"I think so. She won't talk about it. Very scared of big fire and big water. Her Common very good. Chūnko-go first language. Still, no words."

If she had witnessed Fa Shai-Yeh and Charan destroying her home, murdering everyone in it, including her grandfather, and then somehow managed to escape, all at the age of maybe ten…yeah, 'no words' was a good way of putting it. Permanent. Emotional. Damage. Another way.

"I'm so sorry, Lily. So the Peddlerhouse lost its strongest members and its leader. It stopped receiving the Menu. When did that happen?"

"I do not know. Remaining Peddlers left two, three weeks after the fight and the fire. Joined Bleeding Shadow. Ying Seht Yut. Bad gang. Husband left gang, help make Helping Hands. Haha. Help make help. I said funny thing." And she giggled. Such a strangely incongruous reaction to the topic, and to her thus-far solemn attitude. Maybe Littleknife wasn't the only one in here with a bruised psyche thanks to my brother.

"This might be a weird question, but have you had dreams about my brother? Ever?"

She pursed her lips. Weird, yes. But also rude. Now that I thought about it. "I not remember if I did."

"Okay. You'd definitely remember if you had the sorts of dreams I mean." So she hadn't heard his name in her head, or seen any of his dreams. Lily's connection to my brother was likely strictly bound to her existence in Kaifeng. Oddly reassuring.

"Bleeding Shadow gang also break up. Now little gangs, fight each other at night sometimes. City dangerous but no one big danger."

"What about the Guards? They didn't want to let me into the city."

She spread her hands. A form of shrug? "We do not know, only that they do not help anyone. They watch. From the walls. Most are inside Palace area. And they didn't want let you in because all Kasudenjin gone. Scared of gang fights. Scared of Helping Hands too."

"Why would they be scared of you?"

And now she brought those hands together, fingers interlocked. Shook both as one. It hadn't been a shrug after all, but a precursor to meaningful representation. This woman was *good*. "Chūnkojin, Mifūnjin. Not bow to Kasudenjin any more. No Menu. No Peddlers. No Sisters. No…hunting night. Night of hunt. So no more need for Haven. Just us."

I took this in as calmly as possible, which I imagine wasn't very. "How did you stop the hunting night? How?"

"We did not. After few moons, saw no one taken by Night's Own. Kaifeng cursed now. Kasudenjin gone. The Nobles gone. We alone. Alone together. God help us. *Fahm En.*"

I had little desire to engage her faith, even though I could see no logical connection between the seemingly liberated state of the city and it being considered 'cursed'. Then again, that's what faith did. It could convince suddenly free people they were cursed. It could make entering a prison cell in a city where one barely spoke the language seem the smartest move. It could…convert an insolent, precocious but genuinely gifted boy into an instrument of destruction. Was it simply that, little brother? Had you found *faith* in Vachaelle, where you wouldn't listen to either of our real parents, tortuous though their own tenets were? Was all this nothing more than a fucking suicide mission?

Another topic for another time…or never, if the answer proved less important than figuring out how to respond to it.

"Was Fa Shai-Yeh the only Sister in Kaifeng when it happened?"

"No, I saw few others leave after. But Fa Shai-Yeh only Sister to work with us. Only Sister I ever talk to. She put Char in Hands."

"Did you see her around much while Char was here?"

"No. Not more than ten times."

"And after he left?"

"No times. I think she use Kaifeng and move on. Talon Gukh-Fah, I have question now."

"Ask." I refilled both of our tea cups.

"Do you want to find him to stop him, or to help him?"

Eph me, if that wasn't the question I'd been avoiding for years.

I went to answer when a tall and handsome man dressed in various shades of green walked up the stairs (I could see him; Lily could not) and strode our way. I'm sorry, 'tall and handsome' seemed sufficient: he had a neat haircut, well-trimmed beard, defined cheekbones, and moved with a purpose that projected his awareness of all these factors. Besides, you know I'm going to undercut this initial assessment so let's not pretend either of us are new to this.

When he approached our table, I tried to avoid his eye but noticed, as he placed a hand on Lily's shoulder from behind, that 'handsome' might only apply at a certain distance: his nose had been broken at some point, and either he'd failed to get it healed in time or had chosen not to.

Lily turned her head a little to hear him whisper into her ear, smiled and stood up. Gave a small but precise bow. "My duties call, Talon Gukh-Fah. I am sorry for my rude questions. It was good to meet you."

So they were going to take turns with me. Interesting. "And you, Lily. Joi gin."

The man sat, looked over the table. I admired how similar his clothing was to hers. Very practical. He then asked a question that was in neither Common nor Chūnko-go, and I had to strain to register any meaning to it.

But it certainly explained why he looked a little different. Why he moved as though he owned the place. Why I could see others stepping aside for him.

Mifūn-go? Alright, Sariana, your turn.

"Yes, thank you. Very delicious. Delectable even." Show-off.

He smiled without showing any teeth, then nibbled on Lily's leftovers.

I addressed his choice of language. "Not Common then?" If Chūnko-go was the language of the people, then perhaps Mifūn-go was the language of the state. Of the court. The façade of nobility beneath the Nobility.

"Whichever you prefer." He spread his hands magnanimously after demonstrating this mastery of Common. He'd prepared for this moment. Rehearsed it. So there was a script and I didn't know it. Eh, wasn't there always?

"Who are you?" Mifūn-go then.

"Leung Zha-Ku, comrade of the Helping Hands. Did my wife not tell you this?"

"She called you 'husband' and said you could tell me more about what happened. That's all really."

Leung Zha-Ku flagged over an otherwise idle servant girl, directed her to clear the table. "Thank you, Min-Wen." This, in Chūnko-go.

"Your Common and Mifūn-go are both very good." Might as well get that part over with.

"I was not born with the name Leung, and most Mifūnjin raised in Kaifeng received…very good tutelage. My parents made sure of that." Rather than sounding proud, he didn't even bother to conceal his sneer. A self-hating oppressor, or just another case of filial bitterness?

"And yet you were friends with kids from an orphanage?"

"The Society For Disadvantaged Youth was not an orphanage, Talon. It was a thieves…guild, I think the word for it is in Kas'Daen. My predecessor, Leung Guan-Pi, ran it. He was, like me, formerly Mifūnjin. I suppose Mifūnjin who see the system for what it is just feel attracted towards the less-privileged. A system with no assumed privilege would be nice, do you not think?"

Both then.

"But then who would clean up after we've eaten, Leung Zha-Ku?"

"Someone happier to get paid to do that than other things. A place for everyone. All are welcome here." He smirked.

"Everyone has a job."

"Exactly."

"And a job for everyone?"

"Ideally. That is a little more complicated. But you aren't interested in any of that, are you, Talon? You're interested in this." Apparently bored of local politics, he said this in a deeper tone, a natural shift for native Mifūn-go getting down to business it seemed. 'This' was a piece of paper he produced from within the folds of his coat, and he didn't need to slide it over to me, but I accepted it and looked anyway.

And then folded the paper and left it beneath my hand. "Where did you see that?"

"Tsuba of his sword. The guard. Terrible design. Very impractical. But he never did use it the way anyone else does. His sword didn't need a tsuba at all, which is why I always remembered it."

"You got close enough to see this detail?" This man may have been the first to see the crux et luna before Charan's awakening. Would he have known it? Certainly not…but still, he'd seen it. What had it meant to him? Anything? Just a 'bad' guard design?

"He never used his sword against me, Talon. Obviously. I'm still here."

"You were there that night. The Zhengkai Massacre."

"I was the reason he was there. The massacre, the haven fire, the end of the Peddlers. All my fault. If I hadn't obeyed her, and just kept the sword for myself…"

"Fa Shai-Yeh?" Again. Always.

"Dignitary of Kasuden. Sister of the Liquid Night. She left me with a sword, one I could not use, told me if I passed it to him, I would get the city. Me, an underling in the Bloody Shadows. Wong Chu-Deng's lapdog. Hua-Shi's childhood…friend. She said if I didn't give him the sword, I would die, and so would everyone I loved. She didn't say that was going to happen anyway."

"Wong Chu-Deng?" I recognised this name as well, not from that first dream but the later one, in which my brother had committed patricide and made me forgive him for it. What did this man's absence from the first dream signify? Who was he to everyone else? "Who is Wong Chu-Deng?"

"Ah. Leung Guan-Pi's former second. Leader of the Bloody Shadows."

Oh. Definitely still in play then. "And when you gave Char Ah-Ran the sword?"

"You are Half, Talon. You know what happens."

"But it wasn't really like that, was it?" Because I was Half…and he was Half…and neither of us really were.

"No." He closed his eyes. "We thought he was Hua-Shi, and he played on that a little. When we set up a mock duel for him to win his sword back, he tried to resist. But not for long. Once he had it, he started talking to himself, but not in a mad or frantic way. As though he was talking to others we couldn't hear. The Peddlers were fending off the other Shadows there quite well, using their skill to keep casualties to a minimum. But I saw him start to move, and I ran. I couldn't get away. I ran into another Peddler, one I'd once called Brother. We had unfinished business, and were too ignorant, too consumed, to notice that as we brawled, Char Ah-Ran was carving his way through everyone else. Shadows and Peddlers. He was not us or them. He was something else, something alone. He'd just cut down my…lover, and Chang-dailoh rushed in to avenge her. He was Half, I was not. Better him than me. I didn't see much else."

"But you got away? A sole survivor of the Zhengkai Massacre?"

"Three people survived Char Ah-Ran's wrath. Me, Fa Shai-Yeh, and Hua-Shi. They were not part of the main skirmish. I think they…or at least she orchestrated it and always planned to just watch."

So Hua-Shi and Fa Shai-Yeh took refuge in the House of Joyful Goodbyes, Charan found them there, and the disastrous results were written in stone. "And at least one of them died at the nearby Haven. Did you seek help there after the fight as well?"

"No. Hua-Shi carried me back to Kaifeng, to the Benevolent Hand Haven. I was in and out of consciousness, and only remember a few details. Hua-Shi setting me down. Talking to the healer on duty. Then leaving, saying he had to go stop 'The Scourge' before he could find his way to the next city, and the next. And the healer, she knew my name. Later told me that Char Ah-Ran himself had her prepare for my coming. That he had, all along, planned for me to survive. Me and others. So why, I asked. Why would he ready a Haven for the wounded and then very deliberately make sure there were almost none? The healer shrugged, Flailed herself and left me to heal. A few weeks later, I wake up to hear what happened. I learn the healer's name, and together we visit the Malevolent Hand chapterhouse. It is abandoned, so I take over. Use that filthy Mifūnjin wealth and power one last time. Change my name to honour the man who would have changed Kaifeng for the better. Turn Peddlerhouse into a second Haven, but then as time went by, we just stopped obeying any sorts of Haven rules and…this. This is the result."

"I asked Lily if you work here and she said to ask you. Do you own it?"

"I helped create it, but I do not claim ownership. It is for all who need it."

Comrade. Right. "The symbol you saw on Oni-Goroshi's guard. The sword. Have you seen it anywhere else since?"

"No. But you must remember, Kaifeng is isolated now. No outsiders. Just you, and you are not an outsider anymore."

Oh. Yeah, that sounded…less than good.

"Condition of my release? I serve you? Work for you?"

"We will work together, Talon. You are, as far as I know, the only Half in the city now, and if you were going to turn, you would have already. More importantly, you are a Sister, which to my knowledge means you have experience with childbirth. Always more children being born in Kaifeng. I'd like you to help in the old Benevolent Hand Haven. Establish the first Kaifeng Sisterhood. And after that, who knows. Endless jobs for a Half in a city full of normal people."

"A city, Leung Zha-Ku? Don't you mean a 'war'?"

"A war on starvation, yes. On poverty. On social injustice. Very good, Talon. Very, very good."

"And the other Peddlerhouses? The other Havens of Kaifeng? The Bloody Shadows?"

"If we win the real war, they won't be a problem. How can a gang beat a whole city?"

So he really had believed her. He'd given Charan the sword when asked, and now the city was his. Or at least one tiny south-eastern suburb of it. Then again, he apparently had the resources to pluck me from a guardhouse at the other end of the city. Me, the only Half in Kaifeng. The only foreigner. The only Sister. So many things I could do…and he wanted me to play midwife.

Compared to letting a few surly watchmen keep me locked up under their building as an act of faith, this didn't seem even slightly unacceptable. Besides, I still needed Littleknife's testimony, to fill that last gap with what happened in the Haven, and that could take months, or even years of waiting.

But what of Lily's last question? He had to be wondering as well.

"This isn't my war. Or my city. I came here looking for my brother, and now I know he's gone. Why shouldn't I just go after him?"

"Does he need you? We do. Because of what he has done, we need you. Fa Shai-Yeh is a terrible person, but she is also always right. She was right about Char Ah-Ran. About Leung Guan-Pi. About Hua-Shi. About Lily. And she was right about you coming here. She even told me how I would know it was you, just in case I somehow missed all the other signs. You know what I am talking about, yes? He has a guard on his sword…you have a pendant around your neck."

Eph damn her. Eph…Ephin' damn the sly Ephin' gashslitbitchcuntfuuuck! I grit my teeth and replied very…very carefully. "If you knew I was coming, why let me sit in a prison cell for months?"

"Your timing surprised me. Fa Shai-Yeh said you would either arrive a month or two after she left, or maybe just over a year. When it was neither I forgot about all of it. It's now been two, maybe closer to three years. You are very late, at least as far as Fa Shai-Yeh was concerned. I had to move quickly to get through to you. But, I did."

"And what did Fa Shai-Yeh tell you I would do when I arrived?"

"Help. Because she said you are a good person. You would see what Char Ah-Ran had done, and how desperate we would be for someone of your ability. We cannot let Wong Chu-Deng and the Bloody Shadows take over, Talon. This city must be ours, and ready for whatever comes next."

"Lily said the Bloody Shadows broke up." I didn't correct him this time. I had the feeling right now he couldn't see the difference between 'ours' and 'mine'. And whether or not I was a good person…who could judge that? Surely not she. 'Good' from Vachaelle might as well just mean 'useful'.

"Wong Chu-Deng wouldn't let that happen. They operate individually, in each suburb, each district, but I believe he is still in charge. When he reveals that, there may be that other war you mentioned. And it won't be just a gang. And they will not let you just leave. We win, you walk away from a happy, healthy Kaifeng. A new capital of human freedom."

I leaned back against the wall, adjusting my thighs on the bench's cushioning. Even allowed myself a rare moment of vulnerability by reaching up and tapping on the concealed pendant a few times. How I longed for the day when I could just wear it openly…the day I walked out of this city unhindered, maybe even exalted. Sooner or later the Night would return to this place, but maybe not in the form anyone expected. Vachaelle had used this city as a testing ground, to see what happens when the order breaks down. And she remembered so much about Jaydemyr, about our role in implementing and maintaining that order, about how the other clans had reacted to it, that she couldn't but know that the only reason the Night hadn't erased the entire city was my brother now erasing Night's Own in their formerly secure homes. So what was she testing? How this plays out, or whether or not Charan's actions were distraction enough? Or if Kaifeng itself would be a distraction?

I sighed, deciding it was probably all of those, and much more. And my role? Resume the chase, finding him only if she wanted me to find him. Or keep the faith. Follow orders. Believe in the power of the Nightsong.

"I accept. I will help you as I can, hopefully bringing enough stability to convince your enemies their combined brute force cannot defeat your purpose. Failing that, one type of war becomes another. I'm not doing this because I'm a good person, whatever Fa Shai-Yeh might have said. I'm doing this because Kaifeng as a city abandoned by the Night is something new and very interesting to me. How far will this go? Will it establish a new council? Will those holed up in the Palace be deposed? Will your new order overturn even the Twelve? Show me exactly how far you want to take this, Leung Zha-Ku. At the worst, I'll just walk away from the flames one night and turn the whole experience into a fanciful story to be told up and down the Long Way between here and Kas'Daen."

He smiled again, and this time I saw his teeth. He stood up, walked a few steps around the table and thrust out his hand. "I believe this is how Kasudenjin introduce themselves. I am Terasawa Jaku, protégé of Tsukamoto Genma, and I am so very glad to meet you at last, sister of Char Ah-Ran."

I took his hand, shook with the ever-present awareness that he'd want to have the firmer grip, despite knowing how difficult a favour that was for me to grant. "I am Sariana Jaydemyr, sister to Charan Jaydemyr."

These names demanded Common. "But for you, for this city, I will be Sister Talon Gukh-Fah, comrade of the Munnamdun Helping Hands. Your war is now my war.

"Now, how does a girl go about getting her hair styled around here?"

Expectations vs Surreality

"I just can't see it. The Lily I know would never have entertained the Jaku I know, let alone marry the spoiled little ass."

"A lot can happen in a few years, Brother. A few years and over a decade of questionable memories. I find it strange you can't see something despite knowing what you can see is based on a fabrication. I can't see you ever somehow believing you were an abused villager or, of all things, Hua-Shi himself, but I still believe that you believe it because Vachaelle makes everyone strangers to us, especially ourselves. Because that's how we learn to use them…especially our selves."

24 hours until the revelation

Chapter 17: The Ravenous Boar
3/876 to 10/877 A.R.

"So that's what Wong Chu-Deng wants. Everything."

I didn't look up from my work at the main desk, which I made look far more important and engrossing than it really was: scheduled intake and condition of the dozen or so women currently in the care of Happy Deliveries. The former Haven did not lack for healers and even had a hydrotheurge, but I'd had to ask around to coax a few untrained Maliscients out of hiding. They'd lived in fear of being Weeded for so long, I could understand their hesitation. Thankfully 'taking vulnerable people to a happy place in their heads' is one of the easier things for even a raw Maliscient to do, much easier than the sort of memory-change shit Cass had worked on Viera that last time, and nevermind whatever reality-bending madness Vachaelle and our mother had imposed on a worldwide scale. And while Kaifeng hadn't had a functioning Sister abbey in a very long time (if ever), there had been working knowledge of the Sacred Cuts and the Mothergift. So it had taken time, but when spring thawed the city and rain replaced snow, we were open and servicing the needs of south-eastern Kaifeng's female population...give or take.

"I'm sure it's not bad." A lie to stave off Sister Wai-Bahk's tendency to gossip. It was Bladesun, and we had a while before the day's business began. She was cleaning the floor of the entrance hall, where the Sisters usually talked with the guests, explained the procedure, or helped them prepare to leave. My Chūnko-go wasn't yet up to a standard where I took part in comforting the guests, but I understood enough to pick up

Wai-Bahk's teenage prattle more often than not, and to respond. "I will talk with comrade Zha-Ku."

"Has he called a meeting?" She paused to drag some hair out of her face, backed up in a crawl, spread some more water across the floorboards with a focused splaying of fingers, got back to scrubbing. I hadn't made any of them wear the usual Liquid Night garb; Kaifeng was free of all that. Let them wear what they want. Even if most of the time that was the same thing as before: variants on what Lily and Zha-Ku had been wearing when I'd first met them months ago. "He has to have. It's the Shadows, isn't it?"

"I don't know. Just woke up." Another lie came easily enough. "Ask Sister Lily to finish this when she arrives?" Still felt strange calling her that, but she'd insisted, as a former healer of the place, that she'd be involved. Zha-Ku, in turn, had insisted that we use the Sister title rather than the much simpler 'comrade' appellation for all. And, as Lizaveta had once made clear, healers with Haven experience were indispensable. They were the difference between a successful recovery and simply too much blood lost. A typical Delivery wouldn't get to that point, but…eh, what was a typical Delivery?

I closed the book, adjusted my blood-dark robes (because that's what *I* wanted to wear), pulled the hood over my face, concealing my now fashionable (and functional) short hair, and headed for the door. "I'm off to get some breakfast."

"At the Gentle Bouquet?"

"Didn't it close for few days of cleaning?"

"So they say. Maybe it'll reopen today. People will want somewhere to gather and talk."

"Stop caring what people say. We do what we need to do. Tell Sister Littleknife be available to help Sister Lily if we need more healing done than normal days."

"So you do think something's happening!"

"Something always happening, Wai-Bahk. What do Sisters do?"

"Assist. Provide."

"And what do Sisters not do?"

"Ask. Probe."

I always liked the Brothers' tenet far more than the Sisters', so why not?

"Exactly. Do as I say and as I do. For now."

"As you say, Mother."

"Fuck, Wai-Bahk, don't still call me that."

"What then? Aunty? Granny?"

"And you wonder why you're always on cleaning duty." One last lie, this time in Common and to myself, to see me on my way.

The former Haven turned Sisterhood was on the main east-west road of Munnamdun; Lily and I had actually walked right past it when I'd arrived, but without any signage it was easy to miss. I glanced up now at the sign we'd chosen: no bleeding eyes, no wounded hands. No Flail. Just two simple flowers, one yellow and one pink, holding leafy 'hands', each with a smiling face in the middle. Zha-Ku might have requested a traditional Sisterhood abbey, but I knew better than to perpetuate any iconography of a regime this city neither wanted nor needed. I didn't even use the old First Order or Second Hand ranks, and naturally Third Eye was completely unnecessary. No, in the spirit of this nascent postlunar equality, we were all just Sisters serving the people of Kaifeng.

An earlybird merchant sang out my way. "Good morning, Sister! Hear the news?"

"Good morning to you." I slowed but did not stop. "Some. Trying to learn more."

"Here, take these." The fellow held out a few apples.

"Oh no, Dai-Suhk." I waved the 'uncle' off, now backpedaling. "You have given Sisters more than enough."

"Aiyaa, I could provide them a whole orchard and it wouldn't be enough for what you've done for us. Come get them on the way back then, Sister. Promise me."

"I will try. Stay safe."

"Stay safe, Sister."

It was a habitual farewell, but right now, as I neared the corner leading to the Gentle Bouquet, I knew it was also anything but empty. Stationed at said corner were four or five young men, all wearing orange armbands over their black jackets. All armed. They nodded as I passed. No doubt I'd have found similar vigilance at the north end of the street, and likely at most intersections in Munnamdun. Perhaps I should have worn my Fourth Going uniform and the Gildenhammer, something I'd not felt any need to do since meeting Zha-Ku and not leaving Munnamdun even once. As Lily had said, it was home.

"They're inside waiting, Sister." One of the guards at the door nodded me in. Instead of an orange armband, he was wearing a scarf. It wasn't that cold anymore, but with one quick move he could easily hide his face.

"Thank you. Stay safe." Definitely less and less a hollow salutation.

The furniture had been cleared away but for one large oblong table, the length of which cut across the hall. All the chairs at said table faced the entrance, as though anyone entering were immediately being judged and scrutinised. Which, naturally, they were. Only one chair was empty, on the far left end; the other ten or eleven played host to a variety of men and women, some of whom I'd seen around, a few of whom I knew by name.

And they all had those same bands about their upper arms, forearms or wrists.

The conversation that bound them was lively and a little intimidating, and none stopped to acknowledge my entrance. I just stepped around to the left and took that last chair, listening and trying to keep up while pouring myself some tea and nabbing a few dumplings from a plate. I caught maybe one word in three at the time but this is pretty much the flow of the assembly's argumentation.

"We should seal the gates." A gaunt elderly woman had a map spread before her, and she kept stabbing at it. "Roads and water. Keep them out."

"How many guards in the Pagoda district do we have taking coin?" This, from a younger woman dressed not entirely unlike a Peddler. "We will need eyes, ears."

"We might completely lose our supply of Mifūné steel. We must stockpile…"

"I have family in Jinmouzong! We can't just cut them off—"

"Family? It's us or them now!"

Zha-Ku stood from his chair at the other end of the table, walked around to face all the seated members of this sudden council, and just waited for calm.

"For our newly arrived Sister Talon Gukh-Fah's benefit, I will now speak in Common. Don't worry; I am just going to repeat what we know, and will translate anything new." So he began. "A few days ago we heard distressing news: Wong Chu-Deng had amassed sufficient forces in the north to besiege the inner walls of the Five-Fold Palace. I say besiege because unlike the feckless, toothless relics of the Court, we know that the Bloody Shadows do not 'defend' anything, let alone 'noble honour'. We know that were we to attack the Court, it wouldn't be something as patently foolish as a head-on assault. But still, hundreds, probably thousands rallied to his cause once he convinced them that was our plan. So for two days, we have waited to see what happens next. Closed our doors, suppressed information. Business as usual in Munnamdun. Yuwantai. Siu-Tsin. As far as most of our people know, the Five-Fold Palace is conducting a militia-guard training operation. If they know anything about that at all."

Leung Zha-Ku clasped his hands behind his back, started to pace. It almost looked contemplative and collected. Almost. "What they do know, or will very soon, is that Wong Chu-Deng officially no longer exists. Nor do the Bloody Shadows. Expect to see the names 'Ayakawa no Inoh-ueh Kenjiroh' and 'Teikoku Chikagehkidan' on a lot of walls."

"Dogfucking traitor." The maybe-not-Peddler woman called this out to rough jeers of agreement.

Zha-Ku smiled but shook his head. "Closer to wild pig. He might have been granted the lordly Ayakawa connection, but whoever gave him the name Inoh-ueh may have been closer to the truth than they knew. Not a rare family name, but it can also mean 'the boar above'. Kenjiroh, just another name. Mifūnjin are fiercely addicted to long names. As for 'Teikoku Chikagehkidan', equally ridiculous. You all know that Teikoku means imperial. Chi? Blood. Kageh? Shadow. Kidan? Well, I'd say that means 'fanciful tale'...but equally Chikagehkidan can mean "underground attack force". Yet another way of reading Chikage: "a thousand views": usually a woman's name. Wong Chu-Deng likely didn't realise how insulting it was of the Court to write his little army's new name in hiragana and not kanji, inviting all these wonderful interpretations."

The assembled council looked lost at this uninvited language lesson. Zha-Ku's privileged Mifūnjin education was showing and now sure as Shyn' wasn't the time for that. Common or not, I stepped in. "How about we call him Inoh and them Chikageh? Simple. I take it Chūnko-go has been outlawed in the northern half of Kaifeng?"

"It has, Sister Talon. We might want to consider not shutting off the roads and rivers quite yet. Plenty of northerners with little love for Mifūn-go. We would be fools to not take them in or at least get them on our side."

"Once the gates are closed, that'll be it. Those walls are terribly easy to man."

A new voice then, which Jaku translated easily enough but his expression was by the end a little uneasy. "I think someone like you would be able to climb them."

I leaned forward and looked down the table to see who'd spoken. Between me and the flushed middle-aged man dressed like a well-off landowner, a whole row of tight-lipped faces looked very glad they hadn't stepped in it first. "And who are you?"

"Lim Yuen-Boh, comrade. Humble owner of this place, and many others in Kaifeng."

I glanced at Zha-Ku, who was once more inscrutable despite having to play linguistic go-between for what was quickly becoming more than just heated debate. Definitely on a Mifūnjin streak, then.

Fine, I could handle this. "Let me ask you, Comrade Lim. You clearly have a mouth, and I assume you have an arsehole, so why can't you just eat as much as you want?"

The Probably-A-Peddler lady guffawed at what I hoped was an accurate translation, and even Zha-Ku's expression slipped. I revelled in the gasps and let the man fluster for a bit before explaining. "Because there are steps in-between. Chewing. Digestion. Whatever it is that happens after that. Same with being 'someone like me'. I can run fast. I am strong. I am quick. But climbing a district wall or even jumping over it? That's a step in-between I do not know. A combination of steps. Now are you done with assumptions or do you want a show of how fast and strong I can be?"

Zha-Ku interrupted his own translation after a few sentences – his turn to rein someone in, I suppose. "What Sister Talon means to say is that as valuable an asset as she is, her Half nature is not without limits and not to be taken for granted. I am sure once she has mastered more of our language she will be able to speak for herself. Agreed, Sister Talon Gukh-Fah?"

"Yes. Agreed. Sorry." Fuck you too, you slick bastard.

He sat down, as though to remind everyone he wasn't, in fact, completely in charge here. "This has been helpful, but I believe we've kept Sister Talon from her duties long enough." Then he addressed me directly in Common while the others in-between leaned back, as if on cue. "My wife tells me you're almost at the point of needing a second location. And should this conflict escalate…which it will…healers will be beyond precious."

"Thank you for invitation." This, in Chūnko-go to show I hadn't missed what was really being said. But he was right: I knew more than enough to do my part, and I definitely had no time for politicking and logistical minutiae. Back to Common for necessary clarity and accuracy for one last point. "Oh, send some of those orange bands to the Sisterhood please? We wouldn't want innocent people confusing us for the bad guys."

Zha-Ku laughed and, as usual, the sound rang false. "I'm certain they won't be necessary, but sure, I'll have them delivered today. I will make the time for it especially. See you soon, Sister Talon, but not too soon I do hope." Another of his infuriatingly diplomatic chuckles and I couldn't get out of there quickly enough.

Two weeks later the armbands arrived, only about a week after the first casualties.

Sarah-Jade would have called the steady but increasing volume of injured comrades 'messengers'. There were former Havens farther north, between Munnamdun and the Pagoda district, but they likely had their own issues. The victims that reached us were non-critical, mostly the result of frightened citizens crossing Chikageh patrols and not knowing how to properly show respect.

Sisters fluent in Mifūn-go were also moved north-west, closer to the more unstable parts of the city such as Jinmouzong. And whatever else the council decided in that Gentle Bouquet meeting, no roads or rivers were sealed off; no interdistrict gates had been barred. As we headed into a rather warm summer, the so-called Kaifeng Civil Conflict remained decidedly frigid.

I made the armbands optional. Most of the Sisters chose not to wear them. They were of little value this far south, whereas up north they would have been a clear distinction from the appropriately rubricated garb of the Chikageh. Few of us ever even saw a member of the boar's personal army. We just kept on Delivering and healing.

In early autumn, Zha-Ku formalised the establishment of a second Sisterhood facility, this one closer to south-central Kaifeng in the Yuwantai district. A former Respite seemed an appropriate location. The council assigned Lily to be its head Sister, even though I honestly hadn't taught her much about the Sisterhood at all. With her went some very skilled Deliverers, but the main role of Yuwantai branch of Happy Deliveries was to handle other needs. I was surprised when Wai-Bahk and Littleknife chose to stay with me at Munnamdun, but both were valued members and I didn't take their decision for granted.

The first true winter of the conflict had an oddly adverse effect to the heat. I'd imagined tempers would have flared and shortened during the hotter months, but once the snow returned, people started to get desperate for resources. The Chikageh went from being mere northern suburbs thugs and faux-guards to active harassers of shops, stores, stalls and markets across all of Kaifeng. They dared not enter the Gentle Bouquet itself, which was as much a stronghold as anything else by then, but Chikageh members were no longer an unusual sight in Munnamdun, Yuwantai and Siu-Tsin. True to their image as official servants of the Mifūnjin Court, they swaggered about with katana and jitteh thrust through their belts, waving lanterns on sticks through the short frosty days, the long freezing nights. They imposed, demanded, and abused. If we had bedspace, we even put some up in Happy Deliveries, and at first they behaved, perhaps knowing that those who heal can always also harm.

I didn't see many orange armbands that winter.

The Chikageh presence didn't recede with the ice and the snow. Their brutish occupation of Siu-Tsin reduced the southern territory to Yuwantai and Munnamdun. North of Yuwantai was the Palace; north of Munnamdun was the Pagoda. The sporadic nocturnal skirmishing continued, but it seemed the lines had been drawn, and neither side had the resources to affect them.

Late in the spring of 877, I was once again invited to the Bouquet, but this time not for an early morning emergency convention of the South's most influential in response to aggressions up north. No, this came via Lily herself, who was just 'passing by'. Passing by the safely-tucked-away Munnamdun branch of Happy Deliveries in the quickened dark of Risingmoon. Wearing an orange armband. And, much to my surprise, openly carrying a slender but serious-looking sword at her hip.

She noticed my noticing, but said nothing on the matter as we took a very late tea in the dining room.

Still, she did not nibble fingers. "Littleknife still not really talking to you?" *You have yet to hear her story about what happened that night?*

"She obeys orders, is friendly to the other Sisters, but still has these…quiet periods. I haven't approached her for any serious discussion." *Yep. Still waiting.* 'It's the same here as with you. We've all been too busy. Seems what they say about cold nights and warm bodies rings true."

She laughed lightly, almost dutifully. She knew I answered to her husband and his council, but I suppose within the Sisterhood, I was her senior. What a ridiculous situation. "I fear my husband's fervour for what's been coming is warmth enough for him." That, however, just seemed to slip out. She blushed. "I would like a family someday, although it seems irresponsible to consider it at the moment."

"In Kas'Daen, Sisters aren't allowed to have children, and if they are intimate with men, they need to ensure they do not fall pregnant. We called it Honouring the Seventh. In spirit if not reality."

Lily pondered this, and then made a small admission. "I miss the order of the Twelve. The clarity of right and wrong, regardless of personal feelings. But its absence seems an acceptable price for the freedom from the Hunt, from Peddlers. And soon, I truly believe, from the remaining Mifūnjin trying to rule us from behind very tall walls."

Time to address her new accessory. "That lack of order is why you're now going about with a Hands armband and a sword?"

"We will not allow next winter to be anything like the last."

"How bad was it? We are quite self-sufficient here. I rarely venture out."

"You said before that it was the same here as with us. Not entirely true. Munnamdun is of course safe. But anywhere else? Let me just say in Yuwantai, not all of the Deliveries were Happy. And some of them were so early, we simply couldn't save the child."

"Ephin' monsters." My outrage was more comfortable in Common, but I forced myself back into the language we actually had in common. "I wouldn't have let any of them leave this place alive had I known what they'd do. Tending the wounds of a beast doesn't make him any less of one afterwards."

"Sister Talon Gukh-Fah, there's not a…not a damn thing we could have done. Kill one patrol, they'd send three more. We should be thankful most of the Chikageh are still busy putting on a show of guarding the Five-Fold Palace. It seems Wong Chu-Deng…I refuse to call him anything else, I'm sorry, I just won't!…it seems that horrid pig of a man failed to predict how much the Court enjoyed his protection.

But it's not how many or how few he sends. It's the type. The rapacious scum might be here to collect taxes and levy food, but they take so much…well okay. I'm just being dramatic. A few mishaps with a girl here and there aside, they weren't doing any real harm. Just a nuisance, really. Or so Zha-Ku and his council kept saying. Just. A. Nuisance."

I said nothing, letting her loop from despondency to reason, reason to wrath, and then back to that despondency, the source of which she finally failed to conceal. Zha-Ku and *his* council. When it was clear she needed to be eased back into the present, I nodded at her and did just that.

"The armband. That sword. And visiting me, specifically, after dinner. They're not saying the Chikageh 'patrols' are just a nuisance anymore, are they?"

"Not after seeing how much they'd depleted our reserves of rice and coin, no. The loss of such precious resources demands a response. And that's why I'm here. Jaku…" She paused, perhaps wondering if the slip of his real name, his real nature, would be a problem; I just tilted my head a little to indicate it was not. "Jaku wants you to know that one type of war may yet become the other type. He will be expecting you at the headquarters tomorrow night at highmoon, armed and prepared. What he won't be expecting, is this." She pulled an armband from her work bag, placed it on the table.

"That…isn't orange." Not that its colour was the issue.

"No, it's not."

"Why this? Why now?" I took the black armband, examined it. The light grey circle. The black crescent inside it. The black cross inside that. The odd gold tinge to the edges of the crescent and the cross, as though there might have been a sun behind the moon, its luminance almost breaking through.

"You are…unique, Sister Talon." Lily was feeling her way through just that much, but then her words caught up to her beliefs, and her sentiment roused itself towards a series of facts I'd been avoiding. "Unique, just as your brother was when he was here. Jaku doesn't quite know what it means, that symbol, but I do. I saw it on the pendant around your neck the day we met. Something about it is wrong, wrong in this world. But Kaifeng, the Kaifeng Char Ah-Ran…Charan and Fa Shai-Yeh wrought, is not of 'this world'. We no longer Flail ourselves. We no longer fear the full moon. We do not wake and wonder who of us might have been taken to keep the peace. Our rulers have diminished, propped up by bullies and braggarts. We have new rules, and new symbols. And if our right is the world's wrong, then why not this one?"

"You would have me make my family name an icon of terror?" I was only half-worried that I'd let slip precisely what the crux et luna was. Not a symbol, but the name itself.

"We've tried everything else. Coexistence. Obedience. Complacency. Tribute. Tolerance. Hardship. When the Bloody Shadows besieged the Palace, they called it protection. Now the Chikageh besiege us, they are not so vague in their language. Containment, they're calling it. And as long as we stay here, they'll leave us alone. How…generous of them. Until they figure out how to live without us, whatever it is we grubby Chūnkojin provide. And then it'll be over so quickly we won't have time to be afraid. So before that can happen, yes, Sister Talon Gukh-Fah, I think you delivering the Chikageh and anyone affiliated with them unto terror is absolutely our next best option."

What inhumanity this woman must have seen and experienced to reach that conclusion. Reach? Not even that. It just fell into her hands. This…certainty. I was far from unsympathetic; she was right. Jaku's priorities were and likely always had been far too detached, too strategically sterile. But still…How dare she decide for me, their not-so-secret and not-so-willing weapon, my role in this conflict?

"Why in Eph's roiling Hell aren't you on your husband's council?" Contrary to my resistance, I slipped the armband into place. I'd have to change before going – the Gildenhammer demanded its own uniform – but she had at least earned the right to see me do it, before anyone else. Before the rest of the city might learn to fear my family's name. Fear, respect and, maybe, eventually, love.

"I was for a while." She rose to her feet. "They voted me out for being, what was it? Ah. They said I was too bloody-minded." I wanted her to smile, to make clear this was all a bit of a joke at their expense. She *did* smile, but it wasn't in jest. "Maybe you'll help me change their minds."

I stood up as well, and that meant looking down at her. "I like you, Lily. A lot. Would you like it to stay that way?"

She cast her gaze downward as well and gripped the back of her chair, any sort of smile now gone. "If you're even half the monster your brother proved to be, yes. Very much so."

"Then please, never mistake my alliance for allegiance. Nothing bores me more than petty intrigue and politics, and I do really stupid things when I'm bored. Stupid…dangerous things."

She took this well, considering. "Were you really raised by Fa Shai-Yeh?"

"The woman you know as Fa Shai-Yeh is the closest thing to a mother I have. And she went to great lengths to put me here. Now. Like this. Do you really want to find out why? Because I don't."

Another pause. Still no eye contact. And then she released the chair, bowed and didn't rise. "I apologise for my impropriety. I have misspoke and beg your forgiveness. I have done what I came here to do. I shall now with your permission take my leave, Sister."

She was defeat incarnate, so why did I feel like the one who had to concede? "…Lily.…This is fucking idiocy." I wouldn't apologise for chastening her 'impropriety', but something. She deserved something.

The way she held that bow was not something a person could do without a *lot* of practice.

"I'm sorry I threatened you. I'm not like her. You've been through a lot, and I know you think no one's listening. But I am. And I intend to make sure Jaku knows just how poorly he's handled things. Whatever task he sets me next, I promise to do everything I can to protect us. Us, Lily. The Sisterhood. We who do nothing but give our everything, even to those who do not deserve it. Without the Twelve, we have to decide our own ideas of right and wrong. What happened to our sisters this winter, that was absolutely wrong. But it is done. Now we need to figure out the right action from so many other wrong ones. I am not convinced that simply killing every person wearing a Chikageh uniform is that right or our right…and right now, between you and me, it is incredibly tempting. But later. Later we have to live with the past."

I stopped, because she didn't so much as twitch during this atrocious attempt at a concession speech. Fuck.

I stepped around the table and opened my arms. "Can we just hug and you let me go see what the Eph your husband wants from me this time?"

She straightened at my approach, nodded wordlessly and we embraced as Sisters, although her unyielding tension in my too-strong arms said more than I ever could.

Late the next night, I marched towards the Bouquet dressed as a Sister of the Fourth Going, alien attire enabling alien weapon, the red hood concealing my face as much as it concealed those around me from my gaze. Not that said gaze strayed even once. I'd spent the day saying my goodbyes to Munnamdun, whether literally or otherwise.

Overhead, the full moon made for quite the beacon.

It also illuminated something very interesting: the sign above the Gentle Bouquet no longer showed any hands. Just a circle now, orange with a yellow corona. And a new name: The Society for the Advancement of Kaifeng's Youth. A bit clunky but it got the message across.

Inside the Society's headquarters, Leung Zha-Ku looked tired. Of course he did. And he was not alone. I would have wagered he was never alone now.

He guided me into the kitchen, and an office behind that. Guards flanked that door too, Society headbands concealing their brows. We sat, he behind a desk, me in a chair that Sarah-Jade very much did not like.

"A little bit dramatic asking me to come so late, don't you think?" I opened in Common.

He rubbed his coarse cheek, waved the thought away, replied in the same. "We are both busy most of the time. Besides, it's a nice night out there, from what I can tell."

"It's always a nice night, 'out there'. Try seeing for yourself sometime. So, what do you want me to do now, Jaku? Assassinations? Nighttime raids? Spying? Supply line disruption? How shall the city's only Half deliver victory unto you, and terror unto your enemies?"

"I have no idea what my wife told you, but I assure you it's nothing so…uncouth. Is this why you've come dressed like that?"

Oh, Lily.

I almost said yes. It was true.

But it was also true that Jaku, so-called leader of the South, considered the gross mistreatment of his most vulnerable civilians 'a nuisance'.

And that truth, Lily's ultimate stance, was the right one.

"No. I've come dressed like this because even if you are not ready to fight, I am."

"Meaning?"

"Meaning your approach to this conflict is failing to stop the Chikageh from abusing the very people you claim to protect. Abusing, Jaku. Not harassing. Not haranguing. Not 'making a nuisance'. Fucking abuse."

"Ah. The involuntary pregnancies. Very unfortunate."

I gaped at him. Just…gaped.

"What exactly did you expect, Sariana?" He remained unmoved. As though people had been talking to him this way all his life, and it'd long ceased to even register as anything but noise. "That I'd ask you to form a Sisterhood here because…what? That we ignorant, barbaric Chūnkojin suddenly didn't know how to give birth? I'm just one man. I can't stop what those Chikageh thugs do to my people in the deepest dark of night, but I can and did prepare us for what comes the morning after. I gave them *you*. Sister of the Scourge of Kaifeng, a weapon so powerful and terrible, merely loosing you in a war would mean everyone immediately loses…and yet, Sariana Jaydemyr, how many people have you killed here? And how many people…have you *saved*?"

"My God, she has no idea. She was worried you might become a monster. But this. This is worse. You've become a *politician*."

"Without the Sisters, the south would be an abattoir, Sariana. You. My wife. All of you. Healing. Wasted not on the inevitable victims of the Night, but saving the essential casualties of human friction. Wear that battle garb all you want. Display your cursed symbol on a pendant or an armband. Fly it on huge banners for all I care. It doesn't change the fact that I believe you are not here to kill the city as your brother was, but to help it through his grim aftermath. Yours should not be a bloody legacy of short-sighted slaughter and revenge, but a long-lasting one of benevolence and care."

"For Shyn's Ephing sake, stop with the speeches. Just stop."

He did. And that left it to me to say whatever came next. I had no idea what it would be. "All that you said. All of it. It is true. I have no rejoinder. No disagreement. No argument even. You are painfully, brilliantly correct."

He let his face quirk at that, but I wasn't done.

"But just because you're correct, that doesn't mean you're right. She is. She is right. Your idea of acceptable losses, your assumption that atrocities are just going to happen and so all we can do is be ready for them, is abhorrent. Repulsive. I see now that I can't do anything to change that, nothing that won't be catastrophic for all of us. But…you can. All you need to do is reject inevitability. Stop reacting pre-emptively and start acting preventatively. That's the only way you will get through this, Jaku. The only way!"

I expected a smirk. A roll of eyes. A cowering. A disarmament.

Which was stupid of me, given what I'd just called him.

"And if you hadn't come here looking for a fight, you'd know that's exactly what I am doing!" He pushed his voice into an almost-shout, an almost-breaking. It almost convinced me. "Now are you ready to listen or do you want to waste more of my time telling me what I already know?"

I prepared my response when he did something I think he went to great lengths to never do in front of others: he put his face into his palm and rubbed his nose with his middle finger. Even if everything else was performance, that was without doubt his true self crawling into view. He caught himself, made it look like he was just shrugging, not in dismissal but in helplessness. "Do you want to hear me say the hateful word both of us are avoiding? To make perfectly clear that I know what happened to those poor girls this winter? And is probably still happening now? Is that your price, Sariana Jaydemyr?"

"No."

And that was all I could say.

"Then?"

"Then tell me your orders, Leung Zha-Ku, and I might even obey them. Especially if they mean I don't have to go through this again. Send me where you will, and may it be far from your world of truthful wrongness." One last pathetic ramble to confirm he had won a fight I could barely remember trying to start. He had won not because he was smart. Not because he was right. He had won because he knew there was something to win. He knew the rules of this game, and I hadn't even looked at many of the pieces. Because to do so would be to admit that it was a game. That the game had rules. That it had pieces. That they were being played. And I'd thought that although I didn't want to play this game, *his* game, I could remain on the board and not be one of the pieces.

It was as if I'd forgotten absolutely everything Vachaelle had taught me, or…desperately hoped I wouldn't need it.

But, as I'd already said, perhaps not aware of who I really meant: she was right.

"Your wish to be sent afar is one I am more than content to grant. I want you to set up a new Happy Delivery service north of here, just south of Pagoda Park."

At any other time I'd have been ecstatic at this. Expanding our services into the north! But now that he'd made clear what dire services Happy Deliveries *really* delivered in his loathsome eyes, I chose my path through the concept very carefully. "That's past the middle wall."

"Only a little bit. Not exactly a hot zone. Not yet."

"Not yet? I will not allow you to use Happy Deliveries as a front for covert violence, Jaku. Send me alone if you want me to start that sort of fire."

He managed to look insulted. "Sister! I already said this will be a peaceful mission. The people up there are not the enemy. They are victims. Prisoners. Of the old ways of life. Of old beliefs. Of the Twelve. But they have heard how we do things down here. New ways. New beliefs. New freedoms."

"Another speech, Terasawa?" Then I resisted further rejection of his bloviated rhetoric. I thought about what I'd noticed when I first arrived here. Ah. "You mean this, then? The renaming of this place, of your organisation. Wong Chu-Deng has abandoned Guan-Pi's legacy; you're renewing it. Clever. But that's just a start. Get to the point."

"New freedoms, Sister Talon Gukh-Fah. No one likes how the Teikoku Chikagehkidan treat the people. The hypocrisy of their full stomachs, their warm beds. Not down here, and not up there. But it keeps their men in line and their women off their feet. *Voluntarily,* I am sure. So you're going to provide a service the Twelve will not allow, and in their own homes. The Happy Deliveries branch of the Pagoda district will introduce home visits, so get to know the streets up there. Take your most trusted and talented. You'll need someone reliable to run the place as usual, and no you can't take Lily."

"Wouldn't anyway. She needs to stay close to you, and you need to convince her that we should not fight fire with an Ephin' inferno."

"She does tend towards the hysterical, doesn't she?" Amazing how one word can almost be a man's undoing. Almost. "So, to the plan. We will give the women of the north what they want. I am sure they have the means to do it themselves, but not as safely and cleanly as you. Also, there'll be food stalls and stores near the Sisterhood so you can provide them with meals and other supplies at the same time. The Society for the Advancement of Kaifeng's Youth has such a bright future, Sister Talon, and Happy Deliveries will lead the way."

Given what he was asking me to do, the irony of that ludicrous title was beyond question. "And regarding our earlier…chat. Should I go armed and prepared?"

"I don't expect you'll need visible guards outside your doors, but I also don't expect the more devout to agree with the quiet agenda of Happy Deliveries being also, when absolutely needed, Happy Prevention-of-Unwanted-Deliveries. The sight of you, dressed like that, will be deterrent enough. Or so I hope. For them. I imagine it'd be quite humiliating, getting thrashed by that nasty thing you carry, only to be healed by its wielder's employees, so to speak."

This was both unprecedented and a little underwhelming. It was one thing to reject the old Commandments vocally and in small acts of defiance…and another altogether to tempt the Mother's eternal fury for doing the one thing She absolutely…unequivocally forbade. And yet I had a feeling at least one Healer here in the south had risked that fury, in the dread face of an unhappily ruined maid.

"I know this is a difficult decision, but if I didn't think you were the—"

"Shut *up*, Jaku. This isn't about me; it's definitely not about what you think of me. And it's not difficult at all. This will be the ultimate test of whatever new order Kaifeng will accept. If it…we are truly free of the Twelve, then even this is no crime. But I need to stress, iterate and reiterate. It must be absolutely the woman's choice."

"Of course! Mother's Love, Sister, what sort of monster do you take me for?"

"Not the sort of monster needed for this task. No. You are, however, precisely the sort of monster that has no trouble asking it of others. Like I said, you're a politician. But, I do concede…you're not always a poor one. You have won. Don't gloat. Don't expect me to say it again. I just want to hear one thing now. When do I start?"

It was a long night for both of us. I slept for two days afterwards. And then I made arrangements for my departure from the Munnamdun Happy Deliveries branch. Zha-Ku had been right: the place ran itself for the most part. I left Wai-Bahk there, since she was no longer the sole hydrotheurge and her Mifūn-go was atrocious. Littleknife came with me, having had some Haven experience and, well, I think she liked keeping an eye on me. No, not liked. Felt it was her duty. I also took the Tsai twins, Yum-Ying and On-Lam, who were originally from the Pagoda district and could help me figure out how to fit in. They were keen to be reunited with their parents, and both had proven very apt with Deliveries: Yum-Ying, a pyrotic, was almost as good with a blade as Littleknife, and On-Lam was a gifted Maliscient when it came to inducing a compliant state for Delivery. We four would suffice for what Zha-Ku wanted. Finally I recruited a handful of kids, who would make legitimate deliveries to cover for the actual Deliveries. Successful and otherwise.

Just as the south hadn't cut off the north, the north was technically open to the south. Still, when the guards let us through a series of checkpoints, both those wearing the orange and those wearing dark red, I knew Zha-Ku had expended serious resources on me and my task.

What a sight we must have been, this handful of women and children, dragging a cart through the gates and archways, always under the watchful gaze of the men on the walls, the ramparts. I wasn't foolish enough to think any of them saw me and thought 'frail useless woman', but I do think most of them assumed the Gildenhammer was more ceremonial than practical. I was almost embarrassed for them, these sentinels who did a worse job assessing danger than your average Haven doorkeeper.

As for Kaifeng north of its rebellious walls? "This place is beautiful. All these parks. Rivers. A lake. Trees. Trees everywhere. Open air dining areas. And houses. So many more houses than tenements. The Pagoda District really is a different world."

"Sister, you brought us along to teach you, so please consider this your first lesson." This was Yum-Ying. On-Lam was a bit farther back, tending to the equally awestruck children. "Only outsiders call it the Pagoda District. The people we will be helping, they call it the Dragon Pavilion. And yes, it is beautiful. To look at."

More than one lesson there. I thanked her and focussed once more on the destination. On the mission.

On what it would take to make this 'Dragon Pavilion' more than merely 'beautiful to look at'.

"He's there again, Sister. Just watching the entrance."

I conferred with Yum-Ying and Littleknife a little longer, assessing the state of the unconscious young woman on the bed, and then gave

On-Lam the attention she clearly desired. "He's not really doing anything wrong, is he?"

"How would I know? Sometimes spies 'just watch', don't they?"

"Let's go see."

I followed her out of the procedures area into the small but functional entrance. The cushioned benches and seats were empty, which was a good thing for On-Lam given her current job.

"Can you please just go talk to him?" She resumed her place behind the welcoming desk beside the open door.

"Alright." I debated whether or not I should take the Gildenhammer. Or clean the evidence of our operations from my beige-and-greys. No, to both. One would be too intimidating; the other, not intimidating enough.

I hadn't realised it was raining until I stepped out into the late summer afternoon. A drizzle, at most. Across the street, shaded by the buildings behind me as the sun fell behind them, a single member of the Kaifeng Imperial Guard was eating noodles at a noodle stall. Very obviously just eating noodles at a noodle stall and doing nothing else. Complete coincidence that he was facing the Happy Deliveries entrance at the same time.

"That rahmen must be amazing." I stood a respectful number of steps away from him but also off the street. "You keep coming back for it."

The stall owner, for whom we delivered now and then, caught the hint and just kept working.

"So we have been watching each other." He adjusted his position on the stool. The way his left forearm rested on the hilt of his sword while the hand held the bowl conveyed a deceptive relaxation, almost slovenly. But the middle-aged man was clean-shaven, his hair tucked up and under a steel-brimmed cap declaring his rank. "And at least one of us is not breaking the law in the process."

I'd first noticed him a few weeks ago, maybe just over a month since we'd opened. I'd assumed Zha-Ku had used his vaunted resources to keep the Chikageh's eyes elsewhere, either through financial encouragement or more direct means of distraction. This fellow, though, had two things I didn't like: patient eyes, and a uniform from before the so-called war. He wasn't a Chūnkojin recruit, but a progeny of old Mifūnjin supremacy. I hadn't seen it for myself, but it wasn't hard to imagine. His superiority was unspoken and implicit. At least, over the Chūnkojin.

Kasudenjin Halves, on the other hand…

"If you can stomach the details, you are welcome to inspect every inch of the Happy Deliveries establishment anytime…lieutenant." I'd heard Chikageh members call him 'kahshirah', but I figured it was just a nickname. The sort of thing gang members would call *their* lieutenants, the bosses beneath the Boss. Before Wong Chu-Deng's ploy, they likely would have just called him 'sir' to his face and all manner of unpleasant things otherwise. "We might be from the south, but our services are open to all. Food delivery, women's care, occasional child minding. Every community needs these, regardless of their rules and rulers."

"The Ayawaka Administration provides everything Kaifeng needs." I treasured how rote he made it sound, intentionally or not. Was he here out of suspicion, or curiosity? I hoped both. I could work with both, but not either or neither. "For Mifūnjin and Chūnkojin."

He added the last part as though the doctrine were recently changed, which of course it was.

I put my hands on my hips and turned to appraise where we both were. "You know, before I came here, I saw other cities, other cultures. I grew up not in Kasuden but Teriss-Luniir, the capital of it in fact. Good Twelve-abiding city, Teristra, but its citizens are still free to live how they choose, work for whom they want." I mean, as long as the Guilds approve… "Neither half of Kaifeng has that right now. The southerners call each other 'comrade' but mostly fight one man's war, and up here you have to tolerate a Chūnkojin upstart who managed to convince the Ayakawa Administration they needed his protection."

"An inadvisable choice of words for an inadvisable topic."

"I apologise. My Mifūn-go is inadequate at times."

He put the bowl and chopsticks on the counter and rested his right hand on the sword's hilt, fingers and thumb loose. "Adequate enough to know you are not welcome here, Sister Kikuko. Tolerated, but not welcome."

"I feel as though our customers would disagree. Some of whom even the Chikageh and the Guard would be…ill-advised to upset, Lieutenant Kobayashi." Yes, sir. We had indeed been watching each other. So he knew that I'd taken the Mifūn-go name for chrysanthemum. Or close enough. And I knew that he was true Mifūnjin, else I'd have asked for his real name.

"You mistake me, Sister. I never said I was among those who feel that way."

Huh. Okay…"And you're far too professional to tell me how you do feel about us, right?"

"I approve of the concept of you. And if all you are doing is what you claim, I approve of the reality. But I am not fool enough to think a 'guided tour' would reveal anything, nor even might a surprise raid. The worst fighting is to the west of the Pavilion and the Palace, in Shohchin and Enbushoh." Siu-Tsin, and north of that where the Guard held me for months, Jinmouzong. Loose meaning: mock-battle manor. Now not so mock, and not just a manor. "A front for uncivil aggression would be quiet, unnoticed. Happy Deliveries is all the women can talk about. Even my wife has heard of it. And you women just seem too busy to orchestrate any sort of attack."

"So you would be more concerned if I had men on my staff?"

He laughed a little, in that way men do when a woman is right and they are about to disagree in a roundabout way. "I know what you are and what you can do. You didn't need to set up some women's asylum to do significant damage. Why don't you just approach the Palace yourself, appeal to the authorities? Why align with Southern Insurgents?" So that's what the Ayakawa Administration had labelled them. Us. Them?

"Because I think they're right. The Scourge, Char Ah-Ran, disrupted Kaifeng for a reason. His way was fire and sword, mine is water and knife." I paused, annoyed at how my zeal loved to loosen my tongue towards boastful metaphors. "You've been with the Imperial Guard for a long time, I think. A part of this system. You tell me how it stands. What he did to it."

"Take a look around, Sister Kikuko. Your fellow Half, he burned down a Haven out of town. We rebuilt it in a matter of months. He killed a hundred people. Kaifeng has tens of thousands more. The citizens of Dragon Pavilion didn't even know his name. The only reason we have this current…situation is because he somehow knew Terasawa Jaku, who had just been waiting for his chance to stake his claim somewhere, anywhere. South-east Kaifeng, in disarray, was perfect. Did you ever hear about the Nest?"

"The pleasure house a few streets away?" Sure, we'd already visited that place a few times. Easy clientele. Popular with the Chikageh.

He raised an eyebrow, and I realised I'd fucked up again. "You have settled right in, haven't you? No, not that nest. The old thief's headquarters in Shohchin. Someone burned that down too, but not before all the members got out. All but one. Tsukamoto Genma, also known as Leung Guan-Pi."

"Ah. Him."

"Him. And now I hear Terasawa Jaku is trying to revive that man's vision of a Kaifeng without Imperial guidance. A lawless mess of supposed equality. You cannot expect the Kaifeng Imperial Guard to sit back and watch that happen."

"So you side with a glorified gang made up of men too violent, too extreme to be part of Jaku's plan." For now.

The rain went from a mist to unpleasantly fat plops. Before he could answer, the sky itself set the tone.

Lieutenant Kobayashi stood up. "No, young flower." Ugh, really? "They sided with those who give me my orders. There isn't a member of the Guard to my knowledge content with this, but, eh. What can we do?" He shook out his sleeves, scuffed the damp dirt with his sandaled feet. Loosened himself for the walk ahead and, it seemed, what he was to say next. "We let the Chikageh and the 'Society' bloody each other well away from here, hope the wind doesn't turn and blow shit our way."

I laughed, unfeigned and sudden. "Wind is a problem if there's a fire. But water? Healing? All the wind does then is bring the cleansing rain."

He snorted, but was clearly now enjoying the wordplay. "Until the rain collects in the holes and stagnates into filth. A single tainted well can kill a city quicker than any fire or wind. And with much more suffering."

Rare that both parties given to the play of words know precisely when to stop playing, so I did it for us.

"I promise you this, Lieutenant. We will evaporate and disperse long before that can happen. Kaifeng has seen enough stagnation. Enough false peace. Enough imposed occupation. We aren't here to occupy the holes. If anything, the opposite. We don't bring change. We take away the unwanted constant. We *are* change."

And then something did indeed change.

"Blasphemy." I heard rather than saw his left thumb push against the tsuba of his sword. A tiny twinkle of metal almost pulled my attention from his troubled face to the potential trouble it suggested.

Think quick, Sarah. "Your correct is not necessarily right."

I hoped the subtle difference of the two worked in Mifūn-go as well as it did in Common.

I also hoped a certain Mifūnjin-hating hothead with a tendency to cut her way through problems was not watching this from the entrance of Happy Deliveries. I dared not look.

Kobayashi shifted his grip, and applied just the right amount of pressure to the pommel. Pommel, in Mifūn-go: *kashira*. 'Kahshirah'. A connection my brother would have made with a gleeful display of knowingitall, but I knew something he often didn't: when it wasn't my turn to talk.

The movement of Kobayashi's sword made no sound this time, which made what he said next everything I heard. "I told you already, Sister. If this were about my beliefs, I wouldn't be here. This is about what I do. Who I am."

I felt my eyes widen; maybe he'd made that connection for us. "So, Lieutenant Kobayashi of the Kaifeng Imperial Guard, is it about orders? Orders aren't always right either."

"Following orders is always right." I knew he wasn't arguing with me there, and he was about to lose. His self-assurance faltered, and he muttered what was certainly a little blasphemy under his breath. "In this case I think they were. Right for you, maybe not for me. My orders were simply to come here and watch. Not to spy. Not to hide. To be seen."

"And how is that 'right'?" I had started to guess, but let him see this one through. Let him have this one.

"Think on what I wasn't ordered to do. Think on what I am *not*."

I pretended to, because what was important here was that he already had. "It wasn't about what you saw watching us. It was about who saw you watching us."

He nodded. "The Kaifeng Imperial Guard yet strike some deep-seated fear in the watery bowels of the Chikageh. We were, not so long ago, *their* oppressors."

Oh, Jaku.

"I trust you will continue to follow your orders like the good lieutenant you are then."

"It's I do this or they make me do that." He really didn't need to elaborate on what 'that' was.

My turn to nod.

We were quiet for a while, until the first rumble overhead prompted something more.

"This stall is no shelter against a storm. Care to join us across the street? We have tea and cake."

"If I leave now, I'll make it home before the worst of it."

I half-shrugged, the impending weather robbing me of any energy beyond one last jab. "All are welcome here."

"Blasphemy." He shuffled away with his head down, as though heavy with the helm of his office. The rain plinked against the polished metal. "Not that you care much for that, I suppose."

"All are welcome, Kobayashi-*chuu-i*. Even you." I turned this into a shout at his retreating back and its emblem for the Kaifeng Imperial Guard: an Ayakawa-style chrysanthemum, of course. "Especially you."

Kobayashi had been right; the storm was slow in coming. Before it hit, after I watched him amble off, I turned to the old stall owner, who had been impressively quiet the whole time. "Did...did he just walk off without paying?"

"He did."

"Ephin' guards and their free-loading! Same the world over." I blurted this in Common, then quickly reverted to Mifūn-go. "I'm so sorry. How much does he...do I owe you?"

"We have an agreement, Sister." He started to pull the curtain between us. "...And you are wrong. Guards are not the same the world over. Be thankful for that. Stay safe, comrade." With a swish of fabric, he denied any further inquiry.

Fucking. Jaku.

"Ignore him." The Sisters had definitely been trying not to watch, and I told them exactly what they didn't want to hear when I returned. "We have work to do, and so does he."

But Lieutenant Kobayashi's vigil ended a few days later. One day he was simply not there, and then the next. We stepped up our operations and security as a result, but I hoped he remembered what I'd said.

The stall owner remained, but I'd strangely lost any appetite for rahmen.

"Yes, okay, 'Tahtsunoh Hirohmu', I hear you, now please tell me your real name."

The wounded Chikageh man...no, kid, just a kid, grunted and grit his teeth, clutching his gore-soaked belly, barely able to sit upright. The blood was hard to see through the black and red of his haohri, but in the small bedroom, the mess it was making on the straw mat floor was impossible to ignore.

"Wang." The name filled his breath in much clearer Chūnko-go. "Wang Ying."

"Alright, young master Wang, just lie back now." I directed Littleknife to heal the wound after I ran some water over it. "We will get you fixed up and then we'll talk. Relax now please."

As Littleknife's hands emanated a nimbus of flesh-binding energy, Tsai On-Lam placed her fingertips on his temples from her place kneeling near his head. I'd seen far worse but I had the feeling young 'Hirohmu' thought he was going to die.

Waiting at the door, his mother, dressed in a lavish and honestly uncomfortable-looking kimono, just kept Flailing herself and mumbling feverish prayers. The gold *f* about her neck was no small thing. I'd noticed on an earlier visit that it even had a gem of some sort fixed at the intersection of curve and cut.

"Sister Tai, Sister Zan, keep at it. Mrs. Wang and I need to talk outside. Please let me know if anything goes awry." I then remembered this wasn't a Happy Deliveries room, and the mother was right here. "Not that it will, because you're both peerless Sisters. Come, Mrs. Wang. Your son will be fine."

I ushered her out, and went to follow when I remembered just how uncomfortable Wang Ying had been using Mifūn-go. How he'd relaxed into Chūnko-go, almost as though it were the homecoming his physical return couldn't quite manage. And I remembered just how bloody he looked – all of him, not just his shadow.

I stayed in the room and slid the door shut behind me after glancing to make sure Mrs. Wang was well out of earshot. "Littleknife, a moment please."

She took that moment to ensure her healing was satisfactory, wrung her hands out, and shuffled over to me on her knees. "What?"

Amazing how she could look up at me and down at me at the same time. How dare I interrupt her work. And, as always, it was exemplary work. So, as always, I just sighed and sidestepped her acerbic instinct. "In ten minutes, I want you to come find us and tell me that Tatsunoh Hirohmu has taken a turn for the worst and might not make it."

Sharp though she was, this obvious deception wrinkled her brow. Littleknife looked ready to disagree, but then her expression went blank with an amused servant's compliance. "As you command, Mother."

I was too caught in my idea to chastise her lazy insolence. "Those exact words."

"Can you please repeat them? I have trouble remembering single sentences." There was a tiny, tiny smile accompanying her sarcasm, and I couldn't but enjoy it.

"Just fucking do it, you little smartarse." I fell into exasperated Common a moment before I remembered something else. A moment before she rocked back. Now she was as fragile as a raw egg. As a severely troubled, severely withdrawn teenager. What the fuck had I done? I rushed back into Chūnko-go, hoping the cracks weren't severe enough to break a shell I knew I had to shatter someday. Just not this day. "Please. This is extremely important."

"Fine." Once again her more familiar, volatile self, she cocked her head to the side, but remained in Common. "You know, I could do it for real. Isn't he the enemy? Oops, knife slipped a bit, oh no, accidentally slashed his throat. Snick. Splooosh. One less Chikageh shitbag in the world. Such a tragedy."

"Ten minutes, Littleknife. And ten minutes after that, you will return much more loudly and tell us that Wang Ying has made a miraculous recovery."

Like I said. She was sharp. She said nothing else, just pouted and went back to not-killing the boy.

I left them to their tasks, went down the hall and into a larger room where Mrs. Wang awaited. The whole place, from the sliding screen doors to the wooden framework, was desperately Mifūné in design and layout, but at least it wasn't new.

We knelt on cushions around a squat black lacquered table, and an attendant prepared us late night tea. It took at least five minutes. For hot water that tasted like ash and servitude.

"Most excellent tea." I set the cup down. "Mrs. Wang, why did you send for us? There are healers close by. Surely the Chikageh take care of their own."

The old woman fussed over her tea.

"Mrs. Wang?"

She took a long sip, set the cup down, and reclined on her thighs, hands arranged on top. Then, and only then, did she look at me. "My name is Oh Reh-Na."

Oh really. "Forgive me, Lady Oh Reh-Na. My question stands."

Mollified, or maybe realising she'd been rebuked, she slumped a little. "My son might have died had I not."

"Oh surely not, Lady Oh. The son of an esteemed member of the community such as yourself. First class care all the way."

"The Teikoku Chikagehkidan commandeered our Haven months ago, and they've been stretched to breaking point for weeks. One soldier is much like another to them. With the way you've treated my girls, I felt...I simply had no better choice."

Why do the really awful ones always refer to them as 'my girls'?

"We are not some on-call emergency medical service, Lady Oh. Ensuring your girls are able to fulfil their duties is what we do. One way or another. You do realise that it's very likely that an ally of ours did that to your son, don't you? It is not in our interests to heal Chikageh members."

"You will be compensated appropriately, Sister. Aren't you always?"

"Every little bit helps, it's true. We will make an exception. This once. You are not to tell any of your friends or neighbours that we did this. Not even for the right price. Not even though we are, perhaps, far more likely to save their wayward children's lives than their own so-called medics. And with more funding, we could probably open another branch further west, north of the Palace. But, no, we can't make this a habit. Not with our current limited resources. We have only been open for a few months and are still settling in, figuring out how best to serve in these troubled times."

Just as the light of understanding found its way to her heavily made-up eyes, someone completely unexpected tapped on the wooden frame of the door and said my name in an actually unexpected tone of deference and solemnity.

Lady Oh went rigid at just how deferent and solemn it sounded. Littleknife's voice had somehow mastered the creation of an ominous hush.

"What is it, Sister?"

She slid the door open just enough to show her face, and I saw it wasn't just her voice. That was when I knew she'd had to do this before. "I am so sorry to..." She paused, and in the corner of my eye, Lady Oh's mouth fell slack, a single natural lapse in poise she no doubt spent hours assembling. "Tatsunoh Hirohmu of the Chikageh has taken a bad turn—"

"Thank you, Sister." I jumped in, a little more rudely than I'd planned but I had to anticipate any number of reactions from Lady Oh. Had I read her right? If she wailed or screamed I'd have to move even quicker, but…no. That slightly unhinged jaw was it. That was as far as she'd allow her composure to fall, at least in front of servants of the people such as we. "Please return to your duties. I will be there soon."

Littleknife glanced at the stony-faced crone, nodded in what I knew to be her version of deep satisfaction, and left us.

"Mrs. Wang?" The shock held her. No correction of name. No reaction at all. Good. "What you just heard, and what you are feeling, it happens all the time. Every body we see on the street in the morning. Every blood-stained Chikageh haohri. Every shredded orange headband. They all belonged to someone's son. No one's pain is any greater or lesser than anyone else's."

Had he really died, this would be one of the most inappropriate things anyone could say to her, but I was done with appropriateness. Because it was all true. And she, perfumed and preening, had looked the other way and counted her coin, providing for these young manslayers a one-sided comfort they didn't really need. No. What they really needed was us. And she now knew it, knew it almost too late.

"You said nothing would go wrong." I wish I could say her voice was small, cowed, humbled. But I had to settle for it not being a full-voiced screech. And then her far-from-perfect Mifūn-go failed to convey a grief she'd been hiding for a very long time. From when Wang Ying first took the crimson and the black, I suspected. "Oh, Ah-Ying. My boy…"

I'd said what I needed to. Time to wait. Let her fully work through the worst outcome, now that it was very likely the only one.

"I should go see what I can do." A murmur, as I counted the seconds in my head. A much more reliable but less consuming measurement of time than my pulse. She didn't respond, so I rose to my feet as quickly as possible given my goal was to be as slow as possible.

"I will come with you." She started to unfold.

"I'm not sure that's the best idea…"

Any moment now…

"What? You outsiders think you can take better care of him than his own mother?"

Shit. The premature despair and loss was funneling into familiar contempt and indignation. Into rejection. Too soon, too soon. "Now, now, Mrs. Wang—"

"My name is *Lady Oh Reh-Na*, you southern slattern."

Fuuuuuck. "Let me go check, perhaps—"

"MOTHER!" Littleknife came pounding down the hall, balls of her feet all but slipping on the polished wood. "It's a miracle!"

Bit thick there, little monster, but thank you for not waiting until 'Lady Oh Reh-Na' started denouncing our entire cause. "What news, Sister?"

I stepped back from the door to let Mrs. Wang, who had clambered to her feet, see with her own wobbly, angry, confused eyes this bearer of glorious news. Bless the brat, she fair glowed with the ecstasy and exhaustion I knew very well from after any Delivery.

"Wang Ying has recovered. He came to briefly, but now sleeps the healing sleep."

"…My boy…"

"Mrs. Wang." Littleknife addressed her in Chūnko-go.

"Littleknife, no…"

"Yes, child?" Lady Oh Reh-Na was not her name now.

"He only said one thing when his eyes opened. He said: 'Mother. Tell her I'm sorry.' Then a tear fell down his cheek. Now he dreams of you, Mrs. Wang. You who can be there when he wakes."

Littleknife YES.

"A miracle indeed!" I couldn't match Littleknife's theatrics but I could at least affirm them. "Wang Ying has been saved." By us, old woman. Not by the Night. Not by the Teikoku Chikagehkidan. Not by the Ayakawa administration. By this 'southern slattern'. By *us*. "But, if I may say something else, Mrs. Wang?"

"Yes, yes, say what you will, my boy, my dear boy…"

I turned to her and made a little effort at scraping the relief from her face. "We may have saved Wang Ying, but it is truly unfortunate that we could not save yet one more Chikageh member from the incessant violence of his chosen life."

I saw Littleknife smirk in the corner of my eye. Yes, yes. I stole your idea from years ago. You aren't the only one worthy of a new life.

But my focus was Mrs. Wang of the Nightingale Nest. I didn't know why or how her son, surely pampered and sheltered here of all places, came to join the truly heinous Bloody Shadows, but I had a feeling why and how he'd leave them.

"Tatsunoh Hirohmu?" Mrs. Wang wrinkled her nose. "Stupid name for a stupid boy. I am glad he's dead."

"One less Chikageh shitbag in the world." Before Littleknife could react to my indulgent appropriation, I returned my attention to her. "We will check on him one last time before departing. It has been a…turbulent visit, and I am sure Lady Oh Reh-Na will be glad to be rid of us. Is that not so, Lady Oh?"

And she didn't answer immediately. That was when I knew we had won.

"Mrs. Wang? We shall be going now."

"Why, yes. Yes, of course. It was…what was the word? Turbulent. But you saved him…" And of course, she was now just another doting mother clucking away in Chūnko-go. "I will be forever grateful."

"We cannot do this again, Mrs. Wang. Not for anyone who is just going to waste our humble offerings by rushing back into this most pointless of battles. Mifūnjin, Chūnkojin…we do not care. Ours is not the place to perpetuate the savagery of either side. Ours is to assist and provide for those who wish to heal this magnificent city."

Read the room, you wrinkly old sow. Remember what we said before. And tell absolutely everyone.

"This will stay between us, Sister."

"Very well." I made to return to my most talented Sisters. "We will be on our way. Unless any of your girls need our attendance?"

"No, no I couldn't. Let us end this on the highest note possible. Bless you, Sisters. I still have a son thanks to you."

Despite my subterfuge, this was probably true and I let that wash over me. I smiled without pretense. "Well, you know where we are. What we do. And who we'll do it for. Send a messenger anytime."

Once we were back at the Dragon Pavilion Happy Deliveries office, I waited until the others had headed off to bed before tapping Littleknife on the shoulder.

"What?"

…No. It would not be this day after all. Her shell was reinforced, solidifed. Baked hard in whatever heat she'd generated in the kitchen of our collective concoction tonight. "Good work back there."

"Mother?" Common. I knew it was coming and I braced myself and it was going to hurt anyway.

"Yes?"

"Don't ever call me a little smartarse again."

The next day, I took one of the kids aside, a jumpy kitten called Ming-Kee. "I have a message for comrade Leung Zha-Ku. Show him this to prove it's from me." I gave her my crux et luna armband, which I'd only been wearing on and off – mostly house calls, just to stir some mystique into who and what we were. "And tell him we will need more staff very soon."

Zha-Ku's original vision had been curiously myopic. At first, there *had* been a quiet demand for our original plan: we delivered food, Delivered babies and delivered women from unintended circumstances from their encounters with unruly…nuisances. But after responding to that frantic summons to the Nest almost on a whim, I realised we had a much bigger role to play than aiding the women of the North: we could also aid their children, many of whom had been initially lured into the glory found in Chikageh ranks but now had experienced the truth of the Bloody Shadows' opportunistic, self-serving legacy. They, too, needed to be delivered from the boar's gluttonous grasp.

Two weeks later, Mrs. Wang of the Nightingale's Nest paid us triple what we'd requested, which was as close to a direct response as I could expect from her ilk. I thanked her with some fresh fruit from the south, and a we-very-much-look-forward-to-servicing-you-again note.

Word of mouth did the work for us, and for months we weren't bothered by anyone at all despite Kobayashi's troubling absence.

Eventually I sent Ming-Kee off south with another message, this one requesting more than just a staff bolster. We needed to start looking at properties to the north-west. I hoped that Terasawa was keeping track of where we were now servicing, because the map I had set up in the welcoming room made sure everyone visiting couldn't miss the way we were starting to give the Five-Fold Palace a nice, big, Happy hug.

One night maybe a month later, just before my twenty-fourth birthday I think, a wounded man in the now all-but-expected black and reds of the Chikagehkidan turned up on the doorstep of our new West Dragon Pavilion facility. He was holding one hand in the other, which would have been humble – but for the crudely bandaged stump at the end of his left arm.

"Sister…" When he stepped into our light, I knew who it was. "Am I welcome here?"

"Blessed mother! Get in here, Kobayashi-*chuui*."

"Kobayashi-*tai-i*…" And then he rolled his eyes. Rather, his eyes rolled, and he almost buckled. "Promoted to Captain. Night-time patrol. For talking to you. One time. Not part of my orders…"

He fell and I caught him. I rallied the Sisters on duty as best I could, despite not knowing many of them beyond hurried introductions. I was aware of how easy it would be for either side to insert a subversive element now, which is why I made sure Happy Deliveries maintained an image, a modus operandi, of complete neutrality.

"Can you…can you put it back the way it was, Little Flower?" I kept pace as they entered the Procedures area, closed the door behind me. Wouldn't do for the guests to see any of this. Any more than they already had. "Can you make it better?"

Perhaps he was too close to shock to realise those were two very different questions. And perhaps not. His hand was fucked but I said it anyway. "Absolutely, Captain Kobayashi. It's why I'm here. To make it better. All of it. Everything. For everyone."

Nature Against Nature

"What did you do with the evidence of those tragically unsuccessful Deliveries?"

"I ate it."

19 hours until the revelation

Chapter 18: The Wanton Cow
6-7/878 A.R.

"Nothing will change, Talon. We just need you elsewhere."

I shrugged off his attempts at placation. "Horseshit and pigpiss, Jaku."

"Yes, yes, it's great news." He grinned and took hold of my arm. He knew better than to touch me at all, let alone like this. But I knew better than to make a real scene when he was right: this was great news for most of them. "Come, let's discuss this where we can hear each other."

Terasawa Jaku insinuated his way through the crowd in the Gentle Bouquet Community Centre, a crowd that was roughly fifty-six times too jubilant and self-congratulatory for my likes. He'd told me to come dressed for a party, so naturally I was in my old faux-Sisters robe the colour of an extremely unhappy pomegranate. Now and then people clapped him on the shoulder, laughed and even went for a hug. Eventually we made it back into that old office behind the kitchen.

And it all looked the same, but for the map behind his chair. It was exactly what I'd hoped he'd done, and now wished he hadn't. I sat there staring at it. The way he'd marked the location and scope of each Happy Deliveries branch. Not with flowers. Not with smiling faces. No. Of course not.

I hadn't even been wearing the armband much.

"I have no idea how you managed it." He waved at a few candles on the desk, providing a little more light to the room. "Six branches, now servicing almost three quarters of the city. Not the south. Not the north. The entire city. Delivering babies. Food. Taking care of unwanted burdens. And, I hear, healing whoever asks for it. Kaifeng Imperial Guard. Teikoku Chikagehkidan members. Former Rats and Shadows. Thieves. Murderers. Rapists. How charitable of you."

"Whoever asks for it and *pays very well*. Besides, it wasn't a Kaifeng Imperial Guard. Just another bloody Chikageh soldier."

He just looked at me, and I pressed on.

"All are welcome? Shall we resort to that yet again, even in the absence of the Twelve and its Respites?" I gave no room for an answer about which I cared not even a tiny bit. "No. The truth then: very few of the Chikageh and almost none of the Kaifeng Imperial Guard we have treated are thieves, murderers or rapists. Have you forgotten your own words? They are not the enemy. Not like the thugs Chu-Deng...*Inoh* unleashed on the south early on, although I doubt he ever had that much of a hold on their leash. What's left then? Kids and old men, tired and desperate. Your Society has reclaimed Siu-Tsin and Yuwantai, as this very party is celebrating. I have softened the Dragon Pavilion, sorry, the Pagoda District. The Society could just walk on in. They are far too dependent on our services now, our Twelve-defying mission. Let me establish one last branch in the north-west. In Jinmouzong, exclusively for Imperial Guard and Chikagehkidan usage, and you'll have the Five-Fold Palace surrounded. Not by troops or bloodshed, but by benevolence and care."

"You sound just like her." I bristled at this, certain that I knew precisely who he meant, but said nothing, because I wanted to give him every chance to prove me wrong. "You saw what those 'kids' did to the innocent women of our community. Barely a year ago and my wife was ready to claw out all four balls of the first Chikageh mutt she came across. Now you would have her and the other Sisters provide succour for those same animals?"

I simply didn't have the will to point out that he had been the one to call those atrocities a 'nuisance' and 'unfortunate'. He'd just make excuses or, worse, make none at all. "You of all people making me repeat myself. Fine. The Chikageh that Inoh sent down here were truly the lowest of them all. He likely expected them to die, one way or another. I'd wager many of them have by now. Besides, I know for a fact your Society has its share of former Shadows and defecting Chikageh. There's no way you consolidated power down here with the piddling forces I saw barely a year ago."

Jaku inhaled through his nose, loud and slow. A build-up…and then nothing but an exhale, still with his mouth pursed. "Once they dedicated themselves to cleansing Kaifeng of Mifūnjin tyranny, it didn't matter where they came from. Who they were before."

"Or what they'd done."

"Or. What. They'd. Done."

"Or…what they might still do in the frenzy of the moment."

"Tread softly and lightly now, Sariana."

Nah, fuck it, let's dance a lively jig here. "Jaku, some of the women we have treated for what you once so heartlessly called 'involuntary pregnancy' have Chikageh relatives. Some *are* Chikageh. I doubt it was our 'enemy' at fault there. Moreover, some of them were old Mifūné. I know for a fact that some of the women suffering 'involuntary pregnancies' at the hands of *our comrades* had old family names. Oda. Fujiwara…Terasawa."

Terasawa Jaku didn't even blink at this blunt assertion. Honestly, had I dared hope for anything else? "I sent you up there to endear our cause to the vulnerable populace, not endear them to your Sisterhood. You did an excellent job of the former, until the weakness of the latter took over. That's why we're going to let others take over that role, others a little more steeled against the erosion of exposure. And you. I'm sending you at Inoh."

He'd veered so far from the fight I knew he wasn't going to let me have, so deep into other, admittedly important terrain of conflict, that I had no choice but to follow.

"*At* Wong Chu-Deng? A few years and a whole lot of suffering too late to send me 'at' anyone, don't you think? And to my knowledge he's comfortably embedded in the Palace district. Guess I could just kill as many Chikageh as possible. He'll show sooner or later." I forced myself to not dwell on how this had been Lily's most desired plan for me when Jaku had first sent me north. Surely it had been different then. "Is that your level of subtlety, Terasawa Jaku?"

"Leung. Zha. Ku." He cracked his knuckles. The sound only increased my irritation.

"Well, Leung…Zha…Ku. Is it?"

"Of course not. I told you I don't ever want you doing things that way. I'm moving you from Deliveries to Hospitality."

"I…what? What does that mean? I seduce the boar? You would treat me like a piece of succulent beef? Me!?"

"How can you be so quick and so slow all at once? No. It means the Court is ready for the next stage. They have seen how good we are for the people, all people of Kaifeng, and they're tired of Wong Chu-Deng's posturing. He said he'd protect them from us, and not once in over a year have we made a single aggressive move against them. They can see it's all still in-fighting, which was fine for them when it was just Chūnkojin squabbling over scraps. They legitimised Wong Chu-Deng and the leftovers of the Bloody Shadows in a panic, and now they need to figure out a way to free themselves from that arrangement."

So he wasn't that mad that I'd decided to act in…hospitable neutrality. It, and whatever else he'd been up to, had shown the old rulers of the city that the Society for the Advancement of Kaifeng's Youth was a better option than the Chikageh going forward. They clearly couldn't co-exist. And of course this was his approach.

"And so you plan to court the Court. I bet your council for a free Kaifeng is perfectly amenable to this."

"They don't need to know. They don't *want* to know. They trust me to lay the road to victory. Lily trusts me to lay that road. Why do you always find a way to complain about the size or shape or colour of the bricks? We are so close. One last task, Sister. And all you have to do is be there. Dinner. One night. That's it."

"With him? No assassination. No surprise attacks. No wooing. Dinner."

"With him, in a perfectly public place. You said it yourself. I'm a politician. A statesman building the new State. The time of moonlit skirmishes in the streets and gruesome assaults in the alleyways is over. Everyone's ready to come to the table. Please. Don't leave the place I've set for you empty. Think of this as your reward for all the hard work. For…you know." He gestured at the map behind him, the one undeniably announcing who had won this war and how. "All of that."

"And then we are done?" Why weren't we done already? I owed him nothing. He owed me everything. Shit. It wasn't about me or him. It was about Kaifeng. And Eph no I didn't trust him to lay the road to anything. So of course we weren't done.

"If you wish, but I have a feeling you'll want to stick around to see what comes next. But for now, I'm inviting you to another party, Sariana Jaydemyr, and this time I recommend you dress appropriately. And wear some nice jewellery. A pendant, perhaps."

I just shook my head and rose to get out of there.

"Oh, and that Happy Deliveries in Jinmouzong you just mentioned? I approved it a few days ago. Thank you for indulging my petty whims this one last time."

I left the Society's compound with two things: a written invitation to an Audience with Lord Ayakawa no Inoh-ue Kenjiroh in the Outerfold Palace next month ('A modest repast under the midsummer moon'), and a renewed resentment that someone beat me to breaking Terasawa Jaku's nose.

The seventh and final branch of Happy Deliveries opened in Jinmouzong two weeks later. I had no idea who was operating it, and when I visited the other branches, I was met by strangers. Naturally; this wasn't where Jaku wanted me, nor who he wanted me to be. Jaku wanted me in the Dragon Pavilion, preparing for Kaifeng's idea of a royal gathering. He wanted a Half at this meeting in the Five-Fold Palace…No, he wanted a *Jaydemyr* laughing at the pathetic pecking order, so that's what I'd be, that very name dangling around my neck like an Eph-damned collar.

"You can't go wearing that."

I heard Common so rarely up here let alone that fluent that I didn't need to turn and look to see who it was, but the mirror in which I'd been adjusting the cowl and pendant clarified nonetheless.

Littleknife stood just outside my private chambers on the second floor, in the now-open doorway. Why lock it? This was my home. For the time being.

"And why is that? I can't very well go in our work clothes. I imagine the most esteemed swordsmen of the Chikagehkidan would not appreciate the stale old bloodstains."

She graced me with an expression of scathing I almost recognised and hoped she was only borrowing. "Because it makes you look a piece of *fresh* meat, and you are throwing yourself into a pit of dogs and pigs."

I bit back an admonishment about rank and etiquette and just stared at her reflection. It wasn't what she was saying that mattered. It was that she was saying anything at all. Unprompted. This was not her obeying an order or engaging in biting banter. Now was not the time to be formal or petulant. And Lily had been right; Littleknife's Common was excellent. It needed to be. Because she wasn't just Littleknife of Kaifeng.

"Ping-Gwor—"

"Not that name. Happy Apple is dead." Her mocking look hardened into resolution. More familiar, and more frightening in light of what I thought she'd been through. "And I've decided…I'm going to tell you how she died."

I think I actually blinked at this about ten times. Maybe even fifteen. "Now?" Finally. "Right before I'm due to mince and sashay my way into the heart of Kaifeng's corruption?" *Finally.*

I watched her enter and sit on the messy bed behind me as I kept my eyes on the dressing mirror. She fidgeted a little. "You just answered your own question. Could you please close and lock the door?"

She had any number of reasons to get me into a locked room and not let me out. My apparent lack of devotion to Jaku's cause. Or too much of it. My brother's destruction of her childhood, long overdue its due and surely his sister would be a good start. Or maybe she just thought my going tonight was a bad idea. I certainly did.

I complied anyway, and then took a seat at my dresser. Well, since I was wearing my Fourth Going attire, I could turn the chair around, straddle it and rest my hands and chin on its back. If I could relax, maybe she would as well. If only a little.

"Thank you. What I am going to say might help you at the Palace. Help you want to leave there alive. And no one else must know it. Don't worry, it won't take long."

"You have my attention and my time, Littleknife. If anyone knocks I will send them away. Unless you get hungry or thirsty. Are you? We Halves tend to forget how often that happens." I'd meant it as a joke, and oh Shyn's Plundered Buttocks was it a bad move.

"Don't pretend you're even a normal sort of Half. We had those come and go. You're nothing like them. Nothing like him."

"My brother?"

"No. You are *absolutely* like him." Fucking ouch. "I meant Hua-Shi."

Ah. So this was how she'd work herself up to it. "The offer for water stands, but until…" I trailed off.

"Okay. So I will start there, in fact. Because until Hua-Shi and that bitchwoman turned up, life in our Haven had been normal. You know, the occasional draining, a fistfight here and there, pinched bums and cheeks from drunken Dai-Suhk. Fuckin' paradise compared to what those two brought.

"They arrived just after the big fight, the Zhengkai Massacre or whatever people call it. A Kas'Daen woman dressed like some harlot dancer calling herself Fa Shai-Yeh, Priestess of the Liquid Night, and a tall Half in a Respite-style brown robe who looked like he'd lost a fight with an oven. He gave the name Wu Ming, but you know that was just a bad joke.

"They were clearly a couple; she couldn't keep her hands off him, and he made a big display of rejecting most of her affection. I was on desk, and he left a sword with us. Ugly thing, like a too-short katana or an overgrown wakizashi. Keep that one under the desk, she said, and I knew it was somehow special. Stolen maybe. Not my place to ask. Welcome to the Haven have a nice stay. You know the routine. And they did. They just moved in for the rest of the week. Hua-Shi loitered at the bar, got a bit touchy with…the workers. Normally that'd be enough to get them both kicked out, but Grandfather made clear it was important they stay. That we not upset them. Whenever I took food or drink to their room, the Kasudenjin woman found some reason to complain. Not enough rice. Too much sauce. Watered-down wine. She'd slap me about, call me names, but I didn't tell Grandfather. They had to stay, and I was sure if he found out just how bad they were, he'd have to get rid of them. So I said nothing. Did as I was told. Now I'll never know what would have happened if I'd…"

I knew better than to invade the silence into which her flat, detached demeanour had retreated. And she stayed there, until a very small smile indicated she'd found a means of escape, or at least continuing through the darkness.

"But then, on the next Hunting night, another Half came to the Haven, and he was nothing like Hua-Shi. Wong Shah-Long was so…dumb. And funny. And nice. And very, very afraid. He hid himself with a black cloak, and didn't know anything about anything. Said he was called Dog-Ears just because he was Half, as though he was the only Half in the whole world. He made me feel very smart and really seemed to care about what I had to say. Just chatting with him, telling him the rules, I forgot all the bad stuff and just talked and talked. Then I made a huge Ephin' mistake: I forgot he wasn't my really my friend, and hinted at how some of the guests were treating me. I don't know why, Sister Talon. I guess I just wanted to tell someone, y'know?"

"I do. And please, call me Sariana."

"Even in Common, I am Littleknife. In fact, he gave me the name. In a way. It was the only weapon he had, this little knife I later learned my Healing teacher from Kaifeng had given him. I had to show him why he didn't need to hand it over. Eph me but he was such a silly puppy." She shook her head but didn't smile again.

"He got upset when you tried to tell him about the bad guests?"

"Oh. Yeah. And not just upset. He started to glow, Sariana. It was like nothing I'd ever seen. Hua-Shi was nearby, so he noticed it first, and called it out. He was right: Dog-Ears was breaking the rules, and it was my fault. I said no, he's fine, he's okay, and of course Hua-Shi tried to hit me. Dog-Ears stopped him, and I swear by Eph's balls he didn't even move. Grandfather smoothed it over, because they were both very important people. Sariana, you've probably noticed I don't talk much these days. My throat is sore. Can I have some water please?"

I filled her a glass from the dresser now behind me and wiped my hand dry. She accepted it with both hands, took a quick sip, and continued.

"Grandfather and Dog-Ears talked a bit after I was sent back to the desk, and then Dog-Ears ran upstairs. I watched him go and thought, wow, if he knows that woman, maybe he did get my message and is off to scold her. I held onto that hope for a while as the night wore on.

"Then Hua-Shi came over and just said, 'give me his sword'. I remember it, Sariana, the words. Not my sword. Not the sword. HIS sword. I didn't ask whose, and just did as I was told. He took it and went to leave. I hated him but I had a job to do, right? I said, 'don't go out there, the moon is full. It's not safe.' And you know what he told me? Nothing. He just smiled and left anyway, like an idiot. I tried. A true Night's Own would take care of him."

She took another sip, and then a few mouthfuls.

I offered her more water, shocked to discover I was stalling despite receiving exactly that for which I'd waited so very long.

"Maybe in a bit. Anyway, after Hua-Shi left, Grandad asked me what I thought of Mr. Shah-Long. I told him I liked him but that he was kind of useless. He laughed but said that the priestess and Mr. Shah-Long might be leaving tonight. Together. I said that was ridiculous. Grandad said yes it was, but it was true. Ridiculous and true? Grown-up things, I said. Grown-up things, he agreed.

"Then both Dog-Ears and Fa Shai-Yeh came down the stairs. Together. She was wearing a white dress of some sort, and a red hood. Just like that one you've got on—"

"Oh. Shit. I'm…I had no idea. I'm sorry."

"Well, you probably did since you knew she was a Sister of the Liquid Night, just like you. But when you first arrived here? Long blonde hair, red hood. Maybe not. Doesn't matter. You aren't her. You'll never be her."

I apologised for interrupting.

"Mm. So Fa Shai-Yeh had changed into a Sister, but Dog-Ears, well, he hadn't changed clothes at all…but he didn't need to. It was as though she'd done something to him. Awakened him. He no longer stooped. He strode. He stumbled a few times, but I think it was an act. He looked at the room, not the people in it. And his eyes, Sariana. Sometimes they were brown, like Dog-Ears', but sometimes they'd flash? Flicker?…turn to black too. A weird shiny but flat black. No Half's eyes does that, not that I'd ever seen. I made a little show of asking Grandfather where Dog-Ears had gone, but he knew too. This was why it had been so important that Fa Shai-Yeh stay there. She'd been waiting for him.

"Grandad sent me upstairs to 'look for him'. I knew what he was really saying. Something bad was about to happen, and I should hide. So I did. I thought I smelled something burnt up there, meat or something, but I hid anyway. And then I heard yelling, screaming…and the weirdest sound you could ever hear in a Haven miles from a river: water. Rushing water. And then something more familiar: a lot of glass breaking all at once. Or someone smashing ice. I knew if I stayed up there, whatever was happening down there would get me. So I came out of the room, and sure enough there was no one. They were all downstairs. I'm no idiot. I didn't go near those stairs. I went to a window at the end of a hall, opened it, climbed out. Not for the first time, obviously. I'd lived there my whole life, after all. A quick escape from an overcrowded Haven was one of the first things I learned.

"But then I remembered the full moon. What I'd told Hua-Shi. Still safer out there than inside, I decided, or at least out there but nearby. So I climbed down from the window, and crept around to the front of the Haven that was my home. And I looked. Of course I did. And what I saw was worse than anything I'd imagined from those sounds."

She gazed down at the glass in her hands and started to breathe very deeply, very consciously. I noticed the way those hands were causing ripples in the water.

I offered to take it from her.

"No, it's fine. This happens." A moment, maybe three. The ripples subsided, and her breathing eased. "I won't describe it, Sariana." By then, the water was still and she seemed to have regained her composure. "I think I've forgotten enough of it now. But you should know, your brother didn't kill all those people. That was her. He was attacking someone and…doing things to the body, but everyone else was…frozen, or shattered, or drowned. No human should use their Talent that way. I didn't know what to do, where to look.

"Then I saw Grandfather, on the floor and very hurt. He was so near to me, and just as I was about to get to him, to try to heal him, whoever Dog-Ears had become ran towards me. I pulled back behind a pillar. He couldn't be the same person as Dog-Ears. He simply couldn't. Was he trying to escape too? Had she made him do those horrible things? Should I try to talk to him?

"I heard Grandad's voice, so weak and wet, and looked once more. Dog-Ears was kneeling over him. I listened as he swore to protect me, but Grandad said he'd told me to run. He hadn't, but go hide was close enough. I would run, though. That much I knew then. Fa Shai-Yeh wasn't going to stop until everyone in the Haven was dead. But not yet. I had to keep listening.

"Then Grandad stopped talking. Now the blackcloaked monster was back, punching the floor, and he was about to hit Grandad, or…Grandad's body. I looked around the room for the woman, and when I didn't see her, I made my move. I grabbed him from behind and begged him to stop. He did, and I knew he was Dog-Ears again. Because it was him, I let myself go and wept against his back. And he said I could cry as much as I wanted to, and oh I wish he'd been right. He asked where she was, and I guessed upstairs. Then, desperate to keep him close and the blackcloaked monster away, I said such stupid, empty things. You're a good person, Dog-Ears. Be a good grown-up. Shit like that. He said he'd never forget me, which was also stupid: we'd only just met. But the last thing I told him was that he'd have to forget me. What I meant was, please fucking forget me because I don't think Dog-Ears is going to be around much longer. He was already becoming the monster again, so I said goodbye one last time and left him to his fate. I ran out of there, but then stopped in the darkness and turned back, one last look at the only home I'd ever known. That is when he howled her name, but in a way that made my ears sting. I know now it was her real name: Vachaelle.

"I knew if They were hunting, the road would be safest, quickest. I headed towards Zheng City. But I didn't get away quickly enough. I heard the roar of the flames behind me, and turned back to look. Above the trees, I saw the glow. The same glow I'd seen earlier that night. The same glow that had stopped Hua-Shi from hurting me. His. So yes, he did cause the fire. But she made it necessary. Sariana. I know I haven't really been talking that long, but I need to pause for a bit. Okay?"

"Okay, little Sister. You…You take your time." I can't really cry. You know that. We can't. But if I could, I would have been a mess after all that. Not only for what she'd been through. Not only for the revelation that my brother hadn't killed all those people. But mainly because I could see it, how easily and lightly Chaelle turned a full Haven into her glaciated playground. "…Littleknife?"

"Yeah?"

"You deserve about a million hugs. When you're ready, I plan to get started on that."

She snorted. "A million and ten. I'm not finished. I did say pause, not stop."

"So you did." I nodded, although I'd forgotten it. What more could there be?

She held the glass out and I refilled it.

"I watched the sky waver and fade over where my home had been, and then started on my way again. I didn't run very fast because They like it when people do that. And so I was able to see someone standing in the road, tall, dark and holding a sword at their side. I tried to run the other way, then remembered who was probably coming from *that* direction. Sooner or later. So I hid behind a tree. If Hua-Shi had seen me, he didn't acknowledge it. I should have used the cover and his distraction to go the rest of the way to the city, but…what would happen when the man who waited and the man he was waiting for met? Two Halves, one sword. So, idiot I really am, I stayed and I watched."

"And when they met…they fought?"

"One of them fought, Sariana. The other acted like it was a game. Like he was one of Them. The blackcloaked monster seemed to toy with Hua-Shi. Eventually there was that glow again, turning whoever Dog-

Ears had become into a something like a giant firefly. Beautiful and graceful, and soon gone. He took the sword from Hua-Shi and then it was over."

"The blackcloak cut Hua-Shi down?"

"Not then. It was over. As far as he seemed to care, he had the sword, and Hua-Shi didn't matter. He even put his glow, his fire, into the sword, like he was claiming ownership of it. Then, when the blackcloak turned his back to walk away, Hua-Shi tried again…and that was when your brother cut Hua-Shi down. Cut him up, in fact. In half. I'm a healer, Sariana. I know how bones and muscle work. How hard they can be to cut. And somehow he made it look like chopping up a fish with a cleaver. A fiery cleaver that lit up and went dark in a second. I remember thinking, he made that ugly thing so pretty. He made cutting someone in half enthralling and I had never been so scared of another person. Not even of Vachaelle."

"Eph me."

She finished her drink and then her story. "Eph us all, Sariana. And then he and Vachaelle talked, argued really, and then they just walked away, towards Zheng City. To the west. I waited a bit, and followed. Took refuge for a few nights in Zheng but didn't see them there, so I went to Kaifeng to talk to Lily, tell her what happened. We agreed that I should stay with her, and that Happy Apple died in the fire. So for her, that was it. The end. You may now clap."

"How about that hug?" I found my voice, somehow, and definitely didn't clap.

She shrugged, set down the glass, and made the first real expression since she'd entered the room: a crooked smirk that made clear the hug would be entirely one-sided. Something of a pattern with me it seems. "Only if you promise not to wear that fucking red hood tonight."

The Kas'Daen-style carriage groaned and creaked through the streets, some of them compliant, others, with their grooves and dips, far less so. Naturally the ornate design of said carriage prevented me from seeing much beyond the driver in front of me, who was dressed in finery only Sariana-Ra Jaydemyr found a little quaint. Then again, Sariana-Ra Jaydemyr was in a rather quaint mood, after deciding that while the Fourth Going travel clothes were inappropriate and would likely keep me barred from entering even the Five-Fold Palace's outermost gates, something simple would be best. I only lamented that a black cloak and hood made of almost contradictory expensive material, layers and layers of silk and cotton, couldn't accommodate the Gildenhammer. Not that they'd allow that in either, but I would have liked to see the guards' faces when I surrendered it.

One other thing occupied my mind on that short journey: to believe what Littleknife had told me, I needed a new sort of faith. So far, my belief had been in one thing and one thing only: Vachaelle was in control. Whether she was posing as a healer in an abbey dedicated to safe childbirth, grotesque rituals and I suspected creation of inhuman soldiers, a literally charming performer in a big city, or a hydrotheurge with impossible mastery, Vachaelle the Nightsong dictated the music and the words. I listened to my heartbeat, completely independent of any other rhythm such as the wheels bumping over the stones and dirt or the gentle slap of the driver's reins. It made me wonder how many times she'd tried to adjust it to drive a dance I couldn't remember. Had she done the same to Littleknife? To Happy Apple? To what end? How could it benefit Vachaelle to have someone tell the story as Littleknife did? To paint my brother as the victim, and Vachaelle as the mass murderer? As a lustful manipulator hanging onto a low-life cur like Hua-Shi? To Littleknife, she'd been as abusive and unrestrained as Chantal Falkenstrom. Sarah-Jade remembered learning from that. And then, completely unlike Chantal, she'd waxed joyously destructive upon awakening Charan. Vachaelle could afford to display these types of behaviour only if she knew there'd be no one left to talk of it, or could change the minds of those who might.

No matter how I twisted it, turned it, looked at it, Littleknife's account rang true. It was, mildly put, not the best origin story for a would-be breaker of worlds and his divine guide.

"Alright, Littleknife." I traced the design on my pendant out of a habit I no longer cared to conceal. "You beat her. I can do the same."

The carriage slowed – not by much, given the stunted pace so far – and I let the pendant fall, the chain slipping through my fingers like water. It thudded against my chest, and I let out a tiny little "ouch".

Then I laughed at it, at myself. I exited the carriage and looked up at the open Outermost Eastern Gate, lit with torches and lanterns in the deepening dusk, flanked by sentinels dressed as neither Imperial Guards nor Chikageh, their glaives crackling with flame and lightning. I greeted all of it with an immoveable smile on my face and against my heart. Whatever awaited me. Fanfares. Ranks of fanatic soldiers. Dignified names declared across the courtyards. Denunciations. Proclamations. I was ready for anything.

And of course there was nothing. The courtyard past the gate was empty beyond palace defenders prowling its corners. Wide, luxurious stone stairways led off the expanse into other areas, presumably the Women's Quarters to the south-east, the Armoury north of that, and the Inner Palace straight ahead. Walls blocked my view either way.

The Court didn't even bother assigning me an armed escort, just a few shuffling old ladies nattering away in Chūnko-go. So much for that ban.

We walked north along the edge of the sacred space, and then entered a road flanked by stone carvings. Dogs. Lions. Liondogs? And behind those, houses and shopfronts, curtained entranceways announcing noodles and vegetables, stoneware and incense.

Then the truth sank in. There was no great difference between one side of any wall and the other, not in Kaifeng. I should have known this from how similar Munnamdun and the Dragon Pavilion areas were, despite representing ideologically opposed territories and very different socioeconomic strata. And this was the Outer Palace, not the Inner.

Who lived here?

I looked up at the banners flapping on the poles. Black rectangular field. Three dark red stripes near the bottom. Above that, vertical kanji in white confirming that, yes, they really did mean to be called 'Blood Shadow Imperial Guard':

Chikageh-Kin-Eitai. Glad to see they finally got it right.

The two old ladies stopped in front of a dining hall, a 'tanden' not unlike the Gentle Bouquet. Well, no, to be honest it made anything outside the Palace district look rural and rustic. It was bigger, grander than even the All-Trades Inn in Teristra, or at least what Sarah-Jade remembered of it. A broad set of steps narrowed up towards an entrance of carved wood, papered windows, silk screens. And the name, on a board the size of a small footbridge: A Thousand Views Banquet Hall. Oh, Wong Chu-Deng. You just couldn't resist. Well, from the top floor, it might even be true.

An older man, stooped over under the weight of all sorts of ostentatious clothing and jewellery, hobbled over to our little group, crooning a few 'welcome, welcomes' in mushy Mifūn-go. One of the older ladies nodded at his approach, and then both just turned and walked away. He rubbed his hands together, as though weaving strands of opportunity into some clever net of exploitation. "Welcome, welcome! Invitation please." He stopped with the wringing to hold his palms out, looking oddly like the world's best-dressed beggar.

I placed the resealed red envelope onto his fingers, and his thumbs came unpleasantly close to mine. "I am Kikuko of Happ…sorry, Talon Gukh-Fah, Sister of the Liquid Night." No point invoking Jaydemyr to anyone but confirmed nobility or representatives thereof. Certainly not to some wobbly-jowled welcome-worker.

He fumbled with the invitation, squinted at the characters in the torchlight. "I see. I see…Follow me, if please."

Honestly, you'd think they'd bother to get someone fluent in their damn language.

I tucked the pendant back under the robes. This was such a waste of time, but at least I'd get a good meal out of it.

The guide or whatever he was meant to be held my invitation in one hand, and waved his other at the stone steps feebly. I was too busy watching his fingers, shifty as they were, to think anything of this, until I heard the strange sound of rock shifting, grinding, moving.

"My back and feet, stairs not so good." He flashed a chuckle of a few teeth and shuffled up the new ramp in the middle of the stairway. I hurried after him, remembering Volodymyr's effortless manipulation of the fire back in that tiny Haven near the Kas'Daen border with the Karakani wastelands. Age wore down everything in humans, everything except the one thing God Herself gave them to make life that little bit easier. The weaker the body, the stronger the Talent. God and her Ephin' balance yet again. And you and I, defying it yet again.

Once we reached the landing, he didn't even glance back but I knew the makeshift egress would be gone. And why would I waste time checking that? The Thousand Views Banquet Hall demanded every blink of my eyes, every whiff of my nose, every tilt of my head to snatch a sound from within the buzz. So much light, so much talking.

So. Many. Chikageh. Uniforms.

"Any weapon to leave?" We approached what sure as Eph looked just like a Haven doorkeeper's post. "Not Haven, but Haven smart rule."

"No." I stalked past the desk and its distracted attendant. She was probably about Littleknife's age, and reading a book bound by string. Of course they'd have access to the Imperial library here. In a fit of curiosity, I paused, turned to ask her what the book was about. I missed books from the abbey, although a good storyteller with the right tale could do just as well, as Littleknife had proven earlier.

Before I could say a thing, I saw some of the weapons behind the desk. Most of them were katana or dao leaning against wooden racks, neat and well-maintained. Truly these were not the Chikageh getting their pretty kimono dirty and blades dulled out in the streets. I snorted in derision and went to follow the old man, right as I caught sight of a sword that was neither katana nor dao. One with a tsuba Terasawa Jaku would have very much coveted, or possibly feared seeing again. I knew he'd tried to disseminate my name, but this was insulting.

"Who dropped that sword off?" I stopped and pointed at the offending weapon as the old cripple tried to pull me away. "That one, who left it with you?" And the more I looked at it, the more I realised it was either an incredible replica, or…not supposed to be here.

The attendant closed her book, using a finger to keep her place, followed the direction of my now shaky finger, and pressed her lips together. "Was it…no, his has the *manji*…bit like that though…Oh! I remember." You'd think she'd have some system of knowing these things. Maybe that was another book. There were a few on the desk.

"Delightful. Tell me then. Was he like me? Black cloak, kind of tall, dour, a bit self-important? Have a pair of these?" Frustrated, flustered and completely off-guard, I pulled the hood back, revealing ears I hadn't trimmed once since entering Kaifeng. They were, as he would have put it, definitely dog-ears.

"Oh, sorry I didn't realise it was you, Lady Kikuko!" The desk girl started bowing, and I almost took the time to appreciate the fact that apparently they'd heard of my work even in this sheltered little pocket of privilege. "A thousand apologies for my rudeness and inadequate—"

"Come, we must go now." The old fart kept tugging on my sleeve.

"No, I asked her—"

"—and the work you do, it's just wonderful, healing people no matter who they are, we all—"

"Who. Owns. That. Sword?"

"You will not answer that question." The old man switched to quick but stern Chūnko-go. He still held my sleeve, but when I looked down, it was not with fingers of old bones and stretched skin, but a fist of stone, rough in some places, smooth others. "And stop praising the enemy, you simpering twit."

"Yes, sir. Sorry, sir." She stopped bowing, sat down and looked barely a stern glare away from breaking down in tears.

People were watching, but not in surprise or alarm. If I had to pick only one word for their collective demeanour, it'd be 'disconcerted'. But that'd be missing the amused edge, the tension of anticipation. I replaced the hood (too late, far too late) and gave up. Probably just a replica. Some third-rate smith's attempt based on stories of The Scourge. Sure. Phony Goroshi. Hahaha.

It wasn't funny because it wasn't true.

Was *he* here?

Someone was still gripping my sleeve, trying to turn me around.

"Let go of me…Wong Chu-Deng." I'm sure everyone else had known who he was the whole time, but I suspected that name spoken aloud and to his face was an insult now. No need to shout it, not when a directed whisper did the job.

I heard a sound of rock changing again, softer but distinct. Fucking geomantic adepts. But let go of me he did. And then stepped far too close to respond in his broken Mifūn-go. "My name is Ayakawa no Inoue Kenjiroh-*sama*. Say that, no other, or you lose tongue. Now we go, and no more stopping." *This* flappable fop had terrorised Kaifeng for years? Had somehow convinced the powers that remained in a Court forsaken by its true Nobles that he was the strength they needed to stave off a possible rebellion? Or was it all just another facet of the act? Of no matter. If this was how I was going to get my answer about the sword that should not be there – *Was my brother actually here?* – I had no choice but to follow him. In fact, I wanted to do nothing more.

We climbed no stairs, explored no hallways or hidden passages to some secret meeting area. We did enter a small private dining room with a single round table, set with rich, glistening dishes and just big enough for four people. Two of the chairs were occupied already.

I only noticed one of the occupants, facing the Kas'Daen-style door, which the old man closed behind us. She had blonde hair, with a few streaks of grey. Maybe in her mid-twenties, maybe a bit older. Dressed very distinctly as a Sister of the Fourth Going. I didn't recognise her face, but then again, I didn't need to. Littleknife had told me exactly what I'd need to be ready for this. Eph me, had she conditioned the poor girl after all?

"Well, what do you think? Nothing like her brother, hm?"

"How would I know, Fa Shai-Yeh?" Wong Chu-Deng sat beside her, gazing down at a bowl of rice. "I never had the privilege of meeting him. She is a handful though. Different to what people have been saying."

"You." I was still on my feet and unable to move. "It was you. Not him. You have the sword. But why? Why are you here? Why would he leave the sword with you?"

I remembered it then, a moment she'd tried to erase. Back at the abbey, when I was recovering from Zlatina's scorn. She'd…replaced herself. From Chantal Falkenstrom to something else. Someone else. What had she called it? 'Job change'. Of her inexplicable number of abilities, this one seemed most core to who she was. What she was.

"Because he left me." The Sister confirmed with but four words that despite the different-but-same face, the different-but-same name, she was Vachaelle. "Because I wanted to see how you were doing. Because it's a deadly weapon. I do. Nope. Yes. Yes."

I just gawped at her baffling but precise series of answers. Utter nonsense and complete sense all at once. So very her.

"Sit down already, I'm starving." The third person, to my left, Fa Shai-Yeh's right, was of course Terasawa Jaku, dressed less like a street rat posing as a bureaucrat and more like a bureaucrat who mugged a street rat. So here we all were, three pieces in a game with probably only one real player.

So sit I did, in the only chair remaining. Opposite her, and between the two heirs to Leung Guan-Pi's legacy of larceny and interrupted revolution.

"What the fuck am I doing here, Fa Shai-Yeh?"

She shrugged. "I didn't invite you, he did."

Jaku lifted his black chopsticks from a gaudy little serpent and clacked them a few times aggressively. "You are here because Wong Chu-Deng has her. Two brothers, two Sisters."

"Brothers?" Chu-Deng was far less mocking than I'd expected. And he certainly didn't correct the usage of his real name. "You were Leung's little retriever. One of many. Not even good enough to be called a Rat. I was his right-hand man. He left the Bloody Shadows to me. ME. Brother? A boar does not call a pampered puppy, 'Brother'."

"Not this shit again." Shai-Yeh rolled her eyes. Then she faced me, dismissing two of the most powerful men in Kaifeng just like that. Then she switched to Kas'Daenne, just for me. "Here's what you need to know: I only arrived a week ago. I won't be staying. I have…encouraged the local Court to reconsider their tolerance of this puffed-up gaggle in their back yard. Wasn't exactly difficult. Against all laws of mediocrity and incompetence, Wong muscled his way in, claiming Jaku and his tragic ring of rebels were planning an attack from the south-east. Yes, I know you know. What you don't know is it was true. It still is. Well, except that now it won't be from the south-east. It'll be from all five sides. And, gosh, that might actually work."

The two Kaifeng natives, one a traitorous Chūnkojin and the other a self-hating Mifūnjin, glared at each other through words that would have set their world ablaze had they understood them. Instead, they just ate with that restrained, oddly delicate fury unique to enraged men terrified of breaking decorum and admitting defeat. Good. I had no use for their politicking, nor desire to speak with her in any language they might grasp.

"Where is my brother?" I asked this not in Kas'Daenne but Jaydemyrian, knowing better now than to give her a chance to use multiple questions to divert the topic. A quick check ensured the two men were unaware of the shift from a popular western language to a dead northern one.

"On a very special mission, one that the sword would have made impossible. Do you want to keep it for now? He might come looking for it."

"No. He will return to you for it, and you'd better have it ready when he does."

"Good answer, Daughter. Very prudent of you. Surprisingly so, given how spectacularly you've failed to keep your nose out of his sloppy seconds so far. You won't know when he is done anyway. Not that this matters. You're going to be busy by then, and busy after. Do not waste time or energy looking for us until you are sent for. I hate that I have to say it, but I do not blame you for being tempted."

"Can we get started?" Jaku tried Common, perhaps trying to find some middle ground between the conflicting languages. "I want to—"

"Shut up, little dog." Fa Shai-Yeh lashed him into submission with abrupt Mifūn-go. "Or I will leave the sword with *you* again."

He shut up. Wong Chu-Deng smirked, muttered something about Hua-Shi and someone called Jen-Wah or something. Both retreated to the smouldering silence of rage-nibbling.

"We are very far from home, Vachaelle. I have taken the Long Way alone. I know its hardships, how time stretches across the sand and stone. For you to be here now, either you have as well or he is close. You wouldn't leave him out of reach should conditions change."

"I travel the ways of this world quickly, Sariana. Even the long ones."

"No, *I* travel quickly. You…let me guess. Like this new face. Like your impossible array of Talents. It's all…a seeeecret?"

"It's irrelevant is what it is." I love it when you can tell you've struck a sprout of truth she isn't ready to give up. "I've said what I wanted to say. Do not follow us. Do not investigate The Scourge. When you are done here, just…go back the way you came. Quickly, as you said. You shouldn't have left Cassandra like that. Not as she was just starting to remember. But I knew you would, so I prepared the way. Somewhat."

"Have *you* been back there even once? Or too busy gallivanting about with your new toy?"

"Of course I have, Sariana. The abbey was my home, and I care about my girls very much. You should see what they've done with the place! I could describe it, but honestly, not even my words would do it justice."

"They certainly didn't do me any good."

"Oh grow up, Dumpling. You wanted to run away, so I let you. Set that all up. Best mother in the world that I am. Now you've had a taste of that world, had a little fun playing at Nurse Nightingale, it's time to go back and help Cass finish what we started."

As though this entire journey was nothing more than a luxury tour of the provincial countryside. A whim. All the months out there, getting here, what? A single verse in *her* grand epic. And my time in Kaifeng, establishing a city-wide, truly good Sisterhood helping thousands of people? Pointless busywork to keep 'the spare' happy while The Chosen

One's out there dismantling the old ways, imprinting the new with steel and fire? Fuck. That.

But also: fuck letting her goad me into saying any of this. I stewed without a word as she gloated much the same way. Two pairs of chopsticks clacked and rattled together over a single piece of pork.

"I do like the way you've used the family name here, wearing it like that. Much better than his, but both work. Imagine Kaifeng as a free city, flying the Jaydemyr colours. Exquisite. That old snake Tsukamoto would gut himself in shame. Again. Ha!"

As with her teasing me into distracting queries as to who 'Nurse Nightingale' might be, I ignored her pointed insertion of a name of some clearly dead daimyo. Which Tsukamoto? Didn't matter. But talk of the family name? Close enough to the only topic I wanted to discuss. "It wasn't my idea. Jaku remembered it from Oni-Goroshi, and you told him I'd be wearing it as well. Too much a sign for him not to exploit, sooner or later. I'm not sure it'll be the right move. I saw it once or twice on the way here, in some form or another. But who knows if these people remembered Jaydemyr fondly…or otherwise? It must have taken a massive array of forces from all over Kaef're to bring it down."

She smiled at all this. Not an 'aren't you so clever' crescent of barely-exposed teeth, but something that reached her bright brown eyes. Pride? But of whom? In what? "You are right. But Kaifeng is cut off. Only the Third Eye can see it now. It is…Anathema to the Night, is the official term for it, although that certainly would be a strange office, don't you think?"

I contrived an expression that I hoped came across as something like 'I honestly don't give an Eph'. "I still think it's a bad idea, and whatever happens tonight, I won't be glad to see our name on any flag or buildings here. If Kaifeng is to be free, let it be free of even that. Of you and us."

"You know the best way to make that happen? Leave."

"Eph's Scalded Sac, Mother! I will. Okay? I. Will…Soon."

"I suppose it would be futile, punishing you for blasphemy here of all places. Have it your way. One last thing before we let the men do their secret men's business. *I* am leaving tonight and, thank you, will be taking the sword with me. It is in absolutely everyone's best interest if you don't mention that I was h—"

"I wouldn't, Mother Chantal. People might remember this dinner as the beginning of the end of a very civil war, the rebirth of an old alliance, or maybe just one hell of a foodfight, but neither you nor I will be in the accounts. As you said. There are two very important little men in this important little room, about to be given a way out of their very important little squabble. If it works, history will not permit your presence as she who orchestrated it. Me? I'm just here to not take notes and serve the tea. Maybe I will dance for them later. Play some drunken games. I am, at least for tonight, Hospitality. But you? The woman who plunged Kaifeng into a Godless void and is now deigning to lift it out for no reason other than she's bored without her pet project? That woman can not be here at all. And I am done talking to or about someone who isn't here."

"Good, because as much as that little smartarse might think she hates me, I am content to leave her alone here. Out of respect for Charan's feelings and what she may yet do for him. But if the brat comes at me because of something you said, I will create a new Menu, with just one name on it."

"What did you just call her?" *Don't ever call me a little smartarse again*…no, Littleknife. You were wrong. I *am* her after all.

"Brat? Well she is, so why not?" She shrugged.

Littleknife might have *thought* she hated Vachaelle, but I *knew* Vachaelle really hated Happy Apple. Why? And did she really think I'd believe that excuse about your feelings and Littleknife's future utility? No one with her capacity for spite and access to power spares someone they genuinely hate. Is this why she wanted me gone from Kaifeng? Was my presence alone a threat to the poor girl? A maybe for later. For now: one last absolute statement.

"The worst torture even you could inflict wouldn't drag your name from my mouth around her, Vachaelle. I know you can erase memories, but I'm not foolish enough to hope you'd purge me of this entire fucking meeting. I'm here to learn, as usual, and I can't do that if I don't remember. I just want you to know that if it meant that girl's well-being, I'd dive head-first into whatever deformity of memory you could conjure."

She responded with a third type of smile then. Sad. Resigned. Ancient. Defeated…? And then a murmur in Common. "I love this you, unholy get of Jaydemyr. This brilliant, uncompromised you. But it's not the you he will need. You have done well here, but…Please. Go the fuck home, Sariana."

Then she clapped her hands just once, shook them together at those men in a gesture that was both congratulatory and obeisant. "Very well, gentlemen, I have apprised my fellow Sister of the situation." Fa Shai-Yeh in Mifūn-go sounded not expertly fluent but casually native – I wonder what her first language really was? "And you've made quite the mess here. You both want Kaifeng, and neither of you has realised the other doesn't have it. I agree with Terasawa: allying with the Court by accepting their identity was a terrible move. But I also agree with Wong's approach: rebels just surviving in a ghetto is insufficient. My goal here is to ease both of you into the reality that neither of you truly abandoned the old dragon's vision. You merely only see half of it each. The boar craves the clarity of violence encouraged by the apostate Tsukamoto Genma; the dog seeks to honour the wishes of his late master, Leung Guan-Pi, Godfather of Kaifeng's Disadvantaged Youth. My unfortunately erratic young ward incinerated any and all evidence that Leung Guan-Pi meant the Bloody Shadows and the Rats of Siu-Tsin to enable both, each in their way. In Char Ah-Ran's absence, I take responsibility for that. I assure you he suffers for the recklessness. But he was a child, obsessed with childish things, a childish toy. You are not. You are men, and you do not merely play. So, men of talent, now is your time to act as men, and not children.

"I hereby rename you both First Of the Bloody Rats. There, was that so hard? Now, you have a citizenry to unify and an old order to overthrow, so let's get down to business."

In Voluntary Detachment

"Of course I left her when I could. The details of those years remain a haze, and I don't remember going anywhere near the Swords of Heaven nor the Takhla west of Chūnko, despite Zhang's final urging and what you've said people were saying. But this I do recall: at some point, she dragged me all over the North. Perhaps she was trying to prompt certain memories of this, our home realm. But it was abandoned and merely pocked with civility. A village here, a hamlet there. I suppose we demolished some, just passed through most. But then she said, *this* village I want you to enter alone, unarmed. Show them you are no threat, and ask to learn. Just learn about these people. When she said that, I'd already unslung Oni-Goroshi and started to walk toward the nearby scent of woodsmoke and manure. So yes I left her, but she told me to. I could not have done it by myself. Not then. And I remain grateful to this day that she did it for me. Wildflowers Bloom was…well, I'll tell you about that later. When my mind is ready."

"The best time to tell any story. But regarding this one: we are not made to be alone, Brother. I learned that in the bitter winters of Kas'Daen, and the steppes between Karakan and home. A normal Half left alone self-destructs. Us? We inevitably seek out and destroy others. So company, any company, is preferable to none.
  "If Vachaelle takes advantage of anything, it's that."

15 hours until the revelation

Chapter 19: The Furious Bear
10/878 to 11/879 A.R.

"They're calling it The Feast Of the Boar And The Dog."

I half-shrugged at Littleknife's indignation, just kept on scrubbing blood out of the sheets into a large wooden tub. We were sitting on the front steps of the Munnamdun Happy Deliveries branch. It was good to be back there, at least. "As good a name as any for such an auspicious event."

She wrung her hands out, something I'd noticed she did after a taxing amount, duration and intensity of healing, not unlike Jaku's knuckle-cracking. Kaifeng had a way of bringing out everyone's twitches and tics, it seemed. Well, the Kaifeng that was, and soon would not be. "There were three people at the dinner, not two. Not two angry men, but two angry men and one very smart woman. I hate that I can't tell anyone the truth."

Me too, Littleknife. Me too. Even if telling you might help me understand why you are the one person beyond Vachaelle's hateful reach. "Well, you can tell them it was less of a feast and more of a messy pig-out. That much you will know is true, and people can just dismiss it as embellishment."

"But you…damn it, you never take what you deserve."

No, but sometimes I did get it. "All I did was nod, smile, repeat things one or the other had forgotten. And enjoy a great free meal. As you'd expect for the Outer Palace district, The Thousand Views had some of the best food I've had since getting here."

"Shitty bribe for your silence and omission if you ask me."

"I take what I can get. They could have just as easily not included me at all. Not as though any of it required much more than a good memory and a realisation that men like Wong and Terasawa are less likely to come to blows with a woman pouring them tea and pointing out how special they are."

"But let me guess." She scrunched up a slightly pink rag, slapped it a few times against the step. "They'll still be begging for you to take part in the actual assault on the Palace. And you have to admit, you'd probably be saving a lot of lives. Since you're…y'know, like him."

Interesting how it didn't hurt this time she said it. "No." I hefted the full tub sideways (one handed, because I was indeed 'like him'), watched the rosy froth and fluid rush into a channel along the road and then disappear into a Hole. Not for the first time I wondered what was down there, and who'd maintain it after the True Society For Kaifeng's Advancement (final name change, they promised) overthrew and replaced the Court. Sure, it was a necessary upheaval to pry Kaifeng free, but I was very glad I wouldn't have to be part of the next step: deciding who collects the garbage. Who sweeps the streets. Who cleans the Holes…"That's their fight, to win and to lose. To survive, or to die for. My presence would just cheapen the whole affair. I'm just glad they decided not to use my name as their symbol. Moons and crosses, far too…ominous. A sun, though? Much better. I love the sun."

To illustrate this, I tilted my face towards the sky, closed my eyes and sighed. Maybe it was because of the meeting, but I found myself really missing Cass then. And Viera. Hell, even Lizaveta. But I'd settle just for Cass, just one more sunny day in the abbey courtyard. Just waiting for me…if…

"Sariana, I think it's about to piss down."

"Yeah, I know. Just let me pretend for a bit here."

The Feast Of The Boar And The Dog might not have ended the long-smouldering Kaifeng Conflict on the spot, but it ended my involvement with it. Happy Deliveries branches had their own Sisters, all doing more or less what both Jaku and I wanted them to do, had taught them to do. As I'd said to him the last time we spoke alone, the services we provided undermined the already weak infrastructure the Court left in Chikageh hands. Even had the Society and the Shadows not reconciled, the former had won the war by proxy: their enemy had been reduced to a small pen of piglets living off the scraps of the Court in the Outer Palace. Everyone else once sworn to the black and the red now enjoyed the benefits of a social system that wasn't intractably geared to treat a bunch of ruffians like royal guards. For Wong Chu-Deng, the last move was not to surrender but to provide the Society with the one thing it lacked: a force already positioned within the Palace with which to complete the takeover of the city. Happy Deliveries couldn't affect the Palace district, since those living in there already received the best of everything…mostly via Chikageh coercion, extortion, and outright theft. But winter was not far off; denied the influx of these luxuries and necessities, the Palace district would just be a huge, hollow coffin.

That had been the bulk of the Feast. Agreeing on that. Division of power, labour, responsibilities, territory…any time they started to veer in such murky directions, I poured more tea (and later wine) and suggested that we all remember what happened to the carp that thought it was a dragon.

Don't ask me; I just made it up on the spot. Honestly, it was probably more the food and drink that settled them.

History will mark that dinner as a moment, but the real moments were in the weeks that followed, as the comrades of the Society started seeing the effects of that one decision. Chikageh absent from all four corners of the city, said to be hiding in the Five-Fold Palace as the Court prepared to dispose of them. Increased Society presence in the areas near the various gates leading into the Outer Palace, believed to be ready to cut off Chikageh attempts at fleeing the Court's justice. Reports of military drills behind the walls in the courtyards between the Outer Palace and the other segments of the compound. The Society's victory was assured at this point; people were mostly just gossiping about how it'd happen and what they planned to do afterwards, when the Society and the Court finally began peaceful negotiations.

It wasn't how wrong they were that scared me. It was how easy it was for Jaku and his trusted few to make them believe it that really left me rattled.

The real reason I didn't want to take part in what would later be known as the Three Days of Snow And Blood was because I strongly suspected it would be too close to the dream-memory I'd had in Zheng City. The details were still unformed, disconnected, but this much I knew: when Kazan fell, when Clan Jaydemyr stumbled onto the precipice of extermination and chose nigh-complete non-existence instead, it had been snowing and there had been blood. And screaming. And fighting. And…so when Terasawa Jaku and Wong Chu-Deng made their move, when they revealed that the Chikageh would not be retreating from the Outer Palace but assaulting the Inner, and that the Society was not at the gates to stop them but to support them…When the Bloody Rats swarmed the Palace just as Leung Guan-Pi had planned, I proved Jaku wrong yet again: I *didn't* want to stick around to see what came next.

"I hear the Sisters from the Jinmouzong, Siu-Tsin and Yuwantai branches were on the scene the very second the fighting stopped."

Lily nodded, placed a slice of chicken in my bowl for something to do. The aforementioned Yuwantai was her branch, so it was only right that she play the host. "Some of us before even that. It wasn't pleasant but after you've seen what a Noble can and will do to someone…after the past few years of the Chikageh 'patrols'…I suppose it felt oddly satisfying to deal with something as banal as battle wounds."

"I see you've left the sword at home." Banal?

"I left it at the Palace, after it was over. It served its purpose."

She really wanted to tell me, but not without making me ask about it. "Is it, then? Over?" I nibbled the chicken, glad that Lily's deep need to be a healer had quelled her sporadic vengeful urges. The flesh was thin, glistening, moist. Probably alive not that long ago, kept warm and safe in some enclosure away from the snow, but clearly not the blood.

"Mostly. The Bloody Rats struggled the first day, gaining no real ground, but reinforcements from former Kaifeng Imperial Guard members gave them the strength needed to burrow through the remnants of the Court's defences. Then it was just a matter of going building to building, room to room. Join or die, if they found Chūnkojin. No such offer to join if they found anyone else. I suppose a Mifūnjin who spoke fluent Chūnko-go might have been spared. My husband, for all his flaws, is no hypocrite. The main palatial chambers, the so-called forbidden areas, oh Talon Gukh-Fah, they looked as though some righteously angry beast had torn at the walls, shredded the silk banners, smashed the pottery. Burned the furniture. Slaughtered the occupants. Such unrestrained destruction. It's a good thing I was there!"

A righteously angry beast. Like a mother bear seeking retribution for her cubs?

"I, Lily? Not we?" Like you, Brother, I really did want to see the best in her. Unlike you, I wasn't allowed to. This was the woman who had been a Healer in Kaifeng's grisliest Haven. Had worked closely with Kaifeng's most devoted Peddlers and called unstable deviations like La-Ahn and Chang Tong-kut her 'friends', of a sort. Had chosen the perfect puppet, *Terasawa Jaku*, as her partner, romantic and otherwise. Eph's Clamouring Hells, this was the woman who had moulded Littleknife from Happy Apple, whose education certainly didn't start or stop at 'healing'. Hearing Lily's explanation why her presence at a long-awaited slaughter was a 'good thing' could wait. Preferably forever.

Her sanguinary burst subsided, smoothed down like a lady's wrinkled skirt. "I am a healer. One of many, but still one. Surely you understand what that means on the battlefield."

I had asked, and she didn't take the chance to be clear, so I gave a vague escape. To both of us. "What are they doing now? Those warriors. Those Bloody Rats."

"Failing to remember they are human. I…We left after doing what we could for them. The last thing I saw was a group of Rats using their Talents to deface a statue in the Outer Palace courtyard, and then…urinating on it."

She was quite aghast at this harmless vulgarity; I almost reeled at her sincerity. It should have seemed hypocritical, but somehow it fit.

I chose to foil it. To test it. "Men will be boys."

She froze at this, seeming to measure my tone, to…calculate a reaction. Had I been too glib in the face of simmering righteousness? Was she regretting leaving the sword behind? It would have been useless against me, at least physically. She knew that, but the blank canvas that was then her face didn't. Her absence contained every possibility and could choose only one.

Then all life returned to her expression, and brought something new back with it. It was as though there had been no break at all, but something had absolutely broken. "And all we do is wait for them to dribble their smallswords clean and pretend to be impressed that they manage that much. The woes of womanhood!"

I chortled, horrified that *this* was how it was going to end between us. A dirty joke or two and all sorts of innuendos about swords, and no further mention of what she had done with hers. I should have known from extensive experience: Healers are, to the last, fucking scary. How could they not be? All they see is damage that can be repaired, and damage that cannot. They are aware of their power over people with the former and the futility of trying to fix those with the latter. And thanks to us, to me, Kaifeng had all but run out of people worth healing.

When we eventually hugged our goodbye, she was the warm, relaxed one, and I frigid with foreboding.

It was another bad winter. Not 'gangs roaming the streets raping the women and stealing taxes' bad, of course. It was terrible in the sense that no one knew what to do next. Neighbourhoods tightened and fractured, and all anyone cared about was having enough food to get through the week. Everyone was just too cold to think clearly; grander plans and monumental shifts were almost literally frozen. Jaku took up residence in the Dragon Pavilion; Wong Chu-Deng was said to be recovering from wounds sustained in the Three Days. Both probably knew better than to be within yelling distance of each other when any sort of heat was to be measured and rationed very carefully. That would all come later. For now, the city and its frightening, exciting future hibernated, sharing neither dreams nor nightmares.

The Society For Whatever It Was Called Now wasted no time come the spring of 879. Day by day, as I just sort of wandered from one Happy Deliveries branch to the next, I noticed all sorts of 'interesting' changes. There was, of course, no more talk about the North or the South, Chikageh or Rebellion. Of Shadows or Rats. There was just greetings comrade isn't the weather nice comrade and aren't we lucky it's all over – always in Chūnko-go. Each walk I saw fewer Mifūn-go signs, or even Mifūnjin-style stores. Rahmen carts became just a memory, while permanent shop fronts offering soupy dumplings and fluffy rice buns seemed everywhere. Night markets provided a new way for people to meet, eat and make a tidy profit. The Kaifeng Imperial Guard was abolished, and soon the New Kaifeng State Police patrolled the streets. In the wake of the rebellion's violent echoes, no one really seemed all that inclined towards crime anyway so most of the time the new watchfolk, armed not with katana or jitteh but simple three-foot sticks, ambled about, chatted with people, and…well, watched. Now and then they'd have words with someone foolish enough to go out in public with a weapon, especially those of Mifūné make. The police had their own stations of sorts at most major street intersections, their command decentralised now rather than one or two huge guardhouses such as the one I'd called 'home' for a few months almost four years ago. Incidentally, that place had been turned into a Public Grievances building. I think I saw the former Captain Kobayashi in that area dressed in civilian clothing, but made no effort to confirm. He had things to do. They all did.

Even the Holecleaners, whoever they were.

Everyone was busy but me. I had nothing to do but wait. Again. The new council refused to open the city gates until achieving some measure of internal stability. Oh, farmers and the like could come and go, but that was strictly regulated. I hadn't snuck into the city, and after everything I'd done for it, I wasn't about to fucking sneak out either.

Besides, I knew Jaku wasn't done with me.

Sure enough, in the second month of summer, they finally came for me, and humbly requested that I attend a small meeting in what used to be called the Women's Quarters, but was now apparently the Centre for Domestic Affairs. I arrived an hour late, fully-armed and in my road-worn Fourth Going beige-and-greys, just to make my intentions clear.

"No."

"Are you certain?" Terasawa Jaku was resplendent in majestic reds and yellows, so many layers of gleam and shine. He even had his hair pulled into a bun and tucked under a hilariously ornate headpiece with tassles that danced whenever he so much as shifted his weight. "The role is perfect for you, and you for it."

I was on my knees in the middle of the room, flanked by long, low-set tables crowded with various members of…well, I'm nibbling fingers here. It was a court. Of course it Ephin' was. Packed with former society members dressed more or less like cheaper, flappier versions of their grand leader. And there he was, facing me down from a raised platform, dressed like someone who'd chosen to accept that he had to tell the people to grant him the unfortunately necessary title of 'State Chancellor'.

Small meeting. What a fucking farce.

"This might come as a shock, but I am not naturally disposed to caring for people. That was just my training, and I think those who have come after me are much more suited to the position of…what did you call it? 'Grand Mother of Domestic Affairs'? What about your wife?"

The rumble of disapproval from the sycophant assembly told me I probably shouldn't have called her that.

But State Chancellor Leung Zha-Ku merely pursed his lips. "I'm afraid the State Secretary of New Kaifeng is already more than occupied with her existing duties."

"And Wong Chu-Deng? How did you keep him from your shiny new throne, Jaku?"

Gasps now. How dare she so callously and casually address the grand leader! Earned me a glare from His Magnanimousness. Yeah, I don't care. It's a word now, and it describes what he'd become. Or, I think, always thought he'd been. "He will be more than content to assume the role of Commander of Military Affairs. Once he recovers and is fit to return to public life."

Oh, he wouldn't be that stupid…would he? "If." Very deliberate pause. "If he recovers."

He had the grace to look surprised, and then just shrugged. "If…If you prefer. I doubt there are many in this court who care for his legacy, but I do. We were, are brothers, after all. A poor ruler it is who cannot forgive old rivals."

Yeah, he wasn't going to rule shit. Not with this little self-control and not with Lily at his side, give or take.

Still, he'd invited me to this 'small meeting', to pressure me into accepting a happy little role in his happy little regime. Might as well try to show him what he'd *really* invited in, and how he didn't want it. I switched to Common. "Strange, his injuries. Considering how many Healers were present. You'd think he'd have been the first to receive the best care in the city."

"Did you say something, Sister? Come closer and share with me your voice." One hand beckoned after he responded in kind, and the court knew then that this was not a performance for them. I glanced at their bewildered, horrified faces before complying. I did not shuffle on my knees, however, and my stride took me within spitting distance of Terasawa Jaku. On the other hand, for someone like him, I could probably muster quite the force and distance in that regard.

I sank to my knees once more, looked straight up at him and repeated what I'd said, more or less.

This time the shrug was little more than a shift in posture. The two of them hadn't been able to share so much as a small plate of fucking pork and, out of those present, out of everyone in his entire city, only he and I knew this for a fact. "Of course the old man is being well taken care of."

And since we were now hushed and likely unintelligible noise to everyone else there, I poked harder. "But if…If he succumbs to his terrible wounds, who gets this very important job you've promised him, I wonder?"

He leaned forward, one elbow on one knee, finger wagging at me in what I am sure he thought was canny superiority. "Oh ho. And here I thought my wife was the ambitious one. No Grand Mother of Domestic Affairs you, eh? I suppose any number of high-ranking Sisters could warm that seat. But Commander of Military Affairs? Do you really believe you are up to that? I may have all sorts of designs that such a loyal personage would need to enact. Kaifeng strikes me as so terribly small when I look at the maps, and we did find quite a few of those in the Imperial Library. Our vision of New Kaifeng is a vast and glorious one, but not without its sacrifices."

"And you think Wong Chu-Deng is 'up to that'"?

"As I said, not without its sacrifices."

I was the very picture of artless surprise. "But you said he's being taken care of…I don't understand…"

The rising smile of engorged grandiosity faltered. "I would expect my future general to be a *little* more alert than this, Sariana. He isn't 'up to' anything, and never will be again, and I am rather incensed that you'd make me say it so plainly."

"…Oh. Oh you clever man." I raised my voice, switched back to the language of New Kaifeng, an old tongue from a much older one. "Truly, comrade State Chancellor, your wisdom is as bright as the sun. New Kaifeng's future will blaze with untold grandeur and prosperity."

The smile was back, and he basked in my expansive awe. Aware of this unseemly tilt towards arrogance, he fumbled for humility and grasped nothing more than yet another handful of his own shit. "If this is so, it will be a shared glory. I must admit, my esteemed State Secretary had some small hand in the matter."

"You don't say." The teeth of my adulating grin concealed this mutter well.

Jaku went on, oblivious now that he'd Figured It All Out, Including Dumb Old Sister Sariana. "I want to assure you, all of you, none of our roles have any power or influence over anyone else's. All are equal under the new law."

Blessed Mother, he just refused to accept the victory I kept handing him. Sitting there higher than anyone else in the room by a few very distinct inches, and he says that.

What little mercy I had left melted away as though he actually were some sort of sun, but this would remain between us. "I'm going to be very blunt now, State Chancellor." I switched to Mifūn-go for this strike, not even trying to be subdued. If any of the wheel-greasers paying attention understood, they were hopefully smart enough not to show it. This was a forbidden language now, after all. "I will ask one question. Answer truthfully, please, and I may change *my* answer regarding that earlier offer."

He waved in a way that made me wish it had been his hand severed and not poor old Captain Kobayashi's.

"Where did you get these ideas from? This type of governing without Imperial oversight. This…equal dispensation of privileges." He'd already told me, but like I said, I was done being nice.

"Duties, Sister. Not privileges. Duties. Responsibilities. Burdens."

I waved my hand in a way I am sure he recognised, but then saved him any further effort. "You read about it in a book, didn't you? Something in the former Imperial Library, a text I imagine dating back hundreds of years. But instead of an Emperor, you have State Chancellor. Beneath that one change, I can tell a typical court structure when I see one." Well, Sariana could and wanted to nothing to do with it. Sarah-Jade was hungry for something sweet and juicy and Tzara-Min just wanted to go back to Happy Deliveries and clean a really gory operations room. Or take a short walk on The Long Way. I planned to let all three of us have our way soon enough. "And we all know who really rules a court when a weak husband sits on the throne."

A few of the vassals, comrades, courtiers, whatever the Eph they didn't want to be called, took sharp intakes of breath then, but still held their own tongues for fear of losing them.

I stood up without permission and started to leave. The whole point of forcing someone to kneel that long on a stone floor is to deny them a dignified exit, but I did my best.

"Do you have any better ideas, Sariana?" Maybe it was because he'd used Common again, but he didn't sound hostile or rhetorical. "Give the word and the city is yours. Please."

I stopped and lowered my head, as though contemplating this. Let him think I was thinking about it. But what I was really doing was discovering something else. Terasawa Jaku, the man who would be no king, was nothing but compulsively self-destructive and too cowardly to see it through. This is why he married Lily, who might have put down the sword but would never relinquish her little knife. It's why he undermined my very successful and entirely peaceful subjugation of the city with one stupendously bad decision leading to the so-called war's only instance of mass slaughter. It's why he never fixed his nose. He thought he flirted with failure when in fact he was all but dominated by the allure of it, although I didn't know why and didn't care to learn. There was no fixing this damage either, not even with the city's greatest healer sharing its bed. But with her tempering it, I believed Littleknife would be safe. Happy Deliveries would be safe. Maybe even 'New Kaifeng' itself.

But maybe Jaku had meant what he'd said. Maybe there and then, he realised just how tempting it would be to acknowledge his incorrigible self-annihilating tendencies and what effect they'd have on the city-state now that he purportedly controlled it. So in one last fit of compassion, I turned around and lied my face off to save his. In very plain, very clear Chūnko-go. "That's the point you are missing entirely, Your Eminence. If I wanted the city, I wouldn't give you the word. I wouldn't give anything. I wouldn't need to. I'm a Half and sister to the Scourge. If I wanted Kaifeng, I'd just take it. When it came to its future, I swore to you four years ago I'd make your war for a free and prosperous Kaifeng my war. That if it went poorly, I'd just walk away from the flames. It didn't go poorly at all, State Chancellor. There were no district-wide fires, no huge disasters. Certainly, there were incidents. There were unavoidable deaths. Shit happens. But you couldn't call it much of a war. All we had to do was show the so-called enemy a better way to be. Give them meaning and direction in the absence of the Night. Nothing could be simpler, given the absence of Night is…daylight. The Twelve isn't a set of rules for a good life, one that would otherwise be plagued by chaos and anarchy. It's a relic of a system this city no longer needed. Once people understood that, the rest was inevitable. You and Wong Chu-Deng had no choice but to tear down the corrupted Court and cleanse the Palace, but now here you are, adeptly putting the pieces back together in a way that I *know* will work. This time, it will work! Do not lightly offer that which you fought so hard, sacrificed so much, to attain. You can't give away what you've convinced the people they need you to have, State Chancellor. They'd just give it to you again. Only they can take it away, and I pray God you have sense enough by then, and may it be a long time from now, to let them. If not, it may be you waiting for the rats in the shadows. Your blood in the snow. And as much as I'd love to take you up on your offer, I have no intention of making myself a similar target. Let me leave while I still can, because if you wait much longer, I may change my mind about all of this. Decide you are in fact unworthy. And if that happens, I'm going to make what my brother did to that Haven look like a kitchen mishap. Let me be someone else's problem. I did what you asked. Every time. So grant me this. Let me walk away. Far away. It's safer for you. For me. For everyone."

He took all of this with polite calmness, having refound his self-grandeur at some point in my vapid diatribe, and then gave his formal reply in the same language. "Sister Talon Gukh-Fah, we thank you for your service. New Kaifeng owes you an immeasurable debt. You have my leave to go anytime you wish. No one shall rush you and no one shall restrain you. Please know you are welcome in our city, now and in the future. Should you find yourself in Chūnko once again."

Not bad, Jaku. Not bad at all.

I sketched a bow far more elaborate than a typical Mifūné bending of the waist, aversion of eyes. Something I'd learned in the Fourth Going training, standard behaviour in the presence of minor gentry. The warbound gauntlet making of my left hand a weapon itself twirled through the air in effete little flourishes.

Then I retrieved the Gildenhammer from the startled attendant at the door and walked away, not from the flames but definitely some sort of fire.

There were other goodbyes, yes, but I'd spent so long waiting for this opportunity that they seemed almost perfunctory. Small engagements, stopovers, well-wishes.

Mrs. Wang, formerly Lady Oh Reh-Na of the Nightingale's Nest in the Dragon Pavilion, had her son Wang Ying serve me dinner, while some of 'her girls' tried to get me drunk and play silly games; I obliged, because I'm just a good person like that. It was hard to ignore that where once a golden *f* had adorned her throat, now it was a stylised golden lily, shining like the sun.

Captain Kobayashi, now Inspector Siu-Lam, met me for lunch in Jinmouzong; I was duly impressed at how quickly he devoured the slippery noodles with just one hand and one hell of an appetite. We played with words in a way we could not afford until now, and it was foolish and great.

Wai-Bahk and the other Sisters of Munnamdun shared some cake, tea and, of course, gossip. Littleknife asked if she could come with me and fuck this city also would I be seeing Fa Shai-Yeh anytime soon and does she sleep I hear that's a good time to stab people…bless you to the very bottom of your broken heart, Littleknife. Best that you stayed in the city, with the Tsai twins and all those kids. The Disadvantaged Youth of Kaifeng, New or otherwise, could do far worse than have you guiding their Advancement. And when Lily calls on you to do your duty, I am sure you will answer and Eph help anyone standing in your way. You just leave Fa Shai-Yeh to me…

As for the aforementioned State Secretary and Grand Mother of Domestic Affairs Leung Yoon-Fah, she sent me a very nice note on delicate, appropriately orange rice paper. The last few lines reminded me that this woman never said anything of no value: "I asked you when we first met if you meant to help your brother, or stop him. This was foolish of me. I have always known they are often the same thing. This is true of Dog-Ears, as my dear Littleknife calls him, and it is true of boars, as no one calls someone else anymore. But sometimes merely stopping someone just once isn't enough. Sometimes you have to help them a little, and stop them, and help them a little more…and stop them again. Healing is always slow, and a damaged conscience heals slowest of all."

I knew that Wong Chu-Deng was decisively out of Jaku's vision, but it seemed the State Chancellor's wife was not so quick to move on from certain…nuisances.

I asked a local florist why the State Secretary had chosen the formal name Yoon-Fah, and they pointed out that as well as meaning 'orange lily', it can also mean 'mother'. I imagined people would be calling Leung Yoon-Fah something else before long.

The incoming Commander of Military Affairs and reformed leader of the Northern Dissidents, Wong Chu-Deng, remained in the care of the

New Kaifeng Healing Services. He was granted as much privacy as he required to convalesce and recover from injuries earned in the Just and Rightful Struggle Against Imperial Tyranny. Official reports were that he was doing well and would assume his role as a key figure in New Kaifeng's government as soon as he was able. Until then, the State Secretary would graciously see to the poor man's duties.

Perhaps a week after Lily sent her letter, when I was all but ready to leave that truly forsaken city, the announcement of the sudden and completely unexpected death of Wong Chu-Deng dripped from the former Palace and was news for a day. Gossip for a few more. Within a week, a new statue honouring his sacrifice was erected in the Gentle Bouquet Memorial Hall. Both the State Chancellor and Mother Lily (collect enough titles and you earn just one) were in attendance at the unveiling, so naturally was roughly half the city as well. I watched from afar. Very afar. Once all that died down, I snuck in late one night and beheld what would be my final sign that it was time to put Kaifeng into my past.

The statue towered over the main room, easily higher than the second floor where Jaku had once all but sworn *this* sort of thing would never happen. The plaque at its base was as big and long as the table at which he and his council members had decided to violently oppose Wong Chu-Deng's false submission to Mifūnjin culture and the birth of the Chikageh. The writing on the plaque declared that the statue was called "Father Wong's Last Gift". Upon a broad pedestal, a brave old man, maybe three or four times the size he was when I was forced to meet him, shielded a crying child from arrows and spears. I pride myself on noticing these details first, and not the comically tall and muscular Jaku standing over them, one hand on Wong's shoulder, the other gripping what I was sure was a massive version of Lily's sword. His face was wrought in fierce bronze, the stuff of heroes and saviours.

His bold nose was straighter than the arrows, spears and her sword combined.

I didn't even bother reading the description beside it, but it was hard to miss how many times the word 'brother' appeared on it.

Also, there was no Ephing way they made that ridiculous monstrosity in just a week.

The morning before my departure, I dressed for travel and made my final rounds, weaving through Munnamdun and Yuwantai less to see people and more to just…collect a few more memories, I suppose. Eventually I ran out of streets, or maybe just had my fill of those memories, and I found myself on the east-west boulevard. Would it be? Even now? Yep, there it was. That fruit stall. That old uncle.

I removed my hood, ran a hand through recently cut hair and approached him. "Good day, comrade. How are the apples this fine Aftersun?"

"Fresh and juicy, Sister Gukh-Fah, best in the city. Would you like some?"

"I surely would. I am leaving today, and thought I might finally accept your offer for one."

He froze mid-reach. "I…they're two Little Leungs each."

I fished the very newly-minted coins from my pouch. "One then please."

"As you say, comrade." He took the payment before selecting a particularly shiny apple. "Oh, look. This one's rotten. I'd better give you another to make up for it." So it was that he offered me two perfectly not-rotten apples, and I knew not to leave the poor man standing there breaking the law so brazenly.

"This is fair, Dai-Suhk. Thank you."

His expression disagreed, but he replied with a hawker's loud enthusiasm. "Thank you for your custom. And your service. Glory to New Kaifeng. Great health to the Chancellor."

I took a bite of the apple in lieu of my tongue, and left him to his business.

I chose to leave through the Old Zheng Gate on a warm evening under a late summer gibbous moon. One of the guards on duty, a relic of the Kaifeng that was, swung his lantern stick my way and paused. Guards pause a lot when they look at you, so I thought nothing of it. Resisted the urge to tap my foot or fold my arms. I'd waited this long; let the gaffer do his job properly.

And he did. And kept doing it.

"Do you need me to remove my hood? I'm sorry if it seems like I'm concealing my face, and it is quite dark out here."

His voice was slurry, his face sunken. "Five. Five."

Another guard stepped in, trying to assist the clearly absent-minded fellow towards his post beside the gate. "Don't mind him, please."

"Five. Like a hand. Five..."

I waited for the younger guard to return to finish whatever needed finishing to let me out.

"I apologise for that, Lady Gukh-Fah." He avoided my gaze, keeping an eye on his senior. "As you know, we've only recently reopened and haven't had much chance to review our ranks. Old Wen there has been doing this longer than most of us have been alive. Half the time he isn't in the same year as the rest of us, but the other half he tells us stories to pass the time. Tonight...probably no stories."

"What did the 'five' mean?"

"Blessed Mother knows." The guard caught himself a little too late. "I mean, I don't know. He's said it before, usually when it's a Half or someone tall and wearing black. If we don't calm him down he just starts gibbering and shaking his head, five and hands, five and hands. So if there is a story behind it, I haven't heard it and doubt I ever will."

"A shame I'm not wearing black then. Might get him to tell that story. A Half wearing black in Kaifeng is a rare combination."

"It is these days. Back when the Peddlers were in and out, small groups of them weren't unheard of."

Five. Half wearing black. Five. Like a hand. Five...

Ishida Kocho. Ming Tou-Fah. Zhao La-Ahn. Chang Tong-Kut. Char Ah-Ran.

"Thank the Mother those times are over." For some of us, at least. "Can I go now?"

"You may, and sorry again. Safe travels, Sister. Glory to New Kaifeng."

I nodded, and then started to cross through the corridor between inner gate and outer. I looked at the door to my right, into which the guards had escorted me for 'inspection'. Eph that door.

So I looked left and back, and saw the poor old man. What could I possibly say to him, the last person in Kaifeng to see the city's most dangerous Peddlers on their last mission? To talk with the accursed Half, Blackcloak, The Scourge, who only a week later would commit mass murder, and be blamed for the destruction of a Haven?

The same shameless thing I said to everyone I couldn't help. "I am so...so sorry."

He ignored me, clutching his lantern-stick, and I completed my departure of Kaifeng, slow and easy, and glad one last time the crux et luna remained concealed against my chest, and flew over not even one of this endlessly tortured city's ramparts.

I meandered past a fairly busy House of Happy's Departure (definitely the translation I liked most), spent the rest of the night in Zheng City, which was already starting to look and sound a little like a less-developed version of Leung's oh-so-enlightened New Kaifeng…and then, before the sun rose, took off at Half speed northwest, back towards the Jade Gate, and the quickest means to the Long Way back.

Which, naturally, wasn't that quick at all. The *Ozon Yol* itself proved no hindrance; I am the heir to Jaydemyr and I can conjure water at will. I relied on no caravan, not now that I knew the locations of the oases and karavansarays. No, what really stopped me in my tracks a few months later was what I saw in the shadow of Khovakand's twilit city walls. Hoisted beside a huddle of large tents, a familiar standard, that which a certain commander of Jenetchen Kulutchara had reinterpreted as an omen and a threat, fluttered in the warm desert wind.

There was, however, one change I couldn't miss: where a straight sword once pierced the moon's lower curve, a stylised bird seemed to sit upon it. The Harriers finally had a flag worthy of their name.

I smiled at this and trudged towards the campfires and the largest tent. When no one approached, I called out in Common. "Iskendahrl? Is Kuluf Iskendahrl here? It's me, Tzara-Min of the Liquid Night. We travelled together here, years ago…"

A familiar silhouette, tall and graceful, emerged from that tent. "So you have finally found us again." He stepped closer, and now I could see not just the familiar but also the changes brought on by more than five years of wasteland struggle. The more prominent grey in his beard; the fact that he was wearing dusty black clothes now, no sign of anything violet per the Brotherhood. Starkest of all, the thick, unruly mane curling about his face, down his neck and back. He folded his arms, feet shoulderwidth apart, and continued. "You lied to me. About my flag and how you dreamed of it. I see you bear it proudly now, there, around your neck. Why would you wear such a thing, if it were someone else's dream? You lied about being Half, a Kutsahl Melyaz. You are neither holy nor mongrel. You are something else. That is how you knew you wouldn't turn. And you lied about who you are. You are not Tzara-Min."

I nodded in response, all of it true to some extent, and braced to either tell even more lies, or apologise for the first one.

"I appreciate that you had to hide who you are from us, from me. But much has changed since. More dreams. More memories. More reports of attacks being made by those aligned with that symbol. Though we still honour the Twelve, we are now neither Tantamon nor Swords of Heaven. Mercenaries, like or not. And few pay as generously as the Kas'Daen. The Pallid Harriers would gladly serve as your guard and escort, presuming you wish to leave Karakan and return home." He stepped a little closer, and lowered his voice to a conspiratorial growl. "…Lady Sarivashes-ra Kas'Daen."

Fuck. Me. It hadn't been a bird on the Pallid Harriers flag.

It was an *f*.

Situation Nominal

"You said earlier you weren't going to restructure your history to make it any more interesting than it really was, but that, Sister, was a ridiculous place to stop. I said I'd listen. You don't need to tease it out like that, or end on some sort of unresolved mystery."

"Normally I wouldn't, but I wanted you to experience, briefly, just how much that one caught me off-guard. I didn't stutter or falter, or do anything dramatic. I just stood there, trying to find some sort of meaning in that single sentence. All the names I'd had, all the versions of me I'd either chosen or been forced to become, they were part of some until-then believable map of who Vachaelle wanted me to be. But this? I remembered more about our family before the fall, about how the Kas'Daen conspired with Zieger and Tsukamoto. The Three Beasts. And I knew that Mother had left Xenides-ra Kas'Daen before we were born...and I suppose just presumed it was a long time before that. No one had ever called me Sarivashes before but it rang as true as any other name. Xenides-ra Kas'Daen was as affected by Mother's plan as anyone else, and I suspect he heard your name the instant you declared it to Vachaelle in Jaydemyrian as well. What he started to remember, and how, was no doubt personal and unique. It had been six years since. Plenty of time for the shackles to fall loose, the shroud to lift. For names to re-emerge. I wanted to believe it was all a ruse, some ploy to bring an empowered Half under his control...but by then I'd learned one name is as true as any other, and it doesn't change who we are. It only reveals more of it, first and foremost to ourselves.

"Do you know what they call a man with no name? 'The Man With No Name'. To have a name is to be known. To be known is to have a name. The more names we have, the more known we are. The more known we are, the more names we have. Until we have only one.

"Names are about power, Brother. And we both have a long way to go to reach her level there."

11 hours until the revelation

Chapter 20: The Covetous Toad
11/879 to 8/881 A.R.

"Preposterous, 'kuluf'. Mere mercenaries, escorting the likes of *me?*"

I drew back and away, ensuring the folds of my clothing functioned as a shield, spine stiff and chin uplifted as much as the hood would allow. All to project the air of a runaway royal – the sort of thing I'd heard Princess Jade would do when she forgot to be the smartest, most capable thief/assassin/dancer/muffin-eater in the entire world, which was quite often if the plot demanded it.

"I understand your capacity and ability…Sister." He spoke now at a normal volume. "But you are very fortunate you found us before others found you. Not everyone would see you home safely. Kas'Daen has even fewer allies here in Karakan than before, and I hear some of the Brothers of the Tantamon have also declared their independence and serve only The Twelve. I am wasting your time here. I apologise. You likely know most of this, unless you have been truly in the east all this time."

Curious, watching someone adept at desert survival try to fish.

"I found what I was looking for, kuluf, and then I came back. It's that simple."

He grunted, sniffed. "So you left in the shadow of the sun, but should return in the noble mantle of the night. I would not presume to take you all the way; we are ill company in the confines of a city, as you know." Even here in the Karakan. "Far enough to say, 'here she is, gold please.'" He laughed then, cocking his head as a form of proposal. "You don't need our protection, but we could do with the money, now we no longer receive the support of the Kulutchara. And we did do you quite the favour, did we not?"

I looked at the well-maintained tents, the hale horses, the comfortable men sitting around fires further off, eating, chatting, laughing, and decided to entertain his lie with the truth. He'd certainly done the same for me more than once. I wandered to the nearest fire, sat on the ground before it after placing the Gildenhammer next to me. He followed, but crouched instead so that he need not remove his own weapon.

"I am not going to Lybichmisto, Kuluf. That is not my home."

"I'm afraid it's one of the few places in Kas'Daen I know. Nice easy roads, plenty of waystations and Havens."

"Have you actually been there? Into the capital?"

He snorted. "Of course not. We have these useful little magic devices, you may recall. They're called maps."

"Then later we use one of those and I will show you a new trick: the location of a hidden fortress. Now, let me rest a bit in the delightful company of those in whose company I can rest. It has been too long."

It would be two long months, in fact. Closer to three. Definitely not four.

There are two ways to travel the *Ozon Yol*: quickly to get somewhere, and slowly just to keep moving. I'd arrived in Khovokand just before winter, and although the Harriers had their share of pyrotics, it was best not to waste them on basic necessities. So while we did not stay in one place, we did hop from sanctuary to sanctuary, spending days and sometimes weeks at each. Iskendahrl not only agreed with my destination, he seemed more enthusiastic about it given it wasn't a big city or Kas'Daen stronghold. I believe he'd have been less driven had he known it was, in fact, quite the opposite to both.

The rest of the Harriers treated me much the same as they had before, those that had been there, at least. Djuneht was now a subcommander, but still as mistrustful and wary as ever. I no longer found that distasteful or threatening. He didn't approve of my presence but lacked the means to prevent it. Ehvran was older, tougher, and a little quicker to complain. And those Harriers I didn't know, maybe a dozen or so given Iskendahrl kept the company small and elite, were told the truth and didn't even know it: I was to them Tzara-Min, a hydrotheurge Sister of the Liquid Night, secretly returning from a Fourth Going mission to the east. It was in everyone's best interest that I stay safe and out of sight.

But as for that other name, the Kuluf admitted it had been less public knowledge and more an educated guess. By this point, he told me he remembered this much: the symbol had been that of his former lord, who had somehow become the world's enemy; his former lord had been Xenides-ra Kas'Daen; and Xenides had claimed, time and again, that his enemy had stolen his daughter. What a strange, strange mismatch of facts to assemble into a belief. They were, after all, completely true: those serving Jaydemyr who weren't eradicated likely had turned to serving Kas'Daen after our disintegration, and Xenides had always used the daughter-theft as part of his motivation to make war on Dhiana and Charas'z. He had always claimed I was Sarivashes, not Sariana. That much *I* recalled. But he is true Fey, as is Dhiana. So how could I be that daughter, and also Half? What had…Father done to make that possible? Vachaelle wouldn't say, so perhaps one of her closest confidantes might.

When I did spend time outside of our encampment, I made sure to leave the hood behind. Without that, I just looked like any other useless Kas'Daen Half fumbling her way though the intricacies of *Ozon Yol*'s oh so exotic wonders, spending a small fortune on junk at every stop. I hoped.

Publicly, my notoriety was almost purely word-of-mouth. There were no posters up declaring me wanted, no quests tacked to bounty boards in the common halls of the karavansarays to fetch some wayward young female Half – as ridiculous as that sounds now that I say it. All people knew was that a Sister of the Liquid Night had been seen travelling the Long Way after supposedly witnessing a rebellion in the former capital of Chūnko, Kaifeng.

"Former, honoured elder?" It didn't matter where you were on the Long Way, there was always a Knowledgable Stranger happy to share news passed down the roads, especially with gullible milkskins. This Haven in Khivarezem, a town near the western terminus of the *Ozol Yol*, was no different.

"That is what is said, friend. It is well-known, the destruction of all the Havens and karavansarays in and near the city of Khayfuhn. A monster made of fire with swords for arms. A djinn, to be certain. This is the story that is true. And after, the Nobles of the Middle Eastern land flew from the ruined city, made their capital elsewhere, far to the south. This is all that is known of the fate of doomed Khayfuhn."

Eph and Shyn', Vachaelle hadn't been lying when she'd said the Night had forsaken the place. Oh well, anyone brave enough to travel there would be in for quite the surprise.

"Thank you for your wise tale, honoured elder." I let my remaining few Little Leung coins trickle into his bowl before leaving. I entertained myself wondering how things would go when he tried to spend them.

Naturally we bypassed Azak this time; Swords of Heaven turned swords of fortune were even less welcome in that southern stronghold of Tantamon than renegade Sisters. This cut some of the travel time out, but it still took almost two seasons to negotiate our way from the western tip of the *Ozon Yol* to the first towns of south-eastern Kas'Daen. Thankfully those seasons were spring and summer, so this time I didn't have to deal with the crushing solitude of heavy snowfall. A solitude I would have felt even with the Pallid Harriers 'escorting' me, given how poorly the former Swords of Heaven handled anything much colder than arid conditions.

Yes, actually, there was. I suppose it was unavoidable, given what the kuluf was asking of his now coin-motivated company with no real proof of recompense. The few who agreed with Djuneht confronted Iskehdarhl, arguing (fairly, I thought) that desert warriors were a poor fit for Kas'Daen's dense forests and grassy hills. The former was full of threats they didn't understand, and the latter often played host to battles requiring tactics they found bewildering. As good an excuse for a mutiny as any. Iskendahrl, again proving that he was full of good-natured shit, paid them out handsomely rather than risk bloodshed. Perhaps they'd have tried for more with that bloodshed had they been smart or brave enough to attempt a disagreement on company structure in the desert, and not so many miles deep into Kas'Daen territory. Such an event would have been unthinkable for the devout Jenetchen Kulutchara, but now Djuneht and his disgruntled band would do well not to run into their former brothers-in-arms *or* followers of the Tantamon.

Or my future sisters-in-arms, into whose embrace we were about to fold.

"I'm sorry, could you repeat that, good sir?" I looked back at the Harriers, who'd kept their distance at the man's approach down the road. He looked like any other villager with an empty cart heading home after a day's work offloading his goods, and I'd done my best to ensure the dark-skinned mercenaries not frighten him off. Oddly, he just ignored them, and was much more interested in me. In bowing. Almost falling prostrate. I knew better than to help him up, or even touch him. I just waited for him to remember I'd told him I'd been gone a very long time.

"Ain't been called Abbey's Village for a few years now, Sister." The man failed to maintain eye contact. "But y'aint the first to return or arrive not knowin' that. This here's the town of Sparrowsview."

Over his shoulder I could see that, yes, it wasn't just a village anymore, but it also wasn't what I'd normally consider a 'town'. The growth seemed less the result of increased population and more increased demand for certain services. More chimneys; more…thicker columns of sickly yellow smoke. Where once there had been carriagehouses and inns, I now suspected we'd find hectic forges, sweat-drawing kilns, pungent tanneries. Timberyards.

And even from there, I could hear it. The industrious tempo underscoring Sarah-Jade Falkenstrom's happier days in Teristra: the din of hammers. "Looks…sounds busy."

"Surely is. We've always provided for the Sisters' needs, and ever since the Mind-Changer took over, needier than ever."

Needs? All we'd needed was food, some basic craftwork, and a steady supply of the region's pregnant women. The village, Sparrowsview? It was producing a lot more than that. "And who is this Mind-Changer?"

He shook his head and cleared his throat. "I can't be tellin' you much more about it. I don't come here but to sell what I grow and buy what I need to grow more. I am but a simple farmer, Sister." I had heard once that you should believe people when they tell you who they are, but sometimes when they made too much effort, were too specific…

"Then we shall take no more of your time, simple farmer."

"No trouble, good Sister. Safe and swift travels home."

I bent my hooded head in thanks and returned to the Harriers as the farmer's cart creaked past our displaced band. "We should keep going, The abbey isn't far from here. We'll find no rest in this town."

Iskendarhl wrinkled his nose. "It is a strange odour on the breeze. Best not linger in it."

Ehvran ambled our way. "What are they making?"

I tilted my head at his query; surely he'd been close enough to a city to know. Still, maybe he deserved a better answer. "Progress, Brother. They're making progress."

We skirted Sparrowsview. If Roderic's barn was still there, I didn't see it.

This wasn't right. Not at all. This hill was too high. The unfinished walls too thick, too close to the shores of the Little Tranquil river, too far away from the abbey. And the azurite flag hoisted over the uppermost towers…

"Look at that, Tzara-Min." Iskendahrl seemed almost to weep at the sight before us. "The Mother watches over those who keep Her faith. We are here, finally. We have brought you home!"

"That you have." Not. This, this was not my home.

He leaned close to whisper; perhaps the jubilance was just another act? "But tell me, Sarivashes. Why is the Flail on this Kas'Daen design a cross?"

We filed through gaps in the stonework as the sun continued to withdraw. It wasn't long before we reached much more complete fortifications, where the northern border of the abbey's territory used to be. By then I'd realised why the hill seemed higher: they'd lowered the ground around it and flattened the approach, and had done this long enough ago that grass had grown over the displaced rock and dirt. So this was what Vachaelle had been talking about: walls within walls, patrolled gateways, resculpted grounds. This, and what else?

"Wait here." I moved ahead of Iskendarhl and the Harriers, much as I had when we'd encountered the 'simple farmer' a few hours ago.

Three guards emerged from the base of a small watchtower. All bald. All wearing chain and plate. All trailing violet capes.

"You are well met, Sister, but these Swords of Heaven have no business with the Scarlet Sparrows."

"I'm sorry, the what?" I winced inwardly at how someone else here used to apologise before anything else. "No, nevermind. These men are my…escorts from the Karakani wastelands, Brother. The Pallid Harriers are not Swords of Heaven, however. They serve me."

None of them reacted to this surely strange assertion. "They may encamp here in the outer grounds, but naturally only you may enter the keep."

"…Naturally. Is Aunty Cassandra here? I would report to her directly."

"*Lady* Cassandra has been aware of your arrival for some time, Sister, and insisted the Swords of Heaven…your men go no further."

Much had changed, but it seemed the enmity between the Tantamon and the Swords ran deeper than something as superficial as a shift in leadership. Kas'Daen, Jaydemyr, Tsukamoto, Zieger: same thing far enough down the chain. "I will keep them in line."

"We will watch nonetheless. Welcome to the Rouge Eyrie."

The Pallid Harriers were accustomed to being kept outside walls and showed no discomfort at their exclusion. It was too warm for fires, and the outer grounds were well-lit anyway. I chose to linger in the camp; this 'Rouge Eyrie' was as inviting to me as an abandoned childhood home overrun with spiders and vermin.

I only had to wait an hour before I saw a lone woman approach our sad little gathering from the darkness. She was clad in familiar blood-red robes, a deeply-drawn hood. I only knew it was her once she sat down and leaned closer. The Harriers made themselves scarce, knowing a clandestine liaison when they saw one.

"Welcome home, Sariana."

"Thank you, Aunty Cass."

I saw her lips twitch at that, fending off a smile. "That's not my name anymore."

"I could say the same thing."

Awkward silence followed. This wasn't quite the same as I'd felt with Lily, where a laugh and a hug might reaffirm our sisterhood if not resolve a complicated relationship. I could feel a certain…resistance hardening everything about Cassandra, and despite the divide it placed between us, I liked it. As different to how Vachaelle would have behaved as I could imagine.

"Let's take a walk."

"I think I've seen enough of what you've done with the place, Lady Cassandra Mind-Changer. Is there even still grass in the courtyard?"

"Of course, and young Sisters still sit on it and enjoy the sun."

"Sisters. In a fortress. Guarded by Brothers."

"It's always been a fortress. I just made the defences a little more obvious. I lack Vachaelle's skill there. Come on, let's get away from both the keep and the camp. Just a quiet chat, woman to woman."

I'll admit it: I didn't trust Iskendahrl not to set a pair of ears on the matter either. He had every right to. "I expect I won't need that?" I nodded over at the Gildenhammer, detached and on the ground.

"There isn't a person here who wouldn't die for you."

"The guards didn't recognise me. I doubt anyone in that fortress of yours would either."

"They will soon enough. You are safe here."

No I wasn't, but then again, I wasn't safe anywhere, at least not anywhere that really mattered.

So off we went, into and out of the shadows as we paced the interior of this new outer wall.

"I hear you met my brother."

"She first brought him here three or four years ago, yes. But met isn't the word I'd use for it. He wasn't here long and slept most of the time. Kept to himself for the rest. A very different creature than the one I've begun to remember as the rambunctious boy destined to inherit the world's most radical Clan. Well, that's the Nightsong for you. Besides, are you sure he *is* your brother?"

"Not you too, Cass."

"Xenides-ra Kas'Daen may really think you're his daughter. Which is why you should avoid him and his until he knows otherwise. There are few things a Noble desires more than a child they believe to be stolen. Dhivashes was pregnant when she…aligned with your father. The man you called father. So it is possible."

"No it fucking well isn't. Surely you've remembered enough by now to know I am absolutely the child of Dhiana and Charas'z, not Dhivashes and Xenides."

"Ah, that was his name. I could not recall it. I may even forget it later. Charas'z. Hm." She found this as good a means of changing the subject as any. "That happens a lot, have you noticed? Things come, things go. Your presence should prevent it, I think, as a custodian of memories the rest of us can only wait to receive in unreliable trickles. I am so glad you are back. I'm afraid there are few familiar faces — the Sisters either undertook a Fourth Going or…found other callings. Sofiya passed, may the Mother keep her. I fear I've done a terrible job maintaining her legendary management of the fortress. But there are others now, others who served your family across its vast domain. Others whose minds I do not need to change. Much."

"I'm not staying here. Vachaelle told me to come back, but I should have known she'd only do that if it meant seeing more evidence of my brother's activity. This Rouge Eyrie? The Scarlet Sparrows?…Mind-changer? And just having my family name flapping out in the open? Turning Abbey's Village into a fucking weapons factory? Cass, you can't be planning all this without Kas'Daen knowing of it."

"Of course not. The Scarlet Sparrows are unquestionably devoted followers of Kas'Daen; we are preparing to support them in a push north. North, to you know where but as yet they do not. The Kas'Daen are a ways off finding any of it. Even now, you probably remember Jaydemyr-*desne* as immense but mostly empty. It's why they couldn't conquer it with conventional methods. Why only Jaydemyr could bring down Jaydemyr."

"But the flag?" She was veering too close to acting like *her* with these dense, loaded divulgences. "The commander of the group that brought me noticed it immediately. The crux et luna. Surely it's too soon, given what Charan is doing with it out there."

"You still see one symbol…everyone else remembers seeing another. I can't work the perception on a scale even close to my lady's or your mother's, but a few square miles?" She shrugged. "This reminds me. I'll need to work on your new friends here."

"Not new at all. And what do you mean?"

"You won't stay but they can't leave. It's fine, Sariana. They will know only that they brought Sarivashes-ra Kas'Daen home, were paid well for the job, and now happily serve as the Sparrows' advisers on the Karakani, since the Swords of Heaven may yet become a threat to our eastern borders."

"Just like that?"

"Never 'just like that', but like that, yes. You knew, surely. Knew that bringing *anyone* to my, our home would mean they'd have to be…changed, somehow."

I clenched my fists, one naked and the other very much not. "I did not. I expected to return to the same old abbey, same old Sisterhood. But then…the Third Eye has closed, hasn't it? Where I was, where I've been. The Peddlers were defunct; the Haven, converted into, well, a sort of Sisterhood. But I assumed it was a local breakdown in the old order, not a ripple emanating from this…whatever you've built here and thrown into the tranquil surface of the night."

"So you know about the Menu now. About what we really did here."

"Some of it. I really don't care, Cass. Coming here was a mistake, and bringing my friends is a crime for which I need to atone. Is the reward for the return of Sarivashes real?"

"It is. I told you, Xenides may believe the Half reputed to have been seen in Karakan is his lost daughter. That may, of course, change at any time. Dhiana's plan was for sudden erasure and gradual recollection after Charan said his name, out loud and in Jaydemyrian. Not even she could have foreseen *how* the recollection would occur in any individual. If you're going to take advantage of the lord Kas'Daen's muddled beliefs, you'll need to do it immediately."

"So I leave, now. Take my men with me, and they claim their reward. You will *not* 'change' their minds. They came here free, they will leave here free."

"To Lybichmisto then? I say avoid Xenides and you want to go charging up to his capital and let these desert vultures, too wild for even the Swords of Heaven, take payment for delivering you to your doom?"

"You don't have to make it sound so reckless."

"Fucking damn right I don't."

There she was, the Cass of old. Or at least some shade of her. I leaned away from her, knowing just how quickly she could change *my* mind. One touch, perhaps. Were we Halves more resilient in this regard as well? That I did not know. Still don't know. All I know is we are not immune.

"I…I don't know what to do, Cass. I left here so sure I'd find him, and all I found out was how huge this world really is, how full of people just trying to figure out their place in it. How so many of them overestimate their value, while those who don't do the real work. And the closest I ever came to him was watching those he affected struggle to put their lives back together."

"If you trust me, I can get you much closer than that. Not a guaranteed meeting, but…I do know how Kas'Daen is operating, how they're trying to lure him. It's terribly risky, but it's probably better than either waiting here for her to bring him again or trying to find him alone."

"The last time she was here, did she bring him again?"

"Yes."

"When was that?"

"About a year ago."

"And did she visit about a year before that? Without him?"

Cass paused her pondering pace. "Ten months maybe. First and last time I saw her without him. Said she'd given the boy a special mission up north. Left his sword here though, which is how I knew they'd be back."

Not a lie about where he'd been then. Interesting. But how could it be true? From Kas'Daen to Kaifeng in two months? Or even the full *Ozon Yol*, multiple times in a year? "Cass, you know her better than anyone I know. The Third Eye…did it, does it have a way of moving physical things across great distances?"

"Not that I'm aware of. It's purely for divination and communication. I can't really say much more than that. Not even to you, My Lady."

Her formality I was already used to; that title, not at all. Was it because I'd finally asked a question worthy of her future liege? Future. But not yet. Did she truly plan on pivoting this whole operation away from ostensibly serving the Kas'Daen and towards supporting some resurgence of Jaydemyr?

It wasn't about trusting or not-trusting. As with everything, it was about how much. And how little. "I understand, Mind-Changer. You've done so much for me here, and I've acted very much the ingrate. The shock of it was just…too much. All this." I opened my arms to her, realising that what followed would have been impossible with the Gildenhammer slung to my waist. "I trust you."

We both had to step forward to complete the move, during which she could Change my mind at any moment. I'd seen how affectionately she'd done it to Viera, for her own good. For mine. I had to give voice to my thoughts into her ear, so close I could almost feel the tiny hairs against my lips. "Please, Cass, if you're going to do it, get it over with while I still believe I am choosing it for my own good."

"I would never, ever hurt you, My Lady. You will remember when it's time, but until then we need to hide you again. I am so, so very sorry."

What would it feel like? A tingle? A dizziness? A drowsy sag? Nothing at all?

Or maybe just a sun-warm hug from an old friend.

Cassandra Mind-Changer pushed me away to arm's length, nodded emphatically and then fell to her knees, head bowed with words of contrition dribbling from her lips. I looked down at her, thinking whatever she'd done, it surely didn't demand supplication this extreme. These Self-Scrapers and their feigned humility!

"By the Mother, Cassandra, you're so pathetic. Come on, get up." I bent down to help the obsequious *nse'ante* back to her feet. "You don't have to beg. I've been alone for so long. And we Halves are not meant to be alone for too long. So I'll stay, at least until we decide what to do next. Okay? I'll stay. There, you happy? I've changed my mind."

As she walked me back towards the keep, I could barely contain my excitement at being home. At the changes she'd made. Improved defences of the former abbey. Excellent visibility in all directions. Total geomantic overhaul of the surrounding area. Brothers sworn not only to Tantamon but to Kas'Daen patrolling the grounds. No more of that pointless pregnancy business. The Rouge Eyrie was a proper, well-armed and well-built stronghold fit for me and mine. The Scarlet Sparrows would serve as my personal security, a home guard for when I wasn't operating out there alone. When I needed to return to the roost to rest. Sparrowsview provided everything we needed, under the very professional supervision of Fourneval Foundries. Impressive how Cassandra had convinced the finest arms makers and distributors from Teriss-Luniir, so instrumental in the Purge of Teristra, to set up a factory here in the middle of nowhere.

Well, not the middle of nowhere for much longer. I gazed up at the onyx banners draping the walls around the entrance. A full bone-pale circle, a moon, and the garnet *f* almost slicing it in half. Perfect.

"You have quarters set aside and ready under the main keep." We entered what used to be the greeting hall but was now some sort of sparse ambush enclosure. The windows were still there, but now sat safe behind bars on both sides. Guards stood at every doorway.

"Good."

"One last thing, My Lady." Cassandra halted before we headed towards the updown around the corner. "What do you want done with the sellswords who came with you? Pay them and send them away?"

"Preposterous, Cassandra. After what they've seen and heard?" I drew myself up, stiffened my spine and lifted my chin. Let her see just who I was, not merely who she thought I was. "Do what you do best. Change their minds, send them back to the desolation they so love."

"We could just dispose of them, quietly and quickly."

"No. They turned from their faith, and to kill them as heretics might deny them a chance at returning to God's Dark Heart. Restore that faith and let them find their own end as true Jenetchen Kulutchara of Karakan, of the Faighana."

"Your mercy and wisdom astound me, Lady Sarivashes."

"It is only as my father would have done."

The comforts of a real bed, my own bed, waterroom, attendants, fresh food on demand, and of course *Vahm'esta* should I desire it – they didn't wear off for days. Nor for weeks. Nor months. Why did I leave all this? Not that I didn't appreciate what Cassandra had done in my absence, but I would have preferred to oversee it in person.

"You'll remember when it's time." Cassandra just kept repeating this when I complained about the massive gap in my memory. I remembered leaving Mothers Abbey, trained as a Half, a Sister and a hydrotheurge, Fourth Gone to spread the word and assist women in their natural tribulations. Why had I chosen to go into Karakan and then Chūnko? Likely I wanted to be as far from Kas'Daen as possible, and Father had no desire to keep living evidence of his indiscretion with yet another mortal anywhere near his dominion. What had I done there? That I did not know. Enlighten hordes of primitive narrow-eyed, dark-skinned *nse'ante* who didn't even know about the Sacred Cuts, I supposed. And this necklace hidden against my skin? A gift from Father, I believed. A circle encapsulating the holy *f* of Afraen Who Was Ephriem – noble device of Clan Kas'Daen. I couldn't read whatever was inscribed on the back though. Per any other gift from that bastard: pretty and meaningless. Two things I simply couldn't be for him or anyone else, no matter how hard I tried.

Most of the time I spent luxuriating in that which I so richly deserved, earned through years of rejection and then dedication to helping the disadvantaged youth of less-advanced lands. Rats, dogs and pigs as far as I cared. And Cassandra, bless the woman, kept the fort in tight shape. I didn't have to do anything except occasionally sign a document or sit in a meeting that seemed very important to everyone there. Then I could return to my chambers or tour the grounds if the night air called for my presence. I didn't have to see the sun for at least half a year and that was just fine by me.

I'd get bored of this lifestyle sooner or later. But oh, let later not come too soon.

"Lady Sarivashes, it is time for my nightly hug."

I acknowledged Cass without agreeing. I'd been perfectly comfortable on my bed, sipping some *Vahm'esta* and nibbling a nice barely-warm haunch (being Half was truly the greatest of both worlds), and trying to decide on a style for all that luscious golden hair. But if she said it was time, it was time. Just a hug. Just a silly *nse'ante* needing a little proof that her Lady did indeed love and care for her. Who was I to deny her that?

I didn't remember her grabbing me, only the hint of a whisper before she let me go. "Are you ready then, Sarivashes?"

I nodded at her scrutiny in the dim candlelight and ran my fingers through what little hair I'd allowed myself to keep. How could I not be? "I've only waited about seven years for this. And you've ensured I'll have a good party for the task? Well-trained Brothers and Sisters willing to commit their lives to what must be done?"

"Brothers. I've assembled a few old friends of yours with a representative from Azak's Chapterhouse, far from home and determined to take The Scourge at all costs. Their familiar presence might make things a bit easier. But it was Tzara-Min they knew, not Sarivashes. Remember this. Your name is and always has been Tzara-Min. You are a hydrotheurge of the Scarlet Sparrows, formerly of the Liquid Night. You knew these boys before you left, but they only saw you once or twice, and the first time you were not exactly in a state to say much at all."

"You can't possibly mean…The ones who carried me here. And then at the festival. Kendahl? Huysman?" Only met them a few times, might have had…fascinated thoughts about them once or twice in a cruddy little barn after a decidedly unfascinating encounter with a foul-mouthed swineherd…Roderic. Yes. But those…what were their first names? Did I ever learn them?

Jorik. Henri. If that second meeting with Huysman had even been real.

"You remember their names. My oh my. It's been a long time, mind. Don't go throwing yourself at them."

"Aunty Cass! I would never." …Think about what I thought about that night again. Nope. Never…Ever.

"There was a time…hm. Like I said. Long ago. They might not even remember you. Might be best to pretend you've forgotten them too. But if they remember, you remember. If they treat you like a dangerous animal, that's only natural too. It's not every day they see a Half your age eating raw meat and taking all of the night watches. Follow their cues, but only so far. Sarivashes may lead, but Tzara-Min is more comfortable watching people from behind."

"Alright. Cass, you do know I spent years as her right? Before my mission to Kaifeng. Mother drilled me on all of this. It's not as if I am apt to forget. Not something we Halves do very well."

"No, of course not. But still. It would be disastrous were you to slip. Now. Tzara-Min is a Teristran, and has never been to Lybichmisto. Avoid it if at all possible. You may feel some temptation to return, after all this time. Your destination, as the commander will clarify, isn't far from there."

"Commander? Representative of Azak?"

"The same. He *does* know who you are, but don't let him pry too much out of you. His eyes are so turned to facing The Scourge he probably won't do much more than decide how best to use you. And stop changing the subject. What did I say before about Lybichmisto?"

I couldn't but laugh at her fretting. "Avoid if at all possible. Don't worry. I barely remember it and what little I do recall is best left there. One of a few reasons I wish I *could* forget. Or be made to."

The Lady Cassandra, Mind-Changer inclined her face to the side, as though trying to see me in a different light. "I suppose we could try again…"

"No." I sighed, knowing what she offered and lamenting my immunity to it. "There are limits to even your puissance, Cass. Sadly, the mercy of Maliscience is not for me. I am but who the Mother made me." I smirked and let her know I wasn't off-topic at all. "And who I am is Tzara-Min, hydrotheurge Half of Teristra."

"And no one else. And that reminds me. I know you're Half, a weapon unto yourself, but if requested, wear all the same armour as the others. Brothers *love* to keep up appearances. Take your *Vahm'esta* sparingly; it won't be easy to replenish. Let their Healer handle your wounds if possible. If there is any fighting before you get there.

Probably not. But still, don't forget your hammer flail thing. You left it for maintenance at the keep forge, remember?"

"Of course I remember. With Mastersmith Harald, right?"

"Him? No, he's…Look, I can't keep track of all the names of the commonfolk. It doesn't matter. Just get some sleep, get your weapon, and get yourself to the inner gate at Bladesun."

"Alright, Cass. Anything else I should know or do?"

"Oh. The pendant. The one your father gave you. Keep that hidden. I'd suggest leaving it here but I know better."

It's not that I always wore it, but something wouldn't allow me to leave it anywhere I wasn't sure I could reach if need be. Some deep-seated lesson from the time before, I supposed. "Considering it depicts the Kas'Daen name quite clearly, I should think that's a given, Cass."

"You asked, I answered." She pouted a little.

"Always with the fussing. I'm ready for this, and you know it." I softened this with a rising query of foregone conclusion. "Right?" Then I looked around the unfamiliar bedroom. "You know, you really should fuss less over me and more over keeping this place neater. Goodnight and goodbye, Cassandra, Lady Mind-Changer."

No hug this time. We'd been all business for a while by then.

Six men waited for me just outside the inner gate that crisp early summer morning. Five of them were dressed for battle, helms on and visors lowered, purple cloaks marking their faction. Each held the reins of five equally impressive palfreys. These were no ordinary Tantamonian Brothers content to tromp about on mules mending fences and chopping wood for needy widows and spinsters.

"Tzara-Min of the Scarlet Sparrows, ready to depart." I made a show of hefting a pack the weight of which I couldn't even feel. They all knew I wouldn't need to ride anything to keep up. "To whom should I report?"

A wasteful question: the sixth man was already astride his horse, a portly fop of distinct middle age wearing the same armour and cape, but instead of an impressive helmet hiding his face, he preened with a very expressive cap, feathers and all. His moustache was too long and loose, but probably looked a lot less feral when waxed. Something about him reminded me of a boar, but no, with that smooth scalp I knew to be under that ruffled plumage, he was more like a frog. When he opened his mouth I was genuinely surprised he didn't croak, but instead almost bellowed. "I am Lord Vadim of Azak, follower of Tantamon and your commanding officer. Salute and fall in, Sparrow."

I saluted, fell in, and studied the treeline beyond the walls below. A familiar name though, Vadim. Somehow.

"I am aware that you may be acquainted with a few of my soldiers. There'll be time enough when we camp for pointless reminiscing and nostalgia. For now, we depart. Keep the chatter to a minimum."

Oh, this was going to be a *fun* mission.

The Brothers mounted, assumed formation – two in front, Vadim and I next, the remaining three bringing up the rear. When I thought about that, those words, I was inexplicably reminded of the two old Brothers from Azak. Miroslav and…Vladimir? Something like that. Bring up the rear. I stifled a giggle at the wordplay. Remembered Vi used to call them the Brotherhood of the Fist. Eph me raw but she was a lot of fun.

Enough, Sarivashes. I heard my father's disappointed voice in my head, could almost see him waving his wood hammer at me sternly. *This is the most important mission of your otherwise worthless existence. And these good men may just die for it. Show a little respect, Pumpkin.*

Yes, Father. Sorry, Father.

Wait, when did the Lord Xenides-Ra Kas'Daen ever use a hammer? Or any sort of primitive *nse'ante* tool? Or give a shit about 'good men'?

Or call me 'pumpkin'? Preposterous.

I shook my head to clear it and forced my attention onto the scenery. Nothing I hadn't seen many times and it hadn't changed since.

Exactly what I needed. Trees. Clouds. Hills. Trees. Treestreestrees…

"—have your attention, Sparrow."

"Sir?" I looked up at Commander Vadim atop his trotting mare.

"You have likely noticed we are not a typical Brotherhood company. I do not know these men very well and they are mostly strangers to each other. We have not been roaming the realms of Kas'Daen assisting and providing as is the Brotherhood's traditional mandate."

Emphasis on 'man'. Teehee.

Shut UP, Viera.

His pause indicated it was my turn to speak.

"The Lady Cassandra did mention you'd been assembled recently. To my knowledge, Tantamonian brotherhood is a long and hard, I mean, the relationship required to work together is built over years of close…closeness."

I didn't hear that patriarchal admonishment in my head this time, because I wasn't sure if it actually did come from the Kas'Daen patriarch, and Vadim was too busy preparing his next statement to pick up on my childish innuendo. And if any of the grim Brothers flanking us heard it, they certainly didn't react either.

"Indeed. But circumstances as they are, we require a different approach, one that concentrates the best fighting men available to the Brotherhood into a single formidable unit. It is regrettable but undeniable that not all Brothers are inclined to intense melee."

"Sir?" Where was this going?

"Yes, Sparrow Tzara-Min?"

"Where is this…I mean, I fail to comprehend how this relates to me."

He leaned away from me a little, still puffed up but now also maybe as confused as I was. "You are part of that formidable unit now, but are not I would think familiar with Tantamonian company structure and etiquette. That, you will learn. More to the point, you are, unlike us, a Half, just as he is." No need to ask who here. "I have been informed you may even be his sibling."

"Half, as you said. We've never met, but we have the same mother. Wasn't my decision, sir."

That earned a slight snort, and I let him see just a little of the mirth stirring around in my head at his pompous but somehow earnest demeanour. "We are but who the Mother makes us, it is true. Now, I will tell you in brief what is going to happen. Your being Half will not impede this outcome, although I expect you to employ your full strength at any and every moment before that."

"Sir." This was not how people gave orders…

"Our task is simple: proceed to a Chapterhouse not far from Lybichmisto. This should take a month, no more, even with the mountain passes making our path less than direct. There we will be assigned a role that, Mother willing, will bring us the honour of facing The Scourge personally. I do not know what grievances you bear him as a sibling, but he assaulted my home in my absence. Murdered my Brothers, destroyed my Chapterhouse. That was years ago, and I've been working my way towards this very mission ever since. So make no mistake, Sister: when the time comes, I will be the one to land the first blow to his Mother-damned skull. God's justice and my sword arm be true, it may even be the last."

I swallowed a snigger at the man's enormous delusion, this grandiloquent statement delivered as though words were deeds, as though something could be made possible, no, guaranteed, just by saying it with enough gusto and bluster. But then I had something else on my mind, and I gave voice to my concerns with something alarmingly close to sentimentality. "I am so sorry to hear about what happened to Azak. I knew two Brothers from there. Volodymyr and Miroslav. Did The Scourge kill them too?"

It came at great cost, but the enquiry purchased a flash of uncertainty across his pyretic face. "Those two nags? No, they died well before that, in each other's arms as far as anyone knows."

"At least there's that." I surprised myself with a Flail in their memory. I figured it's what Tzara-Min would have done.

Then *he* surprised me by sighing. "Silly old buggers went and fell in love, but they were granted the purple shroud of Tantamon in death nonetheless. Normally I'd not allow that, but, well, they didn't break the code of Tantamon with a woman or try to start a family or anything so obviously heinous. They could have kept it unspoken like everyone else, but…" Lord Vadim shrugged and adjusted his grip on the saddle. "They were too old for much else anyway. Eventually the truth of who you are is all you have left, and they lived and died true to that."

I glanced around at the other Brothers, then returned my eyes to the road ahead. "And I hope the truth of who we are will be the ones to end The Scourge. Finally."

"*Vahm en*, Sister. We'll make a fine Brother out of you yet."

"You're not going to make me shave my head, are you?"

Bless the man, he allowed one lip to quirk, revealing a dimple beneath his large cheeks. "Of course not. How would we know who you are?"

Eh, maybe it wouldn't be so bad an assignment after all.

The first week or two were mostly dull and routine. The gentle hills in which nestled the Rouge Eyrie and towns such as Sparrowsview soon gave way to the lush, densely wooded mountain range that served as a natural north-eastern border with inner Kas'Daen-*desne*. I recalled something I'd read in the library of Mothers Abbey: one of the names for the idyllic area I'd called home after leaving 'home' was 'the realm beyond the forest'. This had baffled me at the time; there were plenty of trees and groves around the abbey. But not, I saw now, actual forests.

Once this may have been a treacherous region, but the roads snaking between the peaks were well-worn and the towns familiar with travellers.

Brother Prickard, pale of skin, dour in mood, and constantly wary of everyone, even his Tantamonian brethren, also hailed from Lybichmisto, and had journeyed this way before. Vadim hadn't openly appointed him as a guide but also didn't disagree when the man, who seemed more built for espionage or skulking than thudding about in full plate, made suggestions as to our route. When to march. When to take refuge indoors. When to camp.

Vadim's words rang true: this was not a close company, but everyone knew their role and fulfilled it with precise minimalism. Resting was practical and efficient; travel was disciplined and…efficient. If we imposed on a Haven or waystation, we slept in barns or stables, eschewing all but the most basic of civilised offerings. Absent that, people acted per their Talents and skills. As usual, most of us were geomancers or aerian. I was the only hydrotheurge, also as usual. Prickard was the only pyrotic. Two rarities but essential for any self-sufficient party. So we worked together a lot, he and I, and said nothing that wasn't in aid of that work. The whole affair made my time with the Pallid Harriers seem intimate and cosy.

Which would have been fine but for the early confirmation that yes, Kendahl and Huysman were also part of the company. I'd never taken either for an elite fighter but it's not as though I were any fair judge of that. They'd been boys I hardly knew. Kids. We all had been. Now, when they removed their helms, unslung their swords, tended to their mounts and set about the necessities of human repast and human relaxation, they did so with scars on their shaven heads, a hollowness to their bony cheeks, and a disturbing amount of nothing in their stares. They did not approach me. Per Cassandra's command, I let them set the beat to this singularly stolid march towards what must for them have seemed certain death. Death at the hands of a Half of unprecedented power…and here they were forced into comradeship with his estranged, volatile Half sister. She who ate raw flesh as they roasted game, barely slept as they snored the fitful slumber of the seasoned soldier, and sipped surreptitiously from a flask of what was surely human blood. All because their vengeance-bent commander was more than willing to risk me turning on them if it meant even a slightly better chance of scoring a single hit on an otherwise untouchable foe.

There was an us and a them, even if 'them' was actually just 'her'.

Until, of course, we had to contend with a more obvious them.

"We cannot help them." One of the other Brothers repeated this at Kendahl in a vaguely familiar accent from far to the south before spurring his horse forward and away into the grey morning haze. I didn't know his name, but everyone called the sun-leathered man 'Pillar'. He wasn't even very tall. Maybe that was why. Maybe it wasn't. His helmet, removed only when required, did have a sort of spike on it. A little pillar, I guess. "Commander's orders, Brother."

This wasn't the first time a Brother had said something to this effect as we trekked away from the alps and down towards yet-distant Lybichmisto, but it would be the last.

"Easy for you to say…Brother." We trod past the smoke-clotted ruins of brick and mud and thatch and wailing survivors that was probably a village not long ago. Maybe even just last night. "You're not even a real follower of Tantamon. We assist. We provide. All *you* do is kill."

Pillar didn't respond to this, but I certainly did. I slowed and half-turned back to see Kendahl in his deliberately plain casque. He was leading his horse through the slop of the road next to his shorter, stockier companion, who was doing the same. Out of respect for those we apparently couldn't help, I assumed.

"Brother Kendahl, what did you mean by that?" I lowered my voice as much as I could and still be heard. Much easier without having a steel grate in front of your mouth. I knew Cass said do as they do, but heavy metal hats and plates just for a long walk nowhere near the length of *The Long Way*? No thanks. And those poor horses. "Not a real follower."

He neither changed pace nor appeared to turn his concealed face my way. "You should know, Half of Kas'Daen. The same applies to you."

"She is not the same as that bastard and you know it very well, Henri." Huysman's raspy voice was done no favours by the visor. Until that very moment, they'd addressed each other by family name or title. Jorik Huysman, after all this time, was as perceptive and, in his own quiet way, thoughtful as ever. I loved him just a little for these seemingly effortless breadcrumbs. "He's a former Sword of Heaven, Tzara-Min. Now a mercenary. But like our commander, he almost definitely has more personal reasons for joining up."

I tried very hard not to appreciate that it had taken a devastated village and the start of a disagreement over what to do about it to get these two talking to me again.

I glanced back to see if our good leader was paying attention to this 'chatter', but he was too transfixed by the tragic scene around us. Not all roads encountered villages, but this one, dirt more than stone at this point, seemed to send us through all of them. Most were fine. Accommodating, even. This was the first to truly test the commander's resolve. He squinted against the smoke under that ridiculous cap, lips pursed in frustration.

But he did not tell us to stop. Soon he and the other company members were pulling away from us. Good. Time to learn a few things now that the 'them' and 'us' was starting to erode.

"Are you…are you two the only actual Brothers of Tantamon other than Commander Vadim?"

"Not that it really matters to him, but I think so, yes." Kendahl didn't clarify who.

"But…the armour. The capes. The shaven heads. The prayers before eating. After eating. Before making mud…*after* making mud…"

Huysman's shoulders under said cape quaked a little, and Kendahl made an amused grunt but said nothing more.

"All easy to imitate, except the prayers. Pillar keeps slipping into what sounds like Kakanic and Tor forgets to so much as Flail himself half the time." Jorik gestured at a somewhat distant Torbjorn. The company healer. Giant of a man. Barrel-chested and more prone to belly laughing than anyone I'd ever known. For some reason he reminded me of a Havenkeeper, and when I found that image in my head, there was a young man at his side. A son I supposed. Weird. Road-life really pushed my imagination to combat the monotony.

"Where is Tor from?"

"Rural Haven somewhere in Teriss-Luniir. Makes for the best combat healers."

How the hell did I know? "Does he have a son?"

"How the hell would I know?" Huysman shrugged with one gauntleted hand. "He's a good Healer and doesn't oppose Tantamonian tenets. Anything else is…banal and impertinent."

I knew he wasn't speaking from his own stance here; 'banal and impertinent' was a Vadimism if I ever heard one.

"And have you honestly ever seen Pricker pray at all?" Kendahl was thankfully warming up to the topic and hopefully the general idea of me as one of 'them'. "Thinks he's above all that, and probably is. Pyrotics." He probably would have spat if he could have.

"His name's Pricker? I kept hearing Prickard." I made the connection right there and then and sized up the group at last. We had me, two true Brothers of Tantamon, a broken Sword of Heaven, a Healer possibly recruited from a Haven, a fucking *Peddler?*...and a displaced nothing-to-lose commander who had clearly made his order's values a coin for revenge. "Blessed Mother, what *is* this company?"

"Perfect for the trial ahead." Commander Vadim, having noticed our stalling, clicked his mare toward us. "Although these two laggards, unlike the rest, seem fit only to shield their more dedicated comrades. If they fall, Sparrow Tzara-Min, the blame is entirely yours."

He was cruel but also possibly right about their limited utility. Compared to the backgrounds of the others, traditional Brothers were more suited to...well, what we should have been doing for those desperate villagers right then. Also: "What? Why? What the fuck did I do?"

"It's not what you did." Vadim started to move away again. "It's who you are."

At some point during this short exchange, both Huysman and Kendahl had removed their helmets and stopped walking altogether. I saw their faces as they gave full attention to the wretched scene now almost but not quite behind us. Tears moistened their cheeks through their slow blinking, and I knew better than assume it was merely a result of irritation from the smoke and ash.

Who I was? Cassandra said she'd assembled this group, but it was clear that Vadim himself picked most of them for their skills and ruthlessness. Which meant...oh no. These two were here simply because I had met them once or twice and Cass knew I'd liked them. Torn from their true company and thrown into a monstrous party of hardened vagabonds. It wasn't me being a threatening Half that they'd resented and shunned. It wasn't even my tenuous connection to our eventual quarry. It was me knowing them at all.

And, I added in bitter admiration, their vulnerability would make for very fine leverage should I find Vadim's command less than agreeable.

This was a move worthy of Vachaelle, but for Cassandra's thoughtful assertion that the whole thing would be 'easier' for me with a few familiar faces. That she was doing me a favour.

But was it a move made with Vadim's help…or his helplessness?

"Stop." I gave the command to only myself at first. Then I looked away from the grieving Brothers and yelled down the road at the not-quite-distant riders. "STOP."

They didn't at first, but once Vadim jerked his mount about, the other three followed suit. Of course I couldn't read their expressions with their helms in place but the body language spoke of exhausted resistance.

"Is there a problem, Sparrow Tzara-Min?" He actually sounded sincere. Again.

"Yes. Me." Because if I'd said something more obvious like 'look around, you turd-on-two-legs, and you tell me', he probably wouldn't have been able to. How had this paragon of Tantamon fallen so hard and so far? "I have decided we are helping these people. It might take a few hours. It might take a few days. It might take weeks. But those in your so-called company of Brothers who are in fact truly Brothers of Tantamon, the only members worthy of donning the purple and bearing the Fist, they deserve to be who they are and do what they do. We stop, Vadim, or you go without us. And by us, I mean me." Close, but not quite there… I lowered my voice for just us two but still almost shouted. "And by me, I mean your only chance at surviving more than three seconds against Charan fucking Jaydemyr!"

There.

"Who?"

Oh. Kinda fucked that one up, Sari.

Wait, who were we talking about?

Oh. Yeah.

"The Scourge, you lackwit. You need me to face down The fucking Scourge."

His typically ruddy face shook as it found an even deeper shade of jowl-rattling red. His lips came together like stormclouds, the thunder of holy wrath and righteousness started to form behind them…and then it all passed. His mouth eased away from spewing fury and he nodded, less in acknowledgement of my hissed outburst and more as though deciding it wasn't worth the fight. "Company, halt!"

I heard in that full-bodied projection the true command of the Father of Tantamon he had once been. Could that be restored somehow, or was this just an echo from the devastation my Brother left him to find at doomed Azak? Or it may have been just habit that made him call it out to the others. "Our services are required here. Brothers. What is it we do?"

Five male voices of varying enthusiasm and volume in ragged chorus: "We assist. We provide."

"And what is it we do not do?"

"Ask. Probe." Equally dissonant.

Vadim sniffed and trotted towards the forward guard to order/convince/cajole the trio back to the afflicted village.

I exhaled slowly having realised I hadn't done that for an uncomfortably long time, whispered the call's response to myself and myself alone. We assist. We provide. Whether it's ravaged commonfolk or friends in having a deep crisis of everyday faith.

I favoured the two Brothers of Tantamon a half smile.

Kendahl lowered his head and began to trudge back to the once-village, his horse nickering in protest.

Huysman gave me a startled look that darkened into angry disbelief before following him. Apparently I had just pissed on his breadcrumbs.

Then came the rest, all passing judgment on the upstart interloper as they had long wished to do.

The likely Peddler paused as he passed me, held out one gloved hand, palm up, almost as though offering me a ride. A small flame erupted between his knuckles, struggled to grow, and then died as he collapsed his fingers into a fist. Then he rode off. Edgy prick.

Torbjorn neither smiled nor frowned, but simply studied me as though trying to figure out what any of this meant. Then he nodded. "Thank you, Sister." His horse was small but remained steady beneath his swaying girth.

Then came Pillar, who made a show of circling me on his stallion. I called him something in rough, wasteland Kakanic that suggested his ancestors had a fondness for pig, and not in terms of food.

"Enough of your twisted tongue, Kudzal Milyaj." He used the weirdly respectful/hateful term for Half, 'Holy Mongrel', not so much in Kakanic but close enough for me to understand. And that's when I figured out who his accent reminded me of. He wasn't Kakanic; he was

Purashenan. And he hadn't understood my insult. In hindsight: good. "Commander orders that we help. We help."

I marvelled at his lack of rebelliousness. No doubt as to who he obeyed, but if Vadim could be turned a little from simply rushing to his demise and taking his men with him, this one might also be salvageable.

Before yanking the reins and pursuing the fragmented party, Vadim addressed me with just one sentence, and I swear if he'd known my full name he'd have used it. "We will discuss this later, Sarivashes."

That answered my earlier question to him in full then:

This is what the fuck I did do.

True to the Tantamonian code, the company didn't investigate what had happened to Radomyr's Rest at first. The offers of assistance may have come late and obviously with some reluctance, but surely the villagers had seen the colour of our passage and known it for what it was, even if five scary helmets and one gaudy cap had concealed shaven-pated devotion to the Tantamon. But such things, as Huysman had pointed out, are easily imitated and just as easily mistrusted, especially by folk who had very recently been grossly mistreated. In a curiously ironic way, it wasn't until the two Brothers divested themselves of almost all Tantamonian trappings and set about clearing the rubble and debris that the villagers began to actively request and direct their help.

Perhaps drawn to the familiarity of devoted exertion and service, even Vadim had dismounted and was helping the wounded over to where Torbjorn had set up a makeshift station. The swiftness and care in the physically intimidating Luniiri's treatment confirmed that not only was he from a rural Haven, he had probably been the head Healer, if not the only. And at that size, he could have been a Doorman as well. As I helped an old woman dig through splintered beams and fractured furniture, I resolved to ask him later.

"Thank you, Brother." The crone mopped her ashen forehead with a threadbare shawl. "Thank you…"

I didnt correct the title; she'd clearly lost enough, let her keep her dignity in being harmlessly wrong. I handed her a mug of freshly made water. "You are welcome. We assist. We provide."

"*Vahm en, vahm en…*"

On the other hand, *I* was not a follower of Tantamon, nor did I need to pretend to be. Pillar, Huysman and Kendahl were all stripped to the waist, bald heads sheened with effort as they hauled rock, restored slats and otherwise put in a grand effort of caring a great deal. None of them employed Talents per the doctrine, which loosely stated physical labour strengthened not just the body, but the soul as well. Such was the way of the Brotherhood. Assist. Provide.

But me...I could also ask. I could probe.

"What happened here, Baba?"

She coughed after a gulp of water. "The smoke woke me up before dawn. The fire kept us awake. The smoke drew you to us, didn't it? I don't know much else. Thank God you are here, Brother..."

"This was your home?" I looked over my shoulder at her as she stood there, a five foot nothing of dejection and misery.

"Was."

I thought about the size of the wrecked cottage. About this broken old woman. And still I had to ask. "Do you live alone?"

"Normally no." She sniffled. "But Yegor, my son, he was in Radomyr's Rest last night. Not busy, not a Hunting night. So he took little Nora along too, for a treat. Music and good food. He's a good father. My good boy. I should have said no..."

Oh. No. *He* always hit the Havens hardest.

No mention of a wife. Or other children. And probing that wasn't going to get me any closer to the deeper truth here. "Baba, I want you to go over to that big bearded man over there with the others. His name is Brother Torbjorn. He used to work in a Haven too. He will look after you."

"But my home, Brother. We haven't found Ilyena yet...Or Drago..."

Didn't know, didn't want to know. "Please. I will keep looking and tell you once I find them, all right?"

It wasn't far from there to Torbjorn's accumulation of barely-moving bodies. Still, I watched her stagger and slosh her way through the gritty slush. It hadn't rained, so there must have been at least one other hydrotheurge around to extinguish the fire. Contrary to what I told the poor old woman, I stopped my search and took in the village as a whole. Thankfully Torbjorn hadn't set up near what looked to be the Haven. He'd have known: largest building, most central, always a stable, usually free-standing waterrooms this far from a city. And, as if to confirm my horrified suspicion, almost certainly the first structure razed.

I checked the Gildenhammer at my waist even though the live threat was definitely long gone, and squelched towards the presumed Haven. It had only two floors, but was fairly large; it could probably have put up a few hundred people at capacity, which thankfully it hadn't been. Above the main entrance, the tell-tale sign teetered back and forth in the same breeze sending the smoke through what was likely called Radomyr's Village, but probably not for much longer. Radomyr's Ruins, maybe.

Pricker was already inside. He wasn't stripped to the waist like the others but his helmet was off and he just stood there in what I surmised was the main hall. Not all the bodies had been removed yet; some weren't body enough anymore for that.

"We shouldn't have stopped." Pricker's face, usually etched with deep creases of doubt and dismissal, was slack, stunned. Dry, but there was something not far from tears wavering in dark, deepset eyes belonging to an older, more weathered man than I'd taken him for. "There's nothing we can do here. We aren't those who fix things or hold those who remain close and whisper false assurances. This place is the past now. Our future is a fight to keep this from happening again. And you…you just said…stop. And now we have."

I bore my gaze straight at him, because it was that or look at something else. "I agree. We shouldn't have stopped. We have a mission and this isn't it. But that's the problem with you Tantamonian brothers. You don't do what you should; you do what you must."

He sucked air through his teeth, an odd inversion of a hiss. Would he maintain the façade, or realise he'd already torn it right off? "Assist and Provide works when the world isn't threatened by something that requires unity and prioritisation. Sometimes you help others by doing that which they cannot. Should not. *Must not.*" Eph me but he really was a Peddler to the depths of his thorn-bound heart. "You're not one of us. Why did you interfere?"

And now he'd turn it on me, because that's what people who get angry in the shadows do when someone forces them to look at the light. "Because if I didn't, I don't think all of us would have made it to Lybichmisto. And while I don't know you, or Pillar, or Torbjorn, I do know and care for those two young men who shouldn't be here. Surely you've noticed that this party of seven professional warriors is in fact barely half that."

"I have, and this isn't how you protect them, Sparrow. This is how you distract them. This is how you undermine their dedication. One village to help, fine. But then another, now the dice have been rolled once. And then another. Four? Five? Then we're far behind schedule, the commander's frothing in rage, and I'm faced with a very difficult choice."

"No." I went back to scanning the interior of the Haven, for fear of looking at him and losing all self-control. "Harm them and I will disassemble you alive."

"You misread me, Sister in Red." That was a new one. Peddler slang or were the Scarlet Sparrows that prolific already? Pricker stepped closer to me, hands empty and eyes on the entrance over my shoulder. He lowered his voice and let some of the emotion just being in here had evoked suffuse his words. "I would die myself before letting them come to harm. They are true servants of God and the only decent thing in this whole mess. No. The choice would be whether or not to kill the commander and be done with this fool's errand."

I'm sure a sound came out of my mouth but it definitely wasn't anything in any language other than the primal tongue of What The Ephin Eph What? "Who *are* you, Pricker?"

"I am that. Pricker, the Peddler. Former. Not by choice. Now sworn to the purple of Brotherly Love Everyone. You know, I miss my hair." A brief reprieve from the grimness then as he rubbed that now-stubbly dome. "But alright. Not what you asked. I served your family long ago. Your real family. Yes, I know who you are."

Vadim and now his subordinate, possibly insubordinate. Might as well have worn the necklace with my name on it for all to see at this rate. "Pricker, I don't even know who I am sometimes. Is that even *your* name?"

"For now it is all the name I need. So, now we share secrets. And we keep them, I hope."

Cassandra must have planted this one. Just as Mother had once tapped the Peddlers to help me escape the turmoil of Teristra. No. That didn't happen. I've never met my mother. But Chrysanthemum. What?

I swallowed as if this somehow might put these flights of fancy deep and out of the way. "If the safety of those two men is your priority, then yes. Even if that is your priority because it's mine."

"Semantics." He shrugged and resumed his remorseful disposition. I want to stress that at no point did I think that facet of him was an act. Peddlers might be pricks, but…well, you would know. They have a difficult relationship with compassion. But it is a relationship. "We shouldn't have stopped, but I am mildly glad we did. Now to tell the commander what I found in here."

He bent his back slightly, narrowed his eyes a little and stalked out. Ephin' Peddlers, I thought, and left not long after, knowing that I'd not find anything in this husk of a Haven that he'd have missed.

A lot can happen when you are intellectually trapped in a burnt-out room with an aggressor who turns out to be an ally. What I'd taken for loud disagreements between understandably upset villagers was, I saw as I made my way from the residue of Radomyr's Rest, past Tor's healing tents and towards the southern exit to the village, only half that.

A small mob had converged on Vadim. Most of the villagers kept wary distance, but a burly man in a leather apron streaked with blackened stains stood no more than two feet from the commander. The presumed smith's face was livid, his scraggly black hair plastered with what I hoped was sweat to his trembling scalp. Vadim, in aloof contrast, appeared intractable and resolute: seated on a bench, hands clasped and elbows on knees, face directed down at the mud.

"We will not be doing that." His voice was hoarse and wrung out, either from the lingering smoke or the previous assistance he provided. "It is not why we are here."

"But now you *know* who did this to us." The de facto spokesman of Radomyr's Village projected this at a spot near Vadim's feet. "He can't be far away." Then he sagged, as though he'd already said something like this and, as before, it hadn't made a difference. "We aren't ungrateful for your help, Lord Brother. But if you stop him now, maybe the destruction of our haven, of Radomyr's Rest, can be his last crime."

So they were past the eye contact stage, having decided passive communication was preferable to direct, which was but an enraged twitch away from the physical. The smith was indeed holding a forge hammer, but at his side. I suspected Vadim had already told him to keep it there, for lack of relinquishing it.

"We have a sign given by someone claiming to be him, and he can indeed be 'far away' by now. In any direction. We are not trackers, good sir. We assist. We provide. *And then we move on.*"

Off to the side, caught somewhere between one menial expression of this conveniently vague devotion and the next, Huysman and Kendahl had paused to watch the fierce collision of intentions and needs. Pillar, even further detached, was crouched down, petting a large dog that looked well cared-for. For now. But even as his hands sought an exchange of comfort with the animal, his now-exposed eyes measured the escalation of the altercation with pale yellow placidity. I noticed that his sword was unbuckled, but no further from reach on the ground than that blissfully panting mutt.

And Pricker, somehow the last piece of this puzzle I noticed, was from my vantage point behind the incited villagers, gripping a scrap of cloth, almost a small flag. I simply knew it not to be incidental. But had he found this evidence…or merely produced it? "The commander is right. This is just a sign. It is his sign, but well-known enough now that anyone might leave it in their murderous wake." His customary cynicism honed an otherwise palatable conclusion: "We would all do well to resist making of The Scourge a scapegoat in desperation. Or, might I say, laziness."

So I'd been right too. He'd 'found' The Scourge's blasphemous signature in the Haven on that piece of fabric. I'd heard tell the breaker of Havens operated a little more messily, cutting the symbol into the skin of his victims, but there was no agreement that this was his *only* way of claiming responsibility. And surely a well-placed kerchief would be easier to plant for later discovery than a wound on bodies bound for immolation. How did sharing this 'discovery' serve Pricker's larger cause? Was he trying to goad Vadim? Remind him of the mission? Was he just giving these hopeless people something to blame? If so, Vadim was doing a poor job ensuring it wasn't him.

"Sparrow Tzara-Min." The commander called out to me then, beckoning. I sniffed in lieu of spoken curses and approached so he wouldn't have to strain his clearly strained voice. "You were in there with Brother Pricker just before, no?"

"Sir. I was." I kept my attention firmly on the now deflated, already dispersing mob; they seemed to realise the conflict was beyond them, and whether or not we provided them justice came down to how this fortuitously placed company proceeded.

And even a glance at Pricker would be too much.

"Did you see any proof of who attacked the Haven?"

"Sir. I did not."

"Did you see Brother Pricker find that scrap of cloth?"

"No sir."

"What in your opinion happened?"

Shit. No avoiding that one with monosyllabic obedience. "I don't think it was The Scourge, sir, but I also don't think that makes this any less tragic nor that whoever did it any less reprehensible. These people needed help. Tantamon teaches that you…we assist and provide that help as we can."

He took this in with a stoicness that once again spoke of how and why he'd been Father at the Azak Chapterhouse, before what Miroslav and Volodymyr called years ago 'very bad times' made him a Commander. I winced to think what words they'd need to describe where such times had ended up. "And why don't you think it was the Scourge, Sparrow?"

Now I did risk a peek at Pricker, left alone after the last of the villagers returned to sifting through the dregs of their home. He knew better than to acknowledge my attention.

"We wouldn't have had a reason to stop had it been him, sir."

This was dangerously close to admiration, but Vadim would hopefully remember what I'd said earlier regarding his chances against the real thing. Or at least see I was giving him precisely what he needed here. He didn't smile, but he did nod a few times and then stand up. "And our mission is not to blindly chase pretenders and imitators, monsters though they also may be. Ours is to put ourselves directly in The Scourge's path and end it entirely. Let us continue to help these people and then be back to a goal we *know* we can achieve."

"We do not need your pity or your pittances." The smith was now certainly their designated leader going forward. Insomuch as any of these wretches were going anywhere at all. "Off with you then, soldiers of ill-fortune. You are no followers of Tantamon. You are charlatans. Shams. Pretenders to the faith! The Night knows not your names!"

He had no idea how right he was, but something in those words stirred the other villagers to bitter assent, and we fled not pitchforks and torches, but indisputable disrepute.

"I hope Drago's all right." Pillar broke the silence a few nights later as we made camp. It was the first thing anyone had said that wasn't in aid of our resumed mission. The only difference from before Radomyr's Rest was I was welcome to sup at their fire, and no one avoided my eye. No one but Vadim, who also joined the loose circle but seemed unable to decide if he were glad to be back on track or dismayed at how incontrovertibly Radomyr's Rest had laid bare his apostasy.

"He'll fare better than the rest of them, Pillar." Pricker caught an ember from the fire between his hands and made it flutter like a firefly.

Just as Vadim had emerged from the village encounter a damaged leader, Pricker was failing to conceal whatever weight our little chat in Radomyr's Rest had lifted from his uncomfortably pauldroned shoulders. "I've seen dogs survive things that would reduce the strongest person to despair."

Drago was the dog? At least the poor old woman still had that.

"Pillai." The Purashenan exposed his teeth with a surprisingly shy smile.

"Pardon?" Pricker let the ember flutter away, into the clear night sky.

"Pillai, not Pillar." Pillai gnawed on a large bone between words. "We did what we could for them. It was good. Brother-good. Brothers should know names."

I could have leapt over the fire and kissed him, and no one would have been more shocked than I. I'd thought it was going to be Tor to do this, not a wayward Sword of Heaven. No matter. As long as someone did it.

"Pillai it is. I am the Pricker, Nikalay. Nik, if you want. Of the names I've had, that one I believe is the oldest. Well met. And you are right. Thanks to Sparrow Tzara-Min, we did something truly good."

I just shook my head, both in gentle denial and because I couldn't remember anyone serving my family named 'Nikalay'. Not even a more common 'Nicholai'. So he was still hiding who he truly was…

"I am Torbjorn. As was my father. As is my son."

Huysman jumped in. "So you do have a son. Why isn't he called Torson?"

Torbjorn explained some nuances of Luniiric patronyms, and then Jorik proceeded to give his full name and some minor details of who he was before as well. As did Henri Kendahl.

Nice to bond over banter and all, but I wasn't sure what I'd say when my turn came. Hadn't really thought it through. Didn't think we'd make it this far so quickly.

Our leader saved me from what was certainly Nikalay's next attempt at putting me front and centre. "Brothers, you say? You heard those people. We are not Brothers of Tantamon. We never were. Perhaps it'd be better if we were Sisters of the Liquid Night instead."

He threw the rest of whatever he'd been drinking into the fire and stalked off to his tent.

The pyrotic reacted quickly and settled the booze-fueled flare. Definitely not for the first time. "Let him fester. We are obeying his orders. He knows he won, and come morning he'll be back to happily yelling at us what we already know. Say. Everyone's had their turn but you, Tzara-Min. Tell us who you are. Really are."

Fucking Pricker. He would get no other name from me from then forward. Still, I was tired of the façade too. "Sarivashes…of the Gildenhammer."

Okay. Half-tired. As good a chance to fulfil a very old promise as any.

There was a pause for this to sink in, then Henri nudged Jorik, making the latter almost spill his drink. "Told you. Didn't I?"

"You did. Can payment wait until after Tza…sorry, Sarivashes has finished telling us her story?"

"What's happening here?" I noticed none of the others seemed moved at all by my name. They, like me, were more intrigued by the Brothers' exchange.

"I wagered Jorik that you'd bring up the name of that flail ball chain thing before we reached inner Kas'Daen-*desne*. And you named it after that fine old man from the abbey. He was a good smith."

Jorik nodded. "He was. Very fine at his craft, was Master Harald Gildenhammer."

Was? Wait, *that* was what they'd taken from my grand confession?

"How do you even use it? I have seen similar weapons long before, when I was Koolatchara, but not…that many spikes. Not metal…"

I fumbled for a response, still back at Harald Gildenhammer 'was'. "Uh. It's a Half thing."

"Ah. Yes." As though it were that bloody obvious.

"Sarivashes of the Gildenhammer." Pricker tried to sound like he was announcing a lady at the ball, then huffed out a laugh. "The sort of name you'd expect to hear in a song, isn't it?"

Not helping at all there, 'servant of my family'.

Jorik handed Henri a few silver coins. "Maybe pick something a little more original than Sarivashes though. Bit on the nose, yet another Half using the name of Lord Xenides-Ra Kas'Daen's lost daughter."

"Bit on the ears might be closer to the bone." Kendahl grunted at his own wit.

"Fuck ya both." Might as well play along. "I just thought Tzara-Min was a bit too exotic to fit in."

Torbjorn spoke up. "Why not just say you are Gildenhammer then?"

How would the apparently deceased smith of Mothers Abbey feel about me using his name? Not to tell people who made what he felt was one of his better works, but…as an identity. I had barely known him. I supposed it was one way to spread his legend…

"You don't think it's a bit of a mouthful?" I was losing impetus to protest an idea I didn't entirely hate.

"Easier to say than Tzara-Min or Sarif…Sarivashes for me."

"Well, Torbjorn son of Torbjorn, father of Torbjorn, call me what you want. I am just glad you choose to call me at all. And that goes for all of you. Don't stay up too late or Dad might give you a wallop for sleeping in." As good a way as any of excusing myself from a conversation dying as overtly as the fire Pricker seemed content to neglect.

"I was thinking, we need a name." Pricker, surely not reading my mind, waved new life into the flames as I found my feet and stretched. "As a company I mean. If we are a band of Brothers. Sorry Sparrow Tzara-Min Sarivashes Gildenhammer Sister In Red but you are one of us now, so congratulations on the newly-grown—"

"Goodnight!" I left them to it. That much, at least, was true.

Or it had been, until Vadim's summons stilled my bedroll-bound saunter.

"It is late, Sister. Or rather, later."

Ah.

I allowed myself one last little smile at the rowdy laughter echoing from the fire and into the darkness, collected my bearings and strode towards Vadim's command tent. No great warband we; it was really just another tent with a few extra bits sewn into the fabric. A fist here. An *f* there.

He was on a little folding stool I knew he kept handy for comfortable isolation, and as I came closer I mused just how small he looked. How small he was acting. Was probably feeling. He *had* won, technically, but technical victories rarely slake an obsessive man's thirst.

"Sit."

I did so after removing the Gildenhammer and placing it beside me. Cross-legged and feeling more than a little juvenile, I prepared for a proper scolding.

"You know…" He took on a volume perfect for self-reflection and transferring secret musings to a nearby Half with unusually large ears. "I do believe Pricker is planning to kill me."

"…Sir?"

"And he probably has a point." He swatted the air with a scowl. "Not sir. My second need not use titles in private."

Oh. Uh. Shit. How would Pricker take this? I didn't even know who Vadim's former second was – he hadn't exactly announced it. But I knew who it wasn't, and it wasn't any of the others.

But I understood. He wanted to talk, really talk, and for that, a commander needs a second.

Sure enough…

"We couldn't help those people at all, not really. A proper company of Brothers could have. Would have. I don't know what we are but we are not Brothers of Tantamon. Not even sons."

I waited for him to work through a set of uneasy expressions before wiggling my way into this 'second' role. "Father Vadim. This mission is important. More important than what we might encounter along the way. The Mother tests us in this way constantly. I do not know the teachings of Tantamon well at all, but isn't the idea of Assisting and Providing weighed down, made a challenge worthy of your faith, when you are not permitted to Ask or Probe? You embody the Eleventh and yet must, I think, be open to some measure of curiosity. 'How can we assist? How can we provide?' Surely you must ask this silently from time to time…because not everyone is going to offer commands or instructions unbidden. Not everyone knows to ask for help. And in my experience, most people don't know how they can be helped until you tease it out of them."

"The Eleventh you say." He considered this, fingers drumming on his thigh. "We are not meant ask questions even if we do know the answer. So we are not afforded…what? Confirmation? It's rubbish. Of course we ask. Of course we probe. The unspoken part is 'not too much'. And what happened in Radomyr's Village, I fear we erred in the other direction. I should have investigated the Haven myself. Not trusted Pricker at his word. Nor you at yours. Even though doing so got us out of there. More or less in one piece."

"It wasn't The Scourge, Vadim. I would have known. And when it is, I will make sure you are the first to know."

"This is all I have left, this task." So now we came to the bone, not quite before blood but before too much cutting away of meat, fat and gristle. "And I will see it to its end. You are key to that, so the Lady Cassandra assures me. You are my bait, my secret weapon. But you are also slowly taking it away from me. You said 'stop' and we did. No one else in this company could do that. And while most of them don't know why, they know it happened."

He paused as another, less uproarious chorus of laughter came from the campfire. I knew not to interrupt that pause. "And that. That. They sound happy, and I am glad of it, I am, but they also sound high-spirited and a little off the leash. How will they react when we come to the next group of needy peasants? Will they throw Brotherly creeds at me? Will you say stop again? Lady Cassandra also made clear that if we weren't at the Chapterhouse near Lybichmisto in good time, the…conditions for my chance at avenging my beloved Azak and all who trusted me to protect them there will change…quite unfavourably."

"I will not say stop again, no. And there'll be no Brotherly creeds hurled your way like accusations or shackles." How was I so certain of any of this? I said it thinking as his so-called 'second', but as the claims came out, I knew them to be true. "I do not lament giving Radomyr's Rest time and attention, but I think you are mistaking what happened tonight. They aren't dancing on your shamed pride or eager to behave like normal Brothers again. They're just glad we didn't turn this difficult but straightforward slog into a complete waste of time. Happy to have learned that, yes, we can stop and help others if we want. But they're celebrating that we won't, because we did it once and it was not the reclamation of purpose they thought it'd be. It was futile and we all know it now. That's what has cleared the air. And you, Father Vadim, don't have to do a thing in response. This company will strike camp in the morning and almost nothing will stop us from following your orders."

"Almost nothing?" I was glad to hear his voice had lost that frayed, self-pitying quaver.

"If *he* crosses our path, then as far as I am concerned, that's just us being granted a shortcut to mission completion."

It was mostly just air expelled through his nose, but it was laugh enough that I inclined a smile of my own. "The destination cannot interrupt the journey." Not sure I agreed, but I liked the simplicity of the saying. Tantamon has some good ones, I decided. "You are already proving a much more capable second than my last. I appreciate your counsel and clarity, Brother Tzara-Min. Or will it be Sarivashes? Sparrow?" To his great credit, he wasn't being facetious here. "A Brother deserves to be called by her preferred name." Or even there.

"I haven't really made a fuss about this but I twinge a little any time someone says 'brother', for reasons I trust I need not explain. Then again, I'm not overly fond of Sister either. Tzara-Min is a cover and one unneeded here. Sparrow is a rank that doesn't exist in this company. Sarivashes is…a defect, a common enough name among the people but in poor taste for a Half. I made a little joke about naming myself after my weapon but, in absence of better alternatives, I think it is a fitting label. You did call me your secret weapon after all. Gildenhammer. In this company, that shall be my name."

"Brother Gildenhammer?"

"Ugh. No. Gildenhammer is mouthful enough. I'll probably be Gilly or Hammergirl by this time tomorrow."

"That you will not. Tomorrow then. Tomorrow will be the beginning of the end of our travails."

"Sir, I have a request." I formalised my rejection of his implicit dismissal. I hesitated, because so far all he'd done was at my expense. A promotion with no benefits. A false start to fatal distraction averted. Helping him out of his ideological nadir. "As your second, and as someone with no small burden of guilt just being here."

He gestured that I continue, less indulgently and more with genuine attention and interest. I had truly misread this man. Oh, he still more than slightly resembled a frog and he was truly avaricious of this mission's success, but I needed to know if that desire extended to something over which he had no true claim.

"When we reach the Chapterhouse and receive our more detailed orders, I want you to strongly consider letting Brothers Huysman and Kendahl stay there, and replace them with more appropriate veterans of combat. Preferably mercenaries. Halves, if at all possible. I would not have the death of those two good men on my conscience. On my heart."

I may have hesitated but he certainly didn't. "I had considered this and am glad to hear you ask for it. I took those fresh lads on with much protestation; they're good Brothers but share not a hint of bloodthirst between them. Lady Cassandra, who as you know is Mother to your Rouge Eyrie as I was once Father to my Azak, said they were essential to your participation and cooperation, should events become complicated. So it was settled. To lay bare my own heart, I expected that the presence of friendly faces might discourage a Half well into adulthood from…succumbing to deeper urges."

This was all true, and I was gratified to hear confirmation of both Cassandra's intentions and his lack thereof. But: "Dread that not, Commander. Whatever you may have heard or experienced with Halves and their…our deeper urges, I feel no urge deeper than confronting and stopping my brother before he and anyone else spreading the same heretical flame levels every Haven in the world. And thank you. For hearing *me* out on the one matter that has pained me from the moment I learned of their companionship. I may have to convince them. I may not have to. And I may have to…convince them. But I do not want them there when we meet The Scourge at last."

"For the best. It sounds like they've finally run out of that exaltant energy you spoke of. And I am tired, Gildenhammer. Bone tired. Body tired. Soul tired. Should I not wake before you, please do ensure my emergence is not one of embarrassing slothfulness."

"Another duty as your second?" I unfolded to my feet and reattached my namesake.

"That. And a favour for a friend."

One last task before turning in.

"His new second? Excellent. All according to plan. How could I, a mere servant of the Nobility and occasional plucker of weeds, possibly stand in the way of Sarivashes-ra assuming her rightful place as second in command over a company of six whole men? Also, this means if he fucks up, *you* have to kill him. And for all my prowess as a Peddler, I'm infinitely less qualified at that than you, My Liege Sister In Red Gildenhammer Sir. Oh, we came up with a company name. I wanted The Roughbuddies but that didn't sit well. How does Sarivashes The Sparrow's Stalwart Slayers sound to you?"

"Fucking stupid."

"See, that's what I said after I suggested it. Guess we'll need to discuss it more in the morning."

"Seriously, Pricker?"

"Nah. Just kidding. The Avengers of Azak. Like it or leave it."

Ephin' Peddlers.

I will not lie; there were other villages, and other situations where a normal company of Brothers would have stopped and stayed for days. The Avengers of…no, I can't, I just can't…we simply rode or walked past them. Judging by the lack of attention we drew despite the others still wearing the purple capes of Tantamon, we were not the first Brothers to pass them and their tribulations by. Vadim confirmed at some point that there was a sort of convergence of purpose in the north, near and in Lybichmisto, and it was probable not only Brothers but forces from many factions had come this way to join what was looking a bit like the start of a holy war. That or, we all agreed, one very impressive vendetta. As we drew closer to the intended Chapterhouse, we did indeed see a lot more…adventurers, I'll call them in the spirit of generosity. Brothers were to be expected, but on roughly the same road as us were knights, elementalists, Peddlers, Swords, Healers…in effect, the company…fine, *The Avengers of Azak* seemed to be built of a very popular template, employed for the sole task of collectively fighting whoever threatened their way of life, be it The Scourge or anyone else.

There were so many others like us, in fact, that when we reached the Chapterhouse and asked to be admitted per our orders, we were told we'd have to wait our turn. It could take days, the apologetic attendant at the monastery gate said.

"Could have bloody taken our time after all." Pricker spoke for us all as we tried to find space to make camp in the fields surrounding the Chapterhouse amid all the others.

It did take days. We stewed in the heat of Inner Kas'Daen's midsummer. There was some talk with neighbours, travellers mostly, but we were all there to be told where to go and fight, not to gossip or forge new bonds with men and women who may well not be around in a week or a month.

When it was time, only Vadim and I as his second were allowed in. I doubt the former Father of the mighty Azak was even a little awed at that little establishment, but for whatever reason it was a de facto center of operations for this concerted anti-Scourge initiative. There was another line. Another set of doors. And then a cramped office with a tall, gaunt Brother and a very large desk strewn with maps and books. He pored over his pages. Asked our names. And then put his quill down and gave us a look of disappointment.

"I'm afraid you've come too late for your initial assignment." He retrieved his quill and ran it down a very long list of very small letters. "But we've many left that yet need filling. Slightly lower priority but still of the utmost import to our efforts."

Before I could catch him, the commander stepped forward. "Are we still being given a chance to face The Scourge?"

"Of course, Brother. There's always a chance." The clerk's expression made clear just how hard he was trying not to answer truthfully, and I wasn't the only one to see it.

Vadim's face fell in a way I'd not seen before, not even after the Radomyr's Village encounter threatened his status as a Father of Tantamon. And then, rubicund and quaking, it started to rise again…

"How late are we?" I intervened before Vadim could succumb to his emerging cacophony of feelings.

"Let me see…hm. Vadim of Azak…oh. That's a pity. Barely a day. Now, now! I do not have any control or jurisdiction over the timing of—"

"We understand." That I had to place one arm in front of the Commander made this something of an exaggeration. "So what task can you set for our company, the Avengers of Azak?"

The next item on his list was so trivial even I almost surrendered to Vadim's bellicose surge. "We'd like you to guard a cottage in the woods near a town called Vazhar about a hundred miles north-west of the capital for one day. Said day may be of your choosing, but please do let me know—"

Vadim all but erupted. "Surely you have something a little more substantial. We did not come all this way to stand outside a house for a day. This can't be how it ends…"

"Lord Vadim, these are orders from Xenides-ra Kas'Daen himself. A task entrusted to only the most well-reputed of Tantamon's followers…"

I turned to Vadim and addressed him and him alone. "Sir, this might be all they have now, but we should see it through, prove our loyalty and willingness to obey even mundane orders. And then, well, who knows? This *isn't* how it ends."

The gargoyle in the guise of a human continued. "Now upon completion, any and all survivors are to report to the Kas'Daen Military Operations records chamber in Lybichmisto. In the event of contact with an enemy, the capes of fallen Brothers are to be returned, assuming they are in such a state as worth returning. Should no one report to claim payment, we will assume contact with the enemy."

"We don't come back here?" I had not forgotten Cassandra's warning about the city.

"Ours is to dispense tasks, not handle the outcome. You may have noticed we're quite inundated with work as it is…"

"We'll take it." Vadim had seen reason. I let my arm fall away from barring his temper's consequences.

"Excellent. Let me just…" Relieved that we'd stopped ruining his day with our concerns, the clerk set to work, writing very neat, small letters. He occasionally paused to ask details. Company name. Commander. Second… Members…

"On that matter, Brother, two of my company require alternative placement. They are ill-fit for this mission."

"Weren't you just complaining that it sounded 'insubstantial'?" He wasn't even bothering to believe his own propaganda anymore. "You are welcome to seek replacements from the other assembled parties but I mislike your chances; few would abandon their own and even fewer for a mission such as yours. The book states The Avengers of Azak will go to Vazhar and guard a cottage for one whole day. Lord Vadim of Azak commanding. Brother Gildenhammer as second. Five party members. That's seven. So you take seven. Or forfeit and let me pass this one on to the next group and you go to the back of the line. Speaking of which…"

The put-upon clerk had been right. Without alerting any of the company members, Vadim and I tested the chances of finding capable replacements. We were met with two overwhelming issues over and again: firstly, it was hypocritical to consider one's own company well-composed and bonded and then ask others to relinquish two of the own members, and secondly, those who might join us were clearly available for a reason.

"It's just one day, Gildenhammer." Vadim was oddly resigned as we returned to camp. "One day and a cottage in the middle of nowhere. Not even a Haven. They're wasting our time and our skills, but orders are orders. Let's get it over with. Besides, where's the harm in bringing the boys along to what is probably going to be little more than a jaunt?"

"What is in this cottage, Brother Commander? It looks abandoned."

"Don't ask that, Huysman; just guard it."

"Do we really have to wear all this armour? I'm melting in here."

"Yes, Torbjorn."

"And the cape?"

"Absolutely the cape. Appearances matter, Brother Pillai."

"How much did you say we were getting for this again?"

"You are doing it for the good of the world, for the glory of Tantamon, and enough gold to buy you a house anywhere but the finer districts of Lybichmisto, Pricker. The Lord Xenides-ra Kas'Daen *really* wants The Scourge found and terminated, and has spared no expense. At least, not as far as we are concerned."

"And keep those visors down." I had to add this, having noticed Kendahl, usually the one happier to grin and bear these things, was starting to fidget with his. I sympathised, having no desire to wear one either, but if the mission was stand guard in full Brother regalia and armour, that's what we'd do. They'd even procured me a sword, which felt...wrong as a symbolic counterpart to the Gildenhammer. "Against this foe, any and all protection is essential."

That was a lie I'd almost convinced myself to believe.

I remember standing there, likely handling the heat better than my very human comrades, hoping a little darkly and with no real belief that whatever was going to happen, it'd happen soon, before one of them passed out from sun stroke.

That hope, at least, was not in vain.

"Someone's watching us." I approached Lord Vadim when I heard what I thought was a scornful laugh. The others kept still, probably because to do much else would risk falling over. Not for the first time I quietly cursed him for not allowing me to cool them down, to maybe lose some of the armour. Appearances, he had said. Appearances matter.

They do, when whoever is watching cares. I knew that wasn't the case here.

"I see nothing, but I trust your Half sensitivity. Is it him? Is it actually him?"

"I can't say. I want to confirm. If it is, I will signal with an upraised fist. You see me do that, run."

"Run?" I don't recall who asked that. It really doesn't matter now.

"Run. Back to camp. Mount. And ride. Ride hard. And don't look back." It wouldn't help. It just wouldn't. "Or draw and make your stand.

If you see The Scourge coming, you can do that much. But I doubt it's him. Not here. So…Please steady your nerves and do nothing that would shame the Tantamon."

"Investigate then, Brother Gildenhammer, but be quick." Now that the *moment* may have come, Vadim had regressed to almost the same pompous croaker I'd met barely a few months ago. I didn't blame him; we all cling to something hilariously underdeveloped when anticipation and actuality collide and we realise, oh fuck, we are *so* not ready for this.

I took a few cautious steps towards where I'd heard the rustling, seen a flap of movement. One tree of many, these unfortunately thick-trunked ancients were perfect for Scourge-sized concealment. Another step, and then a glance back. Couldn't see shit in that damn bucket. I had the worst feeling that the second I put too much attention on where the intruder *had* been, I'd miss where he *was going to be next*. But orders were investigate, so that's what I did.

One last step and I knew my instincts had been right. There was no one here, but there was absolutely someone *there*. By the time I'd turned around, fist and voice half-raised, what I knew to be The Scourge was already halfway through slicing The Avengers of Azak to so many steel-encased bits and pieces. I was Half. I was fast. Strong. Quick. But I was also stuck inside a full suit of armour and, well, not yet like you. I'd managed to move myself to the other side of the clearing, the Gildenhammer free and ready to make the company's puerile name really mean something.

To avenge Henri Kendahl and Jorik Huysman, two happy-go-lucky Brothers who never stood a chance, and as Vadim said, it was all my fault;

To avenge Torbjorn, son of Torbjorn and father of Torbjorn, a Luniiric Healer pulled far from his Haven and his family;

To avenge Pillai, a lost Sword of Heaven who may or may not have been a willing manslayer but definitely loved dogs;

To avenge Nikalay, a sharp-tongued Peddler also known as Pricker who claimed to serve my real family and I wouldn't remember what that really meant until long after this catastrophic morning;

And to avenge Lord Vadim of Azak, fallen Father of Tantamon who said the mission to murder the 'man' who took everything from him was all he had left. He probably died too quickly with his Brothers at his side to realise that this wasn't true.

Then it took over: the tremulation under all that borrowed Brotherly metal, the well-worn robes of a Sisterhood that was now working a metal of its own, and a pendant I kept as close to my skin as possible, even then. That beating: a call to (re)action; the last refrain of a dance to which I was entirely too late. Too late. Too late. Too late. Too late. The hyper-capable Sarivashes-ra Kas'Daen was, by then, almost completely subsumed into an already-grieving Sister Tzara-Min, who was also somewhere, deep down, a scared little girl called Sarah-Jade Falkenstrom trying to be smart, brave, good.

Toolate toolate toolate toolate—

No.

Just enough of Sariana Jaydemyr awakened to stamp out that hollow echo of all that I was not. To kill that false rhythm entirely and replace it with a pulsating impetus ripped from our shared history and set to the beating of a heart that would dictate our shared future:

It's him or it's me
it's him or it's me
it's him and it's me
it's him and it's me
it's him but I'm me
it's him but I'm me
it's him so—

I charged while he was busy using a Tantamonian cape to clean his sword (the sacrilege!), releasing a yell that I knew was both a bad idea and essential. Look at me, you cruel bastard. I am here. I am going to stop you. With everything I am.

He turned at the sound of my inarticulate announcement of this totality.

I finally saw his face under the hood, just for that second, and it was as expressionless as someone else's doll…but as familiar as one of my own. We were both Half, yes, but that alone couldn't justify the resemblance.

It IS him!

And then he was simply not there, vanished into the endlessly obfuscated periphery a mere few inches either side of the tragically small window provided by the helm's visor.

And then I was simply not there either. I don't remember anything but a noise so loud it briefly became an entire world of anarchy within the agonising confines of that Ephin'…silly helmet.

What do you say?

"Thank you. I have been waiting all this time, weeks of your story, to hear your side of my first entry into it. After all, mine is the ego, and so much of your story has been much more mine. But now that we are here, I understand your story is so much more important than mine. Chaelle used my ego to make it all about me, to everyone but me. Making it about me was *my* impetus. And so she made a series of improbable events my stage, all eyes on me. Dreamt or otherwise. But your story has been about avoiding that stage, as improbable in its almost collisions with significance as mine with its absence of anything but everyone else's significance. Fuck. What I'm trying to say is…how to put this…How—"

"How about you shut the fuck up and let me finish? You're right. The whole damn thing has been me missing the big moments of the world, and softening the few I chose not to participate in. This, though. This was a big moment, and I'm not about to cheapen it by drawing out your accomplishment. It was quick and it was probably painless. And where you have the luxury of cremation on command, I had to bury them by hand. I whispered their names. I prayed for them. And then I left them there. Now I'll tell you how my story, and yes it *is* a story, how it will be written, and is then reread to enrich yours. Isn't that what you want, Brother? Huh? To see if the last reflection of my crescent can bring yours full circle? Poetic. Deliberate. Forced. For you, I'd do no less. What do you say?"

"…Sorry."

5 hours until the revelation

Chapter 21: The Lazy Scapegoats
10/881 to 7/882 A.R.

"Can you repeat that name please?"

I stared around at the audience, a mix of Brothers, Kas'Daen representatives, Lybichmistan guards and a few Peddlers, judging by their proclivity for simple black clothing. All that testimony, my presentation of six bloodied capes, a genuine encounter with Kas'Daen's sworn enemy, and all this little official behind his little desk in this Kas'Daenne Military Operations records chamber wanted to hear was a name I'd let slip. Fine.

"Sarivashes-ra Kas'Daen."

His lips twitched and he shook his head. "No no, that one I heard quite clearly. The other. Your superior officer."

"Lord Vadim of Azak. He was our commander."

He made a note in his huge ledger, one of several shelves' worth. The official then gestured at the capes I cradled, with me trying not to think about whose might be on top, whose might be against the skin of my forearm. "Those you can leave with me. That's right, just put them on the floor there with all the others. It says here that Lord Vadim of Azak was assigned to guard a small house near Vazhar. That is quite a distance from here."

Despite the mess of the pile, I tried my best to arrange the last proof of the Avengers' sacrifice reverently, and then stood back up. I'd mulled over his last sentence the whole time. "I fail to see how its distance from here is relevant."

"Not exactly an important locale. And someone who supposedly let The Scourge escape would be wise not to use a word like 'fail' lightly."

I placed my fists on his desk, leaned forward. He had no choice but to push his chair back. And since I was dressed as a Sister of Fourth Going, that also meant the Gildenhammer swung forward at my hip with satisfying weight. "I told you. I did not let him escape. He overpowered us. Knocked me out. And then, I presume, did what he was there to do and moved on by the time I came to."

"A likely story." I didn't bother looking to see who of the many people behind me said this. "The Scourge himself, known to destroy towns and Noble dwellings, suddenly attacking a small group of nobodies in the woods in the middle of nowhere."

"Shut your mouth and wait your turn!" The official yelled past my shoulder, and then actually smiled a syrupy attempt at an apology to me. "Every day, someone comes in with a report like yours. Today The Scourge is in New Spring burning Havens and slaughtering rabbits. Yesterday he was in Ultava, hundreds of miles away from there, killing the livestock and poisoning the wells. Tomorrow, who knows?"

"It was *him*. Look at me. I am Half. I know my own when I see them."

"Or it was another Half wearing a black robe and wielding an eastern-style sabre."

I stood up straight, unable to deny that this may well have been the case. "So what then? You put the deaths of my commander and comrades down as 'killed by unknown forces, might have been The Scourge But Probably Not, oh well?' And I just fuck off back to whatever·I was doing before that?"

He sighed and gestured again, this time at the growing line behind me. "Do you think any of them consider their own reports any less important? You have no proof you actually saw The Scourge, and just these capes as evidence. The record shows you *were* part of this mission. You are Half. You are how old again?"

I hadn't told him at all, but provided nonetheless. "I will be twenty-eight this month."

"A Half, twenty-eight, claiming to be Sarivashes Kas'Daen." He looked down at the ledger, and for all the world it looked just like the one I'd seen at the Chapterhouse. "But you are listed here as Gildenhammer of the ahem, Avengers of Azak. Whatever your name, this remains true: here we have a Half, reporting her entire party is dead, defeated by a black-cloaked stranger who could, I agree, have been The Scourge. But don't you think it a little more realistic that that a Half of such…advanced age as yours might have, perhaps…had an unforeseen and completely understandable lapse in clarity?"

"Fuck your realistic bullshit. Unlikely doesn't mean impossible."

"No, it just means…unlikely. But say I pass on what you claim. Say it puts you in front of Lord Xenides-ra Kas'Daen himself, glory to the Overclan. Is he going to recognise you as some Half cast-off he may have produced in one of what I imagine to be many encounters of divine charity? You would not be the first Half woman to claim to be Sarivashes, but you would be the first to survive it."

It is a strange thing to be told you are merely claiming to be who you know, *know*, yourself to be. Especially after pretending to be other things for so long. I'd called myself Tzara-Min and then Gildenhammer in the party, but upon awakening in the clearing near the cottage, surrounded by the remains of my companions and inexplicably clutching that pendant, I had known I was the Sarivashes, daughter of Xenides-ra. I was done hiding that, and done holding her back. I was also done dealing with self-important little men with little jobs. Time to go home, back to the Eyrie to regroup, maybe mobilise the Sparrows.

"You have no idea who I am, but one day you will, and you won't be so amused then." I knew I'd lost the moment I resorted to such dull-toothed threats. Such weak ire.

"We already know who you are." Another heckle, much laughter. "Sarivashes, long-lost daughter of His Excellency, Lord Xenides-Ra Kas'Daen!"

"Go fuck a horse!" But the laughter just kept going.

The official waited until he had my attention once again. "We appreciate you returning to us. While we cannot verify your account of the task's outcome, I am authorised to issue you a small compensation in exchange for the return of the Tantamonian capes."

The jeers from the now-impatient petitioners had nettled; this, though, *really* stung. "That's why you think I'm here? To sell you the only reminder I have of my Brothers and their sacrifice? Y'know what, you can go fuck a horse too. Preferably the same one as this lot."

Inconsolable and ashamed, I shoved my way out of there, lying to myself it was for their own good. Maybe I was about to turn. Besides, I didn't need the money – I'd sold *our* horses at first opportunity. Had planned to donate it to the Tantamonian Brotherhood, but Eph that. Maybe I'd go piss it away in a gambling house or something. Anything but let these incompetent fools see a single coin of it.

The way we'd been ejected from Radomyr's Village had felt gentle in comparison. Cassandra had been right. Again. Entering Lybichmisto was a mistake. I never should have come back.

The records office was not far from the southern exit of the capital, so I made for the gateway, hoping the city's outbound security was as ineffectual as its military administration. It was still quite warm a week or so after I'd come to outside that unassuming little cottage near Vazhar. I couldn't hear much over my own heavy breathing – Halves handle extreme weather well enough, but I was still irritated by the encounter and working myself into a dangerous state that would not have surprised anyone in the records chamber in the slightest.

And so when someone grabbed me from behind, peeled back the heavy scarlet hood and managed to get their fingers onto my then-exposed temples, I had been mid-huff and mid-curse at the futility of it all. Completely unready for any sort of attack…and ever so briefly just excited that *something* was happening to me. I felt vindicated.

Maybe I was being robbed. But who'd try to rob a Half in public, in daylight…in *Lybichmisto?*

And whatever I felt next was, needless to say, not exactly the sun-warm hug of an old, old friend.

Whoever had me now, they knew what I was. No bed here, no wheeled chair. I was chained to a wall, gagged, and blindfolded. Naked. Can you imagine waking up in those precise conditions after *that* summer? Conscious, able to move, feeling nothing but metal digging into your wrists, your ankles, and ice-cold stone against your back, shoulders, legs, arms…? Sight denied, voice stifled.

But alive, which meant someone had plans. I was part of someone's plans. I mattered. Yep, *that* is what I clung to, even as these chains clung to me. At least someone in Kas'Daen took me seriously.

That hope kept me buoyant for a while, then when nothing else happened, it occurred to me that it probably wasn't that much effort to imprison an unconscious Half this way, and I could be here…a very long time. Or, almost as bad, a very short one.

After even my ignoble, meaningless demise became a boring consideration, I did what anyone does when the present and the future become the same thing: I started to lose myself in the past. In my upbringing as the adopted daughter of a singer and a carpenter in Teristra. Their messy parting. Father leaving me a special medallion, 'Mother' giving it to me and telling me who I really was when I turned fourteen, and then sending me to a Liquid Night abbey in the middle of nowhere Kas'Daen, safe from any who might question my true heritage as a bastard child of Xenides-ra Kas'Daen. My less than happy time there, dealing with *nse'ante* cows and pretending I was just another Sister serving these incessant breeders. Sister Tzara-Min, at your service, you pitiful little lambs. When it was time to leave, to go abroad, I was out the moment I could go. Sure, still wasting my talent and energy on those who, if they were *very* fortunate, would give their lives to sustain the true Nobility, but at least I was able to see the world at the same time. Fuck that desert sun though. And the Chūnko winters. Things happened. I didn't go insane. I left. I came back. Discovered the abbey had been upgraded into a Kas'Daen fortress. Joined a party looking to find this so-called Scourge, figuring a Half might be able to stop a Half.

Obviously not.

What I didn't do was ponder the missing details in all this. What had that party been like? What had I done on my mission east? Were there any Sisters at the abbey I hadn't loathed or had Cassandra been my sole source of warmth and affection? Who had I known in Teristra?

These were not blank spaces in the story I told myself; they were minor headaches I chose not to endure.

"She is not like the rest, My Lord." A woman used very polite Kas'Daenne to describe me with great dispassion. She was close by. Same room. Cell, I assumed. "This one believes she is your daughter. Her history is remarkably unremarkable: there has been some tampering but overall it is plausible. I do not believe she is a threat, only deluded."

"Thank you. Unbind her mouth but nothing else." A deep, sibilant tone, not quite reptilian, just a stress on that 's' sound that lasted a little too long for *nse'ante*. His voice seemed to fill the room, fill the world entire. Was it him? Dare I hope? "And then you may leave."

"Shall I ask to forget, My Lord?"

"You shall."

I felt someone pull my head forward not too roughly and untie the cloth strapped to my cheeks and jaw. I said nothing though, just indulged the ability to breathe more deeply.

As suspected, I heard a metal door of a cell screech open, groan closed.

Then I felt something pressed against my lips.

"Drink."

As the warm sap slid down my throat, I realised a few important things. The first was he knew I was Half, else he wouldn't offer that as a drink. The second was he needed me stronger, else he wouldn't offer *that* as a drink.

He withdrew the small cup. "You may speak." I heard him step back, and then begin to pace.

"How long have I been here?"

"I do not know. Tell me when you came here."

"The worst of summer had passed. I'd just left the records chamber. Reported the mission. So I think it was the ninth month."

"Tell me the year."

"Eight Eighty-One…?"

"Then you have been here five months. It is now the second month of Eight Eighty-Two. The snow is heavy and constant, as it will be for a while yet. Lybichmisto has short summers, very long winters. We like it that way, *kiend're*."

I didn't recognise the word or the language, but it didn't seem like an insult. And 'we'? "I favour neither extremity, My Lord."

"You believe that. That I am your lord."

"I am completely at your mercy, so yes, My Lord, you are."

"Hmm. My mercy is not a factor. Truthfully, I do not know what to do with you, *kien'dre*. You claim many things, but few of them are true. You are not my daughter. You aren't even of my Clan. I know your desire to the contrary but there is proof. That medallion of yours. Tell me about it."

"My father gave it to me. Left it for me. I have had it ever since I left Teristra." My father, not you. My father is not you.

"The same answer as before. I believe you. It is good that I believe you. The other incredulity is that you claim to have fought The Scourge and lost. And yet you walked away, unscathed. That means he let you live."

"I cannot deny that."

"He does not let Halves live. Not that you should still be alive anyway. Nor should he. You saw his face during the encounter."

"I did, very briefly. I have not seen many Halves in my life, My Lord, but none have struck me as familiar until him. I recognised him but know not from where. A dream, perhaps."

"You say you dream of The Scourge."

"I do not know, My Lord. That is just how it felt. Or as though he looked like a childhood friend whom I'd not seen for a long time."

"At some point between incapacitating you and your return to consciousness, he entered that cottage, discovered who was under it and somehow exposed them to sunfire. I tell you this so that you understand the significance of what you were doing. What you failed to do."

"I cannot apologise enough, My Lord."

"True." He also told me because that wasn't something *nse'ante* were meant to know. Not that making a Noble do anything against their wishes was at all easy, but *if* one managed to get them into the daylight, well…that was that. "Your failure was not without some gain, however. Some gain but not much. I will be watching, *kiend're*."

"My Lord…if I am not Sarivashes, not even Kas'Daen, then who am I? What am I?"

No answer.

"My Lord?"

It didn't take long to realise he was gone. I hadn't heard the door open or close.

I just hung there. Scream? Resist? Long past time for any of that. He'd said I wasn't Sarivashes; I wasn't Kas'Daen. He hadn't replied but the implication was clear enough: to him, I was just another broken Half in the grip of inevitable breakdown. Grand delusions, self-actuating beliefs that there was any purpose to our existence beyond that of a by-product of illicit, unnatural interspecies copulation. I remembered Iskendahrl's description of what it looked like from outside, and then considered my behaviour in the records chamber. The way I'd behaved in Kaifeng. The ease with which I'd thought I'd manipulated The Pallid Harriers into taking me where I'd wanted. How I was the only survivor of the party, whose name and members I still couldn't recall. And how I'd ended up here, precisely where Cassandra had said I'd end up if I didn't respect the frailty of the situation. Of course I was Sarivashes; of course I was Kas'Daen. But not even Lord Xenides-ra Kas'Daen could see that, not yet. Had someone as powerful as Cassandra, or even more powerful, changed his mind too?

I was in no position to answer any of this.

So when I did hear someone enter, maybe hours later, probably not days, and then felt fingers on my temples, my forehead, even my nose, I just let it happen.

Still not a warm hug, but not the mental crash of last time either.

The world shook and I was awake yet again.

"Who are you!" Male voice. Not happy. I blinked myself into simple awareness. I was on a bed, dressed in smallclothes. In a room a bit like the isolation cell back at the abbey. There were windows, and it was daylight. I rolled over to look at whoever had roused me.

"Sorry, what?"

"I said, tell me your name, soldier." The square-jawed man in leather armour and a light blue cloak and hood stood over me, hands on his hips.

"Sarah-Jay...Tal...Tzara..." Nope, none of those felt right in my mouth. "Sarivashes...Gildenhammer."

"And what are you, Sarivashes Gildenhammer?"

I closed my eyes to think. I knew what I wasn't. But what I was? "I don't know."

Yes I did. Focus. Remember. There'd been a mission to possibly encounter the infamous Haven-killer, The Scourge. We had encountered him. Mission accomplished. Only I survived and he evaded justice. Mission failed. I'd tried to report this to the Kas'Daen authorities, who called me a liar and an impostor. I was taken into custody for civil disobedience in the military records chamber. Ascertained not to be a threat despite being Half and well past safe age. Questioned briefly by the Lord Kas'Daen himself. In his grace and mercy, he offered me a chance to redeem myself, to be a part of a more concentrated, coordinated assault on The Scourge. And to be among my own, at last. He deposited me with a large company of my fellow Halves, the Sky Vanguard, due to head on north with the coming of spring. North, where reported sightings of the elusive menace seemed to be legitimate, and Lord Kas'Daen required verification more reputable than that from ragamuffin Brothers and never-truly-trusted Peddlers. A Half disgraced, deposited and disposable, predisposed to go berserk at any time now, so best that we be far, far from the city should that happen. Around those who can stop us. That's who we were. That's what I was.

But, as this barracks master of Lybichmisto's military compound had just prompted me to remember, I was also, much more literally:

"Late. Oh fuck, I'm late!"

"That is *exactly* what you are, soldier." He kicked the cot again, rocking the legs and almost tipping it and me over. "So get up, get dressed, get your shit, and get gone. And you'd better pray to the Mother the SkyVan haven't left without you, because you can't stay here."

I became a frantic scramble of dressing, gathering, straightening, tying of ponytail, more gathering. And after placing the Gildenhammer at my waist and its accompanying glove upon my left hand, I went to dash out, still a flurry of curses and disbelief. What had I been doing last night that I'd be this late? Training? Training. Probably. Didn't matter now.

"Hey. Don't forget this."

I wheeled about and saw the barracks master holding out my pendant. If he found its depiction of The Scourge's symbolic signature distasteful, he didn't say anything about it. Best not to excavate the eccentricities of a Half as old and tense as me. "Shit, I almost did. Thank you, sotnik."

Sky Vanguard had left Lybichmisto as a few dozen fighters but gained one or two more at each of the various forts and castles we graced along the way. We didn't talk much on the road, just marched. Camped every few days. Marched some more. An unthinkable pace for any military unit…one that wasn't specifically made up of Halves, at least.

We didn't talk much because no one really wanted to know anyone else's circumstances. Who was what age. Who we thought our parents were. Had been. Unless there was a family of The Quicks or The Deadlies or The Undaunteds out there, I figured most of us used surnames of self-appointed prowess, which in hindsight is a stupid assumption since I'd appropriated a real one. I did hear some first names though; among the hundred or so, there were at least three others named Sarivashes. A couple of men named Xenides in there too, because why wouldn't a famous person's name also be quite popular?

It amused me to think I'd ever considered myself unique or special. That is not what it meant to be Half. It was all in the word, I realised on that long but not so slow march towards a spring none of us expected to survive: we are Half. Not whole, not full, neither neither nor nor. We are essentially unfinished in every way. There might be a world beyond this one where we are complete, but to get there we had to find a way out of this one. Not an easy task when you have just enough power to fend off any aggressor but not enough self-control to avoid eventually becoming one yourself.

And that should tell you more than enough about the attitude of the average member of the Sky Vanguard.

North-east Kas'Daen was immense, thousands of square miles of nigh impenetrable forest. It was also ferociously cold, too cold for even a Half to tolerate, so other than a few truly miserable outposts dotted about the outskirts, the entire expanse was deemed inhospitable, even for the Night's Own. No one really knew how far north or east it extended. Every spring, the Kas'Daenne Military Operations command in Sahmara to the south-east sent a small expedition to clear dead animals, check on the Havens, make sure no one desperate had put upon the isolated outposts and towns. Go much further east or south of Sahmara and you're in hostile Karakani territory, so it was no surprise that even now, even with reports of Scourge presence somewhere in the thousand miles between and north of Sahmara and Lybichmisto, the combined forces from central and eastern Kas'Daen barely numbered five hundred. No one said it when we arrived at the encampment on the southern edge of Viestrada Forest, but common sentiment was that Lord Xenides-ra Kas'Daen, or his mortal administrative representatives, either didn't take these reports very seriously…or took them *very* seriously and didn't want to risk losing too many troops confirming The Scourge's location.

By the time we'd found our place in the main camp, the snow had started to recede. Unlike those rather disciplined Sahmaran forces, consisting mostly of humans in need of order and a few Nobles there to impose it, Sky Vanguard had a very loose structure: we were each assigned a position somewhere within the south-western Viestrada treeline, two or three members on rotation. Typical solitary watch duration: one to three days. And if we somehow actually did make contact with The Scourge, we had two options: fight, or run back to camp and give a report. I had a feeling even the most blood-crazed member of Sky Vanguard would not have struggled with this choice.

"Hey. Xenya." I nudged his woolen cloak with the tip of my boot. He'd curled up at the base of a tree, under where he'd left his bait. "Seen any black-cloaked monsters lately or just the black insides of your eyelids, you toothless prick?"

"Ah, Sarihammer." He sat up, brushed some debris from the fabric. Sarihammer. Better than Gilly or Hammergirl, but still a little…prickly. "You're not late are you?"

"Course not. I'm never late." I stepped past him to examine the notch in the bark above his head. "But this has gone dry. It's getting towards summer you know. Have to reapply it more often."

Xenides stretched, stood up, and shrugged. He was tall, even for a Half. "Shit doesn't work anyway. If it did, we wouldn't still be here. Great for attracting bears and wolves though. Helps pass the time I guess." He gathered his bag, lifted the sheathed sword from its place leaning against the tree. "Right. See you back at base in a few weeks."

"A few weeks?" I glanced over at him after smearing a few drops of blood on the tree and cleaning the small wound on the palm of my right hand. My namesake's gauntlet had some conveniently sharp edges. I then took a sip of *Vahm'esta* to assist with the recovery. "Got a happy little holiday planned?"

"Something like that."

"Eph me, Xenya. We're stretched thin as is, and they're splitting up the Sky Van even more?"

He shrugged again. "One of the *nse'ante* scouts found an abandoned tower somewhere…" He gestured vaguely off into the distance. "Y'know, in there. Said he saw a light inside. Rika Fasz was probably just exhausted and seeing shit. Or they found some lost villager on their last legs. Still, one night to prepare and then off we go. Weeks away from anything resembling a bed, a kitchen or a bath. For a fucking pile of stone. You weren't invited? Be thankful."

"Hm." I settled in for my watch, the Gildenhammer resting across my crossed legs. "Guess I'm too important to risk on such a deadly mission. Don't stub your toe on the rubble and bleed to death."

He kissed his middle finger at me, smiled with an oddly disarming array of teeth, and stalked back towards the main encampment.

All I know is that it was night-time when it happened.

The canopy overhead obscured most of the stars, the clouds, the moon. It was dark, my watch was barely begun, and I was humming to myself, some lullaby Viera had taught me although I'd never learned the words in her native Purashenan. I'd done this so many times before when alone, when lonely, that there was no reason for me to suddenly lose my place. To feel as though someone or something had rammed an entirely different song between one note and the next.

To then clutch my angular but scarred ears, squint and rock back and forth, back and forth. To imagine my face pressed against some unfinished grain. Rough, smooth, Rough. Smooth. Brave. Rough. Smart. Smooth. Rough…

And then keen, trying to drown out the voice desecrating the inside of my head. It started as noise, guttural skull-splintering gibberish, but once uttered became two words I couldn't have understood more if they were my own name. And, of course, one of them was. The first was his, just as I'd heard it back at the abbey while lazing about with Vi and Cass – an event I'd somehow completely forgotten.

Charan Jaydemyr.

The pain was then gone, just gone. All I felt was whole. Full. Neither, nor, both, one and all. Complete. My names, my roles: facets integrated; lines intersecting to form a shape; circles etched into the surface of a sphere. Not fake, not merely imagined. As real as me, the real me. Layers of a single ballad. No, I wouldn't think of myself like that, not in terms the Nightsong would use. Never again. Father's then. Charas'z-ra Jaydemyr, who commited the greatest affront to the impressive Tongue of Revelation. Father: the Night's Own who expressed himself in writing. He would have understood what everyone got wrong about me. My life until that moment had been like loose notes scattered on the ground, written by and about a sequence of 'I' who were never fully me. Every attempt at remembering *me* had been a failure to pick the pages up and put them back in order, because there was no order. Every time the Nightsong, then the Mind-Changer, and most recently the ludicrously inept Self-Scrapers of Kas'Daen, had tried to collate those pages with their own binding, it had been in vain. Even my own adopting of this last title, Gildenhammer, drawn from a dream and then found to be real, had been a false start.

Because we'd all missed the most important step. That which turned diaries into novels. This was how to take a book treasured only in private and turn it into a story to be shared, to be known by others, declared worthy of retelling, *without* compromising its veracity:

You put its real name on the spine.

Sariana Jaydemyr

Jaydemyr-desne

882 A.R.

I just sat there, chanting my name to myself. And then my brother's name. And Mother's name. And Father's name. All our names. My family, returned to me at last.

I thought about this great and unknowable forest around me, enveloping me, and understood why it seemed so great and unknowable: Viestrada was the name used by Kas'Daen, who could never comprehend its depths, know its secrets. For those of us who called it and the vast realm beyond home, it was not Viestrada but Vizstrahtza. A name too old to have clear meaning in any living language but also so old that it gained meaning of its own: the formidable stretch of wilderness dividing the south-western corner of Jaydemyr-*desne* and our once-unimpregnable home. Kazan. Somewhere beyond Vizstrahtza to the north-east, a name that once meant 'cauldron' but of course Charan had co-opted it by pointing out 'Kazan' also meant 'volcano' in Mifūn-go. Almost as though he *wanted* the place to erupt with some sort of catastrophic event...or maybe it was just his usual cleverness. I doubt there was any real correlation between that coincidence and what happened, but in that nascent state, there in the borderlands between what was ours and what was taken from us, between who I'd been and who I would become, the significance of names jolted through me with unpleasant sharpness.

And not just in Jaydemyrian or Mifūn-go.

"Xenides-ra Kas'Daen." He'd had me in his grasp, and he hadn't known it. Father's nemesis would have known better than to think a simplified composite of existing characters would suffice to neuter me, even if that release had kept me within his ultimate employ. Or perhaps he was watching, even now, somehow. No one understood the prowess of Dhiana the Mindwarp more than he, except perhaps Vachaelle the Nightsong and even then I'd seen them argue so often it seemed less an understanding and more of an endless repetition of peace-making and truce-breaking. And if Xenides-ra were watching...

"Xenya." The so-called abandoned tower was neither abandoned nor just a tower. The scout he'd mentioned had very likely seen someone obeying an imperative they didn't fully understand. The preparation for our return. Could I stop them? Should I? Xenya, the others in Sky Vanguard, the entire Sahmaran cohort...now my enemy. Did they have to be? Was Charan already there? I believed sightings of him in this area to be valid, because of course he'd be drawn back here as the last of Mother's locks fell away. And if he'd said his name in Jaydemyrian again tonight, who had extracted it from him? Vachaelle had kept him leashed all this time, and only made him say it once, so long ago now. So this time it was Mother. It had to be.

Was Xenides-ra Kas'Daen watching me as he said he would?

I made my decision. If I remembered who I was now, having heard the very same phrase in my head that had almost done the job so many years ago one sunny day during a perfectly fine lunch with Cass and Vi, then Xenides-ra very likely did too. His curious monitoring of me might immediately become a priority. He already had a scout force heading towards what used to be a known Jaydemyrian outpost, a stronghold in itself. There was no chance it would be the last, but if I were to go there, that would just increase its value as a primary target. No. I had to remove myself from the situation. Methodically. Run too soon and he'd know I knew. Run too late and he'd catch me and this time he would not let me go.

I kissed Father's final gift then, and remembered two last names. Chrysanthemum: a Talon who had given her life ensuring I kept the pendant when we lost almost everything else. And Nikalay: a Talon who had somehow survived the fall, only to fall at the hands of the one person who would never take it from me.

Nikalay!…Oh no.

Oh, Cassandra, why?

No. Later. For now:

"*Erotas'z en fhia'rez,* Chrys *et* Nikalay. *Vahm en.*"

Too late a prayer, far too late. But it would have to suffice. For now.

For now I had bloody work ahead, and would see to it with no further distraction.

I stood up, gathered my stuff, and headed back towards the encampment with no small measure of haste.

As I'd predicted, the Kas'Daen camp was in complete disarray. The sun was still hours away, so I watched from the treeline as human troops scrambled and formed into ranks dictated by dozens of panicked Halves and a handful of impassive Fey. The former stood on platforms, or balconies, while the latter mostly just stood on the air, observing silently; no doubt it had been their own experience this night that had roused them and called them to muster the encampment. And no Fey to my knowledge can truly fly; few are powerful enough to even hover for long. Their presence told me Xenides-ra had suspected this expedition would run into serious opposition, and was willing to expose true Nobles to deal with it.

Hundreds of humans, a sizeable number of Halves and some very potent Fey. More than enough to overrun the watchtower.

I pulled back into the fringe of Vizstrahtza, hidden and waiting for the sun to rise.

Something Xenides-ra never understood about human resources, something he never considered when incorporating them into his military, is they just don't function well without enough sleep. Most of the members of the Sky Vanguard, Halves one and all, had already entered the forest; nothing I could do about that for now. The Fey had left before them, the distance between here and the former stronghold being nothing but a few hundred steps for their terrible stride – Fey move very fast in straight lines, but can be hilariously inefficient if they don't know precisely where they are going. Now they knew, so they moved.

Which left the camp that day comprised mostly of very tired, very weak humans. Father had told me humans would inherit the world, True God willing, and I'd asked him which ones. There were so very many of them.

"'The ones who are ready to'." I whispered to myself his answer, having decided that didn't include anyone enlisted in the Kas'Daen military. And for those who aren't ready, Father?

Don't make me say what you've already figured out, Sariana.

I left no fire, no wake of destruction. Just quick, quiet visits from one barracks to another, tent to tent. Closed mouths and opened throats. I did not keep count and I did not linger. Time enough to pray for them on the road home. No, not home. Not yet.

I don't know if I saw Xenya again but it didn't matter. Whether by me or my brother, he was dead. Unless he had also heard the name in his head and understood it, in which case perhaps he was doing that which I was planning to do. But no. He would have been a child when Jaydemyr fell. He never knew any world but that which Mother had imposed, one of Kas'Daen Overclan supremacy, of Haven/Peddlerhouse balance, of Hunting Nights. Of Halves known not as deliberate assembly but malformed side-effect. I could not save him from what was now going to happen to that world.

I could, however, save him and whichever other blue-caped defects I encountered between the Kas'Daen rear and the Jaydemyrian front from how this resurgent Clan Jaydemyr, my father's final design, would treat them. I went north again, but not too far north. Not too close to the stronghold. I picked off stragglers and slackers. Not as easy to kill as sleeping mortals but I knew Sariana, the Gildenhammer, was to them what Blackcloak, The Scourge, had been to the Avengers of Azak.

The word 'Half' was about to take on a whole new meaning.

But the further south I went from what was, for now at least, north-east Kas'Daen, the fewer signs of anything abnormal I encountered. Had I gone more eastward, towards Sahmara and then the Karakan, I might have intercepted a lot more activity, although of what nature I couldn't guess. Had I veered north a little about halfway back, I might have seen Lybichmisto in very delightful chaos, frenzied by its Lord's sudden call to arms. Or maybe both directions would have been as unaware as this direct route. And I did take the most direct route because everything is a straight line when you understand both 'here' and 'there'. And a creature somehow not Half Fey and Half human but almost fully both moving in a straight line? As Tzara-Min had almost discovered: all but fully unstoppable.

"Good evening, Cassandra." I just crouched on the end of her bed, savouring half a mouthful of muffin.

The first fortress of the Scarlet Sparrows had looked no different from the outside, although I did approach from the south rather than the main road through Sparrowsview to the north. The Mind-Changer had, it seemed, figured the woods, a few walls and ditches and a few more walls would be defence enough from 'behind' the former abbey. An assumption that was probably quite tenable a month ago. I hadn't lied to that idiot in Kaifeng about how speed, strength and dexterity weren't enough to teach a Half how to scale a wall, how there were steps between that unified these raw potencies into functionality. I simply hadn't remembered those steps then.

"Sariana! How did—" She might have been potent herself, but as I said, humans need their sleep. I'd had to say her name three times before she stirred, four to make her sit up and stare at me in gratifying disbelief.

"So you heard it too. He said it again. And again. Dhiana has him. In Vizstrahtza. Right where she said she would."

Now that she was awake, I relocated from peering down at her to a chair at her desk. Squatting to straddling. Not too quickly. "Yep. And I was almost there. Xenides-ra planted me, I think. So I left. Came straight back, more or less."

Leaders, even human ones, are accustomed to this sort of thing. Middle of the night surprises. I appreciated how quickly she went from drowsy to alert. From almost naked in bed to fully robed and seated at her dressing table. And how this also meant she didn't waste time with pointless questions like how did I get in, when did I get back, am I actually wearing a Kas'Daen uniform, and why was I here.

"What happened to Nikalay?"

So I'd been right. The Brothers Huysman and Kendahl she'd intended to be my companions, but a former Talon, so much stronger than any human Peddler, she'd inserted as my protector. And against anyone else, he would have been the perfect choice.

'I'm so sorry, Cass. I didn't know who he was. He tried to tell me, more than once but…you did too good a job. No, no. It's not your fault. Because even if I'd known, we would have seen that mission through. And it wasn't just 'The Scourge' we faced. Not some much-vaunted shadow tearing havoc across Kas'Daen. No. It was Charan that day, completely in Vachaelle's grip. No one walked away from that encounter. Not even me. I fucking crawled."

She swallowed hard. After all this time, surely she must have known what had happened, but oh, to hear it from the only person who could tell her *how*. And she knew I wouldn't. "Until recently, I'd only thought of him as a Peddler ally aware of his old allegiance to Jaydemyr and roughly what had happened." Then came the tears, and oh, how I longed to hold her, but that was her decision to make. And I knew she wouldn't. "Killed by the man he so often swore to give his life to protect. Fucking irony. Fucking…"

Would that Maliscients could work their power on a mirror.

"Is there anything I can do for you?" It is possible that no Night's Own in history had asked this of a mortal, but for all my power it's all I felt I could do.

"No. No. I knew he was gone, of course, but I suppose seeing you here, like this…brings it all back. Thank you for telling me your side, Sariana-ra." She rallied in a way that I remembered not only from this place but so many others. Vachaelle's most trusted servant couldn't be anything but very, very quick to adjust to sudden, intense changes. She didn't bother wiping the tears but no more came either. "You said that Xenides had his eye on you?"

"I think he wasn't sure what I was and didn't like that very much. I was a maybe. But I also think he's now more than busy with definites to confirm a maybe."

"And if you are wrong, if he is still watching you, then the Rouge Eyrie will be under threat. We are not ready for an attack. At all. I've dispatched too many Sparrows. Your presence would be the ruin of all that I've built." Ah, how I had missed that audacity of hers.

I popped the last of the until-then forgotten muffin into my mouth. "That can't be helped, Cass. Places like this are made to be ruined. All that matters is how long they can resist it. I trust it won't crumble like clay at the first stone, or even the twenty-first. I also trust that by the time Xenides could muster any sizeable force, *we* will be ready. Hell, for all I know The Redfox will follow him here. Damn but that'd be funny."

She ran her hands through her hair, held it in a loose ponytail for a moment then let it flop back down. "We. He. Oh, Mother's love. Charan's coming here. Isn't he? You couldn't go to him, but you can come here and wait."

"He's been here before, and while he might have been in the Nightsong's thrall then, he'll know now what to find here. That Vachaelle brought him here multiple times is testament to what she wanted him to know. Learn. And eventually remember."

"Oh, wonderful. So not one Jaydemyrian heir but both. Here."

"We will leave once he arrives. I think Uncle Arius has something for us, something we can do only together. And only in the safety of Jaydemyr-*desne*."

"Barely a month and you're already talking about it as though wresting control back from the Overclan is as easy as snapping one's fingers. Halves go mad with ambition and power, but you two aren't just going to go there; you're taking the rest of us along with you."

"This is how it happens, Cassandra. This is how it starts. By replacing one type of madness with another. Tell me, Lady Cassandra Mind-Changer: do you want to inherit this world or not?"

Please say yes. I like you. So very much.

So I waited, just as I said I would. Out of sight, out of minds, Changed or otherwise. I didn't expect him to know the straight line between us, but I decided I'd give it a few months before trying to meet him halfway. I hoped he wasn't that useless but from what I remembered from before the fall, it was in no way guaranteed.

Five weeks later, I was watching the sun set from my bedroom on the fourth floor (once Third Eye Operations, now mostly storage, mostly inanimate) when Cassandra knocked on the door. I knew it was her because no one else knew I was there, and, well, she wore a very pleasant perfume.

Before I could say anything, she inched the door open. "He has arrived."

"Offer him nothing. Keep him downstairs. I will receive him here in an hour." I glanced away from the window and saw her face. Oh, Cassandra. I'm so sorry. But not as sorry as he'll be. "Make it two. And have him wait in the closest room to a closet you can find." I can't not help the man who murdered yours, Cass; I was made for this very task. But there's no need to hurry his delivery into my oh-so-welcoming embrace.

Cassandra smiled, as though she'd heard every word of that, but surely that was impossible now. Surely. "As you wish, My Lady."

It was all I could do not to laugh or cry out or both when he entered my secret little nest near the peak of the Rouge Eyrie. Here he was, Kaef're's biggest scapegoat, my younger brother. Actually wearing that same black cloak, carrying the same sword, still acting like such an Ephin' mystery.

He leaned against the wall and I stayed on the bed facing him. I chose to start in Common. "You *do* remember what happened the last time I saw you wearing that stupid costume, right? Go on, tell me. Every little detail, you bastard."

"No hello, sister?" He smirked, because that's what smug shitheads in sleek black hoods like him do.

"No hello because there'll be no goodbye. Do you remember or not?"

"I remember. I remember and I remember. It's all I do."

"No, it's not all you do. It's not even half of it. Talk, Brother. Tell me of our last encounter."

The smirk faltered. He sulked into Mifūn-go. "Don't wanna. You can't make me. You're not my mother."

I just sat there then, because this was my room and my domain and my time. Sat and looked at him, and tried not to show just how much it hurt to see him in this state. I was sure he was feeling amazing, because I was too. We were ourselves again. But Vachaelle always treated the world like an anvil and she, the only person to wield the hammer. She hadn't beaten him into the sword he claimed to be; she'd pounded him into just another stupid hammer. This was going to take so much work, and I had to wait for him to start it.

Thankfully he's Charan fucking Jaydemyr, so I didn't have to wait long. He retreated into the Tongue of Revelation. "It was supposed to be just another—"

Thank you, Brother. My turn. "I don't give a rat's diseased fuck what it was supposed to be, Charan-ra Jaydemyr!" Sometimes you have to pretend to be angry to get people going, but it's great when you don't. "It wasn't 'just another' anything for us. For them, there will be no 'another'. And that's true for hundreds, maybe thousands of people. That's on you. So let's start here. Tell me the first thing that went through that rattling void you call a head when you saw us."

Smirk now totally gone. And his voice changed. Timid. Weak. Beaten past submission into trembling Chūnko-go. "I want to stop. Please let me stop. No more…"

Oh, fuck her. Fuck her so much.

I had asked and he had answered. No. The wrong one had answered. Who was this one? So much work ahead. "Charan Jaydemyr." Jaydemyrian for absolute clarity.

"Hmmmm?"

Find it, Sariana. Find the sympathetic pace. Put a pulse to his ears, strike your hammer to the hollow where his heart should be, and make him dance.

I hated how close to a song it had to be, just that first time.

"The day was hot and you were in the woods." I patted on my thigh as I said certain words here: day, hot, in, woods.

He straightened up.

"The house was ahead but they were in the way." House. 'Head. In. Way.

His lips fell slack.

"What did you think when you saw those men?" What. Think. Saw. Men.

All the emotion melted from his conflicted face. There it was. The doll's intense neutrality. I knew it then: I had cut through to the core identity Father had intended me to manage, and would now see what I had exposed. And then I would never do this again.

No further need for the metrical lull. He was mine now. Every word could now be evenly freighted, evenly weighted. A point unto themselves. A compulsion. Every sound a profound cognitive concussion.

"Tell. Me. What. You. Thought. When. You. Saw. *Me.*"

And what he said wasn't a thought at all. The thing called Charan Jaydemyr doesn't think. He also doesn't care for any sort of rhythm. His is the deathless drive for dissonance.

He told me.

"You had to die first."

30 minutes until the revelation

Epilogue

Vizstrahtza (Jaydemyr Stronghold)
Nighmoon
9/882 A.R.

Not long after Sariana's last monologue completes the circle, Uncle Arius himself knocks on their door and has them follow him through the halls and chambers beneath Vizstrahtza with no further discussion. Then there are stairs, curling about the interior of the watchtower, and then a door.

"I apologise for the wait." The Lord Hawkstorm bids the siblings Jaydemyr enter his study. Vachaelle is already there, standing by a window with her arms folded. She acknowledges none of them, just stares out at the forest below.

Charan picks the nearest wall and leans upon it. "It's fine, Uncle. You were expecting me to be gone for months yet. My fault for finding her just down the road, give or take."

Sariana takes her place to his left, but does not lean. "And we used the time well to…fill in some gaps."

"What news of our mother?"

"She continues to rally our scattered faithful in Kas'Daen, Teriss-Lunirr, and Zieger. I hear you ran into one of them on the way here."

"We did. Their 'faith' has a lot to learn about how things are going to work from now on. But he got the message. The time for murdering innocent Haven-dwellers is over. Isn't it, Brother dear?"

"Yes, Sari."

Vachaelle snorts a laugh but still continues to focus on the world below.

"So I suppose we won't be seeing Mother anytime soon, Uncle Mentor?"

"…No, Charan, but *I* can tell you what happened to your father now."

Two pairs of flat, suddenly black eyes alight upon him, and the Hawkstorm's gaze refuses to meet theirs, or has perhaps already met with the accusing glare of another.

"Then?" Charan lets one hand falter somewhere between his hip and *her* hilt. Sariana retains the stoicism of her Sisterly conditioning, but something churns behind her lips, some resistance to interject.

"He is dead." Vachaelle's muted grey-blue eyes remain fastened to the window. "Can you not just leave it at that?"

"We *know* he's dead, Fa Shai-Yeh." Sariana's brother breaks first, although there is that other name, used by the others. Dog-Ears can now snap; Char can now whimper. Charan can still but try to keep them balanced. "But what *happened?* Why isn't he still here? Who. Killed. Father?"

Sariana acts then, because her brother's insistent hand is a fist, smooth and scarred all-at-once. She touches his arm, says nothing.

"He died." Vachaelle looks at Arius.

"God-damn-you, woman, we—" The Half wrenches away from his sister and takes half a step towards Vachaelle.

"No one killed your father." Arius interrupts the silence. And where Vachaelle invites every morsel of indignation and doubt, the fatherly old voice demands unspoken attention. It resonates with the terrible density of immutable truth. The Hawkstorm says the same thing as his former lover, and he says it differently. "He *died,* Charan."

"So he killed himself?" Sariana cannot see the obvious, because it's never been seen before.

"No, sis…it makes sense now." Charan can, because it isn't obvious. "Our mother was never anything but Noble. And yet, we are Half…remember? Not born, but made. We are immune to the madness. We have the strength of the Holy Mongrels, but not the weakness. What was the word you used? Unstoppable. But we are Half…how?"

Vachaelle groans to herself, not in mockery but genuine sympathy, although for what or whom remains unknown.

"Charas'z died because that's what he was looking for." Arius once again takes her place. "Ultimate knowledge of what he thought made the mortals so innovative, so desperate to fill every second of our life…*with life.*"

Charan hears the most important word, but Sariana interrupts with a knowing gasp. "Oh, I can understand that. The first time I felt the sun on my skin, skin that remembered only fearing its disintegrative judgment. Life. So much life…But it was given to me. Father had to take it. Purchase it? He paid the price."

"Aye and he did it without a moment's doubt. And who knows what curses he had to fling at God to be granted this worst of pleas? I remember his final moments. He looked just like any other *man* at the end of his life. Frail, sick, helpless. Who knows, maybe there's something to that *nse'ante* saying about broken hearts. Certainly the rest of him was broken right along with it.

"No one killed the Lord of our clan. Charas'z-ra uncovered all the secrets of his world and whatever lay beyond it. He found exactly what he was looking for. And then, fulfilled, he expelled the peaceful breath no Noble has ever felt and left that world."

"To us." Vachaelle attaches an ellipsis to the end of the story. Hers is not the patience for awestruck epiphanies. "So…Half." She looks at both of them – whole, together, complete – and half-smirks as only she can. "How exactly do you plan to take vengeance on old age?"

"With your help." Charan's hands are no longer fists; now they are ready once more to reach out and take what they want to keep. "After all, you remember now, now that Sari and I have given our accounts. All of it. I know because I do. So…" He mimics the little witch-woman's charade of suspense. "Arius, it's your turn."

The weary retainer glances at Vachaelle but says nothing.

"You're going to tell us all about the night Father died, and every night leading up to it. And then we'll decide what to do about every night yet to come."

"Tell you, no. But you will learn. I'll need two things first." The Hawkstorm looks at Sariana, nods at the pendant, and then back to Charan. "Your mother's lock has played its role, and Jaydemyr has fully returned to the world's awareness, come what may. Your father's lock, designed not to hide the existence of Jaydemyr but keep its truths safe…it's a little more mundane, a little more human."

He ambles over to a cluttered corner, bends over with an unnecessary grunt and retrieves something hefty, wooden. A small chest. Small enough to sit on the desk. "I have always had this. I couldn't remember why or how until Dhiana fully awakened you, Charan. A simple box with a fairly simple design." And it is true, but for two indentations on the lid, one a solid circle, the other their family name. "So the pendant if you will, Sariana-ra. And you, Charan-ra…Oni-Goroshi, please."

"Will this take long?" Charan unslings his precious weapon. Now very deliberately out of the way, Vachaelle titters to herself.

"Depends." Arius holds the sword by the sheath. "Do you have one of those little hammers for removing the handle, or do I have to just break this thing?"

Ten minutes later, a very undignified blade, handle, and various bits and pieces sit on the floor, completely neglected as three sets of eyes peer expectantly at the lid of the casement.

Arius Hawkstorm places the solid pendant on the surface, slides it up and into the first indentation. It's a little loose but makes a satisfying click. Then he hovers the more delicate swordguard over the other, and lets it fall, filling the carved grooves and curves. Another click.

And then…nothing.

"Yeah, I knew it wouldn't work." Charan resists an urge to reach for the tsuba. "Shit sounded like something out of a fantasy story."

"Any half-decent smith could forge the necessary keys to this, if it were that simple." Sariana glares at the puzzle. "This isn't just a game of pegs and holes…"

Vachaelle has a better idea. As usual. "Let's just smash the fucking thing. It can't be any more upsetting for poor old Char here than what we've done to his baby."

"You think I haven't tried that?" Arius thumps the desk less out of anger and more to pre-empt what he says next. "I'm an Eph-damned carpenter, or at least remember being one. This looks like it's made of wood. It is absolutely not made of wood. You could drop it from the top window of this tower and it wouldn't even bounce. I said it was mundane, and compared to Dhiana's power it certainly is. That doesn't mean it's not still the safebox in which rests the Clan's biggest secrets. Possibly even the world's."

"Well now what?" Charan grimaces down at the floor. "Did Father leave you with any instructions at all?"

"He just said keep the box safe, keep you two separate as long as you owned the keys. And on the night of all the pieces coming together…oh, you cunning old crow." Arius removes the tsuba and the pendant. Holding them up, he places the two circles together; the pendant, being smaller than the tsuba, fits within the larger piece's moon. "Hold it like this, Charan."

The younger sibling obliges.

"Now make them one." Arius steps back, gestures for Sariana to do the same. The heat is instant and powerful. "Not too much now, boy. The swordguard is strong metal, but the pendant…much weaker."

Sariana anticipates what comes next, flexing her fingers. Sure enough: "Your turn, Sariana. Cool it down. Again, not too hard or fast."

The elder sibling obliges.

"How is this going to get back onto my sword?"

"Stupid *kind.* You're not going to need that guard if this works. It was a shit design anyway. We'll get you a new one, dear. There, there."

Sariana interrupts before the two of them can start fighting…again. "Alright, should be cool enough now. Now what, Uncle Arius?"

"Now we try again. Actually, one of you do it. It's your name."

Sister shrugs at Brother. "It's still in your hand." So he's the one to do it.

The merged key, either half of which has travelled thousands of miles before joining with its counterpart, fills the slot perfectly. This time there is no click, but the bottom half of the box springs open, like a drawer.

"Huh. So what was the other indentation for?"

"Why do you carve your name into your victim's skin? Why did Sariana use it in Kaifeng even when she knew not to?" Vachaelle knows. "Pure. Fucking. Jaydemyr. Vanity."

"We should be thankful for that vanity." Arius picks up what was in the drawer. "Because nothing says 'vain' like writing a diary you then go to extraordinary lengths to hide." The Hawkstorm places the large book on the desk next to the box. The curled red *f* on the black cover announces that it is meant to look like a Book, Ephriem's Book of Truth, but the *f* sits neatly within a circle, its cut positioned much higher than usual, and the curls at either end of the Flail are almost entirely absent. The whole thing forms the beginning of what they all now know to be 'Jaydemyr'. "This is *his* Book of Truth. Everything recorded, known only to my late Lord and me, forgotten until now. This was for you, heirs to Jaydemyr. See?"

He eases open the cover, flips it back; the spine makes a satisfying if troublesome crackling sound. The siblings Jaydemyr, not bothering to not act very much like children around a new gift, lean in to behold what the first page reveals. The bold cross at the top draws them in, but the handwriting captivates their collective stare. Both recognise it from exactly the same place. Neither can see the horrified pallor to Vachaelle's face behind them. They start to read the dark letters, saying nothing between them.

To the heirs of Jaydemyr,

This account, scribed by me and annotated by my captain and Brother-in-blood Arius Hawkstorm, is my true will; all else is dust, ash and absence. If I leave anything behind, I wish it to be guided by these words. It is ironic that I had to lose my remaining years to learn what I would like to do with them. Forgive me for not being there, my children. But if I were, there would so much more need for your forgiveness. Soon, you will see. You will know. I pray to the True God and to the Cross that you are strong enough to complete my work. Tonight, it begins...with me.

So at last I must say, as no other Nobleborn may,

Yours lovingly,

Charas'z Jaydemyr

'Through death we found life'
Through death I *embrace* life.

W. James Chan

APPENDIX: The Known Timeline of the Siblings Jaydemyr until the Night of Revelation (853-882 AR)

Note: Per the Ahna Raenta calendar, dates are listed as month/year.

Italics denote events that occur in one of Vachaelle's dreamsong scenarios rather than real life, with **bold** denoting which scenario.

853

10/853 – Sariana Jaydemyr born in Kazan, Jaydemyr-*desne*.

Sarah-Jade *Falkenstrom born in a village outside Teristra, Teriss-Luniir (Zieger-desne), daughter of popular Teristran songstress Chantal Falkenstrom and disgraced carpenter/captain of the Teristran Watch Arius Falkenstrom.*

854

1/854 – ***Sarah-Jade****'s mother first performs 'The Curse of Princess Jade' in the All-Trades Inn, a song that describes in its opening passages a heavily stylised version of the events leading up to the Kas'Daen/Jaydemyr Conflict.*

856

4/856 – Charan Jaydemyr born in Kazan, Jaydemyr-*desne*.

Wong Shah-Long *born in Swimming Carp Village, Chūnko.*

Char Ah-Ran *born in Kaifeng, Chūnko.*

*Chantal Falkenstrom miscarries a son, **Sarah-Jade***'s brother.*

W. James Chan

857

11/857 – *Arius Falkenstrom leaves Chantal and* **Sarah-Jade**.

860

9/860 – *Chantal and* **Sarah-Jade** *move into the All-Trades Inn in the AllTrades district, West Teristra.*

863

4/863 – Charan and Sariana visit Kaifeng and Mifūné. A young Half of Kaifeng, Hua-Shi of a thieves guild called The Society for Disadvantaged Youth and its leader Leung Guan-Pi's protege, notices Charan's sword and tries to steal it from the palace. A serving girl called Fa Shai-Yeh stops him. He injures himself falling from a wall and wakes up in The Benevolent Hand in Munnamdun. He is introduced to the Malevolent Hand Peddler Chapterhouse and becomes its youngest Thorn. Not long after this he manifests Maliscient abilities and attracts Fa Shai-Yeh's attention.

868

4/868 – The Night of the Revolution. The Three Beasts (Tsukamoto, Zieger, Kas'Daen) assault Kazan in central Jaydemyr-*desne*. Having prepared for this, Dhiana executes her Plan to wipe Jaydemyr from living memory and conceal her children behind layers of false personality, imposed by her rival Vachaelle the Nightsong, the Witch-Seer of Jaydemyr. A Talon named Chrysanthemum helps Sariana escape the devastation but is killed in Kazan's outer courtyard. Another Talon, Nikalay, assists and survives. Vachaelle spirits both Sariana and Charan away from the destruction in very different directions. Charan is severely wounded in the process.

Charan is taken to Kaifeng by Vachaelle. He is successfully Healed and given the Char Ah-Ran dreamsong. He wakes up in the Benevolent Hand haven under the care of a healer, Lily, and then integrates into the Malevolent Hand under the care of its Thorn, a half Maliscient, and two other Half Peddlers, Chang Tong-Kut (The Knife) and Zhao La-Ahn (Orchid Witherheart). Vachaelle leaves Charan's sword Oni-Goroshi with a street-rat and former friend of Hua-Shi named Terasawa Jaku, promising him if he keeps it secret but gives it to Char Ah-Ran when he comes for it, the city will someday be his. As part of the Char Ah-Ran dreamsong, Charan experiences a series of visions that give him false future experiences with other members of the Benevolent and Malevolent Hands, including one in which he and Orchid are lovers. In another, he marries Lily and has a child, Tzara-Min Jaydemyr, whom he also calls Pumpkin. He watches her grow under Fa Shai-Yeh's tutelage into a bitter warrior named Talon, who eventually comes home to die at his hands. In the last sequence of the dream, he watches all of them fight and die in one final battle against the Night's Own. He wakes up and forgets almost all of it.

Sariana is taken to Mothers Abbey in Western Kas'Daen and given the Sarah-Jade Falkenstrom dreamsong. It fails, and she wakes up knowing she is Sariana Jaydemyr but soon learns no one else does or should. She pretends to be Sarah-Jade pretending to be Tzara-Min, a name she chooses based on what her brother would sometimes call her. She joins the Sisters of the Liquid Night, overseen by Vachaelle in the guise of the healer Mother Chantal. She also experiences Charan's final dream of the end of the world, and also forgets her part in it.

Char Ah-Ran*, A young Half of Kaifeng, member of a thieves guild called The Society for Disadvantaged Youth and its leader Leung Guan-Pi's protege, notices a visiting Noble's sword and tries to steal it from the palace. A serving girl, Fa Shai-Yeh, stops him. He injures himself falling from a wall and wakes up in The Benevolent Hand in Munnamdun. He is introduced to the Malevolent Hand Peddler Chapterhouse.*

Sarah-Jade *Falkenstrom, ostensibly blamed for starting a war in Teristra, is taken from the city to the abbey by a Peddler known as Chrys. Jacqueline Wright, master of the Teristran Guild of Construction Labour and Services, initiates violent unrest in Teristra after the deadly promotion to mentor of Lucy Loudair, Pauper-pyrotic of Convergence. This is the start of the Purge, a civil conflict that later escalates into a war between the Freely Talented (Freetal), led by Lucille Lourdaire, and the Allied Trades and Businesses (Alltrades), led by arms dealer Lady Tiamat*

Fourneval and Abbadonna Jeriksen, the Butcher of Parelle and wife of Leviathan Jeriksen, keeper of the All-Trades Inn.

Wong-Shah Long, *also known as* **Dog-Ears***, is sent to bed with no dinner on his twelfth birthday, and dreams about killing his father, and then everyone else in the world.*

5/868 – Cassandra, a Second Hand Sister of the Liquid Night and personal assistant to Mother Chantal, helps ease Tzara-Min into abbey life. Under the watchful eye of Aunty Sofiya, head administrator of Mothers Abbey, Tzara-Min is placed into the Gold dormitory of first floor below, and begins her life as a Daughter of the First Order.

11/868 – First known attempt by Sister Viera of Gold dorm to initiate intimacy with Tzara-Min.

869

10/869 – Tzara-Min attends the harvest festival in Abbey's Village. At the insistence of Viera, she meets Henri Kendahl and Jorik Huysman of the Tantamon, who helped carry her 'body' into Mothers Abbey on the night of her arrival. After a disappointing attempt at flirting with either boy, Tzara-Min engages in unfulfilling sex with a village boy named Roderic and is then almost killed in an altercation with his jealous lover, Zlatina Ciobanu.

870

3/870 – Char Ah-Ran and Orchid Witherheart become intimate.

4/870 – Tzara-Min is fully healed and receives her ancestral pendant in exchange for confinement to abbey grounds.

Char Ah-Ran's first field operation as a Peddler under the command of Chang Tong-Kut. He assaults two people he thinks are his adopted parents in Siu-Tsin. They are actually Hua-Shi's adopted parents, put on the Menu by Vachaelle herself as a test.

11/870 – Tzara-Min reciprocates Viera's affections.

871

2/871 – Sister Cassandra promoted to Aunty of the Second Hand.

3/871 – Tzara-Min begins training for the Fourth Going, which Sisters enter upon turning twenty to leave the abbey on various assignments and missions.

9/871 – Tzara-Min and Jorik Huysman reunite briefly.

872

2/872 – Tzara-Min assists in the Delivery of Zlatina Ciobanu. The child is Half, so the Sisters of the Third Eye on the Fourth Floor of Mothers Abbey deal with the Delivery exclusively. Zlatina dies in labour. The child is taken by Vachaelle to be adopted into a Peddler house. Tzara-Min realises after this she was not born Half, but instead somehow made. She assumes she will be spared the madness Halves experience as they enter adulthood; Chantal confirms this, and reminds her to keep training. Upon turning twenty, she plans to go forth – far into the east, to find her brother in Kaifeng.

873

3/873 – In Kaifeng, Leung Guan-Pi dies by self-administered poison in a failed attempt at murder-suicide with Char Ah-Ran. Remaining members of the Society for Disadvantaged Youth join the Bloody Shadows gang under Terasawa Jaku and Hua-Shi. Char Ah-Ran burns the now empty Nest, headquarters of the Society for Disadvantaged Youth in Siu-Tsin, to the ground.

4/73 – Under the pretense of a mission, Char Ah-Ran takes four Peddlers and meets with Terasawa Jaku and his psychotic lover Wu Jen-Wah on the Zhengkai road west of Kaifeng. Jaku and Jen mistake him for their former friend Hua-Shi, but Jaku knows to offer the sword. Upon touching the sword, Char Ah-Ran goes insane and slaughters the human Peddlers Ishida Kocho (One-Slash Butterfly) and Ming Tou-Fah (Blossom), as well as dozens of human Bloody Shadows. Jen manages to kill the Half Orchid Witherheart but is at the same time accidentally killed by Char Ah-Ran. Chang and Jaku fight, and Jaku is kicked unconscious. Hua-Shi, now revealed to be the Malevolent Hand's Thorn, kills Chang and takes the sword. This is later known as the Zhengkai Massacre. Char Ah-Ran is then given the Wong Shah-Long/Dog-Ears dreamsong by Vachaelle in person. A day later, thinking he is Dog-Ears, he wins a fight against an unknown Half in Swimming Carp village, his now abandoned childhood home. He learns the Half is called Hua-Shi from Hua-Shi's unnamed lover, who flees the melee. He then wanders the village for a day or so, recollecting more of this persona's history and trying to figure out why the village is empty.

Wong Shah-Long, *aged seventeen, is a downtrodden Half of Swimming Carp village also known as Dog-Ears. He is sent with a message to a nearby village, Bitter Lotus. Here he learns his abusive father, village elder Wong Chu-Deng, has tried to play a cruel trick on Dog-Ears: an arranged marriage with Plump Treat, village elder Leung Guan-Pi's overweight daughter. Plump Treat is actually a powerful Maliscient who tries to read Dog-Ears' mind and goes insane, leaving him with just one clue: a symbol of a cross inside a crescent moon. He returns to Swimming Carp but before entering thinks back on his life. His childhood was mostly being tormented by Terasawa Jaku, village bully, and his mean girlfriend Wu Jen-Wah, also a village bully. At the age of twelve, Dog-Ears also had a dream about becoming a world-famous scholar. At the end of the dream, he accidentally kills his father. Everyone he has ever known turns into monsters and he kills them too. He woke up laughing.*

Wong Shah-Long meets Happy Apple and her grandfather Havenkeeper Zhang at the House of Joyful Leave-Taking. He also meets Fa Shai-Yeh, whom he'd seen as Hua-Shi's supposed lover. He is coaxed into saying his true name in Jaydemyrian, which is heard around the world by anyone who was personally connected to the clan. This is the key to undoing the lock of Dhiana Jaydemyr's Plan and Charan Jaydemyr incorporates both the Wong Shah-Long and Char Ah-Ran scenarios into his psyche. Fa Shai-Yah mutilates the havendwellers including Havenkeeper Zhang, but Happy Apple escapes. Charan incinerates the Haven and then kills Hua-Shi, taking back his sword and going west with Vachaelle. Unbeknownst to him, Happy Apple witnesses all of this but pretends to be dead. She takes refuge in Kaifeng with Lily under the name Siusiudoh (Littleknife).

Tzara-Min hears 'Charan Jaydemyr' in her head in Jaydemyrian during a picnic with her lover, the soon-to-be-leaving Viera, and Aunty Cassandra. Tzara-Min immediately enters the Sarah-Jade Falkenstrom scenario, remembering both a complete childhood in Teristra and the final dream of the end of the world, in which all those who Charan loves die for him. Cassandra reveals herself to be a Jaydemyrian Maliscient and puts Viera to sleep. Chantal assigned her a secret task when Sariana rejected the Sarah-Jade dreamsong: to help her retain the memories of being Sariana and Tzara-Min at the abbey. Cassandra convinces Sariana that the Sarah-Jade scenario is not real, causing Sariana Jaydemyr to be 'complete' the same way Charan Jaydemyr is. She now remembers 19 years of being both Sariana Jaydemyr and Sarah-Jade Falkenstrom, but retains the name Tzara-Min as a cover for both.

10/873 – Tzara-Min graduates from the abbey and goes forth, armed with her signature weapon from the final dream, the spiked-ball-and-chain flail the Gildenhammer.

874

2/874 – Tzara-Min meets two former Tantamonian brothers, Volodymyr and Miroslav, as they wait out a blizzard in a Haven. She has covered a lot of ground moving at 'Half' speed, roughly 30-40 miles a day. They take her to their home, a Tantamonian stronghold at Azak, near the north-west border of Karakan. Here she finds a large gathering of Swords of Heaven, the Jenetchen Kulutchara, who serve as the guards and custodians of the Karakani wastelands.

3/874 – Tzara-Min joins the Pallid Harriers, a party of Swords led by kuluf (sheath, or roughly 'captain') Iskendahrl heading east, aiming to reach their secret home in the Faighana Valley. This is the beginning of her trek on the Long Way.

7/874 – Tzara-Min arrives in Khovokand. The Pallid Harriers depart for the true stronghold of Faighana and leave her at a karavansaray, where she waits out the heat of summer before joining the first of several caravans on the Long Way.

10/874 – Tzara-Min arrives in Ahksu, "White Water" in Kakanic, a town along the northern branch of the Long Way.

11/874 – Tzara-Min arrives in Kutchar, another town along the northern Long Way. She waits out the winter here.

875

3/875 – Tzara-Min arrives in Tulufan.

4/875 – Tzara-Min arrives in Ansichow, "Peaceful West".

5/875 – Tzara-Min passes through the Jade Gate and crosses the Chūnko border. She takes the Mifūné Highroad to Kiuchuan.

6/875 – Tzara-Min arrives in Lanzhou.

7/875 – Tzara-Min arrives in the City of Eternal Peace, future capital of Chūnko.

8/875 – Tzara-Min arrives in Zheng City. Here she recalls her flight from the Jaydemyrian capital of Kazan on the Night of the Revolution, and takes the name 'Talon Gukh-Fah' in honour of her fallen protector, Chrysanthemum.

9/875 – Talon finds the (new) House of Happy's Departure on the Zhengkai road between Zheng City and Kaifeng. She learns that Kaifeng has become a cursed, lawless place unseen by the Night. She also reads the memorial stone to the Joyful Goodbyes Fire and the Zhengkai Massacre. She attempts to enter Kaifeng, but is promptly arrested for lacking proof of identification.

11/875 – Talon is released into the custody of the healer Lily, who Talon recognises as Pai Hei-Wah from Charan's dream of the Final Garden. Lily guides her to Gentle Bouquet Helping Hands House in the Munnamdun district, South-east Kaifeng. Talon sees Zhang Siusiudoh working there, whom she recognises as Littleknife. She also learns why Kaifeng is shut off: the haven/peddler system has broken down in the wake of the Joyful Goodbyes fire and the Zhengkai massacre. She then speaks with Terasawa Jaku, known now as Leung Zha-Ku, leader of the Helping Hands, and Lily's husband. He convinces her to help him in his cause.

876

2/876 – Talon opens the first Happy Deliveries Sisterhood branch in Munnamdun.

3/876 – Wong Chu-Deng convinces the Kaifeng Imperial Court that the Helping Hands are planning an attack on the Palace. He is renamed Ayakawa no Inoh-ue Kenjiroh, and the Bloody Shadows become the Teikoku Chikagehkidan, official defenders of the Palace and northern Kaifeng. The Kaifeng Civil Conflict begins.

9/876 – A second Happy Deliveries branch is opened in Yuwantai, the central-south district of Kaifeng. Lily is assigned as its head Sister.

11/876 – Chikageh soldiers are sent into the southern districts of Siu-Tsin, Yuwantai and some of Munnamdun to collect taxes, food, and resources for the Palace. This represents an unofficial but practical occupation.

877

5/877 – The Helping Hands is renamed to the Society For The Advancement Of Kaifeng's Youth, or The Society. Talon is ordered by Leung Zha-Ku to open a new Happy Deliveries branch in the north-east Dragon Pavilion district. Unlike the other branches, this one is to provide two other services: food delivery, and home-visit terminations of unwanted pregnancy – a clear violation of the Seventh Commandment.

6/877 – Happy Deliveries opens in Dragon Pavilion/the Pagoda district. Sister Talon is assisted by the healer Littleknife, the pyrotic Tsai Yum-Ying and the maliscient Tsai On-Lam. As Chūnko-go is banned in the north, Talon also uses the name Kikuko (Chrysanthemum child).

7/877 – Lieutenant Kobayashi of the Kaifeng Imperial Guard begins surveilling the Happy Deliveries in the Dragon Pavilion.

9/877 – The Sisters of Happy Deliveries in Dragon Pavilion attend a wounded Chikageh soldier at the Nightingale's Nest pleasure house, operated by Lady Oh Reh-Na. The soldier is her son. This is the first time a Sister heals a Chikageh member. Lady Oh Reh-Na, already a client of Happy Deliveries, pays triple the usual sum for her son's treatment and passes word that Happy Deliveries will now treat Chikageh members, for the right price.

10/877 – The Sisters open a second Happy Deliveries in the Dragon Pavilion, this one much closer to the west. Having been wounded while on patrol, Captain Kobayashi of the Chikageh requests medical help from Happy Deliveries.

878

1/878 – The midsouth area of Kaifeng, Yuwantai, is reclaimed by The Society.

6/878 – The south-west suburb of Siu-Tsin reclaimed by The Society. Zha-Ku reassigns Talon from the Happy Deliveries to a new role: Hospitality. He gives her an invitation to a dinner party in the Outer Palace, intimating that Inoh-ue Kenjiroh/Wong Chu-Deng will be there.

7/878 – The Feast Of The Boar And The Dog. The dinner party is actually a private meeting between Leung Zha-Ku and Wong Chu-Deng. Fa Shai-Yeh is also in attendance. The result of the meeting is an agreement that the Chikageh and the Society will assault the Palace together. Fa Shai Yeh urges Talon not to pursue her brother, whom she has left alone for a year in a village called Wildflowers Bloom without his sword to learn about its people. Fa Shai Yeh suggests Talon return to the abbey to help Cassandra.

Charan Jaydemyr investigates Wildflowers Bloom.

10/878 – The Kaifeng Civil Conflict is declared officially over. The Chikageh and the Society assault the Five-Fold Palace as planned, their combined forces operating under the name The Bloody Rats. The massacre and sacking is called The Three Days Of Snow And Blood.

879

4/879 – The Society forms a loose government based largely on an old system of chancellor, departments and ministries. Leung Zha-Ku is named State Chancellor. Wong Chu-Deng is offered the role of Commander of Military Affairs, but is still recovering from wounds sustain in the Three Days. Leung Yoon-Fah, formerly Lily, is named State Secretary.

5/879 – The Kaifeng Imperial Guard is reformed under the name the New Kaifeng State Police, and establish small stations all over Kaifeng. Old Guardhouses are converted into Public Grievances offices. Mifūné-style food, goods and services start to phase out. Carrying weapons in public is banned, especially those of Mifūné style. A new currency, the Leung, is minted, with Little Leungs being the smallest denomination.

6/879 – All civil services and infrastructure are operational in Kaifeng. The city gates remain closed.

7/879 – Leung Zha-Ku summons Talon to the former Women's Quarters in the Palace district, now the Center for Domestic Affairs. He offers her the position of Grand Mother of Domestic Affairs, a role of equal stature as that of State Secretary and Commander of Military Affairs. She refuses and is given permission to leave the city. Lady Yoon-Fah assumes the role of Grand Mother of Domestic Affairs.

8/879 – The city gates of Kaifeng open for the first time in over six years. Wong Chu-Deng dies; Lady Yoon-Fah assumes his role and, effectively the ruler of Kaifeng, takes on the title of Mother Lily. Talon says her farewells and leaves Kaifeng, aiming to return to Mothers Abbey in Kas'Daen.

11/879 – Talon arrives in Khovokand in the Faighana Valley. She reunites with the Pallid Harriers, who are now mercenaries and no longer affiliated with the Jenetchen Kulutchara. Their commander Iskendahrl is convinced she is Sarivashes-ra Kas'Daen, Xenides' long-lost daughter. He proposes escorting her back to Kas'Daen for a reward, but 'Sarivashes' convinces him to take her back to Mothers Abbey instead.

880

8/880 – The Pallid Harriers and 'Sarivashes' arrive at Sparrowsview, formerly Abbey's Village and enter the Rouge Eyrie, formerly Mothers Abbey. Lady Cassandra Mind-Changer has converted the abbey into a fortress, openly supporting Kas'Daen but secretly preparing to serve as a Jaydemyrian stronghold. Those who stayed to serve her became the Scarlet Sparrows. 'Sarivashes' has her mind Changed by Cassandra to believe she really is Sarivashes. The Pallid Harriers are Changed back to faithful Jenetchen Kulutchara and sent back to Karakan.

881

6/881 – Sarivashes is given a mission to join a party of Brothers led by Vadim, former commander of Azak. Both Henri Kendahl and Jorik Huysman are in the party. The party heads north-east towards the Kas'Daen capital of Lybichmisto to investigate The Scourge. The party stops to assist Radomyr's Rest village, where the Haven has been razed to the ground. Consolidated by this Tantamonian act, they take the name 'The Avengers of Azak'.

8/881 – The Avengers of Azak are assigned to guard a cottage near Vazhar village, about a hundred miles north-west of Lybichmisto. The Scourge kills all members but for Sarivashes, whom he knocks out before killing the Noble sleeping beneath the cottage.

10/881 – Sarivashes reports the encounter to a records office in Lybichmisto but is dismissed as a hoax. She attempts to leave the city but is captured by Kas'Daen authorities and imprisoned.

882

2/882 – Xenides-ra Kas'Daen himself interrogates Sarivashes. He confirms she is not his daughter but gives away nothing else. The Self-Scrapers of Kas'Daen combine parts of the Sarah-Jade layer and the

Sarivashes layer to create Sarivashes Gildenhammer, a member of the Sky Vanguard. Comprised entirely of Halves, the Sky Vanguard head for Viestrada to the north-east, acting on reports of Scourge sightings.

3/882 – Sky Vanguard meets with the main military force from the south-east stronghold of Sahmara. Numbering around 400 humans, 100 Halves and a dozen or so Fey, they set up camp on the south-western edge of Viestrada.

4/882 – Dhiana captures The Scourge deep in Viestrada Forest, and begins her week-long Delving of his personae.

5/882 – A Kas'Daen scouting party stumbles upon Viestrada. Charan, Arius Hawkstorm and a small Jaydemyrian contingent repel their attack. Sariana Jaydemyr, having remembered who she truly is as a result of Dhiana's intense Delving and reassembly of Charan Jaydemyr's fractured psyche, hides in Viestrada until the Halves and Nobles have left and then eradicates the rest of the encampment. She decides to return to the Rouge Eyrie rather than seek her brother in Viestrada, assuming Xenides-Ra Kas'Daen might still be watching her.

6/882 – Charan arrives at the Rouge Eyrie and the two set off for Viestrada. Along the way Sariana recounts her story when time permits. They also encounter a Jaydemyr-aligned Half who is mimicking The Scourge's behaviour. Sariana castigates him, saying those old ways are now over, and orders him to Viestrada instead.

7/882 – The Night of the Revelation. The siblings return to Viestrada, which has been well-fortified since the attacks. They unlock the small chest Arius took with him on the night of the Revolution and begin to read their father's Account of Clan Jaydemyr, aided by the Hawkstorm's commentary.

Thanks and Acknowledgments

This book was a much different process to the first, which involved so many people on so many different levels. *Gildenhammer* existed the moment I finished *Blackcloak*, and grew in some fairly diverse soil. Lest we forget the pandemic and the lockdown of 2020-22, a lot of it was done in isolation and solitude, but even then I was never truly alone.

First, Kate. My *sine qua non*. *Alpha* and *omega*. Enough said.

Peter Kawecki, bestie of many years and my cover artist/designer. Two books, two covers. And no sign of stopping.

Benjamin Drake, partner in theological crime and my Other cover artist. To this day I have no idea how he sees what's in my head. Glory to your Great Works, Brother.

John Purvis, my supercritic, whose unyielding, often painful feedback on a first draft that wasn't forced me to really finish the book. I'm sorry I made you jump at shadows, John, and that I can't give you a laser-sword wielding Zaku. Muh arts and all.

David Wood, my superfan, who wanted to see what happens next. Thank you for asking, and thank you for the added help with the timeline. Sorry for taking so long to sign your book – I genuinely couldn't come up with anything worthy of your support.

Dr. Alana Shilling-Janoff, whose erudite feedback on *Blackcloak* as a much more complex work than its fantasy conceits informed *so much* of what I've done here. The Master-Slave dialectic is still very much in play, Alana.

My early readers: Amber Cansler and Alex Blunck. The best feedback either of you gave was what you didn't say about a clearly unfinished draft.

Jane Coleman, the gaming granny. I will be down to get that beer someday.

Dr. Shady Cosgrove, who may never see a word of this but will always be in my head, somewhere, enthusiastic and critical in equal measure.

Alex Cullen, the bitch who made it and believes I should as well.

And finally, any and all Exiles who have wielded Oni-Goroshi, the Goddess of Swords. You have come to know and possibly love a version of Vachaelle that will never exist anywhere else.

W. James Chan
July 20th, 2024

CONTENT WARNING

Potentially upsetting content in this book

adult language
violence between men and women (some domestic)
violence towards children
parental abuse
teenage suicide ideation
body shaming
vomiting and other bodily functions
self-harm
discussion but no depiction of rape and abortion
childbirth and miscarriage
non-graphic sexual scenes
and quite a few very graphic scenes of horror.

There is a *lot* of blood.

I do not in any way espouse the morals or beliefs conveyed by the characters in this book, and frankly would be wary of anyone who does. 'Gildenhammer' aims not to inspire but to provoke. It is unavoidably provocative.